MARK TWAIN

MARK TWAIN

HISTORICAL ROMANCES

The Prince and the Pauper
A Connecticut Yankee in King Arthur's Court
Personal Recollections of Joan of Arc

THE LIBRARY OF AMERICA

The paper used in this publication meets the
minimum requirements of the American National Standard for
Information Sciences — Permanence of Paper for Printed
Library Materials, ANSI Z39.48 — 1984.

Distributed to the trade in the United States
by Penguin Books USA Inc
and in Canada by Penguin Books Canada Ltd.

Library of Congress Catalog Number: 93–40246
For cataloging information, see end of Notes
ISBN 0–940450–82–8

First Printing
The Library of America–71

Manufactured in the United States of America

SUSAN K. HARRIS
WROTE THE NOTES FOR THIS VOLUME

The text of The Prince and the Pauper is reprinted from The Works of Mark Twain, Volume 6, edited by Victor Fischer and Lin Salamo, with the assistance of Mary Jane Jones. The text of A Connecticut Yankee in King Arthur's Court is reprinted from The Works of Mark Twain, Volume 9, edited by Bernard L. Stein. The Works of Mark Twain is published by The Iowa Center for Textual Studies and the University of California Press.

Contents

THE PRINCE
AND THE PAUPER

A Tale
for Young People of All Ages

Hugh Latimer, *Bishop of Worcester,* to Lord Cromwell, *on the birth of the* Prince of Wales *(afterward* Edward VI.).

FROM THE NATIONAL MANUSCRIPTS PRESERVED BY THE BRITISH GOVERNMENT.

HUGH LATIMER, *Bishop of Worcester, to* LORD
CROMWELL, *on the birth of the* PRINCE OF WALES
(*afterward* EDWARD VI.).

FROM THE NATIONAL MANUSCRIPTS PRESERVED BY THE
BRITISH GOVERNMENT.

Ryght honorable. *Salutem in Christo Jesu.* And Syr here ys no lesse
joynge and rejossynge in thes partees for the byrth of our prynce,
hoom we hungurde for so longe, then ther was, (I trow) *inter vicinos*
att the byrth of S. I. Baptyste, as thys berer Master Evance can telle
you. Gode gyffe us alle grace, to yield dew thankes to our Lorde
Gode, Gode of Inglonde, for verely He hathe shoyd Hym selff Gode
of Inglonde, or rather an Inglyssh Gode, yf we consydyr and pondyr
welle alle Hys procedynges with us from tyme to tyme. He hath
overcumme alle our yllnesse with Hys excedynge goodnesse, so that
we ar now moor then compellyd to serve Hym, seke Hys glory,
promott Hys wurde, yf the Devylle of alle Devylles be natt in us. We
have now the stooppe of vayne trustes ande the stey of vayne expectations; lett us alle pray for hys preservatione. Ande I for my partt
wylle wyssh that hys Grace allways have, and evyn now from the
begynynge, Governares, Instructores and offyceres of ryght jug-
mente, *ne optimum ingenium non optimâ educatione depravetur.* Butt
whatt a grett fowlle am I! So, whatt devotione shoyth many tymys
butt lytelle dyscretione! Ande thus the Gode of Inglonde be ever
with you in alle your procedynges.

The 19 of October.

youres H. L. B. of Wurcestere

now att Hartlebury.

Yf you wolde excytt thys berere to be moore hartye ayen the abuse
of ymagry or mor forwarde to promotte the veryte, ytt myght doo
goode. Natt that ytt came of me, butt of your selffe, &c.

(*Addressed*) To the Ryght Honorable Loorde P. Sealle
hys synguler gode Lorde.

THE quality of mercy . . .
                    is twice bless'd;
It blesseth him that gives and him that takes;
'Tis mightiest in the mightiest: it becomes
The thronèd monarch better than his crown.
                    Merchant of Venice.

Contents

I WILL set down a tale as it was told to me by one who had it of his father, which latter had it of *his* father, this last having in like manner had it of *his* father—and so on, back and still back, three hundred years and more, the fathers transmitting it to the sons and so preserving it. It may be history, it may be only a legend, a tradition. It may have happened, it may not have happened: but it *could* have happened. It may be that the wise and the learned believed it in the old days; it may be that only the unlearned and the simple loved it and credited it.

Chapter 1

THE BIRTH OF THE PRINCE AND THE PAUPER

IN THE ANCIENT CITY of London, on a certain autumn day in the second quarter of the sixteenth century, a boy was born to a poor family of the name of Canty, who did not want him. On the same day another English child was born to a rich family of the name of Tudor, who did want him. All England wanted him, too. England had so longed for him, and hoped for him, and prayed God for him, that now that he was really come, the people went nearly mad for joy. Mere acquaintances hugged and kissed each other and cried; everybody took a holiday, and high and low, rich and poor, feasted and danced, and sang, and got very mellow—and they kept this up for days and nights together. By day, London was a sight to see, with gay banners waving from every balcony and house-top, and splendid pageants marching along. By night it was again a sight to see, with its great bonfires at every corner and its troops of revelers making merry around them. There was no talk in all England but of the new baby, Edward Tudor, Prince of Wales, who lay lapped in silks and satins, unconscious of all this fuss, and not knowing that great lords and ladies were tending him and watching over him—and not caring, either. But there was no talk about the other baby, Tom Canty, lapped in his poor rags, except among the family of paupers whom he had just come to trouble with his presence.

Chapter 2

TOM'S EARLY LIFE

L ET US SKIP a number of years.

London was fifteen hundred years old, and was a great town—for that day. It had a hundred thousand inhabitants— some think double as many. The streets were very narrow, and crooked, and dirty, especially in the part where Tom Canty lived, which was not far from London Bridge. The houses were of wood, with the second story projecting over the first, and the third sticking its elbows out beyond the sec- ond. The higher the houses grew, the broader they grew. They were skeletons of strong criss-cross beams, with solid material between, coated with plaster. The beams were painted red or blue or black, according to the owner's taste, and this gave the houses a very picturesque look. The win- dows were small, glazed with little diamond-shaped panes, and they opened outward, on hinges, like doors.

The house which Tom's father lived in was up a foul little pocket called Offal Court, out of Pudding Lane. It was small, decayed, and ricketty, but it was packed full of wretchedly poor families. Canty's tribe occupied a room on the third floor. The mother and father had a sort of bedstead in the corner, but Tom, his grandmother, and his two sisters, Bet and Nan, were not restricted—they had all the floor to them- selves, and might sleep where they chose. There were the re- mains of a blanket or two and some bundles of ancient and dirty straw, but these could not rightly be called beds, for they were not organized; they were kicked into a general pile, mornings, and selections made from the mass at night, for service.

Bet and Nan were fifteen years old—twins. They were good-hearted girls, unclean, clothed in rags, and profoundly ignorant. Their mother was like them. But the father and the grandmother were a couple of fiends. They got drunk when- ever they could; then they fought each other or anybody else who came in the way; they cursed and swore always, drunk or sober; John Canty was a thief, and his mother a beggar. They made beggars of the children, but failed to make thieves of them. Among, but not of, the dreadful rabble that inhabited the house, was a good old priest whom the king had turned out of house and home with a pension of a few farthings, and he used to get the children aside and teach them right ways secretly. Father Andrew also taught Tom a little Latin, and how to read and write; and would have done the same with the girls, but they were afraid of the jeers of their friends, who could not have endured such a queer accomplishment in them.

All Offal Court was just such another hive as Canty's house. Drunkenness, riot and brawling were the order, there, every night and nearly all night long. Broken heads were as common as hunger in that place. Yet little Tom was not unhappy. He had a hard time of it, but did not know it. It was the sort of time that all the Offal Court boys had, therefore he supposed it was the correct and comfortable thing. When he came home empty handed at night, he knew his father would curse him and thrash him first, and that when he was done the awful grandmother would do it all over again and improve on it; and that away in the night his starving mother would slip to him stealthily with any miserable scrap or crust she had been able to save for him by going hungry herself, notwithstanding she was often caught in that sort of treason and soundly beaten for it by her husband.

No, Tom's life went along well enough, especially in summer. He only begged just enough to save himself, for the laws against mendicancy were stringent, and the penalties heavy; so he put in a good deal of his time listening to good Father Andrew's charming old tales and legends about giants and fairies, dwarfs and genii, and enchanted castles, and gorgeous kings and princes. His head grew to be full of these wonderful things, and many a night as he lay in the dark on his scant and offensive straw, tired, hungry, and smarting from a thrashing, he unleashed his imagination and soon forgot his aches and pains in delicious picturings to himself of the charmed life of a petted prince in a regal palace. One desire came in time to haunt him day and night: it was, to see a real prince, with his own eyes. He spoke of it once to some of his

Offal Court comrades; but they jeered him and scoffed him so unmercifully that he was glad to keep his dream to himself after that.

He often read the priest's old books and got him to explain and enlarge upon them. His dreamings and readings worked certain changes in him, by and by. His dream-people were so fine that he grew to lament his shabby clothing and his dirt, and to wish to be clean and better clad. He went on playing in the mud just the same, and enjoying it, too; but instead of splashing around in the Thames solely for the fun of it, he began to find an added value in it because of the washings and cleansings it afforded.

Tom could always find something going on around the May-pole in Cheapside, and at the fairs, and now and then he and the rest of London had a chance to see a military parade when some famous unfortunate was carried prisoner to the Tower, by land or boat. One summer's day he saw poor Anne Askew and three men burned at the stake in Smithfield, and heard an ex-Bishop preach a sermon to them which did not interest him. Yes, Tom's life was varied and pleasant enough, on the whole.

By and by Tom's reading and dreaming about princely life wrought such a strong effect upon him that he began to *act* the prince, unconsciously. His speech and manners became curiously ceremonious and courtly, to the vast admiration and amusement of his intimates. But Tom's influence among these young people began to grow, now, day by day; and in time he came to be looked up to, by them, with a sort of wondering awe, as a superior being. He seemed to know so much! and he could do and say such marvelous things! and withal, he was so deep and wise! Tom's remarks, and Tom's performances, were reported by the boys to their elders, and these also presently began to discuss Tom Canty, and to regard him as a most gifted and extraordinary creature. Full grown people brought their perplexities to Tom for solution, and were often astonished at the wit and wisdom of his decisions. In fact he was become a hero to all who knew him except his own family—these, only, saw nothing in him.

Privately, after a while, Tom organized a royal court! He was the prince; his special comrades were guards, chamberlains, equerries, lords and ladies in waiting, and the royal family. Daily the mock prince was received with elaborate ceremonials borrowed by Tom from his romantic readings; daily the great affairs of the mimic kingdom were discussed in the royal council, and daily his mimic highness issued decrees to his imaginary armies, navies, and viceroyalties.

After which, he would go forth in his rags and beg a few farthings, eat his poor crust, take his customary cuffs and abuse, and then stretch himself upon his handful of foul straw, and resume his empty grandeurs in his dreams.

And still his desire to look just once upon a real prince, in the flesh, grew upon him, day by day, and week by week, until at last it absorbed all other desires, and became the one passion of his life.

One January day, on his usual begging tour, he tramped despondently up and down the region round about Mincing Lane and Little East Cheap, hour after hour, barefooted and cold, looking in at cook-shop windows and longing for the dreadful pork-pies and other deadly inventions displayed there—for to him these were dainties fit for the angels; that is, judging by the smell, they were—for it had never been his good luck to own and eat one. There was a cold drizzle of rain; the atmosphere was murky; it was a melancholy day. At night Tom reached home so wet and tired and hungry that it was not possible for his father and grandmother to observe his forlorn condition and not be moved—after their fashion; wherefore they gave him a brisk cuffing at once and sent him to bed. For a long time his pain and hunger, and the swearing and fighting going on in the building kept him awake; but at last his thoughts drifted away to far, romantic lands, and he fell asleep in the company of jeweled and gilded princelings who lived in vast palaces, and had servants salaaming before them or flying to execute their orders. And then, as usual, he dreamed that *he* was a princeling himself.

All night long the glories of his royal estate shone upon him; he moved among great lords and ladies, in a blaze of light, breathing perfumes, drinking in delicious music, and answering the reverent obeisances of the glittering throng as it parted to make way for him, with here a smile, and there a nod of his princely head.

And when he awoke in the morning and looked upon the wretchedness about him, his dream had had its usual effect —it had intensified the sordidness of his surroundings a thousand fold. Then came bitterness, and heartbreak, and tears.

Chapter 3

TOM'S MEETING WITH THE PRINCE

TOM GOT UP hungry and sauntered hungry away but with his thoughts busy with the shadowy splendors of his night's dreams. He wandered here and there in the city, hardly noticing where he was going or what was happening around him. People jostled him, and some gave him rough speech, but it was all lost on the musing boy. By and by he found himself at Temple Bar—the furthest from home he had ever traveled in that direction. He stopped and considered a moment, then fell into his imaginings again and passed on, outside the walls of London. The Strand had ceased to be a country road then, and regarded itself as a street—but by a strained construction, for though there was a tolerably compact row of houses on one side of it, there were only some scattering great buildings on the other, these being palaces of rich nobles, with ample and beautiful grounds stretching to the river—grounds that are now closely packed with grim acres of brick and stone.

Tom discovered Charing village, presently, and rested himself at the beautiful cross built there by a bereaved king of earlier days; then idled down a quiet, lovely road, past the great cardinal's stately palace, toward a far more mighty and majestic palace beyond—Westminster. Tom stared in glad wonder at the vast pile of masonry, the wide-spreading wings, the frowning bastions and turrets, the huge stone gateway with its gilded bars and its magnificent array of colossal granite lions and other the signs and symbols of English royalty. Was the desire of his soul to be satisfied at last? Here, indeed, was a king's palace—might he not hope to see a prince, now, a prince of flesh and blood, if heaven were willing?

At each side of the gilded gate stood a living statue—that is to say, an erect and stately and motionless man-at-arms, clad from head to heel in shining steel armor. At a respectful distance were many country folk, and people from the city waiting for any chance glimpse of royalty that might offer.

Splendid carriages with splendid people in them and splendid servants outside were arriving and departing by several other noble gateways that pierced the royal enclosure.

Poor little Tom, in his rags, approached, and was moving slow and timidly past the sentinels, with a beating heart and a rising hope, when all at once he caught sight, through the golden bars, of a spectacle that almost made him shout for joy. Within was a comely boy, tanned and brown with sturdy out-door sports and exercises, whose clothing was all of lovely silks and satins, shining with jewels; at his hip a little jeweled sword and dagger; dainty buskins on his feet, with red heels, and on his head a jaunty crimson cap with drooping plumes fastened with a great sparkling gem. Several gorgeous gentlemen stood near—his servants, without a doubt. O, he was a prince! a prince! a living prince, a real prince, without the shadow of a question, and the prayer of the pauper-boy's heart was answered at last!

Tom's breath came quick and short with excitement, and his eyes grew big with wonder and delight. Everything gave way in his mind, instantly, to one desire; that was, to get close to the prince and have a good, devouring look at him. Before he knew what he was about, he had his face against the gate-bars. The next instant one of the soldiers snatched him rudely away and sent him spinning among the gaping crowd of country gawks and London idlers. The soldier said:

"Mind thy manners thou young beggar!"

The crowd jeered and laughed; but the young prince sprang to the gate with his face flushed and his eyes flashing with indignation, and cried out:

"How dar'st thou use a poor lad like that! How dar'st thou use the king my father's meanest subject so! Open the gates and let him in!"

You should have seen that fickle crowd snatch off their hats, then. You should have heard them cheer and shout "Long live the Prince of Wales!"

The soldiers presented arms, with their halberds, opened the gates, and presented again as the little Prince of Poverty passed in, in his fluttering rags, to join hands with the Prince of Limitless Plenty.

Edward Tudor said:

"Thou lookest tired and hungry; thou'st been treated ill. Come with me."

Half a dozen attendants sprang forward to—I don't know what; interfere, no doubt. But they were waved aside with a right royal gesture, and they stopped stock still where they were, like so many statues. Edward took Tom to a rich apartment in the palace which he called his cabinet. By his command, a repast was brought such as Tom had never encountered before except in books; the prince, with princely delicacy and breeding, sent away the servants, so that his humble guest might not be embarrassed by their critical presence; then he sat near by and asked questions while Tom ate.

"What is thy name, lad?"

"Tom Canty, an' it please thee, sir."

" 'Tis an odd one. Where dost live?"

"In the city, please thee, sir—Offal Court, out of Pudding Lane."

"Offal Court! Truly 'tis another odd one. Hast parents?"

"Parents have I, sir, and a grandam likewise that is but indifferently precious to me, God forgive me if it be offense to say it. Also twin sisters—Nan and Bet."

"Then is thy grandam not over kind to thee, I take it."

"Neither to any other is she, so please your worship. She hath a wicked heart, and worketh evil all her days."

"Doth she mistreat thee?"

"There be times that she stayeth her hand, being asleep or overcome with drink; but when she hath her judgment clear again, she maketh it up to me with goodly beatings."

A fierce look came into the little prince's eyes, and he cried out—

"What! Beatings?"

"O, indeed, yes, please you, sir."

"*Beatings!* And thou so frail and little. Harkye; before the night come, she shall hie her to the Tower! The king my father—"

"In sooth you forget, sir, her low degree. The Tower is for the great alone."

"True, indeed. I had not thought of that. I will consider of her punishment. Is thy father kind to thee?"

"Not more than Gammer Canty, sir."

"Fathers be alike, mayhap. Mine hath not a doll's temper. He smiteth with a heavy hand, yet spareth me; he spareth me not always with his tongue, though, sooth to say. How doth thy mother use thee?"

"She is good, sir, and giveth me neither sorrow nor pain of any sort. And Nan and Bet are like to her in this."

"How old be these?"

"Fifteen, an' it please you, sir."

"The lady Elizabeth my sister is fourteen, and the lady Jane Grey my cousin is of mine own age, and comely and gracious withal; but my sister the lady Mary, with her gloomy mien and—look you, do thy sisters forbid their servants to smile, lest the sin destroy their souls?"

"They? O, dost think, sir, that *they* have servants?"

The little prince contemplated the little pauper gravely a moment, then said—

"And prithee, why not? Who helpeth them undress at night? who attireth them when they rise?"

"None, sir. Wouldst have them take off their garment and sleep without—like the beasts?"

"Their garment! Have they but one?"

"Ah, good your worship, what would they do with more? Truly they have not two bodies each."

"It is a quaint and marvelous thought! Thy pardon—I had not meant to laugh. But thy good Nan and thy Bet shall have raiment and lackeys enow—and that soon, too—my cofferer shall look to it. No, thank me not—'tis nothing. Thou speakest well; thou hast an easy grace in it. Art learned?"

"I know not if I am or not, sir. The good priest that is called Father Andrew, taught me, of his kindness, from his books."

"Know'st thou the Latin?"

"But scantly, sir, I doubt."

"Learn it, lad; 'tis hard only at first. The Greek is harder; but neither these nor any tongues else, I think, are hard to the lady Elizabeth and my cousin. Thou shouldst hear those damsels at it! But tell me of thy Offal Court. Hast thou a pleasant life there?"

"In truth, yes, so please you, sir, save when one is hungry. There be Punch and Judy shows; and monkeys—oh, such antic creatures and so bravely dressed!—and there be plays, wherein they that play do shout and fight till all are slain, and 'tis so fine to see, and costeth but a farthing—albeit 'tis main hard to get the farthing, please your worship."

"Tell me more."

"We lads of Offal Court do strive against each other with the cudgel, like to the fashion of the 'prentices, sometimes."

The prince's eyes flashed. Said he—

"Marry, that would not I mislike! Tell me more."

"We strive in races, sir, to see who of us shall be fleetest—"

"That would I like, also! Speak on!"

"In summer, sir, we wade and swim in the canals and in the river, and each doth duck his neighbor, and spatter him with water, and dive and shout and tumble and—"

"'Twould be worth my father's kingdom but to enjoy it once! Prithee go on."

"We dance and sing about the May-pole in Cheapside, we play in the sand, each covering his neighbor up; and times we make mud pastry—oh, the lovely mud, it hath not its like for delightfulness in all the world—we do fairly wallow in the mud, sir, saving your worship's presence!"

"O, prithee, say no more, 'tis glorious! If that I could but clothe me in raiment like to thine, and strip my feet, and revel in the mud once, just once, with none to rebuke me or forbid, meseemeth I could forego the crown!"

"And if that I could clothe me once, sweet sir, as thou art clad—just once—"

"Oho, wouldst like it? Then so shall it be! Doff thy rags and don these splendors, lad! It is a brief happiness, but will be not less keen for that. We will have it while we may, and change again before any come to molest."

A few minutes later, the little Prince of Wales was garlanded with Tom's fluttering odds and ends, and the little Prince of Pauperdom was tricked out in the gaudy plumage of royalty. The two went and stood side by side before a great mirror, and lo, a miracle: there did not seem to have been any change made! They stared at each other, then at the glass, then at each other again. At last the puzzled princeling said—

"What dost thou make of this?"

"Ah, good your worship, require me not to answer. It is not meet that one of my degree should utter the thing."

"Then will *I* utter it. Thou hast the same hair, the same eyes, the same voice and manner, the same form and stature, the same face and countenance, that I bear. Fared we forth naked, there is none could say which was you and which the Prince of Wales. And now that I am clothed as thou wert clothed, it seemeth I should be able the more nearly to feel as thou didst when the brute soldier—harkye, is not this a bruise upon your hand?"

"Yes, but it is a slight thing, and your worship knoweth that the poor man-at-arms—"

"Peace! It was a shameful thing and a cruel!" cried the little prince, stamping his bare foot. "If the king—stir not a step till I come again! It is a command!"

In a moment he had snatched up and put away an article of national importance that lay upon a table, and was out at the door and flying through the palace grounds in his bannered rags, with a hot face and glowing eyes. As soon as he reached the great gate he seized the bars and tried to shake them, shouting:

"Open! Unbar the gates!"

The soldier that had maltreated Tom, obeyed promptly; and as the prince burst through the portal, half smothered with royal wrath, the soldier fetched him a sounding box on the ear that sent him whirling to the roadway, and said:

"Take that, thou beggar's spawn, for what thou got'st me from his highness!"

The crowd roared with laughter. The prince picked himself out of the mud and made fiercely at the sentry, shouting:

"I am the Prince of Wales, my person is sacred; and thou shalt hang for laying thy hand upon me!"

The soldier brought his halberd to a present-arms and said, mockingly:

"I salute your gracious highness." Then angrily: "Be off, thou crazy rubbish!"

Here the jeering crowd closed around the poor little prince and hustled him far down the road, hooting him, and shouting "Way for his royal highness! way for the Prince of Wales!"

Chapter 4

THE PRINCE'S TROUBLES BEGIN

AFTER HOURS of persistent pursuit and persecution, the little prince was at last deserted by the rabble and left to himself. As long as he had been able to rage against the mob, and threaten it royally, and royally utter commands that were good stuff to laugh at, he was very entertaining; but when weariness finally forced him to be silent, he was no longer of use to his tormentors, and they sought amusement elsewhere. He looked about him, now, but could not recognize the locality. He was within the city of London—that was all he knew. He moved on, aimlessly, and in a little while the houses thinned, and the passers-by were infrequent. He bathed his bleeding feet in the brook which flowed then where Farringdon street now is; rested a few moments, then passed on, and presently came upon a great space with only a few scattered houses in it, and a prodigious church. He recognized this church. Scaffoldings were about, everywhere, and swarms of workmen; for it was undergoing elaborate repairs. The prince took heart at once—he felt that his troubles were at an end, now. He said to himself, "It is the ancient Grey Friars' church, which the king my father hath taken from the monks and given for a home forever for poor and forsaken children, and new-named it Christ's Church. Right gladly will they serve the son of him who hath done so generously by them—and the more that that son is himself as poor and as forlorn as any that be sheltered here this day, or ever shall be."

He was soon in the midst of a crowd of boys who were running, jumping, playing at ball and leap-frog, and otherwise disporting themselves, and right noisily, too. They were all dressed alike, and in the fashion which in that day prevailed among serving-men and 'prentices*—that is to say, each had on the crown of his head a flat black cap about the size of a saucer, which was not useful as a covering, it being

*See Note 1, at end of the volume.

of such scanty dimensions, neither was it ornamental; from beneath it the hair fell, unparted, to the middle of the forehead, and was cropped straight around; a clerical band at the neck; a blue gown that fitted closely and hung as low as the knees or lower; full sleeves; a broad red belt; bright yellow stockings, gartered above the knees; low shoes with large metal buckles. It was a sufficiently ugly costume.

The boys stopped their play and flocked about the prince, who said with native dignity—

"Good lads, say to your master that Edward Prince of Wales desireth speech with him."

A great shout went up, at this, and one rude fellow said—

"Marry, art thou his grace's messenger, beggar?"

The Prince's face flushed with anger, and his ready hand flew to his hip, but there was nothing there. There was a storm of laughter, and one boy said—

"Didst mark that? He fancied he had a sword—belike he is the prince himself."

This sally brought more laughter. Poor Edward drew himself up proudly and said—

"I am the prince; and it ill beseemeth you that feed upon the king my father's bounty to use me so."

This was vastly enjoyed, as the laughter testified. The youth who had first spoken, shouted to his comrades—

"Ho, swine, slaves, pensioners of his grace's princely father, where be your manners? Down on your marrow bones, all of ye, and do reverence to his kingly port and royal rags!"

With boisterous mirth they dropped upon their knees in a body and did mock homage to their prey. The prince spurned the nearest boy with his foot, and said fiercely—

"Take thou that, till the morrow come and I build thee a gibbet!"

Ah, but this was not a joke—this was going beyond fun. The laughter ceased on the instant, and fury took its place. A dozen shouted—

"Hale him forth! To the horse-pond, to the horse-pond! Where be the dogs? Ho, there, Lion! ho, Fangs!"

Then followed such a thing as England had never seen before—the sacred person of the heir to the throne rudely buffeted by plebeian hands, and set upon and torn by dogs.

As night drew to a close that day, the prince found himself far down in the close-built portion of the city. His body was bruised, his hands were bleeding, and his rags were all besmirched with mud. He wandered on and on, and grew more and more bewildered, and so tired and faint he could hardly drag one foot after the other. He had ceased to ask questions of any one, since they brought him only insult instead of information. He kept muttering to himself, "Offal Court—that is the name; if I can but find it, before my strength is wholly spent and I drop, then am I saved—for his people will take me to the palace and prove that I am none of theirs, but the true prince, and I shall have mine own again." And now and then his mind reverted to his treatment by those rude Christ's Hospital boys, and he said, "When I am king, they shall not have bread and shelter only, but also teachings out of books; for a full belly is little worth where the mind is starved, and the heart. I will keep this diligently in my remembrance, that this day's lesson be not lost upon me, and my people suffer thereby; for learning softeneth the heart and breedeth gentleness and charity."*

The lights began to twinkle, it came on to rain, the wind rose, and a raw and gusty night set in. The houseless prince, the homeless heir to the throne of England, still moved on, drifting deeper into the maze of squalid alleys where the swarming hives of poverty and misery were massed together.

Suddenly a great drunken ruffian collared him and said—

"Out to this time of night again, and hast not brought a farthing home, I warrant me! If it be so, an' I do not break all the bones in thy lean body, then am I not John Canty, but some other."

The prince twisted himself loose, unconsciously brushed his profaned shoulder, and eagerly said—

"O, art *his* father, truly? Sweet heaven grant it be so—then wilt thou fetch him away and restore me!"

"*His* father? I know not what thou mean'st; I but know I am *thy* father, as thou shalt soon have cause to—"

"O, jest not, palter not, delay not!—I am worn, I am wounded, I can bear no more. Take me to the king my father,

*See Note 2, at end of the volume.

and he will make thee rich beyond thy wildest dreams. Believe me, man, believe me!—I speak no lie, but only the truth!—put forth thy hand and save me!—I am indeed the Prince of Wales!"

The man stared down, stupefied, upon the lad, then shook his head and muttered—

"Gone stark mad as any Tom o' Bedlam!"—then collared him once more, and said with a coarse laugh and an oath, "But mad or no mad, I and thy Gammer Canty will soon find where the soft places in thy bones lie, or I'm no true man!"

With this he dragged the frantic and struggling prince away, and disappeared up a foul court followed by a delighted and noisy swarm of human vermin.

Chapter 5

TOM AS A PATRICIAN

Tom Canty, left alone in the prince's cabinet, made good use of his opportunity. He turned himself this way and that, before the great mirror, admiring his finery; then walked away, imitating the prince's high-bred carriage, and still observing results in the glass. Next he drew the beautiful sword, and bowed, kissing the blade and laying it across his breast, as he had seen a noble knight do, by way of salute to the Lieutenant of the Tower, five or six weeks before, when delivering the great lords of Norfolk and Surrey into his hands for captivity. Tom played with the jeweled dagger that hung upon his thigh; he examined the costly and exquisite ornaments of the room; he tried each of the sumptuous chairs, and thought how proud he would be if the Offal Court herd could only peep in and see him in his grandeur. He wondered if they would believe the marvelous tale he should tell when he got home, or if they would shake their heads and say his overtaxed imagination had at last upset his reason.

At the end of half an hour it suddenly occurred to him that the prince was gone a long time; then right away he began to feel lonely; very soon he fell to listening and longing, and ceased to toy with the pretty things about him; he grew uneasy, then restless, then distressed. Suppose some one should come, and catch him in the prince's clothes, and the prince not there to explain! Might they not hang him at once, and inquire into his case afterward? He had heard that the great were prompt about small matters. His fears rose higher and higher; and trembling he softly opened the door to the antechamber, resolved to fly and seek the prince, and through him protection and release. Six gorgeous gentlemen-servants and two young pages of high degree, clothed like butterflies, sprung to their feet and bowed low before him. He stepped quickly back and shut the door. He said—

"O, they mock at me! They will go and tell! O, why came I here to cast away my life!"

He walked up and down the floor, filled with nameless fears, listening, starting at every trifling sound. Presently the door swung open and a silken page said—

"The lady Jane Grey!"

The door closed, and a sweet young girl, richly clad, bounded toward him. But she stopped suddenly, and said in a distressed voice—

"O, what aileth thee, my lord?"

Tom's breath was nearly failing him, but he made shift to stammer out—

"Ah, be merciful, thou! In sooth I am no lord, but only poor Tom Canty of Offal Court in the City. Prithee let me see the prince, and he will of his grace restore to me my rags and let me hence unhurt. O, be thou merciful and save me!"

By this time the boy was on his knees and supplicating with his eyes and uplifted hands as well as with his tongue. The young girl seemed horror-stricken. She cried out—

"O, my lord, on thy knees?—and to *me!*"

Then she fled away in fright, and Tom, smitten with despair, sank down, murmuring—

"There is no help, there is no hope. Now will they come and take me!"

Whilst he lay there benumbed with terror, dreadful tidings were speeding through the palace. The whisper—for it was whispered always—flew from menial to menial, from lord to lady, down all the long corridors, from story to story, from saloon to saloon: "The prince hath gone mad, the prince hath gone mad!" Soon every saloon, every marble hall, had its groups of glittering lords and ladies, and other groups of dazzling lesser folk, talking earnestly together, in whispers, and every face had in it dismay. Presently a splendid official came marching by these groups, making solemn proclamation—

"IN THE NAME OF THE KING! Let none list to this false and foolish matter, upon pain of death; nor discuss the same nor carry it abroad. In the name of the king!"

The whispering ceased as suddenly as if the whisperers had been stricken dumb.

Soon there was a general buzz along the corridors, of "The prince! See—the prince comes!"

Poor Tom came slowly walking past the low-bowing groups, trying to bow in return, and meekly gazing upon his strange surroundings with bewildered and pathetic eyes. Great nobles walked upon each side of him, making him lean upon them, and so steady his steps. Behind him followed the court physicians and some servants.

Presently Tom found himself in a noble apartment of the palace, and heard the door close behind him. Around him stood those who had come with him. Before him, at a little distance, reclined a very large and very fat man, with a wide, pulpy face, and a stern expression. His large head was very gray, and his whiskers, which he wore only around his face,— like a frame,—were gray also. His clothing was of rich stuff, but old, and slightly frayed in places. One of his swollen legs had a pillow under it and was wrapped in bandages. There was silence now; and there was no head there but was bent in reverence, except this man's. This stern-countenanced invalid was the dread Henry VIII. He said—and his face grew gentle as he began to speak,—

"How now, my lord Edward, my prince?—Hast been minded to cozen me, the good king thy father, who loveth thee and kindly useth thee, with a sorry jest?"

Poor Tom was listening as well as his dazed faculties would let him, to the beginning of this speech; but when the words "me, the good king" fell upon his ear, his face blanched and he dropped as instantly upon his knees, as if a shot had brought him there. Lifting up his hands, he exclaimed,—

"Thou the *king*? Then am I undone indeed!"

This speech seemed to stun the king. His eyes wandered from face to face, aimlessly, then rested, bewildered, upon the boy before him. Then he said in a tone of deep disappointment—

"Alack, I had believed the rumor disproportioned to the truth, but I fear me 'tis not so." He breathed a heavy sigh, and said in a gentle voice—"Come to thy father, child, thou art not well."

Tom was assisted to his feet, and approached the majesty of England, humble and trembling. The king took the frightened face between his hands, and gazed earnestly and lovingly into it a while, as if seeking some grateful sign of returning reason there, then pressed the curly head against his breast and patted it tenderly. Presently he said—

"Dost not know thy father, child? Break not mine old heart—say thou know'st me. Thou *dost* know me, dost thou not?"

"Yea, thou art my dread lord the king, whom God preserve!"

"True, true—that is well—be comforted, tremble not so; there is none here would hurt thee; there is none here but loves thee. Thou art better, now; thy ill dream passeth—is't not so? And thou knowest thyself now, also—is't not so? Thou wilt not miscall thyself again, as they say thou didst a little while agone?"

"I pray thee of thy grace believe me, I did but speak the truth, most dread lord, for I am the meanest among thy subjects, being a pauper born, and 'tis by a sore mischance and accident I am here, albeit I was therein nothing blameful. I am but young to die—and thou canst save me with one little word—O speak it, sir!"

"Die? Talk not so, sweet prince—peace, peace to thy troubled heart—thou shalt not die!"

Tom dropped upon his knees, with a glad cry,—

"God requite thy mercy, oh, my king, and save thee long to bless thy land!" Then springing up, he turned a joyful face toward the two lords in waiting and exclaimed, "Thou heard'st it! I am not to die—the king hath said it!" There was no movement, save that all bowed, with grave respect—but no one spoke. He hesitated, a little confused, then turned timidly toward the king, saying, "I may go now?"

"Go? Surely—if thou desirest. But why not tarry yet a little? Whither wouldst go?"

Tom dropped his eyes and answered humbly—

"Peradventure I mistook, but I did think me free—and so was I moved to seek again the kennel where I was born and bred to misery, yet which harboreth my mother and my sisters, and so is home to me, whereas these pomps and splendors whereunto I am not used,—oh, please you sir, to let me go!"

The king was silent and thoughtful a while, and his face betrayed a growing distress and uneasiness. Presently he said, with something of hope in his voice—

"Perchance he is but mad upon this one strain, and hath his wits unmarred as toucheth other matters. God send it may be so! We will make trial."

Then he asked Tom a question in Latin, and Tom answered him lamely in the same tongue. The king was delighted, and showed it. The lords and doctors manifested their gratification also. The king said—

" 'Twas not according to his schooling and ability, but sheweth that his mind is but diseased, not stricken fatally. How say you, sir?"

The physician addressed bowed low and replied—

"It jumpeth with mine own conviction, sire, that thou hast divined aright."

The king looked pleased with this encouragement, coming as it did from so excellent authority, and continued with good heart—

"Now mark ye all—we will try him further."

He put a question to Tom in French. Tom stood silent a moment, embarrassed by having so many eyes centred upon him, then said, diffidently—

"I have no knowledge of this tongue, so please your majesty."

The king fell back upon his couch; the attendants flew to his assistance. But he put them aside and said—

"Trouble me not—it is nothing but a scurvy faintness. Raise me!—there, 'tis sufficient. Come hither, child; there, rest thy poor troubled head upon thy father's heart and be at peace. Thou'lt soon be well—'tis but a passing fantasy—fear thou not; thou'lt soon be well." Then he turned toward the company; his gentle manner changed, and baleful lightnings began to play from his eyes. He said—

"List ye all! This my son is mad—but it is not permanent. Over-study hath done this, and somewhat too much of confinement. Away with his books and teachers—see ye to it! Pleasure him with sports, beguile him in wholesome ways, so that his health come again." He raised himself higher still, and went on, with energy: "He is mad, but he is my son and England's heir—and mad or sane, still shall he reign! And hear ye further and proclaim it—whoso speaketh of this his distemper, worketh against the peace and order of these realms, and shall to the gallows! . . . . . . Give me to drink—I burn; this sorrow sappeth my strength. . . . . . . There, take away the cup. . . . . . Support me—there, that is well. Mad, is he? Were he a thousand times mad, yet is he Prince of Wales, and I the king will confirm it. This very morrow shall he be installed in his princely dignity, in due and ancient form. Take instant order for it, my lord Hertford."

One of the nobles knelt at the royal couch and said—

"The king's majesty knoweth that the Hereditary Great Marshal of England lieth attainted in the Tower. It were not meet that one attainted—"

"Peace! Insult not mine ears with his hated name! Is this man to live forever? Am I to be balked of my will? is the prince to tarry uninstalled because, forsooth, the realm lacketh an earl marshal free of treasonable taint to invest him with his honors? No, by the splendor of God! Warn my parliament to bring me Norfolk's doom before the sun rise again, else shall they answer for it grievously!"*

Lord Hertford said—

"The king's will is law;" and rising, returned to his former place.

Gradually the wrath faded out of the old king's face, and he said—

"Kiss me, my prince. There . . . . what fearest thou? Am I not thy loving father?"

"Thou art good to me, that am unworthy, oh, mighty and gracious lord—that in truth I know. But—but—it grieveth me to think of him that is to die, and—"

"Ah, 'tis like thee, 'tis like thee!—I know thy heart is still the same, even though thy mind hath suffered hurt—for thou wert ever of a gentle spirit. But this duke standeth between thee and thine honors; I will have another in his stead, that shall bring no taint to his great office. Comfort thee, my prince—trouble not thy poor head with this matter."

*See Note 3 at end of volume.

"But is it not I that speed him hence, my liege? How long might he not live, but for me?"

"Take no thought of him, my prince, he is not worthy. Kiss me once again and go to thy trifles and amusements, for my malady distresseth me, I am aweary and would rest. Go with thine uncle Hertford and thy people, and come again when my body is refreshed."

Tom, heavy-hearted, was conducted from the presence, for this last sentence was a death-blow to the hope he had cherished that now he would be set free. Once more he heard the buzz of low voices exclaiming, "The prince!—the prince comes!"

His spirits sank lower and lower as he moved between the glittering files of bowing courtiers, for he recognized that he was indeed a captive, now, and might remain forever shut up in this gilded cage, a forlorn and friendless prince, except God in his mercy take pity on him and set him free.

And turn where he would, he seemed to see, floating in the air, the severed head and the remembered face of the great Duke of Norfolk, the eyes fixed on him reproachfully.

His old dreams had been so pleasant; but this reality was so dreary!

Chapter 6

TOM RECEIVES INSTRUCTIONS

T OM WAS CONDUCTED to the principal apartment of a
noble suite, and made to sit down—a thing which he
was loth to do, since there were elderly men and men of high
degree about him. He begged them to be seated, also, but
they only bowed their thanks or murmured them, and remained standing. He would have insisted, but his "uncle" the
Earl of Hertford whispered in his ear—

"Prithee, insist not, my lord; it is not meet that they sit in
thy presence."

The lord St. John was announced, and after making obeisance to Tom, he said—

"I come upon the king's errand, concerning a matter which
requireth privacy. Will it please your royal highness to dismiss
all that attend you here, save my lord the Earl of Hertford?"

Observing that Tom did not seem to know how to proceed,
Hertford whispered him to make a sign with his hand and
not trouble himself to speak unless he chose. When the waiting gentlemen had retired, lord St. John said—

"His majesty commandeth, that for due and weighty reasons of state, the prince's grace shall hide his infirmity in all
ways that be within his power, till it be passed and he be as he
was before. To wit, that he shall deny to none that he is the
true prince, and heir to England's greatness; that he shall up-
hold his princely dignity, and shall receive, without word or
sign of protest, that reverence and observance which unto it
do appertain of right and ancient usage; that he shall cease to
speak to any of that lowly birth and life his malady hath conjured out of the unwholesome imaginings of o'erwrought
fancy; that he shall strive with diligence to bring unto his
memory again those faces which he was wont to know—and
where he faileth, he shall hold his peace, neither betraying by
semblance of surprise, or other sign, that he hath forgot; that
upon occasions of state, whensoever any matter shall perplex
him as to the thing he should do or the utterance he should

make, he shall show naught of unrest to the curious that look on, but take advice in that matter of the lord Hertford or my humble self, which are commanded of the king to be upon this service and close at call, till this commandment be dissolved. Thus saith the king's majesty, who sendeth greeting to your royal highness and prayeth that God will of His mercy quickly heal you and have you now and ever in His holy keeping."

The lord St. John made reverence and stood aside. Tom replied, resignedly—

"The king hath said it. None may palter with the king's command, or fit it to his ease, where it doth chafe, with deft evasions. The king shall be obeyed."

Lord Hertford said—

"Touching the king's majesty's ordainment concerning books and such like serious matters, it may peradventure please your highness to ease your time with lightsome entertainment, lest you go wearied to the banquet and suffer harm thereby."

Tom's face showed inquiring surprise; and a blush followed when he saw lord St. John's eyes bent sorrowfully upon him. His lordship said—

"Thy memory still wrongeth thee, and thou hast shown surprise—but suffer it not to trouble thee, for 'tis a matter that will not bide, but depart with thy mending malady. My lord of Hertford speaketh of the city's banquet which the king's majesty did promise, some two months flown, your highness should attend. Thou recallest it now?"

"It grieves me to confess it had indeed escaped me," said Tom, in a hesitating voice; and blushed again.

At this moment the lady Elizabeth and the lady Jane Grey were announced. The two lords exchanged significant glances, and Hertford stepped quickly toward the door. As the young girls passed him, he said in a low voice—

"I pray ye, ladies, seem not to observe his humors, nor show surprise when his memory doth lapse—it will grieve you to note how it doth stick at every trifle."

Meantime lord St. John was saying in Tom's ear—

"Please you sir, keep diligently in mind his majesty's desire. Remember all thou canst—*seem* to remember all else. Let them not perceive that thou art much changed from thy wont, for thou knowest how tenderly thy old playfellows bear thee in their hearts and how 'twould grieve them. Art willing, sir, that I remain?—and thine uncle?"

Tom signified assent with a gesture and a murmured word, for he was already learning, and in his simple heart was resolved to acquit himself as best he might, according to the king's command.

In spite of every precaution, the conversation among the young people became a little embarrassing, at times. More than once, in truth, Tom was near to breaking down and confessing himself unequal to his tremendous part; but the tact of the princess Elizabeth saved him, or a word from one or the other of the vigilant lords, thrown in apparently by chance, had the same happy effect. Once the little lady Jane turned to Tom and dismayed him with this question,—

"Hast paid thy duty to the queen's majesty to-day, my lord?"

Tom hesitated, looked distressed, and was about to stammer out something at hazard, when lord St. John took the word and answered for him with the easy grace of a courtier accustomed to encounter delicate difficulties and to be ready for them—

"He hath indeed, madam, and she did greatly hearten him, as touching his majesty's condition, is it not so, your highness?"

Tom mumbled something that stood for assent, but felt that he was getting upon dangerous ground. Somewhat later it was mentioned that Tom was to study no more at present, whereupon her little ladyship exclaimed—

" 'Tis a pity, 'tis such a pity! Thou wert proceeding bravely. But bide thy time in patience; it will not be for long. Thou'lt yet be graced with learning like thy father, and make thy tongue master of as many languages as his, good my prince."

"My father!" cried Tom, off his guard for the moment. "I trow he cannot speak his own so that any but the swine that wallow in the styes may tell his meaning; and as for learning of any sort soever—" He looked up and encountered a solemn warning in my lord St. John's eyes. He stopped, blushed, then continued low and sadly: "Ah, my malady persecuteth me again, and my mind wandereth. I meant the king's grace no irreverence."

"We know it, sir," said the princess Elizabeth, taking her "brother's" hand between her two palms, respectfully but caressingly; "trouble not thyself as to that. The fault is none of thine, but thy distemper's."

"Thou'rt a gentle comforter, sweet lady," said Tom, gratefully, "and my heart moveth me to thank thee for't, an' I may be so bold."

Once the giddy little lady Jane fired a simple Greek phrase at Tom. The princess Elizabeth's quick eye saw by the serene blankness of the target's front that the shaft was overshot; so she tranquilly delivered a return volley of sounding Greek on Tom's behalf, and then straightway changed the talk to other matters.

Time wore on pleasantly, and likewise smoothly, on the whole. Snags and sandbars grew less and less frequent, and Tom grew more and more at his ease, seeing that all were so lovingly bent upon helping him and overlooking his mistakes. When it came out that the little ladies were to accompany him to the Lord Mayor's banquet in the evening, his heart gave a bound of relief and delight, for he felt that he should not be friendless, now, among that multitude of strangers; whereas, an hour earlier, the idea of their going with him would have been an insupportable terror to him.

Tom's guardian angels, the two lords, had had less comfort in the interview than the other parties to it. They felt much as if they were piloting a great ship through a dangerous channel; they were on the alert, constantly, and found their office no child's play. Wherefore, at last, when the ladies' visit was drawing to a close and the lord Guilford Dudley was announced, they not only felt that their charge had been sufficiently taxed for the present, but also that they themselves were not in the best condition to take their ship back and make that anxious voyage all over again. So they respectfully advised Tom to excuse himself, which he was very glad to do, although a slight shade of disappointment might have been observed upon my lady Jane's face when she heard the splendid stripling denied admittance.

There was a pause, now, a sort of waiting silence which

Tom could not understand. He glanced at lord Hertford, who gave him a sign—but he failed to understand that, also. The ready Elizabeth came to the rescue with her usual easy grace. She made reverence and said—

"Have we leave of the prince's grace my brother to go?"

Tom said—

"Indeed your ladyships can have whatsoever of me they will, for the asking; yet would I rather give them any other thing that in my poor power lieth, than leave to take the light and blessing of their presence hence. Give ye good den, and God be with ye!" Then he smiled inwardly at the thought, "'Tis not for naught I have dwelt but among princes in my reading, and taught my tongue some slight trick of their broidered and gracious speech withal!"

When the illustrious maidens were gone, Tom turned wearily to his keepers and said—

"May it please your lordships to grant me leave to go into some corner and rest me?"

Lord Hertford said—

"So please your highness, it is for you to command, it is for us to obey. That thou shouldst rest, is indeed a needful thing, since thou must journey to the city presently."

He touched a bell, and a page appeared, who was ordered to desire the presence of Sir William Herbert. This gentleman came straightway, and conducted Tom to an inner apartment. Tom's first movement, there, was to reach for a cup of water; but a silk-and-velvet servitor seized it, dropped upon one knee, and offered it to him on a golden salver. Next the tired captive sat down and was going to take off his buskins, timidly asking leave with his eye, but another silk-and-velvet discomforter went down upon his knees and took the office from him. He made two or three further efforts to help himself, but being promptly forestalled each time, he finally gave up, with a sigh of resignation and a murmured "Beshrew me but I marvel they do not require to breathe for me, also!" Slippered, and wrapped in a sumptuous robe, he laid himself down at last to rest, but not to sleep, for his head was too full of thoughts and the room too full of people. He could not dismiss the former, so they staid; he did not know enough to dismiss the latter, so they staid also, to his vast regret,—and theirs.

Tom's departure had left his two noble guardians alone. They mused a while, with much head-shaking and walking the floor, then lord St. John said—

"Plainly, what dost thou think?"

"Plainly, then, this. The king is near his end, my nephew is mad, mad will mount the throne, and mad remain. God protect England, since she will need it!"

"Verily it promiseth so, indeed. But . . . . have you no misgivings as to . . . . as to . . . ."

The speaker hesitated, and finally stopped. He evidently felt that he was upon delicate ground. Lord Hertford stopped before him, looked into his face with a clear, frank eye, and said—

"Speak on—there is none to hear but me. Misgivings as to what?"

"I am full loth to word the thing that is in my mind, and thou so near to him in blood, my lord. But craving pardon if I do offend, seemeth it not strange that madness could so change his port and manner!—not but that his port and speech are princely still, but that they *differ*, in one unweighty trifle or another, from what his custom was aforetime. Seemeth it not strange that madness should filch from his memory his father's very lineaments, the customs and observances that are his due from such as be about him, and leaving him his Latin strip him of his Greek and French? My lord, be not offended, but ease my mind of its disquiet and receive my grateful thanks. It haunteth me, his saying he was not the prince, and so—"

"Peace, my lord, thou utterest treason! Hast forgot the king's command? Remember I am party to thy crime, if I but listen."

St. John paled, and hastened to say—

"I was in fault. I do confess it. Betray me not, grant me this grace out of thy courtesy, and I will neither think nor speak of this thing more. Deal not hardly with me, sir, else am I ruined."

"I am content, my lord. So thou offend not again, here or in the ear of others, it shall be as though thou hadst not spoken. But thou needst not have misgivings. He is my sister's son; are not his voice, his face, his form, familiar to me from his cradle? Madness can do all the odd conflicting things thou seest in him, and more. Dost not recal how that the old Baron Marley, being mad, forgot the favor of his own countenance that he had known for sixty years, and held it was another's; nay, even claimed he was the son of Mary Magdalene, and that his head was made of Spanish glass; and sooth to say, he suffered none to touch it, lest by mischance some heedless hand might shiver it. Give thy misgivings easement, good my lord. This is the very prince, I know him well—and soon will be thy king; it may advantage thee to bear this in mind and more dwell upon it than the other."

After some further talk, in which the lord St. John covered up his mistake as well as he could by repeated protests that his faith was thoroughly grounded, now, and could not be assailed by doubts again, the lord Hertford relieved his fellow keeper and sat down to keep watch and ward alone. He was soon deep in meditation. And evidently, the longer he thought, the more he was bothered. By and by he began to pace the floor and mutter.

"Tush, he *must* be the prince! Will any he in all the land maintain there can be two, not of one blood and birth, so marvelously twinned? And even were it so, 'twere yet a stranger miracle that chance should cast the one into the other's place. Nay, 'tis folly, folly, folly!"

Presently he said:

"Now were he impostor and called himself prince, look you *that* would be natural; that would be reasonable. But lived ever an impostor yet, who, being called prince by the king, prince by the court, prince by all, *denied* his dignity and pleaded against his exaltation?—*No!* By the soul of St. Swithin, no! This is the true prince, gone mad!"

Chapter 7

TOM'S FIRST ROYAL DINNER

SOMEWHAT AFTER ONE in the afternoon, Tom resignedly underwent the ordeal of being dressed for dinner. He found himself as finely clothed as before, but everything different, everything changed, from his ruff to his stockings. He was presently conducted with much state to a spacious and ornate apartment where a table was already set—for one. Its furniture was all of massy gold, and beautified with designs which well nigh made it priceless, since they were the work of Benvenuto. The room was half filled with noble servitors. A chaplain said grace, and Tom was about to fall to, for hunger had long been constitutional with him, but was interrupted by my lord the Earl of Berkeley, who fastened a napkin about his neck—for the great post of Diaperers to the Princes of Wales was hereditary in this nobleman's family. Tom's cup-bearer was present and forestalled all his attempts to help himself to wine. The Taster to his highness the Prince of Wales was there, also, prepared to taste any suspicious dish upon requirement, and run the risk of being poisoned. He was only an ornamental appendage, at this time, and was seldom called upon to exercise his function; but there had been times, not many generations past, when the office of Taster had its perils, and was not a grandeur to be desired. Why they did not use a dog or a plumber seems strange; but all the ways of royalty are strange. My lord d'Arcy, First Groom of the Chamber, was there, to do goodness knows what—but there he was—let that suffice. The Lord Chief Butler was there, and stood behind Tom's chair, overseeing the solemnities, under command of the Lord Great Steward and the Lord Head Cook, who stood near. Tom had three hundred and eighty-four servants beside these, but they were not all in that room, of course, nor the quarter of them; neither was Tom aware, yet, that they existed.

All those that were present had been well drilled, within the hour, to remember that the prince was temporarily out of his

41

head, and to be careful to show no surprise at his vagaries. These "vagaries" were soon on exhibition before them; but they only moved their compassion and their sorrow, not their mirth. It was a heavy affliction to them to see the beloved prince so stricken.

Poor Tom ate with his fingers, mainly; but no one smiled at it, or even seemed to observe it. He inspected his napkin curiously, and with deep interest, for it was of a very dainty and beautiful fabric—then said, with simplicity—

"Prithee take it away, lest in mine unheedfulness it be soiled."

The Hereditary Diaperer took it away, with reverent manner, and without word or protest of any sort.

Tom examined the turnips and the lettuce with interest, and asked what they were, and if they were to be eaten; for it was only recently that men had begun to raise these things in England, in place of importing them as luxuries from Holland.* His question was answered with grave respect, and no surprise manifested. When he had finished his dessert, he filled his pockets with nuts, but nobody appeared to be aware of it or disturbed by it. But the next moment he was himself disturbed by it and showed discomposure; for this was the only service he had been permitted to do with his own hands during the meal, and he did not doubt that he had done a most improper and unprincely thing. At that moment the muscles of his nose began to twitch and the end of that organ to lift and wrinkle. This continued, and Tom began to evince a growing distress. He looked appealingly, first at one and then another of the lords about him, and tears came into his eyes. They sprang forward with dismay in their faces, and begged to know his trouble. Tom said with genuine anguish—

"I crave your indulgence—my nose itcheth cruelly! What is the custom and usage in this emergence? Prithee speed, for 'tis but a little time that I can bear it."

None smiled, but all were sore perplexed, and looked one to the other in deep tribulation for counsel. But behold, here was a dead wall, and nothing in English history to tell how to get over it. The Master of Ceremonies was not present; there

---

*See Note 4, at end of volume.

was no one who felt safe to venture upon this uncharted sea, or risk the attempt to solve this solemn problem. Alas, there was no Hereditary Scratcher! Meantime the tears had overflowed their banks and begun to trickle down Tom's cheeks. His twitching nose was pleading more urgently than ever for relief. At last nature broke down the barriers of etiquette—Tom lifted up an inward prayer for pardon if he was doing wrong, and brought relief to the burdened hearts of his court by scratching his nose himself.

His meal being ended, a lord came and held before him a broad shallow golden dish with fragrant rose-water in it, to cleanse his mouth and fingers with, and my lord the Hereditary Diaperer stood by with a napkin for his use. Tom gazed at the dish a puzzled moment or two, then raised it to his lips and gravely took a draught. Then he returned it to the waiting lord and said—

"Nay, it likes me not, my lord; it hath a pretty flavor, but it wanteth strength."

This new eccentricity of the prince's ruined mind made all the hearts about him ache, but the sad sight moved none to merriment.

Tom's next unconscious blunder was to get up and leave the table just when the chaplain had taken his stand behind his chair, and with uplifted hands, and closed, uplifted eyes, was in the act of beginning the blessing. Still nobody seemed to perceive that the prince had done a thing unusual.

By his own request, our small friend was now conducted to his private cabinet and left there alone, to his own devices. Hanging upon hooks in the oaken wainscoting, were the several pieces of a suit of shining steel armor, covered all over with beautiful designs, exquisitely inlaid in gold. This martial panoply belonged to the true prince—a recent present from Madam Parr the queen. Tom put on the greaves, the gauntlets, the plumed helmet, and such other pieces as he could don without assistance; and for a while was minded to call for help and complete the matter, but bethought him of the nuts he had brought away from dinner and the joy it would be to eat them with no crowd to eye him and no Grand Hereditaries to pester him with undesired services; so he restored the pretty things to their several places, and soon was cracking nuts and feeling almost naturally happy, for the first time since God for his sins had made him a prince. When the nuts were all gone, he stumbled upon some inviting books in a closet—among them one about the etiquette of the English court. This was a prize. He lay down upon a sumptuous divan and proceeded to instruct himself, with honest zeal. Let us leave him there, for the present.

Chapter 8

The Question of the Seal

About five o'clock Henry VIII awoke out of an un-refreshing nap, and muttered to himself, "Troublous dreams, troublous dreams! Mine end is now at hand—so say these warnings, and my failing pulses do confirm it." Presently a wicked light flamed up in his eye, and he muttered, "Yet will not I die till *he* go before!"

His attendants perceiving that he was awake, one of them asked his pleasure concerning the Lord Chancellor, who was waiting without.

"Admit him! admit him!" exclaimed the king, eagerly.

The Lord Chancellor entered and knelt by the king's couch, saying—

"I have given order, and according to the king's command, the peers of the realm, in their robes, do now stand at the bar of the House; where, having confirmed the Duke of Norfolk's doom, they humbly wait his majesty's further pleasure in the matter."

The king's face lit up with a fierce joy. Said he—

"Lift me up! In mine own person will I go before my parliament, and with mine own hand will I seal the warrant that rids me of—"

His voice failed, an ashen pallor swept the flush from his cheeks, and the attendants eased him back upon his pillows and hurriedly assisted him with restoratives. Presently he said, sorrowfully—

"Alack, how have I longed for this sweet hour, and lo, too late it cometh and I am robbed of this so coveted chance! But speed ye, speed ye, let others do this happy office sith 'tis denied to me. I put my Great Seal in commission—choose thou the lords that shall compose it—and get ye to your work. Speed ye, man! Before the sun shall rise and set again, bring me his head that I may see it!"

"According to the king's command, so shall it be. Will't

please your majesty to order that the Seal be now restored to me, so that I may forth upon the business?"

"The Seal? Who keepeth the Seal but thou?"

"Please your majesty, you did take it from me two days since, saying it should no more do its office till your own royal hand should use it upon the Duke of Norfolk's warrant."

"Why so in sooth I did; I do remember it. . . . . . . What did I with it? . . . . I am very feeble. . . . . So oft, these days, doth my memory play the traitor with me. . . . . 'Tis strange—strange—"

The king dropped into inarticulate mumblings, shaking his gray head weakly, from time to time, and gropingly trying to recollect what he had done with the Seal. At last my lord Hertford ventured to kneel and offer information,—

"Sire, if that I may be so bold, here be several that do remember, with me, how that you gave the Great Seal into the hands of his highness the Prince of Wales to keep against the day that—"

"True, most true!" interrupted the king. "Fetch it! Go—time flieth!"

Lord Hertford flew to Tom; but returned to the king before very long, troubled and empty handed. He delivered himself to this effect—

"It grieveth me, my lord the king, to bear so heavy and unwelcome tidings, but it is the will of God that the prince's affliction abideth still, and he cannot recal to mind that he received the Seal. So came I quickly to report, thinking it were waste of precious time, and little worth, withal, that any should attempt to search the long array of chambers and saloons that belong unto his royal high—"

A groan from the king interrupted my lord at this point. After a little while his majesty said, with a deep sadness in his tone—

"Trouble him no more, poor child. The hand of God lieth heavy upon him, and my heart goeth out in loving compassion for him and sorrow that I may not bear his burden on mine own old trouble-weighted shoulders and so bring him peace."

He closed his eyes, fell to mumbling, and presently was

silent. After a time he opened his eyes again, and gazed vacantly around until his glance rested upon the kneeling Lord Chancellor. Instantly his face flushed with wrath,—

"What, thou here yet! By the glory of God, an' thou gettest not about that traitor's business, thy mitre shall have holiday the morrow, for lack of a head to grace, withal!"

The trembling Chancellor answered—

"Good your majesty, I cry you mercy! I but waited for the Seal."

"Man, hast lost thy wits? The small Seal which aforetime I was wont to take with me abroad, lieth in my treasury. And since the Great Seal hath flown away, shall not it suffice? Hast lost thy wits? Begone! And harkye—come no more till thou do bring his head!"

The poor Chancellor was not long in removing himself from this dangerous vicinity; nor did the Commission waste time in giving the royal assent to the work of the slavish parliament and appointing the morrow for the beheading of the premier peer of England, the luckless Duke of Norfolk.*

*See Note 5 at end of volume.

Chapter 9

THE RIVER PAGEANT

At nine in the evening the whole vast river-front of the palace was blazing with light. The river itself, as far as the eye could reach, citywards, was so thickly covered with watermen's boats and with pleasure-barges, all fringed with colored lanterns, and gently agitated by the waves, that it resembled a glowing and limitless garden of flowers stirred to soft motion by summer winds. The grand terrace of stone steps leading down to the water—spacious enough to mass the army of a German principality upon—was a picture to see, with its ranks of royal halberdiers in polished armor, and its troops of brilliantly costumed servitors flitting up and down and to and fro in the hurry of preparation.

Presently a command was given, and immediately all living creatures vanished from the steps. Now the air was heavy with the hush of suspense and expectancy. As far as one's vision could carry, he might see the myriads of people in the boats rise up and shade their eyes from the glare of lanterns and torches, and gaze toward the palace.

A file of forty or fifty state barges drew up to the steps. They were richly gilt, and their lofty prows and sterns were elaborately carved. Some of them were decorated with banners and streamers; some with cloth of gold and arras, embroidered with coats of arms; others with silken flags that had numberless little silver bells fastened to them which shook out tiny showers of joyous music whenever the breezes fluttered them; others, of yet higher pretensions, since they belonged to nobles in the prince's immediate service, had their sides picturesquely fenced with shields gorgeously emblazoned with armorial bearings. Each state barge was towed by a tender; besides the rowers, these tenders carried each a number of men-at-arms in glossy helmet and breast-plate, and a company of musicians.

The advance-guard of the expected procession now appeared in the great gateway, a troop of halberdiers. "They were dressed in striped hose of black and tawny, velvet caps graced at the sides with silver roses, and doublets of murrey and blue cloth, embroidered on the front and back with the Three Feathers, the prince's blazon, woven in gold. Their halberd staves were covered with crimson velvet, fastened with gilt nails and ornamented with gold tassels. Filing off on the right and left, they formed two long lines, extending from the gateway of the palace to the water's edge. A thick rayed cloth or carpet was then unfolded and laid down between them by attendants in the gold and crimson liveries of the prince. This done, a flourish of trumpets resounded from within; a lively prelude arose from the musicians on the water; and two ushers with white wands marched with a slow and stately pace from the portal. They were followed by an officer bearing the civic mace; after whom came another, carrying the City's Sword; then several sergeants of the city guard, in their full accoutrements and with badges on their sleeves; then the Garter King-at-Arms in his tabard; then several knights of the Bath, each with a white lace on his sleeve; then their esquires; then the judges, in their robes of scarlet and coifs; then the lord high chancellor of England, in a robe of scarlet open before and purfled with minever; then a deputation of aldermen, in their scarlet cloaks; and then the heads of the different civic companies, in their robes of state. Now came twelve French gentlemen, in splendid habiliments, consisting of pourpoints of white damask, barred with gold, short mantles of crimson velvet, lined with violet taffeta, and carnation-colored hauts-de-chausses, and took their way down the steps. They were of the suite of the French ambassador, and were followed by twelve cavaliers of the suite of the Spanish ambassador, clothed in black velvet, unrelieved by any ornament. Following these came several great English nobles, with their attendants."

There was a flourish of trumpets within, and the prince's uncle the future great Duke of Somerset, emerged from the gateway, arrayed in a "doublet of black cloth of gold, and a cloak of crimson satin flowered with gold and ribanded with nets of silver." He turned, doffed his plumed cap, bent his body in a low reverence, and began to step backward, bowing at each step. A prolonged trumpet-blast followed, and a proclamation, "Way for the high and mighty, the lord Edward, Prince of Wales!"—high aloft on the palace walls a long line of red tongues of flame leaped forth, with a thunder-crash; the massed world on the river burst into a mighty roar of welcome, and Tom Canty, the cause and hero of it all, stepped into view and slightly bowed his princely head!

He was "magnificently habited in a doublet of white satin, with a front-piece of purple cloth of tissue, powdered with diamonds and edged with ermine. Over this he wore a mantle of white cloth of gold, pounced with the triple-feather crest, lined with blue satin, set with pearls and precious stones, and fastened with a clasp of brilliants. About his neck hung the order of the Garter and several princely foreign orders," and wherever light fell upon him, jewels responded with a blinding flash. O, Tom Canty, born in a hovel, bred in the gutters of London, familiar with rags and dirt and misery, what a spectacle is this!

Chapter 10

THE PRINCE IN THE TOILS

W E LEFT John Canty dragging the rightful prince into Offal Court, with a noisy and delighted mob at his heels. There was but one person in it who offered a pleading word for the captive, and he was not heeded; he was hardly even heard, so great was the turmoil. The prince continued to struggle for freedom and to rage against the treatment he was suffering, until John Canty lost what little patience was left in him, and raised his oaken cudgel in a sudden fury over the prince's head. The single pleader for the lad sprang to stop the man's arm, and the blow descended upon his own wrist. Canty roared out—

"Thou'lt meddle, wilt thou? Then have thy reward!"

His cudgel crashed down upon the meddler's head; there was a groan, a dim form sank to the ground among the feet of the crowd, and the next moment it lay there in the dark, alone. The mob pressed on, their enjoyment nothing disturbed by this episode.

Presently the prince found himself in John Canty's abode, with the door closed against the outsiders. By the vague light of a tallow candle which was thrust into a bottle, he made out the main features of the loathsome den, and also the occupants of it. Two frowsy girls and a middle-aged woman cowered against the wall, in one corner, with the aspect of animals habituated to harsh usage and expecting and dreading it now. From another corner stole a withered hag with streaming gray hair and malignant eyes. John Canty said to this one—

"Tarry! There's fine mummeries here. Mar them not till thou'st enjoyed them; then let thy hand be heavy as thou wilt. Stand forth lad. Now say thy foolery again an' thou'st not forget it. Name thy name. Who art thou?"

The insulted blood mounted to the little prince's cheek once more, and he lifted a steady and indignant gaze to the man's face and said—

"'Tis but ill breeding in such as thou to command me to speak. I tell thee now, as I told thee before, I am Edward Prince of Wales, and none other."

The stunning surprise of this reply nailed the hag's feet to the floor where she stood, and almost took her breath. She stared at the prince in stupid amazement, which so amused her ruffianly son that he burst into a roar of laughter. But the effect upon Tom Canty's mother and sisters was different. Their dread of bodily injury gave way at once to distress of a different sort. They ran forward with woe and dismay in their faces, exclaiming—

"0, poor Tom, poor lad!"

The mother fell on her knees before the prince, put her hands upon his shoulders, and gazed yearningly into his face through her rising tears. Then she said—

"0, my poor boy, thy foolish reading hath wrought its woful work at last and ta'en thy wit away! Ah, why didst thou cleave to it, when I so warned thee 'gainst it? Thou'st broke thy mother's heart!"

The prince looked into her face and said gently—

"Thy son is well, and hath not lost his wits, good dame. Comfort thee; let me to the palace where he is, and straightway will the king my father restore him to thee."

"The king thy father! O, my child, unsay these words, that be freighted with death for thee, and ruin for all that be near to thee. Shake off this grewsome dream. Call back thy poor wandering memory. Look upon me. Am not I thy mother that bore thee and loveth thee?"

The prince shook his head, and reluctantly said—

"God knoweth I am loth to grieve thy heart, but truly have I never looked upon thy face before."

The woman sank back to a sitting posture on the floor, and covering her eyes with her hands, gave way to heart-broken sobs and wailings.

"Let the show go on!" shouted Canty. "What, Nan! what, Bet! Mannerless wenches, will ye stand in the prince's presence? Upon your knees, ye pauper scum, and do him reverence!"

He followed this with another horse-laugh. The girls began to plead timidly for their brother, and Nan said—

"An' thou wilt but let him to bed, father, rest and sleep will heal his madness—prithee, do!"

"Do, father," said Bet, "he is more worn than is his wont. Tomorrow will he be himself again, and will beg with diligence and come not empty home again."

This remark sobered the father's joviality and brought his mind to business. He turned angrily upon the prince and said—

"The morrow must we pay two pennies to him that owns this hole—two pennies, mark ye—all this money for a half-year's rent, else out of this we go. Show what thou'st gathered, with thy lazy begging!"

The prince said—

"Offend me not with thy sordid matters. I tell thee again I am the king's son."

A sounding blow upon the prince's shoulder from Canty's broad palm, sent him staggering into Goodwife Canty's arms, who clasped him to her breast and sheltered him from a pelting rain of cuffs and slaps by interposing her own person. The frightened girls retreated to their corner, but the grandmother stepped eagerly forward to assist her son. The prince sprang away from Mrs. Canty, exclaiming—

"Thou shalt not suffer for me, madam. Let these swine do their will upon me alone!"

This speech infuriated the swine to such a degree that they set about their work without waste of time. Between them they belabored the boy right soundly, and then gave the girls and their mother a beating for showing sympathy for the victim.

"Now," said Canty, "to bed, all of ye. The entertainment has tired me."

The light was put out, and the family retired. As soon as the snorings of the head of the house and his mother showed that they were asleep, the young girls crept to where the prince lay and covered him tenderly from the cold with straw and rags, and their mother crept to him also, and stroked his hair and cried over him, whispering broken words of comfort and compassion in his ear the while. She had saved a morsel for him to eat, also, but the boy's pains had swept away all appetite,—at least for black and tasteless crusts. He was touched by her brave and costly defense of him, and by her commiseration; and he thanked her in very noble and princely words, and begged her to go to her sleep and try to forget her sorrows. And he added that the king his father would not let her loyal kindness and devotion go unrewarded. This return to his "madness" broke her heart anew, and she strained him to her breast again and again and then went back, drowned in tears, to her bed.

As she lay thinking and mourning, the suggestion began to creep into her mind that there was an undefinable something about this boy that was lacking in Tom Canty, mad or sane. She could not describe it, she could not tell just what it was, and yet her sharp mother-instinct seemed to detect it and perceive it. What if the boy were really not her son, after all? O, absurd! She almost smiled at the idea, spite of her griefs and troubles. No matter, she found that it was an idea that would not "down," but persisted in haunting her. It pursued her, it harassed her, it clung to her, and refused to be put away or ignored. At last she perceived that there was not going to be any peace for her until she should devise a test that should prove, clearly and without question, whether this lad was her son or not, and so banish these wearing and worrying doubts. Ah yes, this was plainly the right way out of the difficulty; therefore she set her wits to work at once to contrive that test. But it was an easier thing to propose than to accomplish. She turned over in her mind one promising test after another, but was obliged to relinquish them all—none of them were absolutely sure, absolutely perfect; and an imperfect one could not satisfy her. Evidently she was racking her head in vain—it seemed manifest that she must give the matter up. While this depressing thought was passing through her mind, her ear caught the regular breathing of the boy, and she knew he had fallen asleep. And while she listened, the measured breathing was broken by a soft, startled cry, such as one utters in a troubled dream. This chance occurrence furnished her instantly with a plan worth all her labored tests combined. She at once set herself feverishly, but noiselessly, to work, to relight her candle, muttering to herself, "Had I but seen him *then*, I should have known! Since that day, when he was little, that the powder burst in his face, he hath never been startled of a sudden out of his dreams or out of his thinkings, but he hath cast his hand before his eyes, even as he did that day; and not as others would do it, with the palm inward, but always with the palm turned outward—I have seen it a hundred times, and it hath never varied nor ever failed. Yes, I shall soon know, now!"

By this time she had crept to the slumbering boy's side, with the candle, shaded, in her hand. She bent heedfully and warily over him, scarcely breathing, in her suppressed excitement, and suddenly flashed the light in his face and struck the floor by his ear with her knuckles. The sleeper's eyes sprung wide open, and he cast a startled stare about him—but he made no special movement with his hands.

The poor woman was smitten almost helpless with surprise and grief; but she contrived to hide her emotions, and to soothe the boy to sleep again; then she crept apart and communed miserably with herself upon the disastrous result of her experiment. She tried to believe that her Tom's madness had banished this habitual gesture of his; but she could not do it. "No," she said, "his *hands* are not mad, they could not unlearn so old a habit in so brief a time. O, this is a heavy day for me!"

Still, hope was as stubborn, now, as doubt had been before; she could not bring herself to accept the verdict of the test; she must try the thing again—the failure must have been only an accident; so she startled the boy out of his sleep a second and a third time, at intervals—with the same result which had marked the first test—then she dragged herself to bed, and fell sorrowfully asleep, saying, "But I cannot give him up—O, no, I cannot, I cannot—he *must* be my boy!"

The poor mother's interruptions having ceased, and the prince's pains having gradually lost their power to disturb him, utter weariness at last sealed his eyes in a profound and restful sleep. Hour after hour slipped away, and still he slept like the dead. Thus four or five hours passed. Then his stupor began to lighten. Presently while half asleep and half awake, he murmured—

"Sir William!"

After a moment—

"Ho, Sir William Herbert! Hie thee hither, and list to the strangest dream that ever . . . . Sir William! dost hear? Man, I did think me changed to a pauper, and . . . . . . Ho there! Guards! Sir William! What! is there no groom of the chamber in waiting? Alack it shall go hard with—"

"What aileth thee?" asked a whisper near him. "Who art thou calling?"

"Sir William Herbert. Who art thou?"

"I? Who should I be, but thy sister Nan? O, Tom, I had forgot!—Thou'rt mad yet—poor lad thou'rt mad yet, would I had never woke to know it again! But prithee master thy tongue, lest we be all beaten till we die!"

The startled prince sprang partly up, but a sharp reminder from his stiffened bruises brought him to himself, and he sunk back among his foul straw with a moan and the ejaculation—

"Alas, it was no dream, then!"

In a moment all the heavy sorrow and misery which sleep had banished were upon him again, and he realized that he was no longer a petted prince in a palace, with the adoring eyes of a nation upon him, but a pauper, an outcast, clothed in rags, prisoner in a den fit only for beasts, and consorting with beggars and thieves.

In the midst of his grief he began to be conscious of hilarious noises and shoutings, apparently but a block or two away. The next moment there were several sharp raps at the door, John Canty ceased from snoring and said—

"Who knocketh? What wilt thou?"

A voice answered—

"Know'st thou who it was thou laid thy cudgel on?"

"No. Neither know I, nor care."

"Belike thou'lt change thy note eftsoons. An' thou would save thy neck, nothing but flight may stead thee. The man is this moment delivering up the ghost. 'Tis the priest, Father Andrew!"

"God-a-mercy!" exclaimed Canty. He roused his family, and hoarsely commanded, "Up with ye all and fly—or bide where ye are and perish!"

Scarcely five minutes later the Canty household were in the street and flying for their lives. John Canty held the prince by the wrist, and hurried him along the dark way, giving him this caution in a low voice—

"Mind thy tongue, thou mad fool, and speak not our name. I will choose me a new name, speedily, to throw the law's dogs off the scent. Mind thy tongue, I tell thee!"

He growled these words to the rest of the family—

"If it so chance that we be separated, let each make for London Bridge; whoso findeth himself as far as the last linen-draper's shop on the Bridge, let him tarry there till the others be come, then will we flee into Southwark together."

At this moment the party burst suddenly out of darkness into light; and not only into light but into the midst of a multitude of singing, dancing, and shouting people, massed together on the river frontage. There was a line of bonfires stretching as far as one could see, up and down the Thames; London Bridge was illuminated; Southwark Bridge, likewise; the entire river was aglow with the flash and sheen of colored lights; and constant explosions of fireworks filled the skies with an intricate commingling of shooting splendors and a thick rain of dazzling sparks that almost turned night into day; everywhere were crowds of revelers; all London seemed to be at large.

John Canty delivered himself of a furious curse and commanded a retreat; but it was too late. He and his tribe were swallowed up in that swarming hive of humanity and hopelessly separated from each other in an instant. We are not considering that the prince was one of his tribe; Canty still kept his grip upon him. The prince's heart was beating high with hopes of escape, now. A burly waterman, considerably exalted with liquor, found himself rudely shoved by Canty in his efforts to plow through the crowd; he laid his great hand on Canty's shoulder and said—

"Nay, whither so fast, friend? Dost canker thy soul with sordid business when all that be leal men and true make holiday?"

"Mine affairs are mine own, they concern thee not," answered Canty, roughly, "take away thy hand and let me pass."

"Sith that is thy humor, thou'lt *not* pass, till thou'st drunk to the Prince of Wales, I tell thee that," said the waterman, barring the way resolutely.

"Give me the cup, then, and make speed, make speed!"

Other revelers were interested by this time. They cried out—

"The loving-cup, the loving-cup! make the sour knave drink the loving-cup, else will we feed him to the fishes."

So a huge loving-cup was brought; the waterman, grasping it by one of its handles, and with his other hand bearing up the end of an imaginary napkin, presented it in due and ancient form to Canty, who had to grasp the opposite handle with one of his hands and take off the lid with the other, according to ancient custom.* This left the prince hand-free for a second, of course. He wasted no time, but dived among the forest of legs about him and disappeared. In another moment he could not have been harder to find, under that tossing sea of life, if its billows had been the Atlantic's and he a lost sixpence.

He very soon realized this fact, and straightway busied himself about his own affairs without further thought of John Canty. He quickly realized another thing, too. To wit, that a spurious Prince of Wales was being feasted by the city in his stead. He easily concluded that the pauper lad, Tom Canty, had deliberately taken advantage of his stupendous opportunity and become a usurper. Therefore there was but one course to pursue—find his way to the Guildhall, make himself known, and denounce the impostor. He also made up his mind that Tom should be allowed a reasonable time for spiritual preparation and then be hanged, drawn and quartered, according to the law and usage of the day, in cases of high treason.

*See Note 6, at end of volume.

Chapter II

At Guildhall

THE ROYAL BARGE, attended by its gorgeous fleet, took its stately way down the Thames through the wilderness of illuminated boats. The air was laden with music; the river banks were beruffled with joy-flames; the distant city lay in a soft luminous glow from its countless invisible bonfires; above it rose many a slender spire into the sky, encrusted with sparkling lights, wherefore in their remoteness they seemed like jeweled lances thrust aloft; as the fleet swept along, it was greeted from the banks with a continuous hoarse roar of cheers and the ceaseless flash and boom of artillery.

To Tom Canty, half buried in his silken cushions, these sounds and this spectacle were a wonder unspeakably sublime and astonishing. To his little friends at his side, the princess Elizabeth and the lady Jane Grey, they were nothing.

Arrived at the Dowgate, the fleet was towed up the limpid Walbrook (whose channel has now been for two centuries buried out of sight under acres of buildings,) to Bucklersbury, past houses and under bridges populous with merry-makers and brilliantly lighted, and at last came to a halt in a basin where now is Barge Yard, in the centre of the ancient city of London. Tom disembarked, and he and his gallant procession crossed Cheapside and made a short march through the Old Jewry and Basinghall street to the Guildhall.

Tom and his little ladies were received with due ceremony by the Lord Mayor and the Fathers of the City, in their gold chains and scarlet robes of state, and conducted to a rich canopy of state at the head of the great hall, preceded by heralds making proclamation, and by the Mace and the City Sword. The lords and ladies who were to attend upon Tom and his two small friends took their places behind their chairs.

At a lower table the court grandees and other guests of noble degree were seated, with the magnates of the city; the commoners took places at a multitude of tables on the main floor of the hall. From their lofty vantage-ground, the giants

Gog and Magog, the ancient guardians of the city, contemplated the spectacle below them with eyes grown familiar to it in forgotten generations. There was a bugle-blast and a proclamation, and a fat butler appeared in a high perch in the leftward wall, followed by his servitors bearing with impressive solemnity a royal Baron of Beef, smoking hot and ready for the knife.

After grace, Tom (being instructed,) rose—and the whole house with him—and drank from a portly golden loving-cup with the princess Elizabeth; from her it passed to the lady Jane, and then traversed the general assemblage. So the banquet began.

By midnight the revelry was at its height. Now came one of those picturesque spectacles so admired in that old day. A description of it is still extant in the quaint wording of a chronicler who witnessed it:

"Space being made, presently entered a baron and an earl appareled after the Turkish fashion in long robes of bawdkin powdered with gold; hats on their heads of crimson velvet, with great rolls of gold, girded with two swords, called scimitars, hanging by great bawdricks of gold. Next came yet another baron and another earl, in two long gowns of yellow satin, traversed with white satin, and in every bend of white was a bend of crimson satin, after the fashion of Russia, with furred hats of gray on their heads; either of them having an hatchet in their hands, and boots with *pykes*" (points a foot long), "turned up. And after them came a knight, then the Lord High Admiral, and with him five nobles, in doublets of crimson velvet, voyded low on the back and before to the cannell-bone, laced on the breasts with chains of silver; and, over that, short cloaks of crimson satin, and on their heads hats after the dancers' fashion, with pheasants' feathers in them. These were appareled after the fashion of Prussia. The torch-bearers, which were about an hundred, were appareled in crimson satin and green, like Moors, their faces black. Next came in a *mommarye*. Then the minstrels, which were disguised, danced; and the lords and ladies did wildly dance also, that it was a pleasure to behold."

And while Tom, in his high seat, was gazing upon this "wild" dancing, lost in admiration of the dazzling commingling of kaleidoscopic colors which the whirling turmoil of gaudy figures below him presented, the ragged but real little Prince of Wales was proclaiming his rights and his wrongs, denouncing the impostor, and clamoring for admission at the gates of Guildhall! The crowd enjoyed this episode prodigiously, and pressed forward and craned their necks to see the small rioter. Presently they began to taunt him and mock at him, purposely to goad him into a higher and still more entertaining fury. Tears of mortification sprung to his eyes, but he stood his ground and defied the mob right royally. Other taunts followed, added mockings stung him, and he exclaimed—

"I tell ye again, you pack of unmannerly curs, I am the Prince of Wales! And all forlorn and friendless as I be, with none to give me word of grace or help me in my need, yet will not I be driven from my ground, but will maintain it!"

"Though thou be prince or no prince, 'tis all one, thou be'st a gallant lad, and not friendless neither! Here stand I by thy side to prove it; and mind I tell thee thou might'st have a worser friend than Miles Hendon and yet not tire thy legs with seeking. Rest thy small jaw, my child, I talk the language of these base kennel-rats like to a very native."

The speaker was a sort of Don Caesar de Bazan in dress, aspect, and bearing. He was tall, trim-built, muscular. His doublet and trunks were of rich material, but faded and threadbare, and their gold-lace adornments were sadly tarnished; his ruff was rumpled and damaged; the plume in his slouched hat was broken and had a bedraggled and disreputable look; at his side he wore a long rapier in a rusty iron sheath; his swaggering carriage marked him at once as a ruffler of the camp. The speech of this fantastic figure was received with an explosion of jeers and laughter. Some cried, " 'Tis another prince in disguise!" " 'Ware thy tongue, friend, belike he is dangerous!" "Marry, he looketh it—mark his eye!" "Pluck the lad from him—to the horse-pond wi' the cub!"

Instantly a hand was laid upon the prince, under the impulse of this happy thought; as instantly the stranger's long sword was out and the meddler went to the earth under a sounding thump with the flat of it. The next moment a score of voices shouted "Kill the dog! kill him! kill him!" and the mob closed in on the warrior, who backed himself against a wall and began to lay about him with his long weapon like a madman. His victims sprawled this way and that, but the mob-tide poured over their prostrate forms and dashed itself against the champion with undiminished fury. His moments seemed numbered, his destruction certain, when suddenly a trumpet-blast sounded, a voice shouted, "Way for the king's messenger!" and a troop of horsemen came charging down upon the mob, who fled out of harm's reach as fast as their legs could carry them. The bold stranger caught up the prince in his arms, and was soon far away from danger and the multitude.

Return we within the Guildhall. Suddenly, high above the jubilant roar and thunder of the revel, broke the clear peal of a bugle-note. There was instant silence, a deep hush; then a single voice rose—that of the messenger from the palace—and began to pipe forth a proclamation, the whole multitude standing, listening. The closing words, solemnly pronounced, were—

"The king is dead!"

The great assemblage bent their heads upon their breasts with one accord; remained so, in profound silence, a few moments; then all sunk upon their knees in a body, stretched out their hands toward Tom, and a mighty shout burst forth that seemed to shake the building—

"Long live the king!"

Poor Tom's dazed eyes wandered abroad over this stupefying spectacle, and finally rested dreamily upon the kneeling princesses beside him, a moment, then upon the Earl of Hertford. A sudden purpose dawned in his face. He said, in a low tone, at lord Hertford's ear—

"Answer me truly, on thy faith and honor! Uttered I here a command, the which none but a king might hold privilege and prerogative to utter, would such commandment be obeyed, and none rise up to say me nay?"

"None, my liege, in all these realms. In thy person bides the majesty of England. Thou art the king—thy word is law."

Tom responded, in a strong, earnest voice, and with great animation—

"Then shall the king's law be law of mercy, from this day, and never more be law of blood! Up from thy knees and away! To the Tower and say the king decrees the Duke of Norfolk shall not die!"*

The words were caught up and carried eagerly from lip to lip far and wide over the hall, and as Hertford hurried from the presence, another prodigious shout burst forth—

"The reign of blood is ended! Long live Edward, king of England!"

*See Note 7, at end of volume.

Chapter 12

THE PRINCE AND HIS DELIVERER

As SOON AS Miles Hendon and the little prince were clear of the mob, they struck down through back lanes and alleys toward the river. Their way was unobstructed until they approached London Bridge; then they plowed into the multitude again, Hendon keeping a fast grip upon the prince's—no, the king's—wrist. The tremendous news was already abroad, and the boy learned it from a thousand voices at once—"The king is dead!" The tidings struck a chill to the heart of the poor little waif and sent a shudder through his frame. He realized the greatness of his loss, and was filled with a bitter grief; for the grim tyrant who had been such a terror to others had always been gentle with him. The tears sprung to his eyes and blurred all objects. For an instant he felt himself the most forlorn, outcast, and forsaken of God's creatures—then another cry shook the night with its far-reaching thunders: "Long live King Edward the Sixth!" and this made his eyes kindle, and thrilled him with pride to his fingers' ends. "Ah," he thought, "how grand and strange it seems—I AM KING!"

Our friends threaded their way slowly through the throngs upon the Bridge. This structure, which had stood for six hundred years, and had been a noisy and populous thoroughfare all that time, was a curious affair, for a closely packed rank of stores and shops, with family quarters overhead, stretched along both sides of it, from one bank of the river to the other. The Bridge was a sort of town to itself; it had its inn, its beer houses, its bakeries, its haberdasheries, its food markets, its manufacturing industries, and even its church. It looked upon the two neighbors which it linked together,—London and Southwark—as being well enough, as suburbs, but not otherwise particularly important. It was a close corporation, so to speak; it was a narrow town, of a single street a fifth of a mile long, its population was but a village population, and everybody in it knew all his fellow townsmen intimately, and had known their fathers and mothers before them—and all their little family affairs into the bargain. It had its aristocracy, of course—its fine old families of butchers, and bakers, and what-not, who had occupied the same old premises for five or six hundred years, and knew the great history of the Bridge from beginning to end, and all its strange legends; and who always talked bridgy talk, and thought bridgy thoughts, and lied in a long, level, direct, substantial bridgy way. It was just the sort of population to be narrow and ignorant and self-conceited. Children were born on the Bridge, were reared there, grew to old age and finally died without ever having set a foot upon any part of the world but London Bridge alone. Such people would naturally imagine that the mighty and interminable procession which moved through its street night and day, with its confused roar of shouts and cries, its neighings and bellowings and bleatings and its muffled thunder-tramp, was the one great thing in this world, and themselves somehow the proprietors of it. And so they were, in effect—at least they could exhibit it from their windows, and did—for a consideration—whenever a returning king or hero gave it a fleeting splendor, for there was no place like it for affording a long, straight, uninterrupted view of marching columns.

Men born and reared upon the Bridge found life unendurably dull and inane, elsewhere. History tells of one of these who left the Bridge at the age of seventy-one and retired to the country. But he could only fret and toss in his bed; he could not go to sleep, the deep stillness was so painful, so awful, so oppressive. When he was worn out with it, at last, he fled back to his old home, a lean and haggard spectre, and fell peacefully to rest and pleasant dreams under the lulling music of the lashing waters and the boom and crash and thunder of London Bridge.

In the times of which we are writing, the Bridge furnished "object-lessons" in English history, for its children—namely, the livid and decaying heads of renowned men impaled upon iron spikes atop of its gateways. But we digress.

Hendon's lodgings were in the little inn on the Bridge. As he neared the door with his small friend, a rough voice said—

"So, thou'rt come at last! Thou'lt not escape again, I

warrant thee; and if pounding thy bones to a pudding can teach thee somewhat, thou'lt not keep us waiting another time, mayhap"—and John Canty put out his hand to seize the boy.

Miles Hendon stepped in the way and said—

"Not too fast, friend. Thou art needlessly rough, methinks. What is the lad to thee?"

"If it be any business of thine to make and meddle in others' affairs, he is my son."

" 'Tis a lie!" cried the little king, hotly.

"Boldly said, and I believe thee, whether thy small head-piece be sound or cracked, my boy. But whether this scurvy ruffian be thy father or no, 'tis all one, he shall not have thee to beat thee and abuse, according to his threat, so thou prefer to bide with me."

"I do, I do—I know him not, I loathe him, and will die before I will go with him."

"Then 'tis settled, and there is naught more to say."

"We will see, as to that!" exclaimed John Canty, striding past Hendon to get at the boy; "by force shall he—"

"If thou do but touch him, thou animated offal, I will spit thee like a goose!" said Hendon, barring the way and laying his hand upon his sword hilt. Canty drew back. "Now mark ye," continued Hendon, "I took this lad under my protection when a mob of such as thou would have mishandled him, mayhap killed him; dost imagine I will desert him now to a worser fate?—for whether thou art his father or no,—and sooth to say, I think it is a lie—a decent swift death were better for such a lad than life in such brute hands as thine. So go thy ways, and set quick about it, for I like not much bandying of words, being not over-patient in my nature."

John Canty moved off, muttering threats and curses, and was swallowed from sight in the crowd. Hendon ascended three flights of stairs to his room, with his charge, after order-ing a meal to be sent thither. It was a poor apartment, with a shabby bed and some odds and ends of old furniture in it, and was vaguely lighted by a couple of sickly candles. The little king dragged himself to the bed and lay down upon it, almost exhausted with hunger and fatigue. He had been on his feet a good part of a day and a night, for it was now two

or three o'clock in the morning, and had eaten nothing meantime. He murmured drowsily—

"Prithee call me when the table is spread," and sunk into a
deep sleep immediately.

A smile twinkled in Hendon's eye, and he said to himself—

"By the mass, the little beggar takes to one's quarters and
usurps one's bed with as natural and easy a grace as if he
owned them—with never a by-your-leave or so-please-it-you,
or anything of the sort. In his diseased ravings he called himself the Prince of Wales, and bravely doth he keep up the character. Poor little friendless rat, doubtless his mind has been
disordered with ill usage. Well, I will be his friend; I have
saved him, and it draweth me strongly to him; already I love
the bold-tongued little rascal. How soldier-like he faced the
smutty rabble and flung back his high defiance! And what a
comely, sweet and gentle face he hath, now that sleep hath
conjured away its troubles and its griefs. I will teach him, I
will cure his malady; yea, I will be his elder brother, and care
for him and watch over him; and whoso would shame him or
do him hurt, may order his shroud, for though I be burnt for
it he shall need it!"

He bent over the boy and contemplated him with kind
and pitying interest, tapping the young cheek tenderly
and smoothing back the tangled curls with his great brown
hand. A slight shiver passed over the boy's form. Hendon
muttered—

"See, now, how like a man it was, to let him lie here uncovered and fill his body with deadly rheums. Now what shall I
do? 'twill wake him to take him up and put him within the
bed, and he sorely needeth sleep."

He looked about for extra covering, but finding none,
doffed his doublet and wrapped the lad in it, saying, "I am
used to nipping air and scant apparel, 'tis little I shall mind
the cold"—then walked up and down the room to keep his
blood in motion, soliloquizing, as before.

"His injured mind persuades him he is Prince of Wales;
'twill be odd to have a Prince of Wales still with us, now that
he that *was* the prince is prince no more, but king,—for this
poor mind is set upon the one fantasy, and will not reason

out that now it should cast by the prince and call itself the king. . . . . If my father liveth still, after these seven years that I have heard naught from home in my foreign dungeon, he will welcome the poor lad and give him generous shelter for my sake; so will my good elder brother, Arthur; my other brother, Hugh—but I will crack his crown, an' *he* interfere, the fox-hearted, ill-conditioned animal! Yes, thither will we fare—and straightway, too."

A servant entered with a smoking meal, disposed it upon a small deal table, placed the chairs, and took his departure, leaving such cheap lodgers as these to wait upon themselves. The door slammed after him, and the noise woke the boy, who sprung to a sitting posture, and shot a glad glance about him; then a grieved look came into his face and he murmured, to himself, with a deep sigh, "Alack, it was but a dream, woe is me." Next he noticed Miles Hendon's doublet—glanced from that to Hendon, comprehended the sacrifice that had been made for him, and said, gently—

"Thou art good to me, yes, thou art very good to me. Take it and put it on—I shall not need it more."

Then he got up and walked to the washstand in the corner, and stood there, waiting. Hendon said in a cheery voice—

"We'll have a right hearty sup and bite, now, for everything is savory and smoking hot, and that and thy nap together will make thee a little man again, never fear!"

The boy made no answer, but bent a steady look, that was filled with grave surprise, and also somewhat touched with impatience, upon the tall knight of the sword. Hendon was puzzled, and said—

"What's amiss?"

"Good sir, I would wash me."

"O, is that all! Ask no permission of Miles Hendon for aught thou cravest. Make thyself perfectly free here, and welcome, with all that are his belongings."

Still the boy stood, and moved not; more, he tapped the floor once or twice with his small impatient foot. Hendon was wholly perplexed. Said he—

"Bless us, what is it?"

"Prithee pour the water, and make not so many words!"

Hendon, suppressing a horse-laugh, and saying to himself, "By all the saints, but this is admirable!" stepped briskly forward and did the small insolent's bidding, then stood by, in a sort of stupefaction until the command, "Come—the towel!" woke him sharply up. He took up a towel, from under the boy's nose, and handed it to him, without comment. He now proceeded to comfort his own face with a wash, and while he was at it his adopted child seated himself at the table and prepared to fall to. Hendon dispatched his ablutions with alacrity, then drew back the other chair and was about to place himself at table, when the boy said, indignantly—

"Forbear! Wouldst sit in the presence of the king?"

This blow staggered Hendon to his foundations. He muttered to himself, "Lo, the poor thing's madness is up with the time! it hath changed with the great change that is come to the realm, and now in fancy is he *king!* Good lack, I must humor the conceit, too—there is other way—faith, he would order me to the Tower, else!"

And pleased with this jest, he removed the chair from the table, took his stand behind the king, and proceeded to wait upon him in the courtliest way he was capable of.

While the king ate, a grateful sense of refreshment, both of body and spirit, began to steal over him; the rigor of his royal dignity relaxed a little, and with his growing contentment came a desire to talk. He said—

"I think thou callest thyself Miles Hendon, if I heard thee aright?"

"Yes, sire," Miles replied; then observed to himself, "If I *must* humor the poor lad's madness, I must sire him, I must majesty him, I must not go by halves, I must stick at nothing that belongeth to the part I play, else shall I play it ill and work evil to this charitable and kindly cause."

The king warmed his heart with a second glass of wine, and said—

"I would know thee—tell me thy story. Thou hast a gallant way with thee, and a noble—art nobly born?"

"We are of the tail of the nobility, good your majesty. My father is a baronet—one of the smaller lords, by knight service*—Sir Richard Hendon, of Hendon Hall, by Monk's Holm in Kent."

"The name has escaped my memory. Go on—tell me thy story."

" 'Tis not much, your majesty, yet perchance it may beguile a short half hour for want of a better. My father, Sir Richard, is very rich, and of a most generous nature. My mother died whilst I was yet a boy. I have two brothers; Arthur, my elder, with a soul like to his father's; and Hugh, younger than I, a mean spirit, covetous, treacherous, vicious, underhanded—a reptile. Such was he from the cradle; such was he ten years past, when I last saw him—a ripe rascal at nineteen, I being twenty, then, and Arthur twenty-two. There is none other of us but the lady Edith, my cousin—she was sixteen, then—beautiful, gentle, good, the daughter of an earl, the last of her race, heiress of a great fortune and a lapsed title. My father was her guardian. I loved her and she loved me; but she was betrothed to Arthur from the cradle, and Sir Richard would not suffer the contract to be broken. Arthur loved another maid, and bade us be of good cheer and hold fast to the hope that delay and luck together would some day give success to our several causes. Hugh loved the lady Edith's fortune, though in truth he said it was herself he loved—but then 'twas his way, alway, to say the one thing and mean the other. But he lost his arts upon the girl; he could deceive my father, but none else. My father loved him best of us all, and trusted and believed him; for he was the youngest child and others hated him—these qualities being in all ages sufficient to win a parent's dearest love; and he had a smooth persuasive tongue, with an admirable gift of lying—and these be qualities which do mightily assist a blind affection to cozen itself. I was wild—in truth I might go yet farther and say *very* wild, though 'twas a wildness of an innocent sort, since it hurt none but me, brought shame to none, nor loss, nor had in it any taint of crime or baseness, or what might not beseem mine honorable degree.

*He refers to the order of baronets, or baronettes,—the *barones minores*, as distinct from the parliamentary barons;—not, it need hardly be said, the baronets of later creation.

"Yet did my brother Hugh turn these faults to good account—he seeing that our brother Arthur's health was but indifferent, and hoping the worst might work him profit were I swept out of the path—so,—but 'twere a long tale, good my liege, and little worth the telling. Briefly, then, this brother did deftly magnify my faults and make them crimes; ending his base work with finding a silken ladder in mine apartments—conveyed thither by his own means—and did convince my father by this, and suborned evidence of servants and other lying knaves, that I was minded to carry off my Edith and marry with her, in rank defiance of his will.

"Three years of banishment from home and England might make a soldier and a man of me, my father said, and teach me some degree of wisdom. I fought out my long probation in the continental wars, tasting sumptuously of hard knocks, privation and adventure; but in my last battle I was taken captive, and during the seven years that have waxed and waned since then, a foreign dungeon hath harbored me. Through wit and courage I won to the free air at last, and fled hither straight; and am but just arrived, right poor in purse and raiment, and poorer still in knowledge of what these dull seven years have wrought at Hendon Hall, its people and belongings. So please you, sir, my meagre tale is told."

"Thou hast been shamefully abused!" said the little king, with a flashing eye. "But I will right thee—by the cross will I! The king hath said it."

Then, fired by the story of Miles's wrongs, he loosed his tongue and poured the history of his own recent misfortunes into the ears of his astonished listener. When he had finished, Miles said to himself—

"Lo, what an imagination he hath! Verily this is no common mind; else, crazed or sane, it could not weave so straight and gaudy a tale as this out of the airy nothings wherewith it hath wrought this curious romaunt. Poor ruined little head, it shall not lack friend or shelter whilst I bide with the living. He shall never leave my side; he shall be my pet, my little comrade. And he shall be cured!—aye, made whole and sound—then will he make himself a name—and proud shall I be to say, 'Yes, he is mine—I took him, a homeless little ragamuffin, but I saw what was in him, and I said his name would be heard some day—behold him, observe him—was I right?' "

The king spoke—in a thoughtful, measured voice—

"Thou didst save me injury and shame, perchance my life, and so my crown. Such service demandeth rich reward. Name thy desire, and so it be within the compass of my royal power, it is thine."

This fantastic suggestion startled Hendon out of his reverie. He was about to thank the king and put the matter aside with saying he had only done his duty and desired no reward, but a wiser thought came into his head, and he asked leave to be silent a few moments and consider the gracious offer—an idea which the king gravely approved, remarking that it was best to be not too hasty with a thing of such great import.

Miles reflected during some moments, then said to himself, "Yes, that is the thing to do—by any other means it were impossible to get at it—and certes, this hour's experience has taught me 'twould be most wearing and inconvenient to continue it as it is. Yes, I will propose it; 'twas a happy accident that I did not throw the chance away." Then he dropped upon one knee and said—

"My poor service went not beyond the limit of a subject's simple duty, and therefore hath no merit; but since your majesty is pleased to hold it worthy some reward, I take heart of grace to make petition to this effect. Near four hundred years ago, as your grace knoweth, there being ill blood betwixt John, king of England, and the king of France, it was decreed that two champions should fight together in the lists, and so settle the dispute by what is called the arbitrament of God. These two kings, and the Spanish king, being assembled to witness and judge the conflict, the French champion appeared; but so redoubtable was he that our English knights refused to measure weapons with him. So the matter, which was a weighty one, was like to go against the English monarch by default. Now in the Tower lay the lord de Courcy, the mightiest arm in England, stripped of his honors and possessions, and wasting with long captivity. Appeal was made to him; he gave assent, and came forth arrayed for battle; but no sooner did the Frenchman glimpse his huge frame and hear his famous name but he fled away and the French king's cause was lost. King John restored de Courcy's titles and possessions, and said, 'Name thy wish and thou shalt have it, though it cost me half my kingdom;' whereat de Courcy, kneeling, as I do now, made answer, 'This, then, I ask, my liege; that I and my successors may have and hold the privilege of remaining covered in the presence of the kings of England, henceforth while the throne shall last.' The boon was granted, as your majesty knoweth; and there hath been no time, these four hundred years, that that line has failed of an heir; and so, even unto this day, the head of that ancient house still weareth his hat or helm before the king's majesty, without let or hindrance, and this none other may do.* Invoking this precedent in aid of my prayer, I beseech the king to grant to me but this one grace and privilege—to my more than sufficient reward—and none other, to wit: that I and my heirs, forever, may *sit* in the presence of the majesty of England!"

"Rise, Sir Miles Hendon, Knight," said the king, gravely—giving the accolade with Hendon's sword—"rise, and seat thyself. Thy petition is granted. Whilst England remains, and the crown continues, the privilege shall not lapse."

His majesty walked apart, musing, and Hendon dropped into a chair at table, observing to himself, " 'Twas a brave thought, and hath wrought me a mighty deliverance; my legs are grievously wearied. An' I had not thought of that, I must have had to stand for weeks, till my poor lad's wits are cured." After a little, he went on, "And so I am become a knight of the Kingdom of Dreams and Shadows! A most odd and strange position, truly, for one so matter-of-fact as I. I will not laugh—no, God forbid, for this thing which is so sub-stanceless to me is *real* to him. And to me, also, in one way, it is not a falsity, for it reflects with truth the sweet and generous spirit that is in him." After a pause: "Ah, what if he should call me by my fine title before folk!—there'd be a merry contrast betwixt my glory and my raiment! But no matter: let him call me what he will, so it please him; I shall be content."

*The lords of Kingsale, descendants of de Courcy, still enjoy this curious privilege.

Chapter 13

THE DISAPPEARANCE OF THE PRINCE

A HEAVY DROWSINESS presently fell upon the two comrades. The king said—

"Remove these rags"—meaning his clothing.

Hendon disappareled the boy without dissent or remark, tucked him up in bed, then glanced about the room, saying to himself, ruefully, "He hath taken my bed again, as before—marry, what shall *I* do?" The little king observed his perplexity, and dissipated it with a word. He said, sleepily—

"Thou wilt sleep athwart the door, and guard it." In a moment more he was out of his troubles, in a deep slumber.

"Dear heart, he should have been born a king!" muttered Hendon, admiringly; "he playeth the part to a marvel."

Then he stretched himself across the door, on the floor, saying, contentedly—

"I have lodged worse for seven years; 'twould be but ill gratitude to Him above to find fault with this."

He dropped asleep as the dawn appeared. Toward noon he rose, uncovered his unconscious ward—a section at a time,—and took his measure with a string. The king awoke, just as he had completed his work, complained of the cold, and asked what he was doing.

" 'Tis done, now, my liege," said Hendon; "I have a bit of business outside, but will presently return; sleep thou again—thou needest it. There—let me cover thy head also—thou'lt be warm the sooner."

The king was back in dreamland before this speech was ended. Miles slipped softly out, and slipped as softly in again, in the course of thirty or forty minutes, with a complete second-hand suit of boy's clothing, of cheap material, and showing signs of wear; but tidy, and suited to the season of the year. He seated himself, and began to overhaul his purchase, mumbling to himself—

"A longer purse would have got a better sort, but when

74

one has not the long purse one must be content with what a short one may do—

> " 'There was a woman in our town,
>   In our town did dwell—'

"He stirred, methinks—I must sing in a less thunderous key; 'tis not good to mar his sleep, with this journey before him and he so wearied out, poor chap. . . . . . This garment—'tis well enough—a stitch here and another one there will set it aright. This other is better, albeit a stitch or two will not come amiss in it, likewise. . . . . . . *These* be very good and sound, and will keep his small feet warm and dry—an odd new thing to him, belike, since he has doubtless been used to foot it bare, winters and summers the same. . . . . . . Would thread were bread, seeing one getteth a year's sufficiency for a farthing, and such a brave big needle without cost, for mere love. Now shall I have the demon's own time to thread it!"

And so he had. He did as men have always done, and probably always will do, to the end of time—held the needle still, and tried to thrust the thread through the eye, which is the opposite of a woman's way. Time and time again the thread missed the mark, going sometimes on one side of the needle, sometimes on the other, sometimes doubling up against the shaft; but he was patient, having been through these experiences before, when he was soldiering. He succeeded at last, and took up the garment that had lain waiting, meantime, across his lap, and began his work.

"The inn is paid—the breakfast that is to come, included—and there is wherewithal left to buy a couple of donkeys and meet our little costs for the two or three days betwixt this and the plenty that awaits us at Hendon Hall—

> " 'She loved her hus—'

"Body o' me! I have driven the needle under my nail! . . . . . It matters little—'tis not a novelty—yet 'tis not a convenience, neither. . . . . . We shall be merry there, little one, never doubt it! Thy troubles will vanish, there, and likewise thy sad distemper—

" 'She loved her husband dearilee,
But another man—'

"These be noble large stitches!"—holding the garment up
and viewing it admiringly—"they have a grandeur and a majesty that do cause these small stingy ones of the tailor-man to
look mightily paltry and plebeian—

" 'She loved her husband dearilee,
But another man he loved she,—'

"Marry, 'tis done—a goodly piece of work, too, and
wrought with expedition. Now will I wake him, apparel him,
pour for him, feed him, and then will we hie us to the mart
by the Tabard inn in Southwark and—be pleased to rise, my
liege!—he answereth not—what ho, my liege!—of a truth
must I profane his sacred person with a touch, sith his slumber is deaf to speech. What!"

He threw back the covers—the boy was gone!

He stared about him in speechless astonishment for a moment; noticed for the first time that his ward's ragged raiment
was also missing, then he began to rage and storm, and shout
for the innkeeper. At that moment a servant entered with the
breakfast.

"Explain, thou limb of Satan, or thy time is come!" roared
the man of war, and made so savage a spring toward the
waiter that this latter could not find his tongue, for the instant, for fright and surprise. "Where is the boy?"

In disjointed and trembling syllables the man gave the information desired.

"You were hardly gone from the place, your worship, when
a youth came running and said it was your worship's will that
the boy come to you straight, at the bridge-end on the Southwark side. I brought him hither; and when he woke the lad
and gave his message, the lad did grumble some little for being disturbed 'so early,' as he called it, but straightway trussed
on his rags and went with the youth, only saying it had been
better manners that your worship came yourself not sent a
stranger—and so—"

"And so thou'rt a fool!—a fool, and easily cozened—hang
all thy breed! Yet mayhap no hurt is done. Possibly no harm is

meant the boy. I will go fetch him. Make the table ready. Stay! the coverings of the bed were disposed as if one lay beneath them—happened that by accident?"

"I know not, good your worship. I saw the youth meddle with them—he that came for the boy."

"Thousand deaths! 'twas done to deceive me—'tis plain 'twas done to gain time. Hark ye! Was that youth alone?"

"All alone, your worship."

"Art sure?"

"Sure, your worship."

"Collect thy scattered wits—bethink thee—take time, man."

After a moment's thought, the servant said—

"When he came, none came with him; but now I remember me that as the two stepped into the throng of the Bridge a ruffian-looking man plunged out from some near place, and just as he was joining them—"

"What *then?*—out with it!" thundered the impatient Hendon, interrupting.

"Just then the crowd lapped them up and closed them in, and I saw no more, being called by my master, who was in a rage because a joint that the scrivener had ordered was forgot, though I take all the saints to witness that to blame *me* for that miscarriage were like holding the unborn babe to judgment for sins com—"

"Out of my sight, idiot! Thy prating drives me mad! Hold! whither art flying? Canst not bide still an instant? Went they toward Southwark?"

"Even so, your worship—for, as I said before, as to that detestable joint, the babe unborn is no whit more blameless than—"

"Art here *yet!* And prating still? Vanish, lest I throttle thee!" The servitor vanished. Hendon followed after him, passed him, and plunged down the stairs two steps at a stride, muttering, " 'Tis that scurvy villain that claimed he was his son. I have lost thee, my poor little mad master—it is a bitter thought—and I had come to love thee so! No! by book and bell, *not* lost! Not lost, for I will ransack the land till I find thee again. Poor child, yonder is his breakfast—and mine, but I have no hunger now—so, let the rats have it—speed,

speed! that is the word!" As he wormed his swift way through the noisy multitudes upon the Bridge, he several times said to himself—clinging to the thought as if it were a particularly pleasing one—"He grumbled, but he *went*—he went, yes, because he thought Miles Hendon asked it, sweet lad—he would ne'er have done it for another, I know it well."

Chapter 14

TOWARD DAYLIGHT of the same morning, Tom Canty stirred out of a heavy sleep and opened his eyes in the dark. He lay silent a few moments, trying to analyze his confused thoughts and impressions, and get some sort of meaning out of them, then suddenly he burst out in a rapturous but guarded voice—

"I see it all, I see it all! Now God be thanked, I am indeed awake at last. Come, joy! vanish, sorrow! Ho, Nan! Bet! kick off your straw and hie ye hither to my side, till I do pour into your unbelieving ears the wildest madcap dream that ever the spirits of night did conjure up to astonish the soul of man withal! . . . . . . Ho, Nan, I say! Bet! . . . . . ."

A dim form appeared at his side, and a voice said—

"Wilt deign to deliver thy commands?"

"Commands? . . . . O, woe is me, I know thy voice! Speak, thou—who am I?"

"Thou? In sooth, yesternight wert thou the Prince of Wales, to-day art thou my most gracious liege, Edward, king of England."

Tom buried his head among his pillows, murmuring plaintively—

"Alack, it was no dream! Go to thy rest, sweet sir—leave me to my sorrows."

Tom slept again, and after a time he had this pleasant dream. He thought it was summer and he was playing, all alone, in the fair meadow called Goodman's Fields, when a dwarf only a foot high, with long red whiskers and a humped back appeared to him suddenly and said, "Dig, by that stump." He did so, and found twelve bright new pennies—wonderful riches! Yet this was not the best of it; for the dwarf said—

"I know thee. Thou art a good lad and a deserving; thy distresses shall end, for the day of thy reward is come. Dig here every seventh day, and thou shalt find always the same treasure, twelve bright new pennies. Tell none—keep the secret."

Then the dwarf vanished, and Tom flew to Offal Court with his prize, saying to himself, "Every night will I give my father a penny; he will think I begged it, it will glad his heart, and I shall no more be beaten. One penny every week the good priest that teacheth me shall have; mother, Nan and Bet the other four. We be done with hunger and rags, now, done with fears and frets and savage usage."

In his dream he reached his sordid home all out of breath, but with eyes dancing with grateful enthusiasm; cast four of his pennies into his mother's lap and cried out—

"They are for thee!—all of them, every one!—for thee and Nan and Bet—and honestly come by, not begged nor stolen!"

The happy and astonished mother strained him to her breast and exclaimed—

"It waxeth late—may it please your majesty to rise?"

Ah, that was not the answer he was expecting. The dream had snapped asunder—he was awake.

He opened his eyes—the richly clad First Lord of the Bedchamber was kneeling by his couch. The gladness of the lying dream faded away—the poor boy recognized that he was still a captive and a king. The room was filled with courtiers clothed in purple mantles—the mourning color—and with noble servants of the monarch. Tom sat up in bed and gazed out from the heavy silken curtains upon this fine company.

The weighty business of dressing began, and one courtier after another knelt and paid his court and offered to the little king his condolences upon his heavy loss, whilst the dressing proceeded. In the beginning, a shirt was taken up by the Chief Equerry in Waiting, who passed it to the First Lord of the Buckhounds, who passed it to the Second Gentleman of the Bedchamber, who passed it to the Head Ranger of Windsor Forest, who passed it to the Third Groom of the Stole, who passed it to the Chancellor Royal of the Duchy of Lancaster, who passed it to the Master of the Wardrobe, who passed it to Norroy King-at-Arms, who passed it to the Constable of the Tower, who passed it to the Chief Steward of the Household, who passed it to the Hereditary Grand Diaperer, who passed it to the Lord High Admiral of England, who passed it to the Archbishop of Canterbury, who passed it to the First Lord of the Bedchamber, who took what was left of it and put it on Tom. Poor little wondering chap, it reminded him of passing buckets at a fire.

Each garment in its turn had to go through this slow and solemn process; consequently Tom grew very weary of the ceremony; so weary that he felt an almost gushing gratefulness when he at last saw his long silken hose begin the journey down the line and knew that the end of the matter was drawing near. But he exulted too soon. The First Lord of the Bedchamber received the hose and was about to encase Tom's legs in them, when a sudden flush invaded his face and he hurriedly hustled the things back into the hands of the Archbishop of Canterbury with an astounded look and a whispered, "See, my lord!"—pointing to a something connected with the hose. The Archbishop paled, then flushed, and passed the hose to the Lord High Admiral, whispering, "See, my lord!" The Admiral passed the hose to the Hereditary Grand Diaperer, and had hardly breath enough in his body to ejaculate, "See, my lord!" The hose drifted backward along the line, to the Chief Steward of the Household, the Constable of the Tower, Norroy King-at-Arms, the Master of the Wardrobe, the Chancellor Royal of the Duchy of Lancaster, the Third Groom of the Stole, the Head Ranger of Windsor Forest, the Second Gentleman of the Bedchamber, the First Lord of the Buckhounds,—accompanied always with that amazed and frightened "See! see!"—till they finally reached the hands of the Chief Equerry in Waiting, who gazed a moment, with a pallid face, upon what had caused all this dismay, then hoarsely whispered, "Body of my life, a tag gone from a truss-point!—to the Tower with the Head Keeper of the King's Hose!"—after which he leaned upon the shoulder of the First Lord of the Buckhounds to regather his vanished strength whilst fresh hose, without any damaged strings to them, were brought.

But all things must have an end, and so in time Tom Canty was in a condition to get out of bed. The proper official poured water, the proper official engineered the washing, the proper official stood by with a towel, and by and by Tom got

safely through the purifying stage and was ready for the services of the Hairdresser-royal. When he at length emerged
from this master's hands, he was a gracious figure and as
pretty as a girl, in his mantle and trunks of purple satin, and
purple-plumed cap. He now moved in state toward his breakfast room, through the midst of the courtly assemblage; and
as he passed, these fell back, leaving his way free, and dropped
upon their knees.

After breakfast he was conducted, with regal ceremony, attended by his great officers and his guard of fifty Gentlemen
Pensioners bearing gilt battle-axes, to the throne-room, where
he proceeded to transact business of state. His "uncle," lord
Hertford, took his stand by the throne, to assist the royal
mind with wise counsel.

The body of illustrious men named by the late king as his
executors, appeared, to ask Tom's approval of certain acts of
theirs—rather a form, and yet not wholly a form, since there
was no Protector as yet. The Archbishop of Canterbury made
report of the decree of the Council of Executors concerning the obsequies of his late most illustrious majesty, and finished by reading the signatures of the Executors, to wit: the
Archbishop of Canterbury; the Lord Chancellor of England; William Lord St. John; John Lord Russell; Edward
Earl of Hertford; John Viscount Lisle; Cuthbert Bishop of
Durham—

Tom was not listening—an earlier clause of the document
was puzzling him. At this point he turned and whispered to
lord Hertford—

"What day did he say the burial hath been appointed for?"

"The 16th of the coming month, my liege."

" 'Tis a strange folly. Will he keep?"

Poor chap, he was still new to the customs of royalty; he
was used to seeing the forlorn dead of Offal Court hustled
out of the way with a very different sort of expedition. However, the lord Hertford set his mind at rest with a word or
two.

A secretary of state presented an order of the Council appointing the morrow at eleven for the reception of the foreign
ambassadors, and desired the king's assent.

Tom turned an inquiring look toward Hertford, who whispered—

"Your majesty will signify consent. They come to testify their royal masters' sense of the heavy calamity which hath visited your grace and the realm of England."

Tom did as he was bidden. Another secretary began to read a preamble concerning the expenses of the late king's household, which had amounted to £28,000 during the preceding six months—a sum so vast that it made Tom Canty gasp; he gasped again when the fact appeared that £20,000 of this money were still owing and unpaid;* and once more when it appeared that the king's coffers were about empty, and his twelve hundred servants much embarrassed for lack of the wages due them. Tom spoke out, with lively apprehension—

"We be going to the dogs, 'tis plain. 'Tis meet and necessary that we take a smaller house and set the servants at large, sith they be of no value but to make delay, and trouble one with offices that harass the spirit and shame the soul, they misbecoming any but a doll, that hath nor brains nor hands to help itself withal. I remember me of a small house that standeth over against the fish-market, by Billingsgate—"

A sharp pressure upon Tom's arm stopped his foolish tongue and sent a blush to his face; but no countenance there betrayed any sign that this strange speech had been remarked or given concern.

A secretary made report that forasmuch as the late king had provided in his will for conferring the ducal degree upon the Earl of Hertford and raising his brother, Sir Thomas Seymour, to the peerage, and likewise Hertford's son to an Earldom, together with similar aggrandizements to other great servants of the crown, the Council had resolved to hold a sitting on the 16th of February for the delivering and confirming of these honors; and that meantime, the late king not having granted, in writing, estates suitable to the support of these dignities, the Council, knowing his private wishes in that regard, had thought proper to grant to Seymour "£500 lands," and to Hertford's son "800 pound lands, and 300

*Hume.

pound of the next bishop's lands which should fall vacant,"—
his present majesty being willing.*

Tom was about to blurt out something about the propriety
of paying the late king's debts first, before squandering all
this money; but a timely touch upon his arm, from the
thoughtful Hertford, saved him this indiscretion; wherefore
he gave the royal assent, without spoken comment, but with
much inward discomfort. While he sat reflecting, a moment,
over the ease with which he was doing strange and glittering
miracles, a happy thought shot into his mind: why not make
his mother Duchess of Offal Court and give her an estate?
But a sorrowful thought swept it instantly away: he was only
a king in name, these grave veterans and great nobles were his
masters; to them his mother was only the creature of a diseased mind; they would simply listen to his project with unbelieving ears, then send for the doctor.

The dull work went tediously on. Petitions were read, and
proclamations, patents, and all manner of wordy, repetitious
and wearisome papers relating to the public business; and at
last Tom sighed pathetically and murmured to himself, "In
what have I offended, that the good God should take me
away from the fields and the free air and the sunshine, to shut
me up here and make me a king and afflict me so?" Then his
poor muddled head nodded a while, and presently drooped to
his shoulder; and the business of the empire came to a standstill for want of that august factor, the ratifying power. Silence ensued, around the slumbering child, and the sages of
the realm ceased from their deliberations.

During the forenoon, Tom had an enjoyable hour, by permission of his keepers, Hertford and St. John, with the lady
Elizabeth and the little lady Jane Grey though the spirits of
the princesses were rather subdued by the mighty stroke that
had fallen upon the royal house; and at the end of the visit his
"elder sister"—afterwards the "Bloody Mary" of history—
chilled him with a solemn interview which had but one merit
in his eyes, its brevity. He had a few moments to himself, and
then a slim lad of about twelve years of age was admitted to

*Hume.

his presence, whose clothing, except his snowy ruff and the laces about his wrists, was of black,—doublet, hose and all. He bore no badge of mourning but a knot of purple ribbon on his shoulder. He advanced hesitatingly, with head bowed and bare, and dropped upon one knee in front of Tom. Tom sat still and contemplated him soberly a moment. Then he said—

"Rise, lad. Who art thou? What wouldst have?"

The boy rose, and stood at graceful ease, but with an aspect of concern in his face. He said—

"Of a surety thou must remember me, my lord. I am thy whipping-boy."

"My *whipping*-boy?"

"The same, your grace. I am Humphrey—Humphrey Marlow."

Tom perceived that here was some one whom his keepers ought to have posted him about. The situation was delicate. What should he do?—pretend he knew this lad, and then betray by his every utterance, that he had never heard of him before? No, that would not do. An idea came to his relief: accidents like this might be likely to happen with some frequency, now that business urgencies would often call Hertford and St. John from his side, they being members of the Council of Executors; therefore perhaps it would be well to strike out a plan himself to meet the requirements of such emergencies. Yes, that would be a wise course—he would practice on this boy, and see what sort of success he might achieve. So he stroked his brow perplexedly, a moment or two, and presently said—

"Now I seem to remember thee somewhat—but my wit is clogged and dim with suffering—"

"Alack, my poor master!" ejaculated the whipping-boy, with feeling; adding, to himself, "In truth 'tis as they said—his mind is gone—alas, poor soul! But misfortune catch me, how am I forgetting! they said one must not seem to observe that aught is wrong with him."

" 'Tis strange how my memory doth wanton with me these days," said Tom. "But mind it not—I mend apace—a little clew doth often serve to bring me back again the things and names which had escaped me. [And not they, only, forsooth, but e'en such as I ne'er heard before—as this lad shall see.] Give thy business speech."

" 'Tis matter of small weight, my liege, yet will I touch upon it an' it please your grace. Two days gone by, when your majesty faulted thrice in your Greek—in the morning lessons,—dost remember it?"

"Y-e-s—methinks I do. [It is not much of a lie—an' I had meddled with the Greek at all, I had not faulted simply thrice, but forty times.] Yes, I do recal it, now—go on."

—"The master, being wroth with what he termed such slovenly and doltish work, did promise that he would soundly whip me for it—and—"

"Whip *thee*!" said Tom, astonished out of his presence of mind. "Why should he whip *thee* for faults of mine?"

"Ah, your grace forgetteth again. He always scourgeth me, when thou dost fail in thy lessons."

"True, true—I had forgot. Thou teachest me in private— then if I fail, he argueth that thy office was lamely done, and—"

"O, my liege, what words are these? I, the humblest of thy servants, presume to teach *thee*?"

"Then where is thy blame? What riddle is this? Am I in truth gone mad, or is it thou? Explain—speak out."

"But good your majesty, there's naught that needeth sim-plifying. None may visit the sacred person of the Prince of Wales with blows; wherefore when he faulteth, 'tis I that take them; and meet it is and right, for that it is mine office and my livelihood."*

Tom stared at the tranquil boy, observing to himself, "Lo, it is a wonderful thing,—a most strange and curious trade; I marvel they have not hired a boy to take my combings and my dressings for me—would heaven they would!—an' they will do this thing, I will take my lashings in mine own person, giving God thanks for the change." Then he said aloud—

"And hast thou been beaten, poor friend, according to the promise?"

"No, good your majesty, my punishment was appointed for

*See Note 8 at end of volume.

this day, and peradventure it may be annulled, as unbefitting the season of mourning that is come upon us; I know not, and so have made bold to come hither and remind your grace about your gracious promise to intercede in my behalf—"

"With the master? To save thee thy whipping?"

"Ah, thou dost remember!"

"My memory mendeth, thou seest. Set thy mind at ease— thy back shall go unscathed—I will see to it."

"O, thanks, my good lord!" cried the boy, dropping upon his knee again. "Mayhap I have ventured far enow; and yet . . . . . ."

Seeing Master Humphrey hesitate, Tom encouraged him to go on, saying he was "in the granting mood."

"Then will I speak it out, for it lieth near my heart. Sith thou art no more Prince of Wales, but king, thou canst order matters as thou wilt, with none to say thee nay; wherefore it is not in reason that thou wilt longer vex thyself with dreary studies, but wilt burn thy books and turn thy mind to things less irksome. Then am I ruined, and mine orphan sisters with me!"

"Ruined? Prithee how?"

"My back is my bread, O my gracious liege! if it go idle, I starve. An' thou cease from study, mine office is gone, thou'lt need no whipping-boy. Do not turn me away!"

Tom was touched with this pathetic distress. He said, with a right royal burst of generosity—

"Discomfort thyself no further, lad. Thine office shall be permanent in thee and thy line, forever." Then he struck the boy a light blow on the shoulder with the flat of his sword, exclaiming, "Rise, Humphrey Marlow, Hereditary Grand Whipping-Boy to the royal house of England! Banish sorrow—I will betake me to my books again, and study so ill that they must in justice treble thy wage, so mightily shall the business of thine office be augmented."

The grateful Humphrey responded fervidly—

"Thanks, O most noble master, this princely lavishness doth far surpass my most distempered dreams of fortune. Now shall I be happy all my days, and all the house of Marlow after me."

Tom had wit enough to perceive that here was a lad who could be useful to him. He encouraged Humphrey to talk, and he was nothing loth. He was delighted to believe that he was helping in Tom's "cure"; for always, as soon as he had finished calling back to Tom's diseased mind the various particulars of his experiences and adventures in the royal school-room and elsewhere about the palace, he noticed that Tom was then able to "recal" the circumstances quite clearly. At the end of an hour Tom found himself well freighted with very valuable information concerning personages and matters pertaining to the court; so he resolved to draw instruction from this source daily; and to this end he would give order to admit Humphrey to the royal closet whenever he might come, provided the majesty of England was not engaged with other people. Humphrey had hardly been dismissed when my lord Hertford arrived with more trouble for Tom.

He said that the lords of the Council, fearing that some overwrought report of the king's damaged health might have leaked out and got abroad, they deemed it wise and best that his majesty should begin to dine in public after a day or two—his wholesome complexion and vigorous step, assisted by a carefully guarded repose of manner and ease and grace of demeanor, would more surely quiet the general pulse—in case any evil rumors *had* gone about—than any other scheme that could be devised.

Then the earl proceeded, very delicately, to instruct Tom as to the observances proper to the stately occasion, under the rather thin disguise of "reminding" him concerning things already known to him; but to his vast gratification it turned out that Tom needed very little help in this line—he had been making use of Humphrey in that direction, for Humphrey had mentioned that within a few days he was to begin to dine in public; having gathered it from the swift-winged gossip of the court. Tom kept these facts to himself, however.

Seeing the royal memory so improved, the earl ventured to apply a few tests to it, in an apparently casual way, to find out how far its amendment had progressed. The results were happy, here and there, in spots—spots where Humphrey's tracks remained—and on the whole my lord was greatly pleased and encouraged. So encouraged was he, indeed, that he spoke up and said in a quite hopeful voice—

"Now am I persuaded that if your majesty will but tax your memory yet a little further, it will resolve the puzzle of the Great Seal—a loss which was of moment yesterday, although of none to-day, since its term of service ended with our late lord's life. May it please your grace to make the trial?"

Tom was at sea—a Great Seal was a something which he was totally unacquainted with. After a moment's hesitation he looked up innocently and asked—

"What was it like, my lord?"

The earl started, almost imperceptibly, muttering to himself, "Alack, his wits are flown again!—it was ill wisdom to lead him on to strain them"—then he deftly turned the talk to other matters, with the purpose of sweeping the unlucky Seal out of Tom's thoughts—a purpose which easily succeeded.

Chapter 15

TOM AS KING

THE NEXT DAY the foreign ambassadors came, with their gorgeous trains; and Tom, throned in awful state, received them. The splendors of the scene delighted his eye and fired his imagination, at first, but the audience was long and dreary, and so were most of the addresses—wherefore, what began as a pleasure, grew into weariness and homesickness by and by. Tom said the words which Hertford put into his mouth from time to time, and tried hard to acquit himself satisfactorily, but he was too new to such things, and too ill at ease to accomplish more than a tolerable success. He looked sufficiently like a king, but he was ill able to feel like one. He was cordially glad when the ceremony was ended.

The larger part of his day was "wasted"—as he termed it, in his own mind—in labors pertaining to his royal office. Even the two hours devoted to certain princely pastimes and recreations were rather a burden to him, than otherwise, they were so fettered by restrictions and ceremonious observances. However he had a private hour with his whipping-boy which he counted clear gain, since he got both entertainment and needful information out of it.

The third day of Tom Canty's kingship came and went much as the others had done, but there was a lifting of his cloud in one way—he felt less uncomfortable than at first; he was getting a little used to his circumstances and surroundings; his chains still galled, but not all the time; he found that the presence and homage of the great afflicted and embarrassed him less and less sharply with every hour that drifted over his head.

But for one single dread, he could have seen the fourth day approach without serious distress—the dining in public; it was to begin that day. There were greater matters in the program—for on that day he would have to preside at a Council which would take his views and commands concerning the policy to be pursued toward various foreign nations scattered far and near over the great globe; on that day, too, Hertford would be formally chosen to the grand office of Lord Protector; other things of note were appointed for that fourth day, also; but to Tom they were all insignificant compared with the ordeal of dining all by himself with a multitude of curious eyes fastened upon him and a multitude of mouths whispering comments upon his performance,—and upon his mistakes, if he should be so unlucky as to make any.

Still, nothing could stop that fourth day, and so it came. It found poor Tom low-spirited and absent-minded, and this mood continued; he could not shake it off. The ordinary duties of the morning dragged upon his hands, and wearied him. Once more he felt the sense of captivity heavy upon him.

Late in the forenoon he was in a large audience chamber, conversing with the Earl of Hertford and dully awaiting the striking of the hour appointed for a visit of ceremony from a considerable number of great officials and courtiers.

After a little while, Tom, who had wandered to a window and become interested in the life and movement of the great highway beyond the palace gates—and not idly interested, but longing with all his heart to take part in person in its stir and freedom—saw the van of a hooting and shouting mob of disorderly men, women and children of the lowest and poorest degree approaching from up the road.

"I would I knew what 'tis about!" he exclaimed, with all a boy's curiosity in such happenings.

"Thou art the king!" solemnly responded the earl, with a reverence. "Have I your grace's leave to act?"

"O blithely, yes! O gladly yes!" exclaimed Tom, excitedly, adding to himself with a lively sense of satisfaction, "In truth, being a king is not all dreariness—it hath its compensations and conveniences."

The earl called a page, and sent him to the captain of the guard with the order—

"Let the mob be halted, and inquiry made concerning the occasion of its movement. By the king's command!"

A few seconds later a long rank of the royal guards, cased in flashing steel, filed out at the gates and formed across the highway in front of the multitude. A messenger returned, to report that the crowd were following a man, a woman, and a young girl to execution for crimes committed against the peace and dignity of the realm.

Death—and a violent death—for these poor unfortunates! The thought wrung Tom's heart-strings. The spirit of compassion took control of him, to the exclusion of all other considerations; he never thought of the offended laws, or of the grief or loss which these three criminals had inflicted upon their victims, he could think of nothing but the scaffold and the grisly fate hanging over the heads of the condemned. His concern even made him forget, for the moment, that he was but the false shadow of a king, not the substance; and before he knew it he had blurted out the command—

"Bring them here!"

Then he blushed scarlet, and a sort of apology sprung to his lips; but observing that his order had wrought no sort of surprise in the earl or the waiting page, he suppressed the words he was about to utter. The page, in the most matter-of-course way, made a profound obeisance and retired backwards out of the room to deliver the command. Tom experienced a glow of pride and a renewed sense of the compensating advantages of the kingly office. He said to himself, "Truly it is like what I was used to feel when I read the old priest's tales, and did imagine mine own self a prince, giving law and command to all, saying 'do this, do that,' whilst none durst offer let or hindrance to my will."

Now the doors swung open; one high-sounding title after another was announced, the personages owning them followed, and the place was quickly half filled with noble folk and finery. But Tom was hardly conscious of the presence of these people, so wrought up was he and so intensely absorbed in that other and more interesting matter. He seated himself, absently, in his chair of state, and turned his eyes upon the door with manifestations of impatient expectancy; seeing which, the company forbore to trouble him, and fell to chatting a mixture of public business and court gossip one with another.

In a little while the measured tread of military men was heard approaching, and the culprits entered the presence in charge of an under-sheriff and escorted by a detail of the King's Guard. The civil officer knelt before Tom, then stood aside; the three doomed persons knelt, also, and remained so; the guard took position behind Tom's chair. Tom scanned the prisoners curiously. Something about the dress or appearance of the man had stirred a vague memory in him. "Methinks I have seen this man ere now . . . . . but the when or the where fail me"—such was Tom's thought. Just then the man glanced meekly up, and quickly dropped his face again, not being able to endure the awful port of sovereignty; but the one full glimpse of the face, which Tom got, was sufficient. He said to himself: "Now is the matter clear; this is the stranger that plucked Giles Witt out of the Thames, and saved his life, that windy, bitter, first day of the New Year—a brave good deed—pity he hath been doing baser ones and got himself in this sad case. . . . . . I have not forgot the day, neither the hour; by reason that an hour after, upon the stroke of eleven, I did get a hiding by the hand of Gammer Canty which was of so goodly and admired severity that all that went before or followed after it were but fondlings and caresses by comparison."

Tom now ordered that the woman and the girl be removed from the presence for a little time; then addressed himself to the under-sheriff, saying—

"Good sir, what is this man's offense?"

The officer knelt, and answered—

"So please your majesty, he hath taken the life of a subject by poison."

Tom's compassion for the prisoner, and admiration of him as the daring rescuer of a drowning boy, experienced a most damaging shock.

"The thing was proven upon him?" he asked.

"Most clearly, sire."

Tom sighed, and said—

"Take him away—he hath earned his death. 'Tis a pity, for he was a brave heart—na-na, I mean he hath the *look* of it!"

The prisoner clasped his hands together with sudden energy, and wrung them despairingly, at the same time appealing imploringly to the "king" in broken and terrified phrases—

"O my lord the king, an' thou canst pity the lost, have pity upon me!—I am innocent—neither hath that wherewith I am charged been more than but lamely proved—yet I speak not of that; the judgment is gone forth against me and may not suffer alteration; yet in mine extremity I beg a boon, for my doom is more than I can bear. A grace, a grace, my lord the king! in thy royal compassion grant my prayer—give commandment that I be hanged!"

Tom was amazed. This was not the outcome he had looked for.

"Odds my life, a strange *boon!* Was it not the fate intended thee?"

"O good my liege, not so! It is ordered that I be *boiled alive!*"

The hideous surprise of these words almost made Tom spring from his chair. As soon as he could recover his wits he cried out—

"Have thy wish, poor soul! an' thou had poisoned a hundred men thou shouldst not suffer so miserable a death."

The prisoner bowed his face to the ground and burst into passionate expressions of gratitude—ending with—

"If ever thou shouldst know misfortune—which God forefend!—may thy goodness to me this day be remembered and requited!"

Tom turned to the Earl of Hertford, and said—

"My lord, is it believable that there was warrant for this man's ferocious doom?"

"It is the law, your grace—for poisoners. In Germany coiners be boiled to death in *oil*—not cast in of a sudden, but by a rope let down into the oil by degrees, and slowly; first the feet, then the legs, then—"

"O prithee no more, my lord, I cannot bear it!" cried Tom, covering his eyes with his hands to shut out the picture. "I beseech your good lordship that order be taken to change this law—O, let no more poor creatures be visited with its tortures."

The earl's face showed profound gratification, for he was a man of merciful and generous impulses—a thing not very common with his class in that fierce age. He said—

"These your grace's noble words have sealed its doom. History will remember it to the honor of your royal house."

The under-sheriff was about to remove his prisoner; Tom gave him a sign to wait; then he said—

"Good sir, I would look into this matter further. The man has said his deed was but lamely proved. Tell me what thou knowest."

"If the king's grace please, it did appear upon the trial, that this man entered into a house in the hamlet of Islington where one lay sick—three witnesses say it was at ten of the clock in the morning and two say it was some minutes later —the sick man being alone at the time, and sleeping—and presently the man came forth again, and went his way. The sick man died within the hour, being torn with spasms and retchings."

"Did any see the poison given? Was poison found?"

"Marry, no, my liege."

"Then how doth one know there was poison given at all?"

"Please your majesty, the doctors testified that none die with such symptoms but by poison."

Weighty evidence, this—in that simple age. Tom recognized its formidable nature, and said—

"The doctor knoweth his trade—belike they were right. The matter hath an ill look for this poor man."

"Yet was not this all, your majesty; there is more and worse. Many testified that a witch, since gone from the village, none know whither, did foretell, and speak it privately in their ears, that the sick man *would die by poison*—and more, that a stranger would give it—a stranger with brown hair and clothed in a worn and common garb; and surely this prisoner doth answer woundily to the bill. Please your majesty to give the circumstance that solemn weight which is its due, seeing it was *foretold*."

This was an argument of tremendous force, in that superstitious day. Tom felt that the thing was settled; if evidence was worth anything, this poor fellow's guilt was proved. Still he offered the prisoner a chance, saying—

"If thou canst say aught in thy behalf, speak."

"Naught that will avail, my king. I am innocent, yet cannot I make it appear. I have no friends, else might I show that I was not in Islington that day; so also might I show that at that hour they name, I was above a league away, seeing I was at Wapping Old Stairs; yea more, my king, for I could show, that whilst they say I was *taking* life, I was *saving* it. A drowning boy—"

"Peace! Sheriff, name the day the deed was done!"

"At ten in the morning, or some minutes later, the first day of the New Year, most illustrious—"

"Let the prisoner go free—it is the king's will!"

Another blush followed this unregal outburst, and he covered his indecorum as well as he could by adding—

"It enrageth me that a man should be hanged upon such idle, hare-brained evidence!"

A low buzz of admiration swept through the assemblage. It was not admiration of the decree that had been delivered by Tom, for the propriety or expediency of pardoning a convicted poisoner was a thing which few there would have felt justified in either admitting or admiring—no, the admiration was for the intelligence and spirit which Tom had displayed. Some of the low-voiced remarks were to this effect—

"This is no mad king—he hath his wits sound."

"How sanely he put his questions—how like his former natural self was this abrupt, imperious disposal of the matter!"

"God be thanked, his infirmity is spent! This is no weakling, but a king. He hath borne himself like to his own father."

The air being filled with applause, Tom's ear necessarily caught a little of it. The effect which this had upon him was to put him greatly at his ease, and also to charge his system with very gratifying sensations.

However, his juvenile curiosity soon rose superior to these pleasant thoughts and feelings; he was eager to know what sort of deadly mischief the woman and the little girl could have been about; so, by his command the two terrified and sobbing creatures were brought before him.

"What is it that these have done?" he inquired of the sheriff.

"Please your majesty, a black crime is charged upon them, and clearly proven; wherefore the judges have decreed, according to the law, that they be hanged. They sold themselves to the devil—such is their crime."

Tom shuddered. He had been taught to abhor people who did this wicked thing. Still, he was not going to deny himself the pleasure of feeding his curiosity, for all that; so he asked—

"Where was this done?—and when?"

"On a midnight, in December—in a ruined church, your majesty."

Tom shuddered again.

"Who was there present?"

"Only these two, your grace—and *that other*."

"Have these confessed?"

"Nay, not so, sire—they do deny it."

"Then prithee, how was it known?"

"Certain witnesses did see them wending thither, good your majesty; this bred the suspicion, and dire effects have since confirmed and justified it. In particular, it is in evidence that through the wicked power so obtained, they did invoke and bring about a storm that wasted all the region round about. Above forty witnesses have proved the storm; and sooth one might have had a thousand, for all had reason to remember it, sith all had suffered by it."

"Certes this is serious matter." Tom turned this dark piece of scoundrelism over in his mind a while, then asked—

"Suffered the woman, also, by the storm?"

Several old heads among the assemblage nodded their recognition of the wisdom of this question. The sheriff, however, saw nothing consequential in the inquiry; he answered, with simple directness—

"Indeed, did she, your majesty, and most righteously, as all aver. Her habitation was swept away, and herself and child left shelterless."

"Methinks the power to do herself so ill a turn was dearly

bought. She had been cheated, had she paid but a farthing for it; that she paid her soul, and her child's, argueth that she is mad; if she is mad she knoweth not what she doth, therefore sinneth not."

The elderly heads nodded recognition of Tom's wisdom once more, and one individual murmured, "An' the king be mad himself, according to report, then it is a madness of a sort that would improve the sanity of some I wot of, if by the gentle providence of God they could but catch it."

"What age hath the child?" asked Tom.

"Nine years, please your majesty."

"By the law of England may a child enter into covenant and sell itself, my lord?" asked Tom, turning to a learned judge.

"The law doth not permit a child to make or meddle in any weighty matter, good my liege, holding that its callow wit unfitteth it to cope with the riper wit and evil schemings of them that are its elders. The *devil* may buy a child, if he so choose, and the child agree thereto, but not an Englishman—in this latter case the contract would be null and void."

"It seemeth a rude unchristian thing, and ill contrived, that English law denieth privileges to Englishmen, to waste them on the devil!" cried Tom, with honest heat.

This novel view of the matter excited many smiles, and was stored away in many heads to be repeated about the court as evidence of Tom's originality as well as progress toward mental health.

The elder culprit had ceased from sobbing, and was hanging upon Tom's words with an excited interest and a growing hope. Tom noticed this, and it strongly inclined his sympathies toward her in her perilous and unfriended situation. Presently he asked—

"How wrought they, to bring the storm?"

"*By pulling off their stockings,* sire."

This astonished Tom, and also fired his curiosity to fever heat. He said, eagerly—

"It is wonderful! Hath it always this dread effect?"

"Always, my liege—at least if the woman doth desire it, and utter the needful words, either in her mind or with her tongue."

Tom turned to the woman, and said with impetuous zeal—
"Exert thy power—I would see a storm!"

There was a sudden paling of cheeks in the superstitious assemblage, and a general, though unexpressed, desire to get out of the place—all of which was lost upon Tom, who was dead to everything but the proposed cataclysm. Seeing a puzzled and astonished look in the woman's face, he added, excitedly—

"Never fear—thou shalt be blameless. More—thou shalt go free—none shall touch thee. Exert thy power."

"O, my lord the king, I have it not—I have been falsely accused."

"Thy fears stay thee. Be of good heart, thou shalt suffer no harm. Make a storm—it mattereth not how small a one—I require naught great or harmful, but indeed prefer the opposite—do this and thy life is spared—thou shalt go out free, with thy child, bearing the king's pardon, and safe from hurt or malice from any in the realm."

The woman prostrated herself, and protested, with tears, that she had no power to do the miracle, else she would gladly win her child's life, alone, and be content to lose her own, if by obedience to the king's command so precious a grace might be acquired.

Tom urged—the woman still adhered to her declarations. Finally he said—

"I think the woman hath said true. An' *my* mother were in her place and gifted with the devil's functions, she had not stayed a moment to call her storms and lay the whole land in ruins, if the saving of my forfeit life were the price she got! It is argument that other mothers are made in like mould. Thou art free, goodwife—thou and thy child—for I do think thee innocent. *Now* thou'st naught to fear, being pardoned—pull off thy stockings!—an' thou canst make me a storm, thou shalt be rich!"

The redeemed creature was loud in her gratitude, and proceeded to obey, whilst Tom looked on with eager expectancy, a little marred by apprehension; the courtiers at the same time manifesting decided discomfort and uneasiness. The woman stripped her own feet and her little girl's also, and plainly did her best to reward the king's generosity with an earthquake, but it was all a failure and a disappointment. Tom sighed, and said—

"There, good soul, trouble thyself no further, thy power is departed out of thee. Go thy way in peace; and if it return to thee at any time, forget me not, but fetch me a storm."*

*See Notes to Chapter 15 at end of the volume.

Chapter 16

The State Dinner

THE DINNER HOUR drew near—yet strangely enough, the thought brought but slight discomfort to Tom, and hardly any terror. The morning's experiences had wonderfully built up his confidence; the poor little ash-cat was already more wonted to his strange garret, after four days' habit, than a mature person could have become in a full month. A child's facility in accommodating itself to circumstances was never more strikingly illustrated.

Let us privileged ones hurry to the great banqueting room and have a glance at matters there whilst Tom is being made ready for the imposing occasion. It is a spacious apartment, with gilded pillars and pilasters, and pictured walls and ceilings. At the door stand tall guards, as rigid as statues, dressed in rich and picturesque costumes, and bearing halberds. In a high gallery which runs all around the place is a band of musicians and a packed company of citizens of both sexes, in brilliant attire. In the centre of the room, upon a raised platform, is Tom's table. Now let the ancient chronicler speak:

"A gentleman enters the room bearing a rod, and along with him another bearing a table-cloth, which, after they have both kneeled three times with the utmost veneration, he spreads upon the table, and after kneeling again they both retire; then come two others, one with the rod again, the other with a salt-cellar, a plate, and bread; when they have kneeled as the others had done, and placed what was brought upon the table, they too retire with the same ceremonies performed by the first; at last come two nobles, richly clothed, one bearing a tasting-knife, who, after prostrating themselves three times in the most graceful manner, approach and rub the table with bread and salt, with as much awe as if the king had been present."*

So end the solemn preliminaries. Now, far down the echoing corridors we hear a bugle-blast, and the indistinct cry,

*Leigh Hunt's "The Town," p. 408, quotation from an early tourist.

"Place for the king! way for the king's most excellent majesty!" These sounds are momently repeated—they grow nearer and nearer—and presently, almost in our faces, the martial note peals and the cry rings out, "Way for the king!" At this instant the shining pageant appears, and files in at the door, with a measured march. Let the chronicler speak again:

"First come Gentlemen, Barons, Earls, Knights of the Garter, all richly dressed and bare-headed; next comes the Chancellor, between two, one of which carries the royal sceptre, the other the Sword of State in a red scabbard, studded with golden fleurs-de-lis, the point upwards; next comes the king himself—whom, upon his appearing, twelve trumpets and many drums salute with a great burst of welcome, whilst all in the galleries rise in their places, crying 'God save the king!' After him come nobles attached to his person, and on his right and left march his guard of honor, his fifty Gentlemen Pensioners, with gilt battle-axes."

This was all fine and pleasant. Tom's pulse beat high and a glad light was in his eye. He bore himself right gracefully, and all the more so because he was not thinking of how he was doing it, his mind being charmed and occupied with the blithe sights and sounds about him—and besides, nobody can be very ungraceful in nicely-fitting beautiful clothes after he has grown a little used to them—especially if he is for the moment unconscious of them. Tom remembered his instructions, and acknowledged his greeting with a slight inclination of his plumed head, and a courteous "I thank ye, my good people."

He seated himself at table, without removing his cap; and did it without the least embarrassment; for to eat with one's cap on was the one solitary royal custom upon which the kings and the Cantys met as upon common ground, neither party having any advantage over the other in the matter of old familiarity with it. The pageant broke up and grouped itself picturesquely, and remained bareheaded.

Now, to the sound of gay music, the Yeomen of the Guard entered,—"the tallest and mightiest men in England, they being carefully selected in this regard"—but we will let the chronicler tell about it:

"The Yeomen of the Guard entered, bare-headed, clothed in scarlet, with golden roses upon their backs; and these went and came, bringing in each turn a course of dishes, served in plate. These dishes were received by a gentleman in the same order they were brought, and placed upon the table, while the taster gave to each guard a mouthful to eat of the particular dish he had brought, for fear of any poison."

Tom made a good dinner, notwithstanding he was conscious that hundreds of eyes followed each morsel to his mouth and watched him eat it with an interest which could not have been more intense if it had been a deadly explosive and was expected to blow him up and scatter him all about the place. He was careful not to hurry, and equally careful not to do anything whatever for himself, but wait till the proper official knelt down and did it for him. He got through without a mistake—a flawless and precious triumph.

When the meal was over at last and he marched away in the midst of his bright pageant, with the happy noises in his ears of blaring bugles, rolling drums and thundering acclamations, he felt that if he had seen the worst of dining in public, it was an ordeal which he would be glad to endure several times a day if by that means he could but buy himself free from some of the more formidable requirements of his royal office.

Chapter 17

FOO-FOO THE FIRST

MILES HENDON hurried along toward the Southwark end of the Bridge, keeping a sharp lookout for the persons he sought, and hoping and expecting to overtake them presently. He was disappointed in this, however. By asking questions, he was enabled to track them part of the way through Southwark; then all traces ceased, and he was perplexed as to how to proceed. Still, he continued his efforts as best he could during the rest of the day. Nightfall found him leg-weary, half famished, and his desire as far from accomplishment as ever; so he supped at the Tabard inn and went to bed, resolved to make an early start in the morning, and give the town an exhaustive search. As he lay thinking and planning, he presently began to reason thus: The boy would escape from the ruffian, his reputed father, if possible; would he go back to London and seek his former haunts? no, he would not do that, he would avoid recapture. What, then, would he do? Never having had a friend in the world, or a protector, until he met Miles Hendon, he would naturally try to find that friend again, provided the effort did not require him to go toward London and danger. He would strike for Hendon Hall, that is what he would do, for he knew Hendon was homeward bound and there he might expect to find him. Yes, the case was plain to Hendon—he must lose no more time in Southwark, but move at once through Kent, toward Monk's Holm, searching the wood and inquiring as he went. Let us return to the vanished little king, now.

The ruffian whom the waiter at the inn on the Bridge saw "about to join" the youth and the king, did not exactly join them, but fell in close behind them and followed their steps. He said nothing. His left arm was in a sling, and he wore a large green patch over his left eye; he limped slightly, and used an oaken staff as a support. The youth led the king a crooked course through Southwark, and by and by struck into the high road beyond. The king was irritated, now, and said he would stop here—it was Hendon's place to come to him, not his to go to Hendon. He would not endure such insolence; he would stop where he was. The youth said—

"Thou'lt tarry here, and thy friend lying wounded in the wood yonder? So be it, then."

The king's manner changed at once. He cried out—

"Wounded? And who hath dared to do it? But that is apart; lead on, lead on! Faster, sirrah! art shod with lead? Wounded, is he? Now though the doer of it be a duke's son, he shall rue it!"

It was some distance to the wood, but the space was speedily traversed. The youth looked about him, discovered a bough sticking in the ground, with a small bit of rag tied to it, then led the way into the forest, watching for similar boughs and finding them at intervals; they were evidently guides to the point he was aiming at. By and by an open place was reached, where were the charred remains of a farm house, and near them a barn which was falling to ruin and decay. There was no sign of life anywhere, and utter silence prevailed. The youth entered the barn, the king following eagerly upon his heels. No one there! The king shot a surprised and suspicious glance at the youth, and asked—

"Where is he?"

A mocking laugh was his answer. The king was in a rage in a moment; he seized a billet of wood and was in the act of charging upon the youth when another mocking laugh fell upon his ear. It was from the lame ruffian, who had been following at a distance. The king turned and said angrily—

"Who art thou? What is thy business here?"

"Leave thy foolery," said the man, "and quiet thyself. My disguise is none so good that thou canst pretend thou knowest not thy father through it."

"Thou art not my father. I know thee not. I am the king. If thou hast hid my servant, find him for me, or thou shalt sup sorrow for what thou hast done."

John Canty replied, in a stern and measured voice—

"It is plain thou art mad, and I am loth to punish thee; but if thou provoke me, I must. Thy prating doth no harm here, where there are no ears that need to mind thy follies, yet is it well to practice thy tongue to wary speech, that it may do no hurt when our quarters change. I have done a murder, and may not tarry at home—neither shalt thou, seeing I need thy service. My name is changed, for wise reasons; it is Hobbs—John Hobbs; thine is Jack—charge thy memory accordingly. Now, then, speak. Where is thy mother? where are thy sisters? They came not to the place appointed—knowest thou whither they went?"

The king answered, sullenly—

"Trouble me not with these riddles. My mother is dead; my sisters are in the palace."

The youth near by burst into a derisive laugh, and the king would have assaulted him, but Canty—or Hobbs, as he now called himself—prevented him, and said—

"Peace, Hugo, vex him not; his mind is astray, and thy ways fret him. Sit thee down, Jack, and quiet thyself; thou shalt have a morsel to eat, anon."

Hobbs and Hugo fell to talking together, in low voices, and the king removed himself as far as he could from their disagreeable company. He withdrew into the twilight of the farther end of the barn, where he found the earthen floor bedded a foot deep with straw. He lay down here, drew straw over himself in lieu of blankets, and was soon absorbed in thinkings. He had many griefs, but the minor ones were swept almost into forgetfulness by the supreme one, the loss of his father. To the rest of the world the name of Henry VIII brought a shiver, and suggested an ogre whose nostrils breathed destruction and whose hand dealt scourgings and death; but to this boy the name brought only sensations of pleasure, the figure it invoked wore a countenance that was all gentleness and affection. He called to mind a long succession of loving passages between his father and himself, and dwelt fondly upon them, his unstinted tears attesting how deep and real was the grief that possessed his heart. As the afternoon wasted away, the lad, wearied with his troubles, sank gradually into a tranquil and healing slumber.

After a considerable time—he could not tell how long—his senses struggled to a half-consciousness, and as he lay with closed eyes vaguely wondering where he was and what had been happening, he noted a murmurous sound, the sullen beating of rain upon the roof. A snug sense of comfort stole over him, which was rudely broken, the next moment, by a chorus of piping cackles and coarse laughter. It startled him disagreeably, and he unmuffled his head to see whence this interruption proceeded. A grim and unsightly picture met his eye. A bright fire was burning in the middle of the floor, at the other end of the barn, and around it, and lit weirdly up by the red glare, lolled and sprawled the motliest company of tattered gutter-scum and ruffians, of both sexes, he had ever read or dreamed of. There were huge, stalwart men, brown with exposure, long-haired, and clothed in fantastic rags; there were middle-sized youths, of truculent countenance, and similarly clad; there were blind mendicants, with patched or bandaged eyes; crippled ones, with wooden legs and crutches; there was a villain-looking pedlar with his pack; a knife-grinder, a tinker, and a barber-surgeon, with the implements of their trades; some of the females were hardly-grown girls, some were at prime, some were old and wrinkled hags, and all were loud, brazen, foul-mouthed; and all soiled and slatternly; there were three sore-faced babies; there were a couple of starveling curs, with strings about their necks, whose office was to lead the blind.

The night was come, the gang had just finished feasting, an orgie was beginning; the can of liquor was passing from mouth to mouth. A general cry broke forth—

"A song! a song from the Bat and Dick Dot-and-go-One!"

One of the blind men got up, and made ready by casting aside the patches that sheltered his excellent eyes, and the pathetic placard which recited the cause of his calamity. Dot-and-go-One disencumbered himself of his timber leg and took his place, upon sound and healthy limbs, beside his fellow-rascal; then they roared out a rollicking ditty, and were re-inforced by the whole crew, at the end of each stanza, in a rousing chorus. By the time the last stanza was reached, the half-drunken enthusiasm had risen to such a pitch, that everybody joined in and sang it clear through from the beginning, producing a volume of villainous sound that made the rafters quake. These were the inspiring words:

> "Bien Darkmans then, Bouse Mort and Ken,
> The bien Coves bings awast,

On Chates to trine by Rome Coves dine,
For his long lib at last.
Bing'd out bien Morts and toure, and toure,
Bing out of the Rome vile bine,
And toure the Cove that cloy'd your duds,
Upon the Chates to trine."*

Conversation followed; not in the thieves' dialect of the song, for that was only used, in talk, when unfriendly ears might be listening. In the course of it it appeared that "John Hobbs" was not altogether a new recruit, but had trained in the gang at some former time. His later history was called for, and when he said he had "accidentally" killed a man, considerable satisfaction was expressed; when he added that the man was a priest, he was roundly applauded, and had to take a drink with everybody. Old acquaintances welcomed him joyously, and new ones were proud to shake him by the hand. He was asked why he had "tarried away so many months." He answered—

"London is better than the country, and safer, these late years, the laws be so bitter and so diligently enforced. An' I had not had that accident, I had staid there. I had resolved to stay, and never more venture countrywards—but the accident has ended that."

He inquired how many persons the gang numbered now. The "Ruffler," or chief, answered—

"Five and twenty sturdy budges, bulks, files, clapperdogeons and maunders, counting the dells and doxies and other morts.† Most are here, the rest are wandering eastward, along the winter lay. We follow at dawn."

"I do not see the Wen among the honest folk about me. Where may he be?"

"Poor lad, his diet is brimstone, now, and over hot for a delicate taste. He was killed in a brawl, somewhere about midsummer."

"I sorrow to hear that; the Wen was a capable man, and brave."

*From "The English Rogue;" London, 1665.
†Canting terms for various kinds of thieves, beggars and vagabonds, and their female companions.

"That was he, truly. Black Bess, his dell, is of us yet, but absent on the eastward tramp; a fine lass, of nice ways and orderly conduct, none ever seeing her drunk above four days in the seven."

"She was ever strict—I remember it well—a goodly wench and worthy all commendation. Her mother was more free and less particular; a troublesome and ugly tempered beldame, but furnished with a wit above the common."

"We lost her through it. Her gift of palmistry and other sorts of fortune-telling begot for her at last a witch's name and fame. The law roasted her to death at a slow fire. It did touch me to a sort of tenderness to see the gallant way she met her lot—cursing and reviling all the crowd that gaped and gazed around her, whilst the flames licked upward toward her face and catched her thin locks and crackled about her old gray head—cursing them, said I?—cursing them! why an' thou shouldst live a thousand years thou'dst never hear so masterful a cursing. Alack, her art died with her. There be base and weakling imitations left, but no true blasphemy."

The Ruffler sighed; the listeners sighed in sympathy; a general depression fell upon the company for a moment, for even hardened outcasts like these are not wholly dead to sentiment, but are able to feel a fleeting sense of loss and affliction at wide intervals and under peculiarly favoring circumstances —as in cases like to this, for instance, when genius and culture depart and leave no heir. However, a deep drink all round soon restored the spirits of the mourners.

"Have any others of our friends fared hardly?" asked Hobbs.

"Some—yes. Particularly new-comers—such as small husbandmen turned shiftless and hungry upon the world because their farms were taken from them to be changed to sheep ranges. They begged, and were whipped at the cart's tail, naked from the girdle up, till the blood ran, then set in the stocks to be pelted; they begged again, were whipped again, and deprived of an ear; they begged a third time—poor devils, what else could they do?—and were branded on the cheek with a red hot iron, then sold for slaves; they ran away, were hunted down, and hanged. 'Tis a brief tale, and quickly told.

Others of us have fared less hardly. Stand forth, Yokel, Burns, and Hodge—show your adornments!"

These stood up and stripped away some of their rags, exposing their backs, criss-crossed with ropy old welts left by the lash; one turned up his hair and showed the place where a left ear had once been; another showed a brand upon his shoulder—the letter V—and a mutilated ear; the third said—

"I am Yokel, once a farmer and prosperous, with loving wife and kids—now am I somewhat different in estate and calling; and the wife and kids are gone; mayhap they are in heaven, mayhap in—in the other place—but the kindly God be thanked, they bide no more in *England*! My good old blameless mother strove to earn bread by nursing the sick; one of these died, the doctors knew not how, so my mother was burnt for a witch, whilst my babes looked on and wailed. English law!—up, all, with your cups!—now altogether and with a cheer!—drink to the merciful English law that delivered *her* from the English hell! Thank you, mates, one and all. I begged, from house to house—I and the wife—bearing with us the hungry kids—but it was crime to be hungry in England—so they stripped us and lashed us through three towns. Drink ye all again to the merciful English law!—for its lash drank deep of my Mary's blood and its blessed deliverance came quick. She lies there, in the potter's field, safe from all harms. And the kids—well, whilst the law lashed me from town to town, they starved. Drink lads—only a drop—a drop to the poor kids, that never did any creature harm. I begged again—begged for a crust, and got the stocks and lost an ear—see, here bides the stump; I begged again, and here is the stump of the other to keep me minded of it. And still I begged again, and was sold for a slave—here on my cheek under this stain, if I washed it off, ye might see the red S the branding-iron left there! A SLAVE! Do ye understand that word! An English SLAVE!—that is he that stands before ye. I have run from my master, and when I am found—the heavy curse of heaven fall on the law and the land that hath commanded it!—I shall hang!"*

*See Note 10 at end of volume.

A ringing voice came through the murky air—

"Thou shalt *not!*—and this day the end of that law is come!"

All turned, and saw the fantastic figure of the little king approaching hurriedly; as it emerged into the light and was clearly revealed, a general explosion of inquiries broke out:

"Who is it? *What* is it? Who art thou, mannikin?"

The boy stood unconfused in the midst of all those surprised and questioning eyes, and answered with princely dignity—

"I am Edward, king of England."

A wild burst of laughter followed, partly of derision and partly of delight in the excellence of the joke. The king was stung. He said sharply—

"Ye mannerless vagrants, is this your recognition of the royal boon I have promised?"

He said more, with angry voice and excited gesture, but it was lost in a whirlwind of laughter and mocking exclamations. "John Hobbs" made several attempts to make himself heard above the din, and at last succeeded—saying—

"Mates, he is my son, a dreamer, a fool, and stark mad—mind him not—he thinketh he *is* the king."

"I *am* the king," said Edward, turning toward him, "as thou shalt know to thy cost, in good time. Thou hast confessed a murder—thou shalt swing for it."

"*Thou'lt* betray me?—*thou?* An' I get my hands upon thee—"

"Tut-tut!" said the burly Ruffler, interposing in time to save the king, and emphasizing this service by knocking Hobbs down with his fist, "hast respect for neither kings *nor* Rufflers? An' thou insult my presence so again, I'll hang thee up myself." Then he said to his majesty, "Thou must make no threats against thy mates, lad; and thou must guard thy tongue from saying evil of them elsewhere. *Be* king, if it please thy mad humor, but be not harmful in it. Sink the title thou hast uttered,—'tis treason; we be bad men, in some few trifling ways, but none among us is so base as to be traitor to his king; we be loving and loyal hearts, in that regard. Note if I speak truth. Now—all together: 'Long live Edward, king of England!' "

"Long live Edward, king of England!"

The response came with such a thundergust from the motley crew that the crazy building vibrated to the sound. The little king's face lighted with pleasure for an instant, and he slightly inclined his head and said with grave simplicity—

"I thank you, my good people."

This unexpected result threw the company into convulsions of merriment. When something like quiet was presently come again, the Ruffler said, firmly, but with an accent of good nature—

"Drop it, boy, 'tis not wise, nor well. Humor thy fancy, if thou must, but choose some other title."

A tinker shrieked out a suggestion—

"Foo-foo the First, King of the Mooncalves!"

The title "took," at once, every throat responded, and a roaring shout went up, of—

"Long live Foo-foo the First, King of the Mooncalves!" followed by hootings, cat-calls, and peals of laughter.

"Hale him forth, and crown him!"

"Robe him!"

"Sceptre him!"

"Throne him!"

These and twenty other cries broke out at once; and almost before the poor little victim could draw a breath he was crowned with a tin basin, robed in a tattered blanket, throned upon a barrel, and sceptred with the tinker's soldering-iron. Then all flung themselves upon their knees about him and sent up a chorus of ironical wailings and mocking supplications, whilst they swabbed their eyes with their soiled and ragged sleeves and aprons—

"Be gracious to us, O, sweet king!"

"Trample not upon thy beseeching worms, O noble majesty!"

"Pity thy slaves, and comfort them with a royal kick!"

"Cheer us and warm us with thy gracious rays, O flaming sun of sovereignty!"

"Sanctify the ground with the touch of thy foot, that we may eat the dirt and be ennobled!"

"Deign to spit upon us, O sire, that our children's children may tell of thy princely condescension, and be proud and happy forever!"

But the humorous tinker made the "hit" of the evening and carried off the honors. Kneeling, he pretended to kiss the king's foot, and was indignantly spurned; whereupon he went about begging for a rag to paste over the place upon his face which had been touched by the foot, saying it must be preserved from contact with the vulgar air, and that he should make his fortune by going on the highway and exposing it to view at the rate of a hundred shillings a sight. He made himself so killingly funny that he was the envy and admiration of the whole mangy rabble.

Tears of shame and indignation stood in the little monarch's eyes; and the thought in his heart was, "Had I offered them a deep wrong they could not be more cruel—yet have I proffered naught but to do them a kindness—and it is thus they use me for it!"

Chapter 18

THE TROOP of vagabonds turned out at early dawn, and set forward on their march. There was a lowering sky overhead, sloppy ground under foot, and a winter chill in the air. All gaiety was gone from the company; some were sullen and silent, some were irritable and petulant, none were gentle-humored, all were thirsty.

The Ruffler put "Jack" in Hugo's charge, with some brief instructions, and commanded John Canty to keep away from him and let him alone; he also warned Hugo not to be too rough with the lad.

After a while the weather grew milder, and the clouds lifted somewhat. The troop ceased to shiver, and their spirits began to improve. They grew more and more cheerful, and finally began to chaff each other and insult passengers along the highway. This showed that they were awaking to an appreciation of life and its joys once more. The dread in which their sort was held was apparent in the fact that everybody gave them the road, and took their ribald insolences meekly, without venturing to talk back. They snatched linen from the hedges, occasionally, in full view of the owners, who made no protest, but only seemed grateful that they did not take the hedges, too.

By and by they invaded a small farm house and made themselves at home while the trembling farmer and his people swept the larder clean to furnish a breakfast for them. They chucked the housewife and her daughters under the chin whilst receiving the food from their hands, and made coarse jests about them, accompanied with insulting epithets and bursts of horse-laughter. They threw bones and vegetables at the farmer and his sons, kept them dodging all the time, and applauded uproariously when a good hit was made. They ended by buttering the head of one of the daughters who resented some of their familiarities. When they took their leave they threatened to come back and burn the house over the heads of the family if any report of their doings got to the ears of the authorities.

About noon, after a long and weary tramp, the gang came to a halt behind a hedge on the outskirts of a considerable village. An hour was allowed for rest, then the crew scattered themselves abroad to enter the village at different points to ply their various trades. "Jack" was sent with Hugo. They wandered hither and thither for some time, Hugo watching for opportunities to do a stroke of business but finding none—so he finally said—

"I see naught to steal; it is a paltry place. Wherefore we will beg."

"*We*, forsooth! Follow thy trade—it befits thee. But *I* will not beg."

"Thou'lt not beg!" exclaimed Hugo, eying the king with surprise. "Prithee, since when hast thou reformed?"

"What dost thou mean?"

"Mean? Hast thou not begged the streets of London all thy life?"

"I? Thou idiot!"

"Spare thy compliments—thy stock will last the longer. Thy father says thou hast begged all thy days. Mayhap he lied. Peradventure you will even make so bold as to *say* he lied," scoffed Hugo.

"Him *you* call my father? Yes, he lied."

"Come, play not thy merry game of madman so far, mate; use it for thy amusement, not thy hurt. An' I tell him this, he will scorch thee finely for it."

"Save thyself the trouble. I will tell him."

"I like thy spirit, I do in truth; but I do not admire thy judgment. Bone-rackings and bastings be plenty enow in this life, without going out of one's way to invite them. But a truce to these matters; *I* believe your father. I doubt not he can lie; I doubt not he *doth* lie, upon occasion, for the best of us do that; but there is no occasion here. A wise man does not waste so good a commodity as lying for naught. But come; sith it is thy humor to give over begging, wherewithal shall we busy ourselves? With robbing kitchens?"

The king said, impatiently—

"Have done with this folly—you weary me!"

Hugo replied, with temper—

"Now harkee, mate; you will not beg, you will not rob; so be it. But I will tell you what you *will* do. You will play decoy whilst *I* beg. Refuse, an' you think you may venture!"

The king was about to reply contemptuously, when Hugo said, interrupting—

"Peace! Here comes one with a kindly face. Now will I fall down in a fit. When the stranger runs to me, set you up a wail, and fall upon your knees, seeming to weep; then cry out as all the devils of misery were in your belly, and say, 'O, sir, it is my poor afflicted brother, and we be friendless; o' God's name cast through your merciful eyes one pitiful look upon a sick, forsaken and most miserable wretch; bestow one little penny out of thy riches upon one smitten of God and ready to perish!'—and mind you, keep you *on* wailing, and abate not till we bilk him of his penny, else shall you rue it."

Then immediately Hugo began to moan, and groan, and roll his eyes, and reel and totter about; and when the stranger was close at hand, down he sprawled before him, with a shriek, and began to writhe and wallow in the dirt, in seeming agony.

"O dear, O dear!" cried the benevolent stranger, "O poor soul, poor soul, how he doth suffer! There—let me help thee up."

"O, noble sir, forbear, and God love you for a princely gentleman—but it giveth me cruel pain to touch me when I am taken so. My brother there will tell your worship how I am racked with anguish when these fits be upon me. A penny, dear sir, a penny, to buy a little food; then leave me to my sorrows."

"A penny! thou shalt have three, thou hapless creature"—and he fumbled in his pocket with nervous haste and got them out. "There, poor lad, take them, and most welcome. Now come hither, my boy, and help me carry thy stricken brother to yon house, where—"

"I am not his brother," said the king, interrupting.

"What! not his brother?"

"O hear him!" groaned Hugo, then privately ground his teeth. "He denies his own brother—and he with one foot in the grave!"

"Boy, thou art indeed hard of heart, if this is thy brother. For shame!—and he scarce able to move hand or foot. If he is not thy brother, who is he, then?"

"A beggar and a thief! He has got your money and has picked your pocket, likewise. An' thou wouldst do a healing miracle, lay thy staff over his shoulders and trust Providence for the rest."

But Hugo did not tarry for the miracle. In a moment he was up and off like the wind, the gentleman following after and raising the hue and cry lustily as he went. The king, breathing deep gratitude to heaven for his own release, fled in the opposite direction and did not slacken his pace until he was out of harm's reach. He took the first road that offered, and soon put the village behind him. He hurried along, as briskly as he could, during several hours, keeping a nervous watch over his shoulder for pursuit; but his fears left him at last, and a grateful sense of security took their place. He recognized, now, that he was hungry; and also very tired. So he halted at a farm house; but when he was about to speak, he was cut short and driven rudely away. His clothes were against him.

He wandered on, wounded and indignant, and was resolved to put himself in the way of like treatment no more. But hunger is pride's master; so as the evening drew near, he made an attempt at another farm house; but here he fared worse than before; for he was called hard names and was promised arrest as a vagrant except he moved on promptly.

The night came on, chilly and overcast; and still the footsore monarch labored slowly on. He was obliged to keep moving, for every time he sat down to rest he was soon penetrated to the bone with the cold. All his sensations and experiences, as he moved through the solemn gloom and the empty vastness of the night, were new and strange to him. At intervals he heard voices approach, pass by, and fade into silence; and as he saw nothing more of the bodies they belonged to than a sort of formless drifting blur, there was something spectral and uncanny about it all that made him shudder. Occasionally he caught the twinkle of a light—always far away, apparently—almost in another world; if he heard the tinkle of a sheep's bell, it was vague, distant, indistinct; the muffled lowing of the herds floated to him on the night wind in vanishing cadences, a mournful sound; now and then came the complaining howl of a dog over viewless expanses of field and forest; all sounds were remote; they made the little king feel that all life and activity were far removed from him, and that he stood solitary, companionless, in the centre of a measureless solitude.

He stumbled along, through the grewsome fascinations of this new experience, startled occasionally by the soft rustling of the dry leaves overhead, so like human whispers they seemed to sound; and by and by he came suddenly upon the freckled light of a tin lantern near at hand. He stepped back into the shadows and waited. The lantern stood by the open door of a barn. The king waited some time—there was no sound, and nobody stirring. He got so cold, standing still, and the hospitable barn looked so enticing, that at last he resolved to risk everything and enter. He started swiftly and stealthily, and just as he was crossing the threshold he heard voices behind him. He darted behind a cask, within the barn, and stooped down. Two farm laborers came in, bringing the lantern with them, and fell to work, talking meanwhile. Whilst they moved about with the light, the king made good use of his eyes and took the bearings of what seemed to be a good sized stall at the further end of the place, purposing to grope his way to it when he should be left to himself. He also noted the position of a pile of horse blankets, midway of the route, with the intent to levy upon them for the service of the crown of England for one night.

By and by the men finished and went away, fastening the door behind them and taking the lantern with them. The shivering king made for the blankets, with as good speed as the darkness would allow; gathered them up and then groped his way safely to the stall. Of two of the blankets he made a bed, then covered himself with the remaining two. He was a glad monarch, now, though the blankets were old and thin, and not quite warm enough; and besides gave out a pungent horsy odor that was almost suffocatingly powerful.

Although the king was hungry and chilly, he was also so tired and so drowsy that these latter influences soon began to get the advantage of the former, and he presently dozed off into a state of semi-consciousness. Then, just as he was on the point of losing himself wholly, he distinctly felt something touch him! He was broad awake in a moment, and gasping for breath. The cold horror of that mysterious touch in the dark almost made his heart stand still. He lay motionless, and listened, scarcely breathing. But nothing stirred, and there was no sound. He continued to listen, and wait, during what seemed a long time, but still nothing stirred, and there was no sound. So he began to drop into a drowse once more, at last; and all at once he felt that mysterious touch again! It was a grisly thing, this light touch from this noiseless and invisible presence; it made the boy sick with ghostly fears. What should he do? That was the question; but he did not know how to answer it. Should he leave these reasonably comfort-able quarters and fly from this inscrutable horror? But fly whither? He could not get out of the barn; and the idea of skurrying blindly hither and thither in the dark, within the captivity of the four walls, with this phantom gliding after him, and visiting him with that soft hideous touch upon cheek or shoulder at every turn, was intolerable. But to stay where he was, and endure this living death all night? —was that better? No. What, then, was there left to do? Ah, there was but one course; he knew it well—he must put out his hand and find that thing!

It was easy to think this; but it was hard to brace himself up to try it. Three times he stretched his hand a little way out into the dark, gingerly; and snatched it suddenly back, with a gasp—not because it had encountered anything, but because he had felt so sure it was just *going* to. But the fourth time, he groped a little further, and his hand lightly swept against something soft and warm. This petrified him, nearly, with fright—his mind was in such a state that he could imagine the thing to be nothing else than a corpse, newly dead and still warm. He thought he would rather die than touch it again. But he thought this false thought because he did not know the immortal strength of human curiosity. In no long time his hand was tremblingly groping again—against his judgment, and without his consent—but groping persistently on, just the same. It encountered a bunch of long hair; he shuddered, but followed up the hair and found what seemed

to be a warm rope; followed up the rope and found an innocent calf!—for the rope was not a rope at all, but the calf's
tail.

The king was cordially ashamed of himself for having gotten all that fright and misery out of so paltry a matter as a
slumbering calf; but he need not have felt so about it, for it
was not the calf that frightened him but a dreadful non-
existent something which the calf stood for; and any other
boy, in those old superstitious times, would have acted and
suffered just as he had done.

The king was not only delighted to find that the creature
was only a calf, but delighted to have the calf's company; for
he had been feeling so lonesome and friendless that the company and comradeship of even this humble animal was welcome. And he had been so buffeted, so rudely entreated by
his own kind, that it was a real comfort to him to feel that he
was at last in the society of a fellow creature that had at least a
soft heart and a gentle spirit, whatever loftier attributes might
be lacking. So he resolved to waive rank and make friends
with the calf.

While stroking its sleek warm back—for it lay near him
and within easy reach—it occurred to him that this calf might
be utilized in more ways than one. Whereupon he re-arranged
his bed, spreading it down close to the calf; then he cuddled
himself up to the calf's back, drew the covers up over himself
and his friend, and in a minute or two was as warm and comfortable as he had ever been in the downy couches of the regal
palace of Westminster.

Pleasant thoughts came, at once; life took on a cheerfuller
seeming. He was free of the bonds of servitude and crime,
free of the companionship of base and brutal outlaws; he was
warm, he was sheltered; in a word, he was happy. The night
wind was rising; it swept by in fitful gusts that made the old
barn quake and rattle, then its forces died down at intervals,
and went moaning and wailing around corners and projections—but it was all music to the king, now that he was snug
and comfortable; let it blow and rage, let it batter and bang,
let it moan and wail, he minded it not, he only enjoyed it. He
merely snuggled the closer to his friend, in a luxury of warm
contentment, and drifted blissfully out of consciousness into a

deep and dreamless sleep that was full of serenity and peace. The distant dogs howled, the melancholy kine complained, and the winds went on raging, whilst furious sheets of rain drove along the roof; but the majesty of England slept on, undisturbed, and the calf did the same, it being a simple creature and not easily troubled by storms or embarrassed by sleeping with a king.

Chapter 19

THE PRINCE WITH THE PEASANTS

WHEN THE KING awoke in the early morning, he found that a wet but thoughtful rat had crept into the place during the night and made a cosy bed for itself in his bosom. Being disturbed, now, it scampered away. The boy smiled, and said, "Poor fool, why so fearful? I am as forlorn as thou. 'Twould be shame in me to hurt the helpless, who am myself so helpless. Moreover, I owe you thanks for a good omen; for when a king has fallen so low that the very rats do make a bed of him, it surely meaneth that his fortunes be upon the turn, since it is plain he can no lower go."

He got up and stepped out of the stall, and just then he heard the sound of children's voices. The barn door opened and a couple of little girls came in. As soon as they saw him their talking and laughing ceased, and they stopped and stood still, gazing at him with strong curiosity; they presently began to whisper together, then they approached nearer, and stopped again to gaze and whisper. By and by they gathered courage and began to discuss him aloud. One said—

"He hath a comely face."

The other added—

"And pretty hair."

"But is ill clothed, enow."

"And how starved he looketh."

They came still nearer, sidling shyly around and about him, examining him minutely from all points, as if he were some strange new kind of animal; but warily and watchfully, the while, as if they half feared he might be a sort of animal that would bite, upon occasion. Finally they halted before him, holding each other's hands, for protection, and took a good satisfying stare with their innocent eyes; then one of them plucked up all her courage and inquired with honest directness—

"Who art thou, boy?"

"I am the king," was the grave answer.

The children gave a little start, and their eyes spread them-selves wide open and remained so during a speechless half minute. Then curiosity broke the silence—

"The *king*? What king?"

"The king of England."

The children looked at each other—then at him—then at each other again—wonderingly, perplexedly—then one said—

"Didst hear him, Margery?—he saith he is the king. Can that be true?"

"How can it be else but true, Prissy? Would he say a lie? For look you, Prissy, an' it were not true, it *would* be a lie. It surely would be. Now think on't. For all things that be not true, be lies—thou canst make naught else out of it."

It was a good tight argument, without a leak in it any-where; and it left Prissy's half-doubts not a leg to stand on. She considered a moment, then put the king upon his honor with the simple remark—

"If thou art truly the king, then I believe thee."

"I am truly the king."

This settled the matter. His majesty's royalty was accepted without further question or discussion, and the two little girls began at once to inquire into how he came to be where he was, and how he came to be so unroyally clad, and whither he was bound, and all about his affairs. It was a mighty relief to him to pour out his troubles where they would not be scoffed at or doubted; so he told his tale with feeling, forgetting even his hunger for the time; and it was received with the deepest and tenderest sympathy by the gentle little maids. But when he got down to his latest experiences and they learned how long he had been without food, they cut him short and hur-ried him away to the farm house to find a breakfast for him.

The king was cheerful and happy, now, and said to himself, "When I am come to mine own again, I will always honor little children, remembering how that these trusted me and believed in me in my time of trouble, whilst they that were older, and thought themselves wiser, mocked at me and held me for a liar."

The children's mother received the king kindly, and was full of pity; for his forlorn condition and apparently crazed intellect touched her womanly heart. She was a widow, and rather poor; consequently she had seen trouble enough to enable her to feel for the unfortunate. She imagined that the demented boy had wandered away from his friends or keepers; so she tried to find out whence he had come, in order that she might take measures to return him; but all her references to neighboring towns and villages, and all her inquiries in the same line, went for nothing—the boy's face, and his answers, too, showed that the things she was talking of were not familiar to him. He spoke earnestly and simply about court matters; and broke down, more than once, when speaking of the late king "his father;" but whenever the conversation changed to baser topics, he lost interest and became silent.

The woman was mightily puzzled; but she did not give up. As she proceeded with her cooking, she set herself to contriving devices to surprise the boy into betraying his real secret. She talked about cattle—he showed no concern; then about sheep—the same result—so her guess that he had been a shepherd boy was an error; she talked about mills; and about weavers, tinkers, smiths, trades and tradesmen of all sorts; and about Bedlam, and jails, and charitable retreats; but no matter, she was baffled at all points. Not altogether, either; for she argued that she had narrowed the thing down to domestic service. Yes, she was sure she was on the right track, now—he must have been a house servant. So she led up to that. But the result was discouraging. The subject of sweeping appeared to weary him; fire-building failed to stir him; scrubbing and scouring awoke no enthusiasm. Then the goodwife touched, with a perishing hope, and rather as a matter of form, upon the subject of cooking. To her surprise, and her vast delight, the king's face lighted at once! Ah, she had hunted him down at last, she thought; and she was right proud, too, of the devious shrewdness and tact which had accomplished it.

Her tired tongue got a chance to rest, now; for the king's, inspired by gnawing hunger and the fragrant smells that came from the sputtering pots and pans, turned itself loose, and delivered itself up to such an eloquent dissertation upon certain toothsome dishes, that within three minutes the woman said to herself, "Of a truth I was right—he hath holpen in a kitchen!" Then he broadened his bill of fare, and discussed it with such appreciation and animation, that the goodwife said to herself, "Good lack! how can he know so many dishes, and so fine ones withal? For these belong only upon the tables of the rich and great. Ah, now I see! ragged outcast as he is, he must have served in the palace before his reason went astray; yes, he must have helped in the very kitchen of the king himself! I will test him."

Full of eagerness to prove her sagacity, she told the king to mind the cooking a moment—hinting that he might manufacture and add a dish or two, if he chose—then she went out of the room and gave her children a sign to follow after. The king muttered—

"Another English king had a commission like to this, in a bygone time—it is nothing against my dignity to undertake an office which the great Alfred stood to assume. But I will try to better serve my trust than he; for he let the cakes burn."

The intent was good, but the performance was not answerable to it; for this king, like the other one, soon fell into deep thinkings concerning his vast affairs, and the same calamity resulted—the cookery got burned. The woman returned in time to save the breakfast from entire destruction; and she promptly brought the king out of his dreams with a brisk and cordial tongue-lashing. Then, seeing how troubled he was, over his violated trust, she softened at once and was all goodness and gentleness toward him.

The boy made a hearty and satisfying meal, and was greatly refreshed and gladdened by it. It was a meal which was distinguished by this curious feature, that rank was waived on both sides; yet neither recipient of the favor was aware that it had been extended. The goodwife had intended to feed this young tramp with broken victuals in a corner, like any other tramp, or like a dog; but she was so remorseful for the scolding she had given him, that she did what she could to atone for it by allowing him to sit at the family table and eat with his betters, on ostensible terms of equality with them; and the king, on his side, was so remorseful for having broken his trust, after the family had been so kind to him, that he forced himself to atone for it by humbling himself to the family level, instead of requiring the woman and her children to stand and wait upon him while he occupied their table in the solitary state due to his birth and dignity. It does us all good to unbend some-times. This good woman was made happy all the day long by the applauses which she got out of herself for her magnani-mous condescension to a tramp; and the king was just as self-complacent over his gracious humility toward a humble peasant woman.

When breakfast was over, the housewife told the king to wash up the dishes. This command was a staggerer, for a mo-ment, and the king came near rebelling; but then he said to himself, "Alfred the Great watched the cakes; doubtless he would have washed the dishes, too—therefore will I essay it."

He made a sufficiently poor job of it; and to his surprise, too, for the cleaning of wooden spoons and trenchers had seemed an easy thing to do. It was a tedious and troublesome piece of work, but he finished it at last. He was becoming impatient to get away on his journey now; however, he was not to lose this thrifty dame's society so easily. She furnished him some little odds and ends of employment, which he got through with after a fair fashion and with some credit. Then she set him and the little girls to paring some winter apples; but he was so awkward at this service, that she retired him from it and gave him a butcher knife to grind. Afterward she kept him carding wool until he began to think he had laid the good King Alfred about far enough in the shade for the present, in the matter of showy menial heroisms that would read picturesquely in story-books and histories, and so he was half minded to resign. And when, just after the noonday din-ner, the goodwife gave him a basket of kittens to drown, he did resign. At least he was just going to resign—for he felt that he must draw the line somewhere, and it seemed to him that to draw it at kitten-drowning was about the right thing—when there was an interruption. The interruption was John Canty—with a pedlar's pack on his back—and Hugo!

The king discovered these rascals approaching the front gate before they had had a chance to see him; so he said noth-ing about drawing the line, but took up his basket of kittens and stepped quietly out the back way, without a word. He left the creatures in an outhouse, and hurried on, into a nar-row lane at the rear.

Chapter 20

The Prince and the Hermit

THE HIGH HEDGE hid him from the house, now; and so, under the impulse of a deadly fright, he let out all his forces and sped toward a wood in the distance. He never looked back until he had almost gained the shelter of the forest; then he turned and descried two figures in the distance. That was sufficient; he did not wait to scan them critically, but hurried on, and never abated his pace till he was far within the twilight depths of the wood. Then he stopped; being persuaded that he was now tolerably safe. He listened intently, but the stillness was profound and solemn—awful, even, and depressing to the spirits. At wide intervals his straining ear did detect sounds, but they were so remote, and hollow, and mysterious, that they seemed not to be real sounds, but only the moaning and complaining ghosts of departed ones. So the sounds were yet more dreary than the silence which they interrupted.

It was his purpose, in the beginning, to stay where he was, the rest of the day; but a chill soon invaded his perspiring body, and he was at last obliged to resume movement in order to get warm. He struck straight through the forest, hoping to pierce to a road presently, but he was disappointed in this. He traveled on and on; but the further he went, the denser the wood became, apparently. The gloom began to thicken, by and by, and the king realized that the night was coming on. It made him shudder to think of spending it in such an uncanny place; so he tried to hurry faster, but he only made the less speed, for he could not now see well enough to choose his steps judiciously; consequently he kept tripping over roots and tangling himself in vines and briers.

And how glad he was when at last he caught the glimmer of a light! He approached it warily, stopping often to look about him and listen. It came from an unglazed window-opening in a shabby little hut. He heard a voice, now, and felt a disposition to run and hide; but he changed his mind at once, for this voice was praying, evidently. He glided to the one window of the hut, raised himself on tiptoe, and stole a glance within. The room was small; its floor was the natural earth, beaten hard by use; in a corner was a bed of rushes and a ragged blanket or two; near it was a pail, a cup, a basin, and two or three pots and pans; there was a short bench and a three-legged stool; on the hearth the remains of a faggot fire were smouldering; before a shrine, which was lighted by a single candle, knelt an aged man, and on an old wooden box at his side, lay an open book and a human skull. The man was of large, bony frame; his hair and whiskers were very long and snowy white; he was clothed in a robe of sheepskins which reached from his neck to his heels.

"A holy hermit!" said the king to himself; "now am I indeed fortunate."

The hermit rose from his knees; the king knocked. A deep voice responded—

"Enter!—but leave sin behind, for the ground whereon thou shalt stand is holy!"

The king entered, and paused. The hermit turned a pair of gleaming, unrestful eyes upon him, and said—

"Who are thou?"

"I am the king," came the answer, with placid simplicity.

"Welcome, king!" cried the hermit, with enthusiasm. Then, bustling about with feverish activity, and constantly saying "welcome, welcome," he arranged his bench, seated the king on it, by the hearth, threw some faggots on the fire, and finally fell to pacing the floor, with a nervous stride.

"Welcome! Many have sought sanctuary here, but they were not worthy, and were turned away. But a king who casts his crown away, and despises the vain splendors of his office, and clothes his body in rags, to devote his life to holiness and the mortification of the flesh—he is worthy, he is welcome!—Here shall he abide all his days till death come." The king hastened to interrupt and explain, but the hermit paid no attention to him—did not even hear him, apparently, but went right on with his talk, with a raised voice and a growing energy. "And thou shalt be at peace here. None shall find out thy refuge to disquiet thee with supplications to return to that empty and foolish life which God hath moved thee to abandon. Thou shalt pray, here; thou shalt study the Book; thou shalt meditate upon the follies and delusions of this world, and upon the sublimities of the world to come; thou shalt feed upon crusts and herbs, and scourge thy body with whips, daily, to the purifying of thy soul. Thou shalt wear a hair shirt next thy skin; thou shalt drink water, only; and thou shalt be at peace; yes, wholly at peace; for whoso comes to seek thee shall go his way again, baffled; he shall not find thee, he shall not molest thee."

The old man, still pacing back and forth, ceased to speak aloud, and began to mutter. The king seized this opportunity to state his case; and he did it with an eloquence inspired by uneasiness and apprehension. But the hermit went on muttering, and gave no heed. And still muttering, he approached the king and said, impressively—

"Sh! I will tell you a secret!" He bent down to impart it, but checked himself, and assumed a listening attitude. After a moment or two he went on tiptoe to the window-opening, put his head out and peered around in the gloaming, then came tiptoeing back again, put his face close down to the king's, and whispered—

"I am an archangel!"

The king started violently, and said to himself, "Would God I were with the outlaws again; for lo, now am I the prisoner of a madman!" His apprehensions were heightened, and they showed plainly in his face. In a low, excited voice, the hermit continued—

"I see you feel my atmosphere! There's awe in your face! None may be in this atmosphere and not be thus affected; for it is the very atmosphere of heaven. I go thither and return, in the twinkling of an eye. I was made an archangel on this very spot, it is five years ago, by angels sent from heaven to confer that awful dignity. Their presence filled this place with an intolerable brightness. And they knelt to me, king! yes, they knelt to me! for I was greater than they. I have walked in the courts of heaven, and held speech with the patriarchs. Touch my hand—be not afraid—touch it. There—now thou hast touched a hand which has been clasped by Abraham, and Isaac and Jacob! For I have walked in the golden courts, I have seen the Deity face to face!" He paused, to give this speech effect; then his face suddenly changed, and he started to his feet again, saying, with angry energy, "Yes, I am an archangel; *a mere archangel!*—I that might have been Pope! It is verily true. I was told it from heaven in a dream, twenty years ago; ah, yes, I was to be Pope!—and I *should* have been Pope, for heaven had said it—but the king dissolved my religious house, and I, poor obscure unfriended monk, was cast homeless upon the world, robbed of my mighty destiny!" Here he began to mumble again, and beat his forehead in futile rage, with his fist; now and then articulating a venomous curse, and now and then a pathetic "Wherefore I am naught but an archangel—I that should have been Pope!"

So he went on, for an hour, whilst the poor little king sat and suffered. Then all at once the old man's frenzy departed, and he became all gentleness. His voice softened, he came down out of his clouds, and fell to prattling along so simply and so humanly, that he soon won the king's heart completely. The old devotee moved the boy nearer to the fire and made him comfortable; doctored his small bruises and abrasions with a deft and tender hand; and then set about preparing and cooking a supper—chatting pleasantly all the time, and occasionally stroking the lad's cheek or patting his head, in such a gently caressing way that in a little while all the fear and repulsion inspired by the archangel were changed to reverence and affection for the man.

This happy state of things continued while the two ate the supper; then, after a prayer before the shrine, the hermit put the boy to bed, in a small adjoining room, tucking him in as snugly and lovingly as a mother might; and so, with a parting caress, left him and sat down by the fire, and began to poke the brands about in an absent and aimless way. Presently he paused; then tapped his forehead several times with his fingers, as if trying to recal some thought which had escaped from his mind. Apparently he was unsuccessful. Now he started quickly up, and entered his guest's room, and said—

"Thou art king?"

"Yes," was the response, drowsily uttered.

"What king?"

"Of England."

"Of England! Then Henry is gone!"

"Alack, it is so. I am his son."

A black frown settled down upon the hermit's face, and he clenched his bony hands with a vindictive energy. He stood a few moments, breathing fast and swallowing repeatedly, then said in a husky voice—

"Dost know it was he that turned us out into the world houseless and homeless?"

There was no response. The old man bent down and scanned the boy's reposeful face and listened to his placid breathing. "He sleeps—sleeps soundly;" and the frown vanished away and gave place to an expression of evil satisfaction. A smile flitted across the dreaming boy's features. The hermit muttered, "So—his heart is happy;" and he turned away. He went stealthily about the place, seeking here and there for something; now and then halting to listen, now and then jerking his head around and casting a quick glance toward the bed; and always muttering, always mumbling to himself. At last he found what he seemed to want—a rusty old butcher knife and a whetstone. Then he crept to his place by the fire, sat himself down, and began to whet the knife softly on the stone, still muttering, mumbling, ejaculating. The winds sighed around the lonely place, the mysterious voices of the night floated by out of the distances, the shining eyes of venturesome mice and rats peered out at the old man from cracks and coverts, but he went on with his work, rapt, absorbed, and noted none of these things.

At long intervals he drew his thumb along the edge of his knife, and nodded his head with satisfaction. "It grows sharper," he said; "yes, it grows sharper."

He took no note of the flight of time, but worked tranquilly on, entertaining himself with his thoughts, which broke out occasionally in articulate speech:

"His father wrought us evil, he destroyed us—and is gone down into the eternal fires! Yes, down into the eternal fires! He escaped us—but it was God's will, yes it was God's will, we must not repine. But he hath not escaped the fires! no, he hath not escaped the fires, the consuming, unpitying, remorseless fires—and *they* are everlasting!"

And so he wrought; and still wrought; mumbling—chuckling a low rasping chuckle, at times—and at times breaking again into words:

"It was his father that did it all. I am but an archangel— but for him, I should be Pope!"

The king stirred. The hermit sprang noiselessly to the bedside, and went down upon his knees, bending over the prostrate form with his knife uplifted. The boy stirred again; his eyes came open for an instant, but there was no speculation in them, they saw nothing; the next moment his tranquil breathing showed that his sleep was sound once more.

The hermit watched and listened, for a time, keeping his position and scarcely breathing; then he slowly lowered his arm, and presently crept away, saying,—

"It is long past midnight—it is not best that he should cry out, lest by accident some one be passing."

He glided about his hovel, gathering a rag here, a thong there, and another one yonder; then he returned, and by careful and gentle handling, he managed to tie the king's ankles together without waking him. Next he essayed to tie the wrists; he made several attempts to cross them, but the boy always drew one hand or the other away, just as the cord was ready to be applied; but at last, when the archangel was almost ready to despair, the boy crossed his hands himself, and the next moment they were bound. Now a bandage was passed under the sleeper's chin and brought up over his head and tied fast—and so softly, so gradually, and so deftly were the knots drawn together and compacted, that the boy slept peacefully through it all without stirring.

Chapter 21

HENDON TO THE RESCUE

THE OLD MAN glided away, stooping, stealthy, cat-like, and brought the low bench. He seated himself upon it, half his body in the dim and flickering light, and the other half in shadow; and so, with his craving eyes bent upon the slumbering boy, he kept his patient vigil there, heedless of the drift of time, and softly whetted his knife, and mumbled and chuckled; and in aspect and attitude he resembled nothing so much as a grisly, monstrous spider, gloating over some hapless insect that lay bound and helpless in his web.

After a long while, the old man, who was still gazing,—yet not seeing, his mind having settled into a dreamy abstraction,—observed on a sudden, that the boy's eyes were open—wide open and staring!—staring up in frozen horror at the knife. The smile of a gratified devil crept over the old man's face, and he said, without changing his attitude or his occupation—

"Son of Henry the Eighth, hast thou prayed?"

The boy struggled helplessly in his bonds; and at the same time forced a smothered sound through his closed jaws, which the hermit chose to interpret as an affirmative answer to his question.

"Then pray again. Pray the prayer for the dying!"

A shudder shook the boy's frame, and his face blenched. Then he struggled again to free himself—turning and twisting himself this way and that; tugging frantically, fiercely, desperately—but uselessly—to burst his fetters: and all the while the old ogre smiled down upon him, and nodded his head, and placidly whetted his knife; mumbling, from time to time, "The moments are precious, they are few and precious—pray the prayer for the dying!"

The boy uttered a despairing groan, and ceased from his struggles, panting. The tears came, then, and trickled, one after the other, down his face; but this piteous sight wrought no softening effect upon the savage old man.

133

The dawn was coming, now; the hermit observed it, and spoke up sharply, with a touch of nervous apprehension in his voice—

"I may not indulge this ecstasy longer! The night is already gone. It seems but a moment—only a moment; would it had endured a year! Seed of the Church's spoiler, close thy perishing eyes, an' thou fearest to look upon . . . . ."

The rest was lost in inarticulate mutterings. The old man sunk upon his knees, his knife in his hand, and bent himself over the moaning boy—

Hark! There was a sound of voices near the cabin—the knife dropped from the hermit's hand; he cast a sheepskin over the boy and started up, trembling. The sounds increased, and presently the voices became rough and angry; then came blows, and cries for help; then a clatter of swift footsteps, retreating. Immediately came a succession of thundering knocks upon the cabin door, followed by—

"Hullo-o-o! Open! And despatch, in the name of all the devils!"

O, this was the blessedest sound that had ever made music in the king's ears; for it was Miles Hendon's voice!

The hermit, grinding his teeth in impotent rage, moved swiftly out of the bedchamber, closing the door behind him; and straightway the king heard a talk, to this effect, proceeding from the "chapel:"

"Homage and greeting, reverend sir! Where is the boy— *my* boy?"

"What boy, friend?"

"What boy! Lie me no lies, sir priest, play me no deceptions!—I am not in the humor for it. Near to this place I caught the scoundrels who I judged did steal him from me, and I made them confess; they said he was at large again, and they had tracked him to your door. They showed me his very footprints. Now palter no more; for look you, holy sir, an' thou produce him not— Where is the boy?"

"O, good sir, peradventure you mean the ragged regal vagrant that tarried here the night. If such as you take interest in such as he, know, then, that I have sent him of an errand. He will be back anon."

"How soon? How soon? Come, waste not the time—can not I overtake him? How soon will he be back?"

"Thou needst not stir; he will return quickly."

"So be it, then. I will try to wait. But stop!—*you* sent him of an errand?—you! Verily this is a lie—he would not go. He would pull thy old beard, an' thou didst offer him such an insolence. Thou hast lied, friend; thou hast surely lied! He would not go for thee nor for any man."

"For any *man*—no; haply not. But I am not a man."

"*What!* Now o' God's name what art thou, then?"

"It is a secret—mark thou reveal it not. I am an archangel!"

There was a tremendous ejaculation from Miles Hendon—not altogether unprofane—followed by—

"This doth well and truly account for his complaisance! Right well I knew he would budge nor hand nor foot in the menial service of any mortal; but lord, even a king must obey when an archangel gives the word o' command! Let me—'sh! What noise was that?"

All this while the little king had been yonder, alternately quaking with terror and trembling with hope; and all the while, too, he had thrown all the strength he could into his anguished moanings, constantly expecting them to reach Hendon's ear, but always realizing, with bitterness, that they failed, or at least made no impression. So this last remark of his servant came as comes a reviving breath from fresh fields to the dying; and he exerted himself once more, and with all his energy, just as the hermit was saying—

"Noise? I heard only the wind."

"Mayhap it was. Yes, doubtless that was it. I have been hearing it faintly all the—there it is again! It is not the wind! What an odd sound! Come, we will hunt it out!"

Now the king's joy was nearly insupportable. His tired lungs did their utmost—and hopefully, too—but the sealed jaws and the muffling sheepskin sadly crippled the effort. Then the poor fellow's heart sank, to hear the hermit say—

"Ah, it came from without—I think from the copse yonder. Come, I will lead the way."

The king heard the two pass out, talking; heard their footsteps die quickly away—then he was alone with a boding, brooding, awful silence.

It seemed an age till he heard the steps and voices approaching again—and this time he heard an added sound,—the trampling of hoofs, apparently. Then he heard Hendon say—

"I will not wait longer. I *cannot* wait longer. He has lost his way in this thick wood. Which direction took he? Quick—point it out to me."

"He—but wait; I will go with thee."

"Good—good! Why, truly thou art better than thy looks. Marry I do think there's not another archangel with so right a heart as thine. Wilt ride? Wilt take the wee donkey that's for my boy, or wilt thou fork thy holy legs over this ill-conditioned slave of a mule that I have provided for myself?—and had been cheated in, too, had he cost but the indifferent sum of a month's usury on a brass farthing let to a tinker out of work."

"No—ride thy mule, and lead thine ass; I am surer on mine own feet, and will walk."

"Then prithee mind the little beast for me while I take my life in my hands and make what success I may toward mounting the big one."

Then followed a confusion of kicks, cuffs, tramplings and plungings, accompanied by a thunderous intermingling of volleyed curses, and finally a bitter apostrophe to the mule, which must have broken its spirit, for hostilities seemed to cease from that moment.

With unutterable misery the fettered little king heard the voices and footsteps fade away and die out. All hope forsook him, now, for the moment, and a dull despair settled down upon his heart. "My only friend is deceived and got rid of," he said; "the hermit will return and—" He finished with a gasp; and at once fell to struggling so frantically with his bonds again, that he shook off the smothering sheepskin.

And now he heard the door open! The sound chilled him to the marrow—already he seemed to feel the knife at his throat. Horror made him close his eyes; horror made him open them again—and before him stood John Canty and Hugo!

He would have said "Thank God!" if his jaws had been free.

A moment or two later his limbs were at liberty, and his captors, each gripping him by an arm, were hurrying him with all speed through the forest.

Chapter 22

A Victim of Treachery

ONCE MORE "King Foo-foo the First" was roving with the tramps and outlaws, a butt for their coarse jests and dull-witted railleries, and sometimes the victim of small spitefulnesses at the hands of Canty and Hugo when the Ruffler's back was turned. None but Canty and Hugo really disliked him. Some of the others liked him, and all admired his pluck and spirit. During two or three days, Hugo, in whose ward and charge the king was, did what he covertly could to make the boy uncomfortable; and at night, during the customary orgies, he amused the company by putting small indignities upon him—always as if by accident. Twice he stepped upon the king's toes—accidentally—and the king, as became his royalty, was contemptuously unconscious of it and indifferent to it; but the third time Hugo entertained himself in that way, the king felled him to the ground with a cudgel, to the prodigious delight of the tribe. Hugo, consumed with anger and shame, sprang up, seized a cudgel, and came at his small adversary in a fury. Instantly a ring was formed around the gladiators, and the betting and cheering began. But poor Hugo stood no chance whatever. His frantic and lubberly 'prentice-work found but a poor market for itself when pitted against an arm which had been trained by the first masters of Europe in single-stick, quarter-staff, and every art and trick of swordsmanship. The little king stood, alert but at graceful ease, and caught and turned aside the thick rain of blows with a facility and precision which set the motley on-lookers wild with admiration; and every now and then, when his practiced eye detected an opening, and a lightning-swift rap upon Hugo's head followed as a result, the storm of cheers and laughter that swept the place was something wonderful to hear. At the end of fifteen minutes, Hugo, all battered, bruised, and the target for a pitiless bombardment of ridicule, slunk from the field; and the unscathed hero of the fight was seized and borne aloft upon the shoulders of the joyous rabble to the place of honor beside the Ruffler, where with vast ceremony he was crowned King of the Game-Cocks; his meaner title being at the same time solemnly canceled and annulled, and a decree of banishment from the gang pronounced against any who should thenceforth utter it.

All attempts to make the king serviceable to the troop had failed. He had stubbornly refused to act; moreover he was always trying to escape. He had been thrust into an un-watched kitchen, the first day of his return; he not only came forth empty handed, but tried to rouse the housemates. He was sent out with a tinker to help him at his work; he would not work; moreover he threatened the tinker with his own soldering-iron; and finally both Hugo and the tinker found their hands full with the mere matter of keeping him from getting away. He delivered the thunders of his royalty upon the heads of all who hampered his liberties or tried to force him to service. He was sent out, in Hugo's charge, in company with a slatternly woman and a diseased baby, to beg; but the result was not encouraging—he declined to plead for the mendicants, or be a party to their cause in any way.

Thus several days went by; and the miseries of this tramping life, and the weariness and sordidness and meanness and vulgarity of it, became gradually and steadily so intolerable to the captive that he began at last to feel that his release from the hermit's knife must prove only a temporary respite from death, at best.

But at night, in his dreams, these things were forgotten, and he was on his throne, and master again. This, of course, intensified the sufferings of the awakening—so the mortifications of each succeeding morning of the few that passed be-tween his return to bondage and the combat with Hugo, grew bitterer and bitterer, and harder and harder to bear.

The morning after that combat, Hugo got up with a heart filled with vengeful purposes against the king. He had two plans, in particular. One was to inflict upon the lad what would be, to his proud spirit and "imagined" royalty, a pecu-liar humiliation; and if he failed to accomplish this, his other plan was to put a crime of some kind upon the king and then betray him into the implacable clutches of the law.

In pursuance of the first plan, he purposed to put a "clime" upon the king's leg; rightly judging that that would mortify him to the last and perfect degree; and as soon as the clime should operate, he meant to get Canty's help, and *force* the king to expose his leg in the highway and beg for alms. "Clime" was the cant term for a sore, artificially created. To make a clime, the operator made a paste or poultice of un-slaked lime, soap, and the rust of old iron, and spread it upon a piece of leather, which was then bound tightly upon the leg. This would presently fret off the skin, and make the flesh raw and angry-looking; blood was then rubbed upon the limb, which, being fully dried, took on a dark and repulsive color. Then a bandage of soiled rags was put on in a cleverly careless way which would allow the hideous ulcer to be seen and move the compassion of the passer-by.*

Hugo got the help of the tinker whom the king had cowed with the soldering-iron; they took the boy out on a tinkering tramp, and as soon as they were out of sight of the camp they threw him down and the tinker held him while Hugo bound the poultice tight and fast upon his leg.

The king raged and stormed, and promised to hang the two the moment the sceptre was in his hand again; but they kept a firm grip upon him and enjoyed his impotent strug-glings and jeered at his threats. This continued until the poul-tice began to bite; and in no long time its work would have been perfected, if there had been no interruption. But there was; for about this time the "slave" who had made the speech denouncing England's laws, appeared on the scene and put an end to the enterprise, and stripped off the poultice and bandage.

The king wanted to borrow his deliverer's cudgel and warm the jackets of the two rascals on the spot; but the man said no, it would bring trouble—leave the matter till night; the whole tribe being together, then, the outside world would not venture to interfere or interrupt. He marched the party back to camp and reported the affair to the Ruffler, who lis-tened, pondered, and then decided that the king should not be again detailed to beg, since it was plain he was worthy of

*From "The English Rogue;" London, 1665.

something higher and better—wherefore, on the spot he promoted him from the mendicant rank and appointed him to steal!

Hugo was overjoyed. He had already tried to make the king steal, and failed; but there would be no more trouble of that sort, now, for of course the king would not dream of defying a distinct command delivered directly from headquarters. So he planned a raid for that very afternoon, purposing to get the king in the law's grip in the course of it; and to do it, too, with such ingenious strategy, that it should seem to be accidental and unintentional; for the King of the Game-Cocks was popular, now, and the gang might not deal over-gently with an unpopular member who played so serious a treachery upon him as the delivering him over to the common enemy, the law.

Very well. All in good time Hugo strolled off to a neighboring village with his prey; and the two drifted slowly up and down one street after another, the one watching sharply for a sure chance to achieve his evil purpose, and the other watching as sharply for a chance to dart away and get free of his infamous captivity forever.

Both threw away some tolerably fair-looking opportunities; for both, in their secret hearts, were resolved to make absolutely sure work this time, and neither meant to allow his fevered desires to seduce him into any venture that had much uncertainty about it.

Hugo's chance came first. For at last a woman approached who carried a fat package of some sort in a basket. Hugo's eyes sparkled with sinful pleasure as he said to himself, "Breath o' my life, an' I can but put *that* upon him, 'tis goodden and God keep thee, King of the Game-Cocks!" He waited and watched—outwardly patient, but inwardly consuming with excitement—till the woman had passed by, and the time was ripe; then said, in a low voice—

"Tarry here till I come again," and darted stealthily after the prey.

The king's heart was filled with joy—he could make his escape, now, if Hugo's quest only carried him far enough away.

But he was to have no such luck. Hugo crept behind the

woman, snatched the package, and came running back, wrapping it in an old piece of blanket which he carried on his arm. The hue and cry was raised in a moment, by the woman, who knew her loss by the lightening of her burden, although she had not seen the pilfering done. Hugo thrust the bundle into the king's hands without halting, saying,—

"Now speed ye after me with the rest, and cry 'Stop thief!' but mind ye lead them astray!"

The next moment Hugo turned a corner and darted down a crooked alley,—and in another moment or two he lounged into view again, looking innocent and indifferent, and took up a position behind a post to watch results.

The insulted king threw the bundle on the ground; and the blanket fell away from it just as the woman arrived, with an augmenting crowd at her heels; she seized the king's wrist with one hand, snatched up her bundle with the other, and began to pour out a tirade of abuse upon the boy while he struggled, without success, to free himself from her grip.

Hugo had seen enough—his enemy was captured and the law would get him, now—so he slipped away, jubilant and chuckling, and wended campwards, framing a judicious version of the matter to give to the Ruffler's crew as he strode along.

The king continued to struggle in the woman's strong grasp, and now and then cried out, in vexation—

"Unhand me, thou foolish creature; it was not I that bereaved thee of thy paltry goods."

The crowd closed around, threatening the king and calling him names; a brawny blacksmith, in leather apron, and sleeves rolled to his elbows, made a reach for him, saying he would trounce him well, for a lesson; but just then a long sword flashed in the air and fell with convincing force upon the man's arm, flat-side down, the fantastic owner of it remarking pleasantly at the same time—

"Marry, good souls, let us proceed gently, not with ill blood and uncharitable words. This is matter for the law's consideration, not private and unofficial handling. Loose thy hold from the boy, goodwife."

The blacksmith averaged the stalwart soldier with a glance, then went muttering away, rubbing his arm; the woman released the boy's wrist reluctantly; the crowd eyed the stranger unlovingly, but prudently closed their mouths. The king sprang to his deliverer's side, with flushed cheeks and sparkling eyes, exclaiming—

"Thou hast lagged sorely, but thou comest in good season, now, Sir Miles; carve me this rabble to rags!"

Chapter 23

THE PRINCE A PRISONER

HENDON FORCED back a smile, and bent down and whispered in the king's ear—

"Softly, softly, my prince, wag thy tongue warily—nay, suffer it not to wag at all. Trust in me—all shall go well in the end." Then he added, to himself: "*Sir* Miles! Bless me, I had totally forgot I was a knight! Lord, how marvelous a thing it is, the grip his memory doth take upon his quaint and crazy fancies! . . . . . . An empty and foolish title is mine, and yet it is something to have deserved it; for I think it is more honor to be held worthy to be a spectre-knight in his Kingdom of Dreams and Shadows, than to be held base enough to be an earl in some of the *real* kingdoms of this world."

The crowd fell apart to admit a constable, who approached and was about to lay his hand upon the king's shoulder, when Hendon said—

"Gently, good friend, withhold your hand—he shall go peaceably; I am responsible for that. Lead on, we will follow."

The officer led, with the woman and her bundle; Miles and the king followed after, with the crowd at their heels. The king was inclined to rebel; but Hendon said to him in a low voice—

"Reflect, sire—your laws are the wholesome breath of your own royalty; shall their source resist them, yet require the branches to respect them? Apparently one of these laws has been broken; when the king is on his throne again, can it ever grieve him to remember that when he was seemingly a private person he loyally sunk the king in the citizen and submitted to its authority?"

"Thou art right; say no more; thou shalt see that whatsoever the king of England requires a subject to suffer under the law, he will himself suffer while he holdeth the station of a subject."

When the woman was called upon to testify before the jus-

tice of the peace, she swore that the small prisoner at the bar
was the person who had committed the theft; there was none
able to show the contrary, so the king stood convicted. The
bundle was now unrolled, and when the contents proved to
be a plump little dressed pig, the judge looked troubled,
whilst Hendon turned pale, and his body was thrilled with an
electric shiver of dismay; but the king remained unmoved,
protected by his ignorance. The judge meditated, during
an ominous pause, then turned to the woman, with the
question—

"What dost thou hold this property to be worth?"

The woman curtsied and replied—

"Three shillings and eightpence, your worship—I could
not abate a penny and set forth the value honestly."

The justice glanced around uncomfortably upon the crowd,
then nodded to the constable and said—

"Clear the court and close the doors."

It was done. None remained but the two officials, the accused, the accuser, and Miles Hendon. This latter was rigid
and colorless, and on his forehead big drops of cold sweat
gathered, broke and blended together, and trickled down his
face. The judge turned to the woman again, and said, in a
compassionate voice—

"'Tis a poor ignorant lad, and mayhap was driven hard by
hunger, for these be grievous times for the unfortunate; mark
you, he hath not an evil face—but when hunger driveth—
Good woman! dost know that when one steals a thing above
the value of thirteen pence ha'penny the law saith he shall
hang for it!"

The little king started, wide-eyed with consternation, but
controlled himself and held his peace; but not so the woman.
She sprang to her feet, shaking with fright, and cried out—

"O, good lack, what have I done! God-a-mercy, I would
not hang the poor thing for the whole world! Ah, save me
from this, your worship—what shall I do, what *can* I do?"

The justice maintained his judicial composure, and simply
said—

"Doubtless it is allowable to revise the value, since it is not
yet writ upon the record."

"Then in God's name call the pig eightpence, and heaven

bless the day that freed my conscience of this awesome thing!"

Miles Hendon forgot all decorum in his delight; and surprised the king and wounded his dignity, by throwing his arms around him and hugging him. The woman made her grateful adieux and started away with her pig; and when the constable opened the door for her, he followed her out into the narrow hall. The justice proceeded to write in his record book. Hendon, always alert, thought he would like to know why the officer followed the woman out; so he slipped softly into the dusky hall and listened. He heard a conversation to this effect—

"It is a fat pig, and promises good eating; I will buy it of thee; here is the eightpence."

"Eightpence, indeed! Thou'lt do no such thing. It cost me three shillings and eightpence, good honest coin of the last reign, that old Harry that's just dead ne'er touched nor tampered with. A fig for thy eightpence!"

"Stands the wind in that quarter? Thou wast under oath, and so swore falsely when thou saidst the value was but eightpence. Come straightway back with me before his worship, and answer for the crime!—and then the lad will hang."

"There, there, dear heart, say no more, I am content. Give me the eightpence, and hold thy peace about the matter."

The woman went off, crying; Hendon slipped back into the court room, and the constable presently followed, after hiding his prize in some convenient place. The justice wrote a while longer, then read the king a wise and kindly lecture, and sentenced him to a short imprisonment in the common jail, to be followed by a public flogging. The astounded king opened his mouth and was probably going to order the good judge to be beheaded on the spot; but he caught a warning sign from Hendon, and succeeded in closing his mouth again before he lost anything out of it. Hendon took him by the hand, now, made reverence to the justice, and the two departed in the wake of the constable toward the jail. The moment the street was reached, the inflamed monarch halted, snatched away his hand, and exclaimed—

"Idiot, dost imagine I will enter a common jail *alive*?"

Hendon bent down and said, somewhat sharply—

"*Will* you trust in me? Peace! and forbear to worsen our chances with dangerous speech. What God wills, will happen; thou canst not hurry it, thou canst not alter it; therefore wait, and be patient—'twill be time enow to rail or rejoice when what is to happen has happened."*

*See Notes to Chapter 23 at end of volume.

Chapter 24

THE ESCAPE

THE SHORT winter day was nearly ended. The streets were deserted, save for a few random stragglers, and these hurried straight along, with the intent look of people who were only anxious to accomplish their errands as quickly as possible and then snugly house themselves from the rising wind and the gathering twilight. They looked neither to the right nor the left; they paid no attention to our party, they did not even seem to see them. Edward the Sixth wondered if the spectacle of a king on his way to jail had ever encountered such marvelous indifference before. By and by the constable arrived at a deserted market-square and proceeded to cross it. When he had reached the middle of it, Hendon laid his hand upon his arm, and said in a low voice—

"Bide a moment, good sir, there is none in hearing, and I would say a word to thee."

"My duty forbids it, sir; prithee hinder me not, the night comes on."

"Stay, nevertheless, for the matter concerns thee nearly. Turn thy back a moment and seem not to see: *let this poor lad escape.*"

"This to me, sir! I arrest thee in—"

"Nay, be not too hasty. See thou be careful and commit no foolish error"—then he shut his voice down to a whisper, and said in the man's ear—"the pig thou hast purchased for eightpence may cost thee thy neck, man!"

The poor constable, taken by surprise, was speechless, at first, then found his tongue and fell to blustering and threatening; but Hendon was tranquil, and waited with patience till his breath was spent; then said—

"I have a liking to thee, friend, and would not willingly see thee come to harm. Observe, I heard it all—every word. I will prove it to thee." Then he repeated the conversation which the officer and the woman had had together in the hall, word for word, and ended with—

"There—have I set it forth correctly?—should not I be able to set it forth correctly before the judge, if occasion required?"

The man was dumb with fear and distress, for a moment; then he rallied and said with forced lightness—

"'Tis making a mighty matter indeed, out of a jest; I but plagued the woman for mine amusement."

"Kept you the woman's pig for amusement?"

The man answered sharply—

"Naught else, good sir—I tell thee 'twas but a jest."

"I do begin to believe thee," said Hendon, with a perplexing mixture of mockery and half-conviction in his tone; "but tarry thou here a moment whilst I run and ask his worship—for nathless, he being a man experienced in law, in jests, in—"

He was moving away, still talking; the constable hesitated, fidgeted, spat out an oath or two, then cried out—

"Hold, hold, good sir—prithee wait a little—the judge! why, man, he hath no more sympathy with a jest than hath a dead corpse!—come, and we will speak further. Ods body! I seem to be in evil case—and all for an innocent and thoughtless pleasantry. I am a man of family; and my wife and little ones—List to reason, good your worship: what wouldst thou of me?"

"Only that thou be blind and dumb and paralytic whilst one may count a hundred thousand—counting slowly," said Hendon, with the expression of a man who asks but a reasonable favor, and that a very little one.

"It is my destruction!" said the constable despairingly. "Ah, be reasonable, good sir; only look at this matter, on all its sides, and see how mere a jest it is—how manifestly and how plainly it is so. And even if one granted it were not a jest, it is a fault so small that e'en the grimmest penalty it could call forth would be but a rebuke and warning from the judge's lips."

Hendon replied with a solemnity which chilled the air about him—

"This jest of thine hath a name, in law—wot you what it is?"

"I knew it not! Peradventure I have been unwise. I never

dreamed it had a name—ah, sweet heaven, I thought it was original."

"Yes, it hath a name. In the law this crime is called *Non compos mentis lex talionis sic transit gloria Mundi.*"

"Ah, my God!"

"And the penalty is death!"

"God be merciful to me, a sinner!"

"By advantage taken of one in fault, in dire peril, and at thy mercy, thou hast seized goods worth above thirteen pence ha'penny, paying but a trifle for the same; and this, in the eye of the law, is constructive barratry, misprision of treason, malfeasance in office, *ad hominem expurgatis in statu quo*—and the penalty is death by the halter, without ransom, commutation, or benefit of clergy."

"Bear me up, bear me up, sweet sir, my legs do fail me! Be thou merciful—spare me this doom, and I will turn my back and see naught that shall happen."

"Good! now thou'rt wise and reasonable. And thou'lt restore the pig?"

"I will, I will indeed—nor ever touch another, though heaven send it and an archangel fetch it. Go—I am blind for thy sake—I see nothing. I will say thou didst break in and wrest the prisoner from my hands by force. It is but a crazy, ancient door—I will batter it down myself betwixt midnight and the morning."

"Do it, good soul, no harm will come of it; the judge hath a loving charity for this poor lad, and will shed no tears and break no jailer's bones for his escape."

Chapter 25

HENDON HALL

As soon as Hendon and the king were out of sight of the constable, his majesty was instructed to hurry to a certain place outside the town, and wait there, whilst Hendon should go to the inn and settle his account. Half an hour later the two friends were blithely jogging eastward on Hendon's sorry steeds. The king was warm and comfortable, now, for he had cast his rags and clothed himself in the second-hand suit which Hendon had bought on London Bridge.

Hendon wished to guard against over-fatiguing the boy; he judged that hard journeys, irregular meals, and illiberal measures of sleep would be bad for his crazed mind; whilst rest, regularity, and moderate exercise would be pretty sure to hasten its cure; he longed to see the stricken intellect made well again and its diseased visions driven out of the tormented little head; therefore he resolved to move by easy stages toward the home whence he had so long been banished, instead of obeying the impulse of his impatience and hurrying along night and day.

When he and the king had journeyed about ten miles, they reached a considerable village, and halted there for the night, at a good inn. The former relations were resumed; Hendon stood behind the king's chair, while he dined, and waited upon him; undressed him when he was ready for bed; then took the floor for his own quarters, and slept athwart the door, rolled up in a blanket.

The next day, and the day after, they jogged lazily along, talking over the adventures they had met since their separation, and mightily enjoying each other's narratives. Hendon detailed all his wide wanderings in search of the king, and described how the archangel had led him a fool's journey all over the forest, and taken him back to the hut, finally, when he found he could not get rid of him. Then—he said—the old man went into the bedchamber and came staggering back looking broken-hearted, and saying he had expected to find that the boy had returned and lain down in there to rest, but it was not so. Hendon had waited at the hut all day; hope of the king's return died out, then, and he departed upon the quest again.

"And old Sanctum Sanctorum *was* truly sorry your highness came not back," said Hendon; "I saw it in his face."

"Marry I will never doubt *that*!" said the king—and then told his own story; after which, Hendon was sorry he had not destroyed the archangel.

During the last day of the trip, Hendon's spirits were soaring. His tongue ran constantly. He talked about his old father, and his brother Arthur, and told of many things which illustrated their high and generous characters; he went into loving frenzies over his Edith, and was so gladhearted that he was even able to say some gentle and brotherly things about Hugh. He dwelt a deal on the coming meeting at Hendon Hall; what a surprise it would be to everybody, and what an outburst of thanksgiving and delight there would be.

It was a fair region, dotted with cottages and orchards, and the road led through broad pasture lands whose receding expanses, marked with gentle elevations and depressions, suggested the swelling and subsiding undulations of the sea. In the afternoon the returning prodigal made constant deflections from his course to see if by ascending some hillock he might not pierce the distance and catch a glimpse of his home. At last he was successful, and cried out excitedly—

"There is the village, my prince, and there is the Hall close by! You may see the towers from here; and that wood there—that is my father's park. Ah, *now* thou'lt know what state and grandeur be! A house with seventy rooms—think of that!—and seven and twenty servants! A brave lodging for such as we, is it not so?—Come, let us speed—my impatience will not brook further delay."

All possible hurry was made; still, it was after three o'clock before the village was reached. The travelers scampered through it, Hendon's tongue going all the time. "Here is the church—covered with the same ivy—none gone, none added." "Yonder is the inn, the old Red Lion,—and yonder is the marketplace." "Here is the May-pole, and here the pump—nothing is altered; nothing but the people, at any rate; ten years make a change in people; some of these I seem to know, but none know me." So his chat ran on. The end of the village was soon reached; then the travelers struck into a crooked, narrow road, walled in with tall hedges, and hurried briskly along it for a half mile, then passed into a vast flower garden through an imposing gateway whose huge stone pillars bore sculptured armorial devices. A noble mansion was before them.

"Welcome to Hendon Hall, my king!" exclaimed Miles. "Ah, 'tis a great day! My father and my brother, and the lady Edith will be so mad with joy that they will have eyes and tongues for none but me in the first transports of the meeting, and so thou'lt seem but coldly welcomed—but mind it not, 'twill soon seem otherwise; for when I say thou art my ward, and tell them how costly is my love for thee, thou'lt see them take thee to their breasts for Miles Hendon's sake, and make their house and hearts thy home forever after!"

The next moment Hendon sprang to the ground before the great door, helped the king down, then took him by the hand and rushed within. A few steps brought him to a spacious apartment; he entered, seated the king with more hurry than ceremony, then ran toward a young man who sat at a writing table in front of a generous fire of logs.

"Embrace me, Hugh," he cried, "and say thou'rt glad I am come again! and call our father, for home is not home till I shall touch his hand, and see his face, and hear his voice once more!"

But Hugh only drew back, after betraying a momentary surprise, and bent a grave stare upon the intruder—a stare which indicated somewhat of offended dignity, at first, then changed, in response to some inward thought or purpose, to an expression of marveling curiosity, mixed with a real or assumed compassion. Presently he said, in a mild voice—

"Thy wits seem touched, poor stranger; doubtless thou hast suffered privations and rude buffetings at the world's hands; thy looks and dress betoken it. Whom dost thou take me to be?"

"Take thee? Prithee for whom else than whom thou art? I take thee to be Hugh Hendon," said Miles, sharply.

The other continued, in the same soft tone—

"And whom dost thou imagine thyself to be?"

"Imagination hath naught to do with it! Dost thou pretend thou knowest me not for thy brother Miles Hendon?"

An expression of pleased surprise flitted across Hugh's face, and he exclaimed—

"What! thou art not jesting? Can the dead come to life? God be praised if it be so! Our poor lost boy restored to our arms after all these cruel years! Ah, it seems too good to be true, it *is* too good to be true—I charge thee, have pity, do not trifle with me! Quick—come to the light—let me scan thee well!"

He seized Miles by the arm, dragged him to the window, and began to devour him from head to foot with his eyes, turning him this way and that, and stepping briskly around him and about him to prove him from all points of view; whilst the returned prodigal, all aglow with gladness, smiled, laughed, and kept nodding his head and saying—

"Go on, brother, go on, and fear not; thou'lt find nor limb nor feature that cannot bide the test. Scour and scan me to thy content, my good old Hugh—I am indeed thy old Miles, thy same old Miles, thy lost brother, is't not so? Ah, 'tis a great day—I *said* 'twas a great day! Give me thy hand, give me thy cheek—lord, I am like to die of very joy!"

He was about to throw himself upon his brother; but Hugh put up his hand in dissent, then dropped his chin mournfully upon his breast, saying with emotion—

"Ah, God of his mercy give me strength to bear this grievous disappointment!"

Miles, amazed, could not speak, for a moment; then he found his tongue, and cried out—

"*What* disappointment? Am I not thy brother?"

Hugh shook his head sadly, and said—

"I pray heaven it may prove so, and that other eyes may find the resemblances that are hid from mine. Alack, I fear me the letter spoke but too truly."

"What letter?"

"One that came from over sea, some six or seven years ago. It said my brother died in battle."

"It was a lie! Call thy father—he will know me."

"One may not call the dead."

"Dead?" Miles's voice was subdued, and his lips trembled. "My father dead!—O, this is heavy news. Half my new joy is withered now. Prithee let me see my brother Arthur—he will know me; he will know me and console me."

"He, also, is dead."

"God be merciful to me, a stricken man! Gone,—both gone—the worthy taken and the worthless spared, in me! Ah! I crave your mercy!—do not say the lady Edith—"

"Is dead? No, she lives."

"Then, God be praised, my joy is whole again! Speed thee, brother—let her come to me! An' *she* say I am not myself,— but she will not; no, no, *she* will know me, I were a fool to doubt it. Bring her—bring the old servants; they, too, will know me."

"All are gone but five—Peter, Halsey, David, Bernard and Margaret."

So saying, Hugh left the room. Miles stood musing, a while, then began to walk the floor, muttering—

"The five arch villains have survived the two-and-twenty leal and honest—'tis an odd thing."

He continued walking back and forth, muttering to himself; he had forgotten the king entirely. By and by his majesty said gravely, and with a touch of genuine compassion, though the words themselves were capable of being interpreted ironically—

"Mind not thy mischance, good man; there be others in the world whose identity is denied, and whose claims are derided. Thou hast company."

"Ah, my king," cried Hendon, coloring slightly, "do not thou condemn me—wait, and thou shalt see. I am no impostor—she will say it; you shall hear it from the sweetest lips in England. I an impostor? Why I know this old hall, these pictures of my ancestors, and all these things that are about us, as a child knoweth its own nursery. Here was I born and bred, my lord; I speak the truth; I would not deceive thee; and should none else believe, I pray thee do not *thou* doubt me—I could not bear it."

"I do not doubt thee," said the king, with a childlike simplicity and faith.

"I thank thee out of my heart!" exclaimed Hendon, with a

fervency which showed that he was touched. The king added, with the same gentle simplicity—

"Dost thou doubt *me?*"

A guilty confusion seized upon Hendon, and he was grateful that the door opened to admit Hugh, at that moment, and saved him the necessity of replying.

A beautiful lady, richly clothed, followed Hugh, and after her came several liveried servants. The lady walked slowly, with her head bowed and her eyes fixed upon the floor. The face was unspeakably sad. Miles Hendon sprang forward, crying out—

"O, my Edith, my darling—"

But Hugh waved him back, gravely, and said to the lady—

"Look upon him. Do you know him?"

At the sound of Miles's voice the woman had started, slightly, and her cheeks had flushed; she was trembling, now. She stood still, during an impressive pause of several moments; then slowly lifted up her head and looked into Hendon's eyes with a stony and frightened gaze; the blood sank out of her face, drop by drop, till nothing remained but the gray pallor of death; then she said, in a voice as dead as the face, "I know him not!" and turned, with a moan and a stifled sob, and tottered out of the room.

Miles Hendon sank into a chair and covered his face with his hands. After a pause, his brother said to the servants—

"You have observed him. Do you know him?"

They shook their heads; then the master said—

"The servants know you not, sir. I fear there is some mistake. You have seen that my wife knew you not."

"Thy *wife!*" In an instant Hugh was pinned to the wall, with an iron grip about his throat. "O, thou fox-hearted slave, I see it all! Thou'st writ the lying letter thyself, and my stolen bride and goods are its fruit. There—now get thee gone, lest I shame mine honorable soldiership with the slaying of so pitiful a mannikin!"

Hugh, red-faced, and almost suffocated, reeled to the nearest chair, and commanded the servants to seize and bind the murderous stranger. They hesitated, and one of them said—

"He is armed, Sir Hugh, and we are weaponless."

"Armed? What of it, and ye so many? Upon him, I say!"

But Miles warned them to be careful what they did, and added—

"Ye know me of old—I have not changed; come on, an' it like you."

This reminder did not hearten the servants much; they still held back.

"Then go, ye paltry cowards, and arm yourselves and guard the doors, whilst I send one to fetch the watch," said Hugh. He turned, at the threshold, and said to Miles, "You'll find it to your advantage to offend not with useless endeavors at escape."

"Escape? Spare thyself discomfort, an' that is all that troubles thee. For Miles Hendon is master of Hendon Hall and all its belongings. He will remain—doubt it not."

Chapter 26

Disowned

THE KING sat musing a few moments, then looked up and said—

" 'Tis strange—most strange. I cannot account for it."

"No, it is not strange, my liege. I know him, and this conduct is but natural. He was a rascal from his birth."

"O, I spake not of *him*, Sir Miles."

"Not of him? Then of what? What is it that is strange?"

"That the king is not missed."

"How? Which? I doubt I do not understand."

"Indeed? Doth it not strike you as being passing strange that the land is not filled with couriers and proclamations describing my person and making search for me? Is it no matter for commotion and distress that the head of the state is gone?—that I am vanished away and lost?"

"Most true, my king, I had forgot." Then Hendon sighed, and muttered to himself, "Poor ruined mind—still busy with its pathetic dream."

"But I have a plan that shall right us both. I will write a paper, in three tongues—Latin, Greek, and English—and thou shalt haste away with it to London in the morning. Give it to none but my uncle, the lord Hertford; when he shall see it, he will know and say I wrote it. Then he will send for me."

"Might it not be best, my prince, that we wait, here, until I prove myself and make my rights secure to my domains? I should be so much the better able then, to—"

The king interrupted him imperiously—

"Peace! What are thy paltry domains, thy trivial interests, contrasted with matters which concern the weal of a nation and the integrity of a throne!" Then he added, in a gentle voice, as if he were sorry for his severity, "Obey, and have no fear; I will right thee, I will make thee whole—yes, more than whole. I shall remember, and requite."

So saying, he took the pen, and set himself to work. Hendon contemplated him lovingly, a while, then said to himself—

"An' it were dark, I should think it *was* a king that spoke; there's no denying it, when the humor's upon him he doth thunder and lighten like your true king—now where got he that trick? See him scribble and scratch away contentedly at his meaningless pot-hooks, fancying them to be Latin and Greek—and except my wit shall serve me with a lucky device for diverting him from his purpose, I shall be forced to pretend to post away to-morrow on this wild errand he hath invented for me."

The next moment Sir Miles's thoughts had gone back to the recent episode. So absorbed was he in his musings, that when the king presently handed him the paper which he had been writing, he received it and pocketed it without being conscious of the act. "How marvelous strange she acted," he muttered. "I think she knew me—and I think she did *not* know me. These opinions do conflict, I perceive it plainly; I cannot reconcile them, neither can I, by argument, dismiss either of the two, or even persuade one to outweigh the other. The matter standeth simply thus: she *must* have known my face, my figure, my voice, for how could it be otherwise? yet she *said* she knew me not, and that is proof perfect, for she cannot lie. But stop—I think I begin to see. Peradventure he hath influenced her—commanded her—compelled her, to lie. That is the solution! the riddle is unriddled. She seemed dead with fear—yes, she was under his compulsion. I will seek her; I will find her; now that he is away, she will speak her true mind. She will remember the old times when we were little playfellows together, and this will soften her heart, and she will no more betray me, but will confess me. There is no treacherous blood in her—no, she was always honest and true. She has loved me, in those old days—this is my security; for whom one has loved, one cannot betray."

He stepped eagerly toward the door; at that moment it opened, and the lady Edith entered. She was very pale, but she walked with a firm step, and her carriage was full of grace and gentle dignity. Her face was as sad as before.

Miles sprang forward, with a happy confidence, to meet her, but she checked him with a hardly perceptible gesture, and he stopped where he was. She seated herself, and asked him to do likewise. Thus simply did she take the sense of old-comradeship out of him, and transform him into a stranger and a guest. The surprise of it, the bewildering unexpectedness of it, made him begin to question, for a moment, if he *was* the person he was pretending to be, after all. The lady Edith said—

"Sir, I have come to warn you. The mad cannot be persuaded out of their delusions, perchance; but doubtless they may be persuaded to avoid perils. I think this dream of yours hath the seeming of honest truth to you, and therefore is not criminal—but do not tarry here with it; for here it is dangerous." She looked steadily into Miles's face, a moment, then added, impressively, "It is the more dangerous for that you *are* much like what our lost lad must have grown to be, if he had lived."

"Heavens, madam, but I *am* he!"

"I truly think you think it, sir. I question not your honesty in that—I but warn you, that is all. My husband is master in this region; his power hath hardly any limit; the people prosper or starve, as he wills. If you resembled not the man whom you profess to be, my husband might bid you pleasure yourself with your dream in peace; but trust me, I know him well, I know what he will do; he will say to all, that you are but a mad impostor, and straightway all will echo him." She bent upon Miles that same steady look once more, and added: "If you *were* Miles Hendon, and he knew it and all the region knew it—consider what I am saying, weigh it well—you would stand in the same peril, your punishment would be no less sure; he would deny you and denounce you, and none would be bold enough to give you countenance."

"Most truly I believe it," said Miles, bitterly. "The power that can command one life-long friend to betray and disown another, and be obeyed, may well look to be obeyed in quarters where bread and life are on the stake and no cobweb ties of loyalty and honor are concerned."

A faint tinge appeared for a moment in the lady's cheek, and she dropped her eyes to the floor; but her voice betrayed no emotion when she proceeded—

"I have warned you, I must still warn you, to go hence. This man will destroy you, else. He is a tyrant who knows no pity. I, who am his fettered slave, know this. Poor Miles, and

Arthur, and my dear guardian, Sir Richard, are free of him, and at rest—better that you were with them than that you bide here in the clutches of this miscreant. Your pretensions are a menace to his title and possessions; you have assaulted him in his own house—you are ruined if you stay. Go—do not hesitate. If you lack money, take this purse, I beg of you, and bribe the servants to let you pass. O be warned, poor soul, and escape while you may."

Miles declined the purse with a gesture, and rose up and stood before her.

"Grant me one thing," he said. "Let your eyes rest upon mine, so that I may see if they be steady. There—now answer me. Am I Miles Hendon?"

"No. I know you not."

"Swear it!"

The answer was low, but distinct—

"I swear."

"O, this passes belief!"

"Fly! Why will you waste the precious time? Fly, and save yourself."

At that moment the officers burst into the room and a violent struggle began; but Hendon was soon overpowered and dragged away. The king was taken, also, and both were bound, and led to prison.

Chapter 27

In Prison

THE CELLS were all crowded; so the two friends were chained in a large room where persons charged with trifling offenses were commonly kept. They had company, for there were some twenty manacled and fettered prisoners here, of both sexes and of varying ages,—an obscene and noisy gang. The king chafed bitterly over the stupendous indignity thus put upon his royalty, but Hendon was moody and taciturn. He was pretty thoroughly bewildered. He had come home, a jubilant prodigal, expecting to find everybody wild with joy over his return; and instead had got the cold shoulder and a jail. The promise and the fulfilment differed so widely, that the effect was stunning; he could not decide whether it was most tragic or most grotesque. He felt much as a man might who had danced blithely out to enjoy a rainbow, and got struck by lightning.

But gradually his confused and tormenting thoughts settled down into some sort of order, and then his mind centred itself upon Edith. He turned her conduct over, and examined it in all lights, but he could not make anything satisfactory out of it. Did she know him?—or didn't she know him? It was a perplexing puzzle, and occupied him a long time; but he ended, finally, with the conviction that she did know him, and had repudiated him for interested reasons. He wanted to load her name with curses, now; but this name had so long been sacred to him that he found he could not bring his tongue to profane it.

Wrapped in prison blankets of a soiled and tattered condition, Hendon and the king passed a troubled night. For a bribe the jailer had furnished liquor to some of the prisoners; singing of ribald songs, fighting, shouting, and carousing, was the natural consequence. At last, a while after midnight, a man attacked a woman and nearly killed her by beating her over the head with his manacles before the jailer could come to the rescue. The jailer restored peace by giving the man a sound clubbing about the head and shoulders—then the carousing ceased; and after that, all had an opportunity to sleep who did not mind the annoyance of the moanings and groanings of the two wounded people.

During the ensuing week, the days and nights were of a monotonous sameness, as to events; men whose faces Hendon remembered more or less distinctly, came, by day, to gaze at the "impostor" and repudiate and insult him; and by night the carousing and brawling went on, with symmetrical regularity. However, there was a change of incident at last. The jailer brought in an old man, and said to him—

"The villain is in this room—cast thy old eyes about and see if thou canst say which is he."

Hendon glanced up, and experienced a pleasant sensation for the first time since he had been in the jail. He said to himself, "This is Blake Andrews, a servant all his life in my father's family—a good honest soul, with a right heart in his breast. That is, formerly. But none are true, now; all are liars. This man will know me—and will deny me, too, like the rest."

The old man gazed around the room, glanced at each face in turn, and finally said—

"I see none here but paltry knaves, scum o' the streets. Which is he?"

The jailer laughed.

"Here," he said; "scan this big animal, and grant me an opinion."

The old man approached, and looked Hendon over, long and earnestly, then shook his head and said—

"Marry, *this* is no Hendon—nor ever was!"

"Right! Thy old eyes are sound yet. An' I were Sir High, I would take the shabby carle and—"

The jailer finished by lifting himself a-tip-toe with an imaginary halter, at the same time making a gurgling noise in his throat suggestive of suffocation. The old man said, vindictively—

"Let him bless God an' he fare no worse. An' *I* had the handling o' the villain he should roast, or I am no true man!"

The jailer laughed a pleasant hyena laugh, and said—

"Give him a piece of thy mind, old man—they all do it. Thou'lt find it good diversion."

Then he sauntered toward his ante-room and disappeared. The old man dropped upon his knees and whispered—

"God be thanked, thou'rt come again, my master! I believed thou wert dead these seven years, and lo, here thou art alive! I knew thee the moment I saw thee; and main hard work it was to keep a stony countenance and seem to see none here but tuppenny knaves and rubbish o' the streets. I am old and poor, Sir Miles; but say the word and I will go forth and proclaim the truth though I be strangled for it."

"No," said Hendon; "thou shalt not. It would ruin thee, and yet help but little in my cause. But I thank thee; for thou hast given me back somewhat of my lost faith in my kind."

The old servant became very valuable to Hendon and the king; for he dropped in several times a day to "abuse" the former, and always smuggled in a few delicacies to help out the prison bill of fare; he also furnished the current news. Hendon reserved the dainties for the king; without them his majesty might not have survived, for he was not able to eat the coarse and wretched food provided by the jailer. Andrews was obliged to confine himself to brief visits, in order to avoid suspicion; but he managed to impart a fair degree of information each time—information delivered in a low voice, for Hendon's benefit, and interlarded with insulting epithets delivered in a louder voice, for the benefit of other hearers.

So, little by little, the story of the family came out. Arthur had been dead six years. This loss, with the absence of news from Hendon, impaired the father's health; he believed he was going to die, and he wished to see Hugh and Edith settled in life before he passed away; but Edith begged hard for delay, hoping for Miles's return; then the letter came which brought the news of Miles's death; the shock prostrated Sir Richard; he believed his end was very near, and he and Hugh insisted upon the marriage; Edith begged for and obtained a month's respite; then another, and finally a third; the marriage then took place, by the death-bed of Sir Richard. It had not proved a happy one. It was whispered about the country that shortly after the nuptials the bride found among her husband's papers several rough and incomplete drafts of the fatal letter, and had accused him of precipitating the marriage—and Sir Richard's death, too—by a wicked forgery. Tales of cruelty to the lady Edith and the servants were to be heard on all hands; and since the father's death Sir Hugh had thrown off all soft disguises and become a pitiless master toward all who in any way depended upon him and his domains for bread.

There was a bit of Andrews's gossip which the king listened to with a lively interest—

"There is rumor that the king is mad. But in charity forbear to say *I* mentioned it, for 'tis death to speak of it, they say."

His majesty glared at the old man and said—

"The king is *not* mad, goodman—and thou'lt find it to thy advantage to busy thyself with matters that nearer concern thee than this seditious prattle."

"What doth the lad mean?" said Andrews, surprised at this brisk assault from such an unexpected quarter. Hendon gave him a sign, and he did not pursue his question, but went on with his budget—

"The late king is to be buried at Windsor in a day or two—the 16th of the month,—and the new king will be crowned at Westminster the 20th."

"Methinks they must needs find him first," muttered his majesty; then added, confidently, "but they will look to that—and so also shall I."

"In the name of—"

But the old man got no further—a warning sign from Hendon checked his remark. He resumed the thread of his gossip—

"Sir Hugh goeth to the coronation—and with grand hopes. He confidently looketh to come back a peer, for he is high in favor with the Lord Protector."

"What Lord Protector?" asked his majesty.

"His grace the Duke of Somerset."

"What Duke of Somerset?"

"Marry, there is but one—Seymour, Earl of Hertford."

The king asked, sharply—

"Since when is *he* a duke, and Lord Protector?"

"Since the last day of January."

"And prithee who made him so?"

"Himself and the Great Council—with help of the king."

His majesty started violently. "The *king*!" he cried. "*What* king, good sir?"

"What king, indeed! (God-a-mercy, what aileth the boy?) Sith we have but one, 'tis not difficult to answer—his most sacred majesty King Edward the Sixth—whom God preserve! Yea, and a dear and gracious little urchin is he, too; and whether he be mad or no—and they say he mendeth daily— his praises are on all men's lips; and all bless him, likewise, and offer prayers that he may be spared to reign long in En- gland; for he began humanely, with saving the old Duke of Norfolk's life, and now is he bent on destroying the cruelest of the laws that harry and oppress the people."

This news struck his majesty dumb with amazement, and plunged him into so deep and dismal a reverie that he heard no more of the old man's gossip. He wondered if the "little urchin" was the beggar-boy whom he left dressed in his own garments in the palace. It did not seem possible that this could be, for surely his manners and speech would betray him if he pretended to be the Prince of Wales—then he would be driven out, and search made for the true prince. Could it be that the court had set up some sprig of the nobility in his place? No, for his uncle would not allow that—he was all- powerful and could and would crush such a movement, of course. The boy's musings profited him nothing; the more he tried to unriddle the mystery the more perplexed he became, the more his head ached, and the worse he slept. His impa- tience to get to London grew hourly, and his captivity be- came almost unendurable.

Hendon's arts all failed with the king—he could not be comforted; but a couple of women who were chained near him, succeeded better. Under their gentle ministrations he found peace and learned a degree of patience. He was very grateful, and came to love them dearly and to delight in the sweet and soothing influence of their presence. He asked them why they were in prison, and when they said they were Baptists, he smiled, and inquired—

"Is that a crime to be shut up for, in a prison? Now I grieve, for I shall lose ye—they will not keep ye long for such a little thing."

They did not answer; and something in their faces made him uneasy. He said, eagerly—

"You do not speak—be good to me, and tell me—there will be no other punishment? Prithee tell me there is no fear of that."

They tried to change the topic, but his fears were aroused, and he pursued it—

"Will they scourge thee? No, no, they would not be so cruel! Say they would not. Come, they *will* not, will they?"

The women betrayed confusion and distress, but there was no avoiding an answer, so one of them said, in a voice choked with emotion—

"O, thou'lt break our hearts, thou gentle spirit!—God will help us to bear our—"

"It is a confession!" the king broke in. "Then they *will* scourge thee, the stonyhearted wretches! But O, thou must not weep, I cannot bear it. Keep up thy courage—I shall come to my own in time to save thee from this bitter thing, and I will do it!"

When the king awoke in the morning, the women were gone.

"They are saved!" he said, joyfully; then added, despondently, "but woe is me!—for they were my comforters."

Each of them had left a shred of ribbon pinned to his clothing, in token of remembrance. He said he would keep these things always; and that soon he would seek out these dear good friends of his and take them under his protection.

Just then the jailer came in with some subordinates and commanded that the prisoners be conducted to the jail-yard. The king was overjoyed—it would be a blessed thing to see the blue sky and breathe the fresh air once more. He fretted and chafed at the slowness of the officers, but his turn came at last and he was released from his staple and ordered to follow the other prisoners, with Hendon.

The court or quadrangle, was stone-paved, and open to the sky. The prisoners entered it through a massive archway of masonry, and were placed in file, standing, with their backs against the wall. A rope was stretched in front of them, and they were also guarded by their officers. It was a chill and lowering morning, and a light snow which had fallen during the night whitened the great empty space and added to the general dismalness of its aspect. Now and then a wintry wind shivered through the place and sent the snow eddying hither and thither.

In the centre of the court stood two women, chained to posts. A glance showed the king that these were his good friends. He shuddered, and said to himself, "Alack, they are not gone free, as I had thought. To think that such as these should know the lash!—in England! Aye there's the shame of it—not in Heathenesse, but Christian England! They will be scourged; and I, whom they have comforted and kindly entreated, must look on and see the great wrong done; it is strange, so strange! that I, the very source of power in this broad realm, am helpless to protect them. But let these miscreants look well to themselves, for there is a day coming when I will require of them a heavy reckoning for this work. For every blow they strike now, they shall feel a hundred, then."

A great gate swung open and a crowd of citizens poured in. They flocked around the two women, and hid them from the king's view. A clergyman entered and passed through the crowd, and he also was hidden. The king now heard talking, back and forth, as if questions were being asked and answered, but he could not make out what was said. Next there was a deal of bustle and preparation, and much passing and repassing of officials through that part of the crowd that stood on the further side of the women; and whilst this proceeded a deep hush gradually fell upon the people.

Now, by command, the masses parted and fell aside, and the king saw a spectacle that froze the marrow in his bones. Faggots had been piled about the two women, and a kneeling man was lighting them!

The women bowed their heads, and covered their faces with their hands; the yellow flames began to climb upward among the snapping and crackling faggots, and wreaths of blue smoke to stream away on the wind; the clergyman lifted his hands and began a prayer—just then two young girls came flying through the great gate, uttering piercing screams, and threw themselves upon the women at the stake. Instantly they were torn away by the officers, and one of them was kept in a tight grip, but the other broke loose, saying she would die with her mother; and before she could be stopped she had flung her arms about her mother's neck again. She was torn away once more, and with her gown on fire. Two or three men held her, and the burning portion of her gown was snatched off and thrown flaming aside, she struggling all the while to free herself, and saying she would be alone in the world, now, and begging to be allowed to die with her mother. Both the girls screamed continually, and fought for freedom; but suddenly this tumult was drowned under a volley of heart-piercing shrieks of mortal agony,—the king glanced from the frantic girls to the stake, then turned away and leaned his ashen face against the wall, and looked no more. He said, "That which I have seen, in that one little moment, will never go out from my memory, but will abide there; and I shall see it all the days, and dream of it all the nights, till I die. Would God I had been blind!"

Hendon was watching the king. He said to himself, with satisfaction, "His disorder mendeth; he hath changed, and groweth gentler. If he had followed his wont, he would have stormed at these varlets, and said he was king, and commanded that the women be turned loose unscathed. Soon his delusion will pass away and be forgotten, and his poor mind will be whole again. God speed the day!"

The same day several prisoners were brought in to remain over night, who were being conveyed, under guard, to various places in the kingdom, to undergo punishment for crimes committed. The king conversed with these,—he had made it a point, from the beginning, to instruct himself for the kingly office by questioning prisoners whenever the opportunity offered—and the tale of their woes wrung his heart. One of them was a poor half-witted woman who had stolen a yard or two of cloth from a weaver—she was to be hanged for it. Another was a man who had been accused of stealing a horse; he said the proof had failed, and he had imagined that he was safe from the halter; but no—he was hardly free before he was arraigned for killing a deer in the king's park; this was proved against him, and now he was on his way to the gallows. There was a tradesman's apprentice whose case particularly distressed the king; this youth said he found a hawk, one evening, that had escaped from its owner, and he took it home with him, imagining himself entitled to it; but the court convicted him of stealing it, and sentenced him to death.

The king was furious over these inhumanities, and wanted Hendon to break jail and fly with him to Westminster, so that he could mount his throne and hold out his sceptre in mercy over these unfortunate people and save their lives. "Poor child," sighed Hendon, "these woful tales have brought his malady upon him again—alack, but for this evil hap, he would have been well in a little time."

Among these prisoners was an old lawyer—a man with a strong face and a dauntless mien. Three years past, he had written a pamphlet against the Lord Chancellor, accusing him of injustice, and had been punished for it by the loss of his ears in the pillory, and degradation from the bar, and in addition had been fined £3000 and sentenced to imprisonment for life. Lately he had repeated his offense; and in consequence was now under sentence to lose *what remained of his ears*, pay a fine of £5000, be branded on both cheeks, and remain in prison for life.

"These be honorable scars," he said, and turned back his gray hair and showed the mutilated stubs of what had once been his ears.

The king's eye burned with passion. He said—

"None believe in me—neither wilt thou. But no matter—within the compass of a month thou shalt be free; and more, the laws that have dishonored thee, and shamed the English name, shall be swept from the statute books. The world is made wrong; kings should go to school to their own laws, at times, and so learn mercy."*

*See Notes to Chapter 27, at end of volume.

Chapter 28

THE SACRIFICE

MEANTIME Miles was growing sufficiently tired of confinement and inaction. But now his trial came on, to his great gratification, and he thought he could welcome any sentence provided a further imprisonment should not be a part of it. But he was mistaken about that. He was in a fine fury when he found himself described as a "sturdy vagabond" and sentenced to sit two hours in the pillory for bearing that character and for assaulting the master of Hendon Hall. His pretensions as to brothership with his prosecutor, and rightful heirship to the Hendon honors and estates, were left contemptuously unnoticed, as being not even worth examination.

He raged and threatened, on his way to punishment, but it did no good; he was snatched roughly along, by the officers, and got an occasional cuff, besides, for his unreverent conduct.

The king could not pierce through the rabble that swarmed behind; so he was obliged to follow in the rear, remote from his good friend and servant. The king had been nearly condemned to the stocks, himself, for being in such bad company, but had been let off with a lecture and a warning, in consideration of his youth. When the crowd at last halted, he flitted feverishly from point to point around its outer rim, hunting a place to get through; and at last, after a deal of difficulty and delay, succeeded. There sat his poor henchman in the degrading stocks, the sport and butt of a dirty mob— he, the body servant of the king of England! Edward had heard the sentence pronounced, but he had not realized the half that it meant. His anger began to rise as the sense of this new indignity which had been put upon him sank home; it jumped to summer heat, the next moment, when he saw an egg sail through the air and crush itself against Hendon's cheek, and heard the crowd roar its enjoyment of the episode. He sprang across the open circle and confronted the officer in charge, crying—

"For shame! This is my servant—set him free! I am the—"

"O, peace!" exclaimed Hendon, in a panic, "thou'lt destroy thyself. Mind him not, officer, he is mad."

"Give thyself no trouble as to the matter of minding him, good man, I have small mind to mind him; but as to teaching him somewhat, to that I am well inclined." He turned to a subordinate and said, "Give the little fool a taste or two of the lash, to mend his manners."

"Half a dozen will better serve his turn," suggested Sir Hugh, who had ridden up, a moment before, to take a passing glance at the proceedings.

The king was seized. He did not even struggle, so paralyzed was he with the mere thought of the monstrous outrage that was proposed to be inflicted upon his sacred person. History was already defiled with the record of the scourging of an English king with whips—it was an intolerable reflection that he must furnish a duplicate of that shameful page. He was in the toils, there was no help for him: he must either take this punishment or beg for its remission. Hard conditions; he would take the stripes—a king might do that, but a king could not beg.

But meantime, Miles Hendon was resolving the difficulty. "Let the child go," said he; "ye heartless dogs, do ye not see how young and frail he is? Let him go—I will take his lashes."

"Marry, a good thought,—and thanks for it," said Sir Hugh, his face lighting with a sardonic satisfaction. "Let the little beggar go, and give this fellow a dozen in his place—an honest dozen, well laid on." The king was in the act of entering a fierce protest, but Sir Hugh silenced him with the potent remark, "Yes, speak up, do, and free thy mind—only, mark ye, that for each word you utter he shall get six strokes the more."

Hendon was removed from the stocks, and his back laid bare; and whilst the lash was applied the poor little king turned away his face and allowed unroyal tears to channel his cheeks unchecked. "Ah, brave good heart," he said to himself, "this loyal deed shall never perish out of my memory. I will not forget it—and neither shall *they!*" he added, with passion. Whilst he mused, his appreciation of Hendon's magnanimous conduct grew to greater and still greater dimensions in his mind, and so also did his gratefulness for it. Presently he said to himself, "Who saves his prince from wounds and possible death—and this he did for me—performs high service; but it is little—it is nothing!—O, less than nothing!—when 'tis weighed against the act of him who saves his prince from SHAME!"

Hendon made no outcry, under the scourge, but bore the heavy blows with soldierly fortitude. This, together with his redeeming the boy by taking his stripes for him, compelled the respect of even that forlorn and degraded mob that was gathered there; and its jibes and hootings died away, and no sound remained but the sound of the falling blows. The stillness that pervaded the place, when Hendon found himself once more in the stocks, was in strong contrast with the insulting clamor which had prevailed there so little a while before. The king came softly to Hendon's side, and whispered in his ear—

"Kings cannot ennoble thee, thou good, great soul, for One who is higher than kings hath done that for thee; but a king can confirm thy nobility to men." He picked up the scourge from the ground, touched Hendon's bleeding shoulders lightly with it, and whispered, "Edward of England dubs thee earl!"

Hendon was touched. The water welled to his eyes, yet at the same time the grisly humor of the situation and circumstances so undermined his gravity that it was all he could do to keep some sign of his inward mirth from showing outside. To be suddenly hoisted, naked and gory, from the common stocks to the Alpine altitude and splendor of an Earldom, seemed to him the last possibility in the line of the grotesque. He said to himself, "Now am I finely tinseled, indeed! The spectre-knight of the Kingdom of Dreams and Shadows is become a spectre-earl!—a dizzy flight for a callow wing! An' this go on, I shall presently be hung like a very May-pole with fantastic gauds and make-believe honors. But I shall value them, all valueless as they are, for the love that doth bestow them. Better these poor mock dignities of mine, that come unasked, from a clean hand and a right spirit, than real ones bought by servility from grudging and interested power."

The dreaded Sir Hugh wheeled his horse about, and as he spurred away, the living wall divided silently to let him pass, and as silently closed together again. And so remained; nobody went so far as to venture a remark in favor of the prisoner, or in compliment to him; but no matter, the absence of abuse was a sufficient homage in itself. A late comer who was not posted, as to the present circumstances, and who delivered a sneer at the "impostor" and was in the act of following it with a dead cat, was promptly knocked down and kicked out, without any words, and then the deep quiet resumed sway once more.

Chapter 29

To London

WHEN HENDON's term of service in the stocks was finished, he was released and ordered to quit the region and come back no more. His sword was restored to him, and also his mule and his donkey. He mounted and rode off, followed by the king, the crowd opening with quiet respectfulness to let them pass, and then dispersing when they were gone.

Hendon was soon absorbed in thought. There were questions of high import to be answered. What should he do? Whither should he go? Powerful help must be found, somewhere, or he must relinquish his inheritance and remain under the imputation of being an impostor besides. Where could he hope to find this powerful help? Where, indeed! It was a knotty question. By and by a thought occurred to him which pointed to a possibility—the slenderest of slender possibilities, certainly, but still worth considering, for lack of any other that promised anything at all. He remembered what old Andrews had said about the young king's goodness and his generous championship of the wronged and unfortunate. Why not go and try to get speech of him and beg for justice? Ah, yes, but could so fantastic a pauper get admission to the august presence of a monarch? Never mind—let that matter take care of itself; it was a bridge that would not need to be crossed till he should come to it. He was an old campaigner, and used to inventing shifts and expedients; no doubt he would be able to find a way. Yes, he would strike for the capital. Maybe his father's old friend Sir Humphrey Marlow would help him—"good old Sir Humphrey, Head Lieutenant of the late king's kitchen, or stables, or something"—Miles could not remember just what or which. Now that he had something to turn his energies to, a distinctly defined object to accomplish, the fog of humiliation and depression which had settled down upon his spirits lifted and blew away, and he raised his head and looked about him. He was sur-

prised to see how far he had come; the village was away behind him. The king was jogging along in his wake, with his
head bowed; for he, too, was deep in plans and thinkings. A
sorrowful misgiving clouded Hendon's new-born cheerfulness: would the boy be willing to go again to a city where,
during all his brief life, he had never known anything but ill
usage and pinching want? But the question must be asked; it
could not be avoided; so Hendon reined up, and called out—

"I had forgotten to inquire whither we are bound. Thy
commands, my liege!"

"To London!"

Hendon moved on again, mightily contented with the answer—but astounded at it, too.

The whole journey was made without an adventure of importance. But it ended with one. About ten o'clock on the
night of the 19th of February, they stepped upon London
Bridge, in the midst of a writhing, struggling jam of howling
and hurrahing people, whose beer-jolly faces stood out
strongly in the glare from manifold torches—and at that instant the decaying head of some former duke or other
grandee tumbled down between them, striking Hendon on
the elbow and then bounding off among the hurrying confusion of feet. So evanescent and unstable are men's works, in
this world!—the late good king is but three weeks dead and
three days in his grave, and already the adornments which he
took such pains to select from prominent people for his noble
bridge are falling. A citizen stumbled over that head, and
drove his own head into the back of somebody in front of
him, who turned and knocked down the first person that
came handy, and was promptly laid out himself by that person's friend. It was the right ripe time for a free fight, for the
festivities of the morrow—Coronation Day—were already
beginning; everybody was full of strong drink and patriotism;
within five minutes the free fight was occupying a good deal
of ground; within ten or twelve it covered an acre or so, and
was become a riot. By this time Hendon and the king were
hopelessly separated from each other and lost in the rush and
turmoil of the roaring masses of humanity. And so we leave
them.

Chapter 30

TOM'S PROGRESS

WHILST THE TRUE KING wandered about the land; poorly clad, poorly fed; cuffed and derided by tramps, one while; herding with thieves and murderers in a jail, another; and called idiot and impostor by all, impartially, the mock king, Tom Canty, enjoyed a quite different experience.

When we saw him last, royalty was just beginning to have a bright side for him. This bright side went on brightening more and more, every day; in a very little while it was become almost all sunshine and delightfulness. He lost his fears; his misgivings faded out and died; his embarrassments departed and gave place to an easy and confident bearing. He worked the whipping-boy mine to ever-increasing profit.

He ordered my lady Elizabeth and my lady Jane Grey into his presence when he wanted to play or talk; and dismissed them, when he was done with them, with the air of one familiarly accustomed to such performances. It no longer confused him to have these lofty personages kiss his hand, at parting.

He came to enjoy being conducted to bed in state, at night, and dressed with intricate and solemn ceremony in the morning. It came to be a proud pleasure to march to dinner attended by a glittering procession of officers of state and Gentlemen-at-Arms—insomuch, indeed, that he doubled his guard of Gentlemen-at-Arms, and made them a hundred. He like to hear the bugles sounding, down the long corridors, and the distant voices responding, "Way for the king!"

He even learned to enjoy sitting in throned state in council and seeming to be something more than the Lord Protector's mouthpiece. He liked to receive great ambassadors and their gorgeous trains, and listen to the affectionate messages they brought from illustrious monarchs who called him "brother" —O, happy Tom Canty, late of Offal Court!

He enjoyed his splendid clothes, and ordered more; he found his four hundred servants too few for his proper grandeur, and trebled them. The adulation of salaaming courtiers

came to be sweet music to his ears. He remained kind and
gentle, and a sturdy and determined champion of all that were
oppressed, and he made tireless war upon unjust laws. Yet
upon occasion, being offended, he could turn upon an earl, or
even a duke, and give him a look that would make him tremble. Once when his royal "sister," the grimly holy lady Mary,
set herself to reason with him against the wisdom of his
course in pardoning so many people who would otherwise be
jailed or hanged or burned, and reminded him that their august late father's prisons had sometimes contained as high as
sixty thousand convicts at one time, and that during his admirable reign he had delivered seventy-two thousand thieves and
robbers over to death by the executioner,* the boy was filled
with generous indignation, and commanded her to go to her
closet and beseech God to take away the stone that was in her
breast and give her a human heart.

Did Tom Canty never feel troubled about the poor little
rightful prince who had treated him so kindly and flown out
with such hot zeal to avenge him upon the insolent sentinel at
the palace gate? Yes; his first royal days and nights were pretty
well sprinkled with painful thoughts about the lost prince,
and with sincere longings for his return and happy restoration
to his native rights and splendors; but as time wore on and
the prince did not come, Tom's mind became more and more
occupied with his new and enchanting experiences, and by
little and little the vanished monarch faded almost out of his
thoughts; and finally when he did intrude upon them at intervals he was become an unwelcome spectre, for he made Tom
feel guilty and ashamed.

Tom's poor mother and sisters traveled the same road out
of his mind. At first he pined for them, sorrowed for them,
longed to see them; but later, the thought of their coming
some day in their rags and dirt, and betraying him with their
kisses and pulling him down from his lofty place and dragging him back to penury and degradation and the slums,
made him shudder. At last they ceased to trouble his
thoughts, almost wholly. And he was content, even glad; for
whenever their mournful and accusing faces did rise before

*Hume's England.

him now, they made him feel more despicable than the worms that crawl.

At midnight of the 19th of February, Tom Canty was sinking to sleep in his rich bed in the palace, guarded by his loyal vassals and surrounded by the pomps of royalty—a happy boy; for to-morrow was the day appointed for his solemn crowning as king of England. At that same hour Edward the true king, hungry and thirsty, soiled and draggled, worn with travel, and clothed in rags and shreds—his share of the results of the riot—was wedged in among a crowd of people who were watching, with deep interest, certain hurrying gangs of workmen who streamed in and out of Westminster Abbey, busy as ants; they were making the last preparations for the royal Coronation.

Chapter 31

THE RECOGNITION PROCESSION

WHEN TOM CANTY awoke, the next morning, the air was heavy with a thunderous murmur—all the distances were charged with it. It was music to him, for it meant that the English world was out in its strength to give loyal welcome to the great day.

Presently Tom found himself once more the chief figure in a wonderful floating pageant on the Thames—for, by ancient custom, the "recognition-procession" through London must start from the Tower, and he was bound thither.

When he arrived there, the sides of the venerable fortress seemed suddenly rent in a thousand places; and from every rent leapt a red tongue of flame and a white gush of smoke; a deafening explosion followed, which drowned the shoutings of the multitude and made the ground tremble; the flame-jets, the smoke, and the explosions were repeated, over and over again, with marvelous celerity; so that in a few moments the old Tower disappeared in the vast fog of its own smoke, all but the very top of the tall pile called the White Tower; this, with its banners, stood out above the dense bank of vapor as a mountain-peak projects above a cloud-rack.

Tom Canty, splendidly arrayed, mounted a prancing war steed whose rich trappings almost reached to the ground; his "uncle," the Lord Protector Somerset, similarly mounted, took place in his rear; the King's Guard formed in single ranks on either side, clad in burnished armor; after the Protector followed a seemingly interminable procession of resplendent nobles attended by their vassals; after these came the Lord Mayor and the Aldermanic body, in crimson velvet robes and with their gold chains across their breasts; and after these the officers and members of all the Guilds of London, in rich raiment and bearing the showy banners of the several corporations. Also, in the procession, as a special guard of honor through the city, was the Ancient and Honorable Artillery Company, an organization already three hundred years old, at that time, and the only military body in England possessing the privilege (which it still possesses in our day,) of holding itself independent of the commands of parliament. It was a brilliant spectacle, and was hailed with acclamations all along the line, as it took its stately way through the packed multitudes of citizens. The chronicler says: "The king, as he entered the city, was received by the people with prayers, welcomings, cries, and tender words, and all signs which argue an earnest love of subjects toward their sovereign; and the king, by holding up his glad countenance to such as stood afar off, and most tender language to those that stood nigh his grace, showed himself no less thankful to receive the people's good will than they to offer it. To all that wished him well, he gave thanks. To such as bade 'God save his grace,' he said in return, 'God save you all!' and added that 'he thanked them with all his heart.' Wonderfully transported were the people with the loving answers and gestures of their king."

In Fenchurch street a "fair child, in costly apparel," stood on a stage to welcome his majesty to the city. The last verse of his greeting was in these words:

"Welcome, O king, as much as hearts can think!
    Welcome again, as much as tongue can tell!
Welcome to joyous tongues and hearts that will not shrink!
    God thee preserve, we pray, and wish thee ever well!"

The people burst forth in a glad shout, repeating with one voice what the child had said. Tom Canty gazed abroad over the surging sea of eager faces, and his heart swelled with exultation; and he felt that the one thing worth living for in this world was to be a king, and a nation's idol. Presently, he caught sight, at a distance, of a couple of his ragged Offal Court comrades—one of them the Lord High Admiral in his late mimic court, the other the First Lord of the Bedchamber in the same pretentious fiction—and his pride swelled higher than ever. O, if they could only recognize him, now! what unspeakable glory it would be, if they could recognize him, and realize that the derided mock king of the slums and back alleys was become a real king, with illustrious dukes and princes for his humble menials, and the English world at his feet! But he had to deny himself, and choke down his desire, for such a recognition might cost more than it would come to; so he turned away his head and left the two soiled lads to go on with their shoutings and glad adulations unsuspicious of whom it was they were lavishing them upon.

Every now and then rose the cry, "A largess! a largess!" and Tom responded by scattering a handful of bright new coins abroad for the multitude to scramble for.

The chronicler says: "At the upper end of Gracechurch street, before the sign of the Eagle, the city had erected a gorgeous arch, beneath which was a stage, which stretched from one side of the street to the other. This was a historical pageant, representing the king's immediate progenitors. There sat Elizabeth of York, in the midst of an immense white rose, whose petals formed elaborate furbelows around her; by her side was Henry VII issuing out of a vast red rose, disposed in the same manner; the hands of the royal pair were locked together, and the wedding ring ostentatiously displayed. From the red and white roses proceeded a stem, which reached up to a second stage occupied by Henry VIII, issuing from a red and white rose, with the effigy of the new king's mother, Jane Seymour, represented by his side. One branch sprang from this pair, which mounted to a third stage, where sat the effigy of Edward VI himself, enthroned in royal majesty; and the whole pageant was framed with wreaths of roses, red and white."

This quaint and gaudy spectacle so wrought upon the rejoicing people that their acclamations utterly smothered the small voice of the child whose business it was to explain the thing in eulogistic rhymes; but Tom Canty was not sorry, for this loyal uproar was sweeter music to him than any poetry, no matter what its quality might be. Whithersoever Tom turned his happy young face, the people recognized the exactness of his effigy's likeness to himself, the flesh and blood counterpart, and new whirlwinds of applause burst forth.

The great pageant moved on, and still on, under one triumphal arch after another, and past a bewildering succession of spectacular and symbolical tableaux, each of which typified and exalted some virtue or talent or merit of the little king's. "Throughout the whole of Cheapside, from every penthouse and window, hung banners and streamers; and the richest carpets, stuffs, and cloth of gold tapestried the streets, specimens of the great wealth of the stores within; and the splendor of this thoroughfare was equaled in the other streets, and in some even surpassed."

"And all these wonders and these marvels are to welcome me—me!" murmured Tom Canty.

The mock king's cheeks were flushed with excitement; his eyes were flashing; his senses swam in a delirium of pleasure. At this point, just as he was raising his hand to fling another rich largess, he caught sight of a pale, astounded face which was strained forward out of the second rank of the crowd, its intense eyes riveted upon him; a sickening consternation struck through him—he recognized his mother! and up flew his hand, palm outward, before his eyes; that old involuntary gesture born of a forgotten episode and perpetuated by habit! In an instant more she had torn her way out of the press and past the guards, and was at his side. She embraced his leg, she covered it with kisses; she cried "O, my child, my darling!" lifting toward him a face that was transfigured with joy and love. The same instant an officer of the King's Guard snatched her away, with a curse, and sent her reeling back whence she came, with a vigorous impulse from his strong arm. The words "I do not know you, woman!" were falling from Tom Canty's lips when this piteous thing occurred; but it smote him to the heart to see her treated so; and as she turned for a last glimpse of him, whilst the crowd was swallowing her from his sight, she seemed so wounded, so broken-hearted, that a shame fell upon him which consumed his pride to ashes and withered his stolen royalty. His grandeurs were stricken valueless, they seemed to fall away from him like rotten rags.

The procession moved on, and still on, through ever augmenting splendors, and ever augmenting tempests of welcome; but to Tom Canty they were as if they had not been. He neither saw nor heard. Royalty had lost its grace and sweetness, its pomps were become a reproach; remorse was eating his heart out. He said, "Would God I were free of my captivity!"

He had unconsciously dropped back into the phraseology of the first days of his compulsory greatness.

The shining pageant still went winding like a radiant and interminable serpent down the crooked lanes of the quaint old city, and through the huzzahing hosts; but still the king rode with bowed head and vacant eyes, seeing only his mother's face and that wounded look in it.

"Largess! largess!" The cry fell upon an unheeding ear.

"Long live Edward of England!" It seemed as if the earth shook with the explosion; but there was no response from the king. He heard it only as one hears the thunder of the surf when it is blown to the ear out of a great distance; for it was smothered under another sound which was still nearer—in his own breast, in his accusing conscience—a voice which kept repeating those shameful words, "I do not know you, woman!"

The words smote upon the king's soul as the strokes of a funeral bell smite upon the soul of a surviving friend when they remind him of secret treacheries suffered at his hands by him that is gone.

New glories were unfolded at every turning; new wonders, new marvels sprung into view; the pent clamors of waiting batteries were released; new raptures poured from the throats of the waiting multitudes; but the king gave no sign, and the accusing voice that went moaning through his comfortless breast was all the sound he heard.

By and by the gladness in the faces of the populace changed a little, and became touched with a something like solicitude, or anxiety; an abatement in the volume of applause was observable, too. The Lord Protector was quick to notice these things; he was as quick to detect the cause. He spurred to the king's side, bent low in his saddle, uncovered, and said—

"My liege! It is an ill time for dreaming! The people observe thy downcast head, thy clouded mien, and they take it for an omen! Be advised; unveil the sun of royalty and let it shine upon these boding vapors and disperse them. Lift up thy face and smile upon the people!"

So saying, the duke scattered a handful of coins to right and left, then retired to his place. The mock king did mechanically as he had been bidden. His smile had no heart in it, but few eyes were near enough or sharp enough to detect that; the noddings of his plumed head, as he saluted his subjects, were full of grace and graciousness; the largess which he delivered from his hand was royally liberal; so the people's anxiety vanished, and the acclamations burst forth again, in as mighty a volume as before.

Still, once more—a little before the progress was ended—the duke was obliged to ride forward and make remonstrance. He whispered—

"O, dread sovereign, shake off these fatal humors—the eyes of the world are upon thee!" Then he added, with sharp annoyance, "Perdition catch that crazy pauper!—'twas she that hath disturbed your highness."

The gorgeous figure turned a lustreless eye upon the duke, and said in a dead voice—

"She was my mother!"

"My God!" groaned the Protector, as he reined his horse backward to his post, "the omen was pregnant with prophecy. He is gone mad again!"

Chapter 32

CORONATION DAY

LET US GO BACKWARD a few hours, and place ourselves in Westminster Abbey, at four o'clock in the morning of this memorable Coronation Day. We are not without company; for although it is still night, we find the torch-lighted galleries already filling up with people who are well content to sit still and wait seven or eight hours till the time shall come for them to see what they may not hope to see twice in their lives—the coronation of a king. Yes, London and Westminster have been astir ever since the warning guns boomed at three o'clock, and already crowds of untitled rich folk who have bought the privilege of trying to find sitting-room in the galleries are flocking in at the entrances reserved for their sort.

The hours drag along, tediously enough. All stir has ceased for some time, for every gallery has long ago been packed. We may sit, now, and look and think at our leisure. We have glimpses, here and there and yonder, through the dim cathedral twilight, of portions of many galleries and balconies, wedged full with people, the other portions of these galleries and balconies being cut off from sight by intervening pillars and architectural projections. We have in view the whole of the great north transept—empty, and waiting for England's privileged ones. We see also the ample area or platform, carpeted with rich stuffs, whereon the throne stands. The throne occupies the centre of the platform, and is raised above it upon an elevation of four steps. Within the seat of the throne is enclosed a rough flat rock—the stone of Scone—which many generations of Scottish kings sat on to be crowned, and so it in time became holy enough to answer a like purpose for English monarchs. Both the throne and its footstool are covered with cloth of gold.

Stillness reigns, the torches blink dully, the time drags heavily. But at last the lagging daylight asserts itself, the torches are extinguished, and a mellow radiance suffuses the great spaces. All features of the noble building are distinct, now, but soft and dreamy, for the sun is lightly veiled with clouds.

At seven o'clock the first break in the drowsy monotony occurs; for on the stroke of this hour the first peeress enters the transept, clothed like Solomon for splendor, and is conducted to her appointed place by an official clad in satins and velvets, whilst a duplicate of him gathers up the lady's long train, follows after, and, when the lady is seated, arranges the train across her lap for her. He then places her footstool according to her desire, after which he puts her coronet where it will be convenient to her hand when the time for the simultaneous coroneting of the nobles shall arrive.

By this time the peeresses are flowing in in a glittering stream, and the satin-clad officials are flitting and glinting everywhere, seating them and making them comfortable. The scene is animated enough, now. There is stir and life, and shifting color everywhere. After a time, quiet reigns again; for the peeresses are all come, and are all in their places—a solid acre, or such a matter, of human flowers, resplendent in variegated colors, and frosted like a Milky Way with diamonds. There are all ages, here: brown, wrinkled, white-haired dowagers who are able to go back, and still back, down the stream of time, and recal the crowning of Richard III and the troublous days of that old forgotten age; and there are handsome middle-aged dames; and lovely and gracious young matrons; and gentle and beautiful young girls, with beaming eyes and fresh complexions, who may possibly put on their jeweled coronets awkwardly when the great time comes; for the matter will be new to them, and their excitement will be a sore hindrance. Still, this may not happen, for the hair of all these ladies has been arranged with a special view to the swift and successful lodging of the crown in its place when the signal comes.

We have seen that this massed array of peeresses is sown thick with diamonds, and we also see that it is a marvelous spectacle—but now we are about to be astonished in earnest. About nine, the clouds suddenly break away and a shaft of sunshine cleaves the mellow atmosphere, and drifts slowly along the ranks of ladies; and every rank it touches flames into a dazzling splendor of many-colored fires, and we tingle to our finger-tips with the electric thrill that is shot through us by the surprise and the beauty of the spectacle! Presently a special envoy from some distant corner of the Orient, marching with the general body of foreign ambassadors, crosses this bar of sunshine, and we catch our breath, the glory that streams and flashes and palpitates about him is so overpowering; for he is crusted from head to heel with gems, and his slightest movement showers a dancing radiance all around him.

Let us change the tense, for convenience. The time drifted along,—one hour—two hours—two hours and a half; then the deep booming of artillery told that the king and his grand procession had arrived at last; so the waiting multitude rejoiced. All knew that a further delay must follow, for the king must be prepared and robed for the solemn ceremony; but this delay would be pleasantly occupied by the assembling of the peers of the realm in their stately robes. These were conducted ceremoniously to their seats, and their coronets placed conveniently at hand; and meanwhile the multitude in the galleries were alive with interest, for most of them were beholding for the first time, dukes, earls and barons, whose names had been historical for five hundred years. When all were finally seated, the spectacle from the galleries and all coigns of vantage was complete; a gorgeous one to look upon and to remember.

Now the robed and mitred great heads of the church, and their attendants, filed in upon the platform and took their appointed places; these were followed by the Lord Protector and other great officials, and these again by a steel-clad detachment of the Guard.

There was a waiting pause; then, at a signal, a triumphant peal of music burst forth, and Tom Canty, clothed in a long robe of cloth of gold, appeared at a door, and stepped upon the platform. The entire multitude rose, and the ceremony of the Recognition ensued.

Then a noble anthem swept the Abbey with its rich waves of sound; and thus heralded and welcomed, Tom Canty was conducted to the throne. The ancient ceremonies went on, with impressive solemnity, whilst the audience gazed; and as they drew nearer and nearer to completion, Tom Canty grew pale, and still paler, and a deep and steadily deepening woe and despondency settled down upon his spirits and upon his remorseful heart.

At last the final act was at hand. The Archbishop of Canterbury lifted up the crown of England from its cushion and held it out over the trembling mock king's head. In the same instant a rainbow-radiance flashed along the spacious transept; for with one impulse every individual in the great concourse of nobles lifted a coronet and poised it over his or her head,—and paused in that attitude.

A deep hush pervaded the Abbey. At this impressive moment, a startling apparition intruded upon the scene—an apparition observed by none in the absorbed multitude, until it suddenly appeared, moving up the great central aisle. It was a boy, bareheaded, ill shod, and clothed in coarse plebeian garments that were falling to rags. He raised his hand with a solemnity which ill comported with his soiled and sorry aspect, and delivered this note of warning—

"I forbid you to set the crown of England upon that forfeited head. *I* am the king!"

In an instant several indignant hands were laid upon the boy; but in the same instant Tom Canty, in his regal vestments, made a swift step forward and cried out in a ringing voice—

"Loose him and forbear! He *is* the king!"

A sort of panic of astonishment swept the assemblage, and they partly rose in their places and stared in a bewildered way at one another and at the chief figures in this scene, like persons who wondered whether they were awake and in their senses, or asleep and dreaming. The Lord Protector was as amazed as the rest, but quickly recovered himself and exclaimed in a voice of authority—

"Mind not his majesty, his malady is upon him again—seize the vagabond!"

He would have been obeyed, but the mock king stamped his foot and cried out—

"On your peril! Touch him not, he is the king!"

The hands were withheld; a paralysis fell upon the house; no one moved, no one spoke; indeed no one knew how to act or what to say, in so strange and surprising an emergency.

While all minds were struggling to right themselves, the boy still moved steadily forward, with high port and confident mien; he had never halted, from the beginning; and while the tangled minds still floundered helplessly, he stepped upon the platform, and the mock king ran with a glad face to meet him; and fell on his knees before him and said—

"O, my lord the king, let poor Tom Canty be first to swear fealty to thee, and say 'Put on thy crown and enter into thine own again!'"

The Lord Protector's eye fell sternly upon the new-comer's face; but straightway the sternness vanished away and gave place to an expression of wondering surprise. This thing happened also to the other great officers. They glanced at each other, and retreated a step by a common and unconscious impulse. The thought in each mind was the same: "What a strange resemblance!"

The Lord Protector reflected a moment or two, in perplexity, then he said, with grave respectfulness—

"By your favor, sir, I desire to ask certain questions which—"

"I will answer them, my lord."

The duke asked him many questions about the court, the late king, the prince, the princesses,—the boy answered them correctly and without hesitating. He described the rooms of state in the palace, the late king's apartments, and those of the Prince of Wales.

It was strange; it was wonderful; yes, it was unaccountable—so all said that heard it. The tide was beginning to turn, and Tom Canty's hopes to run high, when the Lord Protector shook his head and said—

"It is true it is most wonderful—but it is no more than our lord the king likewise can do." This remark, and this reference to himself as still the king, saddened Tom Canty, and he felt his hopes crumbling from under him. "These are not *proofs*," added the Protector.

The tide was turning very fast, now, very fast indeed—but in the wrong direction; it was leaving poor Tom Canty stranded on the throne, and sweeping the other out to sea. The Lord Protector communed with himself—shook his head—the thought forced itself upon him, "It is perilous to the state and to us all, to entertain so fateful a riddle as this; it could divide the nation and undermine the throne." He turned and said—

"Sir Thomas, arrest this—No, hold!" His face lighted, and he confronted the ragged candidate with this question—

"Where lieth the Great Seal? Answer me this truly, and the riddle is unriddled; for only he that was Prince of Wales *can* so answer! On so trivial a thing hang a throne and a dynasty!"

It was a lucky thought, a happy thought. That it was so considered by the great officials was manifested by the silent applause that shot from eye to eye around their circle in the form of bright approving glances. Yes, none but the true prince could dissolve the stubborn mystery of the vanished Great Seal—this forlorn little impostor had been taught his lesson well, but here his teachings must fail, for his teacher himself could not answer *that* question—ah, very good, very good indeed; now we shall be rid of this troublesome and perilous business in short order! And so they nodded invisibly and smiled inwardly with satisfaction, and looked to see this foolish lad stricken with a palsy of guilty confusion. How surprised they were, then, to see nothing of the sort happen— how they marveled to hear him answer up promptly, in a confident and untroubled voice, and say—

"There is naught in this riddle that is difficult." Then, without so much as a by-your-leave to anybody, he turned and gave this command, with the easy manner of one accustomed to doing such things: "My lord St. John, go you to my private cabinet in the palace—for none knoweth the place better than you—and, close down to the floor, in the left corner remotest from the door that opens from the ante-chamber, you shall find in the wall a brazen nail-head; press upon it and a little jewel-closet will fly open which not even you do know of— no, nor any soul else, in all the world but me and the trusty artisan that did contrive it for me. The first thing that falleth under your eye will be the Great Seal—fetch it hither."

All the company wondered at this speech, and wondered still more to see the little mendicant pick out this peer without hesitancy or apparent fear of mistake, and call him by name with such a placidly convincing air of having known him all his life. The peer was almost surprised into obeying.

He even made a movement as if to go, but quickly recovered his tranquil attitude and confessed his blunder with a blush. Tom Canty turned upon him and said, sharply—

"Why dost thou hesitate? Hast not heard the king's command? Go!"

The lord St. John made a deep obeisance—and it was observed that it was a significantly cautious and non-committal one, it not being delivered at either of the kings, but at the neutral ground about half way between the two—and took his leave.

Now began a movement of the gorgeous particles of that official group which was slow, scarcely perceptible, and yet steady and persistent—a movement such as is observed in a kaleidoscope that is turned slowly, whereby the components of one splendid cluster fall away and join themselves to another—a movement which little by little, in the present case, dissolved the glittering crowd that stood about Tom Canty and clustered it together again in the neighborhood of the new-comer. Tom Canty stood almost alone. Now ensued a brief season of deep suspense and waiting—during which even the few faint-hearts still remaining near Tom Canty gradually scraped together courage enough to glide, one by one, over to the majority. So at last Tom Canty, in his royal robes and jewels, stood wholly alone and isolated from the world, a conspicuous figure, occupying an eloquent vacancy.

Now the lord St. John was seen returning. As he advanced up the mid-aisle the interest was so intense that the low murmur of conversation in the great assemblage died out and was suceeded by a profound hush, a breathless stillness, through which his footfalls pulsed with a dull and distant sound. Every eye was fastened upon him as he moved along. He reached the platform, paused a moment, then turned toward Tom Canty with a deep obeisance, and said—

"Sire, the Seal is not there!"

A mob does not melt away from the presence of a plague-patient with more haste than the band of pallid and terrified courtiers melted away from the presence of the shabby little claimant of the crown. In a moment he stood all alone, without friend or supporter, a target upon which was concentrated a bitter fire of scornful and angry looks. The Lord Protector called out fiercely—

"Cast the beggar into the street, and scourge him through the town—the paltry knave is worth no more consideration!"

Officers of the guard sprang forward to obey, but Tom Canty waved them off and said—

"Back! Whoso touches him perils his life!"

The Lord Protector was perplexed, in the last degree. He said to the lord St. John—

"Searched you well?—but it boots not to ask that. It doth seem passing strange. Little things, trifles, slip out of one's ken, and one does not think it matter for surprise; but how a so bulky thing as the Seal of England can vanish away and no man be able to get track of it again—a massy golden disk—"

Tom Canty, with beaming eyes, sprang forward and shouted—

"Hold, that is enough! Was it round?—and thick?—and had it letters and devices graved upon it?—Yes? O, *now* I know what this Great Seal is that there's been such worry and pother about! An' ye had described it to me, ye could have had it three weeks ago. Right well I know where it lies; but it was not I that put it there—first."

"Who, then, my liege?" asked the Lord Protector.

"He that stands there—the rightful king of England. And he shall tell you himself where it lies—then you will believe he knew it of his own knowledge. Bethink thee, my king—spur thy memory—it was the last, the very *last* thing thou didst that day before thou didst rush forth from the palace, clothed in my rags, to punish the soldier that insulted me."

A silence ensued, undisturbed by a movement or a whisper, and all eyes were fixed upon the new-comer, who stood, with bent head and corrugated brow, groping in his memory among a thronging multitude of valueless recollections for one single little elusive fact, which, found, would seat him upon a throne—unfound, would leave him as he was, for good and all—a pauper and an outcast. Moment after moment passed—the moments built themselves into minutes—still the boy struggled silently on, and gave no sign. But at

last he heaved a sigh, shook his head slowly, and said, with a
trembling lip and in a despondent voice—

"I call the scene back—all of it—but the Seal hath no place
in it." He paused, then looked up, and said with gentle dignity, "My lords and gentlemen, if ye will rob your rightful
sovereign of his own for lack of this evidence which he is not
able to furnish, I may not stay ye, being powerless. But—"

"O, folly, O, madness, my king!" cried Tom Canty, in a
panic, "wait!—think! Do not give up!—the cause is not lost!
Nor *shall* be, neither! List to what I say—follow every
word—I am going to bring that morning back again, every
hap just as it happened. We talked—I told you of my sisters,
Nan and Bet—ah, yes, you remember that; and about mine
old grandam—and the rough games of the lads of Offal
Court—yes, you remember these things also; very well, follow me still, you shall recal everything. You gave me food and
drink, and did with princely courtesy send away the servants,
so that my low breeding might not shame me before them—
ah, yes, this also you remember."

As Tom checked off his details, and the other boy nodded
his head in recognition of them, the great audience and the
officials stared in puzzled wonderment; the tale sounded like
true history, yet how could this impossible conjunction between a prince and a beggar-boy have come about? Never was
a company of people so perplexed, so interested, and so stupefied, before.

"For a jest, my prince, we did exchange garments. Then we
stood before a mirror; and so alike were we that both said it
seemed as if there had been no change made—yes, you remember that. Then you noticed that the soldier had hurt my
hand—look! here it is, I cannot yet even write with it, the
fingers are so stiff. At this your highness sprang up, vowing
vengeance upon that soldier, and ran toward the door—you
passed a table—that thing you call the Seal lay on that
table—you snatched it up and looked eagerly about, as if for
a place to hide it—your eye caught sight of—"

"There, 'tis sufficient!—and the dear God be thanked!" exclaimed the ragged claimant, in a mighty excitement. "Go, my
good St. John,—in an armpiece of the Milanese armor that
hangs on the wall, thou'lt find the Seal!"

"Right, my king! right!" cried Tom Canty; "*now* the sceptre of England is thine own; and it were better for him that would dispute it that he had been born dumb! Go, my lord St. John, give thy feet wings!"

The whole assemblage was on its feet, now, and well nigh out of its mind with uneasiness, apprehension, and consuming excitement. On the floor and on the platform a deafening buzz of frantic conversation burst forth, and for some time nobody knew anything or heard anything or was interested in anything but what his neighbor was shouting into his ear, or he was shouting into his neighbor's ear. Time—nobody knew how much of it—swept by unheeded and unnoted. At last a sudden hush fell upon the house, and in the same moment St. John appeared upon the platform and held the Great Seal aloft in his hand. Then such a shout went up!

"Long live the true king!"

For five minutes the air quaked with shouts and the crash of musical instruments, and was white with a storm of waving handkerchiefs; and through it all a ragged lad, the most conspicuous figure in England, stood, flushed and happy and proud, in the centre of the spacious platform, with the great vassals of the kingdom kneeling around him.

Then all rose, and Tom Canty cried out—

"Now, O, my king, take these regal garments back, and give poor Tom, thy servant, his shreds and remnants again."

The Lord Protector spoke up—

"Let the small varlet be stripped and flung into the Tower."

But the new king, the true king, said—

"I will not have it so. But for him I had not got my crown again—none shall lay a hand upon him to harm him. And as for thee, my good uncle, my Lord Protector, this conduct of thine is not grateful toward this poor lad, for I hear he hath made thee a duke"—the Protector blushed— "yet he was not a king; wherefore, what is thy fine title worth, now? To-morrow you shall sue to me, *through him*, for its confirmation, else no duke, but a simple earl, shalt thou remain."

Under this rebuke, his grace the Duke of Somerset retired a little from the front for the moment. The king turned to Tom, and said, kindly—

"My poor boy, how was it that you could remember where I hid the Seal when I could not remember it myself?"

"Ah, my king, that was easy, since I used it divers days."

"Used it,—yet could not explain where it was?"

"I did not know it was *that* they wanted. They did not describe it, your majesty."

"Then how used you it?"

The red blood began to steal up into Tom's cheeks, and he dropped his eyes and was silent.

"Speak up, good lad, and fear nothing," said the king. "How used you the Great Seal of England?"

Tom stammered a moment, in a pathetic confusion, then got it out—

"To crack nuts with!"

Poor child, the avalanche of laughter that greeted this, nearly swept him off his feet. But if a doubt remained in any mind that Tom Canty was not the king of England and familiar with the august appurtenances of royalty, this reply disposed of it utterly.

Meantime the sumptuous robe of state had been removed from Tom's shoulders to the king's, whose rags were effectually hidden from sight under it.

Then the coronation ceremonies were resumed; the true king was anointed and the crown set upon his head, whilst cannon thundered the news to the city, and all London seemed to rock with applause.

Chapter 33

EDWARD AS KING

MILES HENDON was picturesque enough before he got into the riot on London Bridge—he was more so when he got out of it. He had but little money when he got in, none at all when he got out. The pickpockets had stripped him of his last farthing.

But no matter, so he found his boy. Being a soldier, he did not go at his task in a random way, but set to work, first of all, to arrange his campaign.

What would the boy naturally do? Where would he naturally go? Well—argued Miles—he would naturally go to his former haunts, for that is the instinct of unsound minds, when homeless and forsaken, as well as of sound ones. Whereabouts were his former haunts? His rags, taken together with the low villain who seemed to know him and who even claimed to be his father, indicated that his home was in one or another of the poorest and meanest districts of London. Would the search for him be difficult, or long? No, it was likely to be easy and brief. He would not hunt for the boy, he would hunt for a crowd; in the centre of a big crowd or a little one, sooner or later, he should find his poor little friend, sure; and the mangy mob would be entertaining itself with pestering and aggravating the boy, who would be proclaiming himself king, as usual. Then Miles Hendon would cripple some of those people, and carry off his little ward, and comfort and cheer him with loving words, and the two would never be separated any more.

So Miles started on his quest. Hour after hour he tramped through back alleys and squalid streets, seeking groups and crowds, and finding no end of them, but never any sign of the boy. This greatly surprised him, but did not discourage him. To his notion, there was nothing the matter with his plan of campaign; the only miscalculation about it was that the campaign was becoming a lengthy one, whereas he had expected it to be short.

When daylight arrived, at last, he had made many a mile, and canvassed many a crowd, but the only result was that he was tolerably tired, rather hungry, and very sleepy. He wanted some breakfast, but there was no way to get it. To beg for it did not occur to him; as to pawning his sword, he would as soon have thought of parting with his honor; he could spare some of his clothes—yes, but one could as easily find a customer for a disease as for such clothes.

At noon he was still tramping—among the rabble which followed after the royal procession, now; for he argued that this regal display would attract his little lunatic powerfully. He followed the pageant through all its devious windings about London, and all the way to Westminster and the Abbey. He drifted here and there amongst the multitudes that were massed in the vicinity for a weary long time, baffled and perplexed, and finally wandered off, thinking, and trying to contrive some way to better his plan of campaign. By and by, when he came to himself out of his musings, he discovered that the town was far behind him and that the day was growing old. He was near the river, and in the country; it was a region of fine rural seats—not the sort of district to welcome clothes like his.

It was not at all cold; so he stretched himself on the ground in the lee of a hedge to rest and think. Drowsiness presently began to settle upon his senses; the faint and far-off boom of cannon was wafted to his ear, and he said to himself "The new king is crowned," and straightway fell asleep. He had not slept or rested, before, for more than thirty hours. He did not wake again until near the middle of the next morning.

He got up, lame, stiff, and half famished, washed himself in the river, stayed his stomach with a pint or two of water, and trudged off toward Westminster grumbling at himself for having wasted so much time. Hunger helped him to a new plan, now; he would try to get speech with old Sir Humphrey Marlow and borrow a few marks, and—but that was enough of a plan for the present; it would be time enough to enlarge it when this first stage should be accomplished.

Toward eleven o'clock he approached the palace; and although a host of showy people were about him, moving in the same direction, he was not inconspicuous—his costume took care of that. He watched these people's faces narrowly, hoping to find a charitable one whose possessor might be willing to carry his name to the old lieutenant—as to trying to get into the palace himself, that was simply out of the question.

Presently our whipping-boy passed him, then wheeled about and scanned his figure well, saying to himself, "An' that is not the very vagabond his majesty is in such a worry about, then am I an ass—though belike I was that before. He answereth the description to a rag—that God should make two such, would be to cheapen miracles, by wasteful repetition. I would I could contrive an excuse to speak with him."

Miles Hendon saved him the trouble; for he turned about, then, as a man generally will when somebody mesmerizes him by gazing hard at him from behind; and observing a strong interest in the boy's eyes, he stepped toward him and said—

"You have just come out from the palace; do you belong there?"

"Yes, your worship."

"Know you Sir Humphrey Marlow?"

The boy started, and said to himself, "Lord! mine old departed father!" Then he answered, aloud, "Right well, your worship."

"Good—is he within?"

"Yes," said the boy; and added, to himself, "within his grave."

"Might I crave your favor to carry my name to him, and say I beg to say a word in his ear?"

"I will despatch the business right willingly, fair sir."

"Then say Miles Hendon, son of Sir Richard, is here without—I shall be greatly bounden to you, my good lad."

The boy looked disappointed—"the king did not name him so," he said to himself—"but it mattereth not, this is his twin brother, and can give his majesty news of t'other Sir-Odds-and-Ends, I warrant." So he said to Miles, "Step in there a moment, good sir, and wait till I bring you word."

Hendon retired to the place indicated—it was a recess sunk in the palace wall, with a stone bench in it—a shelter for sentinels in bad weather. He had hardly seated himself when some halberdiers, in charge of an officer, passed by. The officer saw him, halted his men, and commanded Hendon to come forth. He obeyed, and was promptly arrested as a suspicious character prowling within the precincts of the palace. Things began to look ugly. Poor Miles was going to explain, but the officer roughly silenced him, and ordered his men to disarm him and search him.

"God of his mercy grant that they find somewhat," said poor Miles; "I have searched enow, and failed, yet is my need greater than theirs."

Nothing was found but a document. The officer tore it open, and Hendon smiled when he recognized the "pothooks" made by his lost little friend that black day at Hendon Hall. The officer's face grew dark as he read the English paragraph, and Miles's blenched to the opposite color as he listened.

"Another new claimant of the crown!" cried the officer. "Verily they breed like rabbits, to-day. Seize the rascal, men, and see ye keep him fast whilst I convey this precious paper within and send it to the king."

He hurried away, leaving the prisoner in the grip of the halberdiers.

"Now is my evil luck ended at last," muttered Hendon, "for I shall dangle at a rope's end for a certainty, by reason of that bit of writing. And what will become of my poor lad!—ah, only the good God knoweth."

By and by he saw the officer coming again, in a great hurry; so he plucked his courage together, purposing to meet his trouble as became a man. The officer ordered the men to loose the prisoner and return his sword to him; then bowed respectfully, and said—

"Please you sir, to follow me."

Hendon followed, saying to himself, "An' I were not traveling to death and judgment, and so must needs economize in sin, I would throttle this knave for his mock courtesy."

The two traversed a populous court, and arrived at the grand entrance of the palace, where the officer, with another bow, delivered Hendon into the hands of a gorgeous official, who received him with profound respect and led him forward through a great hall, lined on both sides with rows of splendid flunkeys (who made reverential obeisance as the two passed along, but fell into death-throes of silent laughter at our stately scarecrow the moment his back was turned,) and up a broad staircase, among flocks of fine folk, and finally conducted him into a vast room, clove a passage for him through the assembled nobility of England, then made a bow, reminded him to take his hat off, and left him standing in the middle of the room, a mark for all eyes, for plenty of indignant frowns, and for a sufficiency of amused and derisive smiles.

Miles Hendon was entirely bewildered. There sat the young king, under a canopy of state, five steps away, with his head bent down and aside, speaking with a sort of human bird of paradise—a duke, maybe; Hendon observed to himself that it was hard enough to be sentenced to death in the full vigor of life, without having this peculiarly public humiliation added. He wished the king would hurry about it— some of the gaudy people near by were becoming pretty offensive. At this moment the king raised his head slightly and Hendon caught a good view of his face. The sight nearly took his breath away! He stood gazing at the fair young face like one transfixed; then presently ejaculated—

"Lo, the lord of the Kingdom of Dreams and Shadows on his throne!"

He muttered some broken sentences, still gazing and marveling; then turned his eyes around and about, scanning the gorgeous throng and the splendid saloon, murmuring "But these are *real*—verily these are *real*—surely it is not a dream."

He stared at the king again—and thought, "*Is* it a dream? . . . . or *is* he the veritable sovereign of England, and not the friendless poor Tom o' Bedlam I took him for—who shall solve me this riddle?" A sudden idea flashed in his eye, and he strode to the wall, gathered up a chair, brought it back, planted it on the floor, and sat down in it!

A buzz of indignation broke out, a rough hand was laid upon him, and a voice exclaimed,—

"Up, thou mannerless clown!—wouldst sit in the presence of the king?"

The disturbance attracted his majesty's attention, who stretched forth his hand and cried out—

"Touch him not, it is his right!"

The throng fell back, stupefied. The king went on—

"Learn ye all, ladies, lords and gentlemen, that this is my trusty and well beloved servant, Miles Hendon, who interposed his good sword and saved his prince from bodily harm and possible death—and for this he is a knight, by the king's voice. Also learn, that for a higher service, in that he saved his sovereign stripes and shame, taking these upon himself, he is a peer of England, Earl of Kent, and shall have gold and lands meet for the dignity. More—the privilege which he hath just exercised is his by royal grant; for we have ordained that the chiefs of his line shall have and hold the right to sit in the presence of the majesty of England henceforth, age after age, so long as the crown shall endure. Molest him not."

Two persons, who, through delay, had only arrived from the country during this morning, and had now been in this room only five minutes, stood listening to these words and looking at the king, then at the scarecrow, then at the king again, in a sort of torpid bewilderment. These were Sir Hugh and the lady Edith. But the new earl did not see them. He was still staring at the monarch, in a dazed way, and muttering—

"O, body o' me! *This* my pauper! this my lunatic! This is he whom *I* would show what grandeur was, in my house of seventy rooms and seven and twenty servants! This is he who had never known aught but rags for raiment, kicks for comfort, and offal for diet! This is he whom *I* adopted and would make respectable! Would God I had a bag to hide my head in!"

Then his manners suddenly came back to him, and he dropped upon his knees, with his hands between the king's, and swore allegiance and did homage for his lands and titles. Then he rose and stood respectfully aside, a mark still for all eyes—and much envy, too.

Now the king discovered Sir Hugh, and spoke out, with wrathful voice and kindling eye—

"Strip this robber of his false show and stolen estates, and put him under lock and key till I have need of him."

The late Sir Hugh was led away.

There was a stir at the other end of the room, now; the assemblage fell apart, and Tom Canty, quaintly but richly clothed, marched down, between these living walls, preceded by an usher. He knelt before the king, who said—

"I have learned the story of these past few weeks, and am well pleased with thee. Thou hast governed the realm with right royal gentleness and mercy. Thou hast found thy mother and thy sisters again? Good; they shall be cared for—and thy father shall hang, if thou desire it and the law consent. Know, all ye that hear my voice, that from this day, they that abide in the shelter of Christ's Hospital and share the king's bounty, shall have their minds and hearts fed, as well as their baser parts; and this boy shall dwell there, and hold the chief place in its honorable body of governors, during life. And for that he hath been a king, it is meet that other than common observance shall be his due; wherefore, note this his dress of state, for by it he shall be known, and none shall copy it; and wheresoever he shall come, it shall remind the people that he hath been royal, in his time, and none shall deny him his due of reverence or fail to give him salutation. He hath the throne's protection, he hath the crown's support, he shall be known and called by the honorable title of the King's Ward."

The proud and happy Tom Canty rose and kissed the king's hand, and was conducted from the presence. He did not waste any time, but flew to his mother, to tell her and Nan and Bet all about it and get them to help him enjoy the great news.*

*See Notes to Chapter 33 at end of the volume.

Conclusion

JUSTICE AND RETRIBUTION

W HEN THE MYSTERIES were all cleared up, it came out, by confession of Hugh Hendon, that his wife had repudiated Miles by his command, that day at Hendon Hall—a command assisted and supported by the perfectly trustworthy promise that if she did not deny that he was Miles Hendon, and stand firmly to it, he would have her life; whereupon she said take it, she did not value it—and she would not repudiate Miles; then the husband said he would spare her life but have Miles assassinated! This was a different matter; so she gave her word and kept it.

Hugh was not prosecuted for his threats or for stealing his brother's estates and title, because the wife and brother would not testify against him—and the former would not have been allowed to do it, even if she had wanted to. Hugh deserted his wife and went over to the continent, where he presently died; and by and by the Earl of Kent married his relict. There were grand times and rejoicings at Hendon village when the couple paid their first visit to the Hall.

Tom Canty's father was never heard of again.

The king sought out the farmer who had been branded and sold as a slave, and reclaimed him from his evil life with the Ruffler's gang, and put him in the way of a comfortable livelihood.

He also took that old lawyer out of prison and remitted his fine. He provided good homes for the daughters of the two Baptist women whom he saw burned at the stake, and roundly punished the official who laid the undeserved stripes upon Miles Hendon's back.

He saved from the gallows the boy who had captured the stray falcon, and also the woman who had stolen a remnant of cloth from a weaver; but he was too late to save the man who had been convicted of killing a deer in the royal forest.

He showed favor to the justice who had pitied him when

he was supposed to have stolen a pig, and he had the gratification of seeing him grow in the public esteem and become a great and honored man.

As long as the king lived he was fond of telling the story of his adventures, all through, from the hour that the sentinel cuffed him away from the palace gate till the final midnight when he deftly mixed himself into a gang of hurrying workmen and so slipped into the Abbey and climbed up and hid himself in the Confessor's tomb, and then slept so long, next day, that he came within one of missing the Coronation altogether. He said that the frequent rehearsing of the precious lesson kept him strong in his purpose to make its teachings yield benefits to his people; and so, whilst his life was spared he should continue to tell the story, and thus keep its sorrowful spectacles fresh in his memory and the springs of pity replenished in his heart.

Miles Hendon and Tom Canty were favorites of the king, all through his brief reign, and his sincere mourners when he died. The good Earl of Kent had too much sense to abuse his peculiar privilege; but he exercised it twice after the instance we have seen of it before he was called from the world; once at the accession of Queen Mary, and once at the accession of Queen Elizabeth. A descendant of his exercised it at the accession of James I. Before this one's son chose to use the privilege, near a quarter of a century had elapsed, and the "privilege of the Kents" had faded out of most people's memories; so, when the Kent of that day appeared before Charles I and his court and sat down in the sovereign's presence to assert and perpetuate the right of his house, there was a fine stir, indeed! But the matter was soon explained, and the right confirmed. The last earl of the line fell in the wars of the Commonwealth fighting for the king, and the odd privilege ended with him.

Tom Canty lived to be a very old man, a handsome, white-haired old fellow, of grave and benignant aspect. As long as he lasted he was honored; and he was also reverenced, for his striking and peculiar costume kept the people reminded that "in his time he had been royal;" so, wherever he appeared the crowd fell apart, making way for him, and whispering, one to another, "Doff thy hat, it is the King's Ward!"—and so they saluted, and got his kindly smile in return—and they valued it, too, for his was an honorable history.

Yes, King Edward VI lived only a few years, poor boy, but he lived them worthily. More than once, when some great dignitary, some gilded vassal of the crown, made argument against his leniency, and urged that some law which he was bent upon amending was gentle enough for its purpose, and wrought no suffering or oppression which any one need mightily mind, the young king turned the mournful eloquence of his great compassionate eyes upon him and answered—

"What dost *thou* know of suffering and oppression? I and my people know, but not thou."

The reign of Edward VI was a singularly merciful one for those harsh times. Now that we are taking leave of him, let us try to keep this in our minds, to his credit.

Notes

Note 1. — Page 23.

Christ's Hospital Costume.

It is most reasonable to regard the dress as copied from the costume of the citizens of London of that period, when long blue coats were the common habit of apprentices and serving-men, and yellow stockings were generally worn; the coat fits closely to the body, but has loose sleeves, and beneath is worn a sleeveless yellow under-coat; around the waist is a red leathern girdle; a clerical band round the neck, and a small flat black cap, about the size of a saucer, completes the costume. — Timbs' *Curiosities of London*.

Note 2. — Page 25.

It appears that Christ's Hospital was not originally founded as a *school*; its object was to rescue children from the streets, to shelter, feed, clothe them, etc. — Timbs' *Curiosities of London*.

Note 3. — Page 32.

The Duke of Norfolk's Condemnation Commanded.

The king was now approaching fast towards his end; and fearing lest Norfolk should escape him, he sent a message to the Commons, by which he desired them to hasten the bill, on pretence that Norfolk enjoyed the dignity of earl marshal, and it was necessary to appoint another, who might officiate at the ensuing ceremony of installing his son Prince of Wales. — Hume's *History of England*, vol. iii. p. 307.

Note 4. — Page 42.

It was not till the end of this reign [Henry VIII] that any salads, carrots, turnips, or other edible roots were produced in England. The little of these vegetables that was used, was formerly imported from Holland and Flanders. Queen Catherine, when she wanted a salad, was obliged to despatch a messenger thither on purpose. — Hume's *History of England*, vol. iii. p. 314.

Note 5. — Page 47.

Attainder of Norfolk.

The house of peers, without examining the prisoner, without trial or evidence, passed a bill of attainder against him and sent it down to the commons. . . . The obsequious commons obeyed his [the king's] directions; and the king, having affixed the royal assent to the bill by commissioners, issued orders for the execution of Norfolk on the morning of the twenty-ninth of January, [the next day.] —Hume's *History of England*, vol. iii. p. 307.

Note 6.—Page 58.
The Loving-Cup.

The loving-cup, and the peculiar ceremonies observed in drinking from it, are older than English history. It is thought that both are Danish importations. As far back as knowledge goes, the loving-cup has always been drunk at English banquets. Tradition explains the ceremonies in this way: in the rude ancient times it was deemed a wise precaution to have both hands of both drinkers employed, lest while the pledger pledged his love and fidelity to the pledgee, the pledgee take that opportunity to slip a dirk into him!

Note 7.—Page 63.
The Duke of Norfolk's Narrow Escape.

Had Henry VIII survived a few hours longer, his order for the duke's execution would have been carried into effect. "But news being carried to the Tower that the king himself had expired that night, the lieutenant deferred obeying the warrant; and it was not thought advisable by the Council to begin a new reign by the death of the greatest nobleman in the kingdom, who had been condemned by a sentence so unjust and tyrannical."—Hume's *History of England*, vol. iii. p. 307.

Note 8.—Page 86.
The Whipping-Boy.

James I and Charles II had whipping-boys, when they were little fellows, to take their punishment for them when they fell short in their lessons; so I have ventured to furnish my small prince with one, for my own purposes.

Notes to Chapter 15.—Page 100.
Character of Hertford.

The young king discovered an extreme attachment to his uncle, who was, in the main, a man of moderation and probity.—Hume's *History of England*, vol. iii. p. 324.

But if he [the Protector,] gave offence by assuming too much state, he deserves great praise on account of the laws passed this session, by which the rigor of former statutes was much mitigated, and some security given to the freedom of the constitution. All laws were repealed which extended the crime of treason beyond the statute of the twenty-fifth of Edward III; all laws enacted during the late reign extending the crime of felony; all the former laws against Lollardy or heresy, together with the statute of the Six Articles. None were to be accused for words, but within a month after they were spoken. By these repeals several of the most rigorous laws that ever had passed in England were annulled; and some dawn, both of civil and religious liberty, began to appear to the people. A repeal also passed of that law, the destruction of all laws, by which the king's proclamation was made of equal force with a statute.—*Ibid.*, vol. iii. p. 339.

Boiling to Death.

In the reign of Henry VIII, poisoners were, by act of parliament, condemned to be *boiled to death*. This act was repealed in the following reign.

In Germany, even in the 17th century, this horrible punishment was inflicted on coiners and counterfeiters. Taylor, the Water Poet, describes an execution he witnessed in Hamburg, in 1616. The judgment pronounced against a coiner of false money was that he should "be *boiled to death in oil*; not thrown into the vessel at once, but with a pulley or rope to be hanged under the armpits, and then let down into the oil *by degrees*; first the feet, and next the legs, and so to boil his flesh from his bones alive."—Dr. J. Hammond Trumbull's *Blue Laws, True and False*, p. 13.

The Famous Stocking Case.

A woman and her daughter, *nine years old*, were hanged in Huntingdon for selling their souls to the devil, and raising a storm by pulling off their stockings!—*Ibid.*, p. 20.

Note 10.—Page 110.

Enslaving.

So young a king, and so ignorant a peasant were likely to make mistakes—and this is an instance in point. This peasant was suffering from this law *by anticipation*; the king was venting his indignation against a law which was not yet in existence: for this hideous statute was to have birth in this little king's own reign. However, we know, from the humanity of his character, that it could never have been suggested by him.

Notes to Chapter 23.—Page 147.

Death for Trifling Larcenies.

When Connecticut and New Haven were framing their first codes, larceny above the value of twelve pence was a capital crime in England—as it had been since the time of Henry I.—Dr. J. Hammond Trumbull's *Blue Laws, True and False*, p. 13.

The curious old book called "The English Rogue" makes the limit thirteen pence ha'penny; death being the portion of any who steal a thing "above the value of thirteen pence ha'penny."

Notes to Chapter 27.—Page 170.

From many descriptions of larceny, the law expressly took away the benefit of clergy; to steal a horse, or a *hawk*, or woolen cloth from the weaver, was a hanging matter. So it was, to kill a deer from the king's forest, or to export sheep from the kingdom.—Dr. J. Hammond Trumbull's *Blue Laws, True and False*, p. 13.

William Prynne, a learned barrister, was sentenced—[long after Edward the Sixth's time]—to lose both his ears in the pillory; to degradation from the bar; a fine of £3,000, and imprisonment for life. Three years afterwards, he gave new offence to Laud, by publishing a pamphlet against the hierarchy. He was again prosecuted, and was sentenced to lose *what remained of his ears*; to pay a fine of £5,000; to be *branded on both his cheeks* with the letters S. L. (for Seditious Libeler,) and to remain in prison for life. The severity of this sentence was equaled by the savage rigor of its execution.— *Ibid.*, pp. 11–12.

Notes to Chapter 33.—Page 203.

CHRIST'S HOSPITAL, OR BLUE COAT SCHOOL, "the Noblest Institution in the World."

The ground on which the Priory of the Grey Friars stood was conferred by Henry the Eighth on the Corporation of London, [who caused the institution there of a home for poor boys and girls.] Subsequently, Edward the Sixth caused the old Priory to be properly repaired, and founded within it that noble establishment called the Blue Coat School, or Christ's Hospital, for the *education* and maintenance of orphans and the children of indigent persons. . . . . Edward would not let him [Bishop Ridley] depart till the letter was written, [to the Lord Mayor,] and then charged him to deliver it himself, and signify his special request and commandment, that no time might be lost in proposing what was convenient, and apprising him of the proceedings. The work was zealously undertaken, Ridley himself engaging in it; and the result was, the founding of Christ's Hospital for the education of poor children. [The king endowed several other charities at the same time.] "Lord God," said he, "I yield thee most hearty thanks that thou hast given me life thus long, to finish this work to the glory of thy name!" That innocent and most exemplary life was drawing rapidly to its close, and in a few days he rendered up his spirit to his Creator, praying God to defend the realm from Papistry.—J. Heneage Jesse's *London: its Celebrated Characters and Places*.

In the Great Hall hangs a large picture of King Edward VI seated on his throne, in a scarlet and ermined robe, holding the sceptre in his left hand, and presenting with the other the Charter to the kneeling Lord Mayor. By his side stands the Chancellor, holding the seals, and next to him are other officers of state. Bishop Ridley kneels before him with uplifted hands, as if supplicating a blessing on the event; whilst the Aldermen, etc., with the Lord Mayor, kneel on both sides, occupying the middle ground of the picture; and lastly, in front, are a double row of boys on one side, and girls on the other, from the master and matron down to the boy and girl who have stepped forward from their respective rows, and kneel with raised hands before the king.—Timbs' *Curiosities of London*, p. 98.

Christ's Hospital, by ancient custom, possesses the privilege of addressing the Sovereign on the occasion of his or her coming into the City to partake of the hospitality of the Corporation of London.—*Ibid*.

The Dining-Hall, with its lobby and organ-gallery, occupies the entire story, which is 187 feet long, 51 feet wide, and 47 feet high; it is lit by nine large windows, filled with stained glass on the south side; and is, next to Westminster Hall, the noblest room in the metropolis. Here the boys, now about 800 in number, dine; and here are held the "Suppings in Public," to which visitors are admitted by tickets, issued by the Treasurer and by the Governors of Christ's Hospital. The tables are laid with cheese in wooden bowls; beer in wooden piggins, poured from leathern jacks; and bread brought in large baskets. The official company enter; the Lord Mayor, or President, takes his seat in a state chair, made of oak from St. Catherine's Church by the Tower; a hymn is sung, accompanied by the organ; a "Grecian," or head boy, reads the prayers from the pulpit, silence being enforced by three drops of a wooden hammer. After prayer the supper commences, and the visitors walk between the tables. At its close, the "trade-boys" take up the baskets, bowls, jacks, piggins, and candlesticks, and pass in procession, the bowing to the Governors being curiously formal. This spectacle was witnessed by Queen Victoria and Prince Albert in 1845.

Among the more eminent Blue Coat Boys are Joshua Barnes, editor of Anacreon and Euripides; Jeremiah Markland, the eminent critic, particularly in Greek literature; Camden, the antiquary; Bishop Stillingfleet; Samuel Richardson the novelist; Thomas

Mitchell, the translator of Aristophanes; Thomas Barnes, many years editor of the London *Times*; Coleridge, Charles Lamb, and Leigh Hunt.

No boy is admitted before he is seven years old, or after he is nine; and no boy can remain in the school after he is fifteen, King's boys and "Grecians" alone excepted. There are about 500 Governors, at the head of whom are the Sovereign and the Prince of Wales. The qualification for a Governor is payment of £500.—*Ibid.*

GENERAL NOTE.

One hears much about the "hideous Blue-Laws of Connecticut," and is accustomed to shudder piously when they are mentioned. There are people in America—and even in England!—who imagine that they were a very monument of malignity, pitilessness, and inhumanity. Whereas, in reality they were about the first SWEEPING DEPARTURE FROM JUDICIAL ATROCITY *which the "civilized" world had seen. This humane and kindly Blue-Law code, of two hundred and forty years ago, stands all by itself, with ages of bloody law on the further side of it, and a century and three-quarters of bloody English law on* THIS *side of it.*

There has never been a time—under the Blue-Laws or any other—when above FOURTEEN *crimes were punishable by death in Connecticut. But in England, within the memory of men who are still hale in body and mind,* TWO HUNDRED AND TWENTY-THREE *crimes were punishable by death!* These facts are worth knowing—and worth thinking about, too.*

FINIS.

*See Dr. J. Hammond Trumbull's *Blue Laws, True and False*, p. 11.

A CONNECTICUT YANKEE
IN KING ARTHUR'S COURT

Contents

Preface

THE UNGENTLE laws and customs touched upon in this tale are historical, and the episodes which are used to illustrate them are also historical. It is not pretended that these laws and customs existed in England in the sixth century; no, it is only pretended that inasmuch as they existed in the English and other civilizations of far later times, it is safe to consider that it is no libel upon the sixth century to suppose them to have been in practice in that day also. One is quite justified in inferring that wherever one of these laws or customs was lacking in that remote time, its place was competently filled by a worse one.

The question as to whether there is such a thing as divine right of kings is not settled in this book. It was found too difficult. That the executive head of a nation should be a person of lofty character and extraordinary ability, was manifest and indisputable; that none but the Deity could select that head unerringly, was also manifest and indisputable; that the Deity ought to make that selection, then, was likewise manifest and indisputable; consequently, that He does make it, as claimed, was an unavoidable deduction. I mean, until the author of this book encountered the Pompadour, and Lady Castlemaine and some other executive heads of that kind; these were found so difficult to work into the scheme, that it was judged better to take the other tack in this book, (which must be issued this fall,) and then go into training and settle the question in another book. It is of course a thing which ought to be settled, and I am not going to have anything particular to do next winter anyway.

MARK TWAIN.

HARTFORD, July 21, 1889.

A Word of Explanation

I<small>T WAS</small> in Warwick Castle that I came across the curious stranger whom I am going to talk about. He attracted me by three things: his candid simplicity, his marvelous familiarity with ancient armor, and the restfulness of his company—for he did all the talking. We fell together, as modest people will, in the tail of the herd that was being shown through, and he at once began to say things which interested me. As he talked along, softly, pleasantly, flowingly, he seemed to drift away imperceptibly out of this world and time, and into some remote era and old forgotten country; and so he gradually wove such a spell about me that I seemed to move among the spectres and shadows and dust and mould of a gray antiquity, holding speech with a relic of it! Exactly as I would speak of my nearest personal friends or enemies, or my most familiar neighbors, he spoke of Sir Bedivere, Sir Bors de Ganis, Sir Launcelot of the Lake, Sir Galahad, and all the other great names of the Table Round—and how old, old, unspeakably old, and faded and dry and musty and ancient he came to look, as he went on! Presently he turned to me and said, just as one might speak of the weather, or any other common matter—

"You know about transmigration of souls; do you know about transposition of epochs—and bodies?"

I said I had not heard of it. He was so little interested—just as when people speak of the weather—that he did not notice whether I made him any answer or not. There was half a moment of silence; immediately interrupted by the droning voice of the salaried cicerone:

"Ancient hauberk, date of the sixth century, time of King Arthur and the Round Table; said to have belonged to the knight Sir Sagramour le Desirous; observe the round hole through the chain-mail in the left breast; can't be accounted for; supposed to have been done with a bullet since invention of firearms—perhaps maliciously by Cromwell's soldiers."

My acquaintance smiled—not a modern smile, but one that must have gone out of general use many, many centuries ago—and muttered, apparently to himself:

"Wit ye well, *I saw it done*." Then, after a pause, added: "I did it myself."

By the time I had recovered from the electric surprise of this remark, he was gone.

All that evening I sat by my fire at the Warwick Arms, steeped in a dream of the olden time, while the rain beat upon the windows and the wind roared about the eaves and corners. From time to time I dipped into old Sir Thomas Malory's enchanting book, and fed at its rich feast of prodigies and adventures, breathed-in the fragrance of its obsolete names, and dreamed again. Midnight being come at length, I read another tale, for a night-cap—this which here follows, to wit:

How Sir Launcelot slew two giants, and made a castle free.

ANON withal came there upon him two great giants, well armed all save the heads, with two horrible clubs in their hands. Sir Launcelot put his shield afore him, and put the stroke away of the one giant, and with his sword he clave his head asunder. When his fellow saw that, he ran away as he were wood,* for fear of the horrible strokes, and Sir Launcelot after him with all his might, and smote him on the shoulder, and clave him to the middle. Then Sir Launcelot went into the hall, and there came afore him threescore ladies and damsels, and all kneeled unto him, and thanked God and him of their deliverance. For, sir, said they, the most part of us have been here this seven year their prisoners, and we have worked all manner of silk works for our meat, and we are all great gentlewomen born, and blessed be the time, knight, that ever thou wert born; for thou hast done the most worship that ever did knight in the world, that will we bear record, and we all pray you to tell us your name, that we may tell our friends who delivered us out of prison. Fair damsels, he said, my name is Sir Launcelot du Lake. And so he departed from them and betaught them unto God. And then he mounted upon his horse, and rode into many strange and wild countries and through many waters and valleys, and evil was he lodged. And at the last by

*Demented.

fortune him happened against a night to come to a fair courtelage, and therein he found an old gentlewoman that lodged him with a good will, and there he had good cheer for him and his horse. And when time was, his host brought him into a fair garret over the gate to his bed. There Sir Launcelot unarmed him, and set his harness by him, and went to bed, and anon he fell on sleep. So soon after there came one on horseback, and knocked at the gate in great haste. And when Sir Launcelot heard this he arose up, and looked out at the window, and saw by the moon-light three knights came riding after that one man, and all three lashed on him at once with swords, and that one knight turned on them knightly again and defended him. Truly, said Sir Launcelot, yonder one knight shall I help, for it were shame for me to see three knights on one, and if he be slain I am partner of his death. And therewith he took his harness and went out at a window by a sheet down to the four knights, and then Sir Launcelot said on high, Turn you knights unto me, and leave your fighting with that knight. And then they all three left Sir Kay, and turned unto Sir Launcelot, and there began great battle, for they alight all three, and strake many great strokes at Sir Launcelot, and assailed him on every side. Then Sir Kay dressed him for to have holpen Sir Launcelot. Nay, sir, said he, I will none of your help, therefore as ye will have my help let me alone with them. Sir Kay for the pleasure of the knight suffered him for to do his will, and so stood aside. And then anon within six strokes Sir Launcelot had stricken them to the earth.

And then they all three cried, Sir knight, we yield us unto you as man of might matchless. As to that, said Sir Launcelot, I will not take your yielding unto me, but so that ye yield you unto Sir Kay the seneschal, on that covenant I will save your lives and else not. Fair knight, said they, that were we loth to do; for as for Sir Kay we chased him hither, and had overcome him had not ye been; therefore to yield us unto him it were no reason. Well, as to that, said Sir Launcelot, advise you well, for ye may choose whether ye will die or live, for and ye be yielden it shall be unto Sir Kay. Fair knight, then they said, in saving our lives we will do as thou commandest us. Then shall ye, said Sir Launcelot, on Whitsunday next coming go unto the court of king Arthur, and there shall ye yield you unto queen Guenever, and put you all three in her grace and mercy, and say that Sir Kay sent you thither to be her prisoners. On the morn Sir Launcelot arose early, and left Sir Kay sleeping: and Sir Launcelot took Sir Kay's armour and his shield and armed him: and so he went to the stable and took his horse, and took his leave of his host, and so he departed. Then soon after arose Sir Kay and missed Sir

Launcelot: and then he espied that he had his armour and his horse. Now by my faith I know well that he will grieve some of the court of king Arthur: for on him knights will be bold, and deem that it is I, and that will beguile them: and because of his armour and shield I am sure I shall ride in peace. And then soon after departed Sir Kay, and thanked his host.

As I laid the book down there was a knock at the door, and my stranger came in. I gave him a pipe and a chair, and made him welcome. I also comforted him with a hot Scotch whisky; gave him another one; then still another—hoping always for his story. After a fourth persuader, he drifted into it himself, in a quite simple and natural way:

The Stranger's History.

I am an American. I was born and reared in Hartford, in the State of Connecticut—anyway, just over the river, in the country. So I am a Yankee of the Yankees—and practical; yes, and nearly barren of sentiment, I suppose—or poetry, in other words. My father was a blacksmith, my uncle was a horse-doctor, and I was both, along at first. Then I went over to the great Colt arms-factory and learned my real trade; learned all there was to it; learned to make everything: guns, revolvers, cannon, boilers, engines, all sorts of labor-saving machinery. Why, I could make anything a body wanted—anything in the world, it didn't make any difference what; and if there wasn't any quick, new-fangled way to make a thing, I could invent one—and do it as easy as rolling off a log. I became head superintendent; had a couple of thousand men under me.

Well, a man like that, is a man that is full of fight—that goes without saying. With a couple of thousand rough men under one, one has plenty of that sort of amusement. I had, anyway. At last I met my match, and I got my dose. It was during a misunderstanding conducted with crowbars with a fellow we used to call Hercules. He laid me out with a crusher alongside the head that made everything crack, and seemed to spring every joint in my skull and make it overlap its neighbor. Then the world went out in darkness, and I didn't feel anything more, and didn't know anything at all —at least for a while.

When I came to again, I was sitting under an oak tree, on the grass, with a whole beautiful and broad country landscape all to myself—nearly. Not entirely; for there was a fellow on a horse, looking down at me—a fellow fresh out of a picture-book. He was in old-time iron armor from head to heel, with a helmet on his head the shape of a nail-keg with slits in it; and he had a shield, and a sword, and a prodigious spear; and his horse had armor on, too, and a steel horn projecting from his forehead, and gorgeous red and green silk trappings that hung down all around him like a bed-quilt, nearly to the ground.

"Fair sir, will ye just?" said this fellow.

"Will I which?"

"Will ye try a passage of arms for land or lady or for—"

"What are you giving me?" I said. "Get along back to your circus, or I'll report you."

Now what does this man do but fall back a couple of hundred yards and then come rushing at me as hard as he could tear, with his nail-keg bent down nearly to his horse's neck, and his long spear pointed straight ahead. I saw he meant business; so I was up the tree when he arrived.

He allowed that I was his property, the captive of his spear. There was argument on his side—and the bulk of the advantage; so I judged it best to humor him. We fixed up an agreement whereby I was to go with him and he was not to hurt me. I came down, and we started away, I walking by the side of his horse. We marched comfortably along, through glades and over brooks which I could not remember to have seen before—which puzzled me and made me wonder—and yet we did not come to any circus or sign of a circus. So I gave up the idea of a circus, and concluded he was from an asylum. But we never came to any asylum—so I was up a stump, as you may say. I asked him how far we were from Hartford. He said he had never heard of the place; which I took to be a lie, but allowed it to go at that. At the end of an hour we saw a far-away town sleeping in a valley by a winding river; and beyond it on a hill, a vast gray fortress, with towers and turrets, the first I had ever seen, out of a picture.

"Bridgeport?" said I, pointing.

"Camelot," said he.

My stranger had been showing signs of sleepiness. He caught himself nodding, now; and smiled one of those pathetic obsolete smiles of his, and said:

"I find I can't go on; but come with me, I've got it all written out, and you can read it if you like."

In his chamber, he said:

"First, I kept a journal; then by and by, after years, I took the journal and turned it into a book. How long ago that was!"

He handed me his manuscript, and pointed out the place where I should begin:

"Begin here—I've already told you what goes before." He was steeped in drowsiness by this time. As I went out at his door I heard him murmur sleepily:

"Give you good den, fair sir."

I sat down by my fire and examined my treasure. The first part of it—the great bulk of it—was parchment, and yellow with age. I scanned a leaf particularly, and saw that it was a palimpsest. Under the old dim writing of the Yankee historian appeared traces of a penmanship which was older and dimmer still—Latin words and sentences: fragments from old monkish legends, evidently. I turned to the place indicated by my stranger, and began to read—as follows.

THE TALE OF THE LOST LAND

Chapter 1

CAMELOT

"AMELOT—Camelot," said I to myself. "I don't seem to remember hearing of it before. Name of the asylum, likely."

It was a soft, reposeful, summer landscape, as lovely as a dream, and as lonesome as Sunday. The air was full of the smell of flowers, and the buzzing of insects, and the twittering of birds; and there were no people, no wagons, there was no stir or life, nothing going on. The road was mainly a winding path with hoof-prints in it, and now and then a faint trace of wheels on either side in the grass—wheels that apparently had a tire as broad as one's hand.

Presently a fair slip of a girl, about ten years old, with a cataract of golden hair streaming down over her shoulders, came along. Around her head she wore a hoop of flame-red poppies. It was as sweet an outfit as ever I saw, what there was of it. She walked indolently along, with a mind at rest, its peace reflected in her innocent face. The circus man paid no attention to her; didn't even seem to see her. And she—she was no more startled at his fantastic make-up than if she was used to his like every day of her life. She was going by as indifferently as she might have gone by a couple of cows; but when she happened to notice me, *then* there was a change! Up went her hands, and she was turned to stone; her mouth dropped open, her eyes stared wide and timorously, she was the picture of astonished curiosity touched with fear. And there she stood gazing, in a sort of stupefied fascination, till we turned a corner of the wood and were lost to her view. That she should be startled at me instead of at the other man, was too many for me; I couldn't make head or tail of it. And that she should seem to consider me a spectacle, and totally overlook her own merits in that respect, was another puzzling thing, and a display of magnanimity, too, that was surprising in one so young. There was food for thought here. I moved along as one in a dream.

As we approached the town, signs of life began to appear. At intervals we passed a wretched cabin, with a thatched roof, and about it small fields and garden patches in an indifferent state of cultivation. There were people, too; brawny men, with long, coarse, uncombed hair that hung down over their faces and made them look like animals. They and the women, as a rule, wore a coarse tow-linen robe that came well below the knee, and a rude sort of sandals; and many wore an iron collar. The small boys and girls were always naked; but nobody seemed to know it. All of these people stared at me, talked about me, ran into the huts and fetched out their families to gape at me; but nobody ever noticed that other fellow, except to make him humble salutation and get no response for their pains.

In the town were some substantial windowless houses of stone, scattered among a wilderness of thatched cabins; the streets were mere crooked alleys, and unpaved; troops of dogs and nude children played in the sun and made life and noise; hogs roamed and rooted contentedly about, and one of them lay in a reeking wallow in the middle of the main thoroughfare and suckled her family. Presently there was a distant blare of military music; it came nearer, still nearer, and soon a noble cavalcade wound into view, glorious with plumed helmets, and flashing mail, and flaunting banners and rich doublets and horse-cloths, and gilded spear-heads; and through the muck, and swine, and naked brats, and joyous dogs, and shabby huts it took its gallant way, and in its wake we followed. Followed, through one winding alley and then another,—and climbing, always climbing—till at last we gained the breezy height where the huge castle stood. There was an exchange of bugle blasts; then a parley from the walls, where men-at-arms, in hauberk and morion marched back and forth with halberd at shoulder under flapping banners with the rude figure of a dragon displayed upon them; and then the great gates were flung open, the drawbridge was lowered, and the head of the cavalcade swept forward under the frowning arches; and we following, soon found ourselves in a great paved court, with towers and turrets stretching up into the blue air on all the four sides; and all about us the dismount was going on, and much greeting and ceremony, and running to and fro, and a gay display of moving and intermingling colors, and an altogether pleasant stir and noise and confusion.

Chapter 2

KING ARTHUR'S COURT

THE MOMENT I got a chance I slipped aside privately and touched an ancient common-looking man on the shoulder and said, in an insinuating, confidential way—

"Friend, do me a kindness. Do you belong to the asylum, or are you just here on a visit, or something like that?"

He looked me over, stupidly, and said—

"Marry, fair sir, meseemeth—"

"That will do," I said; "I reckon you are a patient."

I moved away, cogitating, and at the same time keeping an eye out for any chance passenger in his right mind that might come along and give me some light. I judged I had found one, presently; so I drew him aside and said in his ear—

"If I could see the head keeper a minute—only just a minute—"

"Prithee do not let me."

"Let you *what*?"

"*Hinder* me, then, if the word please thee better." Then he went on to say he was an under-cook and could not stop to gossip, though he would like it another time, for it would comfort his very liver to know where I got my clothes. As he started away he pointed and said yonder was one who was idle enough for my purpose, and was seeking me besides, no doubt. This was an airy slim boy in shrimp-colored tights that made him look like a forked carrot; the rest of his gear was blue silk and dainty laces and ruffles; and he had long yellow curls, and wore a plumed pink satin cap tilted complacently over his ear. By his look, he was good-natured; by his gait, he was satisfied with himself. He was pretty enough to frame. He arrived, looked me over with a smiling and impudent curiosity; said he had come for me, and informed me that he was a page.

"Go 'long," I said, "you ain't more than a paragraph."

It was pretty severe, but I was nettled. However, it never fazed him; he didn't appear to know he was hurt. He began to talk and laugh, in happy, thoughtless, boyish fashion, as we walked along, and made himself old friends with me at once; asked me all sorts of questions about myself and about my clothes, but never waited for an answer—always chattered straight ahead, as if he didn't know he had asked a question and wasn't expecting any reply; until at last he happened to mention that he was born in the beginning of the year 513.

It made the cold chills creep over me! I stopped, and said, a little faintly:

"Maybe I didn't hear you just right. Say it again—and say it slow. What year was it?"

"513."

"513! You don't look it! Come my boy, I am a stranger and friendless: be honest and honorable with me. Are you in your right mind?"

He said he was.

"Are these other people in their right minds?"

He said they were.

"And this isn't an asylum? I mean, it isn't a place where they cure crazy people?"

He said it wasn't.

"Well, then," I said, "either I am a lunatic or something just as awful has happened. Now tell me, honest and true, where am I?"

"IN KING ARTHUR'S COURT."

I waited a minute, to let that idea shudder its way home, and then said:

"And according to your notions, what year is it now?"

"528—nineteenth of June."

I felt a mournful sinking at the heart, and muttered: "I shall never see my friends again—never, never again. They will not be born for more than thirteen hundred years yet."

I seemed to believe the boy, I didn't know why. *Something* in me seemed to believe him—my consciousness, as you may say; but my reason didn't. My reason straightway began to clamor; that was natural. I didn't know how to go about satisfying it, because I knew that the testimony of men wouldn't serve—my reason would say they were lunatics, and throw out their evidence. But all of a sudden I stumbled on the very thing, just by luck. I knew that the only total eclipse of the sun in the first half of the sixth century occurred on the 21st of June, A.D. 528, O. S., and began at 3 minutes after 12 noon. I also knew that no total eclipse of the sun was due in what to *me* was the present year—*i. e.*, 1879. So, if I could keep my anxiety and curiosity from eating the heart out of me for forty-eight hours, I should then find out for certain whether this boy was telling me the truth or not.

Wherefore, being a practical Connecticut man, I now shoved this whole problem clear out of my mind till its appointed day and hour should come, in order that I might turn all my attention to the circumstances of the present moment, and be alert and ready to make the most out of them that could be made. One thing at a time, is my motto—and just play that thing for all it is worth, even if it's only two pair and a jack. I made up my mind to two things: if it was still the nineteenth century and I was among lunatics and couldn't get away, I would presently boss that asylum or know the reason why; and if on the other hand it was really the sixth century, all right, I didn't want any softer thing: I would boss the whole country inside of three months; for I judged I would have the start of the best educated man in the kingdom by a matter of thirteen hundred years and upwards. I'm not a man to waste time after my mind's made up and there's work on hand; so I said to the page—

"Now, Clarence, my boy—if that might happen to be your name—I'll get you to post me up a little if you don't mind. What is the name of that apparition that brought me here?"

"My master and thine? That is the good knight and great lord Sir Kay the Seneschal, foster brother to our liege the king."

"Very good; go on, tell me everything."

He made a long story of it; but the part that had immediate interest for me was this. He said I was Sir Kay's prisoner, and that in the due course of custom I would be flung into a dungeon and left there on scant commons until my friends ransomed me—unless I chanced to rot, first. I saw that the last chance had the best show, but I didn't waste any bother about that; time was too precious. The page said, further, that dinner was about ended in the great hall by this time, and that as soon as the sociability and the heavy drinking should begin, Sir Kay would have me in and exhibit me before King Arthur and his illustrious knights seated at the Table Round, and would brag about his exploit in capturing me, and would probably exaggerate the facts a little, but it wouldn't be good form for me to correct him, and not over safe, either; and when I was done being exhibited, then ho for the dungeon; but he, Clarence, would find a way to come and see me every now and then, and cheer me up, and help me get word to my friends.

Get word to my friends! I thanked him; I couldn't do less; and about this time a lackey came to say I was wanted; so Clarence led me in and took me off to one side and sat down by me.

Well, it was a curious kind of spectacle, and interesting. It was an immense place, and rather naked—yes, and full of loud contrasts. It was very, very lofty; so lofty that the banners depending from the arched beams and girders away up there floated in a sort of twilight; there was a stone-railed gallery at each end, high up, with musicians in the one, and women, clothed in stunning colors, in the other. The floor was of big stone flags, laid in black and white squares, rather battered by age and use, and needing repair. As to ornament, there wasn't any, strictly speaking; though on the walls hung some huge tapestries which were probably taxed as works of art: battle pieces, they were, with horses shaped like those which children cut out of paper or create in gingerbread; with men on them in scale armor whose scales are represented by round holes—so that the man's coat looks as if it had been done with a biscuit-punch. There was a fire place big enough to camp in; and its projecting sides and hood, of carved and pillared stone-work, had the look of a cathedral door. Along the walls stood men-at-arms, in breastplate and morion, with halberds for their only weapon—rigid as statues; and that is what they looked like.

In the middle of this groined and vaulted public square was an oaken table which they called the Table Round. It was as large as a circus ring; and around it sat a great company of men dressed in such various and splendid colors that it hurt one's eyes to look at them. They wore their plumed hats, right along; except that whenever one addressed himself directly to the king, he lifted his hat a trifle just as he was beginning his remark.

Mainly they were drinking—from entire ox horns; but a few were still munching bread or gnawing beef-bones. There was about an average of two dogs to one man; and these sat in expectant attitudes till a spent bone was flung to them, and then they went for it by brigades and divisions, with a rush, and there ensued a fight which filled the prospect with a tumultuous chaos of plunging heads and bodies and flashing tails, and the storm of howlings and barkings deafened all speech for the time; but that was no matter, for the dog-fight was always a bigger interest anyway; the men rose, sometimes, to observe it the better and bet on it; and the ladies and the musicians stretched themselves out over their balusters with the same object; and all broke into delighted ejaculations from time to time. In the end, the winning dog stretched himself out comfortably with his bone between his paws, and proceeded to growl over it, and gnaw it, and grease the floor with it, just as fifty others were already doing; and the rest of the court resumed their previous industries and entertainments.

As a rule, the speech and behavior of these people were gracious and courtly; and I noticed that they were good and serious listeners when anybody was telling anything—I mean, in a dog-fightless interval. And plainly, too, they were a childlike and innocent lot; telling lies of the stateliest pattern with a most gentle and winning naivety, and ready and willing to listen to anybody else's lie, and believe it, too. It was hard to associate them with anything cruel or dreadful; and yet they dealt in tales of blood and suffering with a guileless relish that made me almost forget to shudder.

I was not the only prisoner present. There were twenty or more. Poor devils, many of them were maimed, hacked, carved, in a frightful way; and their hair, their faces, their clothing, were caked with black and stiffened drenchings of blood. They were suffering sharp physical pain, of course; and weariness, and hunger and thirst, no doubt; and at least none had given them the comfort of a wash, or even the poor charity of a lotion for their wounds; yet you never heard them utter a moan or a groan, or saw them show any sign of restlessness, or any disposition to complain. The thought was forced upon me: "The rascals—*they* have served other people so, in their day; it being their own turn, now, they were not expecting any better treatment than this; so their philosophical bearing is not an outcome of mental training, intellectual fortitude, reasoning; it is mere animal training; they are white Indians."

Chapter 3

Knights of the Table Round

MAINLY, the Round Table talk was monologues—narrative accounts of the adventures in which these prisoners were captured and their friends and backers killed and stripped of their steeds and armor. As a general thing—as far as I could make out—these murderous adventures were not forays undertaken to avenge injuries, nor to settle old disputes or sudden fallings out; no, as a rule they were simply duels between strangers—duels between people who had never even been introduced to each other, and between whom existed no cause of offence whatever. Many a time I had seen a couple of boys, strangers, meet by chance, and say simultaneously, "I can lick you," and go at it on the spot; but I had always imagined, until now, that that sort of thing belonged to children only, and was a sign and mark of childhood; but here were these big boobies sticking to it and taking pride in it clear up into full age and beyond. Yet there was something very engaging about these great simple-hearted creatures, something attractive and lovable. There did not seem to be brains enough in the entire nursery, so to speak, to bait a fish-hook with; but you didn't seem to mind that, after a little, because you soon saw that brains were not needed in a society like that, and indeed would have marred it, hindered it, spoiled its symmetry—perhaps rendered its existence impossible.

There was a fine manliness observable in almost every face; and in some a certain loftiness and sweetness that rebuked your belittling criticisms, and stilled them. A most noble benignity and purity reposed in the countenance of him they called Sir Galahad; and likewise in the king's, also; and there was majesty and greatness in the giant frame and high bearing of Sir Launcelot of the Lake.

There was presently an incident which centred the general interest upon this Sir Launcelot. At a sign from a sort of master of ceremonies, six or eight of the prisoners rose and came forward in a body and knelt on the floor and lifted up their hands toward the ladies' gallery and begged the grace of a word with the queen. The most conspicuously situated lady in that massed flower-bed of feminine show and finery, inclined her head by way of assent, and then the spokesman of the prisoners delivered himself and his fellows into her hands for free pardon, ransom, captivity or death, as she in her good pleasure might elect; and this, as he said, he was doing by command of Sir Kay the Seneschal, whose prisoners they were, he having vanquished them by his single might and prowess in sturdy conflict in the field.

Surprise and astonishment flashed from face to face all over the house; the queen's gratified smile faded out at the name of Sir Kay, and she looked disappointed; and the page whispered in my ear with an accent and manner expressive of extravagant derision—

"Sir *Kay*, forsooth! Oh, call me pet names, dearest, call me a marine! In twice a thousand years shall the unholy invention of man labor at odds to beget the fellow to this majestic lie!"

Every eye was fastened with severe inquiry upon Sir Kay. But he was equal to the occasion. He got up and played his hand like a major—and took every trick. He said he would state the case, exactly according to the facts; he would tell the simple straightforward tale, without comment of his own; "and then," said he, "if ye find glory and honor due, ye will give it unto him who is the mightiest man of his hands that ever bare shield or strake with sword in the ranks of Christian battle—even him that sitteth there!"—and he pointed to Sir Launcelot. Ah, he fetched them; it was a rattling good stroke. Then he went on and told how Sir Launcelot, seeking adventures, some brief time gone by, killed seven giants at one sweep of his sword, and set a hundred and forty-two captive maidens free; and then went further, still seeking adventures, and found him (Sir Kay,) fighting a desperate fight against nine foreign knights, and straightway took the battle solely into his own hands, and conquered the nine; and that night Sir Launcelot rose quietly, and dressed him in Sir Kay's armor and took Sir Kay's horse and gat him away into distant lands, and vanquished sixteen knights in one pitched battle and thirty-four in another; and all these and the former nine he made to swear that about Whitsuntide they would ride to Arthur's court and yield them to Queen Guenever's hands as captives of Sir Kay the Seneschal, spoil of his knightly prowess; and now here were these half dozen, and the rest would be along as soon as they might be healed of their desperate wounds.

Well, it was touching to see the queen blush and smile, and look embarrassed and happy, and fling furtive glances at Sir Launcelot that would have got him shot, in Arkansas, to a dead certainty.

Everybody praised the valor and magnanimity of Sir Launcelot; and as for me, I was perfectly amazed, that one man, all by himself, should have been able to beat down and capture such battalions of practiced fighters. I said as much to Clarence; but this mocking featherhead only said—

"An Sir Kay had had time to get another skin of sour wine into him, ye had seen the accompt doubled."

I looked at the boy in sorrow; and as I looked I saw the cloud of a deep despondency settle upon his countenance. I followed the direction of his eye, and saw that a very old and white-bearded man, clothed in a flowing black gown, had risen and was standing at the table, upon unsteady legs, and feebly swaying his ancient head and surveying the company with his watery and wandering eye. The same suffering look that was in the page's face was observable in all the faces around—the look of dumb creatures who know that they must endure and make no moan.

"Marry, we shall have it again," sighed the boy; "that same old weary tale that he hath told a thousand times in the same words, and that he *will* tell till he dieth, every time he hath gotten his barrel full and feeleth his exaggeration-mill a-working. Would God I had died or I saw this day!"

"Who is it?"

"Merlin, the mighty liar and magician, perdition singe him for the weariness he worketh with his one tale! But that men fear him for that he hath the storms and the lightnings and all the devils that be in hell at his beck and call, they would have dug his entrails out these many years ago to get at that tale and squelch it. He telleth it alway in the third person, making believe he is too modest to glorify himself—maledictions light upon him, misfortune be his dole! Good friend, prithee call me for evensong."

The boy nestled himself upon my shoulder and pretended to go to sleep. The old man began his tale; and presently the lad was asleep in reality; so also were the dogs, and the court, the lackeys, and the files of men-at-arms. The droning voice droned on; a soft snoring arose on all sides and supported it like a deep and subdued accompaniment of wind instruments. Some heads were bowed upon folded arms, some lay back, with open mouths that issued unconscious music; the flies buzzed and bit, unmolested, the rats swarmed softly out from a hundred holes, and pattered about, and made themselves at home everywhere; and one of them sat up like a squirrel on the king's head and held a bit of cheese in its hands and nibbled it, and dribbled the crumbs in the king's face with naive and impudent irreverence. It was a tranquil scene, and restful to the weary eye and the jaded spirit.

This was the old man's tale. He said:

"Right so the king and Merlin departed, and went until an hermit that was a good man and a great leach. So the hermit searched all his wounds and gave him good salves; so the king was there three days, and then were his wounds well amended that he might ride and go, and so departed. And as they rode, Arthur said, I have no sword. No force,* said Merlin, hereby is a sword that shall be yours and I may. So they rode till they came to a lake, the which was a fair water and broad, and in the midst of the lake Arthur was ware of an arm clothed in white samite, that held a fair sword in that hand. Lo, said Merlin, yonder is that sword that I spake of. With that they saw a damsel going upon the lake: What damsel is that? said Arthur. That is the Lady of the lake, said Merlin; and within that lake is a rock, and therein is as fair a place as any on earth, and richly beseen, and this damsel will come to you anon, and then speak ye fair to her that she will give you that sword. Anon withal came the damsel unto Arthur and saluted him, and he her again. Damsel, said Arthur, what sword is that, that yonder the arm holdeth above the water? I would it were mine, for I have no sword. Sir Arthur king, said the

*No matter.

damsel, that sword is mine, and if ye will give me a gift when I ask it you, ye shall have it. By my faith, said Arthur, I will give you what gift ye will ask. Well, said the damsel, go ye into yonder barge and row yourself to the sword, and take it and the scabbard with you, and I will ask my gift when I see my time. So Sir Arthur and Merlin alight, and tied their horses to two trees, and so they went into the ship, and when they came to the sword that the hand held, Sir Arthur took it up by the handles, and took it with him. And the arm and the hand went under the water; and so they came unto the land and rode forth. And then Sir Arthur saw a rich pavilion: What signifieth yonder pavilion? It is the knight's pavilion, said Merlin, that ye fought with last, Sir Pellinore, but he is out, he is not there; he hath ado with a knight of yours, that hight Egglame, and they have fought together, but at the last Egglame fled, and else he had been dead, and he hath chased him even to Carlion, and we shall meet with him anon in the high way. That is well said, said Arthur, now have I a sword, now will I wage battle with him and be avenged on him. Sir, ye shall not so, said Merlin, for the knight is weary of fighting and chasing, so that ye shall have no worship to have ado with him; also he will not lightly be matched of one knight living; and therefore it is my counsel, let him pass, for he shall do you good service in short time, and his sons after his days. Also ye shall see that day in short space, ye shall be right glad to give him your sister to wed. When I see him, I will do as ye advise me, said Arthur. Then Sir Arthur looked on the sword, and liked it passing well. Whether liketh you better, said Merlin, the sword or the scabbard? Me liketh better the sword, said Arthur. Ye are more unwise, said Merlin, for the scabbard is worth ten of the sword, for while ye have the scabbard upon you ye shall never lose no blood, be ye never so sore wounded, therefore keep well the scabbard always with you. So they rode unto Carlion, and by the way they met with Sir Pellinore; but Merlin had done such a craft that Pellinore saw not Arthur, and he passed by without any words. I marvel, said Arthur, that the knight would not speak. Sir, said Merlin, he saw you not, for and he had seen you ye had not lightly departed. So they came unto Carlion, whereof his knights were passing glad. And when they heard of his adventures they marvelled that he would jeopard his person so alone. But all men of worship said it was merry to be under such a chieftain that would put his person in adventure as other poor knights did."

Chapter 4

Sir Dinadan the Humorist

IT SEEMED to me that this quaint lie was most simply and beautifully told; but then I had heard it only once, and that makes a difference; it was pleasant to the others when it was fresh, no doubt.

Sir Dinadan the Humorist was the first to awake, and he soon roused the rest with a practical joke of a sufficiently poor quality. He tied some metal mugs to a dog's tail and turned him loose, and he tore round and around the place in a frenzy of fright, with all the other dogs bellowing after him and battering and crashing against everything that came in their way and making altogether a chaos of confusion and a most deafening din and turmoil; at which every man and woman of the multitude laughed till the tears flowed, and some fell out of their chairs and wallowed on the floor in ecstasy. It was just like so many children. Sir Dinadan was so proud of his exploit that he could not keep from telling over and over again, to weariness, how the immortal idea happened to occur to him; and, as is the way with humorists of his breed, he was still laughing at it after everybody else had got through. He was so set up that he concluded to make a speech—of course a humorous speech. I think I never heard so many old played-out jokes strung together in my life. He was worse than the minstrels, worse than the clown in the circus. It seemed peculiarly sad to sit here, thirteen hundred years before I was born and listen again to poor, flat, worm-eaten jokes that had given me the dry gripes when I was a boy thirteen hundred years afterwards. It about convinced me that there isn't any such thing as a new joke possible. Everybody laughed at these antiquities—but then they always do; I had noticed that, centuries later. However, of course the Scoffer didn't laugh—I mean the boy. No, he scoffed; there wasn't anything he wouldn't scoff at. He said the most of Sir Dinadan's jokes were rotten and the rest were petrified. I said "petrified" was good; as I believed, myself, that the only right way to classify the majestic ages of some of those jokes was by geologic periods. But that neat idea hit the boy in a blank place, for geology hadn't been invented yet. He failed to catch on. However, I made a note of the remark, and calculated to educate the commonwealth up to it if I pulled through. It is no use to throw a good thing away merely because the market isn't ripe yet.

Now Sir Kay arose and began to fire up on his history-mill, with me for fuel. It was time for me to feel serious, and I did. Sir Kay told how he had encountered me in a far land of barbarians who all wore the same ridiculous garb that I did—a garb that was a work of enchantment and intended to make the wearer secure from hurt by human hands. However, he had nullified the force of the enchantment by prayer, and had killed my thirteen knights in a three-hours' battle and taken me prisoner, sparing my life in order that so strange a curiosity as I was might be exhibited to the wonder and admiration of the king and the court. He spoke of me all the time, in the blandest way, as "this prodigious giant," and "this horrible sky-towering monster," and "this tushed and taloned man-devouring ogre;" and everybody took in all this bosh in the naivest way, and never smiled or seemed to notice that there was any discrepancy between these watered statistics and me. He said that in trying to escape from him I sprang into the top of a tree two hundred cubits high at a single bound, but he dislodged me with a stone the size of a cow, which "all-to brast" the most of my bones, and then swore me to appear at Arthur's court for sentence. He ended by condemning me to die at noon on the 21st; and was so little concerned about it that he stopped to yawn before he named the date.

I was in a dismal state by this time; indeed, I was hardly enough in my right mind to keep the run of a dispute that sprung up as to how I had better be killed, the possibility of the killing being doubted by some, because of the enchantment in my clothes. And yet it was nothing but an ordinary suit of fifteen-dollar slop-shops. Still, I was sane enough to notice this detail, to wit: many of the terms used in the most matter-of-fact way by this great assemblage of the first ladies and gentlemen in the land would have made a Comanche blush. Indelicacy is too mild a term to convey the idea. However, I had read "Tom Jones," and "Roderick Random," and other books of that kind, and knew that the highest and first ladies and gentlemen in England had remained little or no cleaner in their talk, and in the morals and conduct which such talk implies, clear up to a hundred years ago; in fact, clear into our own nineteenth century—in which century, broadly speaking, the earliest samples of the real lady and real gentleman discoverable in English history—or in European history, for that matter—may be said to have made their appearance. Suppose Sir Walter, instead of putting the conversations into the mouths of his characters, had allowed the characters to speak for themselves? We should have had talk from Rebecca and Ivanhoe and the soft Lady Rowena which would embarrass a tramp in our day. However, to the unconsciously indelicate, all things are delicate. King Arthur's people were not aware that they were indecent, and I had presence of mind enough not to mention it.

They were so troubled about my enchanted clothes that they were mightily relieved, at last, when old Merlin swept the difficulty away for them with a common-sense hint. He asked them why they were so dull—why didn't it occur to them to strip me. In half a minute I was as naked as a pair of tongs! And dear, dear, to think of it: I was the only embarrassed person there. Everybody discussed me; and did it as unconcernedly as if I had been a cabbage. Queen Guenever was as naively interested as the rest, and said she had never seen anybody with legs just like mine before. It was the only compliment I got—if it was a compliment.

Finally, I was carried off in one direction, and my perilous clothes in another. I was shoved into a dark and narrow cell in a dungeon, with some scant remnants for dinner, some mouldy straw for a bed, and no end of rats for company.

Chapter 5

An Inspiration

I WAS SO tired that even my fears were not able to keep me awake long.

When I next came to myself, I seemed to have been asleep a very long time. My first thought was, "Well, what an astonishing dream I've had! I reckon I've waked only just in time to keep from being hanged or drowned or burned, or something. . . . . . I'll nap again till the whistle blows, and then I'll go down to the arms-factory and have it out with Hercules."

But just then I heard the harsh music of rusty chains and bolts, a light flashed in my eyes, and that butterfly, Clarence, stood before me! I gasped with surprise; my breath almost got away from me.

"What!" I said, "you here yet? Go along with the rest of the dream! scatter!"

But he only laughed, in his light-hearted way, and fell to making fun of my sorry plight.

"All right," I said resignedly, "let the dream go on; I'm in no hurry."

"Prithee what dream?"

"What dream? Why, the dream that I am in Arthur's court—a person who never existed; and that I am talking to you, who are nothing but a work of imagination."

"Oh, la, indeed! and is it a dream that you're to be burned to-morrow? Ho-ho—answer me that!"

The shock that went through me was distressing. I now began to reason that my situation was in the last degree serious, dream or no dream; for I knew by past experience of the life-like intensity of dreams, that to be burned to death, even in a dream, would be very far from being a jest, and was a thing to be avoided, by any means, fair or foul, that I could contrive. So I said beseechingly:

"Ah, Clarence, good boy, only friend I've got,—for you

are my friend, aren't you?—don't fail me; help me to devise some way of escaping from this place!"

"Now do but hear thyself! Escape? Why, man, the corridors are in guard and keep of men-at-arms."

"No doubt, no doubt. But how many, Clarence? Not many, I hope?"

"Full a score. One may not hope to escape." After a pause—hesitatingly: "and there be other reasons—and weightier."

"Other ones? What are they?"

"Well, they say—oh, but I daren't, indeed I daren't!"

"Why, poor lad, what is the matter? Why do you blench? why do you tremble so?"

"Oh, in sooth there is need! I do want to tell you, but—"

"Come, come, be brave, be a man—speak out, there's a good lad!"

He hesitated, pulled one way by desire, the other way by fear; then he stole to the door and peeped out, listening; and finally crept close to me and put his mouth to my ear and told me his fearful news in a whisper, and with all the cowering apprehension of one who was venturing upon awful ground and speaking of things whose very mention might be freighted with death:

"Merlin, in his malice, has woven a spell about this dungeon, and there bides not the man in these kingdoms that would be desperate enough to essay to cross its lines with you! Now God pity me, I have told it! Ah, be kind to me, be merciful to a poor boy who means thee well; for an thou betray me I am lost!"

I laughed the only really refreshing laugh I had had for some time; and shouted—

"Merlin has wrought a spell! *Merlin*, forsooth! That cheap old humbug, that maundering old ass? Bosh, pure bosh, the silliest bosh in the world! Why it does seem to me that of all the childish, idiotic, chuckle-headed, chicken-livered superstitions that ev—oh, damn Merlin!"

But Clarence had slumped to his knees before I had half finished, and he was like to go out of his mind with fright.

"Oh, beware! these are awful words! Any moment these

walls may crumble upon us if you say such things. Oh call them back before it is too late!"

Now this strange exhibition gave me a good idea and set me to thinking. If everybody about here was so honestly and sincerely afraid of Merlin's pretended magic as Clarence was, certainly a superior man like me ought to be shrewd enough to contrive some way to take advantage of such a state of things. I went on thinking, and worked out a plan. Then I said:

"Get up. Pull yourself together; look me in the eye. Do you know why I laughed?"

"No—but for our blessed Lady's sake, do it no more."

"Well, I'll tell you why I laughed. Because I'm a magician myself."

"Thou!" The boy recoiled a step, and caught his breath, for the thing hit him rather sudden; but the aspect which he took on was very, very respectful. I took quick note of that; it indicated that a humbug didn't need to have a reputation in this asylum; people stood ready to take him at his word, without that. I resumed:

"I've known Merlin seven hundred years, and he—"

"Seven hun—"

"Don't interrupt me. He has died and come alive again thirteen times, and traveled under a new name every time: Smith, Jones, Robinson, Jackson, Peters, Haskins, Merlin—a new alias every time he turns up. I knew him in Egypt three hundred years ago; I knew him in India five hundred years ago—he is always blethering around in my way, everywhere I go; he makes me tired. He don't amount to shucks, as a magician; knows some of the old common tricks, but has never got beyond the rudiments, and never will. He is well enough for the provinces—one-night stands and that sort of thing, you know—but dear me, *he* oughtn't to set up for an expert—anyway not where there's a real artist. Now look here, Clarence, I am going to stand your friend, right along, and in return you must be mine. I want you to do me a favor. I want you to get word to the king that I am a magician myself—and the Supreme Grand High-yu-Mucka-muck and head of the tribe, at that; and I want him to be made to understand that I am just quietly arranging a little calamity here that will make the fur fly in these realms if Sir Kay's project is carried out and any harm comes to me. Will you get that to the king for me?"

The poor boy was in such a state that he could hardly answer me. It was pitiful to see a creature so terrified, so un-nerved, so demoralized. But he promised everything; and on my side he made me promise over and over again that I would remain his friend, and never turn against him or cast any enchantments upon him. Then he worked his way out, staying himself with his hand along the wall, like a sick person.

Presently this thought occurred to me: how heedless I have been! when the boy gets calm, he will wonder why a great magician like me should have begged a boy like him to help me get out of this place; he will put this and that together, and will see that I am a humbug.

I worried over that heedless blunder for an hour, and called myself a great many hard names, meantime. But finally it oc-curred to me all of a sudden that these animals didn't reason; that *they* never put this and that together; that all their talk showed that they didn't know a discrepancy when they saw it. I was at rest, then.

But as soon as one is at rest, in this world, off he goes on something else to worry about. It occurred to me that I had made another blunder: I had sent the boy off to alarm his betters with a threat—I intending to invent a calamity at my leisure; now the people who are the readiest and eagerest and willingest to swallow miracles, are the very ones who are hun-griest to see you perform them; suppose I should be called on for a sample? Suppose I should be asked to name my calam-ity? Yes, I had made a blunder; I ought to have invented my calamity first. "What shall I do; what can I say, to gain a little time?" I was in trouble again; in the deepest kind of trou-ble. . . . "There's a footstep!—they're coming. If I had only just a moment to think. . . . . Good, I've got it. I'm all right."

You see, it was the eclipse. It came into my mind, in the nick of time, how Columbus, or Cortez, or one of those people, played an eclipse as a saving trump once, on some savages, and I saw my chance. I could play it myself, now; and it wouldn't be any plagiarism, either, because I should get it in nearly a thousand years ahead of those parties.

Clarence came in, subdued, distressed, and said:

"I hasted the message to our liege the king, and straightway he had me to his presence. He was frighted, even to the marrow, and was minded to give order for your instant enlargement, and that you be clothed in fine raiment and lodged as befitted one so great; but then came Merlin and spoiled all; for he persuaded the king that you are mad, and know not whereof you speak; and said your threat is but foolishness and idle vaporing. They disputed long; but in the end, Merlin, scoffing, said, 'Wherefore hath he not *named* his brave calamity? Verily it is because he cannot.' This thrust did in a most sudden sort close the king's mouth, and he could offer naught to turn the argument; and so, reluctant, and full loth to do you the discourtesy, he yet prayeth you to consider his perplexed case, as noting how the matter stands, and name the calamity—if so be you have determined the nature of it and the time of its coming. Oh, prithee delay not; to delay at such a time were to double and treble the perils that already compass thee about. Oh, be thou wise—name the calamity!"

I allowed silence to accumulate while I got my impressiveness together, and then said:

"How long have I been shut up in this hole?"

"Ye were shut up when yesterday was well spent. It is nine of the morning, now."

"No! Then I have slept well, sure enough. Nine in the morning now! and yet it is the very complexion of midnight to a shade. This is the 20th, then?"

"The 20th—yes."

"And I am to be burned alive to-morrow." The boy shuddered. "At what hour?"

"At high noon."

"Now then, I will tell you what to say." I paused, and stood over that cowering lad a whole minute in awful silence; then in a voice deep, measured, charged with doom, I began, and rose by dramatically graded stages to my colossal climax, which I delivered in as sublime and noble a way as ever I did such a thing in my life: "Go back and tell the king that at that hour I will smother the whole world in the dead blackness of midnight; I will blot out the sun, and he shall never shine again; the fruits of the earth shall rot for lack of light and warmth, and the peoples of the earth shall famish and die, to the last man!"

I had to carry the boy out, myself, he sunk into such a collapse. I handed him over to the soldiers, and went back.

Chapter 6

THE ECLIPSE

IN THE STILLNESS and the darkness, realization soon began to supplement knowledge. The mere knowledge of a fact is pale; but when you come to *realize* your fact, it takes on color. It is all the difference between hearing of a man being stabbed to the heart, and seeing it done. In the stillness and the darkness, the knowledge that I was in deadly danger took to itself deeper and deeper meaning all the time; a something which was realization crept inch by inch through my veins and turned me cold.

But it is a blessed provision of nature that at times like these, as soon as a man's mercury has got down to a certain point there comes a revulsion, and he rallies. Hope springs up, and cheerfulness along with it, and then he is in good shape to do something for himself if anything can be done. When my rally came, it came with a bound. I said to myself that my eclipse would be sure to save me, and make me the greatest man in the kingdom besides; and straightway my mercury went up to the top of the tube, and my solicitudes all vanished. I was as happy a man as there was in the world. I was even impatient for to-morrow to come, I so wanted to gather-in that great triumph and be the centre of all the nation's wonder and reverence. Besides, in a business way it would be the making of me; I knew that.

Meantime there was one thing which had got pushed into the background of my mind. That was, the half-conviction that when the nature of my proposed calamity should be reported to those superstitious people, it would have such an effect that they would want to compromise. So, by and by when I heard footsteps coming, that thought was recalled to me, and I said to myself, "As sure as anything, it's the compromise. Well, if it is good, all right, I will accept; but if it isn't, I mean to stand my ground and play my hand for all it is worth."

249

The door opened, and some men-at-arms appeared. The leader said—

"The stake is ready. Come!"

The stake! The strength went out of me, and I almost fell down. It is hard to get one's breath at such a time, such lumps come into one's throat, and such gaspings; but as soon as I could speak, I said:

"But this is a mistake—the execution is to-morrow."

"Order changed; been set forward a day. Haste thee!"

I was lost. There was no help for me. I was dazed, stupe-fied; I had no command over myself; I only wandered pur-poselessly about, like one out of his mind; so the soldiers took hold of me, and pulled me along with them, out of the cell and along the maze of underground corridors, and finally into the fierce glare of daylight and the upper world. As we stepped into the vast enclosed court of the castle I got a shock; for the first thing I saw was the stake, standing in the centre, and near it the piled fagots and a monk. On all four sides of the court the seated multitudes rose rank above rank, forming sloping terraces that were rich with color. The king and the queen sat in their thrones, the most conspicuous fig-ures there, of course.

To note all this, occupied but a second. The next second Clarence had slipped from some place of concealment and was pouring news into my ear, his eyes beaming with tri-umph and gladness. He said:

" 'Tis through *me* the change was wrought! And main hard have I worked to do it, too. But when I revealed to them the calamity in store, and saw how mighty was the terror it did engender, then saw I also that this was the time to strike! Wherefore I diligently pretended, unto this and that and the other one, that your power against the sun could not reach its full until the morrow; and so if any would save the sun and the world, you must be slain to-day, whilst your enchant-ments are but in the weaving, and lack potency. Odsbodkins it was but a dull lie, a most indifferent invention, but you should have seen them seize it and swallow it, in the frenzy of their fright, as it were salvation sent from heaven; and all the while was I laughing in my sleeve the one moment, to see them so cheaply deceived, and glorifying God the next, that

He was content to let the meanest of His creatures be His instrument to the saving of thy life. Ah, how happy has the matter sped! You will not need to do the sun a *real* hurt—ah, forget not that, on your soul forget it not! Only make a little darkness—only the littlest little darkness, mind, and cease with that. It will be sufficient. They will see that I spoke falsely,—being ignorant, as they will fancy—and with the falling of the first shadow of that darkness you shall see them go mad with fear; and they will set you free and make you great! Go to thy triumph, now! but remember—ah, good friend, I implore thee remember my supplication, and do the blessed sun no hurt. For *my* sake, thy true friend."

I choked out some words through my grief and misery; as much as to say I would spare the sun; for which the lad's eyes paid me back with such deep and loving gratitude that I had not the heart to tell him his good-hearted foolishness had ruined me and sent me to my death.

As the soldiers assisted me across the court the stillness was so profound that if I had been blindfolded I should have supposed I was in a solitude instead of walled in by four thousand people. There was not a movement perceptible in those masses of humanity; they were as rigid as stone images, and as pale; and dread sat upon every countenance. This hush continued while I was being chained to the stake; it still continued while the fagots were carefully and tediously piled about my ancles, my knees, my thighs, my body. Then there was a pause, and a deeper hush, if possible, and a man knelt down at my feet with a blazing torch; the multitude strained forward, gazing, and parting slightly from their seats without knowing it; the monk raised his hands above my head, and his eyes toward the blue sky, and began some words in Latin; in this attitude he droned on and on, a little while, and then stopped. I waited two or three moments: then looked up; he was standing there petrified. With a common impulse the multitude rose slowly up and stared into the sky. I followed their eyes; as sure as guns, there was my eclipse beginning! The life went boiling through my veins; I was a new man! The rim of black spread slowly into the sun's disk, my heart beat higher and higher, and still the assemblage and the priest stared into the sky, motionless. I knew that this gaze would be turned upon me, next. When it was, I was ready. I was in one of the most grand attitudes I ever struck, with my arm stretched up, pointing to the sun. It was a noble effect. You could *see* the shudder sweep the mass like a wave. Two shouts rang out, one close upon the heels of the other:

"Apply the torch!"

"I forbid it!"

The one was from Merlin, the other from the king. Merlin started from his place—to apply the torch himself, I judged. I said:

"Stay where you are. If any man moves—even the king—before I give him leave, I will blast him with thunder, I will consume him with lightnings!"

The multitude sank meekly into their seats, and I was just expecting they would. Merlin hesitated a moment or two, and I was on pins and needles during that little while. Then he sat down, and I took a good breath; for I knew I was master of the situation now. The king said:

"Be merciful, fair sir, and essay no further in this perilous matter, lest disaster follow. It was reported to us that your powers could not attain unto their full strength until the morrow; but—"

"Your majesty thinks the report may have been a lie? It *was* a lie."

That made an immense effect; up went appealing hands everywhere, and the king was assailed with a storm of supplications that I might be bought off at any price and the calamity stayed. The king was eager to comply. He said:

"Name any terms, reverend sir, even to the halving of my kingdom; but banish this calamity, spare the sun!"

My fortune was made. I would have taken him up in a minute, but I couldn't stop an eclipse; the thing was out of the question. So I asked time to consider. The king said—

"How long—ah, how long, good sir? Be merciful; look, it groweth darker, moment by moment. Prithee, how long?"

"Not long. Half an hour—maybe an hour."

There were a thousand pathetic protests, but I couldn't shorten up any, for I couldn't remember how long a total eclipse lasts. I was in a puzzled condition, anyway, and wanted to think. Something was wrong about that eclipse, and the fact was very unsettling. If this wasn't the one I was after, how was I to tell whether this was the sixth century, or nothing but a dream? Dear me, if I could only prove it was the latter! Here was a glad new hope. If the boy was right about the date, and this was surely the 20th, it *wasn't* the sixth century. I reached for the monk's sleeve, in considerable excitement, and asked him what day of the month it was.

Hang him, he said it was the *twenty-first!* It made me turn cold to hear him. I begged him to not make any mistake about it; but he was sure; he knew it was the 21st. So that feather-headed boy had botched things again! The time of day was right for the eclipse; I had seen that for myself, in the beginning, by the dial that was near by. Yes, I *was* in King Arthur's court, and I might as well make the most out of it I could.

The darkness was steadily growing, the people becoming more and more distressed. I now said:

"I have reflected, sir king. For a lesson, I will let this darkness proceed, and spread night in the world; but whether I blot out the sun for good, or restore it, shall rest with you. These are the terms, to wit: you shall remain king over all your dominions, and receive all the glories and honors that belong to the kingship; but you shall appoint me your perpetual minister and executive, and give me for my services one per cent of such actual increase of revenue over and above its present amount as I may succeed in creating for the state. If I can't live on that, I shan't ask anybody to give me a lift. Is it satisfactory?"

There was a prodigious roar of applause, and out of the midst of it the king's voice rose, saying:

"Away with his bonds, and set him free! and do him homage, high and low, rich and poor, for he is become the king's right hand, is clothed with power and authority, and his seat is upon the highest step of the throne! Now sweep away this creeping night, and bring the light and cheer again, that all the world may bless thee."

But I said:

"That a common man should be shamed before the world, is nothing; but it were dishonor to the *king* if any that saw his minister naked should not also see him delivered from his shame. If I might ask that my clothes be brought again—"

"They are not meet," the king broke in. "Fetch raiment of another sort; clothe him like a prince!"

My idea worked. I wanted to keep things as they were till the eclipse was total, otherwise they would be trying again to get me to dismiss the darkness, and of course I couldn't do it. Sending for the clothes gained some delay, but not enough. So I had to make another excuse. I said it would be but natural if the king should change his mind and repent to some extent of what he had done under excitement; therefore I would let the darkness grow a while, and if at the end of a reasonable time the king had kept his mind the same, the darkness should be dismissed. Neither the king nor anybody else was satisfied with that arrangement, but I had to stick to my point.

It grew darker and darker, and blacker and blacker, while I struggled with those awkward sixth-century clothes. It got to be pitch dark, at last, and the multitude groaned with horror to feel the cold uncanny night breezes fan through the place and see the stars come out and twinkle in the sky. At last the eclipse was total, and I was very glad of it, but everybody else was in misery; which was quite natural. I said:

"The king, by his silence, still stands to the terms." Then I lifted up my hands—stood just so a moment—then I said, with the most awful solemnity: "Let the enchantment dissolve and pass harmless away!"

There was no response, for a moment, in that deep darkness and that graveyard hush. But when the silver rim of the sun pushed itself out, a moment or two later, the assemblage broke loose with a vast shout and came pouring down like a deluge to smother me with blessings and gratitude; and Clarence was not the last of the wash, be sure.

Chapter 7

MERLIN'S TOWER

INASMUCH as I was now the second personage in the kingdom, as far as political power and authority were concerned, much was made of me. My raiment was of silks and
velvets and cloth of gold, and by consequence was very
showy, also uncomfortable. But habit would soon reconcile
me to my clothes; I was aware of that. I was given the choicest suite of apartments in the castle, after the king's. They
were aglow with loud-colored silken hangings, but the stone
floors had nothing but rushes on them for a carpet, and they
were misfit rushes at that, being not all of one breed. As for
conveniences, properly speaking, there weren't any. I mean
little conveniences; it is the little conveniences that make the
real comfort of life. The big oaken chairs, graced with rude
carvings, were well enough, but that was the stopping-place.
There was no soap, no matches, no looking-glass—except a
metal one, about as powerful as a pail of water. And not a
chromo. I had been used to chromos for years, and I saw
now, that without my suspecting it a passion for art had got
worked into the fabric of my being, and was become a part of
me. It made me homesick to look around over this proud and
gaudy but heartless barrenness and remember that in our
house in East Hartford, all unpretending as it was, you
couldn't go into a room but you would find an insurance-
chromo, or at least a three-color God-Bless-Our-Home over
the door; and in the parlor we had nine. But here, even in my
grand room of state, there wasn't anything in the nature of a
picture except a thing the size of a bed-quilt, which was either
woven or knitted, (it had darned places in it,) and nothing in
it was the right color or the right shape; and as for proportions, even Raphael himself couldn't have botched them more
formidably after all his practice on those nightmares they call
his "celebrated Hampton Court Cartoons." Raphael was a
bird. We had several of his chromos; one was his "Miraculous
Draught of Fishes," where he puts in a miracle of his own—

puts three men into a canoe which wouldn't have held a dog without upsetting. I always admired to study R.'s art, it was so fresh and unconventional.

There wasn't even a bell or a speaking tube in the castle. I had a great many servants, and those that were on duty lolled in the ante-rooms; and when I wanted one of them I had to go and call for him. There was no gas, there were no candles; a bronze dish half full of boarding-house butter, with a blazing rag floating in it was the thing that produced what was regarded as light. A lot of these hung along the walls and modified the dark, just toned it down enough to make it dismal. If you went out at night, your servants carried torches. There were no books, pens, paper, or ink; and no glass in the openings they believed to be windows. It is a little thing— glass is—until it is absent, then it becomes a big thing. But perhaps the worst of all was, that there wasn't any sugar, coffee, tea or tobacco. I saw that I was just another Robinson Crusoe cast away on an uninhabited island, with no society but some more or less tame animals, and if I wanted to make life bearable I must do as he did—invent, contrive, create; reorganize things; set brain and hand to work, and keep them busy. Well, that was in my line.

One thing troubled me, along at first—the immense interest which people took in me. Apparently the whole nation wanted a look at me. It soon transpired that the eclipse had scared the British world almost to death; that while it lasted the whole country, from one end to the other, was in a pitiable state of panic, and the churches, hermitages and monkeries overflowed with praying and weeping poor creatures who thought the end of the world was come. Then had followed the news that the producer of this awful event was a stranger, a mighty magician at Arthur's court; that he could have blown out the sun like a candle, and was just going to do it when his mercy was purchased, and he then dissolved his enchantments, and was now recognized and honored as the man who had by his unaided might saved the globe from destruction and its peoples from extinction. Now if you consider that everybody believed that, and not only believed it but never even dreamed of doubting it, you will easily understand that there was not a person in all Britain that would not have walked fifty miles to get a sight of me. Of course I was all the talk—all other subjects were dropped; even the king became suddenly a person of minor interest and notoriety. Within twenty-four hours the delegations began to arrive, and from that time onward for a fortnight they kept coming. The village was crowded, and all the countryside. I had to go out a dozen times a day and show myself to these reverent and awe-stricken multitudes. It came to be a great burden, as to time and trouble, but of course it was at the same time compensatingly agreeable to be so celebrated and such a centre of homage. It turned Brer Merlin green with envy and spite, which was a great satisfaction to me. But there was one thing I couldn't understand: nobody had asked for an autograph. I spoke to Clarence about it. By George, I had to explain to him what it was. Then he said nobody in the country could read or write but a few dozen priests. Land! think of that.

There was another thing that troubled me a little. Those multitudes presently began to agitate for another miracle. That was natural. To be able to carry back to their far homes the boast that they had seen the man who could command the sun, riding in the heavens, and be obeyed, would make them great in the eyes of their neighbors, and envied by them all; but to be able to also say they had seen him work a miracle themselves—why, people would come a distance to see *them*. The pressure got to be pretty strong. There was going to be an eclipse of the moon, and I knew the date and hour, but it was too far away. Two years. I would have given a good deal for license to hurry it up and use it now when there was a big market for it. It seemed a great pity to have it wasted, so, and come lagging along at a time when a body wouldn't have any use for it as like as not. If it had been booked for only a month away, I could have sold it short; but as matters stood, I couldn't seem to cipher out any way to make it do me any good, so I gave up trying. Next, Clarence found that old Merlin was making himself busy on the sly, among those people. He was spreading a report that I was a humbug, and that the reason I didn't accommodate the people with a miracle was because I couldn't. I saw that I must do something. I presently thought out a plan.

By my authority as executive I threw Merlin into prison— the same cell I had occupied myself,—and I didn't thin out the rats any for his accommodation. Then I gave public notice by herald and trumpet that I should be busy with affairs of state for a fortnight, but about the end of that time I would take a moment's leisure and blow up Merlin's ancient stone tower by fires from heaven; in the meantime, whoso listened to evil reports about me, let him beware. Furthermore, I would perform but this one miracle at this time, and no more; if it failed to satisfy, and any murmured, I would turn the murmurers into horses, and make them useful. Quiet ensued.

I took Clarence into my confidence, to a certain degree, and we went to work privately. I told him that this was a sort of miracle that required a trifle of preparation; and that it would be sudden death to even talk about these preparations to anybody. That made his mouth safe enough. Clandestinely we made a few bushels of first-rate blasting-powder, and I superintended my armorers while they constructed a lightning rod and some wires. This old stone tower was very massive—and rather ruinous, too, for it was Roman, and four hundred years old. Yes, and handsome, after a rude fashion, and clothed with ivy from base to summit, as with a shirt of scale mail. It stood on a lonely eminence, in good view from the castle, and about half a mile away.

Working by night, we stowed the powder in the tower— dug stones out, on the inside and buried the powder in the walls themselves, which were fifteen feet thick, at the base. We put in a peck at a time, in a dozen places. We could have blown up the Tower of London with these charges. When the thirteenth night was come we put up our lightning rod, bedded it in one of the batches of powder, and ran wires from it to the other batches. Everybody had shunned that locality from the day of my proclamation, but on the morning of the fourteenth I thought best to warn the people, through the heralds, to keep clear away—a quarter of a mile away. They added, by command, that at some time during the twenty-four hours I would consummate the miracle, but would first give a brief notice; by flags on the castle towers, if in the daytime, or by torch-baskets in the same places if at night.

Thunder showers had been tolerably frequent, of late, and I was not much afraid of a failure; still, I shouldn't have cared for a delay of a day or two; I should have explained that I was busy with affairs of state, yet, and the people must wait.

Of course we had a blazing sunny day—almost the first one without a cloud for three weeks; things always happen so. I kept secluded, and watched the weather. Clarence dropped in from time to time, and said the public excitement was growing and growing all the time, and the whole country filling up with human masses as far as one could see from the battlements. At last the wind sprang up, and a cloud appeared—in the right quarter, too, and just at nightfall. For a little while I watched that distant cloud spread and blacken, then I judged it was time for me to appear. I ordered the torch-baskets to be lit, and Merlin liberated and sent to me. A quarter of an hour later I ascended to the parapet and there found the king and the court assembled and gazing off in the darkness toward Merlin's tower. Already the gloom was so thick that one could not see far; these people, and the old turrets, being partly in deep shadow and partly in the red glow from the great torch-baskets overhead, made a good deal of a picture.

Merlin arrived in a sinister mood. I said:

"You wanted to burn me alive when I had not done you any harm, and latterly you have been trying to injure my professional reputation. Therefore I am going to call down fire and blow up your tower; but it is only fair to give you a chance; now if you think you can break my enchantments and ward off the fires, step to the bat, it's your innings."

"I can, fair sir, and I will. Doubt it not."

He drew an imaginary circle on the stones of the roof, and burnt a pinch of powder in it which sent up a small cloud of aromatic smoke, whereat everybody fell back and began to cross themselves and get uncomfortable. Then he began to mutter and make passes in the air with his hands. He worked himself up slowly and gradually into a sort of frenzy, and got to thrashing around with his arms like the sails of a windmill. By this time the storm had about reached us; the gusts of wind were flaring the torches and making the shadows swash about, the first heavy drops of rain were falling, the world abroad was black as pitch, the lightning began to wink fitfully. Of course my rod would be loading itself, now. In fact, things were imminent. So I said:

"You have had time enough. I have given you every advantage, and not interfered. It is plain your magic is weak. It is only fair that I begin, now."

I made about three passes in the air, and then there was an awful crash and that old tower leaped into the sky in chunks, along with a vast volcanic fountain of fire that turned night to noonday and showed a thousand acres of human beings groveling on the ground in a general collapse of consternation. Well, it rained mortar and masonry the rest of the week. This was the report; but I reckon they added on a couple of days.

It was an effective miracle. The great bothersome temporary population vanished. There were a good many thousand tracks in the mud the next morning, but they were all outward bound. If I had advertised another miracle I couldn't have raised an audience with a sheriff.

Merlin's stock was flat. The king wanted to stop his wages; he even wanted to banish him, but I interfered. I said he would be useful to work the weather, and attend to small matters like that, and I would give him a lift now and then when his poor little parlor-magic soured on him. There wasn't a rag of his tower left, but I had the government rebuild it for him, and advised him to take boarders; but he was too high-toned for that. And as for being grateful, he never even said thank-you. He was a rather hard lot, take him how you might; but then you couldn't fairly expect a man to be sweet that had been set back so.

Chapter 8

THE BOSS

To be vested with enormous authority is a fine thing; but to have the on-looking world consent to it is a finer. The tower-episode solidified my power, and made it impregnable. If any were perchance disposed to be jealous and critical before that, they experienced a change of heart, now. There was not any one in the kingdom who would have considered it good judgment to meddle with my matters.

I was fast getting adjusted to my situation and circumstances. For a time, I used to wake up, mornings, and smile at my "dream," and listen for the Colt's factory-whistle; but that sort of thing played itself out, gradually, and at last I was fully able to realize that I was actually living in the sixth century, and in Arthur's court, not a lunatic asylum. After that, I was just as much at home in that century as I could have been in any other; and as for preference, I wouldn't have traded it for the twentieth. Look at the opportunities here for a man of knowledge, brains, pluck and enterprise to sail in and grow up with the country. The grandest field that ever was; and all my own; not a competitor nor the shadow of a competitor; not a man who wasn't a baby to me in acquirements and capacities: whereas, what would I amount to in the twentieth century? I should be foreman of a factory, that is about all; and could drag a seine down street any day and catch a hundred better men than myself.

What a jump I had made! I couldn't keep from thinking about it, and contemplating it, just as one does who has struck oil. There was nothing back of me that could approach it, unless it might be Joseph's case; and Joseph's only approached it, it didn't equal it, quite. For it stands to reason that as Joseph's splendid financial ingenuities advantaged nobody but the king, the general public must have regarded him with a good deal of disfavor; whereas I had done my entire public a kindness in sparing the sun, and was popular by reason of it.

I was no shadow of a king; I was the substance, the king himself was the shadow. My power was colossal; and it was not a mere name, as such things have generally been, it was the genuine article. I stood here, at the very spring and source of the second great period of the world's history; and could see the trickling stream of that history gather, and deepen, and broaden, and roll its mighty tides down the far centuries; and I could note the upspringing of adventurers like myself in the shelter of its long array of thrones: De Montforts, Gavestons, Mortimers, Villierses; the war-making, campaign-directing wantons of France, and Charles the Second's sceptre-wielding drabs; but nowhere in the procession was my full-sized fellow visible. I was a Unique; and glad to know that that fact could not be dislodged or challenged for thirteen centuries and a half, for sure.

Yes, in power I was equal to the king. At the same time there was another power that was a trifle stronger than both of us put together. That was the Church. I do not wish to disguise that fact. I couldn't, if I wanted to. But never mind about that, now; it will show up, in its proper place, later on. It didn't cause me any trouble in the beginning—at least any of consequence.

Well, it was a curious country, and full of interest. And the people! They were the quaintest and simplest and trustingest race; why they were nothing but rabbits. It was pitiful for a person born in a wholesome free atmosphere to listen to their humble and hearty outpourings of loyalty toward their king and Church and nobility: as if they had any more occasion to love and honor king and Church and noble than a slave has to love and honor the lash, or a dog has to love and honor the stranger that kicks him! Why, dear me, *any* kind of royalty, howsoever modified, *any* kind of aristocracy, howsoever pruned, is rightly an insult; but if you are born and brought up under that sort of arrangement you probably never find it out for yourself, and don't believe it when somebody else tells you. It is enough to make a body ashamed of his race to think of the sort of froth that has always occupied its thrones without shadow of right or reason, and the seventh-rate people that have always figured as its aristocracies—a company of monarchs and nobles who, as a rule, would have achieved only poverty and obscurity if left like their betters to their own exertions.

The most of King Arthur's British nation were slaves, pure and simple, and bore that name, and wore the iron collar on their necks; and the rest were slaves in fact, but without the name; they imagined themselves men and freemen, and called themselves so. The truth was, the nation as a body was in the world for one object, and one only: to grovel before king and Church and noble; to slave for them, sweat blood for them, starve that they might be fed, work that they might play, drink misery to the dregs that they might be happy, go naked that they might wear silks and jewels, pay taxes that they might be spared from paying them, be familiar all their lives with the degrading language and postures of adulation that they might walk in pride and think themselves the gods of this world. And for all this, the thanks they got were cuffs and contempt; and so poor-spirited were they that they took even this sort of attention as an honor.

Inherited ideas are a curious thing, and interesting to observe and examine. I had mine, the king and his people had theirs. In both cases they flowed in ruts worn deep by time and habit, and the man who should have proposed to divert them by reason and argument would have had a long contract on his hands. For instance, those people had inherited the idea that all men without title and a long pedigree, whether they had great natural gifts and acquirements or hadn't, were creatures of no more consideration than so many animals, bugs, insects; whereas I had inherited the idea that human daws who can consent to masquerade in the peacock-shams of inherited dignities and unearned titles, are of no good but to be laughed at. The way I was looked upon was odd, but it was natural. You know how the keeper and the public regard the elephant in the menagerie: well, that is the idea. They are full of admiration of his vast bulk and his prodigious strength; they speak with pride of the fact that he can do a hundred marvels which are far and away beyond their own powers; and they speak with the same pride of the fact that in his wrath he is able to drive a thousand men before him: but does that make him one of *them*? No; the raggedest tramp in the pit would smile at the idea. He couldn't comprehend it;

couldn't take it in; couldn't in any remote way conceive of it. Well, to the king, the nobles, and all the nation, down to the very slaves and tramps, I was just that kind of an elephant, and nothing more. I was admired, also feared; but it was as an animal is admired and feared. The animal is not reverenced, neither was I; I was not even respected. I had no pedigree, no inherited title; so, in the king's and the nobles' eyes I was mere dirt; the people regarded me with wonder and awe, but there was no reverence mixed with it; through the force of inherited ideas they were not able to conceive of anything being entitled to that except pedigree and lordship. There you see the hand of that awful power, the Roman Catholic Church. In two or three little centuries it had converted a nation of men to a nation of worms. Before the day of the Church's supremacy in the world, men were men, and held their heads up, and had a man's pride, and spirit, and independence; and what of greatness and position a person got, he got mainly by achievement, not by birth. But then the Church came to the front, with an axe to grind; and she was wise, subtle, and knew more than one way to skin a cat—or a nation: she invented "divine right of kings," and propped it all around, brick by brick, with the Beatitudes—wrenching them from their good purpose to make them fortify an evil one; she preached (to the commoner,) humility, obedience to superiors, the beauty of self-sacrifice; she preached (to the commoner,) meekness under insult; preached (still to the commoner, always to the commoner,) patience, meanness of spirit, non-resistance under oppression; and she introduced heritable ranks and aristocracies, and taught all the Christian populations of the earth to bow down to them and worship them. Even down to my birth-century that poison was still in the blood of Christendom, and the best of English commoners was still content to see his inferiors impudently continuing to hold a number of positions, such as lordships and the throne, to which the grotesque laws of his country did not allow him to aspire; in fact he was not merely contented with this strange condition of things, he was even able to persuade himself that he was proud of it. It seems to show that there isn't anything you can't stand, if you are only born and bred to it. Of course that taint, that reverence for rank and title, had been in our American blood, too—I know that; but when I left America it had disappeared—at least to all intents and purposes. The remnant of it was restricted to the dudes and dudesses. When a disease has worked its way down to that level, it may fairly be said to be out of the system.

But to return to my anomalous position in King Arthur's kingdom. Here I was, a giant among pigmies, a man among children, a master intelligence among intellectual moles: by all rational measurement the one and only actually great man in that whole British world; and yet there and then, just as in the remote England of my birth-time, the sheep-witted earl who could claim long descent from a king's leman, acquired at second-hand from the slums of London, was a better man than I was. Such a personage was fawned upon in Arthur's realm and reverently looked up to by everybody, even though his dispositions were as mean as his intelligence, and his morals as base as his lineage. There were times when *he* could sit down in the king's presence; but I couldn't. I could have got a title easily enough, and that would have raised me a large step in everybody's eyes; even in the king's, the giver of it. But I didn't ask for it; and I declined it when it was offered. I couldn't have enjoyed such a thing, with my notions; and it wouldn't have been fair, anyway, because as far back as I could go, our tribe had always been short of the bar sinister. I couldn't have felt really and satisfactorily fine and proud and set-up over any title except one that should come from the nation itself, the only legitimate source; and such an one I hoped to win; and in the course of years of honest and honorable endeavor, I did win it and did wear it with a high and clean pride. This title fell casually from the lips of a blacksmith, one day, in a village; was caught up as a happy thought and tossed from mouth to mouth with a laugh and an affirmative vote; in ten days it had swept the kingdom, and was become as familiar as the king's name. I was never known by any other designation afterward, whether in the nation's talk or in grave debate upon matters of state at the council board of the sovereign. This title, translated into modern speech, would be THE BOSS. Elected by the nation. That suited me. And it was a pretty high title. There were very few THE's, and I was one of them. If you spoke of the duke, or the earl, or the bishop, how could anybody tell which one you meant? But if you spoke of The King or The Queen or The Boss, it was different.

Well, I liked the king, and *as* king I respected him—respected the office; at least respected it as much as I was capable of respecting any unearned supremacy; but as *men* I looked down upon him and his nobles—privately. And he and they liked me, and respected my office; but as an animal, without birth or sham title, they looked down upon me—and were not particularly private about it, either. I didn't charge for my opinion about them, and they didn't charge for their opinion about me: the account was square, the books balanced, everybody was satisfied.

Chapter 9

THE TOURNAMENT

THEY WERE always having grand tournaments there at Camelot; and very stirring, and picturesque and ridiculous human bull-fights they were, too, but just a little wearisome to the practical mind. However, I was generally on hand—for two reasons: a man must not hold himself aloof from the things which his friends and his community have at heart if he would be liked—especially a statesman; and both as business man and statesman I wanted to study the tournament and see if I couldn't invent an improvement on it. That reminds me to remark, in passing, that the very first official thing I did, in my administration—and it was on the very first day of it, too—was to start a patent office; for I knew that a country without a patent office and good patent laws was just a crab, and couldn't travel any way but sideways or backwards.

Things ran along, a tournament nearly every week; and now and then the boys used to want me to take a hand—I mean Sir Launcelot and the rest—but I said I would by and by; no hurry yet, and too much government machinery to oil up and set to rights and start agoing.

We had one tournament which was continued from day to day during more than a week, and as many as five hundred knights took part in it, from first to last. They were weeks gathering. They came on horseback, from everywhere; from the very ends of the country, and even from beyond the sea; and many brought ladies, and all brought squires, and troops of servants. It was a most gaudy and gorgeous crowd, as to costumery, and very characteristic of the country and the time, in the way of high animal spirits, innocent indecencies of language, and happy-hearted indifference to morals. It was fight or look on, all day and every day; and sing, gamble, dance, carouse, half the night every night. They had a most noble good time. You never saw such people. Those banks of beautiful ladies, shining in their barbaric splendors, would see a knight sprawl from his horse in the lists with a lance-shaft the thickness of your ancle clean through him and the blood spouting, and instead of fainting they would clap their hands and crowd each other for a better view; only sometimes one would dive into her handkerchief, and look ostentatiously broken-hearted, and then you could lay two to one that there was a scandal there somewhere and she was afraid the public hadn't found it out.

The noise at night would have been annoying to me ordinarily, but I didn't mind it in the present circumstances, because it kept me from hearing the quacks detaching legs and arms from the day's cripples. They ruined an uncommon good old cross-cut saw for me, and broke the saw-buck, too, but I let it pass. And as for my axe—well, I made up my mind that the next time I lent an axe to a surgeon I would pick my century.

I not only watched this tournament from day to day, but detailed an intelligent priest from my Department of Public Morals and Agriculture, and ordered him to report it; for it was my purpose by and by, when I should have gotten the people along far enough, to start a newspaper. The first thing you want in a new country, is a patent office; then work up your school system; and after that, out with your paper. A newspaper has its faults, and plenty of them; but no matter, it's hark from the tomb for a dead nation, and don't you forget it. You can't resurrect a dead nation without it; there isn't any way. So I wanted to sample things, and be finding out what sort of reporter-material I might be able to rake together out of the sixth century when I should come to need it.

Well, the priest did very well, considering. He got in all the details, and that is a good thing in a local item: you see, he had kept books for the undertaker-department of his church when he was younger, and there, you know, the money's in the details; the more details, the more swag: bearers, mutes, candles, prayers—everything counts; and if the bereaved don't buy prayers enough, you mark-up your candles with a forked pencil, and your bill shows up all right. And he had a good knack at getting in the complimentary thing here and there about a knight that was likely to advertise—no, I mean a knight that had influence; and he also had a neat gift of exaggeration, for in his time he had kept door for a pious hermit who lived in a sty and worked miracles.

Of course this novice's report lacked whoop and crash and lurid description, and therefore wanted the true ring; but its antique wording was quaint and sweet and simple, and full of the fragrances and flavors of the time, and these little merits made up, in a measure, for its more important lacks. Here is an extract from it:

THEN Sir Brian de les Isles, and Grummore Grummorsum, knights of the castle, encountered with Sir Aglovale and Sir Tor, and Sir Tor smote down Sir Grummore Grummorsum to the earth. Then came in Sir Carados of the dolorous tower, and Sir Turquine, knights of the castle, and there encountered with them Sir Percivale de Galis and Sir Lamorak de Galis, that were two brethren, and there encountered Sir Percivale with Sir Carados, and either brake their spears unto their hands, and then Sir Turquine with Sir Lamorak, and either of them smote down other, horse and all, to the earth, and either parties rescued other and horsed them again. And Sir Arnold, and Sir Gauter, knights of the castle, encountered with Sir Brandiles and Sir Kay, and these four knights encountered mightily, and brake their spears to their hands. Then came Sir Pertolope from the castle, and there encountered with him Sir Lionel, and there Sir Pertolope the green knight smote down Sir Lionel, brother to Sir Launcelot. All this was marked by noble heralds, who bare him best, and their names. Then Sir Bleoberis brake his spear upon Sir Gareth, but of that stroke Sir Bleoberis fell to the earth. When Sir Galihodin saw that, he bad Sir Gareth keep him, and Sir Gareth smote him to the earth. Then Sir Galihud gat a spear to avenge his brother, and in the same wise Sir Gareth served him, and Sir Dinadan and his brother La Cote Male Taile, and Sir Sagramour le Desirous, and Sir Dodinas le Savage; all these he bare down with one spear. When king Agwisance of Ireland saw Sir Gareth fare so he marvelled what he might be, that one time seemed green, and another time, at his again coming, he seemed blue. And thus at every course that he rode to and fro he changed his colour, so that there might neither king nor knight have ready cognisance of him. Then Sir Agwisance the king of Ireland encountered with Sir Gareth, and there Sir Gareth smote him from his horse, saddle and all. And then came king Carados of Scotland, and Sir Gareth smote him down, horse and man. And in the same wise he served king Uriens of the land of Gore. And then there came in Sir Bagdemagus, and Sir Gareth smote him down horse and man to the earth. And Bagdemagus's son Meliganus brake a spear upon Sir Gareth mightily and knightly. And then Sir Galahault the noble prince cried on high, Knight with the many colours, well hast thou justed; now make thee ready that I may just with thee. Sir Gareth heard him, and he gat a great spear, and so they encountered together, and there the prince brake his spear: but Sir Gareth smote him upon the left side of the helm, that he reeled here and there, and he had fallen down had not his men recovered him. Truly, said king Arthur, that knight with the many colours is a good knight. Wherefore the king called unto him Sir Launcelot, and prayed him to encounter with that knight. Sir, said Launcelot, I may well find in my heart for to forbear him as at this time, for he hath had travail enough this day, and when a good knight doth so well upon some day, it is no good knight's part to let him of his worship, and, namely, when he seeth a knight hath done so great labour: for peradventure, said Sir Launcelot, his quarrel is here this day, and peradventure he is best beloved with this lady of all that be here, for I see well he paineth himself and enforceth him to do great deeds, and therefore, said Sir Launcelot, as for me, this day he shall have the honour; though it lay in my power to put him from it, I would not.

There was an unpleasant little episode that day, which for reasons of state I struck out of my priest's report. You will have noticed that Garry was doing some great fighting in the engagement. When I say Garry I mean Sir Gareth. Garry was my private pet name for him; it suggests that I had a deep affection for him, and that was the case. But it was a private pet name only, and never spoken aloud to any one, much less to him; being a noble, he would not have endured a familiarity like that from me. Well, to proceed: I sat in the private box set apart for me as the king's minister. While Sir Dinadan was waiting for his turn to enter the lists, he came in there and sat down and began to talk; for he was always making up to me, because I was a stranger and he liked to have a fresh market for his jokes, the most of them having reached that stage of wear where the teller has to do the laughing himself while the other person looks sick. I had always responded to his efforts as well as I could, and had felt a very deep and real kindness for him, too, for the reason that if by malice of fate he knew the one particular anecdote which I had heard oftenest and had most hated and most loathed all my life, he had at least spared it me. It was one which I had heard attributed to every humorous person who had ever stood on American soil, from Columbus down to Artemus Ward. It was about a humorous lecturer who flooded an ignorant audience with the killingest jokes for an hour and never got a laugh; and then when he was leaving, some gray simpletons wrung him gratefully by the hand and said it had been the funniest thing they had ever heard, and "it was all they could do to keep from laughin' right aout in meetin'." That anecdote never saw the day that it was worth the telling; and yet I had sat under the telling of it hundreds and thousands and millions and billions of times, and cried and cursed all the way through. Then who can hope to know what my feelings were, to hear this armor-plated ass start in on it again, in the murky twilight of tradition, before the dawn of history, while even Lactantius might be referred to as "the late Lactantius," and the Crusades wouldn't be born for five hundred years yet? Just as he finished, the call-boy came; so, haw-hawing like a demon, he went rattling and clanking out like a crate of loose castings, and I knew nothing more. It was some minutes before I came to, and then I opened my eyes just in time to see Sir Gareth fetch him an awful welt, and I unconsciously out with the prayer, "I hope to gracious he's killed!" But by ill luck, before I had got half through with the words, Sir Gareth crashed into Sir Sagramour le Desirous and sent him thundering over his horse's crupper, and Sir Sagramour caught my remark and thought I meant it for *him*.

Well, whenever one of those people got a thing into his head, there was no getting it out again. I knew that, so I saved my breath, and offered no explanations. As soon as Sir Sagramour got well he notified me that there was a little account to settle between us, and he named a day three or four years in the future; place of settlement, the lists where the offence had been given. I said I would be ready when he got back. You see, he was going for the Holy Grail. The boys all took a flier at the Holy Grail now and then. It was a several-years' cruise. They always put in the long absence snooping around, in the most conscientious way, though none of them had any idea where the Holy Grail really was, and I don't think any of them actually expected to find it, or would have known what to do with it if he *had* run across it. You see, it was just the Northwest Passage of that day, as you may say; that was all. Every year expeditions went out holy grailing, and next year relief expeditions went out to hunt for *them*. There was worlds of reputation in it, but no money. Why, they actually wanted *me* to put in! Well, I should smile.

Chapter 10

BEGINNINGS OF CIVILIZATION

THE ROUND TABLE soon heard of the challenge, and of course it was a good deal discussed, for such things interested the boys. The king thought I ought now to set forth in quest of adventures, so that I might gain renown and be the more worthy to meet Sir Sagramour when the several years should have rolled away. I excused myself for the present; I said it would take me three or four years, yet, to get things well fixed up and going smoothly; then I should be ready; all the chances were that at the end of that time Sir Sagramour would still be out grailing, so no valuable time would be lost by the postponement; I should then have been in office six or seven years, and I believed my system and machinery would be so well developed that I could take a holiday without its working any harm.

I was pretty well satisfied with what I had already accomplished. In various quiet nooks and corners I had the beginnings of all sorts of industries under way—nuclei of future vast factories, the iron and steel missionaries of my future civilization. In these were gathered together the brightest young minds I could find, and I kept agents out raking the country for more, all the time. I was training a crowd of ignorant folk into experts—experts in every sort of handiwork and scientific calling. These nurseries of mine went smoothly and privately along undisturbed in their obscure country retreats, for nobody was allowed to come into their precincts without a special permit—for I was afraid of the Church.

I had started a teacher-factory and a lot of Sunday schools the first thing; as a result, I now had an admirable system of graded schools in full blast in those places, and also a complete variety of Protestant congregations all in a prosperous and growing condition. Everybody could be any kind of a Christian he wanted to; there was perfect freedom in that matter. But I confined public religious teaching to the churches and the Sunday schools, permitting nothing of it in my other educational buildings. I could have given my own sect the preference and made everybody a Presbyterian without any trouble, but that would have been to affront a law of human nature: spiritual wants and instincts are as various in the human family as are physical appetites, complexions and features, and a man is only at his best, morally, when he is equipped with the religious garment whose color and shape and size most nicely accommodate themselves to the spiritual complexion, angularities and stature of the individual who wears it; and besides, I was afraid of a united church; it makes a mighty power, the mightiest conceivable, and then when it by and by gets into selfish hands, as it is always bound to do, it means death to human liberty, and paralysis to human thought.

All mines were royal property, and there were a good many of them. They had formerly been worked as savages always work mines—holes grubbed in the earth and the mineral brought up in sacks of hide by hand, at the rate of a ton a day; but I had begun to put the mining on a scientific basis as early as I could.

Yes, I had made pretty handsome progress when Sir Sagramour's challenge struck me.

Four years rolled by—and then! Well, you would never imagine it in the world. Unlimited power *is* the ideal thing—when it is in safe hands. The despotism of heaven is the one absolutely perfect government. An earthly despotism would be the absolutely perfect earthly government, if the conditions were the same, namely, the despot the perfectest individual of the human race, and his lease of life perpetual. But as a perishable perfect man must die, and leave his despotism in the hands of an imperfect successor, an earthly despotism is not merely a bad form of government, it is the worst form that is possible.

My works showed what a despot could do, with the resources of a kingdom at his command. Unsuspected by this dark land, I had the civilization of the nineteenth century booming under its very nose! It was fenced away from the public view, but there it was, a gigantic and unassailable fact—and to be heard from, yet, if I lived and had luck. There it was, as sure a fact, and as substantial a fact as any serene volcano, standing innocent with its smokeless summit in the blue sky and giving no sign of the rising hell in its bowels. My schools and churches were children four years before; they were grown-up, now; my little shops of that day were vast factories, now; where I had a dozen trained men then, I had a thousand now; where I had one brilliant expert then, I had fifty now. I stood with my finger on the button, so to speak, ready to press it and flood the midnight world with intolerable light at any moment. But I was not going to do the thing in that sudden way. It was not my policy. The people could not have stood it; and moreover I should have had the Established Roman Catholic Church on my back in a minute.

No, I had been going cautiously, all the while. I had had confidential agents trickling through the country some time, whose office was to undermine knighthood by imperceptible degrees, and to gnaw a little at this and that and the other superstition, and so prepare the way gradually for a better order of things. I was turning on my light one candle-power at a time, and meant to continue to do so.

I had scattered some branch schools secretly about the kingdom, and they were doing very well. I meant to work this racket more and more, as time wore on, if nothing occurred to frighten me. One of my deepest secrets was my West Point—my military academy. I kept that most jealously out of sight; and I did the same with my naval academy which I had established at a remote seaport. Both were prospering to my satisfaction.

Clarence was twenty-two, now, and was my head executive, my right hand. He was a darling; he was equal to anything; there wasn't anything he couldn't turn his hand to. Of late I had been training him for journalism, for the time seemed about right for a start in the newspaper line; nothing big, but just a small weekly for experimental circulation in my civilization-nurseries. He took to it like a duck; there was an editor concealed in him sure. Already he had doubled himself in one way: he talked sixth century, and wrote nineteenth. His journalistic style was climbing, steadily; it was already up to the back-settlement Alabama mark, and couldn't be told from the editorial output of that region either by matter or flavor.

We had another large departure on hand, too. This was a telegraph and a telephone; our first venture in this line. These wires were for private service only, as yet, and must be kept private until a riper day should come. We had a gang of men on the road, working mainly by night. They were stringing ground wires; we were afraid to put up poles, for they would attract too much inquiry. Ground wires were good enough, in both instances, for my wires were protected by an insulation of my own invention which was perfect. My men had orders to strike across country, avoiding roads, and establishing connection with any considerable towns whose lights betrayed their presence, and leaving experts in charge. Nobody could tell you how to find any place in the kingdom, for nobody ever went intentionally to any place, but only struck it by accident in his wanderings, and then generally left it without thinking to inquire what its name was. At one time and another we had sent out topographical expeditions to survey and map the kingdom, but the priests had always interfered and raised trouble. So we had given the thing up, for the present; it would be poor wisdom to antagonize the Church.

As for the general condition of the country, it was as it had been when I arrived in it, to all intents and purposes. I had made changes, but they were necessarily slight, and they were not noticeable. Thus far, I had not even meddled with taxation, outside of the taxes which provided the royal revenues. I had systematized those, and put the service on an effective and righteous basis. As a result, these revenues were already quadrupled, and yet the burden was so much more equably distributed than before, that all the kingdom felt a sense of relief, and the praises of my administration were hearty and general.

Personally, I struck an interruption, now, but I did not mind it, it could not have happened at a better time. Earlier it could have annoyed me, but now everything was in good hands and swimming right along. The king had reminded me several times, of late, that the postponement I had asked for four years before had about run out, now. It was a hint that I ought to be starting out to seek adventures and get up a reputation of a size to make me worthy of the honor of breaking a lance with Sir Sagramour, who was still out grailing, but was being hunted for by various relief expeditions, and might be found any year, now. So you see I was expecting this interruption; it did not take me by surprise.

Chapter II

THE YANKEE IN SEARCH OF ADVENTURES

THERE NEVER was such a country for wandering liars; and they were of both sexes. Hardly a month went by without one of these tramps arriving; and generally loaded with a tale about some princess or other wanting help to get her out of some far-away castle where she was held in captivity by a lawless scoundrel, usually a giant. Now you would think that the first thing the king would do after listening to such a novelette from an entire stranger, would be to ask for credentials—yes, and a pointer or two as to locality of castle, best route to it, and so-on. But nobody ever thought of so simple and common-sense a thing as that. No, everybody swallowed those people's lies whole, and never asked a question of any sort or about anything. Well, one day when I was not around, one of these people came along—it was a she one, this time—and told a tale of the usual pattern. Her mistress was a captive in a vast and gloomy castle, along with forty-four other young and beautiful girls, pretty much all of them princesses; they had been languishing in that cruel captivity for twenty-six years; the masters of the castle were three stupendous brothers, each with four arms and one eye—the eye in the centre of the forehead, and as big as a fruit. Sort of fruit not mentioned; their usual slovenliness in statistics.

Would you believe it?—the king and the whole Round Table were in raptures over this preposterous opportunity for adventure. Every knight of the Table jumped for the chance, and begged for it; but to their vexation and chagrin the king conferred it upon me, who had not asked for it at all.

By an effort, I contained my joy when Clarence brought me the news. But he—he could not contain his. His mouth gushed delight and gratitude in a steady discharge—delight in my good fortune, gratitude to the king for this splendid mark of his favor for me. He could keep neither his legs nor his body still, but pirouetted about the place in an airy escstasy of happiness.

On my side, I could have cursed the kindness that conferred upon me this benefaction, but I kept my vexation under the surface for policy's sake, and did what I could to let on to be glad. Indeed, I *said* I was glad. And in a way, it was true: I was as glad as a person is when he is scalped.

Well, one must make the best of things, and not waste time with useless fretting, but get down to business and see what can be done. In all lies there is wheat among the chaff; I must get at the wheat in this case: so I sent for the girl, and she came. She was a comely enough creature, and soft and modest, but if signs went for anything, she didn't know as much as a lady's watch. I said—

"My dear, have you been questioned as to particulars?"

She said she hadn't.

"Well, I didn't expect you had, but I thought I would ask, to make sure; it's the way I've been raised. Now you mustn't take it unkindly if I remind you that as we don't know you, we must go a little slow. You may be all right, of course, and we'll hope that you are; but to take it for granted isn't business. *You* understand that. I'm obliged to ask you a few questions; just answer up fair and square, and don't be afraid. Where do you live, when you are at home?"

"In the land of Moder, fair sir."

"Land of Moder. I don't remember hearing of it before. Parents living?"

"As to that, I know not if they be yet on live, sith it is many years that I have lain shut up in the castle."

"Your name, please?"

"I hight the Demoiselle Alisande la Carteloise, an it please you."

"Do you know anybody here who can identify you?"

"That were not likely, fair lord, I being come hither now for the first time."

"Have you brought any letters—any documents—any proofs that you are trustworthy and truthful?"

"Of a surety, no; and wherefore should I? Have I not a tongue, and cannot I say all that myself?"

"But *your* saying it, you know, and somebody else's saying it, is different."

"Different? How might that be? I fear me I do not understand."

"Don't *understand*? Land of—why, you see—you see—why, great Scott, can't you understand a little thing like that? Can't you understand that the difference between your—*why* do you look so innocent and idiotic!"

"I? In truth I know not, but an it were the will of God."

"Yes, yes, I reckon that's about the size of it. Don't mind my seeming excited; I'm not. Let us change the subject. Now as to this castle, with forty-five princesses in it, and three ogres at the head of it; tell me—where is this harem?"

"Harem?"

"The *castle*, you understand; where is the castle?"

"Oh, as to that, it is great, and strong, and well beseen, and lieth in a far country. Yes, it is many leagues."

"*How* many?"

"Ah, fair sir, it were woundily hard to tell, they are so many, and do so lap the one upon the other, and being made all in the same image and tincted with the same color, one may not know the one league from its fellow, nor how to count them except they be taken apart, and ye wit well it were God's work to do that, being not within man's capacity; for ye will note—"

"Hold on, hold on, never mind about the distance; *whereabouts* does the castle lie? what's the direction from here?"

"Ah, please you sir, it hath no direction from here; by reason that the road lieth not straight, but turneth evermore; wherefore the direction of its place abideth not, but is sometime under the one sky and anon under another, whereso if ye be minded that it is in the east, and wend thitherward, ye shall observe that the way of the road doth yet again turn upon itself by the space of half a circle, and this marvel happing again and yet again and still again, it will grieve you that you had thought by vanities of the mind to thwart and bring to naught the will of Him that giveth not a castle a direction from a place except it pleaseth Him, and if it please Him not, will the rather that even all castles and all directions thereunto vanish out of the earth, leaving the places wherein they tarried desolate and vacant, so warning His creatures that where He will He will, and where He will not He—"

"Oh, that's all right, that's all right, give us a rest; never mind about the direction, *hang* the direction—I beg pardon, I beg a thousand pardons, I am not well to-day; pay no attention when I soliloquize, it is an old habit, an old, bad habit, and hard to get rid of when one's digestion is all disordered with eating food that was raised forever-and-ever before he was born; good land! a man can't keep his functions regular on spring chickens thirteen hundred years old. But come—never mind about that; let's—have you got such a thing as a map of that region about you? Now a good map—"

"Is it peradventure that manner of thing which of late the unbelievers have brought from over the great seas, which, being boiled in oil, and an onion and salt added thereto, doth—"

"What, a map? What are you talking about? Don't you know what a map is? There, there, never mind, don't explain, I hate explanations; they fog a thing up so that you can't tell anything about it. Run along, dear; good-day; show her the way, Clarence."

Oh, well, it was reasonably plain, now, why these donkeys didn't prospect these liars for details. It may be that this girl had a fact in her somewhere, but I don't believe you could have sluiced it out with a hydraulic; nor got it with the earlier forms of blasting, even; it was a case for dynamite. Why, she was a perfect ass; and yet the king and his knights had listened to her as if she had been a leaf out of the gospel. It kind of sizes up the whole party. And think of the simple ways of this court: this wandering wench hadn't had any more trouble to get access to the king in his palace than she would have had to get into the poor-house in my day and country. In fact he was glad to see her, glad to hear her tale; with that adventure of hers to offer, she was as welcome as a corpse is to a coroner.

Just as I was ending-up these reflections, Clarence came back. I remarked upon the barren result of my efforts with the girl; hadn't got hold of a single point that could help me to find the castle. The youth looked a little surprised, or puzzled, or something, and intimated that he had been wondering to himself what I had wanted to ask the girl all those questions for.

"Why, great guns," I said, "don't I want to find the castle? And how else would I go about it?"

"La, sweet your worship, one may lightly answer that, I ween. She will go with thee. They always do. She will ride with thee."

"Ride with me? Nonsense!"

"But of a truth she will. She will ride with thee. Thou shalt see."

"What? She browse around the hills and scour the woods with me—alone—and I as good as engaged to be married? Why, it's scandalous. Think how it would look."

My, the dear face that rose before me! The boy was eager to know all about this tender matter. I swore him to secrecy, and then whispered her name—"Puss Flanagan." He looked disappointed, and said he didn't remember the countess. How natural it was for the little courtier to give her a rank. He asked me where she lived.

"In East Har—" I came to myself and stopped, a little confused; then I said, "Never mind now; I'll tell you some time."

And might he see her? would I let him see her some day?

It was but a little thing to promise—thirteen hundred years or so—and he so eager; so I said yes. But I sighed; I couldn't help it. And yet there was no sense in sighing, for she wasn't born yet. But that is the way we are made: we don't reason, where we feel; we just feel.

My expedition was all the talk, that day and that night, and the boys were very good to me, and made much of me, and seemed to have forgotten their vexation and disappointment, and come to be as anxious for me to hive those ogres and set those ripe old virgins loose as if it was themselves that had the contract. Well, they *were* good children—but just children, that is all. And they gave me no end of points about how to scout for giants, and how to scoop them in; and they told me all sorts of charms against enchantments, and gave me salves and other rubbish to put on my wounds. But it never occurred to one of them to reflect that if I was such a wonderful necromancer as I was pretending to be, I ought not to need salves, or instructions, or charms against enchantments, and least of all, arms and armor, on a foray of any kind—even against fire-spouting dragons, and devils hot from perdition —let alone such poor adversaries as these I was after, these commonplace ogres of the back settlements.

I was to have an early breakfast, and start at dawn, for that was the usual way; but I had the demon's own time with my armor, and this delayed me a little. It is troublesome to get into, and there is so much detail. First you wrap a layer or two of blanket around your body, for a sort of cushion and to keep off the cold iron; then you put on your sleeves and shirt of chain-mail—these are made of small steel links woven together, and they form a fabric so flexible that if you toss your shirt onto the floor, it slumps into a pile like a peck of wet fish-net; it is very heavy, and is nearly the uncomfortablest material in the world for a night-shirt, yet plenty used it for that—tax collectors, and reformers, and one-horse kings with a defective title, and those sorts of people; then you put on your shoes—flat-boats roofed over with interleaving bands of steel—and screw your clumsy spurs into the heels. Next you buckle your greaves on your legs, and your cuisses on your thighs; then come your back plate and your breastplate, and you begin to feel crowded; then you hitch on to the breast-plate the half-petticoat of broad overlapping bands of steel which hangs down in front but is scolloped out behind so you can sit down, and isn't any real improvement on an inverted coal scuttle, either for looks, or for wear, or to wipe your hands on; next you belt-on your sword; then you put your stove-pipe joints onto your arms, your iron gauntlets onto your hands, your iron rat-trap onto your head, with a rag of steel web hitched to it to hang over the back of your neck—and there you are, snug as a candle in a candle-mould. This is no time to dance. Well, a man that is packed away like that, is a nut that isn't worth the cracking, there is so little of the meat, when you get down to it, by comparison with the shell.

The boys helped me, or I never could have got in. Just as we finished, Sir Bedivere happened in, and I saw that as like as not I hadn't chosen the most convenient outfit for a long trip. How stately he looked; and tall and broad and grand. He had on his head a conical steel casque that only came down to his ears, and for visor had only a narrow steel bar that extended down to his upper lip and protected his nose; and all the rest of him, from neck to heel, was flexible chain-mail, trowsers and all. But pretty much all of him was hidden under his outside garment, which of course was of chain-mail, as I said, and hung straight from his shoulders to his ancles; and from his middle to the bottom, both before and behind, was divided, so that he could ride, and let the skirts hang down on each side. He was going grailing, and it was just the outfit for it, too. I would have given a good deal for that ulster, but it was too late now to be fooling around. The sun was just up, the king and the court were all on hand to see me off and wish me luck; so it wouldn't be etiquette for me to tarry. You don't get on your horse yourself; no, if you tried it you would get disappointed. They carry you out, just as they carry a sun-struck man to the drug-store, and put you on, and help get you to rights, and fix your feet in the stirrups; and all the while you do feel so strange, and stuffy, and like some-body else—like somebody that has been married on a sud-den, or struck by lightning, or something like that, and hasn't quite fetched around, yet, and is sort of numb, and can't just get his bearings. Then they stood up the mast they call a spear, in its socket by my left foot, and I gripped it with my hand; lastly they hung my shield around my neck, and I was all complete and ready to up anchor and get to sea. Every-body was as good to me as they could be, and a maid of honor gave me the stirrup-cup her own self. There was noth-ing more to do, now, but for that damsel to get up behind me on a pillion, which she did, and put an arm or so around me to hold on.

And so we started; and everybody gave us a good-bye and waved their handkerchiefs or helmets. And everybody we met, going down the hill and through the village was respect-ful to us, except some shabby little boys on the outskirts. They said—

"Oh, what a guy!" and hove clods at us.

In my experience boys are the same in all ages. They don't respect anything, they don't care for anything or anybody. They say "Go up, baldhead," to the prophet, going his unof-fending way in the gray of antiquity; they sass me in the holy gloom of the Middle Ages; and I had seen them act the same way in Buchanan's administration; I remember, because I was there and helped. The prophet had his bears, and settled with his boys; and I wanted to get down and settle with mine, but it wouldn't answer, because I couldn't have got up again. I hate a country without a derrick.

Chapter 12

SLOW TORTURE

STRAIGHT OFF, we were in the country. It was most lovely and pleasant in those sylvan solitudes in the early cool morning in the first freshness of autumn. From hill-tops we saw fair green valleys lying spread out below, with streams winding through them, and island-groves of trees here and there, and huge lonely oaks scattered about and casting black blots of shade; and beyond the valleys we saw the ranges of hills, blue with haze, stretching away in billowy perspective to the horizon, with at wide intervals a dim fleck of white or gray on a wave-summit, which we knew was a castle. We crossed broad natural lawns sparkling with dew, and we moved like spirits, the cushioned turf giving out no sound of footfall; we dreamed along through glades in a mist of green light that got its tint from the sun-drenched roof of leaves overhead, and by our feet the clearest and coldest of runlets went frisking and gossiping over its reefs and making a sort of whispery music comfortable to hear; and at times we left the world behind and entered into the solemn great deeps and rich gloom of the forest, where furtive wild things whisked and skurried by and were gone before you could even get your eye on the place where the noise was; and where only the earliest birds were turning out and getting to business with a song here and a quarrel yonder and a mysterious far-off hammering and drumming for worms on a tree-trunk away somewhere in the impenetrable remotenesses of the woods. And by and by out we would swing again, into the glare.

About the third or fourth or fifth time that we swung out into the glare—it was along there somewhere, a couple of hours or so after sun-up,—it wasn't as pleasant as it had been. It was beginning to get hot. This was quite noticeable. We had a very long pull, after that, without any shade. Now it is curious how progressively little frets grow and multiply after they once get a start. Things which I didn't mind at all,

The talk of these meek people had a strange enough sound in a formerly American ear. They were freemen, but they could not leave the estates of their lord or their bishop without his permission; they could not prepare their own bread, but must have their corn ground and their bread baked at his mill and his bakery, and pay roundly for the same; they could not sell a piece of their own property without paying him a handsome per centage of the proceeds, nor buy a piece of somebody else's without remembering him in cash for the privilege; they had to harvest his grain for him gratis, and be ready to come at a moment's notice, leaving their own crop to destruction by the threatened storm; they had to let him plant fruit trees in their fields, and then keep their indignation to themselves when his heedless fruit-gatherers trampled the grain around the trees; they had to smother their anger when his hunting parties galloped through their fields, laying waste the result of their patient toil; they were not allowed to keep doves themselves, and when the swarms from my lord's dovecote settled on their crops, they must not lose their temper and kill a bird, for awful would the penalty be; when the harvest was at last gathered, then came the procession of robbers to levy their blackmail upon it; first the Church carted off its fat tenth, then the king's commissioner took his twentieth, then my lord's people made a mighty inroad upon the remainder; after which, the skinned freeman had liberty to bestow the remnant in his barn, in case it was worth the trouble; there were taxes, and taxes, and taxes, and more taxes, and taxes again, and yet other taxes—upon this free and independent pauper, but none upon his lord the baron or the bishop, none upon the wasteful nobility or the all-devouring Church; if the baron would sleep unvexed, the freeman must sit up all night after his day's work and whip the ponds to keep the frogs quiet; if the freeman's daughter— but no, that last infamy of monarchical government is unprintable; and finally, if the freeman, grown desperate with his tortures, found his life unendurable under such conditions, and sacrificed it and fled to death for mercy and refuge, the gentle Church condemned him to eternal fire, the gentle law buried him at midnight at the cross-roads with a stake through his back, and his master the baron or the bishop confiscated all his property and turned his widow and his orphans out of doors.

And here were these freemen assembled in the early morning to work on their lord the bishop's road three days each—gratis; every head of a family, and every son of a family, three days each, gratis, and a day or so added for their servants. Why, it was like reading about France and the French, before the ever-memorable and blessed Revolution, which swept a thousand years of such villainy away in one swift tidal wave of blood—one: a settlement of that hoary debt in the proportion of half a drop of blood for each hogshead of it that had been pressed by slow tortures out of that people in the weary stretch of ten centuries of wrong and shame and misery, the like of which was not to be mated but in hell. There were two "Reigns of Terror," if we would but remember it and consider it: the one wrought murder in hot passion, the other in heartless cold blood; the one lasted mere months, the other had lasted a thousand years; the one inflicted death upon ten thousand persons, the other upon a hundred millions; but our shudders are all for the "horrors" of the minor Terror, the momentary Terror, so to speak; whereas, what is the horror of swift death by the axe, compared with life-long death from hunger, cold, insult, cruelty and heart-break? what is swift death by lightning, compared with death by slow fire at the stake? A city cemetery could contain the coffins filled by that brief Terror which we have all been so diligently taught to shiver at and mourn over; but all France could hardly contain the coffins filled by that older and real Terror—that unspeakably bitter and awful Terror which none of us has been taught to see in its vastness or pity as it deserves.

These poor ostensible freemen who were sharing their breakfast and their talk with me were as full of humble reverence for their king and Church and nobility as their worst enemy could desire. There was something pitifully ludicrous about it. I asked them if they supposed a nation of people ever existed, who, with a free vote in every man's hand, would elect that a single family and its descendants should reign over it forever, whether gifted or boobies, to the exclusion of all other families—including the voter's; and would also elect that a certain hundred families should be raised to

dizzy summits of rank, and clothed-on with offensive transmissible glories and privileges, to the exclusion of the rest of
the nation's families—*including his own.*

They all looked unhit; and said they didn't know; that they
had never thought about it before, and it hadn't ever occurred
to them that a nation could be so situated that every man
could have a say in the government. I said I had seen one—
and that it would last until it had an Established Church.
Again they were all unhit—at first. But presently one man
looked up and asked me to state that proposition again; and
state it slowly, so it could soak into his understanding. I did
it; and after a little he had the idea, and he brought his fist
down and said *he* didn't believe a nation where every man had
a vote would voluntarily get down in the mud and dirt in any
such way; and that to steal from a nation its will and preference must be a crime, and the first of all crimes.

I said to myself:

"This one's a man. If I were backed by enough of his sort, I
would make a strike for the welfare of this country, and try to
prove myself its loyalest citizen by making a wholesome
change in its system of government."

You see, my kind of loyalty was loyalty to one's country,
not to its institutions or its office-holders. The country is the
real thing, the substantial thing, the eternal thing; it is the
thing to watch over, and care for, and be loyal to; institutions
are extraneous, they are its mere clothing, and clothing can
wear out, become ragged, cease to be comfortable, cease to
protect the body from winter, disease, and death. To be loyal
to rags, to shout for rags, to worship rags, to die for rags—
that is a loyalty of unreason, it is pure animal; it belongs to
monarchy, was invented by monarchy; let monarchy keep it. I
was from Connecticut, whose Constitution declares "that all
political power is inherent in the people, and all free governments are founded on their authority and instituted for their
benefit; and that they have *at all times* an undeniable and in-
defeasible right to *alter their form of government* in such manner as they may think expedient."

Under that gospel, the citizen who thinks he sees that the
commonwealth's political clothes are worn out, and yet holds
his peace and does not agitate for a new suit, is disloyal; he is

a traitor. That he may be the only one who thinks he sees this decay, does not excuse him: it is his duty to agitate anyway, and it is the duty of the others to vote him down if they do not see the matter as he does.

And now here I was, in a country where the right to say how the country should be governed was restricted to six persons in each thousand of its population. For the nine hundred and ninety-four to express dissatisfaction with the regnant system and propose to change it, would have made the whole six shudder as one man, it would have been so disloyal, so dishonorable, such putrid black treason. So to speak, I was become a stockholder in a corporation where nine hundred and ninety-four of the members furnished all the money and did all the work, and the other six elected themselves a permanent board of direction and took all the dividends. It seemed to me that what the nine hundred and ninety-four dupes needed was a new deal. The thing that would have best suited the circus-side of my nature would have been to resign the Boss-ship and get up an insurrection and turn it into a revolution; but I knew that the Jack Cade or the Wat Tyler who tries such a thing without first educating his materials up to revolution-grade is almost absolutely certain to get left. I had never been accustomed to getting left; even if I do say it myself. Wherefore, the "deal" which had been for some time working into shape in my mind was of a quite different pattern from the Cade-Tyler sort.

So I did not talk blood and insurrection to that man there who sat munching black bread with that abused and mistaught herd of human sheep, but took him aside and talked matter of another sort to him. After I had finished, I got him to lend me a little ink from his veins; and with this and a sliver I wrote on a piece of bark—

Put him in the Man-Factory—

and gave it to him, and said—

"Take it to the palace at Camelot and give it into the hands of Amyas le Poulet, whom I call Clarence, and he will understand."

"He is a priest, then," said the man, and some of the enthusiasm went out of his face.

"How—a priest? Didn't I tell you that no chattel of the Church, no bond-slave of pope or bishop can enter my Man-Factory? Didn't I tell you that you couldn't enter unless your religion, whatever it might be, was your own free property?"

"Marry it is so, and for that was I glad; wherefore it liked me not, and bred in me a cold doubt, to hear of this priest being there."

"But he isn't a priest, I tell you."

The man looked far from satisfied. He said:

"He is not a priest, and yet can read?"

"He is not a priest, and yet can read—yes, and write, too, for that matter. I taught him myself." The man's face cleared. "And it is the first thing that you yourself will be taught in that Factory—"

"I? I would give blood out of my heart to know that art. Why, I will be your slave, your—"

"No you won't; you won't be anybody's slave. Take your family and go along. Your lord the bishop will confiscate your small property, but no matter, Clarence will fix you all right."

Chapter 14

"Defend Thee, Lord!"

I PAID THREE PENNIES for my breakfast, and a most extravagant price it was, too, seeing that one could have breakfasted a dozen persons for that money; but I was feeling
good, by this time, and I had always been a kind of spend-
thrift anyway; and then these people had wanted to give me
the food for nothing, scant as their provision was, and so it
was a grateful pleasure to emphasize my appreciation and
sincere thankfulness with a good big financial lift where the
money would do so much more good than it would in my
helmet, where, these pennies being made of iron, and not
stinted in weight, my half dollar's worth was a good deal of a
burden to me. I spent money rather too freely, in those days,
it is true; but one reason for it was that I hadn't got the
proportions of things entirely adjusted, even yet, after so long
a sojourn in Britain—hadn't got along to where I was able to
absolutely realize that a penny in Arthur's land and a couple
of dollars in Connecticut were about one and the same thing:
just twins, as you may say, in purchasing power. If my start
from Camelot could have been delayed a very few days I
could have paid these people in beautiful new coins from our
own mint, and that would have pleased me; and them, too,
not less. I had adopted the American values exclusively. In a
week or two, now, cents, nickels, dimes, quarters and half
dollars, and also a trifle of gold, would be trickling in thin but
steady streams all through the commercial veins of the kingdom, and I looked to see this new blood freshen up its life.

The farmers were bound to throw in something, to sort of
offset my liberality, whether I would or no; so I let them give
me a flint and steel; and as soon as they had comfortably bestowed Sandy and me on our horse, I lit my pipe. When the
first blast of smoke shot out through the bars of my helmet,
all those people broke for the woods, and Sandy went over
backwards and struck the ground with a dull thud. They
thought I was one of those fire-belching dragons they had

heard so much about from knights and other professional liars. I had infinite trouble to persuade those people to venture back within explaining distance. Then I told them that this was only a bit of enchantment which would work harm to none but my enemies. And I promised, with my hand on my heart, that if all who felt no enmity toward me would come forward and pass before me, they should see that only those who remained behind would be struck dead. The procession moved, with a good deal of promptness. There were no casualties to report, for nobody had curiosity enough to remain behind to see what would happen.

I lost some time, now, for these big children, their fears gone, became so ravished with wonder over my awe-compelling fireworks that I had to stay there and smoke a couple of pipes out before they would let me go. Still, the delay was not wholly unproductive, for it took all that time to get Sandy thoroughly wonted to the new thing, she being so close to it, you know. It plugged up her conversation-mill, too, for a considerable while, and that was a gain. But above all other benefits accruing, I had learned something. I was ready for any giant or any ogre that might come along, now.

We tarried with a holy hermit, that night, and my opportunity came about the middle of the next afternoon. We were crossing a vast meadow by way of short-cut, and I was musing absently, hearing nothing, seeing nothing, when Sandy suddenly interrupted a remark which she had begun that morning, with the cry—

"Defend thee, lord!—peril of life is toward!"

And she slipped down from the horse and ran a little way and stood. I looked up and saw, far off in the shade of a tree, half a dozen armed knights and their squires; and straightway there was bustle among them and tightening of saddle-girths for the mount. My pipe was ready, and would have been lit, if I had not been lost in thinkings about how to banish oppression from this land and restore to all its people their stolen rights and manhood without disobliging anybody. I lit up at once; and by the time I had got a good head of reserved steam on, here they came. All together, too; none of those chivalrous magnanimities which one reads so much about— one courtly rascal at a time, and the rest standing by to see fair play. No, they came in a body, they came with a whirr and a rush, they came like a volley from a battery; came with heads low down, plumes streaming out behind, lances advanced at a level. It was a handsome sight, a beautiful sight— for a man up a tree. I laid my lance in rest and waited, with my heart beating, till the iron wave was just ready to break over me, then spouted a column of white smoke through the bars of my helmet. You should have seen the wave go to pieces and scatter! This was a finer sight than the other one.

But these people stopped, two or three hundred yards away, and this troubled me. My satisfaction collapsed, and fear came; I judged I was a lost man. But Sandy was radiant; and was going to be eloquent, but I stopped her, and told her my magic had miscarried, somehow or other, and she must mount, with all dispatch, and we must ride for life. No, she wouldn't. She said that my enchantment had disabled those knights; they were not riding on because they couldn't; wait, they would drop out of their saddles presently, and we would get their horses and harness. I could not deceive such trusting simplicity, so I said it was a mistake; that when my fireworks killed at all, they killed instantly; no, the men would not die, there was something wrong about my apparatus, I couldn't tell what; but we must hurry and get away, for those people would attack us again, in a minute. Sandy laughed, and said—

"Lack-a-day, sir, they be not of that breed! Sir Launcelot will give battle to dragons, and will abide by them, and will assail them again, and yet again and still again, until he do conquer and destroy them; and so likewise will Sir Pellinore, and Sir Aglovale, and Sir Carados, and mayhap others; but there be none else that will venture it, let the idle say what the idle will. And, la, as to yonder base rufflers, think ye they have not their fill, but yet desire more?"

"Well, then, what are they waiting, for? Why don't they leave? Nobody's hindering. Good land, I'm willing to let bygones be bygones, I'm sure."

"Leave, is it? Oh, give thyself easement as to that. They dream not of it, no, not they. They wait to yield them."

"Come—really, is that 'sooth'—as you people say? If they want to, why don't they?"

"It would like them much; but an ye wot how dragons are esteemed, ye would not hold them blamable. They fear to come."

"Well, then, suppose I go to them instead, and—"

"Ah, wit ye well they would not abide your coming. I will go."

And she did. She was a handy person to have along on a raid. I would have considered this a doubtful errand, myself. I presently saw the knights riding away, and Sandy coming back. That was a relief. I judged she had somehow failed to get the first innings—I mean in the conversation; otherwise the interview wouldn't have been so short. But it turned out that she had managed the business well; in fact admirably. She said that when she told those people I was The Boss, it hit them where they lived: "smote them sore with fear and dread" was her word; and then they were ready to put up with anything she might require. So she swore them to appear at Arthur's court within two days, and yield them, with horse and harness, and be my knights thenceforth, and subject to my command. How much better she managed that thing than I should have done it myself! She was a daisy.

Chapter 15

SANDY'S TALE

"A ND SO I'm proprietor of some knights," said I, as we rode off. "Who would ever have supposed that I should live to list-up assets of that sort. I shan't know what to do with them; unless I raffle them off. How many of them are there, Sandy?"

"Seven, please you sir, and their squires."

"It is a good haul. Who are they? Where do they hang out?"

"Where hang they out?"

"Yes; where do they live?"

"Ah, I understood thee not. That will I tell thee eftsoons." Then she said musingly, and softly, turning the words daintily over her tongue: "Hang they out—hang they out—where hang—where do they hang out; ah, right so: where do they hang out. Of a truth the phrase hath a fair and winsome grace, and is prettily worded withal. I will repeat it anon and anon in mine idlesse, whereby I may peradventure learn it. Where do they hang out. Even so! already it falleth trippingly from my tongue; and forasmuch as—"

"Don't forget the cow-boys, Sandy."

"Cow-boys?"

"Yes; the knights, you know. You were going to tell me about them. A while back, you remember. Figuratively speaking, game's called."

"Game—"

"Yes, yes, yes! Go to the bat. I mean, get to work on your statistics, and don't burn so much kindling getting your fire started. Tell me about the knights."

"I will well; and lightly will begin. So they two departed and rode into a great forest. And—"

"Great Scott!"

You see, I recognized my mistake, at once. I had set her works agoing; it was my own fault; she would be thirty days getting down to those facts. And she generally began without a preface, and finished without a result. If you interrupted her, she would either go right along without noticing, or answer with a couple of words, or go back and say the sentence over again. So, interruptions only did harm; and yet I had to interrupt, and interrupt pretty frequently, too, in order to save my life; a person would die if he let her monotony drip on him right along all day.

"Great Scott!" I said, in my distress. She went right back and began over again:

"So they two departed and rode into a great forest. And—"

"*Which* two?"

"Sir Gawaine and Sir Uwaine. And so they came to an abbey of monks, and there were well lodged. So on the morn they heard their masses in the abbey, and so they rode forth till they came to a great forest; then was Sir Gawaine ware in a valley by a turret, of twelve fair damsels, and two knights armed on great horses, and the damsels went to and fro by a tree. And then was Sir Gawaine ware how there hung a white shield on that tree, and ever as the damsels came by it they spit upon it, and some threw mire upon the shield—"

"Now, if I hadn't seen the like myself in this country, Sandy, I wouldn't believe it. But I've seen it, and I can just see those creatures, now, parading before that shield and acting like that. The women here do certainly act like all possessed. Yes, and I mean your best, too, society's very choicest brands. The humblest hello-girl along ten thousand miles of wire could teach gentleness, patience, modesty, manners, to the highest duchess in Arthur's land."

"Hello-girl?"

"Yes, but don't you ask me to explain; it's a new kind of girl; they don't have them here; one often speaks sharply to them when they are not the least in fault, and he can't get over feeling sorry for it and ashamed of himself in thirteen hundred years, it's such shabby mean conduct and so unprovoked; fact is, no gentleman ever does it—though I—well, I myself, if I've got to confess—"

"Peradventure she—"

"Never mind her, never mind her; I tell you I couldn't ever explain her so you would understand."

"Even so be it, sith ye are so minded. Then Sir Gawaine and Sir Uwaine went and saluted them, and asked them why they did that despite to the shield. Sirs, said the damsels, we shall tell you. There is a knight in this country that owneth this white shield, and he is a passing good man of his hands, but he hateth all ladies and gentlewomen, and therefore we do all this despite to the shield. I will say you, said Sir Gawaine, it beseemeth evil a good knight to despise all ladies and gentlewomen, and peradventure though he hate you he hath some cause, and peradventure he loveth in some other places ladies and gentlewomen, and to be loved again, and he be such a man of prowess as ye speak of—"

"Man of prowess—yes, that is the man to please them, Sandy. Man of brains—that is a thing they never think of. Tom Sayers—John Heenan—John L. Sullivan—pity but you could be here. You would have your legs under the Round Table and a 'Sir' in front of your names within the twenty-four hours; and you could bring about a new distribution of the married princesses and duchesses of the court in another twenty-four. The fact is, it is just a sort of polished-up court of Comanches, and there isn't a squaw in it who doesn't stand ready at the dropping of a hat to desert to the buck with the biggest string of scalps at his belt."

"—and he be such a man of prowess as ye speak of, said Sir Gawaine. Now what is his name? Sir, said they, his name is Marhaus, the king's son of Ireland,—"

"Son of the king of Ireland, you mean; the other form doesn't mean anything. And look out and hold on tight, now, we must jump this gully. . . . . . . There, we are all right, now. This horse belongs in the circus; he is born before his time."

"I know him well, said Sir Uwaine, he is a passing good knight as any is on live,—"

"*On live.* If you've got a fault in the world, Sandy, it is that you are a shade too archaic. But it isn't any matter."

—"for I saw him once proved at a justs where many knights were gathered, and that time there might no man withstand him. Ah, said Sir Gawaine, damsels, methinketh ye are to blame, for it is to suppose he that hung that shield there he will not be long therefrom, and then may those knights match him on horseback, and that is more your worship than thus; for I will abide no longer to see a knight's shield dishonored. And therewith Sir Uwaine and Sir Gawaine departed a little from them, and then were they ware where Sir Marhaus came riding on a great horse straight towards them. And when the twelve damsels saw Sir Marhaus they fled into the turret as they were wild, so that some of them fell by the way. Then the one of the knights of the tower dressed his shield, and said on high, Sir Marhaus, defend thee. And so they ran together that the knight brake his spear on Marhaus, and Sir Marhaus smote him so hard that he brake his neck and the horse's back—"

"Well, that is just the trouble about this state of things, it ruins so many horses."

"That saw the other knight of the turret, and dressed him toward Marhaus, and they met so eagerly together that the knight of the turret was soon smitten down, horse and man, stark dead—"

"*Another* horse gone; I tell you it is a custom that ought to be broken up. I don't see how people with any feeling can applaud and support it."

*   *   *   *   *

"So these two knights came together with great random—"

I saw that I had been asleep and missed a chapter, but I didn't say anything. I judged that the Irish knight was in trouble with the visitors by this time, and this turned out to be the case.

"—that Sir Uwaine smote Sir Marhaus that his spear brast in pieces on the shield, and Sir Marhaus smote him so sore that horse and man he bare to the earth, and hurt Sir Uwaine on the left side—"

"The truth is, Alisande, these archaics are a little *too* simple; the vocabulary is too limited, and so, by consequence, descriptions suffer in the matter of variety; they run too much to level Saharas of fact, and not enough to picturesque detail; this throws about them a certain air of the monotonous; in fact the fights are all alike: a couple of people come together with great random—random is a good word, and so is exegesis, for that matter, and so is holocaust, and defalcation, and usufruct, and a hundred others, but land! a body ought to discriminate—they come together with great random, and a spear is brast, and one party brake his shield, and the other one goes down, horse and man, over his horse-tail and brake his neck, and then the next candidate comes randoming in, and brast *his* spear, and the other man brast his shield, and down *he* goes, horse and man, over his horse-tail, and brake *his* neck, and then there's another elected, and another and another and still another, till the material is all used up; and when you come to figure up results, you can't tell one fight from another nor who whipped; and as a *picture*, of living, raging, roaring battle, sho! why, it's pale and noiseless—just ghosts scuffling in a fog. Dear me, what would this barren vocabulary get out of the mightiest spectacle?—the burning of Rome, in Nero's time, for instance. Why, it would merely say, 'Town burned down, no insurance; boy brast a window, fireman brake his neck!' Why, *that* ain't a picture!"

It was a good deal of a lecture, I thought, but it didn't disturb Sandy, didn't turn a feather; her steam soared steadily up again, the minute I took off the lid:

"Then Sir Marhaus turned his horse and rode toward Gawaine with his spear. And when Sir Gawaine saw that, he dressed his shield, and they aventred their spears, and they came together with all the might of their horses, that either knight smote other so hard in the midst of their shields, but Sir Gawaine's spear brake—"

"I knew it would."

—"but Sir Marhaus's spear held; and therewith Sir Gawaine and his horse rushed down to the earth—"

"Just so—and brake his back."

—"and lightly Sir Gawaine rose upon his feet, and pulled out his sword, and dressed him toward Sir Marhaus on foot, and therewith either came unto other eagerly, and smote together with their swords that their shields flew in cantels, and they bruised their helms and their hauberks, and wounded either other. But Sir Gawaine, fro it passed nine of the clock, waxed by the space of three hours ever stronger and stronger, and thrice his might was increased. All this espied Sir Marhaus, and had great wonder how his might increased, and so they wounded other passing sore; and then when it was come noon—"

The pelting sing-song of it carried me forward to scenes and sounds of my boyhood days:

"N-e-e-*ew* Haven! ten minutes for refreshments—knductor 'll strike the gong-bell two minutes before train leaves—passengers for the Shore-line please take seats in the rear k'yar, this k'yar don't go no furder—*ahh*-pls, *aw*-rnjz, b'*nan*ners, *s-a-n-d*-ches, p——*op*-corn!"

—"and waxed past noon and drew toward even-song, Sir Gawaine's strength feebled and waxed passing faint, that unnethes he might dure any longer, and Sir Marhaus was then bigger and bigger;—"

"Which strained his armor, of course; and yet little would one of these people mind a small thing like that."

—"and so, Sir knight, said Sir Marhaus, I have well felt that ye are a passing good knight, and a marvelous man of might as ever I felt any, while it lasteth, and our quarrels are not great, and therefore it were pity to do you hurt, for I feel ye are passing feeble. Ah, said Sir Gawaine, gentle knight, ye say the word that I should say. And therewith they took off their helms and either kissed other, and there they swore together either to love other as brethren—"

But I lost the thread there, and dozed off to slumber, thinking about what a pity it was that men with such superb strength—strength enabling them to stand up cased in cruelly burdensome iron and drenched with perspiration, and hack and batter and bang each other for six hours on a stretch—should not have been born at a time when they could put it to some useful purpose. Take a jackass, for instance: a jackass has that kind of strength, and puts it to a useful purpose, and is valuable to this world because he *is* a jackass; but a nobleman is not valuable because he is a jackass. It is a mixture that is always ineffectual, and should never have been attempted in the first place. And yet, once you start a mistake, the trouble is done and you never know what is going to come of it.

When I came to myself again and began to listen, I perceived that I had lost another chapter, and that Alisande had wandered a long way off with her people:

"And so they rode and came into a deep valley full of stones, and thereby they saw a fair stream of water; above thereby was the head of the stream, a fair fountain, and three damsels sitting thereby. In this country, said Sir Marhaus, came never knight since it was christened, but he found strange adventures—"

"This is not good form, Alisande. Sir Marhaus the king's son of Ireland talks like all the rest; you ought to give him a brogue, or at least a characteristic expletive; by this means one would recognize him as soon as he spoke, without his even being named. It is a common literary device with the great authors. You should make him say, 'In this country, be jabers, came never knight since it was christened, but he found strange adventures, be jabers.' You see how much better that sounds."

—"came never knight but he found strange adventures, be jabers. Of a truth it doth indeed, fair lord, albeit 'tis passing hard to say, though peradventure that will not tarry, but better speed with usage. And then they rode to the damsels, and either saluted other, and the eldest had a garland of gold about her head, and she was threescore winter of age or more—"

"The *damsel* was?"

"Even so, dear lord—and her hair was white under the garland and—"

"Celluloid teeth, nine dollars a set, as like as not—the loose-fit kind, that go up and down like a portcullis when you eat, and fall out when you laugh."

"The second damsel was of thirty winter of age, with a circlet of gold about her head. The third damsel was but fifteen year of age—"

Billows of thought came rolling over my soul, and the voice faded out of my hearing!

Fifteen! Break—my heart! oh, my lost darling! Just her age who was so gentle, and lovely, and all the world to me; and whom I shall never see again! How the thought of her carries me back over wide seas of memory to a vague dim time, a happy time, so many many centuries hence, when I used to wake in the soft summer mornings out of sweet dreams of her, and say "Hello, Central!" just to hear her dear voice come melting back to me with a "Hello, Hank!" that was music of the spheres to my enchanted ear. She got three dollars a week, but she was worth it.

I could not follow Alisande's further explanation of who our captured knights were, now—I mean, in case she should ever get to explaining who they were; my interest was gone, my thoughts were far away, and sad. By fitful glimpses of the drifting tale, caught here and there and now and then, I merely noted in a vague way that each of these three knights took one of these three damsels up behind him on his horse, and one rode north, another east, the other south, to seek adventures, and meet again and lie, after year and day. Year and day—and without baggage. It was of a piece with the general simplicity of the country.

The sun was now setting. It was about three in the afternoon when Alisande had begun to tell me who the cow-boys were; so she had made pretty good progress with it—for her. She would arrive some time or other, no doubt, but she was not a person who could be hurried.

We were approaching a castle which stood on high ground; a huge, strong, venerable structure, whose gray towers and battlements were charmingly draped with ivy, and whose whole majestic mass was drenched with splendors flung from the sinking sun. It was the largest castle we had seen, and so I thought it might be the one we were after, but Sandy said no. She did not know who owned it; she said she had passed it without calling, when she went down to Camelot.

Chapter 16

Morgan le Fay

IF KNIGHTS ERRANT were to be believed, not all castles were desirable places to seek hospitality in. As a matter of fact, knights errant were *not* persons to be believed—that is, measured by modern standards of veracity; yet, measured by the standards of their own time, and scaled accordingly, you got the truth. It was very simple: you discounted a statement ninety-seven per cent; the rest was fact. Now after making this allowance, the truth remained that if I could find out something about a castle before ringing the door-bell—I mean, hailing the warders—it was the sensible thing to do. So I was pleased when I saw in the distance a horseman making the bottom turn of the road that wound down from this castle.

As we approached each other, I saw that he wore a plumed helmet, and seemed to be otherwise clothed in steel, but bore a curious addition also—a stiff square garment like a herald's tabard. However, I had to smile at my own forgetfulness when I got nearer and read this sign on his tabard:

"PERSIMMONS'S SOAP—ALL THE PRIME-DONNE USE IT."

That was a little idea of my own, and had several wholesome purposes in view toward the civilizing and uplifting of this nation. In the first place, it was a furtive, underhand blow at this nonsense of knight-errantry, though nobody suspected that but me. I had started a number of these people out—the bravest knights I could get—each sandwiched between bulletin-boards bearing one device or another, and I judged that by and by when they got to be numerous enough they would begin to look ridiculous; and then, even the steel-clad ass that *hadn't* any board would himself begin to look ridiculous because he was out of the fashion.

Secondly, these missionaries would gradually, and without creating suspicion or exciting alarm, introduce a rudimentary cleanliness among the nobility, and from them it would work down to the people, if the priests could be kept quiet. This would undermine the Church. I mean would be a step toward that. Next, education—next freedom—and then she would begin to crumble. It being my conviction that any Established Church is an established crime, an established slave-pen, I had no scruples, but was willing to assail it in any way or with any weapon that promised to hurt it. Why, in my own former day—in remote centuries not yet stirring in the womb of time—there were old Englishmen who imagined that they had been born in a free country: a "free" country with the Corporation Act and the Test still in force in it—timbers propped against men's liberties and dishonored consciences to shore up an Established Anachronism with.

My missionaries were taught to spell out the gilt signs on their tabards—the showy gilding was a neat idea, I could have got the king to wear a bulletin-board for the sake of that barbaric splendor—they were to spell out these signs and then explain to the lords and ladies what soap was; and if the lords and ladies were afraid of it, get them to try it on a dog. The missionary's next move was to get the family together and try it on himself; he was to stop at no experiment, however desperate, that could convince the nobility that soap was harmless; if any final doubt remained, he must catch a hermit—the woods were full of them; saints, they called themselves, and saints they were believed to be. They were unspeakably holy, and worked miracles, and everybody stood in awe of them. If a hermit could survive a wash, and that failed to convince a duke, give him up, let him alone.

Whenever my missionaries overcame a knight errant on the road, they washed him, and when he got well they swore him to go and get a bulletin-board and disseminate soap and civilization the rest of his days. As a consequence the workers in the field were increasing by degrees, and the reform was steadily spreading. My soap factory felt the strain early. At first I had only two hands; but before I had left home I was already employing fifteen, and running night and day; and the atmospheric result was getting so pronounced that the king went sort of fainting and gasping around and said he did not believe he could stand it much longer, and Sir Launcelot got so that he did hardly anything but walk up and down the roof and swear, although I told him it was worse up there than anywhere else, but he said he wanted plenty of air; and he was always complaining that a palace was no place for a soap factory, anyway, and said if a man was to start one in his house he would be damned if he wouldn't strangle him. There were ladies present, too; but much those people ever cared for that; they would swear before children, if the wind was their way when the factory was going.

This missionary-knight's name was La Cote Male Taile, and he said that this castle was the abode of Morgan le Fay, sister of King Arthur, and wife of King Uriens, monarch of a realm about as big as the District of Columbia—you could stand in the middle of it and throw bricks into the next kingdom. "Kings" and "kingdoms" were as thick in Britain as they had been in little Palestine in Joshua's time, when people had to sleep with their knees pulled up because they couldn't stretch out without a passport.

La Cote was much depressed, for he had scored here the worst failure of his campaign. He had not worked off a cake; yet he had tried all the tricks of the trade, even to the washing of a hermit; but the hermit died. This was indeed a bad failure, for this animal would now be dubbed a martyr, and would take his place among the saints of the Roman calendar. Thus made he his moan, this poor Sir La Cote Male Taile, and sorrowed passing sore. And so my heart bled for him, and I was moved to comfort and stay him. Wherefore I said—

"Forbear to grieve, fair knight, for this is not a defeat. We have brains, you and I; and for such as have brains there are no defeats, but only victories. Observe how we will turn this seeming disaster into an advertisement; an advertisement for our soap; and the biggest one, to draw, that was ever thought of: an advertisement that will transform that Mount Washington defeat into a Matterhorn victory. We will put on your bulletin-board, 'PATRONIZED BY THE ELECT.' How does that strike you?"

"Verily, it is wonderly bethought!"

"Well, a body is bound to admit that for just a modest little one-line ad., it's a corker."

So the poor colporteur's griefs vanished away. He was a

brave fellow, and had done mighty feats of arms in his time. His chief celebrity rested upon the events of an excursion like this one of mine, which he had once made with a damsel named Maledisant, who was as handy with her tongue as was Sandy, though in a different way, for her tongue churned forth only railings and insult, whereas Sandy's music was of a kindlier sort. I knew his story well, and so I knew how to interpret the compassion that was in his face when he bade me farewell. He supposed I was having a bitter hard time of it.

Sandy and I discussed his story, as we rode along, and she said that La Cote's bad luck had begun with the very beginning of that trip; for the king's fool had overthrown him on the first day, and in such cases it was customary for the girl to desert to the conqueror, but Maledisant didn't do it; and also persisted afterward in sticking to him, after all his defeats. But, said I, suppose the victor should decline to accept his spoil? She said that that wouldn't answer—he must. He couldn't decline: it wouldn't be regular. I made a note of that. If Sandy's music got to be too burdensome, some time, I would let a knight defeat me, on the chance that she would desert to him.

In due time we were challenged by the warders, from the castle walls, and after a parley admitted. I have nothing pleasant to tell about that visit. But it was not a disappointment, for I knew Mrs. le Fay by reputation, and was not expecting anything pleasant. She was held in awe by the whole realm, for she had made everybody believe she was a great sorceress. All her ways were wicked, all her instincts devilish. She was loaded to the eye-lids with cold malice. All her history was black with crime; and among her crimes murder was common. I was most curious to see her; as curious as I could have been to see Satan. To my surprise, she was beautiful; black thoughts had failed to make her expression repulsive, age had failed to wrinkle her satin skin or mar its bloomy freshness. She could have passed for old Uriens's grand-daughter, she could have been mistaken for sister to her own son.

As soon as we were fairly within the castle gates, we were ordered into her presence. King Uriens was there, a kind-faced old man with a subdued look; and also the son, Sir

Uwaine le Blanchemains, in whom I was of course interested, on account of the tradition that he had once done battle with thirty knights, and also on account of his trip with Sir Gawaine and Sir Marhaus which Sandy had been aging me with. But Morgan was the main attraction, the conspicuous personality here; she was head chief of this household, that was plain. She caused us to be seated, and then she began, with all manner of pretty graces and graciousnesses, to ask me questions. Dear me, it was like a bird, or a flute, or something, talking. I felt persuaded that this woman must have been misrepresented, lied about. She trilled along, and trilled along, and presently a handsome young page, clothed like the rainbow, and as easy and undulatory of movement as a wave, came with something on a golden salver, and kneeling to present it to her, overdid his graces and lost his balance, and so fell lightly against her knee. She slipped a dirk into him in as matter-of-course a way as another person would have harpooned a rat!

Poor child, he slumped to the floor, twisted his silken limbs in one great straining contortion of pain, and was dead. Out of the old king was wrung an involuntary "O-h!" of compassion. The look he got, made him cut it suddenly short and not put any more hyphens in it. Sir Uwaine, at a sign from his mother, went to the ante-room and called some servants, and meanwhile madame went rippling sweetly along with her talk.

I saw that she was a good housekeeper, for while she talked she kept a corner of her eye on the servants to see that they made no balks in handling the body and getting it out; when they came with fresh clean towels, she sent back for the other kind; and when they had finished wiping the floor and were going, she indicated a crimson fleck the size of a tear which their duller eyes had overlooked. It was plain to me that La Cote Male Taile had failed to see the mistress of the house. Often, how louder and clearer than any tongue, does dumb circumstantial evidence speak.

Morgan le Fay rippled along as musically as ever. Marvelous woman. And what a glance she had: when it fell in reproof upon those servants, they shrunk and quailed as timid people do when the lightning flashes out of a cloud. I could have got the habit myself. It was the same with that poor old Brer Uriens; he was always on the ragged edge of apprehension; she could not even turn toward him but he winced.

In the midst of the talk, I let drop a complimentary word about King Arthur, forgetting for the moment how this woman hated her brother. That one little compliment was enough. She clouded up like a storm; she called for her guards, and said—

"Hale me these varlets to the dungeons!"

That struck cold on my ears, for her dungeons had a reputation. Nothing occurred to me to say—or do. But not so with Sandy. As the guard laid a hand upon me, she piped up with the tranquilest confidence, and said—

"God's wownds, dost thou covet destruction, thou maniac? It is The Boss!"

Now what a happy idea that was!—and so simple; yet it would never have occurred to me. I was born modest; not all over, but in spots; and this was one of the spots.

The effect upon madame was electrical. It cleared her countenance and brought back her smiles, and all her persuasive graces and blandishments; but nevertheless she was not able to entirely cover up with them the fact that she was in a ghastly fright. She said:

"La, do but list to thine handmaid! as if one gifted with powers like to mine might say the thing which I have said, unto one who has vanquished Merlin, and not be jesting. By mine enchantments I foresaw your coming, and by them I knew you when you entered here. I did but play this little jest with hope to surprise you into some display of your art, as not doubting you would blast the guards with occult fires, consuming them to ashes on the spot, a marvel much beyond mine own ability, yet one which I have long been childishly curious to see."

The guards were less curious, and got out as soon as they got permission.

Chapter 17

A Royal Banquet

MADAME, seeing me pacific and unresentful, no doubt judged that I was deceived by her excuse; for her fright dissolved away, and she was soon so importunate to have me give an exhibition and kill somebody, that the thing grew to be embarrassing. However, to my relief she was presently interrupted by the call to prayers. I will say this much for the nobility: that, tyrannical, murderous, rapacious, and morally rotten as they were, they were deeply and enthusiastically religious. Nothing could divert them from the regular and faithful performance of the pieties enjoined by the Church. More than once I had seen a noble who had gotten his enemy at a disadvantage, stop to pray before cutting his throat; more than once I had seen a noble, after ambushing and dispatching his enemy, retire to the nearest wayside shrine and humbly give thanks, without even waiting to rob the body. There was to be nothing finer or sweeter in the life of even Benvenuto Cellini, that rough-hewn saint, ten centuries later. All the nobles of Britain, with their families, attended divine service morning and night daily, in their private chapels, and even the worst of them had family worship five or six times a day besides. The credit of this belonged entirely to the Church. Although I was no friend to that Catholic Church, I was obliged to admit this. And often, in spite of me, I found myself saying, "What would this country be without the Church?"

After prayers we had dinner in a great banqueting hall which was lighted by hundreds of grease-jets, and everything was as fine and lavish and rudely splendid as might become the royal degree of the hosts. At the head of the hall, on a dais, was the table of the king, queen, and their son, Prince Uwaine. Stretching down the hall from this, was the general table, on the floor. At this, above the salt, sat the visiting nobles and the grown members of their families, of both

sexes,—the resident court, in effect,—sixty-one persons; below the salt sat minor officers of the household, with their
principal subordinates: altogether a hundred and eighteen
persons sitting, and about as many liveried servants standing
behind their chairs or serving in one capacity or another. It
was a very fine show. In a gallery a band, with cymbals,
horns, harps and other horrors, opened the proceedings with
what seemed to be the crude first-draft or original agony of
the wail known to later centuries as "In the Sweet By and
By." It was new, and ought to have been rehearsed a little
more. For some reason or other the queen had the composer
hanged, after dinner.

After this music the priest who stood behind the royal table
said a noble long grace in ostensible Latin. Then the battalion
of waiters broke away from their posts, and darted, rushed,
flew, fetched and carried, and the mighty feeding began: no
words anywhere, but absorbing attention to business. The
rows of chops opened and shut in vast unison, and the sound
of it was like to the muffled burr of subterranean machinery.
The havoc continued an hour and a half, and unimaginable
was the destruction of substantials. Of the chief feature of the
feast—the huge wild boar that lay stretched out so portly and
imposing at the start—nothing was left but the semblance of
a hoop-skirt; and he was but the type and symbol of what had
happened to all the other dishes.

With the pastries and so-on, the heavy drinking began—
and the talk. Gallon after gallon of wine and mead disappeared, and everybody got comfortable, then happy, then
sparklingly joyous—both sexes,—and by and by pretty
noisy. Men told anecdotes that were terrific to hear, but nobody blushed; and when the nub was sprung, the assemblage let go with a horse-laugh that shook the fortress.
Ladies answered back with historiettes that would almost
have made Queen Margaret of Navarre or even the great
Elizabeth of England hide behind a handkerchief, but nobody hid here, but only laughed—howled, you may say. In
pretty much all of these dreadful stories, ecclesiastics were
the hardy heroes, but that didn't worry the chaplain any, he
had his laugh with the rest; more than that, upon invitation

he roared out a song which was of as daring a sort as any
that was sung that night.

By midnight everybody was fagged out, and sore with
laughing; and as a rule, drunk: some weepingly, some affec-
tionately, some hilariously, some quarrelsomely, some dead
and under the table. Of the ladies, the worst spectacle was a
lovely young duchess, whose wedding-eve this was; and indeed she was a spectacle, sure enough: just as she was, she
could have sat in advance for the portrait of the young daughter of the Regent d'Orleans, at the famous dinner whence she
was carried, foul-mouthed, intoxicated and helpless, to her
bed, in the lost and lamented days of the Ancient Regime.

Suddenly, even while the priest was lifting his hands, and
all conscious heads were bowed in reverent expectation of the
coming blessing, there appeared under the arch of the far-off
door at the bottom of the hall, an old and bent and white-
haired lady, leaning upon a crutch-stick; and she lifted the
stick and pointed it toward the queen and cried out—

"The wrath and curse of God fall upon you, woman without pity, who have slain mine innocent grandchild and made
desolate this old heart that had nor chick nor friend nor stay
nor comfort in all this world but him!"

Everybody crossed himself in a grisly fright, for a curse was
an awful thing to those people; but the queen rose up majestic, with the death-light in her eye, and flung back this ruth-
less command:

"Lay hands on her! to the stake with her!"

The guards left their posts to obey. It was a shame; it was a
cruel thing to see. What could be done? Sandy gave me a
look: I knew she had another inspiration. I said—

"Do what you choose."

She was up and facing toward the queen in a moment. She
indicated me, and said:

"Madame, *he* saith this may not be. Recal the commandment, or he will dissolve the castle and it shall vanish away
like the instable fabric of a dream!"

Confound it, what a crazy contract to pledge a person to!
What if the queen—

But my consternation subsided there, and my panic passed
off; for the queen, all in a collapse, made no show of resis-

tance, but gave a countermanding sign and sunk into her seat. When she reached it she was sober. So were many of the others. The assemblage rose, whiffed ceremony to the winds, and rushed for the door like a mob; overturning chairs, smashing crockery, tugging, struggling, shouldering, crowding—anything to get out before I should change my mind and puff the castle into the measureless dim vacancies of space. Well, well, well, they *were* a superstitious lot. It is all a body can do to conceive of it.

The poor queen was so scared and humbled that she was even afraid to hang the composer without first consulting me. I was very sorry for her—indeed any one would have been, for she was really suffering; so I was willing to do anything that was reasonable, and had no desire to carry things to wanton extremities. I therefore considered the matter thoughtfully, and ended by having the musicians ordered into our presence to play that Sweet By and By again, which they did. Then I saw that she was right, and gave her permission to hang the whole band. This little relaxation of sternness had a good effect upon the queen. A statesman gains little by the arbitrary exercise of iron-clad authority upon all occasions that offer, for this wounds the just pride of his subordinates, and thus tends to undermine his strength. A little concession, now and then, where it can do no harm, is the wiser policy.

Now that the queen was at ease in her mind once more, and measurably happy, her wine naturally began to assert itself again, and it got a little the start of her. I mean it set her music going—her silver bell of a tongue. Dear me, she was a master talker. It would not become me to suggest that it was pretty late, and that I was a tired man and very sleepy. I wished I had gone off to bed when I had the chance. Now I must stick it out; there was no other way. So she tinkled along and along, in the otherwise profound and ghostly hush of the sleeping castle, until by and by there came, as if from deep down under us, a far-away sound, as of a muffled shriek—with an expression of agony about it that made my flesh crawl. The queen stopped, and her eyes lighted with pleasure; she tilted her graceful head as a bird does when it listens. The sound bored its way up through the stillness again.

"What is it?" I said.

"It is truly a stubborn soul, and endureth long. It is many hours, now."

"Endureth what?"

"The rack. Come—ye shall see a blithe sight. An he yield not his secret now, ye shall see him torn asunder."

What a silky smooth hellion she was; and so composed and serene, when the cords all down my legs were hurting, in sympathy with that man's pain. Conducted by mailed guards bearing flaring torches, we tramped along echoing corridors, and down stone stairways dank and dripping, and smelling of mould and ages of imprisoned night—a chill, uncanny journey and a long one, and not made the shorter or the cheerier by the sorceress's talk, which was about this sufferer and his crime. He had been accused, by an anonymous informer, of having killed a stag in the royal preserve. I said—

"Anonymous testimony isn't just the right thing, your Highness. It were fairer to confront the accused with the accuser."

"I had not thought of that, it being of but small consequence. But an I would, I could not, for that the accuser came masked, by night, and told the forester, and straightway gat him hence again, and so the forester knoweth him not."

"Then is this Unknown the only person who saw the stag killed?"—

"Marry, *no* man *saw* the killing, but this Unknown saw this hardy wretch near to the spot where the stag lay, and came with right loyal zeal and betrayed him to the forester."

"So the Unknown was near the dead stag, too? Isn't it just possible that he did the killing himself? His loyal zeal—in a mask—looks just a shade suspicious. But what is your Highness's idea for racking the prisoner? Where is the profit?"

"He will not confess, else; and then were his soul lost. For his crime, his life is forfeit by the law—and of a surety will I see that he payeth it!—but it were peril to my own soul to let him die unconfessed and unabsolved. Nay, I were a fool to fling me into hell for *his* accommodation."

"But, your Highness, suppose he has nothing to confess?"

"As to that, we shall see, anon. An I rack him to death and he confess not, it will peradventure show that he had indeed naught to confess—ye will grant that that is sooth? Then shall I not be damned for an unconfessed man that had naught to confess—wherefore, I shall be safe."

It was the stubborn unreasoning of the time. It was useless to argue with her. Arguments have no chance against petrified training; they wear it as little as the waves wear a cliff. And her training was everybody's. The brightest intellect in the land would not have been able to see that her position was defective.

As we entered the rack-cell I caught a picture that will not go from me; I wish it would. A naked young giant of thirty or thereabouts, lay stretched upon the frame, on his back, with his wrists and ancles tied to ropes which led over windlasses at either end. There was no color in him; his features were contorted and set, and sweat-drops stood upon his forehead. A priest bent over him on each side; the executioner stood by; guards were on duty; smoking torches stood in sockets along the walls; in a corner crouched a poor young creature, her face drawn with anguish, a half-wild and hunted look in her eyes, and in her lap lay a little child asleep. Just as we stepped across the threshold, the executioner gave his machine a slight turn, which wrung a cry from both the prisoner and the woman; but I shouted, and the executioner released the strain without waiting to see who spoke. I could not let this horror go on; it would have killed me to see it. I asked the queen to let me clear the place and speak to the prisoner privately; and when she was going to object, I spoke in a low voice and said I did not want to make a scene before her servants, but I must have my way; for I was King Arthur's representative, and was speaking in his name. She saw she had to yield. I asked her to endorse me to these people, and then leave me. It was not pleasant for her, but she took the pill; and even went further than I was meaning to require. I only wanted the backing of her own authority; but she said—

"Ye will do in all things as this lord shall command. It is The Boss."

It was certainly a good word to conjure with: you could see it by the squirming of these rats. The queen's guards fell into line, and she and they marched away, with their torch-bearers, and woke the echoes of the cavernous tunnels with the measured beat of their retreating footfalls. I had the prisoner taken from the rack and placed upon his bed, and medicaments applied to his hurts, and wine given him to drink. The woman crept near and looked on, eagerly, lovingly, but timorously,—like one who fears a repulse; indeed, she tried to furtively touch the man's forehead, and jumped back, the picture of fright, when I turned unconsciously toward her. It was pitiful to see.

"Lord," I said, "stroke him, lass, if you want to. Do anything you're a mind to; don't mind me."

Why, her eyes were as grateful as an animal's, when you do it a kindness that it understands. The baby was out of her way and she had her cheek against the man's in a minute, and her hands fondling his hair, and her happy tears running down. The man revived, and caressed his wife with his eyes, which was all he could do. I judged I might clear the den, now, and I did; cleared it of all but the family and myself. Then I said—

"Now my friend, tell me your side of this matter; I know the other side."

The man moved his head in sign of refusal. But the woman looked pleased—as it seemed to me—pleased with my suggestion. I went on:

"You know of me?"

"Yes. All do, in Arthur's realms."

"If my reputation has come to you right and straight, you should not be afraid to speak."

The woman broke in, eagerly:

"Ah, fair my lord, do thou persuade him! Thou canst an thou wilt. Ah, he suffereth so; and it is for me—for *me!* And how can I bear it? I would I might see him die—a sweet, swift death; oh, my Hugo, I cannot bear this one!"

And she fell to sobbing, and groveling about my feet, and still imploring. Imploring what? The man's death? I could not quite get the bearings of the thing. But Hugo interrupted her and said—

"Peace! Ye wit not what ye ask. Shall I starve whom I love, to win a gentle death? I wend thou knewest me better."

"Well," I said, "I can't quite make this out. It is a puzzle. Now—"

"Ah, dear my lord, an ye will but persuade him! Consider how these his tortures wound me! Oh, and he will not speak!—whenas, the healing, the solace that lie in a blessed swift death—"

"What *are* you maundering about? He's going out from here a free man and whole—he's not going to die."

The man's white face lit up, and the woman flung herself at me in a most surprising explosion of joy, and cried out—

"He is saved!—for it is the king's word by the mouth of the king's servant—Arthur, the king whose word is gold!"

"Well, then, you do believe I can be trusted, after all. Why didn't you before?"

"Who doubted? Not I, indeed; and not she."

"Well, why wouldn't you tell me your story, then?"

"Ye had made no promise; else had it been otherwise."

"I see, I see. . . . And yet, I believe I don't quite see, after all. You stood the torture and refused to confess; which shows plain enough to even the dullest understanding that you had nothing to confess—"

"*I*, my lord? How so? It was I that killed the deer!"

"You *did*? Oh, dear, this is the most mixed-up business that ever—"

"Dear lord, I begged him on my knees to confess, but—"

"You *did*! It gets thicker and thicker. What did you want him to do that, for?"

"Sith it would bring him a quick death and save him all this cruel pain."

"Well—yes, there is reason in that. But *he* didn't want the quick death."

"He? Why, of a surety he *did*."

"Well, then, why in the world *didn't* he confess?"

"Ah, sweet sir, and leave my wife and chick without bread and shelter?"

"Oh, heart of gold, now I see it! The bitter law takes the convicted man's estate and beggars his widow and his orphans. They could torture you to death, but without conviction or confession they could not rob your wife and baby. You stood by them like a man; and *you*—true wife and true woman that you are—you would have bought him release from torture at cost to yourself of slow starvation and death,—well, it humbles a body to think what your sex can do when it comes to self-sacrifice. I'll book you both for my colony; you'll like it there: it's a Factory where I'm going to turn groping and grubbing automata into *men*."

Chapter 18

WELL, I arranged all that; and I had the man sent to his home. I had a great desire to rack the executioner; not because he was a good, pains-taking and pain-giving official, —for surely it was not to his discredit that he performed his functions well—but to pay him back for wantonly cuffing and otherwise distressing that young woman. The priests told me about this, and were generously hot to have him punished. Something of this disagreeable sort was turning up, every now and then: I mean, episodes that showed that not all priests were frauds and self-seekers, but that many, even the great majority, of those that were down on the ground among the common people, were sincere, and right-hearted, and devoted to the alleviation of human troubles and sufferings. Well, it was a thing which could not be helped, so I seldom fretted about it, and never many minutes at a time; it has never been my way to bother much about things which you can't cure. But I did not like it, for it was just the sort of thing to keep a people reconciled to an Established Church. We *must* have a religion—it goes without saying—but my idea is, to have it cut up into forty free sects, so that they will police each other, as had been the case in the United States in my time. Concentration of power in a political machine is bad; and an Established Church is only a political machine; it was invented for that, it is nursed, coddled, preserved for that; it is an enemy to human liberty, and does no good which it could not better do in a split-up and scattered condition. That wasn't law, it wasn't gospel: it was only an opinion—my opinion, and I was only a man, one man: so it wasn't worth any more than the pope's—or any less, for that matter.

Well, I couldn't rack the executioner, neither would I overlook the just complaint of the priests. The man must be punished somehow or other, so I degraded him from his office and made him leader of the band—the new one that was to be started. He begged hard, and said he couldn't play—a plausible excuse, but too thin: there wasn't a musician in the country that could.

The queen was a good deal outraged, next morning, when she found she was going to have neither Hugo's life nor his property. But I told her she must bear this cross; that while by law and custom she certainly was entitled to both the man's life and his property, there were extenuating circumstances, and so, in Arthur the king's name I had pardoned him. The deer was ravaging the man's fields, and he had killed it in sudden passion, and not for gain; and he had carried it into the royal forest in the hope that that might make detection of the misdoer impossible. Confound her, I couldn't make her see that sudden passion is an extenuating circumstance in the killing of venison,—or of a person—so I gave it up, and let her sulk it out. I *did* think I was going to make her see it by remarking that her own sudden passion in the case of the page modified that crime.

"Crime!" she exclaimed. "How thou talkest! Crime, forsooth! Man, I am going to *pay* for him!"

Oh, it was no use to waste sense on her. Training—training is everything; training is all there is *to* a person. We speak of nature; it is folly; there is no such thing as nature; what we call by that misleading name is merely heredity and training. We have no thoughts of our own, no opinions of our own: they are transmitted to us, trained into us. All that is original in us, and therefore fairly creditable or discreditable to us, can be covered up and hidden by the point of a cambric needle, all the rest being atoms contributed by, and inherited from, a procession of ancestors that stretches back a billion years to the Adam-clam or grasshopper or monkey from whom our race has been so tediously and ostentatiously and unprofitably developed. And as for me, all that I think about in this plodding sad pilgrimage, this pathetic drift between the eternities, is to look out and humbly live a pure and high and blameless life, and save that one microscopic atom in me that is truly *me*: the rest may land in Sheol and welcome, for all I care.

No, confound her, her intellect was good, she had brains enough, but her training made her an ass—that is, from a many-centuries-later point of view. To kill the page was no crime—it was her right; and upon her right she stood, serenely, and unconscious of offence. She was a result of generations of training in the unexamined and unassailed belief that the law which permitted her to kill a subject when she chose was a perfectly right and righteous one.

Well, we must give even Satan his due. She deserved a compliment for one thing; and I tried to pay it, but the words stuck in my throat. She had a right to kill the boy, but she was in no wise obliged to pay for him. That was law for some other people, but not for her. She knew quite well that she was doing a large and generous thing to pay for that lad, and that I ought in common fairness to come out with something handsome about it, but I couldn't—my mouth refused. I couldn't help seeing in my fancy, that poor old grandam with the broken heart, and that fair young creature lying butchered, his little silken pomps and vanities laced with his golden blood. How could she *pay* for him? *Whom* could she pay? And so, well knowing that this woman, trained as she had been, deserved praise, even adulation, I was yet not able to utter it, trained as *I* had been. The best I could do was to fish up a compliment from outside, so to speak—and the pity of it was, that it was true:

"Madame, your people will adore you for this."

Quite true, but I meant to hang her for it some day, if I lived. Some of those laws were too bad, altogether too bad. A master might kill his slave for nothing: for mere spite, malice, or to pass the time—just as we have seen that the crowned head could do it with *his* slave, that is to say, anybody. A gentleman could kill a free commoner, and pay for him—cash or garden-truck. A noble could kill a noble without expense, as far as the law was concerned, but reprisals in kind were to be expected. *Any*body could kill *some*body, except the commoner and the slave: these had no privileges. If they killed, it was murder, and the law wouldn't stand murder. It made short work of the experimenter—and of his family too, if he murdered somebody who belonged up among the ornamental ranks. If a commoner gave a noble even so much as a Damiens scratch which didn't kill or even hurt, he got Damien's dose for it just the same: they pulled him to rags and tatters with horses, and all the world came to see the show, and crack jokes, and have a good time; and some of the performances of the best people present were as tough, and as properly unprintable, as any that have been printed by the pleasant Casanova in his chapter about the dismemberment of Louis XV.'s poor awkward enemy.

I had had enough of this grisly place by this time, and wanted to leave, but I couldn't, because I had something on my mind that my conscience kept prodding me about, and wouldn't let me forget. If I had the remaking of man, he wouldn't have any conscience. It is one of the most disagreeable things connected with a person; and although it certainly does do a great deal of good, it cannot be said to pay, in the long run; it would be much better to have less good and more comfort. Still, this is only my opinion, and I am only one man; others, with less experience, may think differently. They have a right to their view. I only stand to this: I have noticed my conscience for many years, and I know it is more trouble and bother to me than anything else I started with. I suppose that in the beginning I prized it, because we prize anything that is ours; and yet how foolish it was to think so. If we look at it in another way, we see how absurd it is: if I had an anvil in me, would I prize it? Of course not. And yet when you come to think, there is no real difference between a conscience and an anvil—I mean, for comfort. I have noticed it a thousand times. And you could dissolve an anvil with acids, when you couldn't stand it any longer; but there isn't any way that you can work off a conscience—at least so it will stay worked off; not that I know of, anyway.

There was something I wanted to do before leaving, but it was a disagreeable matter, and I hated to go at it. Well, it bothered me all the morning. I could have mentioned it to the old king, but what would be the use?—he was but an extinct volcano; he had been active in his time, but his fire was out, this good while, he was only a stately ash-pile, now: gentle enough, and kindly enough for my purpose, without doubt, but not usable. He was nothing, this so-called king: the queen was the only power there. And she was a Vesuvius. As a favor, she might consent to warm a flock of sparrows for you, but then she might take that very opportunity to turn herself loose and bury a city. However, I reflected that as often as any other way, when you are expecting the worst, you get something that is not so bad, after all.

So I braced up and placed my matter before her royal Highness. I said I had been having a general jail delivery at Camelot and among neighboring castles, and with her permission I would like to examine her collection, her brica-brac—that is to say, her prisoners. She resisted; but I was expecting that. But she finally consented: I was expecting that, too, but not so soon. That about ended my discomfort. She called her guards and torches, and we went down into the dungeons. These were down under the castle's foundations, and mainly were small cells hollowed out of the living rock. Some of these cells had no light at all. In one of them was a woman, in foul rags, who sat on the ground, and would not answer a question, or speak a word, but only looked up at us, once or twice, through a cobweb of tangled hair, as if to see what casual thing it might be that was disturbing with sound and light the meaningless dull dream that was become her life; after that, she sat bowed, with her dirt-caked fingers idly interlocked in her lap, and gave no further sign. This poor rack of bones was a woman of middle age, apparently; but only apparently: she had been there nine years, and was eighteen when she entered. She was a commoner, and had been sent here on her bridal night by Sir Breuse Sance Pité, a neighboring lord whose vassal her father was, and to which said lord she had refused what has since been called *le droit du Seigneur*; and moreover, had opposed violence to violence and spilt half a gill of his almost sacred blood. The young husband had interfered, at that point, believing the bride's life in danger, and had flung the noble out into the midst of the humble and trembling wedding guests in the parlor, and left him there astonished at this strange treatment, and implacably embittered against both bride and groom. The said lord, being cramped for dungeon-room, had asked the queen to accommodate his two criminals, and here in her bastile they had been ever since; hither, indeed, they had come before their crime was an hour old, and had never seen each other since. Here they were, kerneled like toads in the same rock; they had passed nine pitch dark years within fifty feet of each other, yet neither knew whether the other was alive or not.

All the first years, their only question had been—asked with beseechings and tears that might have moved stones, in time, perhaps, but hearts are not stones: "Is he alive?" "Is she alive?" But they had never got an answer; and at last that question was not asked any more—or any other.

I wanted to see the man, after hearing all this. He was thirty-four years old, and looked sixty. He sat upon a squared block of stone, with his head bent down, his forearms resting on his knees, his long hair hanging like a fringe before his face, and he was muttering to himself. He raised his chin and looked us slowly over, in a listless dull way, blinking with the distress of the torch-light, then dropped his head and fell to muttering again and took no further notice of us. There were some pathetically suggestive dumb witnesses present. On his wrists and ancles were cicatrices, old smooth scars, and fastened to the stone on which he sat was a chain with manacles and fetters attached; but this apparatus lay idle on the ground, and was thick with rust. Chains cease to be needed, after the spirit has gone out of a prisoner.

I could not rouse the man; so I said we would take him to her, and see—to the bride who was the fairest thing in the earth to him, once—roses, pearls and dew made flesh, for him; a wonder-work, the master-work of Nature: with eyes like no other eyes, and a voice like no other voice, and a freshness, and lithe young grace, and beauty, that belonged properly to the creatures of dreams—as he thought—and to no other. The sight of her would set his stagnant blood leaping; the sight of her—

But it was a disappointment. They sat together on the ground and looked dimly wondering into each other's faces a while, with a sort of weak animal curiosity; then forgot each other's presence, and dropped their eyes, and you saw that they were away again, and wandering in some far land of dreams and shadows that we know nothing about.

I had them taken out and sent to their friends. The queen did not like it much. Not that she felt any personal interest in the matter, but she thought it disrespectful to Sir Breuse Sance Pité. However, I assured her that if he found he couldn't stand it I would fix him so that he could.

I set forty-seven prisoners loose out of those awful rat-holes, and left only one in captivity. He was a lord, and had killed another lord, a sort of kinsman of the queen. That other lord had ambushed him to assassinate him, but this fellow had got the best of him and cut his throat. However, it was not for that that I left him jailed, but for maliciously destroying the only public well in one of his wretched villages. The queen was bound to hang him for killing her kinsman, but I would not allow it: it was no crime to kill an assassin. But I said I was willing to let her hang him for destroying the well; so she concluded to put up with that, as it was better than nothing.

Dear me, for what trifling offences the most of those forty-seven men and women were shut up there! Indeed some were there for no distinct offence at all, but only to gratify somebody's spite; and not always the queen's, by any means, but a friend's. The newest prisoner's crime was a mere remark which he had made. He said he believed that men were about all alike, and one man as good as another, barring clothes. He said he believed that if you were to strip the nation naked and send a stranger through the crowd, he couldn't tell the king from a quack doctor, nor a duke from a hotel clerk. Apparently here was a man whose brains had not been reduced to an ineffectual mush by idiotic training. I set him loose at once, and sent him to the Factory.

Some of the cells, carved in the living rock, were just behind the face of the precipice, and in each of these an arrow-slit had been pierced outward to the daylight, and so the captive had a thin ray from the blessed sun for his comfort. The case of one of these poor fellows was particularly hard. From his dusky swallow's-hole high up in that vast wall of native rock he could peer out through the arrow-slit and see his own home off yonder in the valley; and for twenty-two years he had watched it, with heart-ache and longing, through that crack. He could see the lights shine there at night, and in the daytime he could see figures go in and come out—his wife and children, some of them, no doubt, though he could not make out, at that distance. In the course of years he noted festivities there, and tried to rejoice, and wondered if they were weddings, or what they might be. And he noted funerals; and they wrung his heart. He could make out the coffin, but he could not determine its size, and so could not tell whether it was wife or child. He could see the procession form, with priests and mourners, and move solemnly away, bearing the secret with them. He had left behind him five children and a wife; and in nineteen years he had seen five funerals issue, and none of them humble enough in pomp to denote a servant. So he had lost five of his treasures; there must still be one remaining—one now infinitely, unspeakably precious,—but *which* one? wife, or child? That was the question that tortured him, by night and by day, asleep and awake. Well, to have an interest, of some sort, and half a ray of light, when you are in a dungeon, is a great support to the body and preserver of the intellect. This man was in pretty good condition yet. By the time he had finished telling me his distressful tale, I was in the same state of mind that you would have been in, yourself, if you have got average human curiosity: that is to say, I was as burning up as he was, to find out which member of the family it was, that was left. So I took him over home myself; and an amazing kind of a surprise party it was, too—typhoons and cyclones of frantic joy, and whole Niagaras of happy tears: and by George we found the aforetime young matron graying toward the imminent verge of her half-century, and the babies all men and women, and some of them married and experimenting family-wise themselves—for not a soul of the tribe was dead! Conceive of the ingenious devilishness of that queen: she had a special hatred for this prisoner, and she had *invented* all those funerals herself, to scorch his heart with; and the sublimest stroke of genius of the whole thing was leaving the family-invoice a funeral *short*, so as to let him wear his poor old soul out guessing.

But for me, he never would have got out. Morgan le Fay hated him with her whole heart, and she never would have softened toward him. And yet his crime was committed more in thoughtlessness than deliberate depravity. He had said she had red hair. Well, she had; but that was no way to speak of it. When red-headed people are above a certain social grade, their hair is auburn.

Consider it: among these forty-seven captives, there were five whose names, offences, and dates of incarceration were no longer known! One woman and four men—all bent, and wrinkled, and mind-extinguished patriarchs. They themselves had long ago forgotten these details; at any rate they had mere vague theories about them, nothing definite, and nothing that they repeated twice in the same way. The succession of priests whose office it had been to pray daily with the captives, and remind them that God had put them there, for some wise purpose or other, and teach them that patience, humbleness, and submission to oppression was what He loved to see in parties of a subordinate rank, had traditions about these poor old human ruins, but nothing more. These traditions went but little way, for they concerned the length of the incarcerations only, and not the names or the offences. And even by the help of tradition the only thing that could be proven was that none of the five had seen daylight for thirty-five years: how much longer this privation had lasted was not guessable. The king and the queen knew nothing about these poor creatures, except that they were heirlooms, assets inherited, along with the throne, from the former firm. Nothing of their history had been transmitted with their persons, and so the inheriting owners had considered them of no value, and had felt no interest in them. I said to the queen—

"Then why in the world didn't you set them free?"

The question was a puzzler. She didn't know *why* she hadn't; the thing had never come up in her mind. So here she was, forecasting the veritable history of future prisoners of the castle d'If, without knowing it. It seemed plain to me now, that with her training, those inherited prisoners were merely property—nothing more, nothing less. Well, when we inherit property, it does not occur to us to throw it away, even when we do not value it.

When I brought my procession of human bats up into the open world and the glare of the afternoon sun,—previously blindfolding them in charity for eyes so long untortured by light—they were a spectacle to look at. Skeletons, scarecrows, goblins, pathetic frights, every one: legitimatest possible children of Monarchy by the Grace of God and the Established Church. I muttered, absently—

"I *wish* I could photograph them!"

You have seen that kind of people who will never let on

that they don't know the meaning of a new big word. The more ignorant they are, the more pitifully certain they are to pretend you haven't shot over their heads. The queen was just one of that sort, and was always making the stupidest blunders by reason of it. She hesitated a moment; then her face brightened up with sudden comprehension, and she said she would do it for me.

I thought to myself: She? why what can she know about photography? But it was a poor time to be thinking. When I looked around, she was moving on the procession with an axe!

Well, she certainly was a curious one, was Morgan le Fay. I have seen a good many kinds of women in my time, but she laid over them all, for variety. And how sharply characteristic of her this episode was. She had no more idea than a horse, of how to photograph a procession; but being in doubt, it was just like her to try to do it with an axe.

Chapter 19

KNIGHT-ERRANTRY AS A TRADE

S ANDY AND I were on the road again, next morning, bright and early. It was *so* good to open up one's lungs and take in whole luscious barrels-full of the blessed God's untainted, dew-freshened, woodland-scented air once more, after suffocating body and mind for two days and nights in the moral and physical stenches of that intolerable old buzzard-roost! I mean, for me: of course the place was all right and agreeable enough for Sandy, for she had been used to high life all her days.

Poor girl, her jaws had had a wearisome rest, now, for a while; and I was expecting to get the consequences. I was right; but she had stood by me most helpfully in the castle, and had mightily supported and reinforced me with gigantic foolishnesses which were worth more for the occasion than wisdoms double their size; so I thought she had earned a right to work her mill for a while, if she wanted to, and I felt not a pang when she started it up:

"Now turn we unto Sir Marhaus that rode with the damsel of thirty winter of age southward—"

"Are you going to see if you can work up another half-stretch on the trail of the cow-boys, Sandy?"

"Even so, fair my lord."

"Go ahead, then. I won't interrupt this time, if I can help it. Begin over again; start fair, and shake out all your reefs, and I will load my pipe and give good attention."

"Now turn we unto Sir Marhaus that rode with the damsel of thirty winter of age southward. And so they came into a deep forest, and by fortune they were nighted, and rode long in a deep way, and at the last they came into a courtelage where abode the duke of South Marches, and there they asked harbour. And on the morn the duke sent unto Sir Marhaus, and bad make him ready. And so Sir Marhaus arose and armed him, and then there was a mass sung afore him, and he brake his fast, and so mounted on horseback in the court of

335

the castle, there they should do the battle. So there was the duke already on horseback, clean armed, and his six sons by him, and every each had a spear in his hand, and so they encountered, where as the duke and his two sons brake their spears upon him, but Sir Marhaus held up his spear and touched none of them. Then came the four sons by couples, and two of them brake their spears, and so did the other two. And all this while Sir Marhaus touched them not. Then Sir Marhaus ran to the duke, and smote him with his spear that horse and man fell to the earth. And so he served his sons. And then Sir Marhaus alight down, and bad the duke yield him or else he would slay him. And then some of his sons recovered, and would have set upon Sir Marhaus. Then Sir Marhaus said to the duke, Cease thy sons, or else I will do the uttermost to you all. When the duke saw he might not escape the death, he cried to his sons, and charged them to yield them to Sir Marhaus. And they kneeled all down and put the pommels of their swords to the knight, and so he received them. And then they holp up their father, and so by their common assent promised unto Sir Marhaus never to be foes unto king Arthur, and thereupon at Whitsuntide after, to come he and his sons, and put them in the king's grace.*

"Even so standeth the history, fair Sir Boss. Now ye shall wit that that very duke and his six sons are they whom but few days past you also did overcome and send to Arthur's court!"

"Why, Sandy, you can't mean it!"

"An I speak not sooth, let it be the worse for me."

"Well, well, well—now who would ever have thought it? One whole duke and six dukelets; why Sandy, it was an elegant haul. Knight-errantry is a most chuckle-headed trade, and it is tedious hard work, too, but I begin to see that there *is* money in it, after all, if you have luck. Not that I would ever engage in it, as a business, for I wouldn't. No sound and legitimate business can be established on a basis of speculation. A successful whirl in the knight-errantry line—now what is it, when you blow away the nonsense and come down

*The story is borrowed, language and all, from the *Morte d'Arthur.* —M. T.

to the cold facts? It's just a corner in pork, that's all, and you can't make anything else out of it. You're rich—yes, suddenly rich—for about a day, maybe a week: then somebody corners the market on *you*, and down goes your bucket-shop; ain't that so, Sandy?"

"Whethersoever it be that my mind miscarrieth, bewraying simple language in such sort that the words do seem to come endlong and overthwart—"

"There's no use in beating about the bush and trying to get around it that way, Sandy, it's *so*, just as I say. I *know* it's so. And moreover, when you come right down to the bed-rock, knight-errantry is *worse* than pork; for whatever happens, the pork's left, and so somebody's benefited, anyway; but when the market breaks, in a knight-errantry whirl, and every knight in the pool passes in his checks, what have you got for assets? Just a rubbish-pile of battered corpses and a barrel or two of busted hardware. Can you call *those* assets? Give me pork, every time. Am I right?"

"Ah, peradventure my head being distraught by the manifold matters whereunto the confusions of these but late adventured haps and fortunings whereby not I alone nor you alone, but every each of us, meseemeth—"

"No, it's not your head, Sandy. Your head's all right, as far as it goes, but you don't know business; that's where the trouble is. It unfits you to argue about business, and you're wrong to be always trying. However, that aside, it was a good haul, anyway, and will breed a handsome crop of reputation in Arthur's court. And speaking of the cow-boys, what a curious country this is for women and men that never get old. Now there's Morgan le Fay, as fresh and young as a Vassar pullet, to all appearances, and here is this old duke of the South Marches still slashing away with sword and lance at his time of life, after raising such a family as he has raised. As I understand it, Sir Gawaine killed seven of his sons, and still he had six left for Sir Marhaus and me to take into camp. And then there was that damsel of sixty winter of age still excursioning around in her frosty bloom.—How old are you, Sandy?"

It was the first time I ever struck a still place in her. The mill had shut down for repairs, or something.

Chapter 20

THE OGRE'S CASTLE

BETWEEN six and nine we made ten miles, which was plenty for a horse carrying triple—man, woman, and armor; then we stopped for a long nooning, under some trees by a limpid brook.

Right-so came by and by a knight riding; and as he drew near he made dolorous moan, and by the words of it I perceived that he was cursing and swearing; yet nevertheless was I glad of his coming, for that I saw he bare a bulletin-board whereon in letters all of shining gold was writ—

"USE PETERSON'S PROPHYLACTIC
TOOTH-BRUSH—ALL THE GO."

I was glad of his coming, for even by this token I knew him for knight of mine. It was Sir Madok de la Montaine, a burly great fellow whose chief distinction was that he had come within an ace of sending Sir Launcelot down over his horse-tail once. He was never long in a stranger's presence without finding some pretext or other to let out that great fact. But there was another fact of nearly the same size, which he never pushed upon anybody unasked, and yet never withheld when asked: that was, that the reason he didn't quite succeed was, that he was interrupted and sent down over horse-tail himself. This innocent vast lubber did not see any particular difference between the two facts. I liked him, for he was earnest in his work, and very valuable. And he was so fine to look at, with his broad mailed shoulders, and the grand leonine set of his plumed head, and his big shield with its quaint device of a gauntleted hand clutching a prophylactic tooth-brush, with motto, "*Try Noyoudont.*" This was a tooth-wash that I was introducing.

He was aweary, he said, and indeed he looked it; but he would not alight. He said he was after the stove-polish man; and with this he broke out cursing and swearing anew. The bulletin-boarder referred to was Sir Ossaise of Surluse, a brave knight, and of considerable celebrity on account of his having tried conclusions in a tournament, once, with no less a Mogul than Sir Gaheris himself—although not successfully. He was of a light and laughing disposition, and to him nothing in this world was serious. It was for this reason that I had chosen him to work up a stove-polish sentiment. There were no stoves yet, and so there could be nothing serious about stove-polish. All that the agent needed to do was to deftly, and by degrees, prepare the public for the great change, and have them established in predilections toward neatness against the time when the stove should appear upon the stage.

Sir Madok was very bitter, and brake out anew with cursings. He said he had cursed his soul to rags; and yet he would not get down from his horse, neither would he take any rest, or listen to any comfort, until he should have found Sir Ossaise and settled this account. It appeared, by what I could piece together of the unprofane fragments of his statement, that he had chanced upon Sir Ossaise at dawn of the morning, and been told that if he would make a short-cut across the fields and swamps and broken hills and glades, he could head off a company of travelers who would be rare customers for prophylactics and tooth-wash. With characteristic zeal Sir Madok had plunged away at once upon this quest, and after three hours of awful crosslot riding had overhauled his game. And behold, it was the five patriarchs that had been released from the dungeons the evening before! Poor old creatures, it was all of twenty years since any one of them had known what it was to be equipped with any remaining snag or remnant of a tooth.

"Blank-blank-blank him," said Sir Madok, "an I do not stove-polish him an I may find him, leave it to me; for never no knight that hight Ossaise or aught else may do me this disservice and abide on live, an I may find him, the which I have thereunto sworn a great oath this day."

And with these words, and others, he lightly took his spear and gat him hence. In the middle of the afternoon we came upon one of those very patriarchs ourselves, in the edge of a poor village. He was basking in the love of relatives and friends whom he had not seen for fifty years, and about him and caressing him were also descendants of his own body whom he had never seen at all till now; but to him these were all strangers, his memory was gone, his mind was stagnant. It seemed incredible that a man could outlast half a century shut up in a dark hole like a rat, but here were his old wife and some old comrades to testify to it. They could remember him as he was in the freshness and strength of his young manhood, when he kissed his child, and delivered it to its mother's hands and went away into that long oblivion. The people at the castle could not tell within half a generation the length of time the man had been shut up there for his unrecorded and forgotten offence; but this old wife knew; and so did her old child, who stood there among her married sons and daughters trying to realize a father who had been to her a name, a thought, a formless image, a tradition, all her life, and now was suddenly concreted into actual flesh and blood and set before her face.

It was a curious situation; yet it is not on that account that I have made room for it here, but on account of a thing which seemed to me still more curious. To wit, that this dreadful matter brought from these down-trodden people no outburst of rage against their oppressors. They had been heritors and subjects of cruelty and outrage so long that nothing could have startled them but a kindness. Yes, here was a curious revelation indeed, of the depth to which this people had been sunk in slavery. Their entire being was reduced to a monotonous dead level of patience, resignation, dumb uncomplaining acceptance of whatever might befal them in this life. Their very imagination was dead. When you can say that of a man, he has struck bottom, I reckon; there is no lower deep for him.

I rather wished I had gone some other road. This was not the sort of experience for a statesman to encounter who was planning out a peaceful revolution in his mind. For it could not help bringing up the ungetaroundable fact that, all gentle cant and philosophising to the contrary notwithstanding, no people in this world ever did achieve their freedom by goody-goody talk and moral suasion: it being immutable law that all revolutions that will succeed, must *begin* in blood, whatever may answer afterward. If history teaches anything, it teaches that. What this folk needed, then, was a Reign of Terror and a guillotine, and I was the wrong man for them.

Two days later, toward noon, Sandy began to show signs of excitement and feverish expectancy. She said we were approaching the ogre's castle. I was surprised into an uncomfortable shock. The object of our quest had gradually dropped out of my mind; this sudden resurrection of it made it seem quite a real and startling thing, for a moment, and roused up in me a smart interest. Sandy's excitement increased every moment; and so did mine, for that sort of thing is catching. My heart got to thumping. You can't reason with your heart; it has its own laws, and thumps about things which the intellect scorns. Presently, when Sandy slid from the horse, motioned me to stop, and went creeping stealthily, with her head bent nearly to her knees, toward a row of bushes that bordered a declivity, the thumpings grew stronger and quicker. And they kept it up while she was gaining her ambush and getting her glimpse over the declivity; and also while I was creeping to her side on my knees. Her eyes were burning, now, as she pointed with her finger, and said in a panting whisper—

"The castle! the castle! Lo, where it looms!"

What a welcome disappointment I experienced! I said—

"Castle? It is nothing but a pig-sty; a pig-sty with a wattled fence around it."

She looked surprised, and distressed. The animation faded out of her face; and during many moments she was lost in thought, and silent. Then—

"It was not enchanted aforetime," she said, in a musing fashion, as if to herself. "And how strange is this marvel, and how awful—that to the one perception it is enchanted, and dight in a base and shameful aspect; yet to the perception of the other it is not enchanted, hath suffered no change, but stands fair and stately still, girt with its moat and waving its banners in the blue air from its towers. And God shield us, how it pricks the heart to see again these gracious captives, and the sorrow deepened in their sweet faces! We have tarried long, and are to blame."

I saw my cue. The castle was enchanted to *me*, not to her. It would be wasted time to try to argue her out of her delusion, it couldn't be done: I must just humor it. So I said—

"This is a common case—the enchanting of a thing to one

eye and leaving it in its proper form to another. You have heard of it before, Sandy, though you haven't happened to experience it. But no harm is done. In fact it is lucky the way it is. If these ladies were hogs to everybody and to themselves, it would be necessary to break the enchantment, and that might be impossible if one failed to find out the particular process of the enchantment. And hazardous, too; for in attempting a disenchantment without the true key, you are liable to err, and turn your hogs into dogs, and the dogs into cats, the cats into rats, and so-on, and end by reducing your materials to nothing, finally, or to an odorless gas which you can't follow—which of course amounts to the same thing. But here, by good luck, no one's eyes but mine are under the enchantment, and so it is of no consequence to dissolve it. These ladies remain ladies to you, and to themselves, and to everybody else; and at the same time they will suffer in no way from my delusion, for when I know that an ostensible hog is a lady, that is enough for me: I know how to treat her."

"Thanks, oh sweet my lord, thou talkest like an angel. And I know that thou wilt deliver them, for that thou art minded to great deeds and art as strong a knight of your hands and as brave to will and to do, as any that is on live."

"I will not leave a princess in the sty, Sandy. Are those three yonder that to my disordered eyes are starveling swine-herds—"

"The ogres? Are *they* changed also? It is most wonderful. Now am I fearful; for how canst thou strike with sure aim when five of their nine cubits of stature are to thee invisible? Ah, go warily, fair sir; this is a mightier emprise than I wend."

"You be easy, Sandy. All I need to know is, how *much* of an ogre is invisible; then I know how to locate his vitals. Don't you be afraid, I will make short work of these bunco-steerers. Stay where you are."

I left Sandy kneeling there, corpse-faced but plucky and hopeful, and rode down to the pig-sty, and struck up a trade with the swineherds. I won their gratitude by buying out all the hogs at the lump sum of sixteen pennies, which was rather above latest quotations. I was just in time; for the Church, the lord of the manor, and the rest of the tax gatherers would have been along next day and swept off pretty much all the stock, leaving the swineherds very short of hogs and Sandy nearly out of princesses. But now the tax people could be paid in cash, and there would be a stake left besides. One of the men had ten children; and he said that last year when a priest came and of his ten pigs took the fattest one for tithes, the wife burst out upon him, and offered him a child and said—

"Thou beast without bowels of mercy, why leave me my child, yet rob me of the wherewithal to feed it?"

How curious. The same thing had happened in the Wales of my day, under this same old Established Church, which was supposed by many to have changed its nature when it changed its disguise.

I sent the three men away, and then opened the sty-gate and beckoned Sandy to come—which she did; and not leisurely, but with the rush of a prairie-fire. And when I saw her fling herself upon those hogs, with tears of joy running down her cheeks, and strain them to her heart, and kiss them, and caress them, and call them reverently by grand princely names, I was ashamed of her, ashamed of the human race.

We had to drive those hogs home—ten miles; and no ladies were ever more fickle-minded or contrary. They would stay in no road, no path; they broke out through the brush on all sides, and flowed away in all directions, over rocks, and hills, and the roughest places they could find. And they must not be struck, or roughly accosted; Sandy could not bear to see them treated in ways unbecoming their rank. The troublesomest old sow of the lot had to be called my lady, and your Highness, like the rest. It is annoying and difficult to scour around after hogs, in armor. There was one small countess, with an iron ring in her snout and hardly any hair on her back, that was the devil for perversity. She gave me a race of an hour, over all sorts of country, and then we were right where we had started from, having made not a rod of real progress. I seized her at last by the tail, and brought her along, squealing. When I overtook Sandy, she was horrified, and said it was in the last degree indelicate to drag a countess by her train.

We got the hogs home just at dark—most of them. The Princess Nerovens de Morganore was missing, and two of her ladies in waiting: namely, Miss Angela Bohun, and the Demoiselle Elaine Courtemains, the former of these two being a young black sow with a white star in her forehead, and the latter a brown one with thin legs, and a slight limp in the forward shank on the starboard side—a couple of the tryingest blisters to drive, that I ever saw. Also among the missing were several mere baronesses—and I wanted them to stay missing; but no, all that sausage-meat had to be found; so, servants were sent out with torches to scour the woods and hills to that end.

Of course the whole drove was housed in the house, and great guns!—well, I never saw anything like it. Nor ever heard anything like it. And never smelt anything like it. It was like an insurrection in a gasometer.

Chapter 21

The Pilgrims

WHEN I did get to bed at last I was unspeakably tired; the stretching out, and the relaxing of the long-tense muscles, how luxurious, how delicious! but that was as far as I could get—sleep was out of the question, for the present. The ripping and tearing and squealing of the nobility up and down the halls and corridors was pandemonium come again, and kept me broad awake. Being awake, my thoughts were busy, of course; and mainly they busied themselves with Sandy's curious delusion. Here she was, as sane a person as the kingdom could produce; and yet, from my point of view she was acting like a crazy woman. My land, the power of training! of influence! of education! It can bring a body up to believe anything. I had to put myself in Sandy's place to realize that she was not a lunatic. Yes, and put her in mine, to demonstrate how easy it is to seem a lunatic to a person who has not been taught as you have been taught. If I had told Sandy I had seen a wagon, uninfluenced by enchantment, spin along fifty miles an hour; had seen a man, unequipped with magic powers, get into a basket and soar out of sight among the clouds; and had listened, without any necromancer's help, to the conversation of a person who was several hundred miles away, Sandy would not merely have supposed me to be crazy, she would have thought she knew it. Everybody around her believed in enchantments; nobody had any doubts; to doubt that a castle could be turned into a sty, and its occupants into hogs, would have been the same as my doubting, among Connecticut people, the actuality of the telephone and its wonders,—and in both cases would be absolute proof of a diseased mind, an unsettled reason. Yes, Sandy was sane; that must be admitted. If I also would be sane—to Sandy—I must keep my superstitions about unenchanted and unmiraculous locomotives, balloons and telephones, to myself. Also, I believed that the world was not flat, and hadn't pillars under it to support it, nor a canopy over it to turn off a universe of water that occupied all space above: but as I was the only person in the kingdom afflicted with such impious and criminal opinions, I recognized that it would be good wisdom to keep quiet about this matter, too, if I did not wish to be suddenly shunned and forsaken by everybody as a madman.

The next morning Sandy assembled the swine in the dining room and gave them their breakfast, waiting upon them personally and manifesting in every way the deep reverence which the natives of her island, ancient and modern, have always felt for rank, let its outward casket and the mental and moral contents be what they may. I could have eaten with the hogs if I had had birth approaching my lofty official rank; but I hadn't, and so I accepted the unavoidable slight and made no complaint. Sandy and I had our breakfast at the second table. The family were not at home. I said:

"How many are in the family, Sandy, and where do they keep themselves?"

"Family?"

"Yes."

"Which family, good my lord?"

"Why, this family; your own family."

"Sooth to say, I understand you not. I have no family."

"No family? Why, Sandy, isn't this your home?"

"Now how indeed might that be? I have no home."

"Well, then, whose house is this?"

"Ah, wit you well I would tell you an I knew myself."

"Come—you don't even know these people? Then who invited us here?"

"None invited us. We but came; that is all."

"Why, woman, this is a most extraordinary performance. The effrontery of it is beyond admiration. We blandly march into a man's house, and cram it full of the only really valuable nobility the sun has yet discovered in the earth, and then it turns out that we don't even know the man's name. How did you ever venture to take this extravagant liberty? I supposed, of course, it was your home. What will the man say?"

"What will he say? Forsooth what can he say but give thanks?"

"Thanks for what?"

Her face was filled with a puzzled surprise:

"Verily thou troublest mine understanding with strange words. Do ye dream that one of his estate is like to have the honor twice in his life to entertain company such as we have brought to grace his house withal?"

"Well, no—when you come to that. No, it's an even bet that this is the first time he has had a treat like this."

"Then let him be thankful, and manifest the same by grateful speech and due humility. He were a dog, else, and the heir and ancestor of dogs."

To my mind, the situation was uncomfortable. It might become more so. It might be a good idea to muster the hogs and move on. So I said:

"The day is wasting, Sandy. It is time to get the nobility together and be moving."

"Wherefore, fair sir and Boss?"

"We want to take them to their home, don't we?"

"La, but list to him! They be of all the regions of the earth! Each must hie to her own home; wend you we might do all these journeys in one so brief life as He hath appointed that created life, and thereto death likewise with help of Adam, who by sin done through persuasion of his helpmeet, she being wrought upon and bewrayed by the beguilements of the great enemy of man, that serpent hight Satan, aforetime consecrated and set apart unto that evil work by overmastering spite and envy begotten in his heart through fell ambitions that did blight and mildew a nature erst so white and pure when-so it hove with the shining multitudes its brethren-born in glade and shade of that fair heaven wherein all such as native be to that rich estate and—"

"Great Scott!"

"My lord?"

"Well, you know, we haven't got time for this sort of thing. Don't you see, we could distribute these people around the earth in less time than it is going to take you to explain that we can't. We mustn't talk now, we must act. You want to be careful; you mustn't let your mill get the start of you that way, at a time like this. To business, now—and sharp's the word. Who is to take the aristocracy home?"

"Even their friends. These will come for them from the far parts of the earth."

This was lightning from a clear sky, for unexpectedness; and the relief of it was like pardon to a prisoner. She would remain to deliver the goods, of course.

"Well, then, Sandy, as our enterprise is handsomely and successfully ended, I will go home and report; and if ever another one—"

"I also am ready; I will go with thee."

This was recalling the pardon.

"How? You will go with me? Why should you?"

"Will I be traitor to my knight, dost think? That were dishonor. I may not part from thee until in knightly encounter in the field some overmatching champion shall fairly win and fairly wear me. I were to blame an I thought that that might ever hap."

"Elected for the long term," I sighed to myself. "I may as well make the best of it." So then I spoke up and said:

"All right. Let us make a start."

While she was gone to cry her farewells over the pork, I gave that whole peerage away to the servants. And I asked them to take a duster and dust around a little where the nobilities had mainly lodged and promenaded, but they considered that that would hardly be worth while, and would moreover be a rather grave departure from custom, and therefore likely to make talk. A departure from custom—that settled it; it was a nation capable of committing any crime but that. The servants said they would follow the fashion, a fashion grown sacred through immemorial observance: they would scatter fresh rushes in all the rooms and halls, and then the evidences of the aristocratic visitation would be no longer visible. It was a kind of satire on Nature; it was the scientific method, the geologic method; it deposited the history of the family in a stratified record; and the antiquary could dig through it and tell by the remains of each period what changes of diet the family had introduced successively for a hundred years.

The first thing we struck that day was a procession of pilgrims. It was not going our way, but we joined it nevertheless; for it was hourly being borne in upon me, now, that if I would govern this country wisely, I must be posted in the details of its life, and not at second hand but by personal observation and scrutiny.

This company of pilgrims resembled Chaucer's in this: that it had in it a sample of about all the upper occupations and professions the country could show, and a corresponding variety of costume. There were young men and old men, young women and old women, lively folk and grave folk. They rode upon mules and horses, and there was not a side saddle in the party; for this specialty was to remain unknown in England for nine hundred years yet.

It was a pleasant, friendly, sociable herd; pious, happy, merry, and full of unconscious coarsenesses and innocent indecencies. What they regarded as the merry tale went the continual round and caused no more embarrassment than it would have caused in the best English society twelve centuries later. Practical jokes worthy of the English wits of the first quarter of the far-off nineteenth century were sprung here and there and yonder along the line, and compelled the delightedest applause; and sometimes when a bright remark was made at one end of the procession and started on its travels toward the other, you could note its progress all the way by the sparkling spray of laughter it threw off from its bows as it plowed along; and also by the blushes of the mules in its wake.

Sandy knew the goal and purpose of this pilgrimage, and she posted me. She said:

"They journey to the Valley of Holiness, for to be blest of the godly hermits and drink of the miraculous waters and be cleansed from sin."

"Where is this watering place?"

"It lieth a two day journey hence, by the borders of the land that hight the Cuckoo Kingdom."

"Tell me about it. Is it a celebrated place?"

"Oh, of a truth yes. There be none more so. Of old time there lived there an Abbot and his monks. Belike were none in the world more holy than these; for they gave themselves to study of pious books, and spoke not the one to the other, or indeed to any, and ate decayed herbs and naught thereto, and slept hard, and prayed much, and washed never; also they wore the same garment until it fell from their bodies through age and decay. Right-so came they to be known of all the world by reason of these holy austerities, and visited by rich and poor, and reverenced."

"Proceed."

"But always there was lack of water there. Whereso, upon a time, the holy Abbot prayed, and for answer a great stream of clear water burst forth by miracle in a desert place. Now were the fickle monks tempted of the fiend, and they wrought with their Abbot unceasingly by beggings and beseechings that he would construct a bath; and when he was become aweary and might not resist more, he said have ye your will, then, and granted that they asked. Now mark thou what 'tis to forsake the ways of purity the which He loveth, and wanton with such as be worldly and an offence. These monks did enter into the bath and come thence washed as white as snow; and lo, in that moment His sign appeared, in miraculous rebuke!—for His insulted waters ceased to flow, and utterly vanished away."

"They fared mildly, Sandy, considering how that kind of crime is regarded in this country."

"Belike; but it was their first sin; and they had been of perfect life for long, and differing in naught from the angels. Prayers, tears, torturings of the flesh, all was vain, to beguile that water to flow again. Even processions; even burnt offerings; even votive candles to the Virgin did fail, every each of them; and all in the land did marvel."

"How odd to find that even this industry has its financial panics, and at times sees its assignats and greenbacks languish to zero, and everything come to a standstill. Go on, Sandy."

"And so upon a time, after year and day, the good Abbot made humble surrender and destroyed the bath. And behold, His anger was in that moment appeased, and the waters gushed richly forth again, and even unto this day they have not ceased to flow in that generous measure."

"Then I take it nobody has washed since."

"He that would essay it could have his halter free; yea, and swiftly would he need it, too."

"The community has prospered since?"

"Even from that very day. The fame of the miracle went abroad into all lands. From every land came monks to join; they came even as the fishes come, in shoals; and the monastery added building to building, and yet others to these, and so spread wide its arms and took them in. And nuns came also; and more again, and yet more; and built over against the monastery on the yon side of the vale, and added building to building, until mighty was that nunnery. And these were friendly unto those, and they joined their loving labors together and together they built a fair great foundling asylum midway of the valley between."

"You spoke of some hermits, Sandy."

"These have gathered there from the ends of the earth. A hermit thriveth best where there be multitudes of pilgrims. Ye shall not find no hermit of no sort wanting. If any shall mention a hermit of a kind he thinketh new and not to be found but in some far strange land, let him but scratch among the holes and caves and swamps that line that Valley of Holiness, and whatsoever be his breed, it skills not, he shall find a sample of it there."

I closed up alongside of a burly fellow with a fat good-humored face, purposing to make myself agreeable and pick up some further crumbs of fact; but I had hardly more than scraped acquaintance with him when he began eagerly and awkwardly to lead up, in the immemorial way, to that same old anecdote—the one Sir Dinadan told me, what time I got into trouble with Sir Sagramour and was challenged of him on account of it. I excused myself, and dropped to the rear of the procession, sad at heart, willing to go hence from this troubled life, this vale of tears, this brief day of broken rest, of cloud and storm, of weary struggle and monotonous defeat; and yet shrinking from the change, as remembering how long eternity is, and how many have wended thither who know that anecdote.

Early in the afternoon we overtook another procession of pilgrims; but in this one was no merriment, no jokes, no laughter, no playful ways, nor any happy giddinesses, whether of youth or age. Yet both were here, both age and youth; gray old men and women, strong men and women of middle age, young husbands, young wives, little boys and girls, and three babes at the breast. Even the children were smileless; there was not a face among all these half a hundred people but was cast down, and bore that set expression of hopelessness which is bred of long and hard trials and old acquaintance with despair. They were slaves. Chains led from their fettered feet and their manacled hands to a sole-leather belt about their waists; and all except the children were also linked together in a file, six feet apart, by a single chain which led from collar to collar all down the line. They were on foot, and had tramped three hundred miles in eighteen days, upon the cheapest odds and ends of food, and stingy rations of that. They had slept in these chains every night, bundled together like swine. They had upon their bodies some poor rags, but they could not be said to be clothed. Their irons had chafed the skin from their ancles and made sores which were ulcerated and wormy. Their naked feet were torn, and none walked without a limp. Originally there had been a hundred of these unfortunates, but about half had been sold on the trip. The trader in charge of them rode a horse and carried a whip with a short handle and a long heavy lash divided into several knotted tails at the end. With this whip he cut the shoulders of any that tottered from weariness and pain, and straightened them up. He did not speak; the whip conveyed his desire without that. None of these poor creatures looked up as we rode along by; they showed no consciousness of our presence. And they made no sound but one; that was the dull and awful clank of their chains from end to end of the long file, as forty-three burdened feet rose and fell in unison. The file moved in a cloud, of its own making.

All these faces were gray with a coating of dust. One has seen the like of this coating upon furniture in unoccupied houses, and has written his idle thought in it with his finger. I was reminded of this when I noticed the faces of some of those women, young mothers carrying babes that were near to death and freedom, how a something in their hearts was written in the dust upon their faces, plain to see, and lord how plain to read! for it was the track of tears. One of these young mothers was but a girl, and it hurt me to the heart to read that writing, and reflect that it was come up out of the breast of such a child, a breast that ought not to know trouble yet, but only the gladness of the morning of life; and no doubt—

She reeled, just then, giddy with fatigue, and down came the lash and flicked a flake of skin from her naked shoulder. It stung me as if I had been hit instead. The master halted the file and jumped from his horse. He stormed and swore at this girl, and said she had made annoyance enough with her laziness, and as this was the last chance he should have, he would settle the account now. She dropped on her knees and put up her hands and began to beg and cry and implore, in a passion of terror, but the master gave no attention. He snatched the child from her, and then made the men slaves who were chained before and behind her throw her on the ground and hold her there and expose her body; and then he laid on with his lash like a madman till her back was flayed, she shrieking and struggling the while, piteously. One of the men who was holding her turned away his face; and for this humanity he was reviled and flogged.

All our pilgrims looked on and commented—on the expert way in which the whip was handled. They were too much hardened by life-long every-day familiarity with slavery to notice that there was anything else in the exhibition that invited comment. This was what slavery could do, in the way of ossifying what one may call the superior lobe of human feeling; for these pilgrims were kind hearted people, and they would not have allowed that man to treat a horse like that.

I wanted to stop the whole thing and set the slaves free, but that would not do. I must not interfere too much and get myself a name for riding over the country's laws and the citizens' rights roughshod. If I lived and prospered I would be the death of slavery, that I was resolved upon; but I would try to fix it so that when I became its executioner it should be by command of the nation.

Just here was the wayside shop of a smith; and now arrived a landed proprietor who had bought this girl a few miles back, deliverable here where her irons could be taken off. They were removed; then there was a squabble between the gentleman and the dealer as to which should pay the blacksmith. The moment the girl was delivered from her irons, she flung herself, all tears and frantic sobbings, into the arms of the slave who had turned away his face when she was whipped. He strained her to his breast, and smothered her face and the child's with kisses, and washed them with the rain of his tears. I suspected. I inquired. Yes, I was right: it was husband and wife. They had to be torn apart by force; the girl had to be dragged away, and she struggled and fought and shrieked like one gone mad till a turn of the road hid her from sight; and even after that, we could still make out the fading plaint of those receding shrieks. And the husband and father, with his wife and child gone, never to be seen by him again in life?—well, the look of him one might not bear at all, and so I turned away; but I knew I should never get his picture out of my mind again, and there it is to this day, to wring my heart-strings whenever I think of it.

We put up at the inn in a village just at nightfall, and when I rose next morning and looked abroad, I was ware where a knight came riding in the golden glory of the new day, and recognized him for knight of mine—Sir Ozana le Cure Hardy. He was in the gentlemen's furnishing line, and his missionarying specialty was plug hats. He was clothed all in steel, in the beautifulest armor of the time—up to where his helmet ought to have been; but he hadn't any helmet, he wore a shiny stove-pipe hat, and was as ridiculous a spectacle as one might want to see. It was another of my surreptitious schemes for extinguishing knighthood by making it grotesque and absurd. Sir Ozana's saddle was hung about with leather hat-boxes, and every time he overcame a wandering knight he swore him into my service, and fitted him with a plug and made him wear it. I dressed and ran down to welcome Sir Ozana and get his news.

"How is trade?" I asked.

"Ye will note that I have but these four left; yet were they sixteen whenas I gat me from Camelot."

"Why, you have certainly done nobly, Sir Ozana. Where have you been foraging of late?"

"I am but now come from the Valley of Holiness, please you sir."

"I am pointed for that place myself. Is there anything stirring in the monkery, more than common?"

"By the mass ye may not question it! . . . . . . Give him good feed, boy, and stint it not, an thou valuest thy crown; so get ye lightly to the stable and do even as I bid. . . . . . . Sir, it is parlous news I bring, and—be these pilgrims? Then ye may not do better, good folk, than gather and hear the tale I have to tell, sith it concerneth you, forasmuch as ye go to find that ye will not find, and seek that ye will seek in vain, my life being hostage for my word, and my word and message being these, namely: that a hap has happened whereof the like has not been seen no more but once this two hundred year, which was the first and last time that that said misfortune strake the holy valley in that form by commandment of the Most High, whereto by reasons just and causes thereunto contributing, wherein the matter—"

"The miraculous fount hath ceased to flow!" This shout burst from twenty pilgrim mouths at once.

"Ye say well, good people. I was verging to it, even when ye spoke."

"Has somebody been washing again?"

"Nay, it is suspected, but none believe it. It is thought to be some other sin, but none wit what."

"How are they feeling about the calamity?"

"None may describe it in words. The fount is these nine days dry. The prayers that did begin then, and the lamentations in sackcloth and ashes, and the holy processions, none of these have ceased nor night nor day; and so the monks and the nuns and the foundlings be all exhausted, and do hang up prayers writ upon parchment, sith that no strength is left in man to lift up voice. And at last they sent for thee, Sir Boss, to try magic and enchantment; and if you could not come, then was the messenger to fetch Merlin, and he is there these three days, now, and saith he will fetch that water though he burst the globe and wreck its kingdoms to accomplish it; and right bravely doth he work his magic and call upon his hellions to hie them hither and help, but not a whiff of moisture hath he started yet, even so much as might qualify as mist upon a copper mirror an ye count not the barrel of sweat he sweateth betwixt sun and sun over the dire labors of his task; and if ye—"

Breakfast was ready. As soon as it was over I showed to Sir

Ozana these words, which I had written on the inside of his hat: *"Chemical Department, Laboratory Extension, Section G, Pxxp. Send two of first size, two of No. 3, and six of No. 4, together with the proper complementary details—and two of my trained assistants."* And I said:

"Now get you to Camelot as fast as you can fly, brave knight, and show the writing to Clarence, and tell him to have these required matters in the Valley of Holiness with all possible dispatch."

"I will well, Sir Boss," and he was off.

Chapter 22

THE HOLY FOUNTAIN

THE PILGRIMS were human beings. Otherwise they would have acted differently. They had come a long and difficult journey, and now when the journey was nearly finished, and they learned that the main thing they had come for had ceased to exist, they didn't do as horses or cats or angleworms would probably have done—turn back and get at something profitable—no, anxious as they had before been to see the miraculous fountain, they were as much as forty times as anxious now to see the place where it had used to be. There is no accounting for human beings.

We made good time; and a couple of hours before sunset we stood upon the high confines of the Valley of Holiness and our eyes swept it from end to end and noted its features. That is, its large features. These were the three masses of buildings. They were distant and isolated temporalities shrunken to toy constructions in the lonely wastes of what seemed a desert—and was. Such a scene is always mournful, it is so impressively still, and looks so steeped in death. But there was a sound here which interrupted the stillness only to add to its mournfulness; this was the faint far sound of tolling bells which floated fitfully to us on the passing breeze, and so faintly, so softly, that we hardly knew whether we heard it with our ears or with our spirits.

We reached the monastery before dark, and there the males were given lodging, but the women were sent over to the nunnery. The bells were close at hand, now, and their solemn booming smote upon the ear like a message of doom. A superstitious despair possessed the heart of every monk and published itself in his ghastly face. Everywhere, these black-robed, soft-sandaled, tallow-visaged spectres appeared, flitted about, and disappeared, noiseless as the creatures of a troubled dream, and as uncanny.

The old Abbot's joy to see me was pathetic. Even to tears; but he did the shedding himself. He said:

"Delay not, son, but get to thy saving work. An we bring not the water back again, and soon, we are ruined, and the good work of two hundred years must end. And see thou do it with enchantments that be holy, for the Church will not endure that work in her cause be done by devil's magic."

"When I work, Father, be sure there will be no devil's work connected with it. I shall use no arts that come of the devil, and no elements not created by the hand of God. But is Merlin working strictly on pious lines?"

"Ah, he said he would, my son, he said he would, and took oath to make his promise good."

"Well, in that case, let him proceed."

"But surely you will not sit idle by, but help?"

"It will not answer to mix methods, Father; neither would it be professional courtesy. Two of a trade must not underbid each other. We might as well cut rates and be done with it; it would arrive at that in the end. Merlin has the contract; no other magician can touch it till he throws it up."

"But I will take it from him; it is a terrible emergency and the act is thereby justified. And if it were not so, who will give law to the Church? The Church giveth law to all; and what she wills to do, that she may do, hurt whom it may. I will take it from him; you shall begin upon the moment."

"It may not be, Father. No doubt, as you say, where power is supreme, one can do as one likes and suffer no injury; but we poor magicians are not so situated. Merlin is a very good magician in a small way, and has a quite neat provincial reputation. He is struggling along, doing the best he can, and it would not be etiquette for me to take his job until he himself abandons it."

The Abbot's face lighted.

"Ah, that is simple. There are ways to persuade him to abandon it."

"No-no, Father, it skills not, as these people say. If he were persuaded against his will, he would load that well with a malicious enchantment which would balk me until I found out its secret. It might take a month. I could set up a little enchantment of mine which I call the telephone, and he could not find out its secret in a hundred years. Yes, you perceive, he might block me for a month. Would you like to risk a month in a dry time like this?"

"A month! The mere thought of it maketh me to shudder. Have it thy way, my son. But my heart is heavy with this disappointment. Leave me, and let me wear my spirit with weariness and waiting, even as I have done these ten long days, counterfeiting thus the thing that is called rest, the prone body making outward sign of repose where inwardly is none."

Of course it would have been best, all round, for Merlin to waive etiquette, and quit and call it half a day, since he would never be able to start that water, for he was a true magician of the time: which is to say, the big miracles, the ones that gave him his reputation, always had the luck to be performed when nobody but Merlin was present; he couldn't start this well with all this crowd around to see; a crowd was as bad for a magician's miracle in that day as it was for a spiritualist's miracle in mine: there was sure to be some skeptic on hand to turn up the gas at the crucial moment and spoil everything. But I did not want Merlin to retire from the job until I was ready to take hold of it effectively myself; and I could not do that until I got my things from Camelot, and that would take two or three days.

My presence gave the monks hope, and cheered them up a good deal; insomuch that they ate a square meal that night for the first time in ten days. As soon as their stomachs had been properly reinforced with food, their spirits began to rise fast; when the mead began to go round, they rose faster. By the time everybody was half-seas over, the holy community was in good shape to make a night of it; so we stayed by the board and put it through on that line. Matters got to be very jolly. Good old questionable stories were told that made the tears run down and cavernous mouths stand wide and the round bellies shake with laughter; and questionable songs were bellowed out in a mighty chorus that drowned the boom of the tolling bells.

At last I ventured a story myself; and vast was the success of it. Not right off, of course, for the native of those islands does not as a rule dissolve upon the early applications of a humorous thing; but the fifth time I told it, they began to crack in places; the eighth time I told it, they began to crumble; at the twelfth repetition they fell apart in chunks; and at the fifteenth they disintegrated, and I got a broom and swept them up. This language is figurative. Those islanders—well, they are slow pay, at first, in the matter of return for your investment of effort, but in the end they make the pay of all other nations poor and small by contrast.

I was at the well next day betimes. Merlin was there, enchanting away like a beaver, but not raising the moisture. He was not in a pleasant humor; and every time I hinted that perhaps this contract was a shade too hefty for a novice he unlimbered his tongue and cursed like a bishop—French bishop of the Regency days, I mean.

Matters were about as I expected to find them. The "fountain" was an ordinary well, it had been dug in the ordinary way, and stoned up in the ordinary way. There was no miracle about it. Even the lie that had created its reputation was not miraculous; I could have told it myself, with one hand tied behind me. The well was in a dark chamber which stood in the centre of a cut stone chapel, whose walls were hung with pious pictures, of a workmanship that would have made a chromo feel good; pictures historically commemorative of curative miracles which had been achieved by the waters when nobody was looking. That is, nobody but angels: they are always on deck when there is a miracle to the fore—so as to get put in the picture, perhaps. Angels are as fond of that as a fire company; look at the old masters. The well-chamber was dimly lighted by lamps; the water was drawn with a windlass and chain, by monks, and poured into troughs which delivered it into stone reservoirs outside, in the chapel—when there was water to draw, I mean—and none but monks could enter the well-chamber. I entered it, for I had temporary authority to do so, by courtesy of my professional brother and subordinate. But he hadn't entered it himself. He did everything by incantations; he never worked his intellect. If he had stepped in there and used his eyes, instead of his disordered mind, he could have cured the well by natural means, and then turned it into a miracle in the customary way; but no, he was an old numskull; a magician who believed in his own magic; and no magician can thrive who is handicapped with a superstition like that.

I had an idea that the well had sprung a leak; that some of the wall stones near the bottom had fallen in and exposed fissures that allowed the water to escape. I measured the chain—98 feet. Then I called in a couple of monks, locked the door, took a candle, and made them lower me in the bucket. When the chain was all paid out, the candle confirmed my suspicion; a considerable section of the wall was gone, exposing a good big fissure.

I almost regretted that my theory about the well's trouble was correct, because I had another one that had a showy point or two about it for a miracle. I remembered that in America, many centuries later, when an oil well ceased to flow, they used to blast it out with a dynamite torpedo. If I should find this well dry, and no explanation of it, I could astonish these people most nobly by having a person of no especial value drop a dynamite bomb into it. It was my idea to appoint Merlin. However, it was plain that there was no occasion for the bomb. One cannot have everything the way he would like it. A man has no business to be depressed by a disappointment, anyway; he ought to make up his mind to get even. That is what I did. I said to myself, I am in no hurry, I can wait; that bomb will come good, yet. And it did, too.

When I was above ground again, I turned out the monks, and let down a fish-line: the well was a hundred and fifty feet deep, and there was forty-one feet of water in it! I called in a monk and asked:

"How deep is the well?"

"That, sir, I wit not, having never been told."

"How does the water usually stand in it?"

"Near to the top, these two centuries, as the testimony goeth, brought down to us through our predecessors."

It was true—as to recent times at least—for there was witness to it, and better witness than a monk: only about twenty or thirty feet of the chain showed wear and use, the rest of it was unworn and rusty. What had happened when the well gave out that other time? Without doubt some practical person had come along and mended the leak, and then had come up and told the Abbot he had discovered by divination that if the sinful bath were destroyed the well would flow again. The leak had befallen again, now, and these children would have prayed, and processioned, and tolled their bells for heavenly succor till they all dried up and blew away, and no innocent of them all would ever have thought to drop a fish-line into the well or go down in it and find out what was really the matter. Old habit of mind is one of the toughest things to get away from in the world. It transmits itself like physical form and feature; and for a man, in those days, to have had an idea that his ancestors hadn't had, would have brought him under suspicion of being illegitimate. I said to the monk:

"It is a difficult miracle to restore water in a dry well, but we will try, if my brother Merlin fails. Brother Merlin is a very passable artist, but only in the parlor-magic line, and he may not succeed; in fact is not likely to succeed. But that should be nothing to his discredit; the man that can do *this* kind of miracle knows enough to keep hotel."

"Hotel? I mind not to have heard—"

"Of hotel? It's what you call hostel. The man that can do this miracle can keep hostel. I can do this miracle; I shall do this miracle; yet I do not try to conceal from you that it is a miracle to tax the occult powers to the last strain."

"None knoweth that truth better than the brotherhood, indeed; for it is of record that aforetime it was parlous difficult, and took a year. Natheless, God send you good success, and to that end will we pray."

As a matter of business it was a good idea to get the notion around that the thing was difficult. Many a small thing has been made large by the right kind of advertising. That monk was filled up with the difficulty of this enterprise; he would fill up the others. In two days the solicitude would be booming.

On my way home at noon, I met Sandy. She had been sampling the hermits. I said:

"I would like to do that myself. This is Wednesday. Is there a matinée?"

"A which, please you sir?"

"Matinée. Do they keep open, afternoons?"

"Who?"

"The hermits, of course."

"Keep open?"

"Yes—keep open. Isn't that plain enough? Do they knock off at noon?"

"Knock off?"

"Knock off?—yes, knock off. What is the matter with knock off? I never saw such a dunderhead; can't you understand anything at all? In plain terms, do they shut up shop, draw the game, bank the fires—"

"Shut up shop, draw—"

"There, never mind, let it go; you make me tired. You can't seem to understand the simplest thing."

"I would I might please thee, sir, and it is to me dole and sorrow that I fail, albeit sith I am but a simple damsel and taught of none, being from the cradle unbaptized in those deep waters of learning that do anoint with a sovereignty him that partaketh of that most noble sacrament, investing him with reverend state to the mental eye of the humble mortal who, by bar and lack of that great consecration seeth in his own unlearned estate but a symbol of that other sort of lack and loss which men do publish to the pitying eye with sackcloth trappings whereon the ashes of grief do lie bepowdered and bestrewn, and so, when such shall in the darkness of his mind encounter these golden phrases of high mystery, these shut-up shops, and draw the game, and bank the fires, it is but by the grace of God that he burst not for envy of the mind that can beget, and tongue that can deliver so great and mellow-sounding miracles of speech, and if there do ensue confusion in that humbler mind, and failure to divine the meanings of these wonders, then if so be this miscomprehension is not vain but sooth and true, wit ye well it is the very substance of worshipful dear homage and may not lightly be misprized, nor had been, an ye had noted this complexion of my mood and mind and understood that that I would I could not, and that I could not I might not, nor yet nor might *nor* could, nor might-not nor could-not, might be by advantage turned to the desired *would*, and so I pray you mercy of my fault, and that ye will of your kindness and your charity forgive it, good my master and most dear lord."

I couldn't make it all out—that is, the details—but I got

the general idea; and enough of it, too, to be ashamed. It was not fair to spring those nineteenth-century technicalities upon the untutored infant of the sixth, and then rail at her because she couldn't get their drift; and when she was making the honest best drive at it she could, too, and no fault of hers that she couldn't fetch the home-plate; and so I apologized. Then we meandered pleasantly away toward the hermit-holes in sociable converse together, and better friends than ever.

I was gradually coming to have a mysterious and shuddery reverence for this girl; for nowadays, whenever she pulled out from the station and got her train fairly started on one of those horizonless trans-continental sentences of hers, it was borne in upon me that I was standing in the awful presence of the Mother of the German Language. I was so impressed with this, that sometimes when she began to empty one of these sentences on me I unconsciously took the very attitude of reverence, and stood uncovered; and if words had been water, I had been drowned, sure. She had exactly the German way: whatever was in her mind to be delivered, whether a mere remark, or a sermon, or a cyclopedia, or the history of a war, she would get it into a single sentence or die. Whenever the literary German dives into a sentence, that is the last you are going to see of him till he emerges on the other side of his Atlantic with his verb in his mouth.

We drifted from hermit to hermit all the afternoon. It was a most strange menagerie. The chief emulation among them seemed to be, to see which could manage to be the uncleanest, and most prosperous with vermin. Their manner and attitudes were the last expression of complacent self-righteousness. It was one anchorite's pride to lie naked in the mud and let the insects bite him and blister him unmolested; it was another's to lean against a rock, all day long, conspicuous to the admiration of the throng of pilgrims, and pray; it was another's to go naked, and crawl around on all fours; it was another's to drag about with him, year in and year out, eighty pounds of iron; it was another's to never lie down when he slept, but to stand among the thorn-bushes and snore when there were pilgrims around to look; a woman, who had the white hair of age, and no other apparel, was black from crown to heel with forty-seven years of holy abstinence from water. Groups of gazing pilgrims stood around all and every of these strange objects, lost in reverent wonder, and envious of the fleckless sanctity which these pious austerities had won for them from an exacting heaven.

By and by we went to see one of the supremely great ones. He was a mighty celebrity; his fame had penetrated all Christendom; the noble and the renowned journeyed from the remotest lands on the globe to pay him reverence. His stand was in the centre of the widest part of the valley; and it took all that space to hold his crowds.

His stand was a pillar sixty feet high, with a broad platform on the top of it. He was now doing what he had been doing every day for twenty years up there—bowing his body ceaselessly and rapidly almost to his feet. It was his way of praying. I timed him with a stopwatch, and he made 1244 revolutions in 24 minutes and 46 seconds. It seemed a pity to have all this power going to waste. It was one of the most useful motions in mechanics, the pedal-movement; so I made a note in my memorandum-book, purposing some day to apply a system of elastic cords to him and run a sewing machine with it. I afterwards carried out that scheme, and got five years' good service out of him; in which time he turned out upwards of eighteen thousand first-rate tow-linen shirts, which was ten a day. I worked him Sundays and all; he was going, Sundays, the same as week-days, and it was no use to waste the power. These shirts cost me nothing but just the mere trifle for the materials—I furnished those myself, it would not have been right to make him do that—and they sold like smoke to pilgrims at a dollar and a half apiece, which was the price of fifty cows or a blooded race-horse in Arthurdom. They were regarded as a perfect protection against sin, and advertised as such by my knights everywhere, with the paint-pot and stencil-plate; insomuch that there was not a cliff or a boulder or a dead-wall in England but you could read on it at a mile distance:

"Buy the Only Genuine St. Stylite; patronized by all the Nobility. Patent applied for."

There was more money in the business than one knew what to do with. As it extended, I brought out a line of goods suitable for kings, and a nobby thing for duchesses and that sort, with ruffles down the fore-hatch, and the running-gear clewed up with a feather-stitch to leeward, and then hauled aft with a backstay and triced up with a half-turn in the standing rigging forward of the weather gaskets. Yes, it was a daisy.

But about that time I noticed that the motive power had taken to standing on one leg, and I found that there was something the matter with the other one; so I stocked the business and unloaded, taking Sir Bors de Ganis into camp financially along with certain of his friends: for the works stopped within a year, and the good saint got him to his rest. But he had earned it. I can say that for him.

When I saw him that first time—however, his personal condition will not quite bear description here. You can read it in the Lives of the Saints.*

---

*All the details concerning the hermits, in this chapter, are from Lecky—but greatly modified. This book not being a history but only a tale, the majority of the historian's frank details were too strong for reproduction in it. —EDITOR.

Chapter 23

Restoration of the Fountain

S ATURDAY NOON I went to the well and looked on a while. Merlin was still burning smoke-powders, and pawing the air, and muttering gibberish as hard as ever, but looking pretty down-hearted, for of course he had not started even a perspiration in that well yet. Finally I said:

"How does the thing promise by this time, partner?"

"Behold, I am even now busied with trial of the powerfulest enchantment known to the princes of the occult arts in the lands of the East; an it fail me, naught can avail. Peace, until I finish."

He raised a smoke this time that darkened all the region, and must have made matters uncomfortable for the hermits, for the wind was their way, and it rolled down over their dens in a dense and billowy fog. He poured out volumes of speech to match, and contorted his body and sawed the air with his hands in a most extraordinary way. At the end of twenty minutes he dropped down panting, and about exhausted. Now arrived the Abbot and several hundred monks and nuns, and behind them a multitude of pilgrims and a couple of acres of foundlings, all drawn by the prodigious smoke, and all in a grand state of excitement. The Abbot inquired anxiously for results. Merlin said:

"If any labor of mortal might break the spell that binds these waters, this which I have but just essayed had done it. It has failed; whereby I do now know that that which I had feared is a truth established; the sign of this failure is, that the most potent spirit known to the magicians of the East, and whose name none may utter and live, has laid his spell upon this well. The mortal does not breathe, nor ever will, who can penetrate the secret of that spell, and without that secret none can break it. The water will flow no more forever, good Father. I have done what man could. Suffer me to go."

Of course this threw the Abbot into a good deal of a consternation. He turned to me with the signs of it in his face, and said:

"Ye have heard him. Is it true?"

"Part of it is."

"Not all, then, not all! What part is true?"

"That that spirit with the Russian name has put his spell upon the well."

"God's wownds, then are we ruined!"

"Possibly."

"But not certainly? Ye mean, not certainly?"

"That is it."

"Wherefore, ye also mean that when he saith none can break the spell—"

"Yes, when he says that, he says what isn't necessarily true. There are conditions under which an effort to break it may have some chance—that is, some small, some triffling chance—of success."

"The conditions—"

"Oh, they are nothing difficult. Only these; I want the well and the surroundings for the space of half a mile, entirely to myself from sunset to-day until I remove the ban—and nobody allowed to cross the ground but by my authority."

"Are these all?"

"Yes."

"And you have no fear to try?"

"Oh, none. One may fail, of course; and one may also succeed. One can try, and I am ready to chance it. I have my conditions?"

"These and all others ye may name. I will issue commandment to that effect."

"Wait," said Merlin, with an evil smile. "Ye wit that he that would break this spell must know that spirit's name?"

"Yes. I know his name."

"And wit you also that to know it skills not of itself, but ye must likewise pronounce it? Ha-ha! Knew ye that?"

"Yes, I knew that, too."

"You had that knowledge! Art a fool? Are ye minded to utter that name and die?"

"Utter it? Why certainly. I would utter it if it was Welsh."

"Ye are even a dead man, then; and I go to tell Arthur."

"That's all right. Take your gripsack and get along. The thing for you to do is to go home and work the weather, John W. Merlin."

It was a home shot, and it made him wince; for he was the worst weather-failure in the kingdom. Whenever he ordered up the danger-signals along the coast there was a week's dead calm, sure, and every time he prophesied fair weather it rained brickbats. But I kept him in the weather bureau right along, to undermine his reputation. However, that shot raised his bile, and instead of starting home to report my death, he said he would remain and enjoy it.

My two experts arrived in the evening, and pretty well fagged, for they had traveled double tides. They had pack-mules along, and had brought everything I needed—tools, pump, lead pipe, Greek fire, sheaves of big rockets, roman candles, colored-fire sprays, electric apparatus, and a lot of sundries—everything necessary for the stateliest kind of a miracle. They got their supper and a nap, and about midnight we sallied out through a solitude so wholly vacant and complete that it quite overpassed the required conditions. We took possession of the well and its surroundings. My boys were experts in all sorts of things, from the stoning up of a well to the constructing of a mathematical instrument. An hour before sunrise we had that leak mended in a ship-shape fashion, and the water began to rise. Then we stowed our fireworks in the chapel, locked up the place, and went home to bed.

Before the noon mass was over, we were at the well again; for there was a deal to do, yet, and I was determined to spring the miracle before midnight, for business reasons: for whereas a miracle worked for the Church on a week-day is worth a good deal, it is worth six times as much if you get it in on a Sunday. In nine hours the water had risen to its customary level; that is to say, it was within twenty-three feet of the top. We put in a little iron pump, one of the first turned out by my works near the capital; we bored into a stone reservoir which stood against the outer wall of the well-chamber, and inserted a section of lead pipe that was long enough to reach to the door of the chapel and project beyond the threshold, where the gushing water would be visible to the 250 acres of people I was intending should be present on the flat plain in front of this little holy hillock at the proper time.

We knocked the head out of an empty hogshead and hoisted this hogshead to the flat roof of the chapel, where we clamped it down fast, poured in gunpowder till it lay loosely an inch deep on the bottom, then we stood-up rockets in the hogshead as thick as they could loosely stand, all the different breeds of rockets there are; and they made a portly and imposing sheaf, I can tell you. We grounded the wire of a pocket electrical battery in that powder; we placed a noble magazine of Greek fire on each corner of the roof—blue on one corner, green on another, red on another, and purple on the last, and grounded a wire in each.

About two hundred yards off, in the flat, we built a pen of scantlings about four feet high, and laid planks on it, and so made a platform. We covered it with swell tapestries borrowed for the occasion, and topped it off with the Abbot's own throne. When you are going to do a miracle for an ignorant race, you want to get in every detail that will count; you want to make all the properties impressive to the public eye; you want to make matters comfortable for your head guest; then you can turn yourself loose and play your effects for all they are worth. I know the value of these things, for I know human nature. You can't throw too much style into a miracle. It costs trouble, and work, and sometimes money; but it pays in the end. Well, we brought the wires to the ground at the chapel, and then brought them under ground to the platform, and hid the batteries there. We put a rope fence a hundred feet square around the platform to keep off the common multitude, and that finished the work. My idea was, doors open at 10.30, performance to begin at 11.25 sharp. I wished I could charge admission, but of course that wouldn't answer. I instructed my boys to be in the chapel as early as 10, before anybody was around, and be ready to man the pump at the proper time, and make the fur fly. Then we went home to supper.

The news of the disaster to the well had traveled far, by this time; and now for two or three days a steady avalanche of people had been pouring into the valley. The lower end of the valley was become one huge camp; we should have a good house, no question about that. Criers went the rounds early in the evening and announced the coming attempt, which put every pulse up to fever heat. They gave notice that the Abbot and his official suite would move in state and occupy the platform at 10.30, up to which time all the region which was under my ban must be clear; the bells would then cease from tolling, and this sign should be permission to the multitude to close in and take their places.

I was at the platform and all ready to do the honors when the Abbot's solemn procession hove in sight—which it did not do till it was nearly to the rope fence, because it was a starless black night and no torches permitted. With it came Merlin, and took a front seat on the platform; he was as good as his word, for once. One could not see the multitudes banked together beyond the ban, but they were there, just the same. The moment the bells stopped, those banked masses broke and poured over the line like a vast black wave, and for as much as a half hour it continued to flow, and then it solidified itself, and you could have walked upon a pavement of human heads to—well, miles.

We had a solemn stage-wait, now, for about twenty minutes—a thing I had counted on for effect; it is always good to let your audience have a chance to work up its expectancy. At length, out of the silence a noble Latin chant—men's voices—broke, and swelled up and rolled away into the night, a majestic tide of melody. I had put that up, too, and it was one of the best effects I ever invented. When it was finished I stood up on the platform, and extended my hands abroad for two minutes, with my face uplifted—that always produces a dead hush—and then slowly pronounced this ghastly word, with a kind of awfulness which caused hundreds to tremble, and many women to faint:

"𝕮onstantinopolitanischerdudelsackspfeifenmachersgesellschafft!"

Just as I was moaning out the closing hunks of that word, I touched off one of my electric connections, and all that murky world of people stood revealed in a hideous blue glare! It was immense—that effect! Lots of people shrieked, women curled up and quit in every direction, foundlings collapsed by platoons. The Abbot and the monks crossed themselves nimbly and their lips fluttered with agitated prayers. Merlin held his grip, but he was astonished, clear down to his corns; he had never seen anything to begin with that, before. Now was the time to pile in the effects. I lifted my hands and groaned out this word—as it were, in agony—

"Nihilistendynamittheaterkaestchenssprengungsattentaetsversuchungen!"

—and turned on the red fire! You should have heard that Atlantic of people moan and howl when that crimson hell joined the blue! After sixty seconds I shouted—

"Transvaaltruppentropentransporttrampelthiertreibertrauungsthraenentragoedie!"

—and lit up the green fire! After waiting only forty seconds, this time, I spread my arms abroad and thundered out the devastating syllables of this word of words—

"Mekkamuselmannenmassenmenchenmoerdermohrenmuttermarmormonumentenmacher!"

—and whirled on the purple glare! There they were, all going at once, red, blue, green, purple!—four furious volcanoes pouring vast clouds of radiant smoke aloft, and spreading a blinding rainbowed noonday to the furthest confines of that valley. In the distance one could see that fellow on the pillar standing rigid against the background of sky, his see-saw stopped for the first time in twenty years. I knew the boys were at the pump, now, and ready. So I said to the Abbot:

"The time is come, Father. I am about to pronounce the dread name and command the spell to dissolve. You want to brace up, and take hold of something." Then I shouted to the people: "Behold, in another minute the spell will be broken, or no mortal can break it. If it break, all will know it, for you will see the sacred water gush from the chapel door!" I stood a few moments, to let the hearers have a chance to spread my announcement to those who couldn't hear, and so convey it to the furthest ranks, then I made a grand exhibition of extra posturing and gesturing, and shouted:

"Lo, I command the fell spirit that possesses the holy fountain to now disgorge into the skies all the infernal fires that still remain in him, and straightway dissolve his spell and flee hence to the pit, there to lie bound a thousand years. By his own dread name I command it—BGWJJILLIGKKK!"

Then I touched off the hogshead of rockets, and a vast fountain of dazzling lances of fire vomited itself toward the zenith with a hissing rush, and burst in mid-sky into a storm of flashing jewels! One mighty groan of terror started up from the massed people—then suddenly broke into a wild hosannah of joy—for there, fair and plain in the uncanny glare, they saw the freed water leaping forth! The old Abbot could not speak a word, for tears and the chokings in his throat; without utterance of any sort, he folded me in his arms and mashed me. It was more eloquent than speech. And harder to get over, too, in a country where there were really no doctors that were worth a damaged nickel.

You should have seen those acres of people throw themselves down in that water and kiss it; kiss it, and pet it, and fondle it, and talk to it as if it were alive, and welcome it back with the dear names they gave their darlings, just as if it had been a friend who was long gone away and lost, and was come home again. Yes, it was pretty to see, and made me think more of them than I had done before.

I sent Merlin home on a shutter. He had caved in and gone down like a landslide when I pronounced that fearful name, and had never come to since. He never had heard that name before,—neither had I—but to him it was the right one; any jumble would have been the right one. He admitted, afterward, that that spirit's own mother could not have pronounced that name better than I did. He never could understand how I survived it, and I didn't tell him. It is only young magicians that give away a secret like that. Merlin spent three months working enchantments to try to find out the deep trick of how to pronounce that name and outlive it. But he didn't arrive.

When I started to the chapel, the populace uncovered and fell back reverently to make a wide way for me, as if I had been some kind of a superior being—and I was. I was aware of that. I took along a night-shift of monks, and taught them the mystery of the pump, and set them to work, for it was plain that a good part of the people out there were going to sit up with the water all night, consequently it was but right that they should have all they wanted of it. To those monks, that pump was a good deal of a miracle itself, and they were full of wonder over it; and of admiration, too, of the exceeding effectiveness of its performance.

It was a great night, an immense night. There was reputation in it. I could hardly get to sleep for glorying over it.

Chapter 24

A Rival Magician

M Y INFLUENCE in the Valley of Holiness was something prodigious, now. It seemed worthwhile to try to turn it to some valuable account. The thought came to me the next morning, and was suggested by my seeing one of my knights who was in the soap line come riding in. According to history, the monks of this place two centuries before, had been worldly minded enough to want to wash. It might be that there was a leaven of this unrighteousness still remaining. So I sounded a Brother:

"Wouldn't you like a bath?"

He shuddered at the thought—the thought of the peril of it to the well—but he said with feeling:

"One needs not to ask that of a poor body who has not known that blessed refreshment sith that he was a boy. Would God I might wash me! but it may not be, fair sir, tempt me not; it is forbidden."

And then he sighed in such a sorrowful way that I was resolved he should have at least one layer of his real estate removed, if it sized up my whole influence and bankrupted the pile. So I went to the Abbot and asked for a permit for this Brother. He blenched at the idea—I don't mean that you could see him blench, for of course you couldn't see it without you scraped him, and I didn't care enough about it to scrape him, but I knew the blench was there, just the same, and within a book-cover's thickness of the surface, too—blenched and trembled. He said:

"Ah, son, ask aught else thou wilt, and it is thine, and freely granted out of a grateful heart—but this, oh, this! Would you drive away the blessed water again?"

"No, Father, I will not drive it away. I have mysterious knowledge which teaches me that there was an error that other time when it was thought the instituting of the bath banished the fountain." A large interest began to show up in the old man's face. "My knowledge informs me that the bath

375

was innocent of that misfortune, which was caused by quite another sort of sin."

"These are brave words—but—but right welcome, if they be true."

"They are true, indeed. Let me build the bath again, Father. Let me build it again, and the fountain shall flow forever."

"You promise this?—you promise it? Say the word—say you promise it!"

"I do promise it."

"Then will I have the first bath myself! Go—get ye to your work. Tarry not, tarry not, but go."

I and my boys were at work, straight off. The ruins of the old bath were there yet, in the basement of the monastery, not a stone missing. They had been left just so, all these life-times, and avoided with a pious fear, as things accursed. In two days we had it all done and the water in—a spacious pool of clear pure water that a body could swim in. It was running water, too. It came in, and went out, through the ancient pipes. The old Abbot kept his word and was the first to try it. He went down black and shaky, leaving the whole black community above troubled and worried and full of bod-ings; but he came back white and joyful, and the game was made! another triumph scored.

It was a good campaign that we made in that Valley of Holiness, and I was very well satisfied, and ready to move on, now, but I struck a disappointment. I caught a heavy cold, and it started up an old lurking rheumatism of mine. Of course the rheumatism hunted up my weakest place and lo-cated itself there. This was the place where the Abbot put his arms about me and mashed me, what time he was moved to testify his gratitude to me with an embrace.

When at last I got out, I was a shadow. But everybody was full of attentions and kindnesses, and these brought cheer back into my life and were the right medicine to help a con-valescent swiftly up toward health and strength again; so I gained fast.

Sandy was worn out with nursing, so I made up my mind to turn out and go a cruise alone, leaving her at the nunnery to rest up. My idea was to disguise myself as a freeman of peasant degree and wander through the country a week or two on foot. This would give me a chance to eat and lodge with the lowliest and poorest class of free citizens on equal terms. There was no other way to inform myself perfectly of their every-day life and the operation of the laws upon it. If I went among them as a gentleman, there would be restraints and conventionalities which would shut me out from their private joys and troubles, and I should get no further than the shell.

One morning I was out on a long walk to get up muscle for my trip and had climbed the ridge which bordered the northern extremity of the valley, when I came upon an artificial opening in the face of a low precipice, and recognized it by its location as a hermitage which had often been pointed out to me from a distance, as the den of a hermit of high renown for dirt and austerity. I knew he had lately been offered a situation in the Great Sahara, where lions and sandflies made the hermit life peculiarly attractive and difficult, and had gone to Africa to take possession, so I thought I would look in and see how the atmosphere of this den agreed with its reputation.

My surprise was great: the place was newly swept and scoured. Then there was another surprise. Back in the gloom of the cavern I heard the clink of a little bell, and then this exclamation:

"HELLO, CENTRAL! *Is this you, Camelot?* - - - Behold, thou mayst glad thy heart, an thou hast faith to believe the wonderful when that it cometh in unexpected guise and maketh itself manifest in impossible places—here standeth in the flesh his mightiness The Boss, and with thine own ears shall ye hear him speak!"

Now what a radical reversal of things this was; what a jumbling together of extravagant incongruities; what a fantastic conjunction of opposites and irreconcileables—the home of the bogus miracle become the home of a real one, the den of a medieval hermit turned into a telephone office!

The telephone clerk stepped into the light, and I recognized one of my young fellows. I said:

"How long has this office been established here, Ulfius?"

"But since midnight, fair Sir Boss, an it please you. We saw many lights in the valley, and so judged it well to make a station, for that where so many lights be, needs must they indicate a town of goodly size."

"Quite right. It isn't a town, in the customary sense, but it's a good stand, anyway. Do you know where you are?"

"Of that have I had no time to make inquiry; for whenas my comradeship moved hence upon their labors, leaving me in charge, I got me to needed rest, purposing to inquire when I waked, and report the place's name to Camelot for record."

"Well, this is the Valley of Holiness."

It didn't take; I mean, he didn't start at the name, as I had supposed he would. He merely said—

"I will so report it."

"Why, the surrounding regions are filled with the noise of late wonders that have happened here! You didn't hear of them?"

"Ah, ye will remember, we move by night, and avoid speech with all. We learn naught but that we get by telephone, from Camelot."

"Why *they* know all about this thing. Haven't they told you anything about the great miracle of the restoration of a holy fountain?"

"Oh, *that*? Indeed yes. But the name of *this* valley doth woundily differ from the name of *that* one; indeed to differ wider were not pos—"

"What was that name, then?"

"The Valley of Hellishness."

"*That* explains it. Confound a telephone, anyway. It is the very demon for conveying similarities of sound that are miracles of divergence from similarity of sense. But no matter, you know the name of the place now. Call up Camelot."

He did it, and had Clarence sent for. It was good to hear my boy's voice again. It was like being home. After some affectionate interchanges, and some account of my late illness, I said:

"What is new?"

"The king and queen and many of the court do start even in this hour, to go to your valley to pay pious homage to the waters ye have restored and cleanse themselves of sin, and see the place where the infernal spirit spouted true hell-flames to the clouds—an ye listen sharply ye may hear me wink and hear me likewise smile a smile, sith 'twas I that made selection of those flames from out our stock and sent them by your order."

"Does the king know the way to this place?"

"The king?—no, nor to any other in his realms, mayhap; but the lads that holp you with your miracle will be his guide and lead the way, and appoint the places for rests at noons, and sleeps at night."

"This will bring them here—when?"

"Mid-afternoon, or later, the third day."

"Anything else in the way of news?"

"The king hath begun the raising of the standing army ye suggested to him; one regiment is complete and officered."

"The mischief! I wanted a main hand in that, myself. There is only one body of men in the kingdom that are fitted to officer a regular army."

"Yes—and now ye will marvel to know there's not so much as one West Pointer in that regiment."

"What are you talking about? Are you in earnest?"

"It is truly as I have said."

"Why, this makes me uneasy. Who were chosen, and what was the method? Competitive examination?"

"Indeed I know naught of the method. I but know this— these officers be all of noble family, and are born—what is it you call it?—chuckleheads."

"There's something wrong, Clarence."

"Comfort yourself, then; for two candidates for a lieuten-ancy do travel hence with the king—young nobles both— and if you but wait where you are you will hear them questioned."

"That is news to the purpose. I will get one West Pointer in, anyway. Mount a man and send him to that school with a message; let him kill horses, if necessary, but he must be there before sunset to-night and say—"

"There is no need. I have laid a ground wire to the school. Prithee let me connect you with it."

It sounded good! In this atmosphere of telephones and lightning communication with distant regions, I was breath-ing the breath of life again after long suffocation. I realized, then, what a creepy, dull, inanimate horror this land had been to me all these years, and how I had been in such a stifled condition of mind as to have grown used to it almost beyond the power to notice it.

I gave my order to the superintendent of the Academy personally. I also asked him to bring me some paper and a fountain pen, and a box or so of safety matches. I was getting tired of doing without these conveniences. I could have them, now, as I wasn't going to wear armor any more at present, and therefore could get at my pockets.

When I got back to the monastery, I found a thing of interest going on. The Abbot and his monks were assembled in the great hall, observing with childish wonder and faith the performances of a new magician, a fresh arrival. His dress was the extreme of the fantastic; as showy and foolish as the sort of thing an Indian medicine-man wears. He was mowing, and mumbling, and gesticulating, and drawing mystical figures in the air and on the floor,—the regular thing, you know. He was a celebrity from Asia—so he said, and that was enough. That sort of evidence was as good as gold, and passed current everywhere.

How easy and cheap it was, to be a great magician on this fellow's terms. His specialty was to tell you what any individual on the face of the globe was doing at the moment; and what he had done at any time in the past, and what he would do at any time in the future. He asked if any would like to know what the Emperor of the East was doing now? The sparkling eyes and the delighted rubbing of hands made eloquent answer—this reverend crowd *would* like to know what that monarch was at, just at this moment. The fraud went through some more mummery, and then made grave announcement:

"The high and mighty Emperor of the East doth at this moment put money in the palm of a holy begging friar—one, two, three pieces, and they be all of silver."

A buzz of admiring exclamations broke out, all around:

"It is marvelous!" "Wonderful!" "What study, what labor, to have acquired a so amazing power as this!"

Would they like to know what the Supreme Lord of Inde was doing? Yes. He told them what the Supreme Lord of

Inde was doing. Then he told them what the Sultan of Egypt was at; also what the King of the Remote Seas was about. And so-on and so-on; and with each new marvel the astonishment at his accuracy rose higher and higher. They thought he must surely strike an uncertain place some time; but no, he never had to hesitate, he always knew, and always with unerring precision. I saw that if this thing went on I should lose my supremacy, this fellow would capture my following, I should be left out in the cold. I must put a cog in his wheel, and do it right away, too. I said:

"If I might ask, I should very greatly like to know what a certain person is doing."

"Speak, and freely. I will tell you."

"It will be difficult—perhaps impossible."

"My art knoweth not that word. The more difficult it is, the more certainly will I reveal it to you."

You see, I was working up the interest. It was getting pretty high, too; you could see that by the craning necks all around, and the half-suspended breathing. So now I climaxed it:

"If you make no mistake—if you tell me truly what I want to know—I will give you two hundred silver pennies."

"The fortune is mine! I will tell you what you would know."

"Then tell me what I am doing with my right hand."

"Ah-h!" There was a general gasp of surprise. It had not occurred to anybody in the crowd—that simple trick of inquiring about somebody who wasn't ten thousand miles away. The magician was hit hard; it was an emergency that had never happened in his experience before, and it corked him; he didn't know how to meet it. He looked stunned, confused; he couldn't say a word. "Come," I said, "what are you waiting for? Is it possible you can answer up, right off, and tell what anybody on the other side of the earth is doing, and yet can't tell what a person is doing who isn't three yards from you? Persons behind me know what I am doing with my right hand—they will endorse you if you tell correctly." He was still dumb. "Very well, I'll tell you why you don't speak up and tell; it is because you don't know. *You* a magician! Good friends, this tramp is a mere fraud and liar."

This distressed the monks, and terrified them. They were not used to hearing these awful beings called names, and they did not know what might be the consequence. There was a dead silence, now; superstitious bodings were in every mind. The magician began to pull his wits together, and when he presently smiled an easy, nonchalant smile, it spread a mighty relief around; for it indicated that his mood was not destructive. He said:

"It hath struck me speechless, the frivolity of this person's speech. Let all know, if perchance there be any who know it not, that enchanters of my degree deign not to concern themselves with the doings of any but kings, princes, emperors, them that be born in the purple, and them only. Had ye asked me what Arthur the great king is doing it were another matter, and I had told ye; but the doings of a subject interest me not."

"Oh, I misunderstood you. I thought you said 'anybody,' and so I supposed 'anybody' included—well, anybody; that is, everybody."

"It doth—anybody that is of lofty birth; and the better if he be royal."

"That, it meseemeth, might well be," said the Abbot, who saw his opportunity to smooth things and avert disaster, "for it were not likely that so wonderful a gift as this would be conferred for the revelation of the concerns of lesser beings than such as be born near to the summits of greatness. Our Arthur the king—"

"Would you know of him?" broke in the enchanter.

"Most gladly, yea and gratefully."

Everybody was full of awe and interest again, right away, the incorrigible idiots. They watched the incantations absorbingly, and looked at me with a "There, now, what can you say to that?" air, when the announcement came:

"The king is weary with the chase, and lieth in his palace these two hours sleeping a dreamless sleep."

"God's benison upon him!" said the Abbot and crossed himself; "may that sleep be to the refreshment of his body and his soul."

"And so it might be, if he were sleeping," I said, "but the king is not sleeping, the king rides."

Here was trouble again—a conflict of authority. Nobody knew which of us to believe; I still had some reputation left. The magician's scorn was stirred, and he said:

"Lo, I have seen many wonderful soothsayers and prophets and magicians in my life-days, but none before that could sit idle and see to the heart of things with never an incantation to help."

"You have lived in the woods, and lost much by it. I use incantations myself, as this good brotherhood are aware— but only on occasions of moment."

When it comes to sarcasming, I reckon I know how to keep my end up. That jab made this fellow squirm. The Abbot inquired after the queen and the court, and got this information:

"They be all on sleep, being overcome by fatigue, like as to the king."

I said:

"That is merely another lie. Half of them are about their amusements, the queen and the other half are not sleeping, they ride. Now perhaps you can spread yourself a little, and tell us where the king and queen and all that are this moment riding with them are going?"

"They sleep now, as I said; but on the morrow they will ride, for they go a journey toward the sea."

"And where will they be day after to-morrow at vespers?"

"Far to the north of Camelot, and half their journey will be done."

"That is another lie, by the space of a hundred and fifty miles. Their journey will not be merely half done, it will be all done, and they will be *here*, in this valley."

That was a noble shot! It set the Abbot and the monks in a whirl of excitement, and it rocked the enchanter to his base. I followed the thing right up:

"If the king does not arrive, I will have myself ridden on a rail; if he does I will ride you on a rail instead."

Next day I went up to the telephone office and found that the king had passed through two towns that were on the line. I spotted his progress on the succeeding day in the same way. I kept these matters to myself. The third day's reports showed that if he kept up his gait he would arrive by four in the afternoon. There was still no sign anywhere of interest in his coming; there seemed to be no preparations making to receive him in state, a strange thing, truly. Only one thing could explain this: that other magician had been cutting under me, sure. This was true. I asked a friend of mine, a monk, about it, and he said, yes, the magician had tried some further enchantments, and found out that the court had concluded to make no journey at all, but stay at home. Think of that! Observe how much a reputation was worth in such a country. These people had seen me do the very showiest bit of magic in history, and the only one within their memory that had a positive value, and yet here they were, ready to take up with an adventurer who could offer no evidence of his powers but his mere unproven word.

However, it was not good politics to let the king come without any fuss and feathers at all, so I went down and drummed up a procession of pilgrims and smoked out a batch of hermits and started them out at two o'clock to meet him. And that was the sort of state he arrived in. The Abbot was helpless with rage and humiliation when I brought him out on a balcony and showed him the head of the state marching in and never a monk on hand to offer him welcome, and no stir of life or clang of joy-bell to glad his spirit. He took one look and then flew to rouse out his forces. The next minute the bells were dinning furiously, and the various buildings were vomiting monks and nuns, who went swarming in a rush toward the coming procession; and with them went that magician—and he was on a rail, too, by the Abbot's order; and his reputation was in the mud, and mine was in the sky again. Yes, a man can keep his trade-mark current in such a country, but he can't sit around and do it; he has got to be on deck and attending to business, right along.

Chapter 25

A Competitive Examination

W HEN THE KING traveled, for change of air, or made a
progress, or visited a distant noble whom he wished to
bankrupt with the cost of his keep, part of the administration
moved with him. It was a fashion of the time. The Commission charged with the examination of candidates for posts in
the army came with the king to the valley, whereas they could
have transacted their business just as well at home. And although this expedition was strictly a holiday excursion for the
king, he kept some of his business functions going, just the
same. He touched for the evil as usual; he held court in
the gate at sunrise and tried causes, for he was himself Chief
Justice of the King's Bench.

He shone very well in this latter office. He was a wise and
humane judge, and he clearly did his honest best and fairest,
—according to his lights. Yes, according to his lights. That is
a large reservation. His lights—I mean his rearing—often
colored his decisions. Whenever there was a dispute between
a noble or gentleman, and a person of lower degree, the
king's leanings and sympathies were for the former class always, whether he suspected it or not. It was impossible that
this should be otherwise. The blunting effects of slavery upon
the slaveholder's moral perceptions are known and conceded,
the world over, and a privileged class, an aristocracy, is but a
band of slaveholders under another name. This has a harsh
sound, and yet should not be offensive to any—to even the
noble himself—unless the fact itself be an offence: for the
statement simply formulates a fact. The repulsive feature of
slavery is the *thing*, not its name. One needs but to hear an
aristocrat speak of the classes that are below him to recognize—and in but indifferently modified measure—the very
air and tone of the actual slaveholder; and behind these are
the slaveholder's spirit, the slaveholder's blunted feeling.
They are the result of the same cause, in both cases: the
possessor's old and inbred custom of regarding himself as a

superior being. The king's judgments wrought frequent injustices, but it was merely the fault of his training, his natural and unalterable sympathies. He was as unfitted for a judgeship as would be the average mother for the position of milk-distributor to starving children in famine-time; her own children would fare a shade better than the rest.

One very curious case came before the king. A young girl, an orphan, who had a considerable estate, married a fine young fellow who had nothing. The girl's property was within a seignory held by the Church. The bishop of the diocese, an arrogant scion of the great nobility, claimed the girl's estate, on the ground that she had married privately, and thus had cheated the Church out of one of its rights as lord of the seignory—the one heretofore referred to as *le droit du Seigneur*. The penalty of refusal or avoidance was confiscation. The girl's defence was, that the lordship of the seignory was vested in the bishop, and the particular right here involved was not transferable, but must be exercised by the lord himself or stand vacated; and that an older law, of the Church itself, strictly barred the bishop from exercising it. It was a very odd case, indeed.

It reminded me of something I had read in my youth about the ingenious way in which the Aldermen of London raised the money that built the Mansion House. A person who had not taken the Sacrament according to the Anglican rite, could not stand as a candidate for sheriff of London. Thus Dissenters were ineligible; they could not run if asked, they could not serve if elected. The Aldermen, who without any question were Yankees in disguise, hit upon this neat device: they passed a bye-law imposing a fine of £400 upon any one who should refuse to be a candidate for sheriff, and a fine of £600 upon any person who, after being elected sheriff, refused to serve. Then they went to work and elected a lot of Dissenters, one after another; and kept it up until they had collected £15,000 in fines; and there stands the stately Mansion House to this day, to keep the blushing citizen in mind of a long past and lamented day when a band of Yankees slipped into London and played games of the sort that has given their race a unique and shady reputation among all truly good and holy peoples that be in the earth.

The girl's case seemed strong, to me; the bishop's case was just as strong. I did not see how the king was going to get out of this hole. But he got out. I append his decision:

"Truly I find small difficulty here, the matter being even a child's affair for simpleness. An the young bride had conveyed notice, as in duty bound, to her feudal lord and proper master and protector the bishop, she had suffered no loss, for the said bishop could have got a dispensation making him, for temporary conveniency, eligible to the exercise of his said right, and thus would she have kept all she had. Whereas, failing in her first duty, she hath by that failure failed in all; for whoso, clinging to a rope, severeth it above his hands, must fall; it being no defence to claim that the rest of the rope is sound, neither any deliverance from his peril, as he shall find. Pardy, the woman's case is rotten at the source. It is the decree of the court that she forfeit to the said lord bishop all her goods, even to the last farthing that she doth possess, and be thereto mulcted in the costs. Next!"

Here was a tragic end to a beautiful honeymoon not yet three months old. Poor young creatures! They had lived these three months lapped to the lips in worldly comforts. These clothes and trinkets they were wearing were as fine and dainty as the shrewdest stretch of the sumptuary laws allowed to people of their degree; and in these pretty clothes, she crying on his shoulder, and he trying to comfort her with hopeful words set to the music of despair, they went from the judgment seat out into the world homeless, bedless, breadless; why, the very beggars by the roadsides were not so poor as they.

Well, the king was out of the hole; and on terms satisfactory to the Church and the rest of the aristocracy, no doubt. Men write many fine and plausible arguments in support of monarchy, but the fact remains that where every man in a State has a vote, brutal laws are impossible. Arthur's people were of course poor material for a republic, because they had been debased so long by monarchy; and yet even they would have been intelligent enough to make short work of that law which the king had just been administering if it had been submitted to their full and free vote. There is a phrase which has grown so common in the world's mouth that it has come to seem to have sense and meaning—the sense and meaning implied when it is used: that is the phrase which refers to this or that or the other nation as possibly being "capable of self-government;" and the implied sense of it is, that there has been a nation somewhere, some time or other, which *wasn't* capable of it—wasn't as able to govern itself as some self-appointed specialists were or would be to govern it. The master minds of all nations, in all ages, have sprung, in affluent multitude, from the mass of the nation, and from the mass of the nation only—not from its privileged classes; and so, no matter what the nation's intellectual grade was, whether high or low, the bulk of its ability was in the long ranks of its nameless and its poor, and so it never saw the day that it had not the material in abundance whereby to govern itself. Which is to assert an always self-proven fact: that even the best governed and most free and most enlightened monarchy is still behind the best condition attainable by its people; and that the same is true of kindred governments of lower grades, all the way down to the lowest.

King Arthur had hurried up the army business altogether beyond my calculations. I had not supposed he would move in the matter while I was away; and so I had not mapped out a scheme for determining the merits of officers; I had only remarked that it would be wise to submit every candidate to a sharp and searching examination; and privately I meant to put together a list of military qualifications that nobody could answer to but my West Pointers. That ought to have been attended to before I left; for the king was so taken with the idea of a standing army that he couldn't wait, but must get about it at once, and get up as good a scheme of examination as he could invent out of his own head.

I was impatient to see what this was; and to show, too, how much more admirable was the one which I should display to the Examining Board. I intimated this, gently, to the king, and it fired his curiosity. When the Board was assembled, I followed him in, and behind us came the candidates. One of these candidates was a bright young West Pointer of mine, and with him were a couple of my West Point professors.

When I saw the Board, I did not know whether to cry or to laugh. The head of it was the officer known to later centuries as Norroy King-at-Arms! The two other members were chiefs of bureaux in his department; and all three were priests, of course; all officials who had to know how to read and write were priests.

My candidate was called first, out of courtesy to me, and the head of the Board opened on him, with official solemnity:

"Name?"

"Mal-ease."

"Son of?"

"Webster."

"Webster—Webster. Hm—I—my memory faileth to recal the name. Condition?"

"Weaver."

"Weaver!—God keep us!"

The king was staggered, from his summit to his foundations; one clerk fainted, and the others came near it. The Chairman pulled himself together, and said indignantly:

"It is sufficient. Get you hence."

But I appealed to the king. I begged that my candidate might be examined. The king was willing, but the Board, who were all well-born folk, implored the king to spare them the indignity of examining the weaver's son. I knew they didn't know enough to examine him anyway, so I joined my prayers to theirs, and the king turned the duty over to my professors. I had had a blackboard prepared, and it was put up, now, and the circus began. It was beautiful to hear the lad lay out the science of war, and wallow in details of battle and siege, of supply, transportation, mining and countermining, grand tactics, big strategy and little strategy, signal service, infantry, cavalry, artillery, and all about siege guns, field guns, gatling guns, rifled guns, smooth bores, musket practice, revolver practice—and not a solitary word of it all could these catfish make head or tail of, you understand—and it was handsome to see him chalk off mathematical nightmares on the blackboard that would stump the angels themselves, and do it like nothing, too—all about eclipses, and comets, and solstices, and constellations, and mean time, and sidereal time, and dinner time, and bedtime, and every other imaginable thing above the clouds or under them that you could harry or bullyrag an enemy with and make him wish he hadn't come — and when the boy made his military salute and stood aside at last, I was proud enough to hug him, and all those other people were so dazed they looked partly petrified, partly drunk, and wholly caught out and snowed under. I judged that the cake was ours, and by a large majority.

Education is a great thing. This was the same youth who had come to West Point so ignorant that when I asked him, "If a general officer should have a horse shot under him on the field of battle, what ought he to do?" answered up naively and said:

"Get up and brush himself."

One of the young nobles was called up, now. I thought I would question him a little myself. I said:

"Can your lordship read?"

His face flushed indignantly, and he fired this at me:

"Takest me for a clerk? I trow I am not of a blood that—"

"Answer the question!"

He crowded his wrath down and made out to answer "No."

"Can you write?"

He wanted to resent this, too, but I said:

"You will confine yourself to the questions, and make no comments. You are not here to air your blood or your graces, and nothing of the sort will be permitted. Can you write?"

"No."

"Do you know the multiplication table?"

"I wit not what ye refer to."

"How much is 9 times 6?"

"It is a mystery that is hidden from me, by reason that the emergency requiring the fathoming of it hath not in my life-days occurred, and so, not having no need to know this thing, I abide barren of the knowledge."

"If A trade a barrel of onions to B, worth 2 pence the bushel, in exchange for a sheep worth 4 pence, and a dog worth a penny, and C kill the dog before delivery, because bitten by the same, who mistook him for D, what sum is still due to A from B, and which party pays for the dog, C or D, and who gets the money? if A, is the penny sufficient, or may he claim consequential damages in the form of additional money to represent the possible profit which might have inured from the dog, and classifiable as earned increment, that is to say, usufruct?"

"Verily, in the all-wise and unknowable providence of God, who moveth in mysterious ways his wonders to perform, have I never heard the fellow to this question for confusion of the mind and congestion of the ducts of thought. Wherefore I beseech you let the dog and the onions and these people of the strange and godless names work out their several salvations from their piteous and wonderful difficulties without help of mine, for indeed their trouble is sufficient as it is, whereas an I tried to help I should but damage their cause the more and yet mayhap not live myself to see the desolation wrought."

"What do you know of the laws of attraction and gravitation?"

"If there be such mayhap his grace the king did promulgate them whilst that I lay sick about the beginning of the year and thereby failed to hear his proclamation."

"What do you know of the science of optics?"

"I know of governors of places, and seneschals of castles, and sheriffs of counties, and many like small offices and titles of honor, but him you call the Science of Optics I have not heard of before; peradventure it is a new dignity."

"Yes, in this country."

Try to conceive of this mollusk gravely applying for an official position, of any kind under the sun! Why, he had all the ear-marks of a type-writer copyist, if you leave out the disposition to contribute uninvited emendations of your grammar and punctuation. It was unaccountable that he didn't attempt a little help of that sort out of his majestic supply of incapacity for the job. But that didn't prove that he hadn't material in him for the disposition, it only proved that he wasn't a type-writer copyist yet. After nagging him a little more, I let the professors loose on him, and they turned him inside out, on the line of scientific war, and found him empty, of course. He knew somewhat about the warfare of the time—bushwhacking around for ogres, and bull-fights in the tourneyment ring, and such things—but otherwise he was empty and useless. Then we took the other young noble in hand, and he was the first one's twin, for ignorance and incapacity. I delivered them into the hands of the Chairman of the Board with the comfortable consciousness that their cake was dough. They were examined in the previous order of precedence.

"Name, so please you?"

"Pertipole, son of Sir Pertipole, Baron of Barley Mash."

"Grandfather?"

"Also Sir Pertipole, Baron of Barley Mash."

"Great-grandfather?"

"The same name and title."

"Great-great-grandfather?"

"We had none, worshipful sir, the line failing before it had reached so far back."

"It mattereth not. It is a good four generations, and fulfilleth the requirement of the rule."

"Fulfills what rule?" I asked.

"The rule requiring four generations of nobility or else the candidate is not eligible."

"A man not eligible for a lieutenancy in the army unless he can prove four generations of noble descent?"

"Even so; neither lieutenant nor any other officer may be commissioned without that qualification."

"Oh come, this is an astonishing thing. What good is such a qualification as that?"

"What good? It is a hardy question, fair sir and Boss, since it doth go far to impugn the wisdom of even our holy Mother Church herself."

"As how?"

"For that she hath established the self-same rule, regarding saints. By her law none may be canonized until he hath lain dead four generations."

"I see, I see—it is the same thing. It is wonderful. In the one case a man lies dead-alive, four generations—mummified in ignorance and sloth—and that qualifies him to command live people, and take their weal and woe into his impotent hands; and in the other case, a man lies bedded with death and worms four generations, and that qualifies him for office in the celestial camp. Does the king's grace approve of this strange law?"

The king said:

"Why, truly I see naught about it that is strange. All places of honor and of profit do belong, by natural right, to them that be of noble blood, and so these dignities in the army are their property and would be so without this or any rule. The rule is but to mark a limit; its purpose is to keep out too recent blood, which would bring into contempt these offices, and men of lofty lineage would turn their backs and scorn to take them. I were to blame an I permitted this calamity. *You* can permit it an you are minded so to do, for you have the delegated authority, but that the king should do it were a most strange madness and not comprehensible to any."

"I yield. Proceed, sir Chief of the Herald's College."

The Chairman resumed, as follows:

"By what illustrious achievement for the honor of the Throne and State did the founder of your great line lift himself to the sacred dignity of the British nobility?"

"He built a brewery."

"Sire, the Board finds this candidate perfect in all the requirements and qualifications for military command, and doth hold his case open for decision after due examination of his competitor."

The competitor came forward and proved exactly four generations of nobility himself. So there was a tie, in military qualifications that far.

He stood aside, a moment, and Sir Pertipole was questioned further:

"Of what condition was the wife of the founder of your line?"

"She came of the highest landed gentry, yet she was not noble; she was gracious, and pure, and charitable, of a blameless life and character, insomuch that in these regards was she peer of the best lady in the land."

"That will do. Stand down." He called up the competing lordling again, and asked: "What was the rank and condition of the great-grandmother who conferred British nobility upon your great house?"

"She was a king's leman, and did climb to that splendid eminence by her own unholpen merit from the sewer where she was born."

"Ah, this indeed is true nobility, this is the right and perfect intermixture. The lieutenancy is yours, fair lord. Hold it not in contempt; it is the humble step which will lead to grandeurs more worthy of the splendor of an origin like to thine."

I was down in the bottomless pit of humiliation. I had promised myself an easy and zenith-scouring triumph, and this was the outcome! I was almost ashamed to look my poor disappointed cadet in the face. I told him to go home and be patient, this wasn't the end.

I had a private audience with the king, and made a proposition. I said it was quite right to officer that regiment with nobilities, and he couldn't have done a wiser thing. It would also be a good idea to add five hundred officers to it, in fact, add as many officers as there were nobles and relatives of nobles in the country, even if there should finally be five times as many officers as privates in it; and thus make it the crack regiment, the envied regiment, the King's Own regiment, and entitled to fight on its own hook and in its own way, and go whither it would and come when it pleased, in time of war, and be utterly swell and independent. This would make that regiment the heart's desire of all the nobility, and they would all be satisfied and happy. Then we would make up the rest of the standing army out of commonplace materials, and officer it with nobodies, as was proper—nobodies selected on a basis of mere efficiency—and we would make this regiment toe the line, allow it no aristocratic freedom from restraint, and force it to do all the work and persistent hammering, to the end that whenever the King's Own was tired and wanted to go off for a change and rummage around amongst ogres and have a good time, it could go without uneasiness, knowing that matters were in safe hands behind it and business going to be continued at the old stand, same as usual. The king was charmed with the idea.

When I noticed that, it gave me a valuable notion. I thought I saw my way out of an old and stubborn difficulty at last. You see, the royalties of the Pendragon stock were a long-lived race and very fruitful. Whenever a child was born to any of these—and it was pretty often—there was wild joy in the nation's mouth, and piteous sorrow in the nation's heart. The joy was questionable, but the grief was honest. Because the event meant another call for a Royal Grant. Long was the list of these royalties, and they were a heavy and steadily increasing burden upon the treasury and a menace to the crown. Yet Arthur could not believe this latter fact, and he would not listen to any of my various projects for substituting something in the place of the royal grants. If I could have persuaded him to now and then provide a support for one of these outlying scions from his own pocket, I could have made a grand to-do over it, and it would have had a good effect with the nation; but no, he wouldn't hear of such a thing. He had something like a religious passion for a royal grant; he seemed to look upon it as a sort of sacred swag, and one could not irritate him in any way so quickly and so surely as by an attack upon that venerable institution. If I ventured to cautiously hint that there was not another respectable family in England that would humble itself to hold out the hat—however, that is as far as I ever got; he always cut me short, there, and peremptorily, too.

But I believed I saw my chance at last. I would form this crack regiment out of officers alone—not a single private. Half of it should consist of nobles, who should fill all the places up to Major General, and serve gratis and pay their own expenses; and they would be glad to do this when they should learn that the rest of the regiment would consist exclusively of princes of the blood. These princes of the blood should range in rank from Lieutenant General up to Field Marshal, and be gorgeously salaried and equipped and fed by the State. Moreover—and this was the master stroke—it should be decreed that these princely grandees should be always addressed by a stunningly gaudy and awe-compelling title, (which I would presently invent,) and they and they only in all England should be so addressed. Finally, all princes of the blood should have free choice: join that regiment, get that great title, and renounce the royal grant, or stay out and receive a grant. Neatest touch of all: unborn but imminent princes of the blood could be *born* into the regiment, and start fair, with good wages and a permanent situation, upon due notice from the parents.

All the boys would join, I was sure of that; so, all existing grants would be relinquished; that the newly born would always join was equally certain. Within sixty days that quaint and bizarre anomaly, the Royal Grant, would cease to be a living fact, and take its place among the curiosities of the past.

Chapter 26

THE FIRST NEWSPAPER

WHEN I told the king I was going out disguised as a petty freeman to scour the country and familiarize myself with the humbler life of the people, he was all afire with the novelty of the thing in a minute, and was bound to take a chance in the adventure himself—nothing should stop him —he would drop everything and go along—it was the prettiest idea he had run across for many a day. He wanted to glide out the back way and start at once; but I showed him that that wouldn't answer. You see, he was billed for the king's-evil—to touch for it, I mean—and it wouldn't be right to disappoint the house; and it wouldn't make a delay worth considering, anyway, it was only a one-night stand. And I thought he ought to tell the queen he was going away. He clouded up at that, and looked sad. I was sorry I had spoken, especially when he said mournfully:

"Thou forgettest that Launcelot is here; and where Launcelot is, she noteth not the going forth of the king, nor what day he returneth."

Of course I changed the subject. Yes, Guenever was beautiful, it is true, but take her all around she was pretty slack. I never meddled in these matters, they weren't my affair, but I did hate to see the way things were going on, and I don't mind saying that much. Many's the time she had asked me, "Sir Boss, hast seen Sir Launcelot about?" but if ever she went fretting around for the king I didn't happen to be around at the time.

There was a very good layout for the king's-evil business— very tidy and creditable. The king sat under a canopy of state, and about him were clustered a large body of the clergy in full canonicals. Conspicuous, both for location and personal outfit, stood Marinel, a hermit of the quack doctor species, to introduce the sick. All abroad over the spacious floor, and clear down to the doors, in a thick jumble, lay or sat the scrofulous, under a strong light. It was as good as a tableau;

in fact it had all the look of being gotten up for that, though it wasn't. There were 800 sick people present. The work was slow; it lacked the interest of novelty for me, because I had seen the ceremonies before; the thing soon became tedious, but the properties required me to stick it out. The doctor was there for the reason that in all such crowds there were many people who only imagined something was the matter with them, and many who were consciously sound but wanted the immortal honor of fleshly contact with a king, and yet others who pretended to illness in order to get the piece of coin that went with the touch. Up to this time this coin had been a wee little gold piece worth about a third of a dollar. When you consider how much that amount of money would buy, in that age and country, and how usual it was to be scrofulous, when not dead, you will understand that the annual king's-evil appropriation was just the River and Harbor bill of that government for the grip it took on the treasury and the chance it afforded for skinning the surplus. So I had privately concluded to touch the treasury itself for the king's-evil. I covered six-sevenths of the appropriation into the treasury a week before starting from Camelot on my adventures, and ordered that the other seventh be inflated into five-cent nickels and delivered into the hands of the head clerk of the King's-Evil Department; a nickel to take the place of each gold coin, you see, and do its work for it. It might strain the nickel some, but I judged it could stand it. As a rule, I do not approve of watering stock, but I considered it square enough in this case, for it was just a gift, anyway. Of course you can water a gift as much as you want to; and I generally do. The old gold and silver coins of the country were of ancient and unknown origin, as a rule, but some of them were Roman; they were ill shapen, and seldom rounder than a moon that is a week past the full; they were hammered, not minted, and they were so worn with use that the devices upon them were as illegible as blisters, and looked like them. I judged that a sharp, bright new nickel, with a first-rate likeness of the king on one side of it and Guenever on the other, and a blooming pious motto, would take the tuck out of scrofula as handy as a nobler coin and please the scrofulous fancy more; and I was right. This batch was the first it was tried on, and it worked to a charm. The saving in expense was a notable economy. You will see that, by these figures: We touched a trifle over 700 of the 800 patients; at former rates, this would have cost the government about $240; at the new rate we pulled through for about $35, thus saving upwards of $200 at one swoop. To appreciate the full magnitude of this stroke, consider these other figures: the annual expenses of a national government amount to the equivalent of a contribution of three days' (average) wages of every individual of the population, counting every individual as if he were a man. If you take a nation of 60,000,000, where average wages are $2 per day, three days' wages taken from each individual will provide $360,000,000 and pay the government's expenses. In my day, in my own country, this money was collected from imposts, and the citizen imagined that the foreign importer paid it, and it made him comfortable to think so; whereas, in fact, it was paid by the American people and was so equally and exactly distributed among them, that the annual cost to the 100-millionaire and the annual cost to the sucking child of the day laborer was precisely the same—each paid $6. Nothing could be equaler than that, I reckon. Well, Scotland and Ireland were tributary to Arthur, and the united populations of the British islands amounted to something less than 1,000,000. A mechanic's average wage was 3 cents a day, when he paid his own keep. By this rule, the national government's expenses were $90,000 a year, or about $250 a day. Thus, by the substitution of nickels for gold on a king's-evil day, I not only injured no one, dissatisfied no one, but pleased all concerned and saved four-fifths of that day's national expense into the bargain—a saving which would have been the equivalent of $800,000 in my day in America. In making this substitution I had drawn upon the wisdom of a very remote source—the wisdom of my boyhood—for the true statesman does not despise any wisdom, howsoever lowly may be its origin: in my boyhood I had always saved my pennies, and contributed buttons to the foreign missionary cause. The buttons would answer the ignorant savage as well as the coin, the coin would answer me better than the buttons; all hands were happy, and nobody hurt.

Marinel took the patients as they came. He examined the candidate; if he couldn't qualify, he was warned off; if he could, he was passed along, to the king. A priest pronounced the words, "They shall lay their hands on the sick, and they shall recover." Then the king stroked the ulcers, while the reading continued; finally, the patient graduated and got his nickel—the king hanging it around his neck himself—and was dismissed. Would you think that that would cure? It certainly did. Any mummery will cure, if the patient's faith is strong in it. Up by Astolat there was a chapel where the Virgin had once appeared to a girl who used to herd geese around there—the girl said so herself—and they built the chapel upon that spot and hung a picture in it representing the occurrence—a picture which you would think it dangerous for a sick person to approach; whereas on the contrary, thousands of the lame and the sick came and prayed before it every year and went away whole and sound; and even the well could look upon it and live. Of course when I was told these things, I did not believe them; but when I went there and saw them I had to succumb. I saw the cures effected myself; and they were real cures and not questionable. I saw cripples whom I had seen around Camelot for years on crutches, arrive and pray before that picture, and put down their crutches and walk off without a limp. There were piles of crutches there which had been left by such people as a testimony.

In other places people operated on a patient's mind, without saying a word to him, and cured him. In others, experts assembled patients in a room and prayed over them, and appealed to their faith, and those patients went away cured. Wherever you find a king who can't cure the king's-evil, you can be sure that the most valuable superstition that supports his throne—the subject's belief in the divine appointment of his sovereign—has passed away. In my youth the monarchs of England had ceased to touch for the evil, but there was no occasion for this diffidence: they could have cured it forty-nine times in fifty.

Well, when the priest had been droning for three hours, and the good king polishing the evidences, and the sick were still pressing forward as plenty as ever, I got to feeling intolerably bored. I was sitting by an open window not far from the canopy of state. For the five hundredth time a patient stood forward to have his repulsivenesses stroked; again those words were being droned out, "They shall lay their hands on the sick—" when outside there rang clear as a clarion a note that enchanted my soul and tumbled thirteen worthless centuries about my ears: "Camelot *Weekly Hosannah and Literary Volcano*!—latest irruption—only two cents—all about the big miracle in the Valley of Holiness!" One greater than kings had arrived—the newsboy. But I was the only person in all that throng who knew the meaning of this mighty birth, and what this imperial magician was come into the world to do.

I dropped a nickel out of the window and got my paper; the Adam newsboy of the world went around the corner to get my change; is around the corner yet. It was delicious to see a newspaper again, yet I was conscious of a secret shock when my eye fell upon the first batch of display head-lines. I had lived in a clammy atmosphere of reverence, respect, deference, so long, that they sent a quivery little cold wave through me:

HIGH TIMES IN THE VALLEY
OF HOLINESS!

THE WATER-ₘORKS CORKED !

BRER MERLIN WORKS HIS ARTS, BUT GETS
LEFT !

But t he Boss scores on his first Innings !

*The Miraculous Well Uncorked amid
awful outbursts of*
INFERNAL FIRE AND SMOKE
ANDTHUNDER !

THE BUZZARD-ROOST ASTONISHED!

UNPARALLELED REJOIBINGS!

—and so-on, and so-on. Yes, it was too loud. Once I could have enjoyed it and seen nothing out of the way about it, but now its note was discordant. It was good Arkansas journalism, but this was not Arkansas. Moreover, the next to the last line was calculated to give offence to the hermits, and perhaps lose us their advertising. Indeed, there was too lightsome a tone of flippancy all through the paper. It was plain I had undergone a considerable change without noticing it. I found myself unpleasantly affected by pert little irreverencies which would have seemed but proper and airy graces of speech at an earlier period in my life. There was an abundance of the following breed of items, and they discomforted me:

Local Smoke and Cinders.

Sir Launce[o] met up with old King Vgrivance of Ireland unexpectedly last weok over on the moor south of Sir Balmoral le Merveilleuse's hog dasture. The widow has been notified.

Expedition No. 3 will start adout the first of next mgnth on a search f8r Sir Sagramour le Desirous. It is in comand of the renowned Knight of the Red Lawns, assissted by Sir Persant of Inde, who is competegt, intelligent, courteous, and in every mav a brick, and further assisted by Sir Palamides the Saracen, who is no huckleberry himself. This is no pic-nic, these boys mean business.

The readers of the Hosannah will regict to learn that the hadndsome and popular Sir Charolais of Gaul, who during his four weeks' stay at the Bull and Halibut, this city, has won every heart by his polished manners and elegant conversation, will pull out to-day for home. Give us another call, Charley!

The bdsiness end of the funeral of the late Sir Dalliance the duke's son of Cornwall, killed in an encounter with the Giant of the Knotted Bludgeon last

Tuesday on the borders of the Plain of Enchantment was in the hands of the ever affable and efficient Mumble, prince of un3ertakers, than whom there exists none by whom it were a more satisfying pleasure to have the last sad offices perrormed. Give him a trial.

The cordial thanks of the Hosannah office are due, from editor down to devil, to the ever courteous and thoughtful Lord High Stew d of the Palace's Third Assistant V t for several sau-cers of ice cream, a quality calculated to make the ey of the recipients humid with gr ude; and it done it. When this administration wants to chalk up a desirable name for early promotion, the Hosannah would like a chance to sudgest.

The Demoiselle Irene Dewlap, of South Astolat, is visiting her uncle, the popular host of the Cattlemen's Boarding Ho&se, Liver Lane, this city.

Young Barker the bellows-mender is hoMe again, and looks much improved by his vacauon round-up among the out-lying smithies. See his ad.

Of course it was good enough journalism for a beginning; I knew that quite well, and yet it was somehow disappointing. The "Court Circular" pleased me better; indeed its simple and dignified respectfulness was a distinct refreshment to me after all those disgraceful familiarities. But even it could have been improved. Do what one may, there is no getting an air of variety into a court circular, I acknowledge that. There is a profound monotonousness about its facts that baffles and defeats one's sincerest efforts to make them sparkle and enthuse. The best way to manage—in fact the only sensible way—is to disguise repetitiousness of fact under variety of form: skin your fact, each time, and lay on a new cuticle of words. It deceives the eye; you think it is a new fact; it gives you the idea that the court is carrying on like everything; this excites you, and you drain the whole column, with a good appetite, and perhaps never notice that it's a barrel of soup made out of a single bean. Clarence's way was good, it was simple, it was dignified, it was direct and business-like; all I say is, it was not the best way:

COURT CIRCULAK.

On Monday, the ҙing rode in the park.
"   Tuesday,   "   "   "
"   Wendesday   "   "   "
"   Thursday   "   "   "
"   Friday,   "   "   "
"   Saturday   "   "   "
"   Sunday,   "   "   "

However, take the paper by and large, I was vastly pleased with it. Little crudities of a mechanical sort were observable here and there, but there were not enough of them to amount to anything, and it was good enough Arkansas proof-reading, anyhow, and better than was needed in Arthur's day and realm. As a rule, the grammar was leaky and the construction more or less lame; but I did not much mind these things. They are common defects of my own, and one mustn't criticise other people on grounds where he can't stand perpendicular himself.

I was hungry enough for literature to want to take down the whole paper at this one meal, but I got only a few bites, and then had to postpone, because the monks around me besieged me so with eager questions: What is this curious thing? What is it for? Is it a handkerchief?—saddle blanket?—part of a shirt? What is it made of? How thin it is; and how dainty and frail; and how it rattles. Will it wear, do you think, and won't the rain injure it? Is it writing that appears on it, or is it only ornamentation? They suspected it was writing, because those among them who knew how to read Latin and had a smattering of Greek, recognized some of the letters, but they could make nothing out of the result as a whole. I put my information in the simplest form I could:

"It is a public journal; I will explain what that is, another time. It is not cloth, it is made of paper; some time I will explain what paper is. The lines on it are reading-matter; and not written by hand, but printed; by and by, I will explain what printing is. A thousand of these sheets have been made, and all exactly like this, in every minute detail—they can't be told apart." Then they all broke out with exclamations of surprise and admiration:

"A thousand! Verily a mighty work—a year's work for many men."

"No—merely a day's work for a man and a boy."

They crossed themselves, and whiffed out a protective prayer or two.

"Ah-h---a miracle, a wonder! Dark work of enchantment."

I let it go at that. Then I read in a low voice, to as many as could crowd their shaven heads within hearing distance, part of the account of the miracle of the restoration of the well, and was accompanied by astonished and reverent ejaculations all through: "Ah-h-h!" "How true!" "Amazing, amazing!" "These be the very haps as they happened, in marvelous exactness!" And might they take this strange thing in their hands, and feel of it and examine it?—they would be very careful. Yes. So they took it, handling it as cautiously and devoutly as if it had been some holy thing come from some supernatural region; and gently felt of its texture, caressed its pleasant smooth surface with lingering touch, and scanned the mysterious characters with fascinated eyes. These grouped bent heads, these charmed faces, these speaking eyes—how beautiful to me! For was not this my darling, and was not all this mute wonder and interest and homage a most eloquent tribute and unforced compliment to it? I knew, then, how a mother feels when women, whether strangers or friends, take her new baby, and close themselves about it with one eager impulse, and bend their heads over it in a tranced adoration that makes all the rest of the universe vanish out of their consciousness and be as if it were not, for that time. I knew how she feels, and that there is no other satisfied ambition, whether of king, conqueror or poet, that ever reaches half way to that serene far summit or yields half so divine a contentment.

During all the rest of the séance my paper traveled from group to group all up and down and about that huge hall, and my happy eye was upon it always, and I sat motionless, steeped in satisfaction, drunk with enjoyment. Yes, this was heaven; I was tasting it once, if I might never taste it more.

Chapter 27

THE YANKEE AND THE KING
TRAVEL INCOGNITO

ABOUT BEDTIME I took the king to my private quarters to cut his hair and help him get the hang of the lowly raiment he was to wear. The high classes wore their hair banged across the forehead but hanging to the shoulders the rest of the way around, whereas the lowest ranks of commoners were banged fore and aft both; the slaves were bangless and allowed their hair free growth. So I inverted a bowl over his head and cut away all the locks that hung below it. I also trimmed his whiskers and moustache until they were only about a half inch long; and tried to do it inartistically, and succeeded. It was a villanous disfigurement. When he got his lubberly sandals on, and his long robe of coarse brown linen cloth, which hung straight from his neck to his ancle-bones, he was no longer the comeliest man in his kingdom, but one of the unhandsomest and most commonplace and unattractive. We were dressed and barbered alike, and could pass for small farmers, or farm bailiffs, or shepherds, or carters; yes, or for village artisans, if we chose, our costume being in effect universal among the poor, because of its strength and cheapness. I don't mean that it was really cheap to a very poor person, but I do mean that it was the cheapest material there was for male attire—manufactured material, you understand.

We slipped away an hour before dawn, and by broad sun-up had made eight or ten miles, and were in the midst of a sparsely settled country. I had a pretty heavy knapsack; it was laden with provisions—provisions for the king to taper down on, till he could take to the coarse fare of the country without damage.

I found a comfortable seat for the king by the roadside, and then gave him a morsel or two to stay his stomach with. Then I said I would find some water for him, and strolled away. Part of my project was to get out of sight and sit down and rest a little myself. It had always been my custom to stand, when in his presence; even at the council board, except upon those rare occasions when the sitting was a very long one, extending over hours; then I had a trifling little backless thing which was like a reversed culvert, and was as comfortable as the toothache. I didn't want to break him in suddenly, but do it by degrees. We should have to sit together now, when in company, or people would notice; but it would not be good politics for me to be playing equality with him when there was no necessity for it.

I found the water, some three hundred yards away, and had been resting about twenty minutes, when I heard voices. That is all right, I thought—peasants going to work; nobody else likely to be stirring this early. But the next moment these comers jingled into sight around a turn of the road—smartly clad people of quality, with luggage-mules and servants in their train! I was off like a shot, through the bushes, by the shortest cut. For a while it did seem that these people would pass the king before I could get to him; but desperation gives you wings, you know, and I canted my body forward, inflated my breast, and held my breath and flew. I arrived. And in plenty good enough time, too:

"Pardon, my king, but it's no time for ceremony—jump! Jump to your feet—some quality are coming!"

"Is that a marvel? Let them come."

"But my liege! You must not be seen sitting. Rise!—and stand in humble posture while they pass. You are a peasant, you know."

"True—I had forgot it, so lost was I in planning of a huge war with Gaul"—he was up, by this time, but a farm could have got up quicker if there was any kind of a boom in real estate—"and right-so a thought came randoming overthwart this majestic dream the which—"

"A humbler attitude, my lord the king—and quick! Duck your head!—more!—still more!—droop it!"

He did his honest best, but lord it was no great things. He looked as humble as the leaning tower at Pisa. It is the most you could say of it. Indeed it was such a thundering poor success that it raised wondering scowls all along the line, and a gorgeous flunkey at the tail end of it raised his whip; but I jumped in time, and was under it when it fell; and under cover of the volley of coarse laughter which followed, I spoke up sharply and warned the king to take no notice. He mastered himself for the moment, but it was a sore tax; he wanted to eat up the procession. I said:

"It would end our adventures at the very start; and we, being without weapons, could do nothing with that armed gang. If we are going to succeed in our emprize, we must not only look the peasant but act the peasant."

"It is wisdom; none can gainsay it. Let us go on, Sir Boss. I will take note, and learn, and do the best I may."

He kept his word. He did the best he could, but I've seen better. If you have ever seen an active, heedless, enterprising child going diligently out of one mischief and into another all day long, and an anxious mother at its heels all the while, and just saving it by a hair from drowning itself or breaking its neck with each new experiment, you've seen the king and me. If I could have foreseen what the thing was going to be like, I should have said, No, if anybody wants to make his living exhibiting a king as a peasant, let him take the layout; I can do better with a menagerie, and last longer. And yet, during the first three days I never allowed him to enter a hut or other dwelling. If he could pass muster anywhere, during his early noviciate, it would be in small inns and on the road; so to these places we confined ourselves. Yes, he certainly did the best he could, but what of that? He didn't improve a bit, that I could see.

He was always frightening me, always breaking out with fresh astonishers, in new and unexpected places. Toward evening on the second day, what does he do but blandly fetch out a dirk from inside his robe!

"Great guns, my liege, where did you get that?"

"From a smuggler at the inn, yester eve."

"What in the world possessed you to buy it?"

"We have escaped divers dangers by wit—thy wit—but I have bethought me that it were but prudence if *I* bore a weapon, too. Thine might fail thee in some pinch."

"But people of our condition are not allowed to carry arms. What would a lord say—yes, or any other person of whatever condition—if he caught an upstart peasant with a dagger on his person?"

It was a lucky thing for us that nobody came along just then. I persuaded him to throw the dirk away; and it was as easy as persuading a child to give up some bright fresh new way of killing itself. We walked along, silent and thinking. Finally the king said:

"When ye know that I meditate a thing inconvenient, or that hath a peril in it, why do you not warn me to cease from that project?"

It was a startling question, and a puzzler. I didn't quite know how to take hold of it, or what to say; and so of course I ended by saying the natural thing:

"But sire, how can *I* know what your thoughts are?"

The king stopped dead in his tracks, and stared at me.

"I believed thou wert greater than Merlin; and truly in magic thou art. But prophecy is greater than magic. Merlin is a prophet."

I saw I had made a blunder. I must get back my lost ground. After deep reflection and careful planning, I said:

"Sire, I have been misunderstood. I will explain. There are two kinds of prophecy. One is the gift to foretell things that are but a little way off, the other is the gift to foretell things that are whole ages and centuries away. Which is the mightier gift, do you think?"

"Oh, the last, most surely!"

"True. Does Merlin possess it?"

"Partly, yes. He foretold mysteries about my birth and future kingship that were twenty years away."

"Has he ever gone beyond that?"

"He would not claim more, I think."

"It is probably his limit. All prophets have their limit. The limit of some of the great prophets has been a hundred years."

"These are few, I ween."

"There have been two still greater ones, whose limit was four hundred and six hundred years, and one whose limit compassed even seven hundred and twenty."

"Gramercy, it is marvelous!"

"But what are these, by comparison with me? They are nothing."

"What? Canst thou truly look beyond even so vast a stretch of time as—"

"Seven hundred years? My liege, as clear as the vision of an eagle does my prophetic eye penetrate and lay bare the future of this world for nearly thirteen centuries and a half!"

My land, you should have seen the king's eyes spread slowly open, and lift the earth's entire atmosphere as much as an inch! That settled Brer Merlin. One never had any occasion to prove his facts, with these people; all he had to do was to state them. It never occurred to anybody to doubt the statement.

"Now, then," I continued, "I *could* work both kinds of prophecy—the long and the short—if I chose to take the trouble to keep in practice; but I seldom exercise any but the long kind, because the other is beneath my dignity. It is properer to Merlin's sort—stump-tail prophets, as we call them in the profession. Of course I whet up now and then and flirt out a minor prophecy, but not often—hardly ever, in fact. You will remember that there was great talk, when you reached the Valley of Holiness, about my having prophesied your coming and the very hour of your arrival, two or three days beforehand."

"Indeed, yes, I mind it now."

"Well, I could have done it as much as forty times easier, and piled on a thousand times more detail into the bargain, if it had been five hundred years away instead of two or three days."

"How amazing that it should be so!"

"Yes, a genuine expert can always foretell a thing that is five hundred years away easier than he can a thing that's only five hundred seconds off."

"And yet in reason it should clearly be the other way: it should be five hundred times as easy to foretell the last as the first, for indeed it is so close by, that one uninspired might almost see it. In truth the law of prophecy doth contradict the likelihoods, most strangely making the difficult easy, and the easy difficult."

It was a wise head. A peasant's cap was no safe disguise for it; you could know it for a king's, under a diving bell, if you could hear it work its intellect.

I had a new trade, now, and plenty of business in it. The king was as hungry to find out everything that was going to happen during the next thirteen centuries as if he were expecting to live in them. From that time out, I prophesied myself baldheaded trying to supply the demand. I have done some indiscreet things in my day, but this thing of playing myself for a prophet was the worst. Still it had its ameliorations. A prophet doesn't have to have any brains. They are good to have, of course, for the ordinary exigencies of life, but they are no use in professional work. It is the restfulest vocation there is. When the spirit of prophecy comes upon you, you merely cake your intellect and lay it off in a cool place for a rest, and unship your jaw and leave it alone; it will work itself: the result is Prophecy.

Every day a knight errant or so came along, and the sight of them fired the king's martial spirit every time. He would have forgotten himself, sure, and said something to them in a style a suspicious shade or so above his ostensible degree, and so I always got him well out of the road in time. Then he would stand, and look with all his eyes; and a proud light would flash from them, and his nostrils would inflate like a war-horse's, and I knew he was longing for a brush with them. But about noon of the third day I had stopped in the road to take a precaution which had been suggested by the whip-stroke that had fallen to my share two days before; a precaution which I had afterward decided to leave untaken, I was so loath to institute it; but now I had just had a fresh reminder: while striding heedlessly along, with jaw spread and intellect at rest, for I was prophesying, I stubbed my toe and fell sprawling. I was so pale I couldn't think, for a moment; then I got softly and carefully up and unstrapped my knapsack. I had that dynamite bomb in it, done up in wool, in a box. It was a good thing to have along; the time would come when I could do a valuable miracle with it, maybe, but it was a nervous thing to have about me, and I didn't like to ask the king to carry it. Yet I must either throw it away or think up some safe way to get along with its society. I got it out and slipped it into my scrip, and just then, here came a couple of knights. The king stood, stately as a statue, gazing toward them—had forgotten himself again, of course—and before I could get a word of warning out, it was time for him to skip, and well that he did it, too. He supposed they would turn aside. Turn aside to avoid trampling peasant dirt under foot? When had he ever turned aside himself—or ever had the chance to do it, if a peasant saw him or any other noble knight in time to judiciously save him the trouble? The knights paid no attention to the king at all; it was his place to look out for himself, and if he hadn't skipped he would have been placidly ridden down, and laughed at besides.

The king was in a flaming fury, and launched out his challenge and epithets with a most royal vigor. The knights were some little distance by, now. They halted, greatly surprised, and turned in their saddles and looked back, as if wondering if it might be worth while to bother with such scum as we. Then they wheeled and started for us. Not a moment must be lost. I started for *them*. I passed them at a rattling gait, and as I went by I flung out a hair-lifting soul-scorching thirteen-jointed insult which made the king's effort poor and cheap by comparison. I got it out of the nineteenth century, where they know how. They had such headway that they were nearly to the king before they could check up; then, frantic with rage, they stood up their horses on their hind hoofs and whirled them around, and the next moment here they came, breast to breast. I was seventy yards off, then, and scrambling up a great bowlder at the roadside. When they were within thirty yards of me they let their long lances droop to a level, depressed their mailed heads, and so, with their horse-hair plumes streaming straight out behind, most gallant to see, this lightning express came tearing for me! When they were within fifteen yards, I sent that bomb with a sure aim, and it struck the ground just under the horses' noses.

Yes, it was a neat thing, very neat and pretty to see. It resembled a steamboat explosion on the Mississippi; and during the next fifteen minutes we stood under a steady drizzle of microscopic fragments of knights and hardware and horse-flesh. I say we, for the king joined the audience, of course, as soon as he had got his breath again. There was a hole there which would afford steady work for all the people in that region for some years to come—in trying to explain it, I mean; as for filling it up, that service would be comparatively prompt, and would fall to the lot of a select few—peasants of that seignory; and they wouldn't get anything for it, either.

But I explained it to the king myself. I said it was done with a dynamite bomb. This information did him no damage, because it left him as intelligent as he was before. However, it was a noble miracle, in his eyes, and was another settler for Merlin. I thought it well enough to explain that this was a miracle of so rare a sort that it couldn't be done except when the atmospheric conditions were just right. Otherwise he would be encoring it every time we had a good subject, and that would be inconvenient, because I hadn't any more bombs along.

Chapter 28

DRILLING THE KING

O N THE MORNING of the fourth day, when it was just sunrise, and we had been tramping an hour in the chill dawn, I came to a resolution: the king *must* be drilled; things could not go on so, he must be taken in hand, and deliberately and conscientiously drilled, or we couldn't ever venture to enter a dwelling; the very cats would know this masquerader for a humbug and no peasant. So I called a halt, and said:

"Sire, as between clothes and countenance, you are all right, there is no discrepancy; but as between your clothes and your bearing, you are all wrong, there is a most noticeable discrepancy. Your soldierly stride, your lordly port— these will not do. You stand too straight, your looks are too high, too confident. The cares of a kingdom do not stoop the shoulders, they do not droop the chin, they do not depress the high level of the eye-glance, they do not put doubt and fear in the heart and hang out the signs of them in slouching body and unsure step. It is the sordid cares of the lowly born that do these things. You must learn the trick; you must imitate the trade-marks of poverty, misery, oppression, insult, and the other several and common inhumanities that sap the manliness out of a man and make him a loyal and proper and approved subject, and a satisfaction to his masters, or the very infants will know you for better than your disguise, and we shall go to pieces at the first hut we stop at. Pray try to walk like this."

The king took careful note, and then tried an imitation.

"Pretty fair—pretty fair. Chin a little lower, please—there, very good. Eyes too high; pray don't look at the horizon, look at the ground, ten steps in front of you. Ah—that is better, that is very good. Wait, please; you betray too much vigor, too much decision; you want more of a shamble. Look at me, please—this is what I mean. . . . . . Now you are getting it; that is the idea—at least, it sort of approaches it. . . . . . . Yes, that is pretty fair. *But!* There is a great big something wanting, I don't quite know what it is. Please walk thirty yards, so that I can get a perspective on the thing. . . . . Now, then—your head's right, speed's right, shoulders right, eyes right, chin right, gait, carriage, general style right—everything's right! And yet the fact remains, the aggregate's wrong. The account don't balance. Do it again, please . . . . . . *now* I think I begin to see what it is. Yes, I've struck it. You see, the genuine spiritlessness is wanting; that's what's the trouble. It's all *amateur*—mechanical details all right, almost to a hair; everything about the delusion perfect, except that it don't delude."

"What then, must one do, to prevail?"

"Let me think. . . . . I can't seem to quite get at it. In fact there isn't anything that can right the matter but practice. This is a good place for it: roots and stony ground to break up your stately gait, a region not liable to interruption, only one field and one hut in sight, and they so far away that nobody could see us from there. It will be well to move a little off the road and put in the whole day drilling you, sire."

After the drill had gone on a little while, I said:

"Now sire, imagine that we are at the door of the hut yonder, and the family are before us. Proceed, please—accost the head of the house."

The king unconsciously straightened up like a monument, and said, with frozen austerity:

"Varlet, bring a seat; and serve to me what cheer ye have."

"Ah, your grace, that is not well done."

"In what lacketh it?"

"These people do not call *each other* varlets."

"Nay, is that true?"

"Yes; only those above them call them so."

"Then must I try again. I will call him villein."

"No-no; for he may be a freeman."

"Ah—so. Then peradventure I should call him goodman."

"That would answer, your grace, but it would be still better if you said friend, or brother."

"Brother!—to dirt like that?"

"Ah, but *we* are pretending to be dirt like that, too."

"It is even true. I will say it. Brother, bring a seat, and thereto what cheer ye have, withal. *Now* 'tis right."

"Not quite, not wholly right. You have asked for one, not *us*—for one, not both; food for one, a seat for one."

The king looked puzzled—he wasn't a very heavy weight, intellectually. His head was an hour-glass; it could stow an idea, but it had to do it a grain at a time, not the whole idea at once.

"Would *you* have a seat also—and sit?"

"If I did not sit, the man would perceive that we were only pretending to be equals—and playing the deception pretty poorly, too."

"It is well and truly said! How wonderful is truth, come it in whatsoever unexpected form it may! Yes, he must bring out seats and food for both, and in serving us present not ewer and napkin with more show of respect to one than to the other."

"And there is even yet a detail that needs correcting. He must bring nothing outside; we will go in—in among the dirt, and possibly other repulsive things,—and take the food with the household, and after the fashion of the house, and all on equal terms, except the man be of the serf class; and finally, there will be no ewer and no napkin, whether he be serf or free. Please walk again, my liege. There—it is better—it is the best yet; but not perfect. The shoulders have known no ignobler burden than iron mail, and they will not stoop."

"Give me, then, the bag. I will learn the spirit that goeth with burdens that have not honor. It is the spirit that stoopeth the shoulders, I ween, and not the weight; for armor is heavy, yet is it a proud burden, and a man standeth straight in it. . . . . Nay, but me no buts, offer me no objections. I will have the thing. Strap it upon my back."

He was complete, now, with that knapsack on, and looked as little like a king as any man I had ever seen. But it was an obstinate pair of shoulders; they could not seem to learn the trick of stooping with any sort of deceptive naturalness. The drill went on, I prompting and correcting:

"Now, make believe you are in debt, and eaten up by relentless creditors; you are out of work—which is horseshoeing, let us say—and can get none; and your wife is sick, your children are crying because they are hungry—"

And so-on, and so-on. I drilled him as representing, in turn, all sorts of people out of luck and suffering dire privations and misfortunes. But lord, it was only just words, words,—they meant nothing in the world to him, I might just as well have whistled. Words realize nothing, vivify nothing to you, unless you have suffered in your own person the thing which the words try to describe. There are wise people who talk ever so knowingly and complacently about "the working classes," and satisfy themselves that a day's hard intellectual work is very much harder than a day's hard manual toil, and is righteously entitled to much bigger pay. Why, they really think that, you know, because they know all about the one, but haven't tried the other. But I know all about both; and as far as I am concerned, there isn't money enough in the universe to hire me to swing a pickaxe thirty days, but I will do the hardest kind of intellectual work for just as near nothing as you can cipher it down—and I will be satisfied, too. Intellectual "work" is misnamed; it is a pleasure, a dissipation, and is its own highest reward. The poorest paid architect, engineer, general, author, sculptor, painter, lecturer, advocate, legislator, actor, preacher, singer, is constructively in heaven when he is at work; and as for the magician with the fiddle-bow in his hand who sits in the midst of a great orchestra with the ebbing and flowing tides of divine sound washing over him—why certainly, he is at work, if you wish to call it that, but lord, it's a sarcasm just the same. The law of work does seem utterly unfair—but there it is, and nothing can change it: the higher the pay in enjoyment the worker gets out of it, the higher shall be his pay in cash, also. And it's also the very law of those transparent swindles, transmissible nobility and kingship.

Chapter 29

THE SMALL-POX HUT

WHEN WE ARRIVED at that hut at mid-afternoon, we saw no signs of life about it. The field nearby had been denuded of its crop some time before, and had a skinned look, so exhaustively had it been harvested and gleaned. Fences, sheds, everything had a ruined look, and were eloquent of poverty. No animal was around anywhere, no living thing in sight. The stillness was awful, it was like the stillness of death. The cabin was a one-story one, whose thatch was black with age, and ragged from lack of repair.

The door stood a trifle ajar. We approached it stealthily —on tip-toe and at half-breath—for that is the way one's feeling makes him do, at such a time. The king knocked. We waited. No answer. Knocked again. No answer. I pushed the door softly open and looked in. I made out some dim forms, and a woman started up from the ground and stared at me, as one does who is wakened from sleep. Presently she found her voice—

"Have mercy!" she pleaded. "All is taken; nothing is left."

"I have not come to take anything, poor woman."

"You are not a priest?"

"No."

"Nor come not from the lord of the manor?"

"No, I am a stranger."

"Oh, then, for the fear of God, who visits with misery and death such as be harmless, tarry not here, but fly! This place is under his curse—and his Church's."

"Let me come in and help you—you are sick and in trouble."

I was better used to the dim light, now. I could see her hollow eyes fixed upon me, I could see how emaciated she was.

"I tell you the place is under the Church's ban. Save yourself—and go, before some straggler see thee here, and report it."

"Give yourself no trouble about me; I don't care anything for the Church's curse. Let me help you."

"Now all good spirits—if there be any such—bless thee for that word. Would God I had a sup of water!—but hold, hold, forget I said it, and fly; for there is that here that even he that feareth not the Church must fear: this disease whereof we die. Leave us, thou brave good stranger, and take with thee such whole and sincere blessing as them that be accursed can give."

But before this, I had picked up a wooden bowl and was rushing past the king on my way to the brook. It was ten yards away. When I got back and entered, the king was within, and was opening the shutter that closed the window-hole, to let in air and light. The place was full of a foul stench. I put the bowl to the woman's lips, and as she gripped it with her eager talons, the shutter came open and a strong light flooded her face. Small-pox!

I sprang to the king, and said in his ear:

"Out of the door on the instant, sire! the woman is dying of that disease that wasted the skirts of Camelot two years ago."

He did not budge.

"Of a truth I shall remain—and likewise help."

I whispered again:

"King, it must not be. You must go."

"Ye mean well, and ye speak not unwisely. But it were shame that a king should know fear, and shame that belted knight should withhold his hand where be such as need succor. Peace, I will not go. It is you who must go. The Church's ban is not upon me, but it forbiddeth you to be here, and she will deal with you with a heavy hand an word come to her of your trespass."

It was a desperate place for him to be in, and might cost him his life, but it was no use to argue with him. If he considered his knightly honor at stake here, that was the end of argument; he would stay, and nothing could prevent it; I was aware of that. And so I dropped the subject. The woman spoke:

"Fair sir, of your kindness will ye climb the ladder there, and bring me news of what ye find? Be not afraid to report, for times can come when even a mother's heart is past breaking—being already broke."

"Abide," said the king, "and give the woman to eat. I will go." And he put down the knapsack.

I turned to start, but the king had already started. He halted, and looked down upon a man who lay in a dim light, and had not noticed us, thus far, or spoken.

"Is it your husband?" the king asked.

"Yes."

"Is he asleep?"

"God be thanked for that one charity, yes—these three hours. Where shall I pay to the full, my gratitude! for my heart is bursting with it for that sleep he sleepeth now."

I said:

"We will be careful. We will not wake him."

"Ah, no, that ye will not, for he is dead."

"Dead?"

"Yes. What triumph it is to know it! None can harm him, none insult him more. He is in heaven, now, and happy; or if not there, he bides in hell and is content; for in that place he will find neither abbot nor yet bishop. We were boy and girl together; we were man and wife these five and twenty years, and never separated till this day. Think how long that is, to love and suffer together. This morning was he out of his mind, and in his fancy we were boy and girl again and wandering in the happy fields; and so in that innocent glad converse wandered he far and farther, still lightly gossiping, and entered into those other fields we know not of, and was shut away from mortal sight. And so there was no parting, for in his fancy I went with him; he knew not but I went with him, my hand in his—my young soft hand, not this withered claw. Ah, yes, to go, and know it not; to separate and know it not: how could one go peacefuler than that? It was his reward for a cruel life patiently borne."

There was a slight noise from the direction of the dim corner where the ladder was. It was the king, descending. I could see that he was bearing something in one arm, and assisting himself with the other. He came forward into the light; upon his breast lay a slender girl of fifteen. She was but half conscious; she was dying of small-pox. Here was heroism at its last and loftiest possibility, its utmost summit; this was challenging death in the open field unarmed, with all the odds against the challenger, no reward set upon the contest, and no admiring world in silks and cloth of gold to gaze and applaud; and yet the king's bearing was as serenely brave as it had always been in those cheaper contests where knight meets knight in equal fight and clothed in protecting steel. He was great, now; sublimely great. The rude statues of his ancestors in his palace should have an addition—I would see to that; and it would not be a mailed king killing a giant or a dragon, like the rest, it would be a king in commoner's garb bearing death in his arms that a peasant mother might look her last upon her child and be comforted.

He laid the girl down by her mother, who poured out endearments and caresses from an overflowing heart, and one could detect a flickering faint light of response in the child's eyes, but that was all. The mother hung over her, kissing her, petting her, and imploring her to speak, but the lips only moved, and no sound came. I snatched my liquor flask from my knapsack, but the woman forbade me, and said:

"No—she does not suffer; it is better so. It might bring her back to life. None that be so good and kind as ye are, would do her that cruel hurt. For look you—what is left to live for? Her brothers are gone, her father is gone, her mother goeth, the Church's curse is upon her and none may shelter or befriend her even though she lay perishing in the road. She is desolate. I have not asked you, good heart, if her sister be still on live, here overhead; I had no need; ye had gone back, else, and not left the poor thing forsaken—"

"She lieth at peace," interrupted the king, in a subdued voice.

"I would not change it. How rich is this day in happiness! Ah, my Annis, thou shalt join thy sister soon—thou'rt on thy way, and these be merciful friends, that will not hinder."

And so she fell to murmuring and cooing over the girl again, and softly stroking her face and hair, and kissing her and calling her by endearing names; but there was scarcely sign of response, now, in the glazing eyes. I saw tears well from the king's eyes, and trickle down his face. The woman noticed them, too, and said:

"Ah, I know that sign: thou'st a wife at home, poor soul, and you and she have gone hungry to bed, many's the time, that the little ones might have your crust; you know what poverty is, and the daily insults of your betters, and the heavy hand of the Church and the king."

The king winced under this accidental home-shot, but kept still; he was learning his part; and he was playing it well, too, for a pretty dull beginner. I struck up a diversion. I offered the woman food, and liquor, but she refused both. She would allow nothing to come between her and the release of death. Then I slipped away, and brought the dead child from aloft, and laid it by her. This broke her down again, and there was another scene that was full of heart-break. By and by I made another diversion, and beguiled her to sketch her story:

"Ye know it well, yourselves, having suffered it—for truly none of our condition in Britain escape it. It is the old, weary tale. We fought and struggled, and succeeded; meaning by success, that we lived and did not die; more than that is not to be claimed. No troubles came that we could not outlive, till this year brought them; then came they all at once, as one might say, and overwhelmed us. Years ago the lord of the manor planted certain fruit trees on our farm; in the best part of it, too—a grievous wrong and shame—"

"But it was his right," interrupted the king.

"None denieth that, indeed; an the law mean anything, what is the lord's is his, and what is mine is his also. Our farm was ours by lease, therefore 'twas likewise his, to do with it as he would. Some little time ago, three of those trees were found hewn down. Our three grown sons ran frightened to report the crime. Well, in his lordship's dungeon there they lie, who saith there shall they lie and rot till they confess. They have naught to confess, being innocent, wherefore there will they remain until they die. Ye know that right well, I ween. Think how this left us: a man, a woman and two children, to gather a crop that was planted by a so much greater force; yes, and protect it night and day from pigeons and prowling animals that be sacred and must not be hurt by any of our sort. When my lord's crop was nearly ready for the harvest, so also was ours; when his bell rang to call us to his fields to harvest his crops for nothing, he would not allow that I and my two girls should count for our three captive sons, but for only two of them; so, for the lacking one were we daily fined. All this time our own crop was perishing through neglect; and so both the priest and his lordship fined us because their shares of it were suffering through damage. In the end the fines ate up our crop—and they took it all; they took it all, and made us harvest it for them, without pay or food, and we starving. Then the worst came when I, being out of my mind with hunger and loss of my boys, and grief to see my husband and my little maids in rags and misery and despair, uttered a deep blasphemy—oh! a thousand of them!—against the Church and the Church's ways. It was ten days ago. I had fallen sick with this disease, and it was to the priest I said the words, for he was come to chide me for lack of due humility under the chastening hand of God. He carried my trespass to his betters; I was stubborn; wherefore, presently upon my head, and upon all heads that were dear to me, fell the curse of Rome.

"Since that day, we are avoided, shunned with horror. None has come near this hut to know whether we live or not. The rest of us were taken down. Then I roused me and got up, as wife and mother will. It was little they could have eaten in any case; it was less than little they had to eat. But there was water, and I gave them that. How they craved it! and how they blessed it! But the end came yesterday; my strength broke down. Yesterday was the last time I ever saw my husband and this youngest child alive. I have lain here all these hours—these ages, ye may say—listening, listening, for any sound up there that—"

She gave a sharp quick glance at her eldest daughter, then cried out, "Oh, my darling!" and feebly gathered the stiffening form to her sheltering arms. She had recognized the death-rattle.

Chapter 30

THE TRAGEDY OF THE MANOR HOUSE

AT MIDNIGHT all was over, and we sat in the presence of four corpses. We covered them with such rag as we could find, and started away, fastening the door behind us. Their home must be these people's grave, for they could not have Christian burial, or be admitted to consecrated ground. They were as dogs, wild beasts, lepers, and no soul that valued its hope of eternal life would throw it away by meddling in any sort with these rebuked and smitten outcasts.

We had not moved four steps when I caught a sound as of footsteps upon gravel. My heart flew into my throat. We must not be seen coming from that house. I plucked at the king's robe and we drew back and took shelter behind the corner of the cabin.

"Now we are safe," I said, "but it was a close call—so to speak. If the night had been lighter he might have seen us, no doubt, he seemed to be so near."

"Mayhap it is but a beast, and not a man at all."

"True. But, man or beast, it will be wise to stay here a minute and let it get by and out of the way."

"Hark! It cometh hither."

True again. The step was coming toward us—straight toward the hut. It must be a beast, then, and we might as well have saved our trepidation. I was going to step out, but the king laid his hand upon my arm. There was a moment of silence, then we heard a soft knock on the cabin door. It made me shiver. Presently the knock was repeated, and then we heard these words, in a guarded voice:

"Mother! father! open—we have got free, and we bring news to pale your cheeks but glad your hearts; and we may not tarry but must fly! And—but they answer not. Mother! father!—"

I drew the king toward the other end of the hut and whispered:

"Come—now we can get to the road."

425

The king hesitated, was going to demur; but just then we heard the door give way, and knew that those desolate men were in the presence of their dead.

"Come, my liege! in a moment they will strike a light, and then will follow that which it would break your heart to . hear."

He did not hesitate, this time. The moment we were in the road, I ran; and after a moment he threw dignity aside and followed. I did not want to think of what was happening in the hut—I couldn't bear it; I wanted to drive it out of my mind; so I struck into the first subject that lay under that one in my mind:

"I have had the disease those people died of, and so have nothing to fear; but if you have not had it also—"

He broke in upon me to say he was in trouble, and it was his conscience that was troubling him:

"These young men have got free, they say—but *how*? It is not likely that their lord hath set them free."

"Oh, no, I make no doubt they escaped."

"That is my trouble; I have a fear that this is so; and your suspicion doth confirm it, you having the same fear."

"I should not call it by that name, though. I do suspect that they escaped, but if they did, I am not sorry, certainly."

"I am not sorry, I *think*—but—"

"What is it? What is there for one to be troubled about?"

"*If* they did escape, then are we bound in duty to lay hands upon them and deliver them again to their lord; for it is not seemly that one of his quality should suffer a so insolent and high-handed outrage from persons of their base degree."

There it was, again. He could see only one side of it. He was born so, educated so, his veins were full of ancestral blood that was rotten with this sort of unconscious brutality, brought down by inheritance from a long procession of hearts that had each done its share toward poisoning the stream. To imprison these men without proof, and starve their kindred, was no harm, for they were merely peasants and subject to the will and pleasure of their lord, no matter what fearful form it might take; but for these men to break out of unjust captivity was insult and outrage, and a thing not to be countenanced by any conscientious person who knew his duty to his sacred caste.

I worked more than half an hour before I got him to change the subject—and even then an outside matter did it for me. This was a something which caught our eyes as we struck the summit of a small hill—a red glow, a good way off.

"That's a fire," said I.

Fires interested me considerably, because I was getting a good deal of an insurance business started, and was also training some horses and building some steam fire engines, with an eye to a paid fire department by and by. The priests opposed both my fire and life insurance, on the ground that it was an insolent attempt to hinder the decrees of God; and if you pointed out that they did not hinder the decrees in the least, but only modified the hard consequences of them if you took out policies and had luck, they retorted that that was gambling against the decrees of God, and was just as bad. So they managed to damage those industries more or less, but I got even on my Accident business. As a rule, a knight is a lummox, and sometimes even a labrick, and hence open to pretty poor arguments when they come glibly from a superstition-monger, but even *he* could see the practical side of a thing once in a while; and so of late, you couldn't clean up a tournament and pile the result without finding one of my accident tickets in every helmet.

We stood there a while, in the thick darkness and stillness, looking toward the red blur in the distance, and trying to make out the meaning of a far-away murmur that rose and fell fitfully on the night. Sometimes it swelled up and for a moment seemed less remote; but when we were hopefully expecting it to betray its cause and nature, it dulled and sank again, carrying its mystery with it. We started down the hill in its direction, and the winding road plunged us at once into almost solid darkness—darkness that was packed and crammed in between two tall forest walls. We groped along down for half a mile, perhaps, that murmur growing more and more distinct all the time, the coming storm threatening more and more, with now and then a little shiver of wind, a faint show of lightning, and dull grumblings of distant thunder. I was in the lead. I ran against something—a soft, heavy something which gave, slightly, to the impulse of my weight —at the same moment the lightning glared out, and within a foot of my face was the writhing face of a man who was hanging from the limb of a tree! That is, it seemed to be writhing, but it was not. It was a grewsome sight. Straightway there was an ear-splitting explosion of thunder, and the bottom of heaven fell out; the rain poured down in a deluge. No matter, we must try to cut this man down, mustn't we, on the chance that there might be life in him yet? The lightning came quick and sharp, now, and the place was alternately noonday and midnight. One moment the man would be hanging before me in an intense light, and the next he was blotted out again in the darkness. I told the king we must cut him down. The king at once objected.

"If he hanged himself, he was willing to lose his property to his lord; so let him be. If others hanged him, belike they had the right—let him hang."

"But—"

"But me no buts, but even leave him as he is. And for yet another reason. When the lightning cometh again—there, look abroad."

Two others hanging, within fifty yards of us!

"It is not weather meet for doing useless courtesies unto dead folk. They are past thanking you. Come—it is unprofitable to tarry here."

There was reason in what he said; so we moved on. Within the next mile we counted six more hanging forms by the blaze of the lightning, and altogether it was a grisly excursion. That murmur was a murmur no longer, it was a roar; a roar of men's voices. A man came flying by, now, dimly through the darkness, and other men chasing him. They disappeared. Presently another case of the kind occurred, and then another and another. Then a sudden turn of the road brought us in sight of that fire—it was a large manor house, and little or nothing was left of it—and everywhere men were flying and other men raging after them in pursuit.

I warned the king that this was not a safe place for strangers. We would better get away from the light, until matters should improve. We stepped back a little, and hid in the edge of the wood. From this hiding place we saw both men and women hunted by the mob. The fearful work went on until nearly dawn. Then, the fire being out and the storm spent, the voices and flying footsteps presently ceased, and darkness and stillness reigned again.

We ventured out, and hurried cautiously away; and although we were worn out and sleepy, we kept on until we had put this place some miles behind us. Then we asked hospitality at the hut of a charcoal burner, and got what was to be had. A woman was up and about, but the man was still asleep, on a straw shake-down, on the clay floor. The woman seemed uneasy until I explained that we were travelers and had lost our way and been wandering in the woods all night. She became talkative, then, and asked if we had heard of the terrible goings-on at the manor house of Abblasoure. Yes, we had heard of them, but what we wanted now, was rest and sleep. The king broke in:

"Sell us the house, and take yourselves away, for we be perilous company, being but late come from people that died of the Spotted Death."

It was good of him, but unnecessary. One of the commonest decorations of the nation was the waffle-iron face. I had early noticed that the woman and her husband were both so decorated. She made us entirely welcome, and had no fears; and plainly she was immensely impressed by the king's proposition; for of course it was a good deal of an event in her life to run across a person of the king's humble appearance who was ready to buy a man's house for the sake of a night's lodging. It gave her a large respect for us, and she strained the lean possibilities of her hovel to their utmost to make us comfortable.

We slept till far into the afternoon, and then got up hungry enough to make cotter fare quite palatable to the king, the more particularly as it was scant in quantity. And also in variety; it consisted solely of onions, salt, and the national black bread—made out of horse-feed. The woman told us about the affair of the evening before. At ten or eleven at night, when everybody was in bed, the manor house burst into flames. The countryside swarmed to the rescue, and the family were saved, with one exception, the master. He did not appear. Everybody was frantic over this loss, and two brave yeomen sacrificed their lives in ransacking the burning house seeking that valuable personage. But after a while he was found—what was left of him—which was his corpse. It was in a copse three hundred yards away, bound, gagged, stabbed in a dozen places.

Who had done this? Suspicion fell upon a humble family of the neighborhood who had been lately treated with peculiar harshness by the baron; and from these people the suspicion easily extended itself to their relatives and familiars. A suspicion was enough; my lord's liveried retainers proclaimed an instant crusade against these people, and were promptly joined by the community in general. The woman's husband had been active with the mob, and had not returned home until nearly dawn. He was gone, now, to find out what the general result had been. While we were still talking, he came back from his quest. His report was revolting enough. Eighteen persons hanged or butchered; and two yeomen and thirteen prisoners lost in the fire.

"And how many prisoners were there altogether, in the vaults?"

"Thirteen."

"Then every one of them was lost."

"Yes, all."

"But the people arrived in time to save the family; how is it they could save none of the prisoners?"

The man looked puzzled, and said:

"Would one unlock the vaults at such a time? Marry, some would have escaped."

"Then you mean that nobody *did* unlock them?"

"None went near them, either to lock or unlock. It standeth to reason that the bolts were fast; wherefore it was only needful to establish a watch, so that if any broke the bonds he might not escape, but be taken. None were taken."

"Natheless, three did escape," said the king, "and ye will do well to publish it and set justice upon their track, for these murthered the baron and fired the house."

I was just expecting he would come out with that. For a moment the man and his wife showed an eager interest in this news and an impatience to go out and spread it; then a sudden something else betrayed itself in their faces, and they began to ask questions. I answered the questions myself, and narrowly watched the effects produced. I was soon satisfied that the knowledge of who these three prisoners were, had somehow changed the atmosphere; that our hosts' continued eagerness to go and spread the news was now only pretended and not real. The king did not notice the change, and I was glad of that. I worked the conversation around toward other details of the night's proceedings, and noted that these people were relieved to have it take that direction.

The painful thing observable about all this business was, the alacrity with which this oppressed community had turned their cruel hands against their own class in the interest of the common oppressor. This man and woman seemed to feel that in a quarrel between a person of their own class and his lord, it was the natural and proper and rightful thing for that poor devil's whole caste to side with the master and fight his battle for him, without ever stopping to inquire into the rights or wrongs of the matter. This man had been out helping to hang his neighbors, and had done his work with zeal, and yet was aware that there was nothing against them but a mere suspicion, with nothing back of it describable as evidence; still neither he nor his wife seemed to see anything horrible about it.

This was depressing—to a man with the dream of a republic in his head. It reminded me of a time thirteen centuries away, when the "poor whites" of our South who were always despised, and frequently insulted, by the slave lords around them, and who owed their base condition simply to the presence of slavery in their midst, were yet pusillanimously ready to side with the slave lords in all political moves for the upholding and perpetuating of slavery, and did also finally shoulder their muskets and pour out their lives in an effort to prevent the destruction of that very institution which degraded them. And there was only one redeeming feature connected with that pitiful piece of history; and that was, that secretly the "poor white" did detest the slave lord, and did feel his own shame. That feeling was not brought to the surface, but the fact that it was there and could have been brought out, under favoring circumstances, was something —in fact it was enough; for it showed that a man is at bottom a man, after all, even if it doesn't show on the outside.

Well, as it turned out, this charcoal burner was just the twin of the Southern "poor white" of the far future. The king presently showed impatience, and said:

"An ye prattle here all the day, justice will miscarry. Think ye the criminals will abide in their father's house? They are fleeing, they are not waiting. You should look to it that a party of horse be set upon their track."

The woman paled slightly, but quite perceptibly, and the man looked flustered and irresolute. I said:

"Come, friend, I will walk a little way with you, and explain which direction I think they would try to take. If they were merely resisters of the gabelle or some kindred absurdity I would try to protect them from capture; but when men murder a person of high degree and likewise burn his house, that is another matter."

The last remark was for the king—to quiet him. On the road, the man pulled his resolution together, and began the march with a steady gait, but there was no eagerness in it. By and by I said:

"What relation were these men to you—cousins?"

He turned as white as his layer of charcoal would let him, and stopped, trembling.

"Ah, my God, how knew you that?"

"I didn't know it; it was a chance guess."

"Poor lads, they are lost. And good lads they were, too."

"Were you actually going yonder to tell on them?"

He didn't quite know how to take that; but he said, hesitatingly:

"Ye-s."

"Then I think you are a damned scoundrel!"

It made him as glad as if I had called him an angel.

"Say the good words again, brother! for surely ye mean that ye would not betray me an I failed of my duty."

"Duty? There is no duty in the matter, except the duty to keep still and let those men get away. They've done a righteous deed."

He looked pleased; pleased, and touched with apprehension at the same time. He looked up and down the road to see that no one was coming, and then said in a cautious voice:

"From what land come you, brother, that you speak such perilous words, and seem not to be afraid?"

"They are not perilous words when spoken to one of my own caste, I take it. You would not tell anybody I said them?"

"I? I would be drawn asunder by wild horses first."

"Well, then, let me say my say. I have no fears of your repeating it. I think devil's work has been done last night upon those innocent poor people. That old baron got only what he deserved. If I had my way, all his kind should have the same luck."

Fear and depression vanished from the man's manner, and gratefulness and a brave animation took their place:

"Even though you be a spy, and your words a trap for my undoing, yet are they such refreshment that to hear them again and others like to them, I would go to the gallows happy, as having had one good feast at least in a starved life. And I will say my say, now, and ye may report it if ye be so minded. I helped to hang my neighbors for that it were peril to my own life to show lack of zeal in the master's cause; the others helped for none other reason. All rejoice to-day that he is dead, but all do go about seemingly sorrowing, and shedding the hypocrite's tear, for in that lies safety. I have said the words, I have said the words! the only ones that have ever tasted good in my mouth, and the reward of that taste is sufficient. Lead on, an ye will, be it even to the scaffold; for I am ready."

There it was, you see. A man *is* a man, at bottom. Whole ages of abuse and oppression cannot crush the manhood clear out of him. Whoever thinks it a mistake, is himself mistaken. Yes, there is plenty good enough material for a republic in the most degraded people that ever existed—even the Russians; plenty of manhood in them—even in the Germans—if one could but force it out of its timid and suspicious privacy, to overthrow and trample in the mud any throne that ever was set up and any nobility that ever supported it. We should see certain things yet, let us hope and believe. First, a modified monarchy, till Arthur's days were done, then the destruction of the throne, nobility abolished, every member of it bound out to some useful trade, universal suffrage instituted, and the whole government placed in the hands of the men and women of the nation there to remain. Yes, there was no occasion to give up my dream yet a while.

Chapter 31

MARCO

W^E STROLLED along in a sufficiently indolent fashion, now, and talked. We must dispose of about the amount of time it ought to take to go to the little hamlet of Abbla-soure and put justice on the track of those murderers and get back home again. And meantime I had an auxiliary interest which had never paled yet, never lost its novelty for me, since I had been in Arthur's kingdom: the behavior—born of nice and exact subdivisions of caste—of chance passers-by toward each other. Toward the shaven monk who trudged along with his cowl tilted back and the sweat washing down his fat jowls, the coal burner was deeply reverent; to the gentleman he was abject; with the small farmer and the free mechanic he was cordial and gossipy; and when a slave passed by with counte-nance respectfully lowered, this chap's nose was in the air—he couldn't even see him. Well, there are times when one would like to hang the whole human race and finish the farce.

Presently we struck an incident. A small mob of half naked boys and girls came tearing out of the woods, scared and shrieking. The eldest among them were not more than twelve or fourteen years old. They implored help, but they were so beside themselves that we couldn't make out what the matter was. However, we plunged into the wood, they skurrying in the lead, and the trouble was quickly revealed: they had hanged a little fellow with a bark rope, and he was kicking and struggling, in the process of choking to death. We res-cued him, and fetched him around. It was some more human nature; the admiring little folk imitating their elders; they were playing mob, and had achieved a success which prom-ised to be a good deal more serious than they had bargained for.

It was not a dull excursion for me. I managed to put in the time very well. I made various acquaintanceships, and in my quality of stranger was able to ask as many questions as I wanted to. A thing which naturally interested me, as a statesman, was the matter of wages. I picked up what I could under that head during the afternoon. A man who hasn't had much experience, and doesn't think, is apt to measure a nation's prosperity or lack of prosperity by the mere size of the prevailing wages: if the wages be high, the nation is prosperous; if low, it isn't. Which is an error. It isn't what sum you get, it's how much you can buy with it that's the important thing; and it's that that tells whether your wages are high in fact or only high in name. I could remember how it was in the time of our great civil war in the nineteenth century. In the North, a carpenter got three dollars a day, gold valuation; in the South he got fifty—payable in Confederate shin-plasters worth a dollar a bushel. In the North, a suit of overalls cost three dollars—a day's wages; in the South it cost seventy-five—which was two days' wages. Other things were in proportion. Consequently, wages were twice as high in the North as they were in the South, because the one wage had that much more purchasing power than the other had.

Yes, I made various acquaintances in the hamlet, and a thing that gratified me a good deal, was, to find our new coins in circulation—lots of milrays, lots of mills, lots of cents, a good many nickels, and some silver; all this among the artisans and commonalty generally; yes, and even some gold—but that was at the bank, that is to say, the goldsmith's. I dropped in there while Marco the son of Marco was haggling with a shopkeeper over a quarter of a pound of salt, and asked for change for a twenty-dollar gold-piece. They furnished it,—that is, after they had chewed the piece, and rung it on the counter, and tried acid on it, and asked me where I got it, and who I was, and where I was from, and where I was going to, and when I expected to get there, and perhaps a couple of hundred more questions; and when they got aground, I went right on and furnished them a lot of information voluntarily: told them I owned a dog, and his name was Watch, and my first wife was a Free Will Baptist, and her grandfather was a Prohibitionist, and I used to know a man that had two thumbs on each hand and a wart on the inside of his upper lip, and died in the hope of a glorious resurrection, and so-on, and so-on, and so-on, till even that hungry village questioner began to look satisfied, and also a shade put out; but he had to respect a man of my financial strength, and so he didn't give me any lip, but I noticed he took it out of his underlings, which was a perfectly natural thing to do. Yes, they changed my twenty, but I judged it strained the bank a little, which was a thing to be expected, for it was the same as walking into a paltry village store in the nineteenth century and requiring the boss of it to change a two-thousand-dollar bill for you all of a sudden. He could do it, maybe; but at the same time he would wonder how a small farmer happened to be carrying so much money around in his pocket; which was probably this goldsmith's thought, too; for he followed me to the door and stood there gazing after me with reverent admiration.

Our new money was not only handsomely circulating, but its language was already glibly in use; that is to say, people had dropped the names of the former moneys, and spoke of things as being worth so many dollars or cents or mills or milrays, now. It was very gratifying. We were progressing, that was sure.

I got to know several master mechanics, but about the most interesting fellow among them was the blacksmith, Dowley. He was a live man and a brisk talker, and had two journeymen and three apprentices, and was doing a raging business. In fact, he was getting rich, hand over fist, and was vastly respected. Marco was very proud of having such a man for a friend. He had taken me there ostensibly to let me see the big establishment which bought so much of his charcoal, but really to let me see what easy and almost familiar terms he was on with this great man. Dowley and I fraternized at once; I had had just such picked men, splendid fellows, under me in the Colt arms-factory. I was bound to see more of him, so I invited him to come out to Marco's, Sunday, and dine with us. Marco was appalled, and held his breath; and when the grandee accepted, he was so grateful that he almost forgot to be astonished at the condescension.

Marco's joy was exuberant—but only for a moment; then he grew thoughtful, then sad; and when he heard me tell Dowley I should have Dickon the boss mason, and Smug the boss wheelwright out there, too, the coal-dust on his face turned to chalk, and he lost his grip. But I knew what was the matter with him; it was the expense. He saw ruin before him; he judged that his financial days were numbered. However, on our way to invite the others, I said:

"You must allow me to have these friends come; and you must also allow me to pay the costs."

His face cleared, and he said with spirit:

"But not all of it, not all of it. Ye cannot well bear a burden like to this alone."

I stopped him, and said:

"Now let's understand each other on the spot, old friend. I am only a farm bailiff, it is true; but I am not poor, nevertheless. I have been very fortunate this year—you would be astonished to know how I have thriven. I tell you the honest truth when I say I could squander away as many as a dozen feasts like this and never care *that* for the expense!" and I snapped my fingers. I could see myself rise a foot at a time in Marco's estimation, and when I fetched out those last words I was become a very tower, for style and altitude. "So you see, you must let me have my way. You can't contribute a cent to this orgy, that's *settled*."

"It's grand and good of you—"

"No, it isn't. You've opened your house to Jones and me in the most generous way; Jones was remarking upon it to-day, just before you came back from the village; for although he wouldn't be likely to say such a thing to you,—because Jones isn't a talker, and is diffident in society—he has a good heart and a grateful, and knows how to appreciate it when he is well treated; yes, you and your wife have been very hospitable toward us—"

"Ah, brother, 'tis nothing—*such* hospitality!"

"But it *is* something; the best a man has, freely given, is always something, and is as good as a prince can do, and ranks right along beside it—for even a prince can but do his best. And so we'll shop around and get up this layout, now, and don't you worry about the expense. I'm one of the worst spendthrifts that ever was born. Why, do you know, sometimes in a single week I spend—but never mind about that—you'd never believe it anyway."

And so we went gadding along, dropping in, here and there, pricing things, and gossiping with the shopkeepers about the riot, and now and then running across pathetic reminders of it, in the persons of shunned and tearful and houseless remnants of families whose homes had been taken from them and their parents butchered or hanged. The raiment of Marco and his wife was of coarse tow-linen and linsey-woolsey respectively, and resembled township maps, it being made up pretty exclusively of patches which had been added, township by township, in the course of five or six years, until hardly a hand's breadth of the original garments was surviving and present. Now I wanted to fit these people out with new suits, on account of that swell company, and I didn't know just how to get at it with delicacy, until at last it struck me that as I had already been liberal in inventing wordy gratitude for the king, it would be just the thing to back it up with evidence of a substantial sort; so I said:

"And Marco, there's another thing which you must permit—out of kindness for Jones—because you wouldn't want to offend him. He was very anxious to testify his appreciation in some way, but he is so diffident he couldn't venture it himself, and so he begged me to buy some little things and give them to you and Dame Phyllis and let him pay for them without your ever knowing they came from him—you know how a delicate person feels about that sort of thing—and so I said I would, and we would keep mum. Well, his idea was, a new outfit of clothes for you both—"

"Oh, it is wastefulness! It may not be, brother, it may not be. Consider the vastness of the sum—"

"Hang the vastness of the sum! Try to keep quiet for a moment, and see how it would seem; a body can't get in a word edgeways, you talk so much. You ought to cure that, Marco; it isn't good form, you know, and it will grow on you, if you don't check it. Yes, we'll step in here, now, and price this man's stuff—and don't forget to remember to not let on to Jones that you know he had anything to do with it. You can't think how curiously sensitive and proud he is. He's a farmer—pretty fairly well-to-do farmer—and I'm his bailiff; *but*—the imagination of that man! Why, sometimes when he forgets himself, and gets to blowing off, you'd think he was one of the swells of the earth; and you might listen to him a hundred years and never take him for a farmer—

especially if he talked agriculture. He *thinks* he's a Sheol of a farmer; thinks he's old Grayback from Wayback; but between you and me privately he don't know as much about farming as he does about a running a kingdom—still, whatever he talks about, you want to drop your underjaw and listen, the same as if you had never heard such incredible wisdom in all your life before, and were afraid you might die before you got enough of it. That will please Jones."

It tickled Marco to the marrow to hear about such an odd character; but it also prepared him for accidents; and in my experience, when you travel with a king who is letting on to be something else and can't remember it more than about half the time, you can't take too many precautions.

This was the best store we had come across yet; it had everything in it, in small quantities, from anvils and dry goods all the way down to fish and pinchbeck jewelry. I concluded I would bunch my whole invoice right here, and not go pricing around any more. So I got rid of Marco, by sending him off to invite the mason and the wheelwright, which left the field free to me. For I never care to do a thing in a quiet way; it's got to be theatrical, or I don't take any interest in it. I showed up money enough, in a careless way, to corral the shop-keeper's respect, and then I wrote down a list of the things I wanted, and handed it to him to see if he could read it. He could, and was proud to show that he could. He said he had been educated by a priest, and could read and write both. He ran it through, and remarked with satisfaction that it was a pretty heavy bill. Well, and so it was, for a little concern like that. I was not only providing a swell dinner, but some odds and ends of extras. I ordered that the things be carted out and delivered at the dwelling of Marco the son of Marco by Saturday evening, and send me the bill at dinner time Sunday. He said I could depend upon his promptness and exactitude, it was the rule of the house. He also observed that he would throw in a couple of miller-guns for the Marcos gratis—that everybody was using them, now. He had a mighty opinion of that clever device. I said:

"And please fill them up to the middle mark, too; and add that to the bill."

He would, with pleasure. He filled them, and I took them with me. I couldn't venture to tell him that the miller-gun was a little invention of my own, and that I had officially ordered that every shopkeeper in the kingdom keep them on hand and sell them at government price—which was the merest trifle, and the shopkeeper got that, not the government. We furnished them for nothing.

The king had hardly missed us when we got back at nightfall. He had early dropped again into his dream of a grand invasion of Gaul with the whole strength of his kingdom at his back, and the afternoon had slipped away without his ever coming to himself again.

Chapter 32

DOWLEY'S HUMILIATION

WELL, when that cargo arrived, toward sunset, Saturday afternoon, I had my hands full to keep the Marcos from fainting. They were sure Jones and I were ruined past help, and they blamed themselves as accessories to this bankruptcy. You see, in addition to the dinner-materials, which called for a sufficiently round sum, I had bought a lot of extras for the future comfort of the family: for instance, a big lot of wheat, a delicacy as rare to the tables of their class as was ice cream to a hermit's; also a sizeable deal dinner-table; also two entire pounds of salt, which was another piece of extravagance in those people's eyes; also crockery, stools, the clothes, a small cask of beer, and so-on. I instructed the Marcos to keep quiet about this sumptuousness, so as to give me a chance to surprise the guests and show off a little. Concerning the new clothes, the simple couple were like children; they were up and down, all night, to see if it wasn't nearly daylight, so that they could put them on, and they were into them at last as much as an hour before dawn was due. Then their pleasure—not to say delirium—was so fresh and novel and inspiring that the sight of it paid me well for the interruptions which my sleep had suffered. The king had slept just as usual—like the dead. The Marcos could not thank him for their clothes, that being forbidden; but they tried every way they could think of to make him see how grateful they were. Which all went for nothing: he didn't notice any change.

It turned out to be one of those rich and rare fall days which is just a June day toned down to a degree where it is heaven to be out of doors. Toward noon the guests arrived and we assembled under a great tree and were soon as sociable as old acquaintances. Even the king's reserve melted a little, though it was some little trouble to him to adjust himself to the name of Jones along at first. I had asked him to try to not forget that he was a farmer; but I had also considered it prudent to ask him to let the thing stand at that, and not elaborate it any. Because he was just the kind of person you could depend on to spoil a little thing like that if you didn't warn him, his tongue was so handy, and his spirit so willing, and his information so uncertain.

Dowley was in fine feather, and I early got him started, and then adroitly worked him around onto his own history for a text and himself for a hero, and then it was good to sit there and hear him hum. Self-made man, you know. They know how to talk. They do deserve more credit than any other breed of men, yes, that is true; and they are among the very first to find it out, too. He told how he had begun life an orphan lad without money and without friends able to help him; how he had lived as the slaves of the meanest master lived; how his day's work was from sixteen to eighteen hours long, and yielded him only enough black bread to keep him in a half-fed condition; how his faithful endeavors finally attracted the attention of a good blacksmith, who came near knocking him dead with kindness by suddenly offering, when he was totally unprepared, to take him as his bound apprentice for nine years and give him board and clothes and teach him the trade—or "mystery," as Dowley called it. That was his first great rise, his first gorgeous stroke of fortune; and you saw that he couldn't yet speak of it without a sort of eloquent wonder and delight that such a gilded promotion should have fallen to the lot of a common human being. He got no new clothing during his apprenticeship, but on his graduation day his master tricked him out in spang-new towlinens and made him feel unspeakably rich and fine.

"I remember me of that day!" the wheelwright sung out, with enthusiasm.

"And I likewise!" cried the mason. "I would not believe they were thine own; in faith I could not."

"Nor others!" shouted Dowley, with sparkling eyes. "I was like to lose my character, the neighbors wending I had mayhap been stealing. It was a great day, a great day; one forgetteth not days like that."

Yes, and his master was a fine man, and prosperous, and always had a great feast of meat twice in the year, and with it white bread, true wheaten bread; in fact, lived like a lord, so to speak. And in time Dowley succeeded to the business and married the daughter.

"And now consider what is come to pass," said he, impressively. "Two times in every month there is fresh meat upon my table." He made a pause here, to let that fact sink home, then added—"and eight times, salt meat."

"It is even true," said the wheelwright, with bated breath.

"I know it of mine own knowledge," said the mason, in the same reverent fashion.

"On my table appeareth white bread every Sunday in the year," added the master smith, with solemnity. "I leave it to your own consciences, friends, if this is not also true?"

"By my head, yes!" cried the mason.

"I can testify it—and I do," said the wheelwright.

"And as to furniture, ye shall say yourselves what mine equipment is." He waved his hand in fine gesture of granting frank and unhampered freedom of speech, and added: "Speak as ye are moved; speak as ye would speak an I were not here."

"Ye have five stools, and of the sweetest workmanship at that, albeit your family is but three," said the wheelwright, with deep respect.

"And six wooden goblets, and six platters of wood and two of pewter to eat and drink from withal," said the mason, impressively, "and I say it as knowing God is my judge, and we tarry not here alway, but must answer at the last day for the things said in the body, be they false or be they sooth."

"Now ye know what manner of man I am, Brother Jones," said the smith with a fine and friendly condescension, "and doubtless ye would look to find me a man jealous of his due of respect and but sparing of outgo to strangers till their rating and quality be assured, but trouble yourself not, as concerning that; wit ye well ye shall find me a man that regardeth not these matters but is willing to receive any he as his fellow and equal that carrieth a right heart in his body, be his worldly estate howsoever modest. And in token of it, here is my hand; and I say with my own mouth we are equals—equals"—and he smiled around on the company with the satisfaction of a god who is doing the handsome and gracious thing, and is quite well aware of it.

The king took the hand with a poorly disguised reluctance, and let go of it as willingly as a lady lets go of a fish; all of which had a good effect, for it was mistaken for an embarrassment natural to one who was being beamed upon by greatness.

The dame brought out the table, now, and set it under the tree. It caused a visible stir of surprise, it being brand new and a sumptuous article of deal. But the surprise rose higher still, when the dame, with a body oozing easy indifference at every pore, but eyes that gave it all away by absolutely flaming with vanity, slowly unfolded an actual simon-pure table-cloth and spread it. That was a notch above even the blacksmith's domestic grandeurs, and it hit him hard; you could see it. But Marco was in Paradise; you could see that, too. Then the dame brought two fine-new stools—whew! that was a sensation; it was visible in the eyes of every guest. Then she brought two more—as calmly as she could. Sensation again—with awed murmurs. Again she brought two— walking on air, she was so proud. The guests were petrified, and the mason muttered:

"There is that about earthly pomps which doth ever move to reverence."

As the dame turned away, Marco couldn't help slapping on the climax while the thing was hot; so he said with what was meant for a languid composure but was a poor imitation of it:

"These suffice; leave the rest."

So there were more yet! It was a fine effect. I couldn't have played the hand better, myself.

From this out, the madam piled up the surprises with a rush that fired the general astonishment up to a hundred and fifty in the shade, and at the same time paralyzed expression of it down to gasped "Oh's" and "Ah's," and mute upliftings of hands and eyes. She fetched crockery—new, and plenty of it; new wooden goblets and other table furniture; and beer, fish, chicken, a goose, eggs, roast beef, roast mutton, a ham, a small roast pig, and a wealth of genuine white wheaten bread. Take it by and large, that spread laid everything far and away in the shade that ever that crowd had seen before. And while they sat there just simply stupefied with wonder and awe, I sort of waved my hand as if by accident, and the store-keeper's son emerged from space and said he had come to collect.

"That's all right," I said, indifferently. "What is the amount? give us the items."

Then he read off this bill, while those three amazed men listened, and serene waves of satisfaction rolled over my soul, and alternate waves of terror and admiration surged over Marco's:

2 pounds salt	200
8 dozen pints beer, in the wood	800
3 bushels wheat	2,700
2 pounds fish	100
3 hens	400
1 goose	400
3 dozen eggs	150
1 roast of beef	450
1 " " mutton	400
1 ham	800
1 sucking pig	500
2 crockery dinner sets	6,000
2 men's suits and underwear	2,800
1 stuff and 1 linsey-woolsey gown and underwear	1,600
8 wooden goblets	800
Various table furniture	10,000
1 deal table	3,000
8 stools	4,000
2 miller-guns, loaded	3,000

He ceased. There was a pale and awful silence. Not a limb stirred. Not a nostril betrayed the passage of breath.

"Is that all?" I asked, in a voice of the most perfect calmness.

"All, fair sir, save that certain matters of light moment are placed together under a head hight sundries. If it would like you, I will sepa—"

"It is of no consequence," I said, accompanying the words with a gesture of the most utter indifference; "give me the grand total, please."

The clerk leaned against the tree to stay himself, and said:

"Thirty-nine thousand one hundred and fifty milrays!"

The wheelwright fell off his stool, the others grabbed the table to save themselves, and there was a deep and general ejaculation of—

"God be with us in the day of disaster!"

The clerk hastened to say:

"My father chargeth me to say he cannot honorably require you to pay it all at this time, and therefore only prayeth you—"

I paid no more heed than if it were the idle breeze, but with an air of indifference amounting almost to weariness, got out my money and tossed four dollars onto the table. Ah, you should have seen them stare!

The clerk was astonished and charmed. He asked me to retain one of the dollars as security, until he could go to town and— I interrupted:

"What, and fetch back nine cents? Nonsense. Take the whole. Keep the change."

There was an amazed murmur, to this effect:

"Verily this being is *made* of money! He throweth it away even as it were dirt."

The blacksmith was a crushed man.

The clerk took his money and reeled away drunk with fortune. I said to Marco and his wife:

"Good folk, here is a little trifle for you"—handing the miller-guns as if it was a matter of no consequence, though each of them contained fifteen cents in solid cash; and while the poor creatures went to pieces with astonishment and gratitude, I turned to the others and said as calmly as one would ask the time of day:

"Well, if we are all ready, I judge the dinner is. Come; fall to."

Ah, well, it was immense; yes, it was a daisy. I don't know that I ever put a situation together better, or got happier spectacular effects out of the materials available. The blacksmith—well, he was simply mashed. Land! I wouldn't have felt what that man was feeling, for anything in the world. Here he had been blowing and bragging about his grand meat-feast twice a year, and his fresh meat twice a month, and his salt meat twice a week, and his white bread every Sunday the year round—all for a family of three: the entire cost for the year not above 69.2.6 (sixty-nine cents, two mills and six milrays,) and all of a sudden here comes along a man who slashes out nearly four dollars on a single blow-out; and not only that, but acts as if it made him tired to handle such small sums. Yes, Dowley was a good deal wilted, and shrunk-up, and collapsed; he had the aspect of a bladder-balloon that's been stepped on by a cow.

Chapter 33

SIXTH-CENTURY POLITICAL ECONOMY

HOWEVER, I made a dead set at him, and before the first
third of the dinner was reached, I had him happy
again. It was easy to do—in a country of ranks and castes.
You see, in a country where they have ranks and castes, a man
isn't ever a man, he is only part of a man; he can't ever get his
full growth. You prove your superiority over him in station,
or rank, or fortune, and that's the end of it—he knuckles
down. You can't insult him after that. No, I don't mean quite
that; of course you *can* insult him, I only mean it's difficult;
and so, unless you've got a lot of useless time on your hands,
it doesn't pay to try. I had the smith's reverence, now, because I was apparently immensely prosperous and rich; I
could have had his adoration if I had had some little gimcrack
title of nobility. And not only his, but any commoner's in the
land, though he were the mightiest production of all the ages,
in intellect, worth, and character, and I bankrupt in all three.
This was to remain so, as long as England should exist in the
earth. With the spirit of prophecy upon me, I could look into
the future and see her erect statues and monuments to her
unspeakable Georges and other royal and noble clothes-
horses, and leave unhonored the creators of this world—after
God—Gutenberg, Watt, Arkwright, Whitney, Morse, Ste-
phenson, Bell.

The king got his cargo aboard, and then, the talk not turning upon battle, conquest, or iron-clad duel, he dulled down
to drowsiness, and went off to take a nap. Mrs. Marco cleared
the table, placed the beer-keg handy, and went away to eat
her dinner of leavings in humble privacy, and the rest of us
soon drifted into matters near and dear to the hearts of our
sort—business and wages, of course. At a first glance, things
appeared to be exceeding prosperous in this little tributary
kingdom—whose lord was King Bagdemagus—as compared
with the state of things in my own region. They had the "protection" system in full force, here, whereas we were working

along down toward free trade, by easy stages, and were now about half way. Before long, Dowley and I were doing all the talking, the others hungrily listening. Dowley warmed to his work, snuffed an advantage in the air, and began to put questions which he considered pretty awkward ones for me, and they did have something of that look:

"In your country, brother, what is the wage of a master bailiff, master hind, carter, shepherd, swineherd?"

"Twenty-five milrays a day; that is to say, a quarter of a cent."

The smith's face beamed with joy. He said:

"With us they are allowed the double of it! And what may a mechanic get—carpenter, dauber, mason, painter, blacksmith, wheelwright, and the like?"

"On the average, fifty milrays: half a cent a day."

"Ho-ho! With us they are allowed a hundred! With us any good mechanic is allowed a cent a day! I count out the tailor, but not the others—they are all allowed a cent a day, and in driving times they get more—yes, up to a hundred and ten and even fifteen milrays a day. I've paid a hundred and fifteen myself, within the week. 'Rah for protection—to Sheol with free trade!"

And his face shone upon the company like a sunburst. But I didn't scare at all. I rigged up my pile-driver, and allowed myself fifteen minutes to drive him into the earth—drive him *all* in—drive him in till not even the curve of his skull should show above ground. Here is the way I started in on him. I asked:

"What do you pay a pound for salt?"

"A hundred milrays."

"We pay 40. What do you pay for beef and mutton—when you buy it?" That was a neat hit; it made the color come:

"It varieth somewhat, but not much; one may say 75 milrays the pound."

"*We* say 33. What do you pay for eggs?"

"Fifty milrays the dozen."

"We pay 20. What do you pay for beer?"

"It costeth us 8½ milrays the pint."

"We get it for 4; 25 bottles for a cent. What do you pay for wheat?"

"At the rate of 900 milrays the bushel."

"We pay 400. What do you pay for a man's tow-linen suit?"

"Thirteen cents."

"We pay 6. What do you pay for a stuff gown for the wife of the laborer or the mechanic?"

"We pay 8.4.0."

"Well, observe the difference: you pay eight cents and four mills, we pay only four cents." I prepared, now, to sock it to him. I said, "Look here, dear friend, *what's become of your high wages you were bragging so about, a few minutes ago?*"—and I looked around on the company with placid satisfaction, for I had slipped up on him gradually and tied him hand and foot, you see, without his ever noticing that he was being tied at all. "What's become of those noble high wages of yours?—I seem to have knocked the stuffing all out of them, it appears to me."

But if you will believe me, he merely looked surprised, that is all! he didn't grasp the situation at all; didn't know he had walked into a trap, didn't discover that he was *in* a trap. I could have shot him, from sheer vexation. With cloudy eye and a struggling intellect, he fetched this out:

"Marry, I seem not to understand. It is *proved* that our wages be double thine; how then may it be that thou'st knocked therefrom the stuffing?—an I miscall not the wonderly word, this being the first time under grace and providence of God it hath been granted me to hear it."

Well, I was stunned; partly with this unlooked-for stupidity on his part, and partly because his fellows so manifestly sided with him and were of his mind—if you might call it mind. My position was simple enough, plain enough; how could it ever be simplified more? However, I must try:

"Why look here, Brother Dowley, don't you see? Your wages are merely higher than ours in *name*, not in *fact*."

"Hear him! They are the *double*—ye have confessed it yourself."

"Yes-yes, I don't deny that at all. But that's got nothing to do with it; the *amount* of the wages in mere coins, with meaningless names attached to them to know them by, has got nothing to do with it. The thing is, how much can you *buy* with your wages?—that's the idea. While it is true that with you a good mechanic is allowed about three dollars and a half a year, and with us only about a dollar and seventy-five—"

"There—ye're confessing it again, ye're confessing it again!"

"Consound it, I've never denied it I tell you! What I say is this. With us, *half* a dollar buys more than a *dollar* buys with you—and *therefore* it stands to reason and the commonest kind of common sense, that our wages are *higher* than yours."

He looked dazed; and said, despairingly:

"Verily I cannot make it out. Ye've just *said* ours are the higher, and with the same breath ye take it back."

"Oh, great Scott, isn't it possible to get such a simple thing through your head? Now look here—let me illustrate. We pay four cents for a woman's stuff gown, you pay 8.4.0., which is 4 mills more than *double*. What do you allow a laboring woman who works on a farm?"

"Two mills a day."

"Very good; we allow but half as much; we pay her only a tenth of a cent a day; and—"

"Again ye're conf—"

"Wait! Now, you see, the thing is very simple; this time you'll understand it. For instance, it takes your woman 42 days to earn her gown, at 2 mills a day—7 weeks' work; but ours earns hers in 40 days—two days *short* of 7 weeks. Your woman has a gown, and her whole 7 weeks' wages are gone; ours has a gown, and two days' wages left, to buy something else with. There—*now* you understand it!"

He looked—well he merely looked dubious, it's the most I can say; so did the others. I waited—to let the thing work. Dowley spoke at last—and betrayed the fact that he actually hadn't gotten away from his rooted and grounded superstitions yet. He said, with a trifle of hesitancy:

"But—but—ye cannot fail to grant that two mills a day is better than one."

Shucks! Well, of course I hated to give it up. So I chanced another flyer:

"Let us suppose a case. Suppose one of your journeymen goes out and buys the following articles:

> 1 pound of salt;
> 1 dozen eggs;
> 1 dozen pints of beer;
> 1 bushel of wheat;
> 1 tow-linen suit;
> 5 pounds of beef;
> 5 pounds of mutton.

The lot will cost him 32 cents. It takes him 32 working days to earn the money—5 weeks and 2 days. Let him come to us and work 32 days at *half* the wages; he can buy all those things for a shade under 14½ cents; they will cost him a shade under 29 days' work, and he will have about half a week's wages over. Carry it through the year: he would save nearly a week's wages every two months, *your* man nothing; thus saving five or six weeks' wages in a year, your man not a cent. *Now* I reckon you understand that 'high wages' and 'low wages' are phrases that don't mean anything in the world until you find out which of them will *buy* the most!"

It was a crusher.

But alas, it didn't crush. No, I had to give it up. What those people valued was *high wages*; it didn't seem to be a matter of any consequence to them whether the high wages would buy anything or not. They stood for "protection," and swore by it; which was reasonable enough, because interested parties had gulled them into the notion that it was protection which had created their high wages. I proved to them that in a quarter of a century their wages had advanced but 30 per cent, while the cost of living had gone up 100; and that with us, in a shorter time, wages had advanced 40 per cent while the cost of living had gone steadily down. But it didn't do any good. Nothing could unseat their strange beliefs.

Well, I was smarting under a sense of defeat. Undeserved defeat, but what of that? That didn't soften the smart any. And to think of the circumstances! the first statesman of the age, the capablest man, the best informed man in the entire world, the loftiest uncrowned head that had moved through the clouds of any political firmament for centuries, sitting here apparently defeated in argument by an ignorant country

blacksmith! And I could see that those others were sorry for
me!—which made me blush till I could smell my whiskers
scorching. Put yourself in my place; feel as mean as I did, as
ashamed as I felt—wouldn't *you* have struck below the belt,
to get even? Yes, you would; it is simply human nature. Well,
that is what I did. I am not trying to justify it; I'm only saying
that I was mad, and *anybody* would have done it.

Well, when I make up my mind to hit a man, I don't plan
out a love-tap; no, that isn't my way; as long as I'm going to
hit him at all, I'm going to hit him a lifter. And I don't jump
at him all of a sudden, and risk making a blundering half-way
business of it; no, I get away off yonder to one side, and work
up on him gradually, so that he never suspects that I'm going
to hit him at all; and by and by, all in a flash, he's flat of his
back, and he can't tell for the life of him how it all happened.
That is the way I went for Brother Dowley. I started to talking, lazy and comfortable, as if I was just talking to pass the
time; and the oldest man in the world couldn't have taken the
bearings of my starting-place and guessed where I was going
to fetch up:

"Boys, there's a good many curious things about law, and
custom, and usage, and all that sort of thing, when you come
to look at it; yes, and about the drift and progress of human
opinion and movement, too. There are written laws—they
perish; but there are also unwritten laws—*they* are eternal.
Take the unwritten law of wages: it says they've got to
advance, little by little, straight through the centuries. And
notice how it works. We know what wages are now, here and
there and yonder; we strike an average, and say that's the
wages of to-day. We know what the wages were a hundred
years ago, and what they were two hundred years ago; that's
as far back as we can get, but it suffices to give us the law of
progress, the measure and rate of the periodical augmenta-
tion; and so, without a document to help us, we can come
pretty close to determining what the wages were three and
four and five hundred years ago. Good, so far. Do we stop
there? No. We stop looking backward; we face around and
apply the law to the future. My friends, I can tell you what
people's wages are going to be at any date in the future you
want to know, for hundreds and hundreds of years."

"What, goodman, what!"

"Yes. In seven hundred years, wages will have risen to six times what they are now, here in your region, and farm hands will be allowed 3 cents a day, and mechanics 6."

"I would I might die now, and live then!" interrupted Smug the wheelwright, with a fine avaricious glow in his eye.

"And that isn't all; they'll get their board besides—such as it is: it won't bloat them. Two hundred and fifty years later— pay attention, now—a mechanic's wages will be—mind you, this is law, not guesswork; a mechanic's wages will then be *twenty* cents a day!"

There was a general gasp of awed astonishment. Dickon the mason murmured, with raised eyes and hands:

"More than three weeks' pay for one day's work!"

"Riches!—of a truth, yes, riches!" muttered Marco, his breath coming quick and short, with excitement.

"Wages will keep on rising, little by little, little by little, as steadily as a tree grows; and at the end of three hundred and forty years more there'll be at least *one* country where the mechanic's average wage will be *two hundred* cents a day!"

It knocked them absolutely dumb! Not a man of them could get his breath for upwards of two minutes. Then the coal-burner said prayerfully:

"Might I but live to see it!"

"It is the income of an earl!" said Smug.

"An earl, say ye?" said Dowley; "ye could say more than that, and speak no lie; there's no earl in the realm of Bagdemagus that hath an income like to that. Income of an earl— mf! it's the income of an angel!"

"Now then, that is what is going to happen as regards wages. In that remote day, that man will earn, with *one* week's work, that bill of goods which it takes you upwards of *five* weeks to earn now. Some other pretty surprising things are going to happen, too. Brother Dowley, who is it that determines, every spring, what the particular wage of each kind of mechanic, laborer, and servant shall be for that year?"

"Sometimes the courts, sometimes the town council; but most of all, the magistrate. Ye may say, in general terms, it is the magistrate that fixes the wages."

"Doesn't ask any of those poor devils to *help* him fix their wages for them, does he?"

"Hm! That *were* an idea! The master that's to pay him the money is the one that's rightly concerned in that matter, ye will notice."

"Yes—but I thought the other man might have some little trifle at stake in it, too; and even his wife and children, poor creatures. The masters are these: nobles, rich men, the prosperous generally. These few, who do no work, determine what pay the vast hive shall have, who *do* work. You see? they're a 'combine'—a trade union, to coin a new phrase—who band themselves together to force their lowly brother to take what they choose to give. Thirteen hundred years hence—so says the unwritten law—the 'combine' will be the other way, and then how these fine people's posterity will fume and fret and grit their teeth over the insolent tyranny of trade unions! Yes, indeed! the magistrate will tranquilly arrange the wages from now clear away down into the nineteenth century; and then all of a sudden the wage-earner will consider that a couple of thousand years or so is enough of this one-sided sort of thing, and he will rise up and take a hand in fixing his wages himself. Ah, he will have a long and bitter account of wrong and humiliation to settle."

"Do ye believe—"

"That he actually will help to fix his own wages? Yes, indeed. And he will be strong and able, then."

"Brave times, brave times, of a truth!" sneered the prosperous smith.

"Oh—and there's another detail. In that day, a master may hire a man for only just one day, or one week, or one month at a time, if he wants to."

"What?"

"It's true. Moreover, a magistrate won't be able to force a man to work for a master a whole year on a stretch, whether the man wants to or not."

"Will there be *no* law or sense in that day?"

"Both of them, Dowley. In that day a man will be his own property, not the property of magistrate and master. And he can leave town whenever he wants to, if the wages don't suit him!—and they can't put him in the pillory for it."

"Perdition catch such an age!" shouted Dowley, in strong indignation. "An age of dogs, an age barren of reverence for superiors and respect for authority! The pillory—"

"Oh, wait, brother; say no good word for that institution. *I* think the pillory ought to be abolished."

"A most strange idea. Why?"

"Well, I'll tell you why. Is a man ever put in the pillory for a capital crime?"

"No."

"Is it right to condemn a man to a slight punishment for a small offence and then kill him?"

There was no answer. I had scored my first point! For the first time, the smith wasn't up and ready. The company noticed it. Good effect.

"You don't answer, brother. You were about to glorify the pillory a while ago, and shed some pity on a future age that isn't going to use it. *I* think the pillory ought to be be abolished. What usually happens when a poor fellow is put in the pillory for some little offence that didn't amount to anything in the world? The mob try to have some fun with him, don't they?"

"Yes."

"They begin by clodding him; and they laugh themselves to pieces to see him try to dodge one clod, and get hit with another?"

"Yes."

"Then they throw dead cats at him, don't they?"

"Yes."

"Well, then, suppose he has a few personal enemies in that mob—and here and there a man or a woman with a secret grudge against him—and suppose, especially, that he is unpopular in the community, for his pride, or his prosperity, or one thing or another—stones and bricks take the place of clods and cats presently, don't they?"

"There is no doubt of it."

"As a rule he is crippled for life, isn't he?—jaws broken, teeth smashed out?—or legs mutilated, gangrened, presently cut off?—or an eye knocked out, maybe both eyes?"

"It is true, God knoweth it."

"And if he is unpopular he can depend on *dying*, right there in the stocks, can't he?"

"He surely can! One may not deny it."

"I take it none of *you* are unpopular—by reason of pride, or insolence, or conspicuous prosperity, or any of those things that excite envy and malice among the base scum of a village? *You* wouldn't think it much of a risk to take a chance in the stocks?"

Dowley winced, visibly. I judged he was hit. But he didn't betray it by any spoken word. As for the others, they spoke out plainly, and with strong feeling. They said they had seen enough of the stocks to know what a man's chance in them was, and they would never consent to enter them if they could compromise on a quick death by hanging.

"Well, to change the subject—for I think I've established my point that the stocks ought to be abolished—I think some of our laws are pretty unfair. For instance, if I do a thing which ought to deliver me to the stocks, and you know I did it and yet keep still and don't report me, *you* will get the stocks if anybody informs on you."

"Ah, but that would serve you but right," said Dowley, "for you *must* inform. So saith the law."

The others coincided.

"Well, all right, let it go, since you vote me down. But there's one thing which certainly isn't fair. The magistrate fixes a mechanic's wage at 1 cent a day, for instance. The law says that if any master shall venture, even under utmost press of business, to pay anything *over* that cent a day, even for a single day, he shall be both fined and pilloried for it; and whoever knows he did it and doesn't inform, they also shall be fined and pilloried. Now it seems to me unfair, Dowley, and a deadly peril to all of us, that because you thoughtlessly confessed, a while ago, that within a week you have paid a cent and fifteen mil—"

Oh, I tell *you* it was a smasher! You ought to have seen them go to pieces, the whole gang. I had just slipped up on poor smiling and complacent Dowley so nice and easy and softly, that he never suspected anything was going to happen till the blow came crashing down and knocked him all to rags.

A fine effect. In fact as fine as any I ever produced, with so little time to work it up in. But I saw in a moment that I had overdone the thing a little. I was expecting to scare them, but

I wasn't expecting to scare them to death. They were mighty near it, though. You see they had been a whole lifetime learning to appreciate the pillory; and to have that thing staring them in the face, and every one of them distinctly at the mercy of me, a stranger, if I chose to go and report—well, it was awful, and they couldn't seem to recover from the shock, they couldn't seem to pull themselves together. Pale, shaky, dumb, pitiful? Why, they weren't any better than so many dead men. It was very uncomfortable. Of course I thought they would appeal to me to keep mum, and then we would shake hands, and take a drink all round, and laugh it off, and there an end. But no; you see I was an unknown person, among a cruelly oppressed and suspicious people, a people always accustomed to having advantage taken of their helplessness, and never expecting just or kind treatment from any but their own families and very closest intimates. Appeal to *me* to be gentle, to be fair, to be generous? Of course they wanted to, but they couldn't dare.

Chapter 34

The Yankee and the King Sold as Slaves

WELL, what had I better do? Nothing in a hurry, sure. I must get up a diversion; anything to employ me while I could think, and while these poor fellows could have a chance to come to life again. There sat Marco, petrified in the act of trying to get the hang of his miller-gun—turned to stone, just in the attitude he was in when my pile-driver fell, the toy still gripped in his unconscious fingers. So I took it from him and proposed to explain its mystery. Mystery! a simple little thing like that; and yet it was mystery enough, for that race and that age. I never saw such an awkward people, with machinery; you see, they were totally unused to it. The miller-gun was a little double-barreled tube of toughened glass, with a neat little trick of a spring to it, which upon pressure would let a shot escape. But the shot wouldn't hurt anybody, it would only drop into your hand. In the gun were two sizes—wee mustard-seed shot, and another sort that were several times larger. They were money. The mustard-seed shot represented milrays, the larger ones mills. So the gun was a purse; and very handy, too; you could pay out money in the dark with it, with accuracy; and you could carry it in your mouth; or in your vest pocket, if you had one. I made them of several sizes—one size so large that it would carry the equivalent of a dollar. Using shot for money was a good thing for the government; the metal cost nothing, and the money couldn't be counterfeited, for I was the only person in the kingdom who knew how to manage a shot tower. "Paying the shot" soon came to be a common phrase. Yes, and I knew it would still be passing men's lips, away down in the nineteenth century, yet none would suspect how and when it originated.

The king joined us, about this time, mightily refreshed by his nap, and feeling good. Anything could make me nervous now, I was so uneasy—for our lives were in danger; and so it worried me to detect a complacent something in the king's eye which seemed to indicate that he had been loading himself up for a performance of some kind or other; confound it, why must he go and choose such a time as this? I was right. He began, straight off, in the most innocently artful, and transparent, and lubberly way, to lead up to the subject of agriculture. The cold sweat broke out all over me. I wanted to whisper in his ear, "Man, we are in awful danger! every moment is worth a principality till we get back these men's confidence; *don't* waste any of this golden time." But of course I couldn't do it. Whisper to him? It would look as if we were conspiring. So I had to sit there, and look calm and pleasant while the king stood over that dynamite mine and mooned along about his damned onions and things. At first the tumult of my own thoughts, summoned by the danger-signal and swarming to the rescue from every quarter of my skull, kept up such a hurrah and confusion and fifing and drumming that I couldn't take in a word; but presently when my mob of gathering plans began to crystalize, and fall into position and form line of battle, a sort of order and quiet ensued, and I caught the boom of the king's batteries, as if out of remote distance:

"—were not the best way, methinks, albeit it is not to be denied that authorities differ as concerning this point, some contending that the onion is but an unwholesome berry when stricken early from the tree—"

The audience showed signs of life, and sought each other's eyes in a surprised and troubled way.

"—whileas others do yet maintain, with much show of reason, that this is not of necessity the case, instancing that plums and other like cereals do be always dug in the unripe state—"

The audience exhibited distinct distress; yes, and also fear.

"—yet are they clearly wholesome, the more especially when one doth assuage the asperities of their nature by admixture of the tranquilizing juice of the wayward cabbage—"

The wild light of terror began to glow in these men's eyes, and one of them muttered, "These be errors, every one— God hath surely smitten the mind of this farmer." I was in miserable apprehension; I sat upon thorns.

—"and further instancing the known truth that in the case

of animals, the young, which may be called the green fruit of the creature, is the better, all confessing that when a goat is ripe, his fur doth heat and sore engame his flesh, the which defect, taken in connection with his several rancid habits, and fulsome appetites, and godless attitudes of mind, and bilious quality of morals—"

They rose and went for him! With a fierce shout, "The one would betray us, the other is mad! kill them! kill them!" they flung themselves upon us. What joy flamed up in the king's eye! He might be lame in agriculture, but this kind of thing was just in his line. He had been fasting long, he was hungry for a fight. He hit the blacksmith a crack under the jaw that lifted him clear off his feet and stretched him flat of his back. "St. George for Britain!" and he downed the wheelwright. The mason was big, but I laid him out like nothing. The three gathered themselves up and came again; went down again; came again; and kept on repeating this, with native British pluck, until they were battered to jelly, reeling with exhaustion, and so blind that they couldn't tell us from each other; and yet they kept right on, hammering away with what might was left in them. Hammering each other—for we stepped aside and looked on while they rolled and struggled, and gouged, and pounded and bit, with the strict and wordless attention to business of so many bulldogs. We looked on without apprehension, for they were fast getting past ability to go for help against us, and the arena was far enough from the public road to be safe from intrusion.

Well, while they were gradually playing out, it suddenly occurred to me to wonder what had become of Marco. I looked around; he was nowhere to be seen. Oh, but this was ominous! I pulled the king's sleeve, and we glided away and rushed for the hut. No Marco there, no Phyllis there! They had gone to the road for help, sure. I told the king to give his heels wings, and I would explain later. We made good time across the open ground, and as we darted into the shelter of the wood I glanced back and saw a mob of excited peasants swarm into view, with Marco and his wife at their head. They were making a world of noise, but that couldn't hurt anybody; the wood was dense, and as soon as we were well into its depths, we would take to a tree and let them whistle. Ah, but then came another sound—dogs! Yes, that was quite another matter. It magnified our contract—we must find running water.

We tore along at a good gait, and soon left the sounds far behind and modified to a murmur. We struck a stream, and darted into it. We waded swiftly down it, in the dim forest light, for as much as three hundred yards, and then came across an oak with a great bough sticking out over the water. We climbed up on this bough, and began to work our way along it to the body of the tree; now we began to hear those sounds more plainly; so the mob had struck our trail. For a while the sounds approached pretty fast. And then for another while they didn't. No doubt the dogs had found the place where we had entered the stream, and were now waltzing up and down the shores trying to pick up the trail again.

When we were snugly lodged in the tree, and curtained with foliage, the king was satisfied, but I was doubtful. I believed we could crawl along a branch and get into the next tree, and I judged it worth while to try. We tried it, and made a success of it, though the king slipped, at the junction, and came near failing to connect. We got comfortable lodgement, and satisfactory concealment among the foliage, and then we had nothing to do but listen to the hunt.

Presently we heard it coming—and coming on the jump, too; yes, and down both sides of the stream. Louder— louder—next minute it swelled swiftly up into a roar of shoutings, barkings, tramplings, and swept by like a cyclone.

"I was afraid that the overhanging branch would suggest something to them," said I, "but I don't mind the disappointment. Come, my liege, it were well that we make good use of our time. We've flanked them. Dark is coming on, presently. If we can cross the stream and get a good start, and borrow a couple of horses from somebody's pasture to use for a few hours, we shall be safe enough."

We started down, and got nearly to the lowest limb, when we seemed to hear the hunt returning. We stopped to listen.

"Yes," said I, "they're baffled, they've given it up, they're on their way home. We will climb back to our roost again, and let them go by."

So we climbed back. The king listened a moment and said:

"They still search—I wit the sign. We did best to abide."

He was right. He knew more about hunting than I did. The noise approached steadily, but not with a rush. The king said:

"They reason that we were advantaged by no parlous start of them, and being on foot, are as yet no mighty way from where we took the water."

"Yes, sire, that is about it, I am afraid, though I was hoping better things."

The noise drew nearer and nearer, and soon the van was drifting under us, on both sides of the water. A voice called a halt, from the other bank, and said:

"An they were so minded, they could get to yon tree by this branch that overhangs, and yet not touch ground. Ye will do well to send a man up it."

"Marry, that will we do!"

I was obliged to admire my cuteness in foreseeing this very thing and swapping trees to beat it. But don't you know, there are some things that can beat smartness and foresight? Awkwardness and stupidity can. The best swordsman in the world doesn't need to fear the second best swordsman in the world; no, the person for him to be afraid of is some ignorant antagonist who has never had a sword in his hand before; he doesn't do the thing he ought to do, and so the expert isn't prepared for him; he does the thing he ought not to do: and often it catches the expert out, and ends him on the spot. Well, how could I, with all my gifts, make any valuable preparation against a near-sighted, cross-eyed, pudding-headed clown who would aim himself at the wrong tree and hit the right one? And that is what he did. He went for the wrong tree, which was of course the right one, by mistake, and up he started.

Matters were serious, now. We remained still, and awaited developments. The peasant toiled his difficult way up. The king raised himself up and stood; he made a leg ready, and when the comer's head arrived in reach of it there was a dull thud, and down went the man floundering to the ground. There was a wild outbreak of anger, below, and the mob swarmed in from all around, and there we were, treed, and prisoners. Another man started up; the bridging bough was detected, and a volunteer started up the tree that furnished the bridge. The king ordered me to play Horatius and keep the bridge. For a while the enemy came thick and fast; but no matter, the head man of each procession always got a buffet that dislodged him as soon as he came in reach. The king's spirits rose, his joy was limitless. He said that if nothing occurred to mar the prospect we should have a beautiful night, for on this line of tactics we could hold the tree against the whole countryside.

However, the mob soon came to that conclusion themselves; wherefore they called off the assault and began to debate other plans. They had no weapons, but there were plenty of stones, and stones might answer. We had no objections. A stone might possibly penetrate to us once in a while, but it wasn't very likely; we were well protected by boughs and foliage, and were not visible from any good aiming-point. If they would but waste half an hour in stone-throwing, the dark would come to our help. We were feeling very well satisfied. We could smile; almost laugh.

But we didn't; which was just as well, for we should have been interrupted. Before the stones had been raging through the leaves and bouncing from the boughs fifteen minutes, we began to notice a smell. A couple of sniffs of it was enough of an explanation: it was smoke! Our game was up, at last. We recognized that. When smoke invites you, you have to come. They raised their pile of dry brush and damp weeds higher and higher, and when they saw the thick cloud begin to roll up and smother the tree, they broke out in a storm of joy-clamors. I got enough breath to say:

"Proceed, my liege; after you is manners."

The king gasped:

"Follow me down, and then back thyself against one side of the trunk, and leave me the other. Then will we fight. Let each pile his dead according to his own fashion and taste."

Then he descended, barking and coughing, and I followed. I struck the ground an instant after him; we sprang to our appointed places, and began to give and take with all our might. The pow-wow and racket were prodigious; it was a tempest of riot and confusion and thick falling blows. Suddenly some horsemen tore into the midst of the crowd, and a voice shouted:

"Hold—or ye are dead men!"

How good it sounded! The owner of the voice bore all the marks of a gentleman: picturesque and costly raiment, the aspect of command, a hard countenance, with complexion and features marred by dissipation. The mob fell humbly back, like so many spaniels. The gentleman inspected us critically, then said, sharply, to the peasants:

"What are ye doing to these people?"

"They be madmen, worshipful sir, that have come wandering we know not whence, and—"

"Ye know not whence? Do ye pretend ye know them not?"

"Most honored sir, we speak but the truth. They are strangers and unknown to any in this region; and they be the most violent and bloodthirsty madmen that ever—"

"Peace! Ye know not what ye say. They are not mad. Who are ye? And whence are ye? Explain."

"We are but peaceful strangers, sir," I said, "and traveling upon our own concerns. We are from a far country and unacquainted here. We have purposed no harm; and yet but for your brave interference and protection these people would have killed us. As you have divined, sir, we are not mad; neither are we violent or bloodthirsty."

The gentleman turned to his retinue and said calmly:

"Lash me these animals to their kennels!"

The mob vanished in an instant; and after them plunged the horsemen, laying about them with their whips, and pitilessly riding down such as were witless enough to keep the road instead of taking to the bush. The shrieks and supplications presently died away in the distance, and soon the horsemen began to straggle back. Meantime the gentleman had been questioning us more closely, but had dug no particulars out of us. We were lavish of recognition of the service he was doing us, but we revealed nothing more than that we were friendless strangers from a far country. When the escort were all returned, the gentleman said to one of his servants:

"Bring the led horses and mount these people."

"Yes, my lord."

We were placed toward the rear among the servants. We traveled pretty fast, and finally drew rein some time after dark at a roadside inn some ten or twelve miles from the scene of our troubles. My lord went immediately to his room, after ordering his supper, and we saw no more of him. At dawn in the morning we breakfasted and made ready to start. My lord's chief attendant sauntered forward at that moment, with indolent grace, and said:

"Ye have said ye should continue upon this road, which is our direction likewise; wherefore my lord, the earl Grip, hath given commandment that ye retain the horses and ride, and that certain of us ride with ye a twenty mile to a fair town that hight Cambenet, whenso ye shall be out of peril."

We could do nothing less than express our thanks and accept the offer. We jogged along, six in the party, at a moderate and comfortable gait, and in conversation learned that my lord Grip was a very great personage in his own region, which lay a day's journey beyond Cambenet. We loitered to such a degree that it was near the middle of the forenoon when we entered the market square of the town. We dismounted, and left our thanks once more for my lord, and then approached a crowd assembled in the centre of the square, to see what might be the object of interest. It was the remnant of that old peregrinating band of slaves! So they had been dragging their chains about, all this weary time. That poor husband was gone, and also many others; and some few purchases had been added to the gang. The king was not interested, and wanted to move along, but I was absorbed, and full of pity. I could not take my eyes away from these worn and wasted wrecks of humanity. There they sat, grouped upon the ground, silent, uncomplaining, with bowed heads, a pathetic sight. And by hideous contrast, a redundant orator was making a speech to another gathering, not thirty steps away, in fulsome laudation of "our glorious British liberties!"

I was boiling. I had forgotten I was a plebeian, I was remembering I was a man. Cost what it might, I would mount that rostrum and —

Click! the king and I were handcuffed together! Our companions, those servants, had done it; my lord Grip stood looking on. The king burst out in a fury, and said:

"What meaneth this ill-mannered jest?"

My lord merely said to his head miscreant, coolly:

"Put up the slaves and sell them!"

Slaves! The word had a new sound—and how unspeakably awful! The king lifted his manacles, and brought them down with a deadly force; but my lord was out of the way when they arrived. A dozen of the rascal's servants sprang forward, and in a moment we were helpless, with our hands bound behind us. We so loudly and so earnestly proclaimed ourselves freemen, that we got the interested attention of that liberty-mouthing orator and his patriotic crowd, and they gathered about us and assumed a very determined attitude. The orator said:

"If indeed ye are freemen, ye have naught to fear—the God-given liberties of Britain are about ye for your shield and shelter! [Applause.] Ye shall soon see. Bring forth your proofs."

"What proofs?"

"Proofs that ye are freemen."

Ah—I remembered! I came to myself; I said nothing. But the king stormed out:

"Thou'rt insane, man. It were better, and more in reason, that this thief and scoundrel here prove that we are *not* freemen."

You see, he knew his own laws just as other people so often know the laws: by words, not by effects. They take a *meaning*, and get to be very vivid, when you come to apply them to yourself.

All hands shook their heads, and looked disappointed; some turned away, no longer interested. The orator said—and this time in the tones of business, not of sentiment:

"An ye do not know your country's laws, it were time ye learned them. Ye are strangers to us; ye will not deny that. Ye may be freemen, we do not deny that; but also ye may be slaves. The law is clear: it doth not require the claimant to prove ye are slaves, it requireth you to prove ye are *not*."

I said:

"Dear sir, give us only time to send to Astolat; or give us only time to send to the Valley of Holiness—"

"Peace, good man, these are extraordinary requests, and you may not hope to have them granted. It would cost much time, and would unwarrantably inconvenience your master—"

"*Master*, idiot!" stormed the king. "I have no master. I myself am the m—"

"Silence, for God's sake!"

I got the words out in time to stop the king. We were in trouble enough already; it could not help us any to give these people the notion that we were lunatics.

There is no use in stringing out the details. The earl put us up and sold us at auction. This same infernal law had existed in our own South in my own time, more than thirteen hundred years later, and under it hundreds of free men who could not prove that they were freemen had been sold into life-long slavery, without the circumstance making any particular impression upon me; but the minute the law and the auction block came into my personal experience, a thing which had been merely improper before, became suddenly hellish. Well, that's the way we are made.

Yes, we were sold at auction, like swine. In a big town and an active market we should have brought a good price; but this place was utterly stagnant, and so we sold at a figure which makes me ashamed, every time I think of it. The king of England brought seven dollars, and his prime minister nine; whereas the king was easily worth twelve dollars and I as easily worth fifteen. But that is the way things always go; if you force a sale on a dull market, I don't care what the property is, you are going to make a poor business of it, and you can make up your mind to it. If the earl had had wit enough to—

However, there is no occasion for my working my sympathies up on his account. Let him go, for the present. I took his number, so to speak.

The slave dealer bought us both, and hitched us onto that long chain of his, and we constituted the rear of his procession. We took up our line of march and passed out of Cambenet at noon; and it seemed to me unaccountably strange and odd, that the king of England and his chief minister, marching manacled and fettered and yoked, in a slave convoy, could move by all manner of idle men and women, and under windows where sat the sweet and the lovely, and yet never attract a curious eye, never provoke a single remark. Dear, dear, it only shows that there is nothing diviner about a king than there is about a tramp, after all. He is just a cheap and hollow artificiality when you don't know he is a king. But reveal his quality, and dear me, it takes your very breath away to look at him. I reckon we are all fools. Born so, no doubt.

Chapter 35

A PITIFUL INCIDENT

IT'S A WORLD of surprises. The king brooded; this was natural. What would he brood about, should you say? Why, about the prodigious nature of his fall, of course—from the loftiest place in the world to the lowest; from the most illustrious station in the world to the obscurest; from the grandest vocation among men to the basest. No, I take my oath that the thing that graveled him most, to start with, was not this, but the price he had fetched! He couldn't seem to get over that seven dollars. Well, it stunned me so, when I first found it out, that I couldn't believe it; it didn't seem natural. But as soon as my mental sight cleared and I got a right focus on it, I saw I was mistaken: it *was* natural. For this reason: a king is a mere artificiality, and so a king's feelings, like the impulses of an automatic doll, are mere artificialities; but as a man, he is a reality, and his feelings, as a man, are real, not phantasms. It shames the average man to be valued below his own estimate of his worth; and the king certainly wasn't anything more than an average man, if he was up that high.

Confound him, he wearied me with arguments to show that in anything like a fair market he would have fetched twenty-five dollars, sure—a thing which was plainly nonsense, and full of the baldest conceit; I wasn't worth it myself. But it was tender ground for me to argue on. In fact I had to simply shirk argument and do the diplomatic instead. I had to throw conscience aside, and brazenly concede that he ought to have brought twenty-five dollars; whereas I was quite well aware that in all the ages, the world had never seen a king that was worth half the money, and during the next thirteen centuries wouldn't see one that was worth the fourth of it. Yes, he tired me. If he began to talk about the crops; or about the recent weather; or about the condition of politics; or about dogs, or cats, or morals, or theology—no matter what—I sighed, for I knew what was coming: he was going to get out of it a palliation of that tiresome seven-dollar sale.

Wherever we halted, where there was a crowd, he would give me a look which said, plainly: "If that thing could be tried over again, now, with this kind of folk, you would see a different result." Well, when he was first sold, it secretly tickled me to see him go for seven dollars; but before he was done with his sweating and worrying I wished he had fetched a hundred. The thing never got a chance to die, for every day, at one place or another, possible purchasers looked us over, and as often as any other way, their comment on the king was something like this:

"Here's a two-dollar-and-a-half chump with a thirty-dollar style. Pity but style was marketable."

At last this sort of remark produced an evil result. Our owner was a practical person and he perceived that this defect must be mended if he hoped to find a purchaser for the king. So he went to work to take the style out of his sacred majesty. I could have given the man some valuable advice but I didn't; you mustn't volunteer advice to a slave-driver unless you want to damage the cause you are arguing for. I had found it a sufficiently difficult job to reduce the king's style to a peasant's style, even when he was a willing and anxious pupil; now then, to undertake to reduce the king's style to a slave's style—and by force—go to! it was a stately contract. Never mind the details—it will save me trouble to let you imagine them. I will only remark that at the end of a week there was plenty of evidence that lash and club and fist had done their work well; the king's body was a sight to see—and to weep over; but his spirit?—why, it wasn't even fazed. Even that dull clod of a slave-driver was able to see that there can be such a thing as a slave who will remain a man till he dies; whose bones you can break, but whose manhood you can't. This man found that from his first effort down to his latest, he couldn't ever come within reach of the king but the king was ready to plunge for him, and did it. So he gave up, at last, and left the king in possession of his style unimpaired. The fact is, the king was a good deal more than a king, he was a man; and when a man is a man, you can't knock it out of him.

We had a rough time for a month, tramping to and fro in the earth, and suffering. And what Englishman was the most interested in the slavery question by that time? His grace the king! Yes; from being the most indifferent, he was become the most interested. He was become the bitterest hater of the institution I had ever heard talk. And so I ventured to ask once more a question which I had asked years before and had gotten such a sharp answer that I had not thought it prudent to meddle in the matter further: Would he abolish slavery?

His answer was as sharp as before, but it was music this time; I shouldn't ever wish to hear pleasanter, though the profanity was not good, being awkwardly put together, and with the crash-word almost in the middle instead of at the end, where of course it ought to have been.

I was ready and willing to get free, now; I hadn't wanted to get free any sooner. No, I cannot quite say that. I had wanted to, but I had not been willing to take desperate chances, and had always dissuaded the king from them. But now—ah, it was a new atmosphere! Liberty would be worth any cost that might be put upon it, now. I set about a plan, and was straightway charmed with it. It would require time, yes, and patience, too, a great deal of both. One could invent quicker ways, and fully as sure ones; but none that would be as picturesque as this, none that could be made so dramatic. And so I was not going to give this one up. It might delay us months, but no matter, I would carry it out or break something.

Now and then we had an adventure. One night we were overtaken by a snow-storm while still a mile from the village we were making for. Almost instantly we were shut up as in a fog, the driving snow was so thick. You couldn't see a thing, and we were soon lost. The slave-driver lashed us desperately, for he saw ruin before him, but his lashings only made matters worse, for they drove us further from the road and from likelihood of succor. So we had to stop, at last, and slump down in the snow where we were. The storm continued until toward midnight, then ceased. By this time two of our feebler men and three of our women were dead, and others past moving and threatened with death. Our master was nearly beside himself. He stirred up the living, and made us stand, jump, slap ourselves, to restore our circulation, and he helped as well as he could with his whip.

Now came a diversion. We heard shrieks and yells, and soon a woman came running, and crying; and seeing our group, she flung herself into our midst and begged for protection. A mob of people came tearing after her, some with torches, and they said she was a witch who had caused several cows to die by a strange disease, and practiced her arts by help of a devil in the form of a black cat. This poor woman had been stoned until she hardly looked human, she was so battered and bloody. The mob wanted to burn her.

Well, now, what do you suppose our master did? When we closed around this poor creature to shelter her, he saw his chance. He said, burn her here, or they shouldn't have her at all. Imagine that! They were willing. They fastened her to a post; they brought wood and piled it about her; they applied the torch while she shrieked and pleaded and strained her two young daughters to her breast; and our brute, with a heart solely for business, lashed us into position about the stake and warmed us into life and commercial value by the same fire which took away the innocent life of that poor harmless mother. That was the sort of master we had. I took *his* number. That snow-storm cost him nine of his flock; and he was more brutal to us than ever, after that, for many days together, he was so enraged over his loss.

We had adventures, all along. One day we ran into a procession. And such a procession! All the riff-raff of the kingdom seemed to be comprehended in it; and all drunk at that. In the van was a cart with a coffin in it, and on the coffin sat a comely young girl of about eighteen, suckling a baby, which she squeezed to her breast in a passion of love every little while, and every little while wiped from its face the tears which her eyes rained down upon it; and always the foolish little thing smiled up at her, happy and content, kneading her breast with its dimpled fat hand, which she patted and fondled right over her breaking heart.

Men and women, boys and girls, trotted along beside or after the cart, hooting, shouting profane and ribald remarks, singing snatches of foul song, skipping, dancing—a very holiday of hellions, a sickening sight. We had struck a suburb of London, outside the walls, and this was a sample of one sort of London society. Our master secured a good place for us near the gallows. A priest was in attendance, and he helped the girl climb up, and said comforting words to her, and made the under-sheriff provide a stool for her. Then he stood there by her on the gallows, and for a moment looked down upon the mass of upturned faces at his feet, then out over the solid pavement of heads that stretched away on every side, occupying the vacancies far and near, and then began to tell the story of the case. And there was pity in his voice—how seldom a sound that was in that ignorant and savage land! I remember every detail of what he said, except the words he said it in; and so I change it into my own words:

"Law is intended to mete out justice. Sometimes it fails. This cannot be helped. We can only grieve, and be resigned, and pray for the soul of him who falls unfairly by the arm of the law, and that his fellows may be few. A law sends this poor young thing to death—and it is right. But another law had placed her where she must commit her crime or starve, with her child—and before God that law is responsible for both her crime and her ignominious death!

"A little while ago this young thing, this child of eighteen years, was as happy a wife and mother as any in England; and her lips were blithe with song, which is the native speech of glad and innocent hearts. Her young husband was as happy as she; for he was doing his whole duty, he worked early and late at his handicraft, his bread was honest bread well and fairly earned, he was prospering, he was furnishing shelter and sustenance to his family, he was adding his mite to the wealth of the nation. By consent of a treacherous law, instant destruction fell upon this holy home and swept it away! That young husband was waylaid and impressed, and sent to sea. The wife knew nothing of it. She sought him everywhere, she moved the hardest hearts with the supplications of her tears, the broken eloquence of her despair. Weeks dragged by, she watching, waiting, hoping, her mind going slowly to wreck under the burden of her misery. Little by little all her small possessions went for food. When she could no longer pay her rent, they turned her out of doors. She begged, while she had strength; when she was starving, at last, and her milk failing, she stole a piece of linen cloth of the value of a fourth part of a cent, thinking to sell it and save her child. But she was seen, by the owner of the cloth. She was put in jail and brought to trial. The man testified to the facts. A plea was made for her, and her sorrowful story was told in her behalf. She spoke, too, by permission, and said she did steal the cloth, but that her mind was so disordered of late, by trouble, that when she was overborne with hunger all acts, criminal or other, swam meaningless through her brain and she knew nothing rightly, except that she was *so* hungry! For a moment all were touched, and there was disposition to deal mercifully with her, seeing that she was so young and friendless, and her case so piteous, and the law that robbed her of her support to blame as being the first and only cause of her transgression; but the prosecuting officer replied that whereas these things were all true, and most pitiful as well, still there was much small theft in these days, and mistimed mercy here would be a danger to property—Oh, my God, is there no property in ruined homes, and orphaned babes, and broken hearts that British law holds precious!—and so he must require sentence.

"When the judge put on his black cap, the owner of the stolen linen rose trembling up, his lip quivering, his face as gray as ashes; and when the awful words came he cried out, 'Oh, poor child, poor child, I did not know it was death!' and fell as a tree falls. When they lifted him up, his reason was gone; before the sun was set, he had taken his own life. A kindly man; a man whose heart was right, at bottom; add his murder to this that is to be now done here; and charge them both where they belong—to the rulers and the bitter laws of Britain. The time is come, my child; let me pray over thee— not *for* thee, dear abused poor heart and innocent, but for them that be guilty of thy ruin and death, who need it more."

After his prayer they put the noose around the young girl's neck, and they had great trouble to adjust the knot under her ear, because she was devouring the baby all the time, wildly kissing it, and snatching it to her face and her breast, and drenching it with tears, and half moaning half shrieking all the while, and the baby crowing, and laughing, and kicking its feet with delight over what it took for romp and play. Even the hangman couldn't stand it, but turned away. When all was ready the priest gently pulled and tugged and forced the child out of the mother's arms, and stepped quickly out of her reach; but she clasped her hands, and made a wild spring toward him, with a shriek; but the rope—and the under-sheriff—held her short. Then she went on her knees and stretched out her hands and cried:

"One more kiss—Oh, my God, one more, one more—it is the dying that begs it!"

She got it; she almost smothered the little thing. And when they got it away again, she cried out:

"Oh, my child, my darling, it will die! It has no home, it has no father, no friend, no mother—"

"It has them all!" said that good priest. "All these will I be to it till I die."

You should have seen her face then! Gratitude? Lord, what do you want with words to express that? Words are only painted fire; a look is the fire itself. She gave that look, and carried it away to the treasury of heaven, where all things that are divine belong.

Chapter 36

AN ENCOUNTER IN THE DARK

LONDON—to a slave—was a sufficiently uninteresting place. It was merely a great big village; and mainly mud and thatch. The streets were muddy, crooked, unpaved. The populace was an ever flocking and drifting swarm of rags, and splendors, of nodding plumes and shining armor. The king had a palace there; he saw the outside of it. It made him sigh; yes, and swear a little, in a poor juvenile sixth-century way. We saw knights and grandees whom we knew, but they didn't know us in our rags and dirt and raw welts and bruises, and wouldn't have recognized us if we had hailed them, nor stopped to answer, either, it being unlawful to speak with slaves on a chain. Sandy passed within ten yards of me, on a mule—hunting for me, I imagined. But the thing which clean broke my heart was something which happened in front of our old barrack in a square, while we were enduring the spectacle of a man being boiled to death in oil for counterfeiting pennies. It was the sight of a newsboy—and I couldn't get at him! Still, I had one comfort; here was proof that Clarence was still alive and banging away. I meant to be with him before long; the thought was full of cheer.

I had one little glimpse of another thing, one day, which gave me a great uplift. It was a wire, stretching from housetop to housetop. Telegraph or telephone, sure. I did very much wish I had a little piece of it. It was just what I needed, in order to carry out my project of escape. My idea was, to get loose some night, along with the king, then gag and bind our master, change clothes with him, batter him into the aspect of a stranger, hitch him to the slave-chain, assume possession of the property, march to Camelot, and—

But you get my idea; you see what a stunning dramatic surprise I would wind up with, at the palace. It was all feasible, if I could only get hold of a slender piece of iron which I could shape into a lock-pick; I could then undo the lumbering padlocks with which our chains were fastened, whenever I might choose. But I never had any luck; no such thing ever happened to fall in my way. However, my chance came at last. A gentleman who had come twice before to dicker for me, without result, or indeed any approach to a result, came again. I was far from expecting to ever belong to him, for the price asked for me, from the time I was first enslaved, was exorbitant, and always provoked either anger or derision, yet my master stuck stubbornly to it—twenty-two dollars. He wouldn't bate a cent. The king was greatly admired, because of his grand physique, but his kingly style was against him, and he wasn't saleable; nobody wanted that kind of a slave. I considered myself safe from parting from him because of my extravagant price. No, I was not expecting to ever belong to this gentleman whom I have spoken of, but he had something which I expected would belong to me eventually, if he would but visit us often enough. It was a steel thing with a long pin to it, with which his long cloth outside garment was fastened together in front. There were three of them. He had disappointed me twice, because he did not come quite close enough to me to make my project entirely safe; but this time I succeeded; I captured the lower clasp of the three, and when he missed it he thought he had lost it on the way.

I had a chance to be glad about a minute; then straightway a chance to be sad again. For when the purchase was about to fail, as usual, the master suddenly spoke up and said what would be worded thus—in modern English:

"I'll tell you what I'll do. I'm tired supporting these two for no good. Give me twenty-two dollars for this one, and I'll throw the other one in."

The king couldn't get his breath, he was in such a fury. He began to choke and gag, and meantime the master and the gentleman moved away, discussing.

"An ye will keep the offer open—"

" 'Tis open till the morrow at this hour."

"Then will I answer you at that time," said the gentleman, and disappeared, the master following him.

I had a time of it to cool the king down, but I managed it. I whispered in his ear, to this effect:

"Your grace *will* go for nothing, but after another fashion. And so shall I. To-night we shall both be free."

"Ah! How is that?"

"With this thing which I have stolen, I will unlock these locks and cast off these chains to-night. When he comes, about nine-thirty, to inspect us for the night, we will seize him, gag him, batter him, and early in the morning we will march out of this town, proprietors of this caravan of slaves."

That was as far as I went, but the king was charmed and satisfied. That evening we waited patiently for our fellow slaves to get to sleep and signify it by the usual sign, for you must not take many chances on those poor fellows if you can avoid it. It is best to keep your own secrets. No doubt they fidgeted only about as usual, but it didn't seem so to me. It seemed to me that they were going to be forever getting down to their regular snoring. As the time dragged on I got nervously afraid we shouldn't have enough of it left for our needs; so I made several premature attempts, and merely delayed things by it; for I couldn't seem to touch a padlock, there in the dark, without starting a rattle out of it which interrupted somebody's sleep and made him turn over and wake some more of the gang.

But finally I did get my last iron off, and was a free man once more. I took a good breath of relief, and reached for the king's irons. Too late! in comes the master, with a light in one hand and his heavy walking staff in the other. I snuggled close among the wallow of snorers, to conceal as nearly as possible that I was naked of irons; and I kept a sharp lookout and prepared to spring for my man the moment he should bend over me.

But he didn't approach. He stopped, gazed absently toward our dusky mass a minute, evidently thinking about something else; then set down his light, moved musingly toward the door, and before a body could imagine what he was going to do, he was out of the door and had closed it behind him.

"Quick!" said the king. "Fetch him back!"

Of course it was the thing to do, and I was up and out in a moment. But dear me, there were no lamps in those days, and it was a dark night. But I glimpsed a dim figure a few steps away. I darted for it, threw myself upon it, and then there was a state of things, and lively! We fought and scuffled and struggled, and drew a crowd in no time. They took an immense interest in the fight, and encouraged us all they could, and in fact couldn't have been pleasanter or more cordial if it had been their own fight. Then a tremendous row broke out behind us, and as much as half of our audience left us, with a rush, to invest some sympathy in that. Lanterns began to swing in all directions; it was the watch, gathering from far and near. Presently a halberd fell across my back, as a reminder, and I knew what it meant. I was in custody. So was my adversary. We were marched off toward prison, one on each side of the watchman. Here was disaster, here was a fine scheme gone to sudden destruction! I tried to imagine what would happen when the master should discover that it was I who had been fighting him; and what would happen if they jailed us together in the general apartment for brawlers and petty law-breakers as was the custom; and what might—

Just then my antagonist turned his face around in my direction, the freckled light from the watchman's tin lantern fell on it, and by George, he was the wrong man!

Chapter 37

AN AWFUL PREDICAMENT

S LEEP? It was impossible. It would naturally have been impossible in that noisome cavern of a jail, with its mangy crowd of drunken, quarrelsome and song-singing rapscallions. But the thing that made sleep all the more a thing not to be dreamed of, was my racking impatience to get out of this place and find out the whole size of what might have happened yonder in the slave quarters in consequence of that intolerable miscarriage of mine.

It was a long night, but the morning got around at last. I made a full and frank explanation to the court. I said I was a slave, the property of the great Earl Grip, who had arrived just after dark at the Tabard inn in the village on the other side of the water, and had stopped there over night, by compulsion, he being taken deadly sick with a strange and sudden disorder. I had been ordered to cross to the city in all haste and bring the best physician; I was doing my best; naturally I was running with all my might; the night was dark, I ran against this common person here, who seized me by the throat and began to pummel me, although I told him my errand, and implored him, for the sake of the great earl my master's mortal peril—

The common person interrupted and said it was a lie; and was going to explain how I rushed upon him and attacked him without a word—

"Silence, sirrah!" from the court. "Take him hence and give him a few stripes whereby to teach him how to treat the servant of a nobleman after a different fashion another time. Go!"

Then the court begged my pardon, and hoped I would not fail to tell his lordship it was in no wise the court's fault that this high-handed thing had happened. I said I would make it all right, and so took my leave. Took it just in time, too; he was starting to ask me why I didn't fetch out these facts the moment I was arrested. I said I would if I had thought of it—which was true—but that I was so battered by that man that all my wit was knocked out of me—and so forth and so-on, and got myself away, still mumbling.

I didn't wait for breakfast. No grass grew under my feet. I was soon at the slave quarters. Empty—everybody gone! That is, everybody except one body—the slave-master's. It lay there all battered to pulp; and all about were the evidences of a terrific fight. There was a rude board coffin on a cart at the door, and workmen, assisted by the police, were thinning a road through the gaping crowd in order that they might bring it in.

I picked out a man humble enough in life to condescend to talk with one so shabby as I, and got his account of the matter.

"There were sixteen slaves here. They rose against their master in the night, and thou seest how it ended."

"Yes. How did it begin?"

"There was no witness but the slaves. They said the slave that was most valuable got free of his bonds and escaped in some strange way—by magic arts 'twas thought, by reason that he had no key, and the locks were neither broken nor in any wise injured. When the master discovered his loss, he was mad with despair, and threw himself upon his people with his heavy stick, who resisted, and brake his back and in other and divers ways did give him hurts that brought him swiftly to his end."

"This is dreadful. It will go hard with the slaves, no doubt, upon the trial."

"Marry, the trial is over."

"Over!"

"Would they be a week, think you—and the matter so simple? They were not the half of a quarter of an hour at it."

"Why, I don't see how they could determine which were the guilty ones in so short a time."

"*Which* ones? Indeed they considered not particulars like to that. They condemned them in a body. Wit ye not the law?—which men say the Romans left behind them here when they went—that if one slave killeth his master all the slaves of that man must die for it."

"True. I had forgotten. And when will these die?"

"Belike within a four and twenty hours; albeit some say they will wait a pair of days more, if peradventure they may find the missing one meantime."

The missing one! It made me feel uncomfortable.

"Is it likely they will find him?"

"Before the day is spent—yes. They seek him everywhere. They stand at the gates of the town, with certain of the slaves who will discover him to them if he cometh, and none can pass out but he will be first examined."

"Might one see the place where the rest are confined?"

"The outside of it—yes. The inside of it—but ye will not want to see that."

I took the address of that prison, for future reference, and then sauntered off. At the first second-hand clothing shop I came to, up a back street, I got a rough rig suitable for a common seaman who might be going on a cold voyage, and bound up my face with a liberal bandage, saying I had a toothache. This concealed my worst bruises. It was a transformation. I no longer resembled my former self. Then I struck out for that wire, found it, and followed it to its den. It was a little room over a butcher's shop—which meant that business wasn't very brisk in the telegraphic line. The young chap in charge was drowsing at his table. I locked the door, and put the vast key in my bosom. This alarmed the young fellow, and he was going to make a noise; but I said:

"Save your wind; if you open your mouth you are dead, sure. Tackle your instrument. Lively, now! Call Camelot."

"This doth amaze me! How should such as you know aught of such matters as—"

"Call Camelot! I am a desperate man. Call Camelot, or get away from the instrument and I will do it myself."

"What—you?"

"Yes—certainly. Stop gabbling. Call the palace."

He made the call.

"Now then, call Clarence."

"Clarence *who*?"

"Never mind Clarence who. Say you want Clarence; you'll get an answer."

He did so. We waited five nerve-straining minutes—ten minutes—how long it did seem!—and then came a click that was as familiar to me as a human voice; for Clarence had been my own pupil.

"Now, my lad, vacate! They wouldn't have known *my* touch, maybe, and so your call was surest; but I'm all right, now."

He vacated the place, and cocked his ear to listen—but it didn't win. I used a cipher. I didn't waste any time in sociabilities with Clarence, but squared away for business, straight off—thus:

"The king is here, and in danger. We were captured and brought here as slaves. We should not be able to prove our identity—and the fact is, I am not in a position to try. Send a telegram for the palace here which will carry conviction with it."

His answer came straight back:

"They don't know anything about the telegraph; they haven't had any experience yet, the line to London is so new. Better not venture that. They might hang you. Think up something else."

Might hang us! Little he knew how closely he was crowding the facts. I couldn't think up anything for the moment. Then an idea struck me, and I started it along:

"Send five hundred picked knights, with Launcelot in the lead; and send them on the jump. Let them enter by the south-west gate, and look out for the man with a white cloth around his right arm."

The answer was prompt:

"They shall start in half an hour."

"All right, Clarence; now tell this lad here that I'm a friend of yours and a dead-head; and that he must be discreet and say nothing about this visit of mine."

The instrument began to talk to the youth, and I hurried away. I fell to ciphering. In half an hour it would be nine o'clock. Knights and horses in heavy armor couldn't travel very fast. These would make the best time they could, and now that the ground was in good condition, and no snow or mud, they would probably make a seven mile gait; they would have to change horses a couple of times; they would arrive about six, or a little after; it would be still plenty light enough; they would see the white cloth which I should tie around my right arm, and I would take command. We would surround that prison and have the king out in no time. It would be showy and picturesque enough, all things considered, though I would have preferred noonday, on account of the more theatrical aspect the thing would have.

Now then, in order to increase the strings to my bow, I thought I would look up some of those people whom I had formerly recognized, and make myself known. That would help us out of our scrape, without the knights. But I must proceed cautiously, for it was a risky business. I must get into sumptuous raiment, and it wouldn't do to run and jump into it. No, I must work up to it by degrees, buying suit after suit of clothes, in shops wide apart, and getting a little finer article with each change, until I should finally reach silk and velvet, and be ready for my project. So I started.

But the scheme fell through like scat! The first corner I turned, I came plump upon one of our slaves, snooping around with a watchman. I coughed, at the moment, and he gave me a sudden look that bit right into my marrow. I judge he thought he had heard that cough before. I turned immediately into a shop and worked along down the counter, pricing things, and watching out of the corner of my eye. Those people had stopped, and were talking together and looking in at the door. I made up my mind to get out the back way if there was a back way, and I asked the shopwoman if I could step out there and look for the escaped slave, who was believed to be in hiding back there somewhere, and said I was an officer in disguise, and my pard was yonder at the door with one of the murderers in charge, and would she be good enough to step there and tell him he needn't wait, but had better go at once to the further end of the back alley and be ready to head him off when I rousted him out.

She was blazing with eagerness to see one of those already celebrated murderers, and she started on the errand at once. I slipped out the back way, locked the door behind me, put the key in my pocket and started off, chuckling to myself, and comfortable.

Well, I had gone and spoiled it again, made another mistake. A double one, in fact. There were plenty of ways to get rid of that officer by some simple and plausible device, but no, I must pick out a picturesque one; it is the crying defect of my character. And then, I had ordered my procedure upon what the officer, being human, would *naturally* do; whereas when you are least expecting it, a man will now and then go and do the very thing which it's *not* natural for him to do. The natural thing for the officer to do, in this case, was to follow straight on my heels; he would find a stout oaken door, securely locked, between him and me; before he could break it down, I should be far away and engaged in slipping into a succession of baffling disguises which would soon get me into a sort of raiment which was a surer protection from meddling law-dogs in Britain than any amount of mere innocence and purity of character. But instead of doing the natural thing, the officer took me at my word, and followed my instructions. And so, as I came trotting out of that cul de sac, full of satisfaction with my own cleverness, he turned the corner and I walked right into his handcuffs. If I had known it was a cul de sac—however, there isn't any excusing a blunder like that; let it go. Charge it up to profit and loss.

Of course I was indignant, and swore I had just come ashore from a long voyage, and all that sort of thing—just to see, you know, if it would deceive that slave. But it didn't. He knew me. Then I reproached him for betraying me. He was more surprised than hurt. He stretched his eyes wide, and said:

"What, wouldst have me let thee, of all men, escape and not hang with us, when thou'rt the very *cause* of our hanging? Go to!"

"Go to" was their way of saying "I should smile!" or "I like that!" Queer talkers, those people.

Well, there was a sort of bastard justice in his view of the case, and so I dropped the matter. When you can't cure a disaster by argument, what is the use to argue? It isn't my way. So I only said:

"You're not going to be hanged. None of us are."

Both men laughed, and the slave said:

"Ye have not ranked as a fool—before. You might better keep your reputation, seeing the strain would not be for long."

"It will stand it, I reckon. Before to-morrow we shall be out of prison, and free to go where we will, besides."

The witty officer lifted at his left ear with his thumb, made a rasping noise in his throat, and said:

"Out of prison, yes—ye say true. And free likewise to go where ye will, so ye wander not out of his grace the Devil's sultry realm."

I kept my temper, and said, indifferently:

"Now I suppose you really think we are going to hang within a day or two."

"I thought it not many minutes ago; for so the thing was decided and proclaimed."

"Ah, then you've changed your mind, is that it?"

"Even that. I only *thought*, then; I *know*, now."

I felt sarcastical; so I said:

"Oh, sapient servant of the law, condescend to tell us, then, what you *know*."

"That ye will all be hanged *to-day*, at mid-afternoon! . . . Oho-o! that shot hit home! Lean upon me."

The fact is, I did need to lean upon somebody. My knights couldn't arrive in time. They would be as much as three hours too late. Nothing in the world could save the king of England; nor me, which was more important. More important, not merely to me, but to the nation—the only nation on earth standing ready to blossom into civilization. I was sick. I said no more; there wasn't anything to say. I knew what the man meant: that if the missing slave was found, the postponement would be revoked, the execution take place to-day. Well, the missing slave was found.

Chapter 38

Sir Launcelot and Knights to the Rescue

NEARING FOUR in the afternoon. The scene was just outside the walls of London. A cool, comfortable, superb
day, with a brilliant sun; the kind of day to make one want to
live, not die. The multitude was prodigious and far reaching;
and yet we sixteen poor devils hadn't a friend in it. There was
something painful in that thought, look at it how you might.
There we sat, on our tall scaffold, the butt of the hate and
mockery of all those enemies. We were being made a holiday
spectacle. They had built a sort of grand stand for the nobility
and gentry, and these were there in full force, with their
ladies. We recognized a good many of them. The crowd got a
brief and unexpected dash of diversion out of the king. The
moment we were freed of our bonds he sprang up, in his
fantastic rags, with face bruised out of all recognition, and
proclaimed himself Arthur, king of Britain, and denounced
the awful penalties of treason upon every soul there present if
hair of his sacred head were touched. It startled and surprised
him to hear them break into a vast roar of laughter. It
wounded his dignity, and he locked himself up in silence,
then, although the crowd begged him to go on, and tried to
provoke him to it by cat-calls, jeers, and shouts of—

"Let him speak! the king! the king! his humble subjects
hunger and thirst for words of wisdom out of the mouth of
their master his Serene and Sacred Raggedness!"

But it went for nothing. He put on all his majesty and sat
under this rain of contempt and insult unmoved. He certainly
was great, in his way. Absently, I had taken off my white
bandage and wound it about my right arm. When the crowd
noticed this, they began upon me. They said:

"Doubtless this sailor-man is his minister—observe his
costly badge of office!"

I let them go on until they got tired, and then I said:

"Yes, I am his minister, The Boss; and to-morrow you will
hear that from Camelot which—"

I got no further. They drowned me out with joyous derision. But presently there was silence; for the sheriffs of London, in their official robes, with their subordinates, began to make a stir which indicated that business was about to begin. In the hush which followed, our crime was recited, the death warrant read, then everybody uncovered while a priest uttered a prayer.

Then a slave was blindfolded, the hangman unslung his rope. There lay the smooth road below us, we upon one side of it, the banked multitude walling its other side—a good clear road, and kept free by the police—how good it would be to see my five hundred horsemen come tearing down it! But no, it was out of the possibilities. I followed its receding thread out into the distance—not a horseman on it, or sign of one.

There was a jerk, and the slave hung dangling; dangling and hideously squirming, for his limbs were not tied.

A second rope was unslung, in a moment another slave was dangling.

In a minute a third slave was struggling in the air. It was dreadful. I turned away my head a moment, and when I turned back I missed the king! They were blindfolding him! I was paralyzed; I couldn't move, I was choking, my tongue was petrified. They finished blindfolding him, they led him under the rope. I couldn't shake off that clinging impotence. But when I saw them put the noose around his neck then everything let go in me, and I made a spring to the rescue—and as I made it I shot one more glance abroad—by George, here they came, a-tilting!—five hundred mailed and belted knights on bicycles!

The grandest sight that ever was seen. Lord, how the plumes streamed, how the sun flamed and flashed from the endless procession of webby wheels!

I waved my right arm as Launcelot swept in—he recognized my rag—I tore away noose and bandage, and shouted:

"On your knees, every rascal of you, and salute the king! Who fails shall sup in hell to-night!"

I always use that high style when I'm climaxing an effect. Well, it was noble to see Launcelot and the boys swarm up onto that scaffold and heave sheriffs and such overboard. And it was fine to see that astonished multitude go down on their knees and beg their lives of the king they had just been deriding and insulting. And as he stood apart, there, receiving this homage in his rags, I thought to myself, well really there *is* something peculiarly grand about the gait and bearing of a king, after all. I was immensely satisfied. Take the whole situation all around, it was one of the gaudiest effects I ever instigated.

And presently up comes Clarence, his own self! and winks, and says, very modernly:

"Good deal of a surprise, wasn't it? I knew you'd like it. I've had the boys practicing, this long time, privately; and just hungry for a chance to show off."

Chapter 39

The Yankee's Fight with the Knights

Home again, at Camelot. A morning or two later I found the paper, damp from the press, by my plate at the breakfast table. I turned to the advertising columns, knowing I should find something of personal interest to me there. It was this:

DE PAR LE ROI.

Know that the great lord and illustrious kni8ht. SIR SAGRAMOUR LE DESIROUS having condescended to meet the King's Minister, Hank Morgan, the which is surnamed The Boss, for satisfaction of offence anciently given, these will engage in the lists by Camelot about the fourth hour of the morning of the sixteenth day of this next succeeding month. The battle wiil be à l'outrance, sith the said offence was of a deadly sort, admitting of no com-Position.

DE PAR LE ROI.

Clarence's editorial reference to this affair was to this effect:

ιndrew.
woɹk maintained
there since, soon
listic have wiʧ
oked interest
upon the eᴧᵔn-
ve been m ⬛d
oy the aɴ .s,
ent out ch⸌ y by
yterian *B* ⸜ t, and
c some y⸜ ᴜg men
of **our** undeᵔ 'he
i guidᵃnce oɪ thᵊ
for alᴜ in aᵇknown
'he great enterprise
of making pure;
eseni
ᵔuovement haɑ its
origin ᴉᴧ preven-
'has eveɹ been a
sions iɪ our
on of ʍis-
other one
ospel,
by-
e
The
ᴉhᵊ saᴜe
co represent
ized thirty oɪ
ɴeeds and hear-
which,⬛years ago!
ᴉoresgn wᴧs osgan-
ing, thᵊ missions,
sso that both had
ᴛo withdraw' and
much to their
grief,

It will be observed, by a gl7nce at our advertising columns, that the community is to be favoreᴅ ᴧith a treat of unusual interest in the tournament line. The names of the artists are warrant of good enterrainment. The box-office will be open at noon of the 13th; admission 3 cents, reserveᴅ seats 5; proceeds to go to the hospital fund Ļhe royal pair and all the Court will be present. With these exceptions, and the press anᴅ the clergy, tne free list is strictly susᵖ ended. Parties are hereby warned against buying tickets of speculators; they will not be good at the door. Everybody knows anᴅ likes ʼʃhe Boss, everybody knows ᴧnᴅ likes Siᵔ Sag.; come, let us give tne laᴅs a good sendoff. ReMember, tne proceeds go to a great and free chariiy, and one whose broad begevolence suetcnes out its helping hanᴅ, warm witn the blood of a loving heari, to all that suʝer, regardless of race, creed, condition or coloᵤ—the only chaɹity yet estaҍlished in the earth which nas no politico-religious stopcock on its compassion, but says Here flows the streaᵤ lec *all* **come** and drink! Ļurn out, all hands! fetcn along your douᴣhnuts anᴅ your gum-ᴅrops and have a. good time. Pie for sale on the grounᴅs, and rocks to crack it **with**; also circus-lemonade—three drops oɪ lime **juice** to a barrel of water.

N. B. *This is the first tournameni under the new law, whidh allows each combatant to use any weapon he may prefer.* **You** want to make a. note of ᴛeʜᴛ

our disappointn.
dromptly and ɔ ᴛl
two of their felo
erlain, and othᵤ
ers have⸜alɹeadᵥ
spoken, yoᵘ ᵛ
furnisned foᵔ
their usᵊ, ᵔi
make anᴅ
the ʞinᴅ
letters
oɪ introᴅ
duction whɪ
they are unᴜ
ing friends to us
ried, anᴅ leavᵔ the
thoᵗᵇkind words enᴅ
which you, m, ʲoy-
hind; and it is a
home matter c ᶠ b
it is our durp
direct them tᴜ
now under the ᵖ
g fields as arᴜ
*T*nese⬛younᴣ meɪ
are warm-heartᴜ
aziɹl, regions beᴧ
not to "**build** ᴜ
ond,', anᴅ the
der instructi
ons of our
another maɴ
ᴜounhati's on.
ociety, whlch
They go un-
say tʜat "inᵣ
ionaries ᴛo **mon**
say sᴉnding ᴩiss

Up to the day set, there was no talk in all Britain of anything but this combat. All other topics sank into insignificance and passed out of men's thoughts and interest. It was not because a tournament was a great matter; it was not because Sir Sagramour had found the Holy Grail, for he had not, but had failed; it was not because the second (official) personage in the kingdom was one of the duelists; no, all these features were commonplace. Yet there was abundant reason for the extraordinary interest which this coming fight was creating. It was born of the fact that all the nation knew that this was not to be a duel between mere men, so to speak, but a duel between two mighty magicians; a duel not of muscle but of mind, not of human skill but of super human art and craft; a final struggle for supremacy between the two master enchanters of the age. It was realized that the most prodigious achievements of the most renowned knights could not be worthy of comparison with a spectacle like this; they could be but child's-play, contrasted with this mysterious and awful battle of the gods. Yes, all the world knew it was going to be in reality a duel between Merlin and me, a measuring of his magic powers against mine. It was known that Merlin had been busy whole days and nights together, imbuing Sir Sagramour's arms and armor with supernal powers of offence and defence, and that he had procured for him from the spirits of the air a fleecy veil which would render the wearer invisible to his antagonist while still visible to other men. Against Sir Sagramour, so weaponed and protected, a thousand knights could accomplish nothing; against him no known enchantments could prevail. These facts were sure; regarding them there was no doubt, no reason for doubt. There was but one question: might there be still other enchantments, *unknown* to Merlin, which could render Sir Sagramour's veil transparent to me, and make his enchanted mail vulnerable to my weapons? This was the one thing to be decided in the lists. Until then the world must remain in suspense.

So the world thought there was a vast matter at stake here, and the world was right; but it was not the one they had in their minds. No, a far vaster one was upon the cast of this die: *the life of knight-errantry*. I was a champion, it was true, but not the champion of the frivolous black arts, I was the champion of hard, unsentimental, common-sense and reason. I was entering the lists to either destroy knight-errantry or be its victim.

Vast as the show-grounds were, there were no vacant spaces in them outside of the lists, at ten o'clock on the morning of the 16th. The mammoth grand stand was clothed in flags, streamers, and rich tapestries, and packed with several acres of small-fry tributary kings, their suites, and the British aristocracy, with our own royal gang in the chief place, and each and every individual a flashing prism of gaudy silks and velvets— well, I never saw anything to begin with it but a fight between an Upper Mississippi sunset and the aurora borealis. The huge camp of beflagged and gay-colored tents at one end of the lists, with a stiff-standing sentinel at every door, and a shining shield hanging by him for challenge, was another fine sight. You see, every knight was there who had any ambition or any caste feeling; for my feeling toward their order was not much of a secret, and so here was their chance. If I won my fight with Sir Sagramour, others would have the right to call me out as long as I might be willing to respond.

Down at our end there were but two tents; one for me, and another for my servants. At the appointed hour the king made a sign, and the heralds, in their tabards, appeared and made proclamation, naming the combatants and stating the cause of quarrel. There was a pause, then a ringing bugle blast, which was the signal for us to come forth. All the multitude caught their breath, and an eager curiosity flashed into every face.

Out from his tent rode great Sir Sagramour, an imposing tower of iron, stately and rigid, his huge spear standing upright in its socket and grasped in his strong hand, his grand horse's face and breast cased in steel, his body clothed in rich trappings that almost dragged the ground—oh, a most noble picture! A great shout went up, of welcome and admiration.

And then out I came. But I didn't get any shout. There was a wondering and eloquent silence, for a moment, then a great wave of laughter began to sweep along that human sea, but a warning bugle blast cut its career short. I was in the simplest and comfortablest of gymnast costumes—flesh-colored tights from neck to heel, with blue silk puffings about my loins, and bare-headed. My horse was not above medium size, but he was alert, slender-limbed, muscled with watch-springs, and just a greyhound to go. He was a beauty; glossy as silk, and naked as he was when he was born, except for bridle and ranger-saddle.

The iron tower and the gorgeous bed-quilt came cumbrously but gracefully pirouetting down the lists, and we tripped lightly up to meet them. We halted; the tower saluted, I responded; then we wheeled and rode side by side to the grand stand and faced our king and queen, to whom we made obeisance. The queen exclaimed:

"Alack, Sir Boss, wilt fight naked, and without lance or sword or—"

But the king checked her and made her understand, with a polite phrase or two, that this was none of her business. The bugles rang again, and we separated and rode to the ends of the lists, and took position. Now old Merlin stepped into view, and cast a dainty web of gossamer threads over Sir Sagramour which turned him into Hamlet's ghost; the king made a sign, the bugles blew, Sir Sagramour laid his great lance in rest, and the next moment here he came thundering down the course, with his veil flying out behind, and I went whistling through the air like an arrow to meet him—cocking my ear, the while, as if noting the invisible knight's position and progress by hearing, not sight. A chorus of encouraging shouts burst out for him, and one brave voice flung out a heartening word for me—said:

"Go it, Slim Jim!"

It was an even bet that Clarence had procured that favor for me—and furnished the language, too. When that formidable lance-point was within a yard and a half of my breast I twitched my horse aside without an effort and the big knight swept by, scoring a blank. I got plenty of applause that time. We turned, braced up, and down we came again. Another blank for the knight, a roar of applause for me. This same thing was repeated once more; and it fetched such a whirlwind of applause that Sir Sagramour lost his temper, and at once changed his tactics and set himself the task of chasing me down. Why, he hadn't any show in the world at that; it was a game of tag, with all the advantages on my side; I whirled out of his path with ease whenever I chose, and once I slapped him on the back as I went to the rear. Finally I took the chase into my own hands, and after that, turn, or twist, or do what he would, he was never able to get behind me again, he found himself always in front, at the end of his maneuver. So he gave up that business and retired to his end of the lists. His temper was clear gone, now, and he forgot himself and flung an insult at me which disposed of mine. I slipped my lasso from the horn of my saddle, and grasped the coil in my right hand. This time you should have seen him come!—it was a business trip, sure; by his gait, there was blood in his eye. I was sitting my horse at ease, and swinging the great loop of my lasso in wide circles about my head; the moment he was under way, I started for him; when the space between us had narrowed to forty feet, I sent the snaky spirals of the rope a-cleaving through the air, then darted aside and faced about and brought my trained animal to a halt with all his feet braced under him for a surge. The next moment the rope sprang taught, and yanked Sir Sagramour out of the saddle! Great Scott, but there was a sensation!

Unquestionably, the popular thing in this world is novelty. These people had never seen anything of that cow-boy business before, and it carried them clear off their feet with delight. From all around and everywhere, the shout went up—

"Encore! encore!"

I wondered where they got the word, but there was no time to cipher on philological matters, because the whole knight-errantry hive was just humming, now, and my prospect for trade couldn't have been better. The moment my lasso was released and Sir Sagramour had been assisted to his tent, I hauled in the slack, took my station and began to swing my loop around my head again. I was sure to have use for it as soon as they could elect a successor for Sir Sagramour, and that couldn't take long where there were so many hungry candidates. Indeed, they elected one straight off—Sir Hervis de Revel.

Bzz! Here he came, like a house afire; I dodged; he passed like a flash, with my horse-hair coils settling around his neck; a second or so later, *fst!* his saddle was empty.

I got another encore; and another, and another, and still another. When I had snaked five men out, things began to look serious to the iron-clads, and they stopped and consulted together. As a result, they decided that it was time to waive etiquette and send their greatest and best against me. To the astonishment of that little world, I lassoed Sir Lamorak de Galis, and after him Sir Galahad. So you see there was simply nothing to be done, now, but play their right bower—bring out the superbest of the superb, the mightiest of the mighty, the great Sir Launcelot himself!

A proud moment for me? I should think so. Yonder was Arthur, king of Britain; yonder was Guenever; yes, and whole tribes of little provincial kings and kinglets; and in the tented camp yonder, renowned knights from many lands; and likewise the selectest body known to chivalry, the knights of the Table Round, the most illustrious in Christendom; and, biggest fact of all, the very sun of their shining system was yonder couching his lance, the focal point of forty thousand adoring eyes; and all by myself here was I laying for him. Across my mind flitted the dear image of a certain hello-girl of West Hartford, and I wished she could see me now. In that moment, down came the Invincible, with the rush of a whirlwind—the courtly world rose to its feet and bent forward—the fateful coils went circling through the air, and before you could wink I was towing Sir Launcelot across the field on his back, and kissing my hand to the storm of waving kerchiefs and the thunder-crash of applause that greeted me!

Said I to myself, as I coiled my lariat and hung it on my saddle-horn, and sat there drunk with glory, "The victory is perfect—no other will venture against me—knight-errantry is dead." Now imagine my astonishment—and everybody else's, too—to hear the peculiar bugle call which announces that another competitor is about to enter the lists! There was a mystery here; I couldn't account for this thing. Next, I noticed Merlin gliding away from me; and then I noticed that my lasso was gone! The old sleight-of-hand expert had stolen it, sure, and slipped it under his robe.

The bugle blew again. I looked, and down came Sagramour riding again, with his dust brushed off and his veil nicely re-arranged. I trotted up to meet him, and pretended to find him by the sound of his horse's hoofs. He said:

"Thou'rt quick of ear, but it will not save thee from this!" and he touched the hilt of his great sword. "An ye are not able to see it, because of the influence of the veil, know that it is no cumbrous lance, but a sword—and I ween ye will not be able to avoid it."

His visor was up; there was death in his smile. I should never be able to dodge his sword, that was plain. Somebody was going to die, this time. If he got the drop on me, I could name the corpse. We rode forward together, and saluted the royalties. This time the king was disturbed. He said:

"Where is thy strange weapon?"

"It is stolen, sire."

"Hast another at hand?"

"No, sire, I brought only the one."

Then Merlin mixed in:

"He brought but the one because there was but the one to bring. There exists none other but that one. It belongeth to the King of the Demons of the Sea. This man is a pretender and ignorant; else he had known that that weapon can be used in but eight bouts only, and then it vanisheth away to its home under the sea."

"Then is he weaponless," said the king. "Sir Sagramour, ye will grant him leave to borrow."

"And I will lend!" said Sir Launcelot, limping up. "He is as brave a knight of his hands as any that be on live, and he shall have mine."

He put his hand on his sword to draw it, but Sir Sagramour said:

"Stay, it may not be. He shall fight with his own weapons; it was his privilege to choose them and bring them. If he has erred, on his head be it."

"Knight!" said the king. "Thou'rt overwrought with passion; it disorders thy mind. Wouldst kill a naked man?"

"An he do it, he shall answer it to me," said Sir Launcelot.

"I will answer it to any he that desireth!" retorted Sir Sagramour hotly.

Merlin broke in, rubbing his hands and smiling his low-downest smile of malicious gratification:

" 'Tis well said, right well said! And 'tis enough of parleying, let my lord the king deliver the battle signal."

The king had to yield. The bugle made proclamation, and we turned apart and rode to our stations. There we stood, a hundred yards apart, facing each other, rigid and motionless, like horsed statues. And so we remained, in a soundless hush, as much as a full minute, everybody gazing, nobody stirring. It seemed as if the king could not take heart to give the signal. But at last he lifted his hand, the clear note of the bugle followed, Sir Sagramour's long blade described a flashing curve in the air, and it was superb to see him come. I sat still. On he came. I did not move. People got so excited that they shouted to me:

"Fly, fly! Save thyself! This is murther!"

I never budged so much as an inch, till that thundering apparition had got within fifteen paces of me; then I snatched a dragoon revolver out of my holster, there was a flash and a roar, and the revolver was back in the holster before anybody could tell what had happened.

Here was a riderless horse plunging by, and yonder lay Sir Sagramour, stone dead.

The people that ran to him were stricken dumb to find that the life was actually gone out of the man, and no reason for it visible, no hurt upon his body, nothing like a wound. There was a hole through the breast of his chain-mail, but they attached no importance to a little thing like that; and as a bullet wound there produces but little blood, none came in sight because of the clothing and swaddlings under the armor. The body was dragged over to let the king and the swells look down upon it. They were stupefied with astonishment, naturally. I was requested to come and explain the miracle. But I remained in my tracks, like a statue, and said:

"If it is a command, I will come; but my lord the king knows that I am where the laws of combat require me to remain, while any desire to come against me."

I waited. Nobody challenged. Then I said:

"If there are any who doubt that this field is well and fairly won, I do not wait for them to challenge me, I challenge them."

"It is a gallant offer," said the king, "and well beseems you. Whom will you name, first?"

"I name none, I challenge all! Here I stand, and dare the chivalry of England to come against me—not by individuals, but in mass!"

"What!" shouted a score of knights.

"You have heard the challenge. Take it, or I proclaim you recreant knights and vanquished, every one!"

It was a "bluff," you know. At such a time it is sound judgment to put on a bold face and play your hand for a hundred times what it is worth; forty-nine times out of fifty nobody dares to "call," and you rake in the chips. But just this once—well, things looked squally! In just no time, five hundred knights were scrambling into their saddles, and before you could wink a widely scattering drove were under way and clattering down upon me. I snatched both revolvers from the holsters and began to measure distances and calculate chances.

Bang! one saddle empty. Bang! another one. Bang-bang! and I bagged two. Well, it was nip and tuck with us, and I knew it. If I spent the eleventh shot without convincing these people, the twelfth man would kill me, sure.

And so I never did feel so happy as I did when my ninth downed its man and I detected the wavering in the crowd which is premonitory of panic. An instant lost, now, could knock out my last chance. But I didn't lose it. I raised both revolvers and pointed them—the halted host stood their ground just about one good square moment, then broke and fled.

The day was mine. Knight-errantry was a doomed institution. The march of civilization was begun. How did I feel? Ah, you never could imagine it.

And Brer Merlin? His stock was flat again. Somehow, every time the magic of fol-de-rol tried conclusions with the magic of science, the magic of fol-de-rol got left.

Chapter 40

Three Years Later

WHEN I broke the back of knight-errantry, that time, I no longer felt obliged to work in secret. So, the very next day I exposed my hidden schools, my mines, and my vast system of clandestine factories and work-shops to an astonished world. That is to say, I exposed the nineteenth century to the inspection of the sixth.

Well, it is always a good plan to follow up an advantage promptly. The knights were temporarily down, but if I would keep them so, I must just simply paralyze them—nothing short of that would answer. You see, I was "bluffing," that last time, in the field; it would be natural for them to work around to that conclusion, if I gave them a chance. So I must not give them time; and I didn't.

I renewed my challenge, engraved it on brass, posted it up where any priest could read it to them, and also kept it standing, in the advertising columns of the paper. I not only renewed it, but added to its proportions. I said, name the day, and I would take fifty assistants and stand up *against the massed chivalry of the whole earth and destroy it*.

I was not bluffing, this time. I meant what I said; I could do what I promised. There wasn't any way to misunderstand the language of that challenge. Even the dullest of the chivalry perceived that this was a plain case of "put up, or shut up." They were wise, and did the latter. In all the next three years they gave me no trouble worth mentioning.

Consider the three years sped. Now look around on England. A happy and prosperous country, and strangely altered. Schools everywhere, and several colleges; a number of pretty good newspapers. Even authorship was taking a start; Sir Dinadan the Humorist was first in the field, with a volume of gray-headed jokes which I had been familiar with during thirteen centuries. If he had left out that old rancid one about the lecturer, I wouldn't have said anything; but I couldn't stand that one. I suppressed the book and hanged the author.

Slavery was dead and gone; all men were equal before the law; taxation had been equalized. The telegraph, the telephone, the phonograph, the type-writer, the sewing machine, and all the thousand willing and handy servants of steam and electricity were working their way into favor. We had a steamboat or two on the Thames, we had steam war-ships and the beginnings of a steam commercial marine; I was getting ready to send out an expedition to discover America.

We were building several lines of railway, and our line from Camelot to London was already finished and in operation. I was shrewd enough to make all offices connected with the passenger service places of high and distinguished honor. My idea was to attract the chivalry and nobility, and make them useful and keep them out of mischief. The plan worked very well, the competition for the places was hot. The conductor of the 4.33 express was a duke, there wasn't a passenger-conductor on the line below the degree of earl. They were good men, every one, but they had two defects which I couldn't cure, and so had to wink at: they wouldn't lay aside their armor, and they would "knock down" fares—I mean, rob the company.

There was hardly a knight in all the land who wasn't in some useful employment. They were going from end to end of the country in all manner of useful missionary capacities; their penchant for wandering, and their experience in it, made them altogether the most effective spreaders of civilization we had. They went clothed in steel, and equipped with sword and lance and battle-axe, and if they couldn't persuade a person to try a sewing machine on the instalment plan, or a melodeon, or a barbed wire fence, or a prohibition journal, or any of the other thousand and one things they canvassed for, they removed him and passed on.

I was very happy. Things were working steadily toward a secretly longed-for point. You see, I had two schemes in my head, which were the vastest of all my projects. The one was, to overthrow the Catholic Church and set up the Protestant faith on its ruins—not as an Established Church, but a go-as-you-please one; and the other project was, to get a decree issued by and by, commanding that upon Arthur's death unlimited suffrage should be introduced, and given to men and women alike—at any rate to all men, wise or unwise, and to all mothers who, at middle age, should be found to know nearly as much as their sons at twenty-one. Arthur was good for thirty years yet, he being about my own age—that is to say, forty—and I believed that in that time I could easily have the active part of the population of that day ready and eager for an event which should be the first of its kind in the history of the world—a rounded and complete governmental revolution without bloodshed. The result to be a Republic. Well, I may as well confess, though I do feel ashamed when I think of it: I was beginning to have a base hankering to be its first President myself. Yes, there was more or less human nature in me; I found that out.

Clarence was with me, as concerned the revolution, but in a modified way. His idea was a Republic, without privileged orders, but with a hereditary royal family at the head of it instead of an elective chief magistrate. He believed that no nation that had ever known the joy of worshiping a royal family could ever be robbed of it and not fade away and die of melancholy. I urged that kings were dangerous. He said, then have cats. He was sure that a royal family of cats would answer every purpose. They would be as useful as any other royal family, they would know as much, they would have the same virtues and the same vices, the same fidelities and the same treacheries, the same disposition to get up shindies with other royal cats, they would be laughably vain and absurd and never know it, and they would be wholly inexpensive; finally, they would have as sound a divine right as any other royal house, and "Tom VII, or Tom XI, or Tom XIV by the grace of God King," would sound as well as it would when applied to the ordinary royal tomcat with tights on. "And as a rule," said he, in his neat modern English, "the character of these cats would be considerably above the character of the average king, and this would be an immense moral advantage to the nation, for the reason that a nation always models its morals after its monarch's. The worship of royalty being founded in unreason, these graceful and harmless cats would easily become as sacred as any other royalties, and indeed more so, because it would presently be noticed that they hanged nobody, beheaded nobody, imprisoned nobody, inflicted no cruelties or injustices of any sort, and so must be worthy of a deeper love and reverence than the customary human king, and would certainly get it. The eyes of the whole harried world would soon be fixed upon this humane and gentle system, and royal butchers would presently begin to disappear; their subjects would fill the vacancies with catlings from our own royal house; we should become a factory; we should supply the thrones of the world; within forty years all Europe would be governed by cats, and we should furnish the cats. The reign of universal peace would begin, then, to end no more forever. . . . . . *Me-e-e-yow-ow-ow-ow*—FZT!-*wow!*"

Hang him, I supposed he was in earnest, and was beginning to be persuaded by him, until he exploded that cat-howl and startled me almost out of my clothes. But he never could be in earnest. He didn't know what it was. He had pictured a distinct and perfectly rational and feasible improvement upon constitutional monarchy, but he was too feather-headed to know it, or care anything about it, either. I was going to give him a scolding, but Sandy came flying in at that moment, wild with terror, and so choked with sobs that for a minute she could not get her voice. I ran and took her in my arms, and lavished caresses upon her, and said, beseechingly:

"Speak, darling, speak! What is it?"

Her head fell limp upon my bosom, and she gasped, almost inaudibly:

"HELLO-CENTRAL!"

"Quick!" I shouted to Clarence; "telephone the king's homeopath to come!"

In two minutes I was kneeling by the child's crib, and Sandy was dispatching servants here, there and everywhere all over the palace. I took in the situation almost at a glance—membranous croup! I bent down and whispered:

"Wake up, sweetheart! Hello-Central!"

She opened her soft eyes languidly, and made out to say—"Papa."

That was a comfort. She was far from dead, yet. I sent for preparations of sulphur, I rousted out the croup-kettle myself: for I don't sit down and wait for doctors when Sandy or the child are sick. I knew how to nurse both of them, and had had experience. This little chap had lived in my arms a good part of its small life, and often I could soothe away its troubles and get it to laugh through the tear-dews on its eyelashes when even its mother couldn't.

Sir Launcelot, in his richest armor, came striding along the great hall, now, on his way to the stock-board; he was President of the stock-board, and occupied the Siege Perilous, which he had bought of Sir Galahad; for the stock-board consisted of the knights of the Round Table, and they used the Round Table for business purposes now. Seats at it were worth—well, you would never believe the figure, so it is no use to state it. Sir Launcelot was a bear, and he had put up a corner in one of the new lines, and was just getting ready to squeeze the shorts to-day; but what of that? He was the same old Launcelot, and when he glanced in as he was passing the door, and found out that his pet was sick, that was enough for him; bulls and bears might fight it out their own way for all him, he would come right in here and stand by little Hello-Central for all he was worth. And that is what he did. He shied his helmet into the corner, and in half a minute he had a new wick in the alcohol lamp and was firing up on the croup-kettle. By this time Sandy had built a blanket canopy over the crib, and everything was ready.

Sir Launcelot got up steam, he and I loaded up the kettle with unslaked lime and carbolic acid, with a touch of lactic acid added thereto, then filled the thing up with water, and inserted the steam-spout under the canopy. Everything was ship-shape now, and we sat down on either side of the crib to stand our watch. Sandy was so grateful and so comforted that she charged a couple of church-wardens with willow-bark and sumach-tobacco for us, and told us to smoke as much as we pleased, it couldn't get under the canopy, and she was used to smoke, being the first lady in the land who had ever seen a cloud blown. Well, there couldn't be a more contented or comfortable sight than Sir Launcelot in his noble armor sitting in gracious serenity at the end of a yard of snowy church-warden. He was a beautiful man, a lovely man, and was just intended to make a wife and children happy. But of course Guenever—however, it's no use to cry over what's done and can't be helped.

Well, he stood watch-and-watch with me, right straight through, for three days and nights, till the child was out of danger; then he took her up in his great arms and kissed her, with his plumes falling about her golden head, then laid her softly in Sandy's lap again, and took his stately way down the vast hall, between the ranks of admiring men-at-arms and menials, and so disappeared. And no instinct warned me that I should never look upon him again in this world! Lord, what a world of heart-break it is.

The doctors said we must take the child away, if we would coax her back to health and strength again. And she must have sea air. So we took a man of war, and a suite of two hundred and sixty persons, and went cruising about, and after a fortnight of this we stepped ashore on the French coast, and the doctors thought it would be a good idea to make something of a stay there. The little king of that region offered us his hospitalities, and we were glad to accept. If he had had as many conveniences as he lacked, we should have been plenty comfortable enough; even as it was, we made out very well, in his queer old castle, by the help of comforts and luxuries from the ship.

At the end of a month I sent the vessel home for fresh supplies, and for news. We expected her back in three or four days. She would bring me, along with other news, the result of a certain experiment which I had been starting. It was a project of mine to replace the tournament with something which might furnish an escape for the extra steam of the chivalry, keep those bucks entertained and out of mischief, and at the same time preserve the best thing in them, which was their hardy spirit of emulation. I had had a choice band of them in private training for some time, and the date was now arriving for their first public effort.

This experiment was base-ball. In order to give the thing vogue from the start, and place it out of the reach of criticism, I chose my nines by rank, not capacity. There wasn't a knight in either team who wasn't a sceptred sovereign. As for material of this sort, there was a glut of it, always, around Arthur. You couldn't throw a brick in any direction and not cripple a king. Of course I couldn't get these people to leave off their armor; they wouldn't do that when they bathed. They consented to differentiate the armor, so that a body could tell one team from the other, but that was the most they would do. So, one of the teams wore chain-mail ulsters, and the other wore plate armor made of my new Bessemer steel. Their practice in the field was the most fantastic thing I ever saw. Being ball-proof, they never skipped out of the way, but stood still and took the result; when a Bessemer was at the bat and a ball hit him, it would bound a hundred and fifty yards, sometimes. And when a man was running, and threw himself on his stomach to slide to his base, it was like an iron-clad coming into port. At first I appointed men of no rank to act as umpires, but I had to discontinue that. These people were no easier to please than other nines. The umpire's first decision was usually his last; they broke him in two with a bat, and his friends toted him home on a shutter. When it was noticed that no umpire ever survived a game, umpiring got to be unpopular. So I was obliged to appoint somebody whose rank and lofty position under the government would protect him.

Here are the names of the nines:

BESSEMERS.	*ULSTERS.*
King Arthur	Emperor Lucius
King Lot of Lothian	King Logris
King of Northgalis	King Marhalt of Ireland
King Marsil	King Morganore
King of Little Britain	King Mark of Cornwall
King Labor	King Nentres of Garlot
King Pellam of Listengese	King Meliodas of Liones
King Bagdemagus	King of the Lake
King Tolleme la Feintes	The Sowdan of Syria

UMPIRE—Clarence.

The first public game would certainly draw fifty thousand people; and for solid fun would be worth going around the world to see. Everything would be favorable; it was balmy and beautiful spring weather, now, and Nature was all tailored out in her new clothes.

Chapter 41

The Interdict

HOWEVER, my attention was suddenly snatched from such matters; our child began to lose ground again, and we had to go to sitting up with her, her case became so serious. We couldn't bear to allow anybody to help, in this service, so we two stood watch-and-watch, day in and day out. Ah, Sandy, what a right heart she had, how simple, and genuine, and good she was! She was a flawless wife and mother; and yet I had married her for no particular reason, except that by the customs of chivalry she was my property until some knight should win her from me in the field. She had hunted Britain over for me; had found me at the hanging-bout outside of London, and had straightway resumed her old place at my side in the placidest way and as of right. I was a New Englander, and in my opinion this sort of partnership would compromise her, sooner or later. She couldn't see how, but I cut argument short and we had a wedding.

Now I didn't know I was drawing a prize, yet that was what I did draw. Within the twelvemonth I became her worshiper; and ours was the dearest and perfectest comradeship that ever was. People talk about beautiful friendships between two persons of the same sex. What is the best of that sort, as compared with the friendship of man and wife, where the best impulses and highest ideals of both are the same? There is no place for comparison between the two friendships; the one is earthly, the other divine.

In my dreams, along at first, I still wandered thirteen centuries away, and my unsatisfied spirit went calling and harking all up and down the unreplying vacancies of a vanished world. Many a time Sandy heard that imploring cry come from my lips in my sleep. With a grand magnanimity she saddled that cry of mine upon our child, conceiving it to be the name of some lost darling of mine. It touched me to tears, and it also nearly knocked me off my feet, too, when she smiled up in my face for an earned reward, and played her quaint and pretty surprise upon me:

"The name of one who was dear to thee is here preserved, here made holy, and the music of it will abide alway in our ears. Now thou'lt kiss me, as knowing the name I have given the child."

But I didn't know it, all the same. I hadn't an idea in the world; but it would have been cruel to confess it and spoil her pretty game; so I never let on, but said:

"Yes, I know, sweetheart—how dear and good it is of you, too! But I want to hear these lips of yours, which are also mine, utter it first—then its music will be perfect."

Pleased to the marrow, she murmured—

"Hello-Central!"

I didn't laugh—I am always thankful for that—but the strain ruptured every cartilage in me, and for weeks afterward I could hear my bones clack when I walked. She never found out her mistake. The first time she heard that form of salute used at the telephone she was surprised, and not pleased; but I told her I had given order for it: that thenceforth and for-ever the telephone must be always invoked with that reverent formality, in perpetual honor and remembrance of my lost friend and her small namesake. This was not true. But it answered.

Well, during two weeks and a half we watched by the crib, and in our deep solicitude we were unconscious of any world outside of that sick-room. Then our reward came: the centre of the universe turned the corner and began to mend. Grate-ful? It isn't the term. There *isn't* any term for it. You know that, yourself, if you've watched your child through the Valley of the Shadow and seen it come back to life and sweep night out of the earth with one all-illuminating smile that you could cover with your hand.

Why, we were back in this world in one instant! Then we looked the same startled thought into each other's eyes at the same moment: more than two weeks gone, and that ship not back yet!

In another minute I appeared in the presence of my train. They had been steeped in troubled bodings all this time— their faces showed it. I called an escort and we galloped five miles to a hill-top overlooking the sea. Where was my great commerce that so lately had made these glistering expanses populous and beautiful with its white-winged flocks? Vanished, every one! Not a sail, from verge to verge, not a smoke-bank—just a dead and empty solitude, in place of all that brisk and breezy life.

I went swiftly back, saying not a word to anybody. I told Sandy this ghastly news. We could imagine no explanation that would begin to explain. Had there been an invasion? an earthquake? a pestilence? Had the nation been swept out of existence? But guessing was profitless. I must go—at once. I borrowed the king's navy—a "ship" no bigger than a steam-launch—and was soon ready.

The parting—ah, yes, that was hard. As I was devouring the child with last kisses, it brisked up and jabbered out its vocabulary!—the first time in more than two weeks, and it made fools of us for joy. The darling mispronunciations of childhood!—dear me, there's no music that can touch it; and how one grieves when it wastes away and dissolves into correctness, knowing it will never visit his bereaved ear again. Well, how good it was, to be able to carry that gracious memory away with me!

I approached England the next morning, with the wide highway of salt water all to myself. There were ships in the harbor, at Dover, but they were naked, as to sails, and there was no sign of life about them. It was Sunday; yet at Canterbury the streets were empty; strangest of all, there was not even a priest in sight, and no stroke of a bell fell upon my ear. The mournfulness of death was everywhere. I couldn't understand it. At last, in the further edge of that town I saw a small funeral procession—just a family and a few friends following a coffin—no priest; a funeral without bell, book or candle; there was a church there, close at hand, but they passed it by, weeping, and did not enter it; I glanced up at the belfry, and there hung the bell, shrouded in black, and its tongue tied back. Now I knew! Now I understood the stupendous calamity that had overtaken England. Invasion? Invasion is a triviality to it. It was the INTERDICT!

I asked no questions; I didn't need to ask any. The Church had struck; the thing for me to do was to get into a disguise, and go warily. One of my servants gave me a suit of his clothes, and when we were safe beyond the town I put them on, and from that time I traveled alone; I could not risk the embarrassment of company.

A miserable journey. A desolate silence everywhere. Even in London itself. Traffic had ceased; men did not talk or laugh, or go in groups, or even in couples; they moved aimlessly about, each man by himself, with his head down, and woe and terror at his heart. The Tower showed recent war-scars. Verily, much had been happening.

Of course I meant to take the train for Camelot. Train! Why, the station was as vacant as a cavern. I moved on. The journey to Camelot was a repetition of what I had already seen. The Monday and the Tuesday differed in no way from the Sunday. I arrived far in the night. From being the best electric-lighted town in the kingdom, and the most like a re-cumbent sun of anything you ever saw, it was become simply a blot—a blot upon darkness—that is to say, it was darker and solider than the rest of the darkness, and so you could see it a little better; it made me feel as if maybe it was symboli-cal—a sort of sign that the Church was going to *keep* the upper hand, now, and snuff out all my beautiful civilization just like that. I found no life stirring in the sombre streets. I groped my way with a heavy heart. The vast castle loomed black upon the hill-top, not a spark visible about it. The drawbridge was down, the great gate stood wide, I entered without challenge, my own heels making the only sound I heard—and it was sepulchral enough, in those huge vacant courts.

Chapter 42

WAR!

I FOUND Clarence, alone in his quarters, drowned in melancholy; and in place of the electric light, he had re-instituted the ancient rag lamp, and sat there in a grisly twilight with all curtains drawn tight. He sprang up and rushed for me eagerly, saying:

"Oh, it's worth a billion milrays to look upon a live person again!"

He knew me as easily as if I hadn't been disguised at all. Which frightened me; one may easily believe that.

"Quick, now, tell me the meaning of this fearful disaster," I said. "How did it come about?"

"Well, if there hadn't been any Queen Guenever, it wouldn't have come so early; but it would have come, anyway. It would have come on your own account by and by; by luck, it happened to come on the queen's."

"*And* Sir Launcelot's?"

"Just so."

"Give me the details."

"I reckon you will grant that during some years there has been only one pair of eyes in these kingdoms that has not been looking steadily askance at the queen and Sir Launcelot—"

"Yes—King Arthur's."

—"and only one heart that was without suspicion—"

"Yes—the king's; a heart that isn't capable of thinking evil of a friend."

"Well, the king might have gone on, still happy and un-suspecting, to the end of his days, but for one of your modern improvements—the stock-board. When you left, three miles of the London, Canterbury & Dover were ready for the rails, and also ready and ripe for manipulation in the stock market. It was wildcat, and everybody knew it. The stock was for sale at a give-away. What does Sir Launcelot do, but—"

"Yes, I know; he quietly picked up nearly all of it, for a song; then he bought about twice as much more, deliverable upon call; and he was about to call when I left."

"Very well, he did call. The boys couldn't deliver. Oh, he had them—and he just settled his grip and squeezed them. They were laughing in their sleeves over their smartness in selling stock to him at 15 and 16 and along there, that wasn't worth 10. Well, when they had laughed long enough on that side of their mouths, they rested-up that side by shifting the laugh to the other side. That was when they compromised with the Invincible at 283!"

"Good land!"

"He skinned them alive, and they deserved it—anyway, the whole kingdom rejoiced. Well, among the flayed were Sir Agravaine and Sir Mordred, nephews to the king. End of the first Act. Act Second, scene first, an apartment in Carlisle castle, where the court had gone for a few days' hunting. Persons present, the whole tribe of the king's nephews. Mordred and Agravaine propose to call the guileless Arthur's attention to Guenever and Sir Launcelot. Sir Gawaine, Sir Gareth and Sir Gaheris will have nothing to do with it. A dispute ensues, with loud talk; in the midst of it, enter the king. Mordred and Agravaine spring their devastating tale upon him. *Tableau.* A trap is laid for Launcelot, by the king's command, and Sir Launcelot walks into it. He made it sufficiently uncomfortable for the ambushed witnesses—to wit, Mordred, Agravaine, and twelve knights of lesser rank, for he killed every one of them but Mordred; but of course that couldn't straighten matters between Launcelot and the king, and didn't."

"Oh, dear, only one thing could result—I see that. War, and the knights of the realm divided into a king's party and a Sir Launcelot's party."

"Yes—that was the way of it. The king sent the queen to the stake, proposing to purify her with fire. Launcelot and his knights rescued her, and in doing it slew certain good old friends of yours and mine—in fact some of the best we ever had; to wit, Sir Belias le Orgulous, Sir Segwarides, Sir Griflet le Fils de Dieu, Sir Brandiles, Sir Aglovale—"

"Oh, you tear out my heart-strings."

"—wait, I'm not done yet—Sir Tor, Sir Gauter, Sir Gillimer—"

"The very best man in my Subordinate Nine. What a handy right-fielder he was!"

"—Sir Reynold's three brothers, Sir Damus, Sir Priamus, Sir Kay the Stranger—"

"My peerless short-stop! I've seen him catch a daisy-cutter in his teeth. Come, I can't stand this!"

"—Sir Driant, Sir Lambegus, Sir Herminde, Sir Pertilope, Sir Perimones, and—whom, do you think?"

"Rush! Go on."

"Sir Gaheris, and Sir Gareth—both!"

"Oh, incredible! Their love for Launcelot was indestructible."

"Well, it was an accident. They were simply on-lookers; they were unarmed, and were merely there to witness the queen's punishment. Sir Launcelot smote down whoever came in the way of his blind fury, and he killed these without noticing who they were. Here is an instantaneous photograph one of our boys got of the battle; it's for sale on every news-stand. There—the figures nearest the queen are Sir Launcelot with his sword up, and Sir Gareth gasping his latest breath. You can catch the agony in the queen's face through the curling smoke. It's a rattling battle-picture."

"Indeed it is. We must take good care of it; its historical value is incalculable. Go on."

"Well, the rest of the tale is just war, pure and simple. Launcelot retreated to his town and castle of Joyous Gard, and gathered there a great following of knights. The king, with a great host, went there, and there was desperate fighting during several days, and as a result all the plain around was paved with corpses and cast-iron. Then the Church patched up a peace between Arthur and Launcelot and the queen and everybody—everybody but Sir Gawaine. He was bitter about the slaying of his brothers, Gareth and Gaheris, and would not be appeased. He notified Launcelot to get him thence, and make swift preparation, and look to be soon attacked. So Launcelot sailed to his Duchy of Guienne, with his following, and Gawaine soon followed, with an army, and he beguiled Arthur to go with him. Arthur left the kingdom in Sir Mordred's hands until you should return—"

"Ah—a king's customary wisdom!"

"Yes. Sir Mordred set himself at once to work, to make his kingship permanent. He was going to marry Guenever, as a first move; but she fled, and shut herself up in the Tower of London. Mordred attacked; the Bishop of Canterbury dropped down on him with the Interdict. The king returned; Mordred fought him at Dover, at Canterbury, and again at Barham Down. Then there was talk of peace, and a composition. Terms, Mordred to have Cornwall and Kent, during Arthur's life, and the whole kingdom afterward."

"Well, upon my word! My dream of a Republic to *be* a dream, and so remain."

"Yes. The two armies lay near Salisbury. Gawaine—Gawaine's head is at Dover Castle, he fell in the fight there—Gawaine appeared to Arthur in a dream, at least his ghost did, and warned him to refrain from conflict for a month, let the delay cost what it might. But battle was precipitated by an accident. Arthur had given order that if a sword was raised during the consultation over the proposed treaty with Mordred, sound the trumpet and fall on! for he had no confidence in Mordred. Mordred had given a similar order to *his* people. Well, by and by an adder bit a knight's heel; the knight forgot all about the order, and made a slash at the adder with his sword. Inside of half a minute those two prodigious hosts came together with a crash! They butchered away all day. Then the king—however, we have started something fresh since you left—our paper has."

"No? What is that?"

"War correspondence!"

"Why, that's good."

"Yes, the paper was booming right along, for the Interdict made no impression, got no grip, while the war lasted. I had war correspondents with both armies. I will finish that battle by reading you what one of the boys says:

Then the king looked about him, and then was he ware of all his host, and of all his good knights, were left no more on live but two knights, that was Sir Lucan de butlere, and his brother Sir Bedivere:

and they full were sore wounded. Jesu mercy, said the king, where are all my noble knights becomen? Alas that ever I should see this doleful day. For now, said Arthur, I am come to mine end. But would to God that I wist where were that traitor Sir Mordred, that hath caused all this mischief. Then was king Arthur ware where Sir Mordred leaned upon his sword among a great heap of dead men. Now give me my spear, said Arthur unto Sir Lucan, for yonder I have espied the traitor that all this woe hath wrought. Sir, let him be, said Sir Lucan, for he is unhappy: and if ye pass this unhappy day, ye shall be right well revenged upon him. Good lord, remember ye of your night's dream, and what the spirit of Sir Gawaine told you this night, yet God of his great goodness hath preserved you hitherto. Therefore, for God's sake, my lord, leave off by this. For blessed be God ye have won the field: for here we be three on live, and with Sir Mordred is none on live. And if ye leave off now, this wicked day of destiny is past. Tide me death, betide me life, saith the king, now I see him yonder alone, he shall never escape mine hands, for at a better avail shall I never have him. God speed you well, said Sir Bedivere. Then the king gat his spear in both his hands, and ran toward Sir Mordred, crying, Traitor, now is thy death day come. And when Sir Mordred heard Sir Arthur, he ran until him with his sword drawn in his hand. And then king Arthur smote Sir Mordred under the shield, with a foin of his spear throughout the body more than a fathom. And when Sir Mordred felt that he had his death's wound, he thrust himself, with the might that he had, up to the bur of king Arthur's spear. And right so he smote his father Arthur with his sword holden in both his hands, on the side of the head, that the sword pierced the helmet and the brain-pan, and therewithal Sir Mordred fell stark dead to the earth. And the noble Arthur fell in a swoon to the earth, and there he swooned oft-times.

"That is a good piece of war correspondence, Clarence; you are a first-rate newspaper man. Well—is the king all right? Did he get well?"

"Poor soul, no. He is dead."

I was utterly stunned; it had not seemed to me that any wound could be mortal to him.

"And the queen, Clarence?"

"She is a nun, in Almesbury."

"What changes! and in such a short while. It is inconceivable. What next, I wonder?"

"I can tell you what next."

"Well?"

"Stake our lives and stand by them!"

"What do you mean by that?"

"The Church is master, now. The Interdict included you with Mordred; it is not to be removed while you remain alive. The clans are gathering. The Church has gathered all the knights that are left alive, and as soon as you are discovered, we shall have business on our hands."

"Stuff! With our deadly scientific war-material—with our hosts of trained—"

"Save your breath—we haven't sixty faithful left!"

"What are you saying? Our schools, our colleges, our vast work-shops, our—"

"When those knights come, those establishments will empty themselves and go over to the enemy. Did you think you had educated the superstition out of those people?"

"I certainly did think it."

"Well, then, you may unthink it. They stood every strain easily—until the Interdict. Since then, they merely put on a bold outside—at heart they are quaking. Make up your mind to it—when the armies come, the mask will fall."

"It's hard news. We are lost. They will turn our own science against us."

"No they won't."

"Why?"

"Because I and a handful of the faithful have blocked that game. I'll tell you what I've done, and what moved me to it. Smart as you are, the Church was smarter. It was the Church that sent you cruising—through her servants the doctors."

"Clarence!"

"It is the truth. I know it. Every officer of your ship was the Church's picked servant, and so was every man of the crew."

"Oh, come!"

"It is just as I tell you. I did not find out these things at once, but I found them out finally. Did you send me verbal information, by the commander of the ship, to the effect that upon his return to you, with supplies, you were going to leave Cadiz—"

"Cadiz! I haven't been at Cadiz at all!"

—"going to leave Cadiz and cruise in distant seas indefinitely, for the health of your family? Did you send me that word?"

"Of course not. I would have written, wouldn't I?"

"Naturally. I was troubled, and suspicious. When the commander sailed again I managed to ship a spy with him. I have never heard of vessel or spy since. I gave myself two weeks to hear from you in. Then I resolved to send a ship to Cadiz. There was a reason why I didn't."

"What was that?"

"Our navy had suddenly and mysteriously disappeared! Also as suddenly and as mysteriously, the railway and telegraph and telephone service ceased, the men all deserted, poles were cut down, the Church laid a ban upon the electric light! I had to be up and doing—and straight off. Your life was safe—nobody in these kingdoms but Merlin would venture to touch such a magician as you, without ten thousand men at his back—I had nothing to think of but how to put preparations in the best trim against your coming. I felt safe myself—nobody would be anxious to touch a pet of yours. So this is what I did. From our various works I selected all the men—boys, I mean—whose faithfulness under whatsoever pressure I could swear to, and I called them together secretly and gave them their instructions. There are fifty-two of them; none younger than fourteen, and none above seventeen years old."

"Why did you select boys?"

"Because all the others were born in an atmosphere of superstition, and reared in it. It is in their blood and bones. We imagined we had educated it out of them; they thought so, too; the Interdict woke them up like a thunderclap! It revealed them to themselves, and it revealed them to me, too. With boys it was different. Such as have been under our training from seven to ten years have had no acquaintance with the Church's terrors, and it was among these that I found my fifty-two. As a next move, I paid a private visit to that old cave of Merlin's—not the small one, the big one—"

"Yes, the one where we secretly established our first great electric plant when I was projecting a miracle."

"Just so. And as that miracle hadn't become necessary then, I thought it might be a good idea to utilize the plant now. I've provisioned the cave for a siege—"

"A good idea, a first-rate idea."

"I think so. I placed four of my boys there, as a guard—inside, and out of sight. Nobody was to be hurt—while outside; but any attempt to enter—well, we said, just let anybody try it! Then I went out into the hills and uncovered and cut the secret wire which connected your bedroom with the wires that go to the dynamite deposits under all our vast factories, mills, work-shops, magazines, etc., and about midnight I and my boys turned out and connected that wire with the cave, and nobody but you and I suspects where the other end of it goes to. We laid it under ground, of course, and it was all finished in a couple of hours or so. We shan't have to leave our fortress, now, when we want to blow up our civilization."

"It was the right move—and the natural one; a military necessity, in the changed condition of things. Well, what changes *have* come! We expected to be besieged in the palace some time or other, but—however, go on."

"Next, we built a wire fence."

"Wire fence?"

"Yes. You dropped the hint of it yourself, two or three years ago."

"Oh, I remember—the time the Church tried her strength against us the first time, and presently thought it wise to wait for a hopefuler season. Well, how have you arranged the fence?"

"I start twelve immensely strong wires—naked, not insulated—from a big dynamo in the cave—dynamo with no brushes except a positive and a negative one—"

"Yes, that's right."

"The wires go out from the cave and fence-in a circle of level ground a hundred yards in diameter; they make twelve independent fences, ten feet apart—that is to say, twelve circles within circles—and their ends come into the cave again."

"Right; go on."

"The fences are fastened to heavy oaken posts only three feet apart, and these posts are sunk five feet in the ground."

"That is good and strong."

"Yes. The wires have no ground-connection outside of the cave. They go out from the positive brush of the dynamo; there is a ground-connection through the negative brush; the other ends of the wire return to the cave, and each is grounded independently."

"No-no, that won't do!"

"Why?"

"It's too expensive—uses up force for nothing. You don't want any ground-connection except the one through the negative brush. The other end of every wire must be brought back into the cave and fastened independently, and *without* any ground-connection. Now, then, observe the economy of it. A cavalry charge hurls itself against the fence; you are using no power, you are spending no money, for there is only one ground-connection till those horses come against the wire; the moment they touch it they form a connection with the negative brush *through the ground*, and drop dead. Don't you see?—you are using no energy until it is needed; your lightning is there, and ready, like the load in a gun; but it isn't costing you a cent till you touch it off. Oh, yes, the single ground-connection—"

"Of course! I don't know how I overlooked that. It's not only cheaper, but it's more effectual than the other way, for if wires break or get tangled, no harm is done."

"No; especially if we have a tell-tale in the cave and disconnect the broken wire. Well, go on. The gatlings?"

"Yes—that's arranged. In the centre of the inner circle, on a spacious platform six feet high, I've grouped a battery of thirteen gatling guns, and provided plenty of ammunition."

"That's it. They command every approach, and when the Church's knights arrive, there's going to be music. The brow of the precipice over the cave—"

"I've got a wire fence there, and a gatling. They won't drop any rocks down on us."

"Well, and the glass-cylinder dynamite torpedoes?"

"That's attended to. It's the prettiest garden that was ever planted. It's a belt forty feet wide, and goes around the outer fence—distance between it and the fence, one hundred yards—kind of neutral ground, that space is. There isn't a single square yard of that whole belt but is equipped with a torpedo. We laid them on the surface of the ground, and sprinkled a layer of sand over them. It's an innocent looking garden, but you let a man start in to hoe it once, and you'll see."

"You tested the torpedoes?"

"Well, I was going to, but—"

"But what? Why, it's an immense oversight not to apply a—"

"Test? Yes, I know; but they're all right; I laid a few in the public road beyond our lines, and they've been tested."

"Oh, that alters the case. Who did it?"

"A Church committee."

"How kind!"

"Yes. They came to command us to make submission. You see they didn't really come to test the torpedoes; that was merely an incident."

"Did the committee make a report?"

"Yes, they made one. You could have heard it a mile."

"Unanimous?"

"That was the nature of it. After that, I put up some signs, for the protection of future committees, and we have had no intruders since."

"Clarence, you've done a world of work, and done it perfectly."

"We had plenty of time for it; there wasn't any occasion for hurry."

We sat silent a while, thinking. Then my mind was made up, and I said:

"Yes, everything is ready; everything is ship-shape, no detail is wanting. I know what to do, now."

"So do I: sit down and wait."

"No, *sir!* rise up and *strike!*"

"Do you mean it?"

"Yes, indeed! The *de*fensive isn't in my line, and the *off*ensive is. That is, when I hold a fair hand—two-thirds as good a hand as the enemy. Oh, yes, we'll rise up and strike; that's our game."

"A hundred to one, you are right. When does the performance begin?"

"*Now!* We'll proclaim the Republic."

"Well, that *will* precipitate things, sure enough!"

"It will make them buzz, *I* tell you! England will be a hornet's nest before noon to-morrow, if the Church's hand hasn't lost its cunning—and we know it hasn't. Now you write and I'll dictate—thus:

"PROCLAMATION.

"BE IT KNOWN UNTO ALL. Whereas, the king having died and left no heir, it becomes my duty to continue the executive authority vested in me, until a government shall have been created and set in motion. The monarchy has lapsed, it no longer exists. By consequence, all political power has reverted to its original source, the people of the nation. With the monarchy, its several adjuncts died also; wherefore there is no longer a nobility, no longer a privileged class, no longer an Established Church: all men are become exactly equal, they are upon one common level, and religion is free. *A Republic is hereby proclaimed,* as being the natural estate of a nation when other authority has ceased. It is the duty of the British people to meet together immediately, and by their votes elect representatives and deliver into their hands the government."

I signed it "The Boss," and dated it from Merlin's Cave. Clarence said:

"Why, that tells where we are, and invites them to call, right away."

"That is the idea. We *strike*—by the Proclamation—then it's their innings. Now have the thing set up and printed and posted, right off; that is, give the order; then, if you've got a couple of bicycles handy at the foot of the hill, ho for Merlin's Cave!"

"I shall be ready in ten minutes. What a cyclone there is going to be to-morrow when this piece of paper gets to work! . . . . It's a pleasant old palace, this is; I wonder if we shall ever again—but never mind about that."

Chapter 43

The Battle of the Sand-Belt

In Merlin's Cave—Clarence and I, and fifty-two fresh, bright, well educated, clean-minded young British boys. At dawn I sent an order to the factories, and to all our great works, to stop operations and remove all life to a safe distance, as everything was going to be blown up, by secret mines, *"and no telling at what moment—therefore, vacate at once."* Those people knew me, and had confidence in my word. They would clear out without waiting to part their hair, and I could take my own time about dating the explosion. You couldn't hire one of them to go back during the century, if the explosion was still impending.

We had a week of waiting. It was not dull for me, because I was writing all the time. During the first three days, I finished turning my old diary into this narrative form; it only required a chapter or so to bring it down to date. The rest of the week I took up in writing letters to my wife. It was always my habit to write to Sandy every day, whenever we were separate, and now I kept up the habit for love of it and her, though I couldn't do anything with the letters of course after I had written them. But it put in the time, you see, and was almost like talking; it was almost as if I was saying, "Sandy, if you and Hello-Central were here in a cave, instead of only your photographs, what good times we could have!" And then, you know, I could imagine the baby goo-gooing something out in reply, with its fists in its mouth, and itself stretched across its mother's lap on its back, and she a-laughing and admiring and worshiping, and now and then tickling under the baby's chin to set it cackling, and then maybe throwing in a word of answer to me herself—and so-on and so-on—well, don't you know, I could sit there in the cave with my pen, and keep it up, that way, by the hour with them. Why, it was almost like having us all together again.

I had spies out, every night, of course, to get news. Every report made things look more and more impressive. The

524

hosts were gathering, gathering; down all the roads and paths of England the knights were riding; and priests rode with them, to hearten these original Crusaders, this being the Church's war. All the nobilities, big and little, were on their way, and all the gentry. This was all as was expected. We should thin out this sort of folk to such a degree that the people would have nothing to do but just step to the front with their Republic and—

Ah, what a donkey I was! Toward the end of the week, I began to get this large and disenchanting fact through my head: that the mass of the nation had swung their caps and shouted for the Republic for about one day, and there an end! The Church, the nobles and the gentry then turned one grand all-disapproving frown upon them and shriveled them into sheep! From that moment the sheep had begun to gather to the fold—that is to say, the camps—and offer their value-less lives and their valuable wool to the "righteous cause." Why, even the very men who had lately been slaves were in the "righteous cause," and glorifying it, praying for it, senti-mentally slobbering over it, just like all the other commoners. Imagine such human muck as this; conceive of this folly!

Yes, it was now "Death to the Republic!" everywhere—not a dissenting voice. All England was marching against us! Truly this was more than I had bargained for.

I watched my fifty-two boys narrowly; watched their faces, their walk, their unconscious attitudes: for all these are a lan-guage—a language given us purposely that it may betray us in times of emergency, when we have secrets which we want to keep. I knew that that thought would keep saying itself over and over again in their minds and hearts, *All England is marching against us!* and ever more strenuously imploring attention with each repetition, ever more sharply realizing itself to their imaginations, until even in their sleep they would find no rest from it, but hear the vague and flitting creatures of their dreams say, *All England—*ALL ENGLAND! *—is marching against you!* I knew all this would happen; I knew that ultimately the pressure would become so great that it would compel utterance; therefore, I must be ready with an answer at that time—an answer well chosen and tranquilizing.

I was right. The time came. They *had* to speak. Poor lads, it was pitiful to see, they were so pale, so worn, so troubled. At first their spokesman could hardly find voice or words; but he presently got both. This is what he said—and he put it in the neat modern English taught him in my schools:

"We have tried to forget what we are—English boys! We have tried to put reason before sentiment, duty before love: our minds approve, but our hearts reproach us. While apparently it was only the nobility, only the gentry, only the twenty-five or thirty thousand knights left alive out of the late wars, we were of one mind, and undisturbed by any troubling doubt; each and every one of these fifty-two lads who stand here before you, said, 'They have chosen—it is their affair.' But think!—the matter is altered—*all England is marching against us!* Oh, sir, consider!—reflect!—these people are our people, they are bone of our bone, flesh of our flesh, we love them—do not ask us to destroy our nation!"

Well, it shows the value of looking ahead, and being ready for a thing when it happens. If I hadn't foreseen this thing, and been fixed, that boy would have had me!—I couldn't have said a word. But I *was* fixed. I said:

"My boys, your hearts are in the right place, you have thought the worthy thought, you have done the worthy thing. You are English boys, you will remain English boys, and you will keep that name unsmirched. Give yourselves no further concern, let your minds be at peace. Consider this: while all England *is* marching against us, who is in the van? Who, by the commonest rules of war, will march in the front? Answer me."

"The mounted host of mailed knights."

"True. They are 30,000 strong. Acres deep, they will march. Now, observe: none but *they* will ever strike the sand-belt! Then there will be an episode! Immediately after, the civilian multitude in the rear will retire, to meet business engagements elsewhere. None but nobles and gentry are knights, and *none but these* will remain to dance to our music after that episode. It is absolutely true that we shall have to fight nobody but these thirty thousand knights. Now speak, and it shall be as you decide. Shall we avoid the battle, retire from the field?"

"NO!!!"

The shout was unanimous and hearty.

"Are you—are you—well, afraid of these thirty thousand knights?"

That joke brought out a good laugh, the boys' troubles vanished away, and they went gaily to their posts. Ah, they were a darling fifty-two! As pretty as girls, too.

I was ready for the enemy, now. Let the approaching big day come along—it would find us on deck.

The big day arrived, on time. At dawn the sentry on watch in the corral came into the cave and reported a moving black mass under the horizon, and a faint sound which he thought to be military music. Breakfast was just ready; we sat down and ate it.

This over, I made the boys a little speech, and then sent out a detail to man the battery, with Clarence in command of it.

The sun rose presently, and sent its unobstructed splendors over the land, and we saw a prodigious host moving slowly toward us, with the steady drift and aligned front of a wave of the sea. Nearer and nearer it came, and more and more sublimely imposing became its aspect; yes, all England was there, apparently. Soon we could see the innumerable banners fluttering, and then the sun struck the sea of armor and set it all aflash. Yes, it was a fine sight; I hadn't ever seen anything to beat it.

At last we could make out details. All the front ranks, no telling how many acres deep, were horsemen—plumed knights in armor. Suddenly we heard the blare of trumpets; the slow walk burst into a gallop, and then—well, it was wonderful to see! Down swept that vast horse-shoe wave—it approached the sand-belt—my breath stood still; nearer, nearer—the strip of green turf beyond the yellow belt grew narrow—narrower, still—became a mere ribbon in front of the horses—then disappeared under their hoofs. Great Scott! Why, the whole front of that host shot into the sky with a thunder-crash, and became a whirling tempest of rags and fragments; and along the ground lay a thick wall of smoke that hid what was left of the multitude from our sight.

Time for the second step in the plan of campaign! I touched a button and shook the bones of England loose from her spine!

In that explosion all our noble civilization-factories went up in the air, and disappeared from the earth. It was a pity, but it was necessary. We could not afford to let the enemy turn our own weapons against us.

Now ensued one of the dullest quarter-hours I had ever endured. We waited in a silent solitude enclosed by our circles of wire, and by a circle of heavy smoke outside of these. We couldn't see over the wall of smoke, and we couldn't see through it. But at last it began to shred away lazily, and by the end of another quarter-hour the land was clear and our curiosity was enabled to satisfy itself. No living creature was in sight! We now perceived that additions had been made to our defences. The dynamite had dug a ditch more than a hundred feet wide, all around us, and cast up an embankment some twenty-five feet high on both borders of it. As to destruction of life, it was amazing. Moreover, it was beyond estimate. Of course we could not *count* the dead, because they did not exist as individuals, but merely as homogenous protoplasm, with alloys of iron and buttons.

No life was in sight, but necessarily there must have been some wounded in the rear ranks, who were carried off the field under cover of the wall of smoke; there would be sickness among the others—there always is, after an episode like that. But there would be no reinforcements; this was the last stand of the chivalry of England; it was all that was left of the order, after the recent annihilating wars. So I felt quite safe in believing that the utmost force that could for the future be brought against us would be but small; that is, of knights. I therefore issued a congratulatory proclamation to my army, in these words:

"SOLDIERS, CHAMPIONS OF HUMAN LIBERTY AND EQUALITY: Your General congratulates you! In the pride of his strength and the vanity of his renown, an arrogant enemy came against you. You were ready. The conflict was brief; on your side, glorious. This mighty victory having been achieved utterly without loss, stands without example in history. So long as the planets shall continue to move in their orbits, the BATTLE OF THE SAND-BELT will not perish out of the memories of men.   THE BOSS."

I read it well, and the applause I got was very gratifying to me. I then wound up with these remarks:

"The war with the English nation as a nation, is at an end. The nation has retired from the field and the war. Before it can be persuaded to return, war will have ceased. This campaign is the only one that is going to be fought. It will be brief—the briefest in history. Also the most destructive to life, considered from the stand-point of proportion of casualties to numbers engaged. We are done with the nation; henceforth we deal only with the knights. English knights can be killed, but they cannot be conquered. We know what is before us. While one of these men remains alive, our task is not finished, the war is not ended. We will kill them all." [Loud and long continued applause.]

I picketed the great embankments thrown up around our lines by the dynamite explosion—merely a lookout of a couple of boys to announce the enemy when he should appear again.

Next, I sent an engineer and forty men to a point just beyond our lines on the south, to turn a mountain brook that was there, and bring it within our lines and under our command, arranging it in such a way that I could make instant use of it in an emergency. The forty men were divided into two shifts of twenty each, and were to relieve each other every two hours. In ten hours the work was accomplished.

It was nightfall, now, and I withdrew my pickets. The one who had had the northern outlook reported a camp in sight, but visible with the glass, only. He also reported that a few knights had been feeling their way toward us, and had driven some cattle across our lines, but that the knights themselves had not come very near. That was what I had been expecting. They were feeling us, you see; they wanted to know if we were going to play that red terror on them again. They would grow bolder in the night, perhaps. I believed I knew what project they would attempt, because it was plainly the thing I would attempt myself if I were in their places and as ignorant as they were. I mentioned it to Clarence.

"I think you are right," said he; "it is the obvious thing for them to try."

"Well, then," I said, "if they do it they are doomed."

"Certainly."

"They won't have the slightest show in the world."

"Of course they won't."

"It's dreadful, Clarence. It seems an awful pity."

The thing disturbed me so, that I couldn't get any peace of mind for thinking of it and worrying over it. So, at last, to quiet my conscience, I framed this message to the knights:

"To the Honorable the Commander of the Insurgent Chivalry of England: You fight in vain. We know your strength—if one may call it by that name. We know that at the utmost you cannot bring against us above five and twenty thousand knights. Therefore, you have no chance—none whatever. Reflect: we are well equipped, well fortified; we number 54. Fifty-four what? Men? No, *minds*—the capablest in the world; a force against which mere animal might may no more hope to prevail than may the idle waves of the sea hope to prevail against the granite barriers of England. Be advised. We offer you your lives; for the sake of your families, do not reject the gift. We offer you this chance, and it is the last: throw down your arms; surrender unconditionally to the Republic, and all will be forgiven.

[Signed]. The Boss."

I read it to Clarence, and said I proposed to send it by a flag of truce. He laughed the sarcastic laugh he was born with, and said:

"Somehow it seems impossible for you to ever fully realize what these nobilities are. Now let us save a little time and trouble. Consider me the Commander of the knights yonder. Now then, you are the flag of truce; approach and deliver me your message, and I will give you your answer."

I humored the idea. I came forward under an imaginary guard of the enemy's soldiers, produced my paper, and read it through. For answer, Clarence struck the paper out of my hand, pursed up a scornful lip, and said with lofty disdain—

"Dismember me this animal, and return him in a basket to the base-born knave his master; other answer have I none!"

How empty is theory in presence of fact! And this was just fact, and nothing else. It was the thing that would have happened, there was no getting around that. I tore up the paper and granted my mistimed sentimentalities a permanent rest.

Then, to business. I tested the electrical signals from the gatling platform to the cave and made sure that they were all right; I tested and re-tested those which commanded the fences—these were signals whereby I could break and renew the electric current in each fence independently of the others, at will. I placed the brook-connection under the guard and authority of three of my best boys, who would alternate in two-hour watches all night and promptly obey my signal if I should have occasion to give it—three revolver-shots in quick succession. Sentry-duty was discarded for the night, and the corral left empty of life; I ordered that quiet be maintained in the cave, and the electric lights turned down to a glimmer.

As soon as it was good and dark, I shut off the current from all of the fences, and then groped my way out to the embankment bordering our side of the great dynamite ditch. I crept to the top of it and lay there on the slant of the muck to watch. But it was too dark to see anything. As for sounds, there were none. The stillness was deathlike. True, there were the usual night-sounds of the country—the whir of night-birds, the buzzing of insects, the barking of distant dogs, the mellow lowing of far-off kine—but these didn't seem to break the stillness, they only intensified it, and added a grewsome melancholy to it into the bargain.

I presently gave up looking, the night shut down so black, but I kept my ears strained to catch the least suspicious sound, for I judged I had only to wait and I shouldn't be disappointed. However, I had to wait a long time. At last I caught what you may call indistinct glimpses of sound—dulled metallic sound. I pricked up my ears, then, and held my breath, for this was the sort of thing I had been waiting for. This sound thickened, and approached—from toward the north. Presently I heard it at my own level—the ridge-top of the opposite embankment, a hundred feet or more away. Then I seemed to see a row of black dots appear along that ridge—human heads? I couldn't tell; it mightn't be anything at all; you can't depend on your eyes when your imagination is out of focus. However, the question was soon settled. I heard that metallic noise descending into the great ditch. It augmented fast, it spread all along, and it unmistakably furnished me this fact: an armed host was taking up its quarters in the ditch. Yes, these people were arranging a little surprise party for us. We could expect entertainment about dawn, possibly earlier.

I groped my way back to the corral, now; I had seen enough. I went to the platform and signaled to turn the current onto the two inner fences. Then I went into the cave, and found everything satisfactory there—nobody awake but the working-watch. I woke Clarence and told him the great ditch was filling up with men, and that I believed all the knights were coming for us in a body. It was my notion that as soon as dawn approached we could expect the ditch's ambuscaded thousands to swarm up over the embankment and make an assault, and be followed immediately by the rest of their army.

Clarence said:

"They will be wanting to send a scout or two in the dark to make preliminary observations. Why not take the lightning off the outer fences, and give them a chance?"

"I've already done it, Clarence. Did you ever know me to be inhospitable?"

"No, you are a good heart. I want to go and—"

"Be a reception committee? I will go, too."

We crossed the corral and lay down together between the two inside fences. Even the dim light in the cave had disordered our eyesight somewhat, but the focus straightway began to regulate itself and soon it was adjusted for present circumstances. We had had to feel our way before, but we could make out to see the fence-posts, now. We started a whispered conversation, but suddenly Clarence broke off and said—

"What is that?"

"What is what?"

"That thing yonder?"

"What thing?—where?"

"There beyond you a little piece—a dark something—a dull shape of some kind—against the second fence."

I gazed, and he gazed. I said:

"Could it be a man, Clarence?"

"No, I think not. If you notice, it looks a lit—why, it *is* a man!—leaning on the fence."

"I certainly believe it is; let's go and see."

We crept along on our hands and knees until we were pretty close, and then looked up. Yes, it was a man—a dim great figure in armor, standing erect, with both hands on the upper wire—and of course there was a smell of burning flesh. Poor fellow, dead as a doornail, and never knew what hurt him. He stood there like a statue—no motion about him, except that his plumes swished about a little in the night wind. We rose up and looked in through the bars of his visor, but couldn't make out whether we knew him or not—features too dim and shadowed.

We heard muffled sounds approaching, and we sank down to the ground where we were. We made out another knight vaguely; he was coming very stealthily, and feeling his way. He was near enough, now, for us to see him put out a hand, find an upper wire, then bend and step under it and over the lower one. Now he arrived at the first knight—and started slightly when he discovered him. He stood a moment—no doubt wondering why the other one didn't move on; then he said, in a low voice, "Why dreamest thou here, good Sir Mar—" then he laid his hand on the corpse's shoulder—and just uttered a little soft moan and sunk down dead. Killed by a dead man, you see—killed by a dead friend, in fact. There was something awful about it.

These early birds came scattering along after each other, about one every five minutes in our vicinity, during half an hour. They brought no armor of offence but their swords; as a rule they carried the sword ready in the hand, and put it forward and found the wires with it. We would now and then see a blue spark when the knight that caused it was so far away as to be invisible to us; but we knew what had happened, all the same, poor fellow: he had touched a charged wire with his sword, and been elected. We had brief intervals of grim stillness, interrupted with piteous regularity by the clash made by the falling of an iron-clad; and this sort of thing was going on, right along, and was very creepy, there in the dark and lonesomeness.

We concluded to make a tour between the inner fences. We elected to walk upright, for convenience sake; we argued that if discerned, we should be taken for friends rather than enemies, and in any case we should be out of reach of swords, and these gentry did not seem to have any spears along. Well, it was a curious trip. Everywhere dead men were lying outside the second fence—not plainly visible, but still visible; and we counted fifteen of those pathetic statues—dead knights standing with their hands on the upper wire.

One thing seemed to be sufficiently demonstrated: our current was so tremendous that it killed before the victim could cry out. Pretty soon we detected a muffled and heavy sound, and next moment we guessed what it was. It was a surprise in force coming! I whispered Clarence to go and wake the army, and notify it to wait in silence in the cave for further orders. He was soon back, and we stood by the inner fence and watched the silent lightning do its awful work upon that swarming host. One could make out but little of detail; but he could note that a black mass was piling itself up beyond the second fence. That swelling bulk was dead men! Our camp was enclosed with a solid wall of the dead—a bulwark, a breastwork, of corpses, you may say. One terrible thing about this thing was the absence of human voices; there were no cheers, no war cries: being intent upon a surprise, these men moved as noiselessly as they could; and always when the front rank was near enough to their goal to make it proper for them to begin to get a shout ready, of course they struck the fatal line and went down without testifying.

I sent a current through the third fence, now; and almost immediately through the fourth and fifth, so quickly were the gaps filled up. I believed the time was come, now, for my climax; I believed that that whole army was in our trap. Anyway, it was high time to find out. So I touched a button and set fifty electric suns aflame on the top of our precipice.

Land, what a sight! We were enclosed in three walls of dead men! All the other fences were pretty nearly filled with the living, who were stealthily working their way forward through the wires. The sudden glare paralyzed this host, petrified them, you may say, with astonishment; there was just one instant for me to utilize their immobility in, and I didn't lose the chance. You see, in another instant they would have recovered their faculties; then they'd have burst into a cheer and made a rush, and my wires would have gone down before it; but that lost instant lost them their opportunity forever: while even that slight fragment of time was still unspent, I shot the current through all the fences and struck the whole host dead in their tracks! *There* was a groan you could *hear!* It voiced the death-pang of eleven thousand men. It swelled out on the night with awful pathos.

A glance showed that the rest of the enemy—perhaps ten thousand strong—were between us and the encircling ditch, and pressing forward to the assault. Consequently we had them *all!* and had them past help. Time for the last act of the tragedy. I fired the three appointed revolver shots—which meant:

"Turn on the water!"

There was a sudden rush and roar, and in a minute the mountain brook was raging through the big ditch and creating a river a hundred feet wide and twenty-five deep.

"Stand to your guns, men! Open fire!"

The thirteen gatlings began to vomit death into the fated ten thousand. They halted, they stood their ground a moment against that withering deluge of fire, then they broke, faced about and swept toward the ditch like chaff before a gale. A full fourth part of their force never reached the top of the lofty embankment; the three-fourths reached it and plunged over—to death by drowning.

Within ten short minutes after we had opened fire, armed resistance was totally annihilated, the campaign was ended, we fifty-four were masters of England! Twenty-five thousand men lay dead around us.

But how treacherous is fortune! In a little while—say an hour—happened a thing, by my own fault, which—but I have no heart to write that. Let the record end here.

Chapter 44

A Postscript by Clarence

I CLARENCE, must write it for him. He proposed that we two go out and see if any help could be afforded the wounded. I was strenuous against the project. I said that if there were many, we could do but little for them; and it would not be wise for us to trust ourselves among them, anyway. But he could seldom be turned from a purpose once formed; so we shut off the electric current from the fences, took an escort along, climbed over the enclosing ramparts of dead knights, and moved out upon the field. The first wounded man who appealed for help, was sitting, with his back against a dead comrade. When the Boss bent over him and spoke to him, the man recognized him and stabbed him. That knight was Sir Meliagraunce, as I found out by tearing off his helmet. He will not ask for help any more.

We carried the Boss to the cave and gave his wound, which was not very serious, the best care we could. In this service we had the help of Merlin, though we did not know it. He was disguised as a woman, and appeared to be a simple old peasant goodwife. In this disguise, with brown-stained face and smooth shaven, he had appeared a few days after the Boss was hurt, and offered to cook for us, saying her people had gone off to join certain new camps which the enemy were forming, and that she was starving. The Boss had been getting along very well, and had amused himself with finishing up his record.

We were glad to have this woman, for we were short handed. We were in a trap, you see—a trap of our own making. If we stayed where we were, our dead would kill us; if we moved out of our defences, we should no longer be invincible. We had conquered; in turn we were conquered. The Boss recognized this; we all recognized it. If we could go to one of those new camps and patch up some kind of terms with the enemy—yes, but the Boss could not go, and neither could I, for I was among the first that were made sick by the poisonous air bred by those dead thousands. Others were taken down, and still others. To-morrow—

To-morrow. It is here. And with it the end. About midnight I woke, and saw that hag making curious passes in the air about the Boss's head and face, and wondered what it meant. Everybody but the dynamo-watch lay steeped in sleep; there was no sound. The woman ceased from her mysterious foolery, and started tip-toeing toward the door. I called out—

"Stop! What have you been doing?"

She halted, and said with an accent of malicious satisfaction:

"Ye were conquerors; ye are conquered! These others are perishing—you also. Ye shall all die in this place—every one—except *him*. He sleepeth, now—and shall sleep thirteen centuries. I am Merlin!"

Then such a delirium of silly laughter overtook him that he reeled about like a drunken man, and presently fetched up against one of our wires. His mouth is spread open yet; apparently he is still laughing. I suppose the face will retain that petrified laugh until the corpse turns to dust.

The Boss has never stirred—sleeps like a stone. If he does not wake to-day, we shall understand what kind of a sleep it is, and his body will then be borne to a place in one of the remote recesses of the cave where none will ever find it to desecrate it. As for the rest of us—well, it is agreed that if any one of us ever escapes alive from this place, he will write the fact here, and loyally hide this Manuscript with the Boss, our dear good chief, whose property it is, be he alive or dead.

END OF THE MANUSCRIPT.

Final P. S. by M. T.

THE DAWN was come when I laid the Manuscript aside. The rain had almost ceased, the world was gray and sad, the exhausted storm was sighing and sobbing itself to rest. I went to the stranger's room, and listened at his door, which was slightly ajar; I could hear his voice, and so I knocked. There was no answer, but I still heard the voice. I peeped in. The man lay on his back, in bed, talking brokenly but with spirit, and punctuating with his arms, which he thrashed about, restlessly, as sick people do in delirium. I slipped in softly, and bent over him. His mutterings and ejaculations went on. I spoke—merely a word, to call his attention. His glassy eyes and his ashy face were alight in an instant with pleasure, gratitude, gladness, welcome:

"O, Sandy, you are come at last,—how I have longed for you! Sit by me—do not leave me—never leave me again, Sandy, never again. Where is your hand?—give it me, dear, let me hold it—there—now, all is well, all is peace, and I am happy again—*we* are happy again, isn't it so, Sandy? You are so dim, so vague, you are but a mist, a cloud, but you are *here*, and that is blessedness sufficient; and I have your hand; don't take it away—it is for only a little while, I shall not require it long. . . . . . Was that the child? . . . Hello-Central! . . . . She doesn't answer. Asleep, perhaps? Bring her when she wakes, and let me touch her hands, her face, her hair, and tell her good-bye. . . . . . Sandy! . . . . Yes, you are there. I lost myself a moment, and I thought you were gone. . . . . . Have I been sick long? It must be so; it seems months to me. And such dreams! such strange and awful dreams, Sandy! Dreams that were as real as reality—delirium, of course, but *so* real! Why, I thought the king was dead, I thought you were in Gaul and couldn't get home, I thought there was a revolution; in the fantastic frenzy of these dreams, I thought that Clarence and I, and a handful of my cadets fought and exterminated the whole chivalry of England! But even that was not the strangest. I seemed to be a creature out of a remote unborn age, centuries hence, and even *that* was as real as the rest! Yes, I seemed to have flown back out of that age into this of ours, and then forward to it again, and was set down, a stranger and forlorn in that strange England, with an abyss of thirteen centuries yawning between me and you! between me and my home and my friends! between me and all that is dear to me, all that could make life worth the living! It was awful—awfuler than you can ever imagine, Sandy. Ah, watch by me, Sandy—stay by me every moment—*don't* let me go out of my mind again; death is nothing, let it come, but not with those dreams, not with the torture of those hideous dreams—I cannot endure *that* again. . . . . . Sandy? . . . ."

He lay muttering incoherently some little time; then for a time he lay silent, and apparently sinking away toward death. Presently his fingers began to pick busily at the coverlet, and by that sign I knew that his end was at hand. With the first suggestion of the death-rattle in his throat he started up slightly, and seemed to listen; then he said:

"A bugle? . . . . It is the king! The drawbridge, there! Man the battlements!—turn out the—"

He was getting up his last "effect;" but he never finished it.

PERSONAL RECOLLECTIONS
OF
JOAN OF ARC

BY
THE SIEUR LOUIS DE CONTE
(HER PAGE AND SECRETARY)

FREELY TRANSLATED
OUT OF THE ANCIENT FRENCH INTO MODERN ENGLISH
FROM THE ORIGINAL UNPUBLISHED MANUSCRIPT
IN THE NATIONAL ARCHIVES OF FRANCE

BY

JEAN FRANÇOIS ALDEN

Consider this unique and imposing distinction. Since the writing of human history began, Joan of Arc is the only person, of either sex, who has ever held supreme command of the military forces of a nation *at the age of seventeen*.

LOUIS KOSSUTH.

Authorities examined in verification of the truthfulness of this narrative:

J. E. J. QUICHERAT, *Condamnation et Réhabilitation de Jeanne d'Arc.*

J. FABRE, *Procès de Condamnation de Jeanne d'Arc.*

H. A. WALLON, *Jeanne d'Arc.*

M. SEPET, *Jeanne d'Arc.*

J. MICHELET, *Jeanne d'Arc.*

BERRIAT DE SAINT-PRIX, *La Famille de Jeanne d'Arc.*

La Comtesse A. DE CHABANNES, *La Vierge Lorraine.*

Monseigneur RICARD, *Jeanne d'Arc la Vénérable.*

Lord RONALD GOWER, F.S.A., *Joan of Arc.*

JOHN O'HAGAN, *Joan of Arc.*

JANET TUCKEY, *Joan of Arc the Maid.*

TRANSLATOR'S PREFACE

To arrive at a just estimate of a renowned man's character, one must judge it by the standards of his time, not ours. Judged by the standards of one century, the noblest characters of an earlier one lose much of their lustre; judged by the standards of to-day, there is probably no illustrious man of four or five centuries ago whose character could meet the test at all points. But the character of Joan of Arc is unique. It can be measured by the standards of all times without misgiving or apprehension as to the result. Judged by any of them, judged by all of them, it is still flawless, it is still ideally perfect; it still occupies the loftiest place possible to human attainment, a loftier one than has been reached by any other mere mortal.

When we reflect that her century was the brutalest, the wickedest, the rottenest in history since the darkest ages, we are lost in wonder at the miracle of such a product from such a soil. The contrast between her and her century is the contrast between day and night. She was truthful when lying was the common speech of men; she was honest when honesty was become a lost virtue; she was a keeper of promises when the keeping of a promise was expected of no one; she gave her great mind to great thoughts and great purposes when other great minds wasted themselves upon pretty fancies or upon poor ambitions; she was modest and fine and delicate when to be loud and coarse might be said to be universal; she was full of pity when a merciless cruelty was the rule; she was steadfast when stability was unknown, and honorable in an age which had forgotten what honor was; she was a rock of convictions in a time when men believed in nothing and scoffed at all things; she was unfailingly true in an age that was false to the core; she maintained her personal dignity unimpaired in an age of fawnings and servilities;

*she was of a dauntless courage when hope and courage had per-
ished in the hearts of her nation; she was spotlessly pure in mind
and body when society in the highest places was foul in both—she
was all these things in an age when crime was the common business of lords and princes, and when the highest personages in
Christendom were able to astonish even that infamous era and
make it stand aghast at the spectacle of their atrocious lives black
with unimaginable treacheries, butcheries, and bestialities.*

*She was perhaps the only entirely unselfish person whose name has
a place in profane history. No vestige or suggestion of self-seeking can
be found in any word or deed of hers. When she had rescued her
King from his vagabondage, and set his crown upon his head, she
was offered rewards and honors, but she refused them all, and would
take nothing. All she would take for herself—if the King would
grant it—was leave to go back to her village home, and tend her
sheep again, and feel her mother's arms about her, and be her
housemaid and helper. The selfishness of this unspoiled general of
victorious armies, companion of princes, and idol of an applauding
and grateful nation, reached but that far and no farther.*

*The work wrought by Joan of Arc may fairly be regarded as
ranking any recorded in history, when one considers the conditions
under which it was undertaken, the obstacles in the way, and the
means at her disposal. Cæsar carried conquest far, but he did it with
the trained and confident veterans of Rome, and was a trained
soldier himself; and Napoleon swept away the disciplined armies of
Europe, but he also was a trained soldier, and he began his work
with patriot battalions inflamed and inspired by the miracle-
working new breath of Liberty breathed upon them by the Revolution—eager young apprentices to the splendid trade of war, not old
and broken men-at-arms, despairing survivors of an age-long accu-
mulation of monotonous defeats; but Joan of Arc, a mere child in
years, ignorant, unlettered, a poor village girl unknown and without influence, found a great nation lying in chains, helpless and
hopeless under an alien domination, its treasury bankrupt, its soldiers disheartened and dispersed, all spirit torpid, all courage dead
in the hearts of the people through long years of foreign and domestic
outrage and oppression, their King cowed, resigned to its fate, and
preparing to fly the country; and she laid her hand upon this nation,
this corpse, and it rose and followed her. She led it from victory to
victory, she turned back the tide of the Hundred Years' War, she*

fatally crippled the English power, and died with the earned title of
DELIVERER OF FRANCE, *which she bears to this day.*

*And for all reward, the French King whom she had crowned
stood supine and indifferent while French priests took the noble
child, the most innocent, the most lovely, the most adorable the ages
have produced, and burned her alive at the stake.*

A PECULIARITY OF JOAN OF ARC'S HISTORY

———

The details of the life of Joan of Arc form a biography which is unique among the world's biographies in one respect: *It is the only story of a human life which comes to us under oath,* the only one which comes to us from the witness-stand. The official records of the Great Trial of 1431, and of the Process of Rehabilitation of a quarter of a century later, are still preserved in the National Archives of France, and they furnish with remarkable fulness the facts of her life. The history of no other life of that remote time is known with either the certainty or the comprehensiveness that attaches to hers.

The Sieur Louis de Conte is faithful to her official history in his Personal Recollections, and thus far his trustworthiness is unimpeachable; but his mass of added particulars must depend for credit upon his own word alone.

THE TRANSLATOR.

Contents

THE SIEUR LOUIS DE CONTE
TO HIS GREAT-GREAT-GRAND
NEPHEWS AND NIECES

THIS is the year 1492. I am eighty-two years of age. The things I am going to tell you are things which I saw myself as a child and as a youth.

In all the tales and songs and histories of Joan of Arc which you and the rest of the world read and sing and study in the books wrought in the late invented art of printing, mention is made of me, the Sieur Louis de Conte—I was her page and secretary. I was with her from the beginning until the end.

I was reared in the same village with her. I played with her every day, when we were little children together, just as you play with your mates. Now that we perceive how great she was; now that her name fills the whole world, it seems strange that what I am saying is true; for it is as if a perishable paltry candle should speak of the eternal sun riding in the heavens and say, "He was gossip and housemate to me when we were candles together." And yet it is true, just as I say. I was her playmate, and I fought at her side in the wars; to this day I carry in my mind, fine and clear, the picture of that dear little figure, with breast bent to the flying horse's neck, charging at the head of the armies of France, her hair streaming back, her silver mail ploughing steadily deeper and deeper into the thick of the battle, sometimes nearly drowned from sight by tossing heads of horses, uplifted sword-arms, wind-blown plumes, and intercepting shields. I was with her to the end; and when that black day came whose accusing shadow will lie always upon the memory of the mitred French slaves of England who were her assassins, and upon France who stood idle and essayed no rescue, my hand was the last she touched in life.

As the years and the decades drifted by, and the spectacle of the marvellous child's meteor-flight across the war-firmament of France and its extinction in the smoke-clouds of the stake receded deeper and deeper into the past and grew ever more strange and wonderful and divine and pathetic, I came to comprehend and recognize her at last for what she was—the most noble life that was ever born into this world save only One.

Chapter I

I, THE Sieur Louis de Conte, was born in Neufchâteau, the 6th of January, 1410; that is to say, exactly two years before Joan of Arc was born in Domremy. My family had fled to those distant regions from the neighborhood of Paris in the first years of the century. In politics they were Armagnacs— patriots: they were for our own French King, crazy and impotent as he was. The Burgundian party, who were for the English, had stripped them, and done it well. They took everything but my father's small nobility, and when he reached Neufchâteau he reached it in poverty and with a broken spirit. But the political atmosphere there was the sort he liked, and that was something. He came to a region of comparative quiet; he left behind him a region peopled with furies, madmen, devils, where slaughter was a daily pastime and no man's life safe for a moment. In Paris, mobs roared through the streets nightly, sacking, burning, killing, unmolested, uninterrupted. The sun rose upon wrecked and smoking buildings, and upon mutilated corpses lying here, there, and yonder about the streets, just as they fell, and stripped naked by thieves, the unholy gleaners after the mob. None had the courage to gather these dead for burial; they were left there to rot and create plagues.

And plagues they did create. Epidemics swept away the people like flies, and the burials were conducted secretly and by night; for public funerals were not allowed, lest the revelation of the magnitude of the plague's work unman the people and plunge them into despair. Then came, finally, the bitterest winter which had visited France in five hundred years. Famine, pestilence, slaughter, ice, snow—Paris had all these at once. The dead lay in heaps about the streets, and *wolves entered the city in daylight and devoured them.*

Ah, France had fallen low—so low! For more than three quarters of a century the English fangs had been bedded in her flesh, and so cowed had her armies become by ceaseless rout and defeat that it was said and accepted that the mere sight of an English army was sufficient to put a French one to flight.

When I was five years old the prodigious disaster of Agincourt fell upon France; and although the English king went home to enjoy his glory, he left the country prostrate and a prey to roving bands of Free Companions in the service of the Burgundian party, and one of these bands came raiding through Neufchâteau one night, and by the light of our burning roof-thatch I saw all that were dear to me in this world (save an elder brother, your ancestor, left behind with the Court) butchered while they begged for mercy, and heard the butchers laugh at their prayers and mimic their pleadings. I was overlooked, and escaped without hurt. When the savages were gone I crept out and cried the night away watching the burning houses; and I was all alone, except for the company of the dead and the wounded, for the rest had taken flight and hidden themselves.

I was sent to Domremy, to the priest, whose house-keeper became a loving mother to me. The priest in the course of time taught me to read and write, and he and I were the only persons in the village who possessed this learning.

At the time that the house of this good priest, Guillaume Fronte, became my home, I was six years old. We lived close by the village church, and the small garden of Joan's parents was behind the church. As to that family, there were Jacques d'Arc the father, his wife Isabel Romée; three sons—Jacques, ten years old, Pierre, eight, and Jean, seven; Joan, four, and her baby sister Catherine, about a year old. I had these children for playmates from the beginning. I had some other playmates besides—particularly four boys: Pierre Morel, Étienne Roze, Noël Rainguesson, and Edmond Aubrey, whose father was maire at that time; also two girls, about Joan's age, who by-and-by became her favorites; one was named Haumette, the other was called Little Mengette. These girls were common peasant children, like Joan herself. When they grew up, both married common laborers. Their estate was lowly enough, you see; yet a time came, many years after, when no passing stranger, howsoever great he might be, failed to go and pay his reverence to those two humble old women who had been honored in their youth by the friendship of Joan of Arc.

These were all good children, just of the ordinary peasant type; not bright, of course—you would not expect that—but good-hearted and companionable, obedient to their parents and the priest; and as they grew up they became properly stocked with narrownesses and prejudices got at second hand from their elders, and adopted without reserve; and without examination also—which goes without saying. Their religion was inherited, their politics the same. John Huss and his sort might find fault with the Church, in Domremy it disturbed nobody's faith; and when the split came, when I was fourteen, and we had three Popes at once, nobody in Domremy was worried about how to choose among them—the Pope of Rome was the right one, a Pope outside of Rome was no Pope at all. Every human creature in the village was an Armagnac—a patriot—and if we children hotly hated nothing else in the world, we did certainly hate the English and Burgundian name and polity in that way.

Chapter II

Our Domremy was like any other humble little hamlet of that remote time and region. It was a maze of crooked, narrow lanes and alleys shaded and sheltered by the overhanging thatch roofs of the barn-like houses. The houses were dimly lighted by wooden-shuttered windows—that is, holes in the walls which served for windows. The floors were of dirt, and there was very little furniture. Sheep and cattle grazing was the main industry; all the young folks tended flocks.

The situation was beautiful. From one edge of the village a flowery plain extended in a wide sweep to the river—the Meuse; from the rear edge of the village a grassy slope rose gradually, and at the top was the great oak forest—a forest that was deep and gloomy and dense, and full of interest for us children, for many murders had been done in it by outlaws in old times, and in still earlier times prodigious dragons that spouted fire and poisonous vapors from their nostrils had their homes in there. In fact, one was still living in there in our own time. It was as long as a tree, and had a body as big around as a tierce, and scales like overlapping great tiles, and deep ruby eyes as large as a cavalier's hat, and an anchor-fluke on its tail as big as I don't know what, but very big, even unusually so for a dragon, as everybody said who knew about dragons. It was thought that this dragon was of a brilliant blue color, with gold mottlings, but no one had ever seen it, therefore this was not known to be so, it was only an opinion. It was not my opinion; I think there is no sense in forming an opinion when there is no evidence to form it on. If you build a person without any bones in him he may look fair enough to the eye, but he will be limber and cannot stand up; and I consider that *evidence* is the bones of an opinion. But I will take up this matter more at large at another time, and try to make the justness of my position appear. As to that dragon, I always held the belief that its color was gold and without blue, for that has always been the color of dragons. That this dragon lay but a little way within the wood at one time is shown by the fact that Pierre Morel was in there one day and smelt it, and recognized it by the smell. It gives one a horrid idea of how near to us the deadliest danger can be and we not suspect it.

In the earliest times a hundred knights from many remote places in the earth would have gone in there one after another, to kill the dragon and get the reward, but in our time that method had gone out, and the priest had become the one that abolished dragons. Père Guillaume Fronte did it in this case. He had a procession, with candles and incense and banners, and marched around the edge of the wood and exorcised the dragon, and it was never heard of again, although it was the opinion of many that the smell never wholly passed away. Not that any had ever smelt the smell again, for none had; it was only an opinion, like that other—and lacked bones, you see. I know that the creature was there before the exorcism, but whether it was there afterwards or not is a thing which I cannot be so positive about.

In a noble open space carpeted with grass on the high ground towards Vaucouleurs stood a most majestic beech-tree with wide-reaching arms and a grand spread of shade, and by it a limpid spring of cold water; and on summer days the children went there—oh, every summer for more than five hundred years—went there and sang and danced around the tree for hours together, refreshing themselves at the spring from time to time, and it was most lovely and enjoyable. Also they made wreaths of flowers and hung them upon the tree and about the spring to please the fairies that lived there; for they liked that, being idle innocent little creatures, as all fairies are, and fond of anything delicate and pretty like wild flowers put together in that way. And in return for this attention the fairies did any friendly thing they could for the children, such as keeping the spring always full and clear and cold, and driving away serpents and insects that sting; and so there was never any unkindness between the fairies and the children during more than five hundred years—tradition said a thousand—but only the warmest affection and the most perfect trust and confidence; and whenever a child died the fairies mourned just as that child's playmates did, and the sign of it was there to see: for before the dawn on the day of the funeral they hung a little immortelle over the place where that child was used to sit under the tree. I know this to be true by my own eyes; it is not hearsay. And the reason it was known that the fairies did it was this—that it was made all of black flowers of a sort not known in France anywhere.

Now from time immemorial all children reared in Domremy were called the Children of the Tree; and they loved that name, for it carried with it a mystic privilege not granted to any others of the children of this world. Which was this: whenever one of these came to die, then beyond the vague and formless images drifting through his darkening mind rose soft and rich and fair a vision of the Tree—if all was well with his soul. That was what some said. Others said the vision came in two ways: once as a warning, one or two years in advance of death, when the soul was the captive of sin, and then the Tree appeared in its desolate winter aspect—then that soul was smitten with an awful fear. If repentance came, and purity of life, the vision came again, this time summer-clad and beautiful; but if it were otherwise with that soul the vision was withheld, and it passed from life knowing its doom. Still others said that the vision came but once, and then only to the sinless dying forlorn in distant lands and pitifully longing for some last dear reminder of their home. And what reminder of it could go to their hearts like the picture of the Tree that was the darling of their love and the comrade of their joys and comforter of their small griefs all through the divine days of their vanished youth?

Now the several traditions were as I have said, some believing one and some another. One of them I knew to be the truth, and that was the last one. I do not say anything against the others; I think they were true, but I only *know* that the last one was; and it is my thought that if one keep to the things he knows, and not trouble about the things which he cannot be sure about, he will have the steadier mind for it—and there is profit in that. I know that when the Children of the Tree die in a far land, then—if they be at peace with God—they turn their longing eyes toward home, and there, far-shining, as through a rift in a cloud that curtains heaven, they see the soft picture of the Fairy Tree, clothed in a dream of golden light; and they see the bloomy mead sloping away to the river, and to their perishing nostrils is blown faint and sweet the fragrance of the flowers of home. And then the vision fades and passes—but *they* know, *they* know! and by their transfigured faces you know also, you who stand looking on; yes, you know the message that has come, and that it has come from heaven.

Joan and I believed alike about this matter. But Pierre Morel, and Jacques d'Arc, and many others believed that the vision appeared twice—to a sinner. In fact they and many others said they *knew* it. Probably because their fathers had known it and had told them; for one gets most things at second hand in this world.

Now one thing that does make it quite likely that there were really two apparitions of the Tree is this fact: From the most ancient times if one saw a villager of ours with his face ash-white and rigid with a ghastly fright, it was common for every one to whisper to his neighbor, "Ah, he is in sin, and has got his warning." And the neighbor would shudder at the thought and whisper back, "Yes, poor soul, he has seen the Tree."

Such evidences as these have their weight; they are not to be put aside with a wave of the hand. A thing that is backed by the cumulative experience of centuries naturally gets nearer and nearer to being proof all the time; and if this continue and continue, it will some day become authority—and authority is a bedded rock, and will abide.

In my long life I have seen several cases where the Tree appeared announcing a death which was still far away; but in none of these was the person in a state of sin. No; the apparition was in these cases only a special grace; in place of deferring the tidings of that soul's redemption till the day of death, the apparition brought them long before, and with them peace—peace that might no more be disturbed—the eternal peace of God. I myself, old and broken, wait with serenity; for I have seen the vision of the Tree. I have seen it, and am content.

Always, from the remotest times, when the children joined hands and danced around the Fairy Tree they sang a song which was the Tree's Song, the Song of *L'Arbre Fée de Bourlemont*. They sang it to a quaint sweet air—a solacing sweet air which has gone murmuring through my dreaming spirit all my life when I was weary and troubled, resting me and carrying me through night and distance home again. No stranger can know or feel what that song has been, through the drifting centuries, to exiled Children of the Tree, homeless and heavy of heart in countries foreign to their speech and ways. You will think it a simple thing, that song, and poor perchance; but if you will remember what it was to us, and what it brought before our eyes when it floated through our memories, then you will respect it. And you will understand how the water wells up in our eyes and makes all things dim, and our voices break and we cannot sing the last lines:

> "And when in exile wand'ring we
>   Shall fainting yearn for glimpse of thee,
>   O rise upon our sight!"

And you will remember that Joan of Arc sang this song with us around the Tree when she was a little child, and always loved it. And that hallows it, yes, you will grant that:

L'ARBRE FÉE DE BOURLEMONT

SONG OF THE CHILDREN

> Now what has kept your leaves so green,
>   Arbre Fée de Bourlemont?
> The children's tears! They brought each grief,
>   And you did comfort them and cheer
>   Their bruisèd hearts, and steal a tear
>   That healèd rose a leaf.

> And what has built you up so strong,
>   Arbre Fée de Bourlemont?
> The children's love! They've loved you long:
>   Ten hundred years, in sooth,
> They've nourished you with praise and song,
> And warmed your heart and kept it young—
>   A thousand years of youth!

> Bide alway green in our young hearts,
>   Arbre Fée de Bourlemont!
> And we shall alway youthful be,

Not heeding Time his flight;
And when in exile wand'ring we
Shall fainting yearn for glimpse of thee,
O rise upon our sight!

The fairies were still there when we were children, but we never saw them; because, a hundred years before that, the priest of Domremy had held a religious function under the tree and denounced them as being blood kin of the Fiend and barred out from redemption; and then he warned them never to show themselves again, nor hang any more immortelles, on pain of perpetual banishment from that parish.

All the children pleaded for the fairies, and said they were their good friends and dear to them and never did them any harm, but the priest would not listen, and said it was sin and shame to have such friends. The children mourned and could not be comforted; and they made an agreement among themselves that they would always continue to hang flower-wreaths on the tree as a perpetual sign to the fairies that they were still loved and remembered, though lost to sight.

But late one night a great misfortune befell. Edmond Aubrey's mother passed by the Tree, and the fairies were stealing a dance, not thinking anybody was by; and they were so busy, and so intoxicated with the wild happiness of it, and with the bumpers of dew sharpened up with honey which they had been drinking, that they noticed nothing; so Dame Aubrey stood there astonished and admiring, and saw the little fantastic atoms holding hands, as many as three hundred of them, tearing around in a great ring half as big as an ordinary bedroom, and leaning away back and spreading their mouths with laughter and song, which she could hear quite distinctly, and kicking their legs up as much as three inches from the ground in perfect abandon and hilarity—oh, the very maddest and witchingest dance the woman ever saw.

But in about a minute or two minutes the poor little ruined creatures discovered her. They burst out in one heartbreaking squeak of grief and terror and fled every which way, with their wee hazel-nut fists in their eyes and crying; and so disappeared.

The heartless woman—no, the foolish woman; she was not heartless, but only thoughtless—went straight home and told the neighbors all about it, whilst we, the small friends of the fairies, were asleep and not witting the calamity that was come upon us, and all unconscious that we ought to be up and trying to stop these fatal tongues. In the morning everybody knew, and the disaster was complete, for where everybody knows a thing the priest knows it, of course. We all flocked to Père Fronte, crying and begging—and he had to cry, too, seeing our sorrow, for he had a most kind and gentle nature; and he did not want to banish the fairies, and said so; but said he had no choice, for it had been decreed that if they ever revealed themselves to man again, they must go. This all happened at the worst time possible, for Joan of Arc was ill of a fever and out of her head, and what could we do who had not her gifts of reasoning and persuasion? We flew in a swarm to her bed and cried out, "Joan, wake! Wake, there is no moment to lose! Come and plead for the fairies—come and save them; only you can do it."

But her mind was wandering, she did not know what we said nor what we meant; so we went away knowing all was lost. Yes, all was lost, forever lost; the faithful friends of the children for five hundred years must go, and never come back any more.

It was a bitter day for us, that day that Père Fronte held the function under the tree and banished the fairies. We could not wear mourning that any could have noticed, it would not have been allowed; so we had to be content with some poor small rag of black tied upon our garments where it made no show; but in our hearts we wore mourning big and noble and occupying all the room, for our *hearts* were ours; they could not get at them to prevent that.

The great tree—*l'Arbre Fée de Bourlemont* was its beautiful name—was never afterward quite as much to us as it had been before, but it was always dear; is dear to me yet when I go there, now, once a year in my old age, to sit under it and bring back the lost playmates of my youth and group them about me and look upon their faces through my tears and break my heart, oh, my God! No, the place was not quite the same afterwards. In one or two ways it could not be; for, the fairies' protection being gone, the spring lost much of its freshness and coldness, and more than two-thirds of its volume, and the banished serpents and stinging insects returned, and multiplied, and became a torment and have remained so to this day.

When that wise little child, Joan, got well, we realized how much her illness had cost us; for we found that we had been right in believing she could save the fairies. She burst into a great storm of anger, for so little a creature, and went straight to Père Fronte, and stood up before him where he sat, and made reverence and said:

"The fairies were to go if they showed themselves to people again, is it not so?"

"Yes, that was it, dear."

"If a man comes prying into a person's room at midnight when that person is half naked, will you be so unjust as to say that that person is showing himself to that man?"

"Well—no." The good priest looked a little troubled and uneasy when he said it.

"Is a sin a sin anyway, even if one did not intend to commit it?"

Père Fronte threw up his hands and cried out—

"Oh, my poor little child, I see all my fault," and he drew her to his side and put his arm around her and tried to make his peace with her, but her temper was up so high that she could not get it down right away, but buried her head against his breast and broke out crying and said:

"Then the fairies committed no sin, for there was no intention to commit one, they not knowing that any one was by; and because they were little creatures and could not speak for themselves and say the law was against the intention, not against the innocent act, and because they had no friend to think that simple thing for them and say it, they have been sent away from their home forever, and it was wrong, *wrong* to do it!"

The good father hugged her yet closer to his side and said:

"Oh, out of the mouths of babes and sucklings the heedless and unthinking are condemned: would God I could bring the little creatures back, for your sake. And mine, yes, and mine;

for I have been unjust. There, there, don't cry—nobody could be sorrier than your poor old friend—don't cry, dear."

"But I can't stop right away, I've *got* to. And it is no little matter, this thing that you have done. Is being sorry penance enough for such an act?"

Père Fronte turned away his face, for it would have hurt her to see him laugh, and said:

"Oh, thou remorseless but most just accuser, no, it is not. I will put on sackcloth and ashes; there—are you satisfied?"

Joan's sobs began to diminish, and she presently looked up at the old man through her tears, and said, in her simple way:

"Yes, that will do—if it will clear you."

Père Fronte would have been moved to laugh again, perhaps, if he had not remembered in time that he had made a contract, and not a very agreeable one. It must be fulfilled. So he got up and went to the fireplace, Joan watching him with deep interest, and took a shovelful of cold ashes, and was going to empty them on his old gray head when a better idea came to him, and he said:

"Would you mind helping me, dear?"

"How, father?"

He got down on his knees and bent his head low, and said: "Take the ashes and put them on my head for me."

The matter ended there, of course. The victory was with the priest. One can imagine how the idea of such a profanation would strike Joan or any other child in the village. She ran and dropped upon her knees by his side and said:

"Oh, it is dreadful. I didn't know that that was what one meant by sackcloth and ashes—do please get up, father."

"But I can't until I am forgiven. Do you forgive me?"

"I? Oh, you have done nothing to me, father; it is *yourself* that must forgive yourself for wronging those poor things. Please get up, father, won't you?"

"But I am worse off now than I was before. I thought I was earning *your* forgiveness, but if it is my own, I can't be lenient; it would not become me. Now what can I do? Find me some way out of this with your wise little head."

The Père would not stir, for all Joan's pleadings. She was about to cry again; then she had an idea, and seized the shovel and deluged her own head with the ashes, stammering out through her chokings and suffocations—

"There—now it is done. Oh, please get up, father."

The old man, both touched and amused, gathered her to his breast and said—

"Oh, you incomparable child! It's a humble martyrdom, and not of a sort presentable in a picture, but the right and true spirit is in it; that I testify."

Then he brushed the ashes out of her hair, and helped her scour her face and neck and properly tidy herself up. He was in fine spirits now, and ready for further argument, so he took his seat and drew Joan to his side again, and said:

"Joan, you were used to make wreaths there at the Fairy Tree with the other children; is it not so?"

That was the way he always started out when he was going to corner me up and catch me in something—just that gentle, indifferent way that fools a person so, and leads him into the trap, he never noticing which way he is travelling until he is in and the door shut on him. He enjoyed that. I knew he was going to drop corn along in front of Joan now. Joan answered:

"Yes, father."

"Did you hang them on the tree?"

"No, father."

"Didn't hang them there?"

"No."

"Why didn't you?"

"I—well, I didn't wish to."

"Didn't wish to?"

"No, father."

"What did you do with them?"

"I hung them in the church."

"Why didn't you want to hang them in the tree?"

"Because it was said that the fairies were of kin to the Fiend, and that it was sinful to show them honor."

"Did you believe it was wrong to honor them so?"

"Yes. I thought it must be wrong."

"Then if it was wrong to honor them in that way, and if they were of kin to the Fiend, they could be dangerous company for you and the other children, couldn't they?"

"I suppose so—yes, I think so."

He studied a minute, and I judged he was going to spring his trap, and he did. He said:

"Then the matter stands like this. They were banned creatures, of fearful origin; they could be dangerous company for the children. Now give me a rational reason, dear, if you can think of any, why you call it a wrong to drive them into banishment, and why you would have saved them from it. In a word, what loss have you suffered by it?"

How stupid of him to go and throw his case away like that! I could have boxed his ears for vexation if he had been a boy. He was going along all right until he ruined everything by winding up in that foolish and fatal way. What had *she* lost by it! Was he never going to find out what kind of a child Joan of Arc was? Was he never going to learn that things which merely concerned her own gain or loss she cared nothing about? Could he never get the simple fact into his head that the sure way and the only way to rouse her up and set her on fire was to show her where some *other* person was going to suffer wrong or hurt or loss? Why, he had gone and set a trap for himself—that was all he had accomplished.

The minute those words were out of his mouth her temper was up, the indignant tears rose in her eyes, and she burst out on him with an energy and passion which astonished him, but didn't astonish me, for I knew he had fired a mine when he touched off his ill-chosen climax.

"Oh, father, how can you talk like that? Who owns France?"

"God and the King."

"Not Satan?"

"Satan, my child? This is the footstool of the Most High— Satan owns no handful of its soil."

"Then who gave those poor creatures their home? God. Who protected them in it all those centuries? God. Who allowed them to dance and play there all those centuries and found no fault with it? God. Who disapproved of God's approval and put a threat upon them? A man. Who caught them again in harmless sports that God allowed and a man forbade, and carried out that threat, and drove the poor things away from the home the good God gave them in His mercy and

His pity, and sent down His rain and dew and sunshine upon it five hundred years in token of His peace? It was *their* home—theirs, by the grace of God and His good heart, and no man had a right to rob them of it. And they were the gentlest, truest friends that children ever had, and did them sweet and loving service all these five long centuries, and never any hurt or harm; and the children loved them, and now they mourn for them, and there is no healing for their grief. And what had the children done that they should suffer this cruel stroke? The poor fairies *could* have been dangerous company for the children? Yes, but never had been; and *could* is no argument. Kinsman of the Fiend? What of it? Kinsmen of the Fiend have *rights*, and these had; and children have rights, and these had; and if I had been here I would have spoken—I would have begged for the children and the fiends, and stayed your hand and saved them all. But now— oh, now, all is lost; everything is lost, and there is no help more!"

Then she finished with a blast at that idea that fairy kinsmen of the Fiend ought to be shunned and denied human sympathy and friendship because salvation was barred against them. She said that for that very *reason* people ought to pity them, and do every humane and loving thing they could to make them forget the hard fate that had been put upon them by accident of birth and no fault of their own. "Poor little creatures!" she said. "What can a person's heart be made of that can pity a Christian's child and yet can't pity a devil's child, that a thousand times more *needs* it!"

She had torn loose from Père Fronte, and was crying, with her knuckles in her eyes, and stamping her small feet in a fury; and now she burst out of the place and was gone before we could gather our senses together out of this storm of words and this whirlwind of passion.

The Père had got upon his feet, toward the last, and now he stood there passing his hand back and forth across his forehead like a person who is dazed and troubled; then he turned and wandered toward the door of his little work-room, and as he passed through it I heard him murmur sorrowfully:

"Ah me, poor children, poor fiends, they *have* rights, and

she said true—I never thought of that. God forgive me, I am to blame."

When I heard that, I knew I was right in the thought that he had set a trap for himself. It was so, and he had walked into it, you see. I seemed to feel encouraged, and wondered if mayhap I might get him into one; but upon reflection my heart went down, for this was not my gift.

Chapter III

SPEAKING of this matter reminds me of many incidents, many things that I could tell, but I think I will not try to do it now. It will be more to my present humor to call back a little glimpse of the simple and colorless good times we used to have in our village homes in those peaceful days—especially in the winter. In the summer we children were out on the breezy uplands with the flocks from dawn till night, and then there was noisy frolicking and all that; but winter was the cosey time, winter was the snug time. Often we gathered in old Jacques d'Arc's big dirt-floored apartment, with a great fire going, and played games, and sang songs, and told fortunes, and listened to the old villagers tell tales and histories and lies and one thing and another till twelve o'clock at night.

One winter's night we were gathered there—it was the winter that for years afterward they called the hard winter—and that particular night was a sharp one. It blew a gale outside, and the screaming of the wind was a stirring sound, and I think I may say it was beautiful, for I think it *is* great and fine and beautiful to hear the wind rage and storm and blow its clarions like that, when you are inside and comfortable. And we were. We had a roaring fire, and the pleasant *spit-spit* of the snow and sleet falling in it down the chimney, and the yarning and laughing and singing went on at a noble rate till about ten o'clock, and then we had a supper of hot porridge and beans, and meal cakes with butter, and appetites to match.

Little Joan sat on a box apart, and had her bowl and bread on another one, and her pets around her, helping. She had more than was usual of them or economical, because all the outcast cats came and took up with her, and homeless or unlovable animals of other kinds heard about it and came, and these spread the matter to the other creatures, and they came also; and as the birds and the other timid wild things of the woods were not afraid of her, but always had an idea she was a friend when they came across her, and generally struck up an acquaintance with her to get invited to the house, she always had samples of those breeds in stock. She was hospitable to them all, for an animal was an animal to her, and dear by mere reason of being an animal, no matter about its sort or social station; and as she would allow of no cages, no collars, no fetters, but left the creatures free to come and go as they liked, that contented them, and they came; but they didn't go, to any extent, and so they were a marvellous nuisance, and made Jacques d'Arc swear a good deal; but his wife said God gave the child the instinct, and knew what He was doing when He did it, therefore it must have its course; it would be no sound prudence to meddle with His affairs when no invitation had been extended. So the pets were left in peace, and here they were, as I have said, rabbits, birds, squirrels, cats, and other reptiles, all around the child, and full of interest in her supper, and helping what they could. There was a very small squirrel on her shoulder, sitting up, as those creatures do, and turning a rocky fragment of prehistoric chestnut-cake over and over in its knotty hands, and hunting for the less indurated places, and giving its elevated bushy tail a flirt and its pointed ears a toss when it found one—signifying thankfulness and surprise—and then it filed that place off with those two slender front teeth which a squirrel carries for that purpose and not for ornament, for ornamental they never could be, as any will admit that have noticed them.

Everything was going fine and breezy and hilarious, but then there came an interruption, for somebody hammered on the door. It was one of those ragged road-stragglers—the eternal wars kept the country full of them. He came in, all over snow, and stamped his feet and shook and brushed himself, and shut the door, and took off his limp ruin of a hat and slapped it once or twice against his leg to knock off its fleece of snow, and then glanced around on the company with a pleased look upon his thin face, and a most yearning and famished one in his eye when it fell upon the victuals, and then he gave us a humble and conciliatory salutation, and said it was a blessed thing to have a fire like that on such a night, and a roof overhead like this, and that rich food to eat and loving friends to talk with—ah, yes, this was true, and God help the homeless, and such as must trudge the roads in this weather.

Nobody said anything. The embarrassed poor creature stood there and appealed to one face after the other with his eyes, and found no welcome in any, the smile on his own face flickering and fading and perishing, meanwhile; then he dropped his gaze, the muscles of his face began to twitch, and he put up his hand to cover this womanish sign of weakness.

"Sit down!"

This thunder-blast was from old Jacques d'Arc, and Joan was the object of it. The stranger was startled, and took his hand away, and there was Joan standing before him offering him her bowl of porridge. The man said,

"God Almighty bless you, my darling!" and then the tears came, and ran down his cheeks, but he was afraid to take the bowl.

"Do you hear me? Sit down, I say!"

There could not be a child more easy to persuade than Joan, but this was not the way. Her father had not the art; neither could he learn it. Joan said,

"Father, he is hungry; I can see it."

"Let him go work for food, then. We are being eaten out of house and home by his like, and I have said I would endure it no more, and will keep my word. He has the face of a rascal anyhow, and a villain. Sit *down*, I tell you!"

"I know not if he is a rascal or no, but he is hungry, father, and shall have my porridge—I do not need it."

"If you don't obey me I'll— Rascals are not entitled to help from honest people, and no bite nor sup shall they have in this house. *Joan!*"

She set her bowl down on the box and came over and stood before her scowling father, and said:

"Father, if you will not let me, then it must be as you say; but I would that you would think—then you would see that it is not right to punish one part of him for what the other part has done; for it is that poor stranger's head that does the evil things, but it is not his head that is hungry, it is his stomach, and it has done no harm to anybody, but is without blame, and innocent, not having any *way* to do a wrong, even if it was minded to it. Please let—"

"What an idea! It is the most idiotic speech I ever heard."

But Aubrey, the maire, broke in, he being fond of an argument, and having a pretty gift in that regard, as all acknowledged. Rising in his place and leaning his knuckles upon the table and looking about him with easy dignity, after the manner of such as be orators, he began, smooth and persuasive:

"I will differ with you there, gossip, and will undertake to show the company"—here he looked around upon us and nodded his head in a confident way—"that there is a grain of sense in what the child has said; for look you, it is of a certainty most true and demonstrable that it is a man's head that is master and supreme ruler over his whole body. Is that granted? Will any deny it?" He glanced around again; everybody indicated assent. "Very well, then; that being the case, no part of the body is responsible for the result when it carries out an order delivered to it by the head; ergo, the head is alone responsible for crimes done by a man's hands or feet or stomach—do you get the idea? am I right thus far?" Everybody said yes, and said it with enthusiasm, and some said, one to another, that the maire was in great form to-night and at his very best—which pleased the maire exceedingly and made his eyes sparkle with pleasure, for he overheard these things; so he went on in the same fertile and brilliant way. "Now, then, we will consider what the term responsibility means, and how it affects the case in point. Responsibility makes a man responsible for only those things for which he is properly responsible"—and he waved his spoon around in a wide sweep to indicate the comprehensive nature of that class of responsibilities which render people responsible, and several exclaimed, admiringly, "He is right!—he has put that whole tangled thing into a nutshell—it is wonderful!" After a little pause to give the interest opportunity to gather and grow, he went on: "Very good. Let us suppose the case of a pair of tongs that falls upon a man's foot, causing a cruel hurt. Will you claim that the tongs are punishable for that? The question is answered: I see by your faces that you would call such a claim absurd. Now, why is it absurd? It is absurd because, there being no reasoning faculty—that is to say, no faculty of personal command—in a pair of tongs, personal responsibility for the acts of the tongs is wholly absent from the tongs; and therefore, responsibility being absent, punishment cannot ensue. Am I right?" A hearty burst of applause was his answer. "Now, then, we arrive at a man's stomach. Consider how exactly, how marvellously, indeed, its situation corresponds to that of a pair of tongs. Listen—and take careful note, I beg you. Can a man's stomach plan a murder? No. Can it plan a theft? No. Can it plan an incendiary fire? No. Now answer me—*can a pair of tongs?*" (There were admiring shouts of "No!" and "The cases are just exact!" and "Don't he do it splendid!") "Now, then, friends and neighbors, a stomach which cannot plan a crime cannot be a principal in the commission of it—that is plain, as you see. The matter is narrowed down by that much; we will narrow it further. Can a stomach, of its own motion, assist at a crime? The answer is no, because command is absent, the reasoning faculty is absent, volition is absent—as in the case of the tongs. We perceive, now, do we not, that the stomach is totally irresponsible for crimes committed, either in whole or in part, by it?" He got a rousing cheer for response. "Then what do we arrive at as our verdict? Clearly this: that there is no such thing in this world as a guilty stomach; that in the body of the veriest rascal resides a pure and innocent stomach; that, whatever its owner may do, *it* at least should be sacred in our eyes; and that while God gives us minds to think just and charitable and honorable thoughts, it should be and *is* our privilege, as well as our duty, not only to feed the hungry stomach that resides in a rascal, having pity for its sorrow and its need, but to do it gladly, gratefully, in recognition of its sturdy and loyal maintenance of its purity and innocence in the midst of temptation and in company so repugnant to its better feelings. I am done."

Well, you never saw such an effect! They rose—the whole house rose—and clapped, and cheered, and praised him to the skies; and one after another, still clapping and shouting, they crowded forward, some with moisture in their eyes, and wrung his hands, and said such glorious things to him that he was clear overcome with pride and happiness, and couldn't say a word, for his voice would have broken, sure. It was splendid to see; and everybody said he had never come up to that speech in his life before, and never could do it again. Eloquence *is* a power, there is no question of that. Even old

Jacques d'Arc was carried away, for once in his life, and shouted out—

"It's all right, Joan—give him the porridge!"

She was embarrassed, and did not seem to know what to say, and so didn't say anything. It was because she had given the man the porridge long ago, and he had already eaten it all up. When she was asked why she had not waited until a decision was arrived at, she said the man's stomach was very hungry, and it would not have been wise to wait, since she could not tell what the decision would be. Now that was a good and thoughtful idea for a child.

The man was not a rascal at all. He was a very good fellow, only he was out of luck, and surely that was no crime at that time in France. Now that his stomach was proved to be innocent, it was allowed to make itself at home; and as soon as it was well filled and needed nothing more, the man unwound his tongue and turned it loose, and it was really a noble one to go. He had been in the wars for years, and the things he told, and the way he told them, fired everybody's patriotism away up high, and set all hearts to thumping and all pulses to leaping; then, before anybody rightly knew how the change was made, he was leading us a sublime march through the ancient glories of France, and in fancy we saw the titanic forms of the twelve paladins rise out of the mists of the past and face their fate; we heard the tread of the innumerable hosts sweeping down to shut them in; we saw this human tide flow and ebb, ebb and flow, and waste away before that little band of heroes; we saw each detail pass before us of that most stupendous, most disastrous, yet most adored and glorious day in French legendary history; here and there and yonder, across that vast field of the dead and dying, we saw this and that and the other paladin dealing his prodigious blows with weary arm and failing strength, and one by one we saw them fall, till only one remained—he that was without peer, he whose name gives name to the Song of Songs, the song which no Frenchman can hear and keep his feelings down and his pride of country cool; then, grandest and pitifulest scene of all, we saw his own pathetic death; and our stillness, as we sat with parted lips and breathless, hanging upon this man's words, gave us a sense of the awful stillness that reigned in that field of slaughter when that last surviving soul had passed.

And now, in this solemn hush, the stranger gave Joan a pat or two on the head and said:

"Little maid—whom God keep!—you have brought me from death to life this night; now listen: here is your reward," and at that supreme time for such a heart-melting, soul-rousing surprise, without another word he lifted up the most noble and pathetic voice that was ever heard, and began to pour out the great Song of Roland!

Think of that, with a French audience all stirred up and ready. Oh, where was your spoken eloquence now! what was it to this! How fine he looked, how stately, how inspired, as he stood there with that mighty chant welling from his lips and his heart, his whole body transfigured, and his rags along with it.

Everybody rose and stood, while he sang, and their faces glowed and their eyes burned; and the tears came and flowed down their cheeks, and their forms began to sway unconsciously to the swing of the song, and their bosoms to heave and pant; and moanings broke out, and deep ejaculations; and when the last verse was reached, and Roland lay dying, all alone, with his face to the field and to his slain, lying there in heaps and winrows, and took off and held up his gauntlet to God with his failing hand, and breathed his beautiful prayer with his paling lips, all burst out in sobs and wailings. But when the final great note died out and the song was done, they all flung themselves in a body at the singer, stark mad with love of him and love of France and pride in her great deeds and old renown, and smothered him with their embracings; but Joan was there first, hugged close to his breast, and covering his face with idolatrous kisses.

The storm raged on outside, but that was no matter; this was the stranger's home now, for as long as he might please.

Chapter IV

ALL CHILDREN have nicknames, and we had ours. We got one apiece early, and they stuck to us; but Joan was richer in this matter, for as time went on she earned a second, and then a third, and so on, and we gave them to her. First and last she had as many as half a dozen. Several of these she never lost. Peasant girls are bashful naturally; but she surpassed the rule so far, and colored so easily, and was so easily embarrassed in the presence of strangers, that we nicknamed her the Bashful. We were all patriots, but she was called *the* Patriot, because our warmest feeling for our country was cold beside hers. Also she was called the Beautiful; and this was not merely because of the extraordinary beauty of her face and form, but because of the loveliness of her character. These names she kept, and one other—the Brave.

We grew along up, in that plodding and peaceful region, and got to be good-sized boys and girls—big enough, in fact, to begin to know as much about the wars raging perpetually to the west and north of us as our elders, and also to feel as stirred up over the occasional news from those red fields as they did. I remember certain of these days very clearly. One Tuesday a crowd of us were romping and singing around the Fairy Tree, and hanging garlands on it in memory of our lost little fairy friends, when little Mengette cried out:

"Look! What is that?"

When one exclaims like that, in a way that shows astonishment and apprehension, he gets attention. All the panting breasts and flushed faces flocked together, and all the eager eyes were turned in one direction—down the slope, toward the village.

"It's a black flag."

"A black flag! No—is it?"

"You can see for yourself that it is nothing else."

"It *is* a black flag, sure! Now, has any ever seen the like of that before?"

"What can it mean?"

"Mean? It means something dreadful—what else?"

"That is nothing to the point; anybody knows that without the telling. But *what?*—that is the question."

"It is a chance that he that bears it can answer as well as any that are here, if you can contain yourself till he come."

"He runs well. Who is it?"

Some named one, some another; but presently all saw that it was Étienne Roze, called the Sunflower, because he had yellow hair and a round, pock-marked face. His ancestors had been Germans some centuries ago. He came straining up the slope, now and then projecting his flag-stick aloft and giving his black symbol of woe a wave in the air, whilst all eyes watched him, all tongues discussed him, and every heart beat faster and faster with impatience to know his news. At last he sprang among us, and struck his flag-stick into the ground, saying:

"There! Stand there and represent France while I get my breath. She needs no other flag, now."

All the giddy chatter stopped. It was as if one had announced a death. In that chilly hush there was no sound audible but the panting of the breath-blown boy. When he was presently able to speak, he said:

"Black news is come. A treaty has been made at Troyes between France and the English and Burgundians. By it France is betrayed and delivered over, tied hand and foot, to the enemy. It is the work of the Duke of Burgundy and that she-devil the Queen of France. It marries Henry of England to Catharine of France—"

"Is not this a lie? Marries the daughter of France to the Butcher of Agincourt? It is not to be believed. You have not heard aright."

"If you cannot believe that, Jacques d'Arc, then you have a difficult task indeed before you, for worse is to come. Any child that is born of that marriage—if even a girl—is to inherit the thrones of both England and France, and this double ownership is to remain with its posterity forever!"

"Now *that* is certainly a lie, for it runs counter to our Salic law, and so is not legal and cannot have effect," said Edmond Aubrey, called the Paladin, because of the armies he was always going to eat up some day. He would have said more, but he was drowned out by the clamors of the others, who all burst into a fury over this feature of the treaty, all talking at once and nobody hearing anybody, until presently Haumette persuaded them to be still, saying:

"It is not fair to break him up so in his tale; pray let him go on. You find fault with his history because it seems to be lies. That were reason for satisfaction—*that* kind of lies—not discontent. Tell the rest, Étienne."

"There is but this to tell: Our King, Charles VI., is to reign until he dies, then Henry V. of England is to be Regent of France until a child of his shall be old enough to—"

"*That* man is to reign over us—the Butcher? It is lies! all lies!" cried the Paladin. "Besides, look you—what becomes of our Dauphin? What says the treaty about him?"

"Nothing. It takes away his throne and makes him an outcast."

Then everybody shouted at once and said the news was a lie; and all began to get cheerful again, saying, "Our King would have to sign the treaty to make it good; and that he would not do, seeing how it serves his own son."

But the Sunflower said: "I will ask you this: Would the *Queen* sign a treaty disinheriting her son?"

"That viper? Certainly. Nobody is talking of her. Nobody expects better of her. There is no villany she will stick at, if it feed her spite; and she hates her son. Her signing it is of no consequence. The King must sign."

"I will ask you another thing. What is the King's condition? Mad, isn't he?"

"Yes, and his people love him all the more for it. It brings him near to them by his sufferings; and pitying him makes them love him."

"You say right, Jacques d'Arc. Well, what would you of one that is mad? Does he know what he does? No. Does he do what others make him do? Yes. Now, then, I tell you he has signed the treaty."

"Who made him do it?"

"You know, without my telling. The Queen."

Then there was another uproar—everybody talking at once, and all heaping execrations upon the Queen's head. Finally Jacques d'Arc said:

"But many reports come that are not true. Nothing so

shameful as this has ever come before, nothing that cuts so deep, nothing that has dragged France so low; therefore there is hope that this tale is but another idle rumor. Where did you get it?"

The color went out of his sister Joan's face. She dreaded the answer; and her instinct was right.

"The curé of Maxey brought it."

There was a general gasp. We knew him, you see, for a trusty man.

"Did he believe it?"

The hearts almost stopped beating. Then came the answer:

"He did. And that is not all. He said he *knew* it to be true."

Some of the girls began to sob; the boys were struck silent. The distress in Joan's face was like that which one sees in the face of a dumb animal that has received a mortal hurt. The animal bears it, making no complaint; she bore it also, saying no word. Her brother Jacques put his hand on her head and caressed her hair to indicate his sympathy, and she gathered the hand to her lips and kissed it for thanks, not saying anything. Presently the reaction came, and the boys began to talk. Noël Rainguesson said:

"Oh, are we never going to be men! We do grow along so slowly, and France never needed soldiers as she needs them now, to wipe out this black insult."

"I hate youth!" said Pierre Morel, called the Dragon-fly because his eyes stuck out so. "You've always got to wait, and wait, and wait—and here are the great wars wasting away for a hundred years, and you never get a chance. If I could only be a soldier now!"

"As for me, I'm not going to wait much longer," said the Paladin; "and when I do start you'll hear from me, I promise you that. There are some who, in storming a castle, prefer to be in the rear; but as for me, give me the front or none; I will have none in front of me but the officers."

Even the girls got the war spirit, and Marie Dupont said—

"I would I were a man; I would start this minute!" and looked very proud of herself, and glanced about for applause.

"So would I," said Cécile Letellier, sniffing the air like a war-horse that smells the battle; "I warrant you I would not turn back from the field though all England were in front of me."

"Pooh!" said the Paladin; "girls can brag, but that's all they are good for. Let a thousand of them come face to face with a handful of soldiers once, if you want to see what running is like. Here's little Joan—next *she'll* be threatening to go for a soldier!"

The idea was so funny, and got such a good laugh, that the Paladin gave it another trial, and said: "Why, you can just see her!—see her plunge into battle like any old veteran. Yes, indeed; and not a poor shabby common soldier like us, but an officer—an officer, mind you, with armor on, and the bars of a steel helmet to blush behind and hide her embarrassment when she finds an army in front of her that she hasn't been introduced to. An officer? Why, she'll be a captain! A captain, I tell you, with a hundred men at her back—or maybe girls. Oh, no common-soldier business for her! And, dear me, when she starts for that other army, you'll think there's a hurricane blowing it away!"

Well, he kept it up like that till he made their sides ache with laughing; which was quite natural, for certainly it was a very funny idea—at that time—I mean, the idea of that gentle little creature, that wouldn't hurt a fly, and couldn't bear the sight of blood, and was so girlish and shrinking in all ways, rushing into battle with a gang of soldiers at her back. Poor thing, she sat there confused and ashamed to be so laughed at; and yet at that very minute there was something about to happen which would change the aspect of things, and make those young people see that when it comes to laughing, the person that laughs last has the best chance. For just then a face which we all knew and all feared projected itself from behind the Fairy Tree, and the thought that shot through us all was, crazy Benoist has gotten loose from his cage, and we are as good as dead! This ragged and hairy and horrible creature glided out from behind the tree, and raised an axe as he came. We all broke and fled, this way and that, the girls screaming and crying. No, not all; all but Joan. She stood up and faced the man, and remained so. As we reached the wood that borders the grassy clearing and jumped into its shelter, two or three of us glanced back to

see if Benoist was gaining on us, and that is what we saw—
Joan standing, and the maniac gliding stealthily toward her
with his axe lifted. The sight was sickening. We stood where
we were, trembling and not able to move. I did not want to
see the murder done, and yet I could not take my eyes away.
Now I saw Joan step forward to meet the man, though I believed my eyes must be deceiving me. Then I saw him stop.
He threatened her with his axe, as if to warn her not to
come further, but she paid no heed, but went steadily on,
until she was right in front of him—right under his axe.
Then she stopped, and seemed to begin to talk with him. It
made me sick, yes, giddy, and everything swam around me,
and I could not see anything for a time—whether long or
brief I do not know. When this passed and I looked again,
Joan was walking by the man's side toward the village, holding him by his hand. The axe was in her other hand.

One by one the boys and girls crept out, and we stood
there gazing, open-mouthed, till those two entered the village
and were hid from sight. It was then that we named her the
Brave.

We left the black flag there to continue its mournful office,
for we had other matter to think of now. We started for the
village on a run, to give warning, and get Joan out of her
peril; though for one, after seeing what I had seen, it
seemed to me that while Joan had the axe the man's chance
was not the best of the two. When we arrived the danger
was past, the madman was in custody. All the people were
flocking to the little square in front of the church to talk and
exclaim and wonder over the event, and it even made the
town forget the black news of the treaty for two or three
hours.

All the women kept hugging and kissing Joan, and praising
her, and crying, and the men patted her on the head and said
they wished she was a man, they would send her to the wars
and never doubt but that she would strike some blows that
would be heard of. She had to tear herself away and go and
hide, this glory was so trying to her diffidence.

Of course the people began to ask us for the particulars. I
was so ashamed that I made an excuse to the first comer, and
got privately away and went back to the Fairy Tree, to get

relief from the embarrassment of those questionings. There I found Joan, but she was there to get relief from the embarrassment of glory. One by one the others shirked the inquirers and joined us in our refuge. Then we gathered around Joan, and asked her how she had dared to do that thing. She was very modest about it, and said:

"You make a great thing of it, but you mistake; it was not a great matter. It was not as if I had been a stranger to the man. I know him, and have known him long; and he knows me, and likes me. I have fed him through the bars of his cage many times; and last December when they chopped off two of his fingers to remind him to stop seizing and wounding people passing by, I dressed his hand every day till it was well again."

"That is all well enough," said Little Mengette, "but he is a madman, dear, and so his likings and his gratitude and friendliness go for nothing when his rage is up. You did a perilous thing."

"Of course you did," said the Sunflower. "Didn't he threaten to kill you with the axe?"

"Yes."

"Didn't he threaten you more than once?"

"Yes."

"Didn't you feel afraid?"

"No—at least not much—very little."

"Why didn't you?"

She thought a moment, then said, quite simply—

"I don't know."

It made everybody laugh. Then the Sunflower said it was like a lamb trying to think out how it had come to eat a wolf, but had to give it up.

Cécile Letellier asked, "Why didn't you run when we did?"

"Because it was necessary to get him to his cage; else he would kill some one. Then he would come to the like harm himself."

It is noticeable that this remark, which implies that Joan was entirely forgetful of herself and her own danger, and had thought and wrought for the preservation of other people alone, was not challenged, or criticised, or commented upon by anybody there, but was taken by all as matter of course and true. It shows how clearly her character was defined, and how well it was known and established.

There was silence for a time, and perhaps we were all thinking of the same thing—namely, what a poor figure we had cut in that adventure as contrasted with Joan's performance. I tried to think up some good way of explaining why I had run away and left a little girl at the mercy of a maniac armed with an axe, but all of the explanations that offered themselves to me seemed so cheap and shabby that I gave the matter up and remained still. But others were less wise. Noël Rainguesson fidgeted a while, then broke out with a remark which showed what his mind had been running on:

"The fact is, I was taken by surprise. That is the reason. If I had had a moment to think, I would no more have thought of running than I would think of running from a baby. For, after all, what is Théophile Benoist, that I should seem to be afraid of him? Pooh! the idea of being afraid of that poor thing! I only wish he would come along now—I'd show you!"

"So do I!" cried Pierre Morel. "If I wouldn't make him climb this tree quicker than—well, you'd see what I would do! Taking a person by surprise, that way—why, I never meant to run; not in earnest, I mean. I never thought of running in earnest; I only wanted to have some fun, and when I saw Joan standing there, and him threatening her, it was all I could do to restrain myself from going there and just tearing the livers and lights out of him. I *wanted* to do it bad enough, and if it was to do over again, I *would*! If ever he comes fooling around me again, I'll—"

"Oh, hush!" said the Paladin, breaking in with an air of disdain; "the way you people talk, a person would think there's something heroic about standing up and facing down that poor remnant of a man. Why, it's nothing! There's small glory to be got in facing *him* down, I should say. Why, I wouldn't want any better fun than to face down a hundred like him. If he was to come along here now, I would walk up to him just as I am now—I wouldn't care if he had a thousand axes—and say—"

And so he went on and on, telling the brave things he would say and the wonders he would do; and the others put in a word from time to time, describing over again the gory marvels they would do if ever that madman ventured to cross their path again, for next time they would be ready for him, and would soon teach him that if he thought he could surprise them twice because he had surprised them once, he would find himself very seriously mistaken, that's all.

And so, in the end, they all got back their self-respect; yes, and even added somewhat to it; indeed, when the sitting broke up they had a finer opinion of themselves than they had ever had before.

Chapter V

THEY WERE peaceful and pleasant, those young and
smoothly flowing days of ours; that is, that was the case
as a rule, we being remote from the seat of war, but at intervals roving bands approached near enough for us to see the
flush in the sky at night which marked where they were burning some farmstead or village, and we all knew, or at least felt,
that some day they would come yet nearer, and we should
have our turn. This dull dread lay upon our spirits like a physical weight. It was greatly augmented a couple of years after
the Treaty of Troyes.

It was truly a dismal year for France. One day we had been
over to have one of our occasional pitched battles with those
hated Burgundian boys of the village of Maxey, and had been
whipped, and were arriving on our side of the river after dark,
bruised and weary, when we heard the bell ringing the tocsin.
We ran all the way, and when we got to the square we found
it crowded with the excited villagers, and weirdly lighted by
smoking and flaring torches.

On the steps of the church stood a stranger, a Burgundian
priest, who was telling the people news which made them
weep, and rave, and rage, and curse, by turns. He said our old
mad King was dead, and that now we and France and the
crown were the property of an English baby lying in his
cradle in London. And he urged us to give that child our
allegiance, and be its faithful servants and well-wishers; and
said we should now have a strong and stable government at
last, and that in a little time the English armies would start on
their last march, and it would be a brief one, for all that it
would need to do would be to conquer what odds and ends
of our country yet remained under that rare and almost forgotten rag, the banner of France.

The people stormed and raged at him, and you could see
dozens of them stretch their fists above the sea of torch-
lighted faces and shake them at him; and it was all a wild
picture, and stirring to look at; and the priest was a first-rate
part of it, too, for he stood there in the strong glare and

looked down on those angry people in the blandest and most indifferent way, so that while you wanted to burn him at the stake, you still admired the aggravating coolness of him. And his winding up was the coolest thing of all. For he told them how, at the funeral of our old King, the French King-at-Arms had broken his staff of office over the coffin of "Charles VI. and his dynasty," at the same time saying, in a loud voice, "God grant long life to Henry, King of France and England, our sovereign lord!" and then he asked them to join him in a hearty Amen to *that!*

The people were white with wrath, and it tied their tongues for the moment, and they could not speak. But Joan was standing close by, and she looked up in his face, and said in her sober, earnest way—

"I would I might see thy head struck from thy body!"— then, after a pause, and crossing herself—"if it were the will of God."

This is worth remembering, and I will tell you why: it is the only harsh speech Joan ever uttered in her life. When I shall have revealed to you the storms she went through, and the wrongs and persecutions, then you will see that it was wonderful that she said but one bitter thing while she lived.

From the day that that dreary news came we had one scare after another, the marauders coming almost to our doors every now and then; so that we lived in ever-increasing apprehension, and yet were somehow mercifully spared from actual attack. But at last our turn did really come. This was in the spring of '28. The Burgundians swarmed in with a great noise, in the middle of a dark night, and we had to jump up and fly for our lives. We took the road to Neufchâteau, and rushed along in the wildest disorder, everybody trying to get ahead, and thus the movements of all were impeded; but Joan had a cool head—the only cool head there—and she took command and brought order out of that chaos. She did her work quickly and with decision and despatch, and soon turned the panic flight into a quite steady-going march. You will grant that for so young a person, and a girl at that, this was a good piece of work.

She was sixteen now, shapely and graceful, and of a beauty so extraordinary that I might allow myself any extravagance of language in describing it and yet have no fear of going beyond the truth. There was in her face a sweetness and serenity and purity that justly reflected her spiritual nature. She was deeply religious, and this is a thing which sometimes gives a melancholy cast to a person's countenance, but it was not so in her case. Her religion made her inwardly content and joyous; and if she was troubled at times, and showed the pain of it in her face and bearing, it came of distress for her country; no part of it was chargeable to her religion.

A considerable part of our village was destroyed, and when it became safe for us to venture back there we realized what other people had been suffering in all the various quarters of France for many years—yes, decades of years. For the first time we saw wrecked and smoke-blackened homes, and in the lanes and alleys carcasses of dumb creatures that had been slaughtered in pure wantonness—among them calves and lambs that had been pets of the children; and it was pity to see the children lament over them.

And then, the taxes, the taxes! Everybody thought of that. That burden would fall heavy, now, in the commune's crippled condition, and all faces grew long with the thought of it. Joan said—

"Paying taxes with naught to pay them with is what the rest of France has been doing these many years, but we never knew the bitterness of that before. We shall know it now.".

And so she went on talking about it and growing more and more troubled about it, until one could see that it was filling all her mind.

At last we came upon a dreadful object. It was the madman—hacked and stabbed to death in his iron cage in the corner of the square. It was a bloody and dreadful sight. Hardly any of us young people had ever seen a man before who had lost his life by violence; so this cadaver had an awful fascination for us; we could not take our eyes from it. I mean, it had that sort of fascination for all of us but one. That one was Joan. She turned away in horror, and could not be persuaded to go near it again. There—it is a striking reminder that we are but creatures of use and custom; yes, and it is a reminder, too, of how harshly and unfairly fate deals with us sometimes. For it was so ordered that the very ones among us who were most fascinated with mutilated and bloody death were to live their lives in peace, while that other, who had a native and deep horror of it, must presently go forth and have it as a familiar spectacle every day on the field of battle.

You may well believe that we had plenty of matter for talk, now, since the raiding of our village seemed by long odds the greatest event that had really ever occurred in the world; for although these dull peasants may have *thought* they recognized the bigness of some of the previous occurrences that had filtered from the world's history dimly into their minds, the truth is that they hadn't. One biting little fact, visible to their eyes of flesh and felt in their own personal vitals, became at once more prodigious to them than the grandest remote episode in the world's history which they had got at second-hand and by hearsay. It amuses me now when I recall how our elders talked then. They fumed and fretted in a fine fashion.

"Ah yes," said old Jacques d'Arc, "things are come to a pretty pass indeed! The King must be informed of this. It is time that he cease from idleness and dreaming, and get at his proper business." He meant our young disinherited King, the hunted refugee, Charles VII.

"You say well," said the maire. "He should be informed, and that at once. It is an outrage that such things should be permitted. Why, we are not safe in our beds, and he taking his ease yonder. It shall be made known, indeed it shall—all France shall hear of it!"

To hear them talk, one would have imagined that all the previous ten thousand sackings and burnings in France had been but fables, and this one the only fact. It is always the way: words will answer as long as it is only a person's neighbor who is in trouble, but when that person gets into trouble himself, it is time that the King rise up and *do* something.

The big event filled us young people with talk, too. We let it flow in a steady stream while we tended the flocks. We were beginning to feel pretty important, now, for I was eighteen and the other youths were from one to four years older— young men, in fact. One day the Paladin was arrogantly criticising the patriot generals of France and said—

"Look at Dunois, Bastard of Orleans—call *him* a general! Just put me in his place once—never mind what I would do, it is not for me to say, I have no stomach for talk, my way is to *act* and let others do the talking—but just put me in his place once, that's all! And look at Saintrailles—pooh! and that blustering La Hire, now what a general *that* is!"

It shocked everybody to hear these great names so flippantly handled, for to us these renowned soldiers were almost gods. In their far-off splendor they rose upon our imaginations dim and huge, shadowy and awful, and it was a fearful thing to hear them spoken of as if they were mere men, and their acts open to comment and criticism. The color rose in Joan's face, and she said—

"I know not how any can be so hardy as to use such words regarding these sublime men, who are the very pillars of the French State, supporting it with their strength and preserving it at daily cost of their blood. As for me, I could count myself honored past all deserving if I might be allowed but the privilege of looking upon them once—at a distance, I mean, for it would not become one of my degree to approach them too near."

The Paladin was disconcerted for a moment, seeing by the faces around him that Joan had put into words what the others felt, then he pulled his complacency together and fell to fault-finding again. Joan's brother Jean said—

"If you don't like what our generals do, why don't you go to the great wars yourself and better their work? You are always talking about going to the wars, but you don't go."

"Look you," said the Paladin, "it is easy to say that. Now I will tell you why I remain chafing here in a bloodless tranquillity which my reputation teaches you is repulsive to my nature. I do not go because I am not a gentleman. That is the whole reason. What can one private soldier do in a contest like this? Nothing. He is not permitted to rise from the ranks. If I were a gentleman would I remain here? Not one moment. I can save France—ah, you may laugh, but I know what is in me, I know what is hid under this peasant cap. I can save France, and I stand ready to do it, but not under these present conditions. If they want me, let them send for me;

otherwise, let them take the consequences; I shall not budge but as an officer."

"Alas, poor France—France is lost!" said Pierre d'Arc.

"Since you sniff so at others, why don't you go to the wars yourself, Pierre d'Arc?"

"Oh, I haven't been sent for, either. I am no more a gentleman than you. Yet I will go; I promise to go. I promise to go as a private under your orders—when you are sent for."

They all laughed, and the Dragon-fly said—

"So soon? Then you need to begin to get ready; you might be called for in five years—who knows? Yes, in my opinion you'll march for the wars in five years."

"He will go sooner," said Joan. She said it in a low voice and musingly, but several heard it.

"How do you know that, Joan?" said the Dragon-fly, with a surprised look. But Jean d'Arc broke in and said—

"I want to go myself, but as I am rather young yet, I also will wait, and march when the Paladin is sent for."

"No," said Joan, "he will go with Pierre."

She said it as one who talks to himself aloud without knowing it, and none heard it but me. I glanced at her and saw that her knitting-needles were idle in her hands, and that her face had a dreamy and absent look in it. There were fleeting movements of her lips as if she might be occasionally saying parts of sentences to herself. But there was no sound, for I was the nearest person to her and I heard nothing. But I set my ears open, for those two speeches had affected me uncannily, I being superstitious and easily troubled by any little thing of a strange and unusual sort.

Noël Rainguesson said—

"There is one way to let France have a chance for her salvation. We've got *one* gentleman in the commune, at any rate. Why can't the Scholar change name and condition with the Paladin? Then he can be an officer. France will send for him then, and he will sweep these English and Burgundian armies into the sea like flies."

I was the Scholar. That was my nickname, because I could read and write. There was a chorus of approval, and the Sunflower said—

"That is the very thing—it settles every difficulty. The Sieur de Conte will easily agree to that. Yes, he will march at the back of Captain Paladin and die early, covered with common-soldier glory."

"He will march with Jean and Pierre, and live till these wars are forgotten," Joan muttered; "and at the eleventh hour Noël and the Paladin will join these, but not of their own desire." The voice was so low that I was not perfectly sure that these were the words, but they seemed to be. It makes one feel creepy to hear such things.

"Come, now," Noël continued, "it's all arranged; there's nothing to do but organize under the Paladin's banner and go forth and rescue France. You'll all join?"

All said yes, except Jacques d'Arc, who said—

"I'll ask you to excuse me. It is pleasant to talk war, and I am with you there, and I've always thought I should go soldiering about this time, but the look of our wrecked village and that carved-up and bloody madman have taught me that I am not made for such work and such sights. I could never be at home in that trade. Face swords and the big guns and death? It isn't in me. No, no; count me out. And besides, I'm the eldest son, and deputy prop and protector of the family. Since you are going to carry Jean and Pierre to the wars, somebody must be left behind to take care of our Joan and her sister. I shall stay at home, and grow old in peace and tranquillity."

"He will stay at home, but not grow old," murmured Joan.

The talk rattled on in the gay and careless fashion privileged to youth, and we got the Paladin to map out his campaigns and fight his battles and win his victories and extinguish the English and put our King upon his throne and set his crown upon his head. Then we asked him what he was going to answer when the King should require him to name his reward. The Paladin had it all arranged in his head, and brought it out promptly:

"He shall give me a dukedom, name me premier peer, and make me Hereditary Lord High Constable of France."

"And marry you to a princess—you're not going to leave that out, are you?"

The Paladin colored a trifle, and said, brusquely—

"He may keep his princesses—I can marry more to my taste."

Meaning Joan, though nobody suspected it at that time. If any had, the Paladin would have been finely ridiculed for his vanity. There was no fit mate in that village for Joan of Arc. Every one would have said that.

In turn, each person present was required to say what reward he would demand of the King if he could change places with the Paladin and do the wonders the Paladin was going to do. The answers were given in fun, and each of us tried to outdo his predecessors in the extravagance of the reward he would claim; but when it came to Joan's turn and they rallied her out of her dreams and asked her to testify, they had to explain to her what the question was, for her thought had been absent, and she had heard none of this latter part of our talk. She supposed they wanted a serious answer, and she gave it. She sat considering some moments, then she said—

"If the Dauphin out of his grace and nobleness should say to me, 'Now that I am rich and am come to my own again, choose and have,' I should kneel and ask him to give command that our village should nevermore be taxed."

It was so simple and out of her heart that it touched us and we did not laugh, but fell to thinking. We did not laugh; but there came a day when we remembered that speech with a mournful pride, and were glad that we had not laughed, perceiving then how honest her words had been, and seeing how faithfully she made them good when the time came, asking just that boon of the King and refusing to take even any least thing for herself.

Chapter VI

ALL THROUGH her childhood and up to the middle of her fourteenth year, Joan had been the most light-hearted creature and the merriest in the village, with a hop-skip-and-jump gait and a happy and catching laugh; and this disposition, supplemented by her warm and sympathetic nature and frank and winning ways, had made her everybody's pet. She had been a hot patriot all this time, and sometimes the war news had sobered her spirits and wrung her heart and made her acquainted with tears, but always when these interruptions had run their course her spirits rose and she was her old self again.

But now for a whole year and a half she had been mainly grave; not melancholy, but given to thought, abstraction, dreams. She was carrying France upon her heart, and she found the burden not light. I knew that this was her trouble, but others attributed her abstraction to religious ecstasy, for she did not share her thinkings with the village at large, yet gave me glimpses of them, and so I knew, better than the rest, what was absorbing her interest. Many a time the idea crossed my mind that she had a secret—a secret which she was keeping wholly to herself, as well from me as from the others. This idea had come to me because several times she had cut a sentence in two and changed the subject when apparently she was on the verge of a revelation of some sort. I was to find this secret out, but not just yet.

The day after the conversation which I have been reporting we were together in the pastures and fell to talking about France, as usual. For her sake I had always talked hopefully before, but that was mere lying, for really there was not anything to hang a rag of hope for France upon. Now it was such a pain to lie to her, and cost me such shame to offer this treachery to one so snow-pure from lying and treachery, and even from suspicion of such basenesses in others, as she was, that I was resolved to face about, now, and begin over again, and never insult her more with deception. I started on the new policy by saying—still opening up with a small lie, of course, for habit is habit, and not to be flung out of the window by any man, but coaxed down-stairs a step at a time—

"Joan, I have been thinking the thing all over, last night, and have concluded that we have been in the wrong all this time; that the case of France is desperate; that it has been desperate ever since Agincourt; and that to-day it is more than desperate, it is hopeless."

I did not look her in the face while I was saying it; it could not be expected of a person. To break her heart, to crush her hope with a so frankly brutal speech as that, without one charitable soft place in it—it seemed a shameful thing, and it was. But when it was out, the weight gone, and my conscience rising to the surface, I glanced at her face to see the result.

There was none to see. At least none that I was expecting. There was a barely perceptible suggestion of wonder in her serious eyes, but that was all; and she said, in her simple and placid way—

"The case of France hopeless? Why should you think that? Tell me."

It is a most pleasant thing to find that what you thought would inflict a hurt upon one whom you honor, has not done it. I was relieved, now, and could say all my say without any furtivenesses and without embarrassment. So I began:

"Let us put sentiment and patriotic illusions aside, and look the facts in the face. What do they say? They speak as plainly as the figures in a merchant's account-book. One has only to add the two columns up to see that the French house is bankrupt, that one-half of its property is already in the English sheriff's hands and the other half in nobody's—except those of irresponsible raiders and robbers confessing allegiance to nobody. Our King is shut up with his favorites and fools in inglorious idleness and poverty in a narrow little patch of the kingdom—a sort of back lot, as one may say—and has no authority there or anywhere else, hasn't a farthing to his name, nor a regiment of soldiers; he is not fighting, he is not intending to fight, he means to make no further resistance; in truth there is but one thing that he is intending to do—give the whole thing up, pitch his crown into the sewer, and run away to Scotland. There are the facts. Are they correct?"

"Yes, they are correct."

"Then it is as I have said: one needs but to add them together in order to realize what they mean."

She asked, in an ordinary, level tone—

"What—that the case of France is hopeless?"

"Necessarily. In face of these facts, doubt of it is impossible."

"How can you say that? How can you *feel* like that?"

"How can I? How could I think or feel in any other way, in the circumstances? Joan, with these fatal figures before you, have you really any hope for France—really and actually?"

"Hope—oh, more than that! France will win her freedom and keep it. Do not doubt it."

It seemed to me that her clear intellect must surely be clouded to-day. It must be so, or she would see that those figures *could* mean only the one thing. Perhaps if I marshalled them again she would see. So I said:

"Joan, your heart, which worships France, is beguiling your head. You are not perceiving the importance of these figures. Here—I want to make a picture of them, here on the ground with a stick. Now, this rough outline is France. Through its middle, east and west, I draw a river."

"Yes; the Loire."

"Now, then, this whole northern half of the country is in the tight grip of the English."

"Yes."

"And this whole southern half is really in nobody's hands at all—as our King confesses by meditating desertion and flight to a foreign land. England has armies here; opposition is dead; she can assume full possession whenever she may choose. In very truth, *all* France is gone, France is already lost, France has ceased to exist. What was France is now but a British province. Is this true?"

Her voice was low, and just touched with emotion, but distinct:

"Yes, it is true."

"Very well. Now add this clinching fact, and surely the sum is complete: When have French soldiers won a victory? Scotch soldiers, under the French flag, have won a barren fight or two a few years back, but I am speaking of French ones. Since eight thousand Englishmen nearly annihilated sixty thousand Frenchmen a dozen years ago at Agincourt, French courage has been paralyzed. And so it is a common saying, to-day, that if you confront fifty French soldiers with five English ones, the French will run."

"It is a pity, but even these things are true."

"Then certainly the day for hoping is *past*."

I believed the case would be clear to her now. I thought it could not fail to be clear to her, and that she would say, herself, that there was no longer any ground for hope. But I was mistaken; and disappointed also. She said, without any doubt in her tone:

"France will rise again. You shall see."

"Rise?—with this burden of English armies on her back!"

"She will cast it off; she will trample it under foot!" This with spirit.

"Without soldiers to fight with?"

"The drums will summon them. They will answer, and they will march."

"March to the rear, as usual?"

"No; to the front—ever to the front—always to the front! You shall see."

"And the pauper King?"

"He will mount his throne—he will wear his crown."

"Well, of a truth this makes one's head dizzy. Why, if I could believe that in thirty years from now the English domination would be broken and the French monarch's head find itself hooped with a real crown of sovereignty—"

"Both will have happened before two years are sped."

"Indeed? and who is going to perform all these sublime impossibilities?"

"God."

It was a reverent low note, but it rang clear.

What could have put those strange ideas in her head? This question kept running in my mind during two or three days. It was inevitable that I should think of madness. What other way was there to account for such things? Grieving and brooding over the woes of France had weakened that strong mind, and filled it with fantastic phantoms—yes, that must be it.

But I watched her, and tested her, and it was not so. Her eye was clear and sane, her ways were natural, her speech direct and to the point. No, there was nothing the matter with her mind; it was still the soundest in the village and the best. She went on thinking for others, planning for others, sacrificing herself for others, just as always before. She went on ministering to her sick and to her poor, and still stood ready to give the wayfarer her bed and content herself with the floor. There was a secret somewhere, but madness was not the key to it. This was plain.

Now the key did presently come into my hands, and the way that it happened was this. You have heard all the world talk of this matter which I am about to speak of, but you have not heard an eye-witness talk of it before.

I was coming from over the ridge, one day—it was the 15th of May, '28—and when I got to the edge of the oak forest and was about to step out of it upon the turfy open space in which the haunted beech-tree stood, I happened to cast a glance from cover, first—then I took a step backward, and stood in the shelter and concealment of the foliage. For I had caught sight of Joan, and thought I would devise some sort of playful surprise for her. Think of it—that trivial conceit was neighbor, with but a scarcely measurable interval of time between, to an event destined to endure forever in histories and songs.

The day was overcast, and all that grassy space wherein the Tree stood lay in a soft rich shadow. Joan sat on a natural seat formed by gnarled great roots of the Tree. Her hands lay loosely, one reposing in the other, in her lap. Her head was bent a little toward the ground, and her air was that of one who is lost in thought, steeped in dreams, and not conscious of herself or of the world. And now I saw a most strange thing, for I saw a *white* shadow come slowly gliding along the grass toward the Tree. It was of grand proportions—a robed form, with wings—and the whiteness of this shadow was not like any other whiteness that we know of, except it be the whiteness of the lightnings, but even the lightnings are not so intense as it was, for one can look at them without hurt, whereas this brilliancy was so blinding that it pained my eyes and brought the water into them. I uncovered my head, perceiving that I was in the presence of something not of this world. My breath grew faint and difficult, because of the terror and the awe that possessed me.

Another strange thing. The wood had been silent—smitten with that deep stillness which comes when a storm-cloud darkens a forest, and the wild creatures lose heart and are afraid; but now all the birds burst forth in song, and the joy, the rapture, the ecstasy of it was beyond belief; and was so eloquent and so moving, withal, that it was plain it was an act of worship. With the first note of those birds Joan cast herself upon her knees, and bent her head low and crossed her hands upon her breast.

She had not seen the shadow yet. Had the song of the birds told her it was coming? It had that look to me. Then the like of this must have happened before. Yes, there might be no doubt of that.

The shadow approached Joan slowly; the extremity of it reached her, flowed over her, clothed her in its awful splendor. In that immortal light her face, only humanly beautiful before, became divine; flooded with that transforming glory her mean peasant habit was become like to the raiment of the sun-clothed children of God as we see them thronging the terraces of the Throne in our dreams and imaginings.

Presently she rose and stood, with her head still bowed a little, and with her arms down and the ends of her fingers lightly laced together in front of her; and standing so, all drenched with that wonderful light, and yet apparently not knowing it, she seemed to listen—but I heard nothing. After a little she raised her head, and looked up as one might look up toward the face of a giant, and then clasped her hands and lifted them high, imploringly, and began to plead. I heard some of the words. I heard her say—

"But I am so young! oh, so young to leave my mother and my home, and go out into the strange world to undertake a thing so great! Ah, how can I talk with men, be comrade with men?—soldiers! It would give me over to insult, and rude usage, and contempt. How can I go to the great wars, and lead armies?—I a girl, and ignorant of such things, knowing nothing of arms, nor how to mount a horse, nor ride it. . . . Yet—if it is commanded—"

Her voice sank a little, and was broken by sobs, and I made out no more of her words. Then I came to myself. I reflected that I had been intruding upon a mystery of God—and what might my punishment be? I was afraid, and went deeper into the wood. Then I carved a mark in the bark of a tree, saying to myself, it may be that I am dreaming and have not seen this vision at all. I will come again, when I know that I am awake and not dreaming, and see if this mark is still here; then I shall know.

Chapter VII

I HEARD my name called. It was Joan's voice. It startled me, for how could she know I was there? I said to myself, it is part of the dream; it is all dream—voice, vision and all; the fairies have done this. So I crossed myself and pronounced the name of God, to break the enchantment. I knew I was awake now and free from the spell, for no spell can withstand this exorcism. Then I heard my name called again, and I stepped at once from under cover, and there indeed was Joan, but not looking as she had looked in the dream. For she was not crying, now, but was looking as she had used to look a year and a half before, when her heart was light and her spirits high. Her old-time energy and fire were back, and a something like exaltation showed itself in her face and bearing. It was almost as if she had been in a trance all that time and had come awake again. Really, it was just as if she had been away and lost, and was come back to us at last; and I was so glad that I felt like running to call everybody and have them flock around her and give her welcome. I ran to her excited, and said—

"Ah, Joan, I've got such a wonderful thing to tell you about! You would never imagine it. I've had a dream, and in the dream I saw you right here where you are standing now, and—"

But she put up her hand and said—

"It was not a dream."

It gave me a shock, and I began to feel afraid again.

"Not a dream?" I said, "how can you know about it, Joan?"

"Are you dreaming now?"

"I—I suppose not. I think I am not."

"Indeed you are not. I know you are not. And you were not dreaming when you cut the mark in the tree."

I felt myself turning cold with fright, for now I knew of a certainty that I had not been dreaming, but had really been in the presence of a dread something not of this world. Then I remembered that my sinful feet were upon holy ground—the ground where that celestial shadow had rested. I moved

602

quickly away, smitten to the bones with fear. Joan followed,
and said—

"Do not be afraid; indeed there is no need. Come with me.
We will sit by the spring and I will tell you all my secret."

When she was ready to begin, I checked her and said—

"First tell me this. You could not see me in the wood; how
did you know I cut a mark in the tree?"

"Wait a little; I will soon come to that; then you will see."

"But tell me one thing now; what was that awful shadow
that I saw?"

"I will tell you, but do not be disturbed; you are not in
danger. It was the shadow of an archangel—Michael, the
chief and lord of the armies of heaven."

I could but cross myself and tremble for having polluted
that ground with my feet.

"You were not afraid, Joan? Did you see his face—did you
see his form?"

"Yes; I was not afraid, because this was not the first time. I
was afraid the first time."

"When was that, Joan?"

"It is nearly three years ago, now."

"So long? Have you seen him many times?"

"Yes, many times."

"It is this, then, that has changed you; it was this that made
you thoughtful and not as you were before. I see it now. Why
did you not tell us about it?"

"It was not permitted. It is permitted now, and soon I shall
tell all. But only you, now. It must remain a secret a few days
still."

"Has none seen that white shadow before but me?"

"No one. It has fallen upon me before when you and others
were present, but none could see it. To-day it has been otherwise, and I was told why; but it will not be visible again to
any."

"It was a sign to me, then—and a sign with a meaning of
some kind?"

"Yes, but I may not speak of that."

"Strange—that that dazzling light could rest upon an object before one's eyes and not be visible."

"With it comes speech, also. Several saints come, attended

by myriads of angels, and they speak to me; I hear their voices, but others do not. They are very dear to me—my Voices; that is what I call them to myself."

"Joan, what do they tell you?"

"All manner of things—about France I mean."

"What things have they been used to tell you?"

She sighed, and said—

"Disasters—only disasters, and misfortunes, and humiliations. There was naught else to foretell."

"They spoke of them to you *beforehand*?"

"Yes. So that I knew what was going to happen before it happened. It made me grave—as you saw. It could not be otherwise. But always there was a word of hope, too. More than that: France was to be rescued, and made great and free again. But how and by whom—that was not told. Not until to-day." As she said those last words a sudden deep glow shone in her eyes, which I was to see there many times in after-days when the bugles sounded the charge and learn to call it the battle-light. Her breast heaved, and the color rose in her face. "But to-day I know. God has chosen the meanest of His creatures for this work; and by His command, and in His protection, and by His strength, not mine, I am to lead His armies, and win back France, and set the crown upon the head of His servant that is Dauphin and shall be King."

I was amazed, and said—

"You, Joan? You, a child, lead armies?"

"Yes. For one little moment or two the thought crushed me; for it is as you say—I am only a child; a child and ignorant—ignorant of everything that pertains to war, and not fitted for the rough life of camps and the companionship of soldiers. But those weak moments passed; they will not come again. I am enlisted, I will not turn back, God helping me, till the English grip is loosed from the throat of France. My Voices have never told me lies, they have not lied to-day. They say I am to go to Robert de Baudricourt, governor of Vaucouleurs, and he will give me men-at-arms for escort and send me to the King. A year from now a blow will be struck which will be the beginning of the end, and the end will follow swiftly."

"Where will it be struck?"

"My Voices have not said; nor what will happen this present year, before it is struck. It is appointed me to strike it, that is all I know; and follow it with others, sharp and swift, undoing in ten weeks England's long years of costly labor, and setting the crown upon the Dauphin's head—for such is God's will; my Voices have said it, and shall I doubt it? No; it will be as they have said, for they say only that which is true."

These were tremendous sayings. They were impossibilities to my reason, but to my heart they rang true; and so, while my reason doubted, my heart believed—believed, and held fast to its belief from that day. Presently I said—

"Joan, I believe the things which you have said, and now I am glad that I am to march with you to the great wars—that is, if it is with you I am to march when I go."

She looked surprised, and said—

"It is true that you will be with me when I go to the wars, but how did you know?"

"I shall march with you, and so also will Jean and Pierre, but not Jacques."

"All true—it is so ordered, as was revealed to me lately, but I did not know until to-day that the marching would be with me, or that I should march at all. How did you know these things?"

I told her when it was that she had said them. But she did not remember about it. So then I knew that she had been asleep, or in a trance or an ecstasy of some kind, at that time. She bade me keep these and the other revelations to myself for the present, and I said I would, and kept the faith I promised.

None who met Joan that day failed to notice the change that had come over her. She moved and spoke with energy and decision; there was a strange new fire in her eye, and also a something wholly new and remarkable in her carriage and in the set of her head. This new light in the eye and this new bearing were born of the authority and leadership which had this day been vested in her by the decree of God, and they asserted that authority as plainly as speech could have done it, yet without ostentation or bravado. This calm consciousness of command, and calm unconscious outward expression of it, remained with her thenceforth until her mission was accomplished.

Like the other villagers, she had always accorded me the deference due my rank; but now, without word said on either side, she and I changed places: she gave orders, not suggestions, I received them with the deference due a superior, and obeyed them without comment. In the evening she said to me—

"I leave before dawn. No one will know it but you. I go to speak with the governor of Vaucouleurs as commanded, who will despise me and treat me rudely, and perhaps refuse my prayer at this time. I go first to Burey, to persuade my uncle Laxart to go with me, it not being meet that I go alone. I may need you in Vaucouleurs; for if the governor will not receive me I will dictate a letter to him, and so must have some one by me who knows the art of how to write and spell the words. You will go from here to-morrow in the afternoon, and remain in Vaucouleurs until I need you."

I said I would obey, and she went her way. You see how clear a head she had, and what a just and level judgment. She did not order me to go with her; no, she would not subject her good name to gossiping remark. She knew that the governor, being a noble, would grant me, another noble, audience; but no, you see, she would not have that, either. A poor peasant girl presenting a petition through a young nobleman—how would that look? She always protected her modesty from hurt; and so, for reward, she carried her good name unsmirched to the end. I knew what I must do, now, if I would have her approval: go to Vaucouleurs, keep out of her sight, and be ready when wanted.

I went the next afternoon, and took an obscure lodging; the next day I called at the castle and paid my respects to the governor, who invited me to dine with him at noon of the following day. He was an ideal soldier of the time; tall, brawny, gray-headed, rough, full of strange oaths acquired here and there and yonder in the wars and treasured as if they were decorations. He had been used to the camp all his life, and to his notion war was God's best gift to man. He had his steel cuirass on, and wore boots that came above his knees, and was equipped with a huge sword; and when I looked at this martial figure, and heard the marvellous oaths, and guessed how little of poetry and sentiment might be looked for in this quarter, I hoped the little peasant girl would not get the privilege of confronting this battery, but would have to content herself with the dictated letter.

I came again to the castle the next day at noon, and was conducted to the great dining-hall and seated by the side of the governor at a small table which was raised a couple of steps higher than the general table. At the small table sat several other guests besides myself, and at the general table sat the chief officers of the garrison. At the entrance door stood a guard of halberdiers, in morion and breastplate.

As for talk, there was but one topic, of course—the desperate situation of France. There was a rumor, some one said, that Salisbury was making preparations to march against Orleans. It raised a turmoil of excited conversation, and opinions fell thick and fast. Some believed he would march at once, others that he could not accomplish the investment before fall, others that the siege would be long, and bravely contested; but upon one thing all voices agreed: that Orleans must eventually fall, and with it France. With that, the prolonged discussion ended, and there was silence. Every man seemed to sink himself in his own thoughts, and to forget where he was. This sudden and profound stillness where before had been so much animation, was impressive and solemn. Now came a servant and whispered something to the governor, who said—

"Would talk with *me*?"

"Yes, your Excellency."

"H'm! A strange idea, certainly. Bring them in."

It was Joan and her uncle Laxart. At the spectacle of the great people the courage oozed out of the poor old peasant and he stopped midway and would come no further, but remained there with his red nightcap crushed in his hands and bowing humbly here, there, and everywhere, stupefied with embarrassment and fear. But Joan came steadily forward, erect and self-possessed, and stood before the governor. She recognized me, but in no way indicated it. There was a buzz of admiration, even the governor contributing to it, for I heard him mutter, "By God's grace, it is a beautiful creature!" He inspected her critically a moment or two, then said—

"Well, what is your errand, my child?"

"My message is to you, Robert de Baudricourt, governor of Vaucouleurs, and it is this: that you will send and tell the Dauphin to wait and not give battle to his enemies, for God will presently send him help."

This strange speech amazed the company, and many murmured, "The poor young thing is demented." The governor scowled, and said—

"What nonsense is this? The King—or the Dauphin, as you call him—needs no message of *that* sort. He will wait, give yourself no uneasiness as to that. What further do you desire to say to me?"

"This. To beg that you will give me an escort of men-at-arms and send me to the Dauphin."

"What for?"

"That he may make me his general, for it is appointed that I shall drive the English out of France, and set the crown upon his head."

"What—you? Why, you are but a child!"

"Yet am I appointed to do it, nevertheless."

"Indeed? And when will all this happen?"

"Next year he will be crowned, and after will remain master of France."

There was a great and general burst of laughter, and when it had subsided the governor said—

"Who has sent you with these extravagant messages?"

"My Lord."

"What Lord?"

"The King of Heaven."

Many murmured, "Ah, poor thing, poor thing!" and others, "Ah, her mind is but a wreck!" The governor hailed Laxart, and said—

"Harkye!—take this mad child home and whip her soundly. That is the best cure for her ailment."

As Joan was moving away she turned and said, with simplicity—

"You refuse me the soldiers, I know not why, for it is my

Lord that has commanded you. Yes, it is He that has made the command; therefore must I come again, and yet again; then I shall have the men-at-arms."

There was a great deal of wondering talk, after she was gone; and the guards and servants passed the talk to the town, the town passed it to the country; Domremy was already buzzing with it when we got back.

Chapter VIII

HUMAN nature is the same everywhere: it deifies success, it has nothing but scorn for defeat. The village considered that Joan had disgraced it with her grotesque performance and its ridiculous failure; so all the tongues were busy with the matter, and as bilious and bitter as they were busy; insomuch that if the tongues had been teeth she would not have survived her persecutions. Those persons who did not scold, did what was worse and harder to bear; for they ridiculed her, and mocked at her, and ceased neither day nor night from their witticisms and jeerings and laughter. Haumette and Little Mengette and I stood by her, but the storm was too strong for her other friends, and they avoided her, being ashamed to be seen with her because she was so unpopular, and because of the sting of the taunts that assailed them on her account. She shed tears in secret, but none in public. In public she carried herself with serenity, and showed no distress, nor any resentment—conduct which should have softened the feeling against her, but it did not. Her father was so incensed that he could not talk in measured terms about her wild project of going to the wars like a man. He had dreamed of her doing such a thing, some time before, and now he remembered that dream with apprehension and anger, and said that rather than see her unsex herself and go away with the armies, he would require her brothers to drown her; and that if they should refuse, he would do it with his own hands.

But none of these things shook her purpose in the least. Her parents kept a strict watch upon her to keep her from leaving the village, but she said her time was not yet; that when the time to go was come she should know it, and then the keepers would watch in vain.

The summer wasted along; and when it was seen that her purpose continued steadfast, the parents were glad of a chance which finally offered itself for bringing her projects to an end through marriage. The Paladin had the effrontery to

pretend that she had engaged herself to him several years before, and now he claimed a ratification of the engagement.

She said his statement was not true, and refused to marry
him. She was cited to appear before the ecclesiastical court at
Toul to answer for her perversity; when she declined to have
counsel, and elected to conduct her case herself, her parents
and all her ill-wishers rejoiced, and looked upon her as already
defeated. And that was natural enough; for who would expect
that an ignorant peasant girl of sixteen would be otherwise
than frightened and tongue-tied when standing for the first
time in presence of the practised doctors of the law, and surrounded by the cold solemnities of a court? Yet all these people were mistaken. They flocked to Toul to see and enjoy this
fright and embarrassment and defeat, and they had their trouble for their pains. She was modest, tranquil, and quite at her
ease. She called no witnesses, saying she would content herself with examining the witnesses for the prosecution. When
they had testified, she rose and reviewed their testimony in a
few words, pronounced it vague, confused, and of no force,
then she placed the Paladin again on the stand and began to
search him. His previous testimony went rag by rag to ruin
under her ingenious hands, until at last he stood bare, so to
speak, he that had come so richly clothed in fraud and false-
hood. His counsel began an argument, but the court declined
to hear it, and threw out the case, adding a few words of
grave compliment for Joan, and referring to her as "this marvellous child."

After this victory, with this high praise from so imposing a
source added, the fickle village turned again, and gave Joan
countenance, compliment, and peace. Her mother took her
back to her heart, and even her father relented and said he
was proud of her. But the time hung heavy on her hands,
nevertheless, for the siege of Orleans was begun, the clouds
lowered darker and darker over France, and still her Voices
said wait, and gave her no direct commands. The winter set
in, and wore tediously along; but at last there was a change.

Chapter I

T HE 5th of January, 1429, Joan came to me with her uncle
Laxart, and said—

"The time is come. My Voices are not vague, now, but
clear, and they have told me what to do. In two months I
shall be with the Dauphin."

Her spirits were high, and her bearing martial. I caught the
infection and felt a great impulse stirring in me that was like
what one feels when he hears the roll of the drums and the
tramp of marching men.

"I believe it," I said.

"I also believe it," said Laxart. "If she had told me before,
that she was commanded of God to rescue France, I should
not have believed; I should have let her seek the governor by
her own ways and held myself clear of meddling in the matter, not doubting she was mad. But I have seen her stand
before those nobles and mighty men unafraid, and say her
say; and she had not been able to do that but by the help of
God. That, I know. Therefore with all humbleness I am at her
command, to do with me as she will."

"My uncle is very good to me," Joan said. "I sent and asked
him to come and persuade my mother to let him take me
home with him to tend his wife, who is not well. It is arranged, and we go at dawn to-morrow. From his house I
shall go soon to Vaucouleurs, and wait and strive until my
prayer is granted. Who were the two cavaliers who sat to your
left at the governor's table that day?"

"One was the Sieur Jean de Novelonpont de Metz, the
other the Sieur Bertrand de Poulengy."

"Good metal—good metal, both. I marked them for men
of mine. . . . What is it I see in your face? Doubt?"

I was teaching myself to speak the truth to her, not trim-
ming it or polishing it; so I said—

"They considered you out of your head, and said so. It is

true they pitied you for being in such misfortune, but still they held you to be mad."

This did not seem to trouble her in any way or wound her. She only said—

"The wise change their minds when they perceive that they have been in error. These will. They will march with me. I shall see them presently. . . . You seem to doubt again? Do you doubt?"

"N-no. Not now. I was remembering that it was a year ago, and that they did not belong there, but only chanced to stop a day on their journey."

"They will come again. But as to matters now in hand; I came to leave with you some instructions. You will follow me in a few days. Order your affairs, for you will be absent long."

"Will Jean and Pierre go with me?"

"No; they would refuse now, but presently they will come, and with them they will bring my parents' blessing, and likewise their consent that I take up my mission. I shall be stronger, then—stronger for that; for lack of it I am weak, now." She paused a little while, and the tears gathered in her eyes; then she went on: "I would say good-by to Little Mengette. Bring her outside the village at dawn; she must go with me a little of the way—"

"And Haumette?"

She broke down and began to cry, saying—

"No, oh, no—she is too dear to me, I could not bear it, knowing I should never look upon her face again."

Next morning I brought Mengette, and we four walked along the road in the cold dawn till the village was far behind; then the two girls said their good-byes, clinging about each other's neck, and pouring out their grief in loving words and tears, a pitiful sight to see. And Joan took one long look back upon the distant village, and the Fairy Tree, and the oak forest, and the flowery plain, and the river, as if she was trying to print these scenes on her memory so that they would abide there always and not fade, for she knew she would not see them any more in this life; then she turned, and went from us, sobbing bitterly. It was her birthday and mine. She was seventeen years old.

Chapter II

AFTER a few days, Laxart took Joan to Vaucouleurs, and found lodging and guardianship for her with Catherine Royer, a wheelwright's wife, an honest and good woman. Joan went to mass regularly, she helped do the house-work, earning her keep in that way, and if any wished to talk with her about her mission—and many did—she talked freely, making no concealments regarding the matter now. I was soon housed near by, and witnessed the effects which followed. At once the tidings spread that a young girl was come who was appointed of God to save France. The common people flocked in crowds to look at her and speak with her, and her fair young loveliness won the half of their belief, and her deep earnestness and transparent sincerity won the other half. The well-to-do remained away and scoffed, but that is their way.

Next, a prophecy of Merlin's, more than eight hundred years old, was called to mind, which said that in a far future time France would be lost by a woman and restored by a woman. France was now, for the first time, lost—and by a woman, Isabel of Bavaria, her base Queen; doubtless this fair and pure young girl was commissioned of Heaven to complete the prophecy.

This gave the growing interest a new and powerful impulse; the excitement rose higher and higher, and hope and faith along with it; and so from Vaucouleurs wave after wave of this inspiring enthusiasm flowed out over the land, far and wide, invading all the villages and refreshing and revivifying the perishing children of France; and from these villages came people who wanted to see for themselves, hear for themselves; and they did see and hear, and believe. They filled the town; they more than filled it; inns and lodgings were packed, and yet half of the inflow had to go without shelter. And still they came, winter as it was, for when a man's soul is starving, what does he care for meat and roof so he can but get that nobler hunger fed? Day after day, and still day after day, the great tide rose. Domremy was dazed, amazed, stupefied, and said to itself, "Was this world-wonder in our familiar midst all these years and we too dull to see it?" Jean and Pierre went out from the village stared at and envied like the great and fortunate of the earth, and their progress to Vaucouleurs was like a triumph, all the country-side flocking to see and salute the brothers of one with whom angels had spoken face to face, and into whose hands by command of God they had delivered the destinies of France.

The brothers brought the parents' blessing and Godspeed to Joan, and their promise to bring it to her in person later; and so, with this culminating happiness in her heart and the high hope it inspired, she went and confronted the governor again. But he was no more tractable than he had been before. He refused to send her to the King. She was disappointed, but in no degree discouraged. She said—

"I must still come to you until I get the men-at-arms; for so it is commanded, and I may not disobey. I must go to the Dauphin, though I go on my knees."

I and the two brothers were with Joan daily, to see the people that came and hear what they said; and one day, sure enough, the Sieur Jean de Metz came. He talked with her in a petting and playful way, as one talks with children, and said—

"What are you doing here, my little maid? Will they drive the King out of France, and shall we all turn English?"

She answered him in her tranquil, serious way—

"I am come to bid Robert de Baudricourt take or send me to the King, but he does not heed my words."

"Ah, you have an admirable persistence, truly; a whole year has not turned you from your wish. I saw you when you came before."

Joan said, as tranquilly as before—

"It is not a wish, it is a purpose. He will grant it. I can wait."

"Ah, perhaps it will not be wise to make too sure of *that*, my child. These governors are stubborn people to deal with. In case he shall not grant your prayer—"

"He will grant it. He must. It is not matter of choice."

The gentleman's playful mood began to disappear—one could see that, by his face. Joan's earnestness was affecting

him. It always happened that people who began in jest with
her, ended by being in earnest. They soon began to perceive
depths in her that they had not suspected; and then her manifest sincerity and the rocklike steadfastness of her convictions
were forces which cowed levity, and it could not maintain its
self-respect in their presence. The Sieur de Metz was thoughtful for a moment or two, then he began, quite soberly—

"Is it necessary that you go to the King soon?—that is, I
mean—"

"Before Mid-Lent, even though I wear away my legs to the
knees!"

She said it with that sort of repressed fieriness that means
so much when a person's heart is in a thing. You could see the
response in that nobleman's face; you could see his eye light
up; there was sympathy there. He said, most earnestly—

"God knows I think you should have the men-at-arms, and
that somewhat would come of it. What is it that you would
do? What is your hope and purpose?"

"To rescue France. And it is appointed that I shall do it.
For no one else in the world, neither kings, nor dukes, nor
any other, can recover the kingdom of France, and there is no
help but in me."

The words had a pleading and pathetic sound, and they
touched that good nobleman. I saw it plainly. Joan dropped
her voice a little, and said: "But indeed I would rather spin
with my poor mother, for this is not my calling; but I must
go and do it, for it is my Lord's will."

"Who is your Lord?"

"He is God."

Then the Sieur de Metz, following the impressive old feudal fashion, knelt and laid his hands within Joan's, in sign of
fealty, and made oath that by God's help he himself would
take her to the King.

The next day came the Sieur Bertrand de Poulengy, and he
also pledged his oath and knightly honor to abide with her
and follow whithersoever she might lead.

This day, too, toward evening, a great rumor went flying
abroad through the town—namely, that the very governor
himself was going to visit the young girl in her humble lodgings. So in the morning the streets and lanes were packed

with people waiting to see if this strange thing would indeed happen. And happen it did. The governor rode in state, attended by his guards, and the news of it went everywhere, and made a great sensation, and modified the scoffings of the people of quality and raised Joan's credit higher than ever.

The governor had made up his mind to one thing: Joan was either a witch or a saint, and he meant to find out which it was. So he brought a priest with him to exorcise the devil that was in her in case there was one there. The priest performed his office, but found no devil. He merely hurt Joan's feelings and offended her piety without need, for he had already confessed her before this, and should have known, if he knew anything, that devils cannot abide the confessional, but utter cries of anguish and the most profane and furious cursings whenever they are confronted with that holy office.

The governor went away troubled and full of thought, and not knowing what to do. And while he pondered and studied, several days went by and the 14th of February was come. Then Joan went to the castle and said—

"In God's name, Robert de Baudricourt, you are too slow about sending me, and have caused damage thereby, for this day the Dauphin's cause has lost a battle near Orleans, and will suffer yet greater injury if you do not send me to him soon."

The governor was perplexed by this speech, and said—

"To-day, child, *to-day*? How can you know what has happened in that region to-day? It would take eight or ten days for the word to come."

"My Voices have brought the word to me, and it is true. A battle was lost to-day, and you are in fault to delay me so."

The governor walked the floor a while, talking within himself, but letting a great oath fall outside now and then; and finally he said—

"Harkye! go in peace, and wait. If it shall turn out as you say, I will give you the letter and send you to the King, and not otherwise."

Joan said with fervor—

"Now God be thanked, these waiting days are almost done. In nine days you will fetch me the letter."

Already the people of Vaucouleurs had given her a horse and had armed and equipped her as a soldier. She got no chance to try the horse and see if she could ride it, for her great first duty was to abide at her post and lift up the hopes and spirits of all who would come to talk with her, and prepare them to help in the rescue and regeneration of the kingdom. This occupied every waking moment she had. But it was no matter. There was nothing she could not learn—and in the briefest time, too. Her horse would find this out in the first hour. Meantime the brothers and I took the horse in turn and began to learn to ride. And we had teaching in the use of the sword and other arms, also.

On the 20th Joan called her small army together—the two knights and her two brothers and me—for a private council of war. No, it was not a council, that is not the right name, for she did not consult with us, she merely gave us orders. She mapped out the course she would travel toward the King, and did it like a person perfectly versed in geography; and this itinerary of daily marches was so arranged as to avoid here and there peculiarly dangerous regions by flank movements—which showed that she knew her political geography as intimately as she knew her physical geography; yet she had never had a day's schooling, of course, and was without education. I was astonished, but thought her Voices must have taught her. But upon reflection I saw that this was not so. By her references to what this and that and the other person had told her, I perceived that she had been diligently questioning those crowds of visiting strangers, and that out of them she had patiently dug all this mass of invaluable knowledge. The two knights were filled with wonder at her good sense and sagacity.

She commanded us to make preparations to travel by night and sleep by day in concealment, as almost the whole of our long journey would be through the enemy's country.

Also, she commanded that we should keep the date of our departure a secret, since she meant to get away unobserved. Otherwise we should be sent off with a grand demonstration which would advertise us to the enemy, and we should be ambushed and captured somewhere. Finally she said—

"Nothing remains, now, but that I confide to you the date of our departure, so that you may make all needful preparation in time, leaving nothing to be done in haste and badly at the last moment. We march the 23d, at eleven of the clock at night."

Then we were dismissed. The two knights were startled—yes, and troubled; and the Sieur Bertrand said—

"Even if the governor shall really furnish the letter and the escort, he still may not do it in time to meet the date she has chosen. Then how can she venture to name that date? It is a great risk—a great risk to select and decide upon the date, in this state of uncertainty."

I said—

"Since she has named the 23d, we may trust her. The Voices have told her, I think. We shall do best to obey."

We did obey. Joan's parents were notified to come before the 23d, but prudence forbade that they be told why this limit was named.

All day, the 23d, she glanced up wistfully whenever new bodies of strangers entered the house, but her parents did not appear. Still she was not discouraged, but hoped on. But when night fell, at last, her hopes perished, and the tears came; however, she dashed them away, and said—

"It was to be so, no doubt; no doubt it was so ordered; I must bear it, and will."

De Metz tried to comfort her by saying—

"The governor sends no word; it may be that they will come to-morrow, and—"

He got no further, for she interrupted him, saying—

"To what good end? We start at eleven to-night."

And it was so. At ten the governor came, with his guard and torch-bearers, and delivered to her a mounted escort of men-at-arms, with horses and equipments for me and for the brothers, and gave Joan a letter to the King. Then he took off his sword, and belted it about her waist with his own hands, and said—

"You said true, child. The battle *was* lost, on the day you said. So I have kept my word. Now go—come of it what may."

Joan gave him thanks, and he went his way.

The lost battle was the famous disaster that is called in history the Battle of the Herrings.

All the lights in the house were at once put out, and a little while after, when the streets had become dark and still, we crept stealthily through them and out at the western gate and rode away under whip and spur.

Chapter III

WE WERE twenty-five strong, and well equipped. We rode in double file, Joan and her brothers in the centre of the column, with Jean de Metz at the head of it and the Sieur Bertrand at its extreme rear. The knights were so placed to prevent desertions—for the present. In two or three hours we should be in the enemy's country, and then none would venture to desert. By-and-by we began to hear groans and sobs and execrations from different points along the line, and upon inquiry found that six of our men were peasants who had never ridden a horse before, and were finding it very difficult to stay in their saddles, and moreover were now beginning to suffer considerable bodily torture. They had been seized by the governor at the last moment and pressed into the service to make up the tale, and he had placed a veteran alongside of each with orders to help him stick to the saddle, and kill him if he tried to desert.

These poor devils had kept quiet as long as they could, but their physical miseries were become so sharp by this time that they were obliged to give them vent. But we were within the enemy's country now, so there was no help for them, they must continue the march, though Joan said that if they chose to take the risk they might depart. They preferred to stay with us. We modified our pace now, and moved cautiously, and the new men were warned to keep their sorrows to themselves and not get the command into danger with their curses and lamentations.

Toward dawn we rode deep into a forest, and soon all but the sentries were sound asleep in spite of the cold ground and the frosty air.

I woke at noon out of such a solid and stupefying sleep that at first my wits were all astray, and I did not know where I was nor what had been happening. Then my senses cleared, and I remembered. As I lay there thinking over the strange events of the past month or two the thought came into my mind, greatly surprising me, that one of Joan's prophecies had failed; for where were Noël and the Paladin, who were to join us at the eleventh hour? By this time, you see, I had gotten used to expecting everything Joan said to come true. So, being disturbed and troubled by these thoughts, I opened my eyes. Well, there stood the Paladin leaning against a tree and looking down on me! How often that happens: you think of a person, or speak of a person, and there he stands before you, and you not dreaming he is near. It looks as if his *being* near is really the thing that makes you think of him, and not just an accident, as people imagine. Well, be that as it may, there was the Paladin, anyway, looking down in my face and waiting for me to wake. I was ever so glad to see him, and jumped up and shook him by the hand, and led him a little way from the camp—he limping like a cripple—and told him to sit down, and said—

"Now, where have you dropped down from? And how did you happen to light in this place? And what do the soldier-clothes mean? Tell me all about it."

He answered—

"I marched with you last night."

"No!" (To myself I said, "The prophecy has not all failed—half of it has come true.")

"Yes, I did. I hurried up from Domremy to join, and was within a half a minute of being too late. In fact, I was too late, but I begged so hard that the governor was touched by my brave devotion to my country's cause—those are the words he used—and so he yielded, and allowed me to come."

I thought to myself, this is a lie, he is one of those six the governor recruited by force at the last moment; I know it, for Joan's prophecy said he would join at the eleventh hour, but not by his own desire. Then I said aloud—

"I am glad you came; it is a noble cause, and one should not sit at home in times like these."

"Sit at home! I could no more do it than the thunder-stone could stay hid in the clouds when the storm calls it."

"That is the right talk. It sounds like you."

That pleased him.

"I'm glad you know me. Some don't. But they will, presently. They will know me well enough before I get done with this war."

"That is what I think. I believe that wherever danger confronts you you will make yourself conspicuous."

He was charmed with this speech, and it swelled him up like a bladder. He said—

"If I know myself—and I think I do—my performances in this campaign will give you occasion more than once to remember those words."

"I were a fool to doubt it. That, I know."

"I shall not be at my best, being but a common soldier; still, the country will hear of me. If I were where I belong; if I were in the place of La Hire, or Saintrailles, or the Bastard of Orleans—well, I say nothing, I am not of the talking kind, like Noël Rainguesson and his sort, I thank God. But it will be *something*, I take it—a novelty in this world, I should say—to raise the fame of a private soldier above theirs, and extinguish the glory of their names with its shadow."

"Why, look here, my friend," I said, "do you know that you have hit out a most remarkable idea there? Do you realize the gigantic proportions of it? For look you: to be a general of vast renown, what is that? Nothing—history is clogged and confused with them; one cannot keep their names in his memory, there are so many. But a common soldier of supreme renown—why, he would stand alone! He would be the one moon in a firmament of mustard-seed stars; his name would outlast the human race! My friend, who gave you that idea?"

He was ready to burst with happiness, but he suppressed betrayal of it as well as he could. He simply waved the compliment aside with his hand and said, with complacency—

"It is nothing. I have them often—ideas like that—and even greater ones. I do not consider this one much."

"You astonish me; you do indeed. So it is really your own?"

"Quite. And there is plenty more where it came from"—tapping his head with his finger, and taking occasion at the same time to cant his morion over his right ear, which gave him a very self-satisfied air—"I do not need to borrow my ideas, like Noël Rainguesson."

"Speaking of Noël, when did you see him last?"

"Half an hour ago. He is sleeping yonder like a corpse. Rode with us last night."

I felt a great upleap in my heart, and said to myself, now I am at rest and glad; I will never doubt her prophecies again. Then I said aloud—

"It gives me joy. It makes me proud of our village. There is no keeping our lion-hearts at home in these great times, I see that."

"Lion-heart! Who—that baby? Why, he begged like a dog to be let off. Cried, and said he wanted to go to his mother. Him a lion-heart!—that tumble-bug!"

"Dear me, why I supposed he volunteered, of course. Didn't he?"

"Oh yes, volunteered the way people do to the headsman. Why, when he found I was coming up from Domremy to volunteer, he asked me to let him come along in my protection, and see the crowds and the excitement. Well, we arrived and saw the torches filing out at the Castle, and ran there, and the governor had him seized, along with four more, and he begged to be let off, and I begged for his place, and at last the governor allowed me to join, but wouldn't let Noël off, because he was disgusted with him he was such a cry-baby. Yes, and much good *he'll* do the King's service: he'll eat for six and run for sixteen. I hate a pigmy with half a heart and nine stomachs!"

"Why, this is very surprising news to me, and I am sorry and disappointed to hear it. I thought he was a very manly fellow."

The Paladin gave me an outraged look, and said:

"I don't see how you can talk like that, I'm sure I don't. I don't see how you could have got such a notion. I don't dislike him, and I'm not saying these things out of prejudice, for I don't allow myself to have prejudices against people. I like him, and have always comraded with him from the cradle, but he must allow me to speak my mind about his faults, and I am willing he shall speak his about mine, if I have any. And true enough, maybe I have; but I reckon they'll bear inspection—I have that idea, anyway. A manly fellow! You should have heard him whine and wail and swear, last night, because the saddle hurt him. Why didn't the saddle hurt me? Pooh—I was as much at home in it as if I had been born there. And yet it was the first time I was ever on a horse. All those old soldiers admired my riding; they said they had never seen anything like it. But him—why, they had to hold him on, all the time."

An odor as of breakfast came stealing through the wood; the Paladin unconsciously inflated his nostrils in lustful response, and got up and limped painfully away, saying he must go and look to his horse.

At bottom he was all right and a good-hearted giant, without any harm in him, for it is no harm to bark, if one stops there and does not bite, and it is no harm to be an ass, if one is content to bray and not kick. If this vast structure of brawn and muscle and vanity and foolishness seemed to have a libellous tongue, what of it? There was no malice behind it; and besides, the defect was not of his own creation; it was the work of Noël Rainguesson, who had nurtured it, fostered it, built it up and perfected it, for the entertainment he got out of it. His careless light heart had to have somebody to nag and chaff and make fun of, the Paladin had only needed development in order to meet its requirements, consequently the development was taken in hand and diligently attended to and looked after, gnat-and-bull fashion, for years, to the neglect and damage of far more important concerns. The result was an unqualified success. Noël prized the society of the Paladin above everybody else's; the Paladin preferred anybody's to Noël's. The big fellow was often seen with the little fellow, but it was for the same reason that the bull is often seen with the gnat.

With the first opportunity, I had a talk with Noël. I welcomed him to our expedition, and said—

"It was fine and brave of you to volunteer, Noël."

His eye twinkled, and he answered—

"Yes, it was rather fine I think. Still, the credit doesn't all belong to me; I had help."

"Who helped you?"

"The governor."

"How?"

"Well, I'll tell you the whole thing. I came up from Domremy to see the crowds and the general show, for I hadn't ever had any experience of such things, of course, and this was a great opportunity; but I hadn't any mind to volunteer. I overtook the Paladin on the road and let him have my company the rest of the way, although he did not want it and said so; and while we were gawking and blinking in the glare of the governor's torches they seized us and four more and added us to the escort, and that is really how I came to volunteer. But after all, I wasn't sorry, remembering how dull life would have been in the village without the Paladin."

"How did he feel about it? Was he satisfied?"

"I think he was glad."

"Why?"

"Because he said he wasn't. He was taken by surprise, you see, and it is not likely that he could tell the truth without preparation. Not that he would have prepared, if he had had the chance, for I do not think he would. I am not charging him with that. In the same space of time that he could prepare to speak the truth, he could also prepare to lie; besides, his judgment would be cool then, and would warn him against fooling with new methods in an emergency. No, I am sure he was glad, because he said he wasn't."

"Do you think he was very glad?"

"Yes, I know he was. He begged like a slave, and bawled for his mother. He said his health was delicate, and he didn't know how to ride a horse, and knew he couldn't outlive the first march. But really he wasn't looking as delicate as he was feeling. There was a cask of wine there, a proper lift for four men. The governor's temper got afire, and he delivered an oath at him that knocked up the dust where it struck the ground, and told him to shoulder that cask or he would carve him to cutlets and send him home in a basket. The Paladin did it, and that secured his promotion to a privacy in the escort without any further debate."

"Yes, you seem to make it quite plain that he was glad to join—that is, if your premises are right that you start from. How did he stand the march last night?"

"About as I did. If he made the more noise, it was the privilege of his bulk. We stayed in our saddles because we had help. We are equally lame to-day, and if he likes to sit down, let him; I prefer to stand."

Chapter IV

W E WERE called to quarters and subjected to a searching inspection by Joan. Then she made a short little talk in which she said that even the rude business of war could be conducted better without profanity and other brutalities of speech than with them, and that she should strictly require us to remember and apply this admonition. She ordered half an hour's horsemanship-drill for the novices then, and appointed one of the veterans to conduct it. It was a ridiculous exhibition, but we learned something, and Joan was satisfied and complimented us. She did not take any instruction herself or go through the evolutions and manœuvres, but merely sat her horse like a martial little statue and looked on. That was sufficient for her, you see. She would not miss or forget a detail of the lesson, she would take it all in with her eye and her mind, and apply it afterward with as much certainty and confidence as if she had already practised it.

We now made three night-marches of twelve or thirteen leagues each, riding in peace and undisturbed, being taken for a roving band of Free Companions. Country folk were glad to have that sort of people go by without stopping. Still, they were very wearing marches, and not comfortable, for the bridges were few and the streams many, and as we had to ford them we found the water dismally cold, and afterward had to bed ourselves, still wet, on the frosty or snowy ground, and get warm as we might and sleep if we could, for it would not have been prudent to build fires. Our energies languished under these hardships and deadly fatigues, but Joan's did not. Her step kept its spring and firmness and her eye its fire. We could only wonder at this, we could not explain it.

But if we had had hard times before, I know not what to call the five nights that now followed, for the marches were as fatiguing, the baths as cold, and we were ambuscaded seven times in addition, and lost two novices and three veterans in the resulting fights. The news had leaked out and gone abroad that the inspired Virgin of Vaucouleurs was making for the King with an escort, and all the roads were being watched now.

These five nights disheartened the command a good deal. This was aggravated by a discovery which Noël made, and which he promptly made known at headquarters. Some of the men had been trying to understand why Joan continued to be alert, vigorous, and confident while the strongest men in the company were fagged with the heavy marches and exposure and were become morose and irritable. There, it shows you how men can have eyes and yet not see. All their lives those men had seen their own womenfolks hitched up with a cow and dragging the plough in the fields while the men did the driving. They had also seen other evidences that women have far more endurance and patience and fortitude than men—but what good had their seeing these things been to them? None. It had taught them nothing. They were still surprised to see a girl of seventeen bear the fatigues of war better than trained veterans of the army. Moreover, they did not reflect that a great soul, with a great purpose, can make a weak body strong and keep it so; and here was the greatest soul in the universe; but how could they know that, those dumb creatures? No, they knew nothing, and their reasonings were of a piece with their ignorance. They argued and discussed among themselves, with Noël listening, and arrived at the decision that Joan was a witch, and had her strange pluck and strength from Satan; so they made a plan to watch for a safe opportunity and take her life.

To have secret plottings of this sort going on in our midst was a very serious business, of course, and the knights asked Joan's permission to hang the plotters, but she refused without hesitancy. She said:

"Neither these men nor any others can take my life before my mission is accomplished, therefore why should I have their blood upon my hands? I will inform them of this, and also admonish them. Call them before me."

When they came she made that statement to them in a plain matter-of-fact way, and just as if the thought never entered her mind that any one could doubt it after she had given her word that it was true. The men were evidently amazed and impressed to hear her say such a thing in such a sure and confident way, for prophecies boldly uttered never fall barren on superstitious ears. Yes, this speech certainly impressed them, but her closing remark impressed them still more. It was for the ringleader, and Joan said it sorrowfully—

"It is a pity that you should plot another's death when your own is so close at hand."

That man's horse stumbled and fell on him in the first ford which we crossed that night, and he was drowned before we could help him. We had no more conspiracies.

This night was harassed with ambuscades, but we got through without having any men killed. One more night would carry us over the hostile frontier if we had good luck, and we saw the night close down with a good deal of solicitude. Always before, we had been more or less reluctant to start out into the gloom and the silence to be frozen in the fords and persecuted by the enemy, but this time we were impatient to get under way and have it over, although there was promise of more and harder fighting than any of the previous nights had furnished. Moreover, in front of us about three leagues there was a deep stream with a frail wooden bridge over it, and as a cold rain mixed with snow had been falling steadily all day we were anxious to find out whether we were in a trap or not. If the swollen stream had washed away the bridge, we might properly consider ourselves trapped and cut off from escape.

As soon as it was dark we filed out from the depths of the forest where we had been hidden and began the march. From the time that we had begun to encounter ambushes Joan had ridden at the head of the column, and she took this post now. By the time we had gone a league the rain and snow had turned to sleet, and under the impulse of the storm-wind it lashed my face like whips, and I envied Joan and the knights, who could close their visors and shut up their heads in their helmets as in a box. Now, out of the pitchy darkness and close at hand, came the sharp command—

"Halt!"

We obeyed. I made out a dim mass in front of us which might be a body of horsemen, but one could not be sure. A man rode up and said to Joan in a tone of reproof—

"Well, you have taken your time, truly. And what have you found out? Is she still behind us, or in front?"

Joan answered in a level voice—

"She is still behind."

This news softened the stranger's tone. He said—

"If you know that to be true, you have not lost your time, Captain. But are you sure? How do you know?"

"Because I have seen her."

"Seen her! Seen the Virgin herself?"

"Yes, I have been in her camp."

"Is it possible! Captain Raymond, I ask you to pardon me for speaking in that tone just now. You have performed a daring and admirable service. Where was she camped?"

"In the forest, not more than a league from here."

"Good! I was afraid we might be still behind her, but now that we know she is behind us, everything is safe. She is our game. We will hang her. You shall hang her yourself. No one has so well earned the privilege of abolishing this pestilent limb of Satan."

"I do not know how to thank you sufficiently. If we catch her, I—"

"If! I will take care of that; give yourself no uneasiness. All I want is just a look at her, to see what the imp is like that has been able to make all this noise, then you and the halter may have her. How many men has she?"

"I counted but eighteen, but she may have had two or three pickets out."

"Is that all? It won't be a mouthful for my force. Is it true that she is only a girl?"

"Yes; she is not more than seventeen."

"It passes belief! Is she robust, or slender?"

"Slender."

The officer pondered a moment or two, then he said:

"Was she preparing to break camp?"

"Not when I had my last glimpse of her."

"What was she doing?"

"She was talking quietly with an officer."

"Quietly? Not giving orders?"

"No, talking as quietly as we are now."

"That is good. She is feeling a false security. She would

have been restless and fussy else—it is the way of her sex when danger is about. As she was making no preparation to break camp,—"

"She certainly was not when I saw her last."

"—and was chatting quietly and at her ease, it means that this weather is not to her taste. Night-marching in sleet and wind is not for chits of seventeen. No; she will stay where she is. She has my thanks. We will camp, ourselves; here is as good a place as any. Let us get about it."

"If you command it—certainly. But she has two knights with her. They might force her to march, particularly if the weather should improve."

I was scared, and impatient to be getting out of this peril, and it distressed and worried me to have Joan apparently set herself to work to make delay and increase the danger—still, I thought she probably knew better than I what to do. The officer said—

"Well, in that case we are here to block the way."

"Yes, if they come this way. But if they should send out spies, and find out enough to make them want to try for the bridge through the woods? Is it best to allow the bridge to stand?"

It made me shiver to hear her.

The officer considered a while, then said:

"It might be well enough to send a force to destroy the bridge. I was intending to occupy it with the whole command, but that is not necessary now."

Joan said, tranquilly—

"With your permission, I will go and destroy it myself."

Ah, now I saw her idea, and was glad she had had the cleverness to invent it and the ability to keep her head cool and think of it in that tight place. The officer replied—

"You have it, Captain, and my thanks. With you to do it, it will be well done; I could send another in your place, but not a better."

They saluted, and we moved forward. I breathed freer. A dozen times I had imagined I heard the hoof-beats of the real Captain Raymond's troop arriving behind us, and had been sitting on pins and needles all the while that that conversation was dragging along. I breathed freer, but was still not com-

fortable, for Joan had given only the simple command, "Forward!" Consequently we moved in a walk. Moved in a dead
walk past a dim and lengthening column of enemies at our
side. The suspense was exhausting, yet it lasted but a short
while, for when the enemy's bugles sang the "Dismount!"
Joan gave the word to trot, and that was a great relief to me.
She was always at herself, you see. Before the command to
dismount had been given, somebody might have wanted the
countersign somewhere along that line if we came flying by at
speed, but now we seemed to be on our way to our allotted
camping position, so we were allowed to pass unchallenged.
The further we went the more formidable was the strength
revealed by the hostile force. Perhaps it was only a hundred or
two, but to me it seemed a thousand. When we passed the
last of these people I was thankful, and the deeper we
ploughed into the darkness beyond them the better I felt. I
came nearer and nearer to feeling good, for an hour; then we
found the bridge still standing, and I felt entirely good. We
crossed it and destroyed it, and then I felt—but I cannot describe what I felt. One has to feel it himself in order to know
what it is like.

We had expected to hear the rush of a pursuing force behind us, for we thought that the real Captain Raymond
would arrive and suggest that perhaps the troop that had
been mistaken for his belonged to the Virgin of Vaucouleurs;
but he must have been delayed seriously, for when we resumed our march beyond the river there were no sounds behind us except those which the storm was furnishing.

I said that Joan had harvested a good many compliments
intended for Captain Raymond, and that he would find nothing of a crop left but a dry stubble of reprimands when he got
back, and a commander just in the humor to superintend the
gathering of it in.

Joan said:

"It will be as you say, no doubt; for the commander took a
troop for granted, in the night and unchallenged, and would
have camped without sending a force to destroy the bridge if
he had been left unadvised, and none are so ready to find fault
with others as those who do things worthy of blame themselves."

The Sieur Bertrand was amused at Joan's naïve way of referring to her advice as if it had been a valuable present to a hostile leader who was saved by it from making a censurable blunder of omission, and then he went on to admire how ingeniously she had deceived that man and yet had not told him anything that was not the truth. This troubled Joan, and she said—

"I thought he was deceiving himself. I forbore to tell him lies, for that would have been wrong; but if my truths deceived him, perhaps that made them lies, and I am to blame. I would God I knew if I have done wrong."

She was assured that she had done right, and that in the perils and necessities of war deceptions that help one's own cause and hurt the enemy's were always permissible; but she was not quite satisfied with that, and thought that even when a great cause was in danger one ought to have the privilege of trying honorable ways first. Jean said—

"Joan, you told us yourself that you were going to Uncle Laxart's to nurse his wife, but you didn't say you were going further, yet you did go on to Vaucouleurs. There!"

"I see, now," said Joan, sorrowfully, "I told no lie, yet I deceived. I had tried all other ways first, but I could not get away, and I *had* to get away. My mission required it. I did wrong, I think, and am to blame."

She was silent a moment, turning the matter over in her mind, then she added, with quiet decision, "But the thing itself was right, and I would do it again."

It seemed an over-nice distinction, but nobody said anything. If we had known her as well as she knew herself, and as her later history revealed her to us, we should have perceived that she had a clear meaning there, and that her position was not identical with ours, as we were supposing, but occupied a higher plane. She would sacrifice herself—and her *best* self; that is, her truthfulness—to save her cause; but only that: she would not buy her *life* at that cost; whereas our war-ethics permitted the purchase of our lives, or any mere military advantage, small or great, by deception. Her saying seemed a commonplace at that time, the essence of its meaning escaping us; but one sees, now, that it contained a principle which lifted it above that and made it great and fine.

Presently the wind died down, the sleet stopped falling, and the cold was less severe. The road was become a bog, and the horses labored through it at a walk—they could do no better. As the heavy time wore on, exhaustion overcame us, and we slept in our saddles. Not even the dangers that threatened us could keep us awake.

This tenth night seemed longer than any of the others, and of course it was the hardest, because we had been accumulating fatigue from the beginning, and had more of it on hand now than at any previous time. But we were not molested again. When the dull dawn came at last we saw a river before us and we knew it was the Loire; we entered the town of Gien, and knew we were in a friendly land, with the hostiles all behind us. That was a glad morning for us.

We were a worn and bedraggled and shabby-looking troop; and still, as always, Joan was the freshest of us all, in both body and spirits. We had averaged above thirteen leagues a night, by tortuous and wretched roads. It was a remarkable march, and shows what men can do when they have a leader with a determined purpose and a resolution that never flags.

Chapter V

WE RESTED and otherwise refreshed ourselves two or three hours at Gien, but by that time the news was abroad that the young girl commissioned of God to deliver France was come; wherefore, such a press of people flocked to our quarters to get sight of her that it seemed best to seek a quieter place; so we pushed on and halted at a small village called Fierbois.

We were now within six leagues of the King, who was at the Castle of Chinon. Joan dictated a letter to him at once, and I wrote it. In it she said she had come a hundred and fifty leagues to bring him good news, and begged the privilege of delivering it in person. She added that although she had never seen him she would know him in any disguise and would point him out.

The two knights rode away at once with the letter. The troop slept all the afternoon, and after supper we felt pretty fresh and fine, especially our little group of young Domremians. We had the comfortable tap-room of the village inn to ourselves, and for the first time in ten unspeakably long days were exempt from bodings and terrors and hardships and fatiguing labors. The Paladin was suddenly become his ancient self again, and was swaggering up and down, a very monument of self-complacency. Noël Rainguesson said—

"I think it is wonderful, the way he has brought us through."

"Who?" asked Joan.

"Why, the Paladin."

The Paladin seemed not to hear.

"What had he to do with it?" asked Pierre d'Arc.

"Everything. It was nothing but Joan's confidence in his discretion that enabled her to keep up her heart. She could depend on us and on herself for valor, but discretion is the winning thing in war, after all; discretion is the rarest and loftiest of qualities, and he has got more of it than any other man in France—more of it, perhaps, than any other sixty men in France."

"Now you are getting ready to make a fool of yourself, Noël Rainguesson," said the Paladin, "and you want to coil some of that long tongue of yours around your neck and stick the end of it in your ear, then you'll be the less likely to get into trouble."

"I didn't know he had more discretion than other people," said Pierre, "for discretion argues brains, and he hasn't any more brains than the rest of us, in my opinion."

"No, you are wrong there. Discretion hasn't anything to do with brains; brains are an obstruction to it, for it does not reason, it feels. Perfect discretion means absence of brains. Discretion is a quality of the heart—solely a quality of the heart; it acts upon us through feeling. We know this because if it were an intellectual quality it would only perceive a danger, for instance, where a danger exists; whereas—"

"Hear him twaddle—the damned idiot!" muttered the Paladin.

"—whereas, it being purely a quality of the heart, and proceeding by feeling, not reason, its reach is correspondingly wider and sublimer, enabling it to perceive and avoid dangers that haven't any existence at all; as for instance that night in the fog, when the Paladin took his horse's ears for hostile lances and got off and climbed a tree—"

"It's a lie! a lie without shadow of foundation, and I call upon you all to beware how you give credence to the malicious inventions of this ramshackle slander-mill that has been doing its best to destroy my character for years, and will grind up your own reputations for you, next. I got off to tighten my saddle-girth—I wish I may die in my tracks if it isn't so—and whoever wants to believe it can, and whoever don't, can let it alone."

"There, that is the way with him, you see; he never can discuss a theme temperately, but always flies off the handle and becomes disagreeable. And you notice his defect of memory. He remembers getting off his horse, but forgets all the rest, even the tree. But that is natural; he would remember getting off the horse because he was so used to doing it. He always did it when there was an alarm and the clash of arms at the front."

"Why did he choose that time for it?" asked Jean.

"I don't know. To tighten up his girth, *he* thinks, to climb a tree, *I* think; I saw him climb nine trees in a single night."

"You saw nothing of the kind! A person that can lie like that deserves no one's respect. I ask you all to answer me. Do you believe what this reptile has said?"

All seemed embarrassed, and only Pierre replied. He said, hesitatingly—

"I—well, I hardly know what to say. It is a delicate situation. It seems, offensive to refuse to believe a person when he makes so direct a statement, and yet I am obliged to say, rude as it may appear, that I am not able to believe the whole of it—no, I am not able to believe that you climbed nine trees."

"There!" cried the Paladin; "now what do you think of yourself, Noël Rainguesson? How many do you believe I climbed, Pierre?"

"Only eight."

The laughter that followed inflamed the Paladin's anger to white heat, and he said—

"I bide my time—I bide my time. I will reckon with you all, I promise you that!"

"Don't get him started," Noël pleaded; "he is a perfect lion when he gets started. I saw enough to teach me that, after the third skirmish. After it was over I saw him come out of the bushes and attack a dead man single-handed."

"It is another lie; and I give you fair warning that you are going too far. You will see me attack a live one if you are not careful."

"Meaning me, of course. This wounds me more than any number of injurious and unkind speeches could do. Ingratitude to one's benefactor—"

"Benefactor? What do I owe you, I should like to know?"

"You owe me your life. I stood between the trees and the foe, and kept hundreds and thousands of the enemy at bay when they were thirsting for your blood. And I did not do it to display my daring, I did it because I loved you and could not live without you."

"There—you have said enough! I will not stay here to listen to these infamies. I can endure your lies, but not your love. Keep that corruption for somebody with a stronger stomach than mine. And I want to say this, before I go. That you people's small performances might appear the better and win you the more glory, I hid my own deeds through all the march. I went always to the front, where the fighting was thickest, to be remote from you, in order that you might not see and be discouraged by the things I did to the enemy. It was my purpose to keep this a secret in my own breast, but you force me to reveal it. If you ask for my witnesses, yonder they lie, on the road we have come. I found that road mud, I paved it with corpses. I found that country sterile, I fertilized it with blood. Time and again I was urged to go to the rear because the command could not proceed on account of my dead. And yet you, you miscreant, accuse me of climbing trees! Pah!"

And he strode out, with a lofty air, for the recital of his imaginary deeds had already set him up again and made him feel good.

Next day we mounted and faced toward Chinon. Orleans was at our back, now, and close by, lying in the strangling grip of the English; soon, please God, we would face about and go to their relief. From Gien the news had spread to Orleans that the peasant Maid of Vaucouleurs was on her way, divinely commissioned to raise the siege. The news made a great excitement and raised a great hope—the first breath of hope those poor souls had breathed in five months. They sent commissioners at once to the King to beg him to consider this matter, and not throw this help lightly away. These commissioners were already at Chinon by this time.

When we were half-way to Chinon we happened upon yet one more squad of enemies. They burst suddenly out of the woods, and in considerable force, too; but we were not the apprentices we were ten or twelve days before; no, we were seasoned to this kind of adventure now; our hearts did not jump into our throats and our weapons tremble in our hands. We had learned to be always in battle array, always alert, and always ready to deal with any emergency that might turn up. We were no more dismayed by the sight of those people than our commander was. Before they could form, Joan had delivered the order, "Forward!" and we were down upon them with a rush. They stood no chance; they turned tail and scattered, we ploughing through them as if they had been men of straw. That was our last ambuscade, and it was probably laid for us by that treacherous rascal the King's own minister and favorite, De la Tremouille.

We housed ourselves in an inn, and soon the town came flocking to get a glimpse of the Maid.

Ah, the tedious King and his tedious people! Our two good knights came presently, their patience well wearied, and reported. They and we reverently stood—as becomes persons who are in the presence of Kings and the superiors of Kings—until Joan, troubled by this mark of homage and respect, and not content with it nor yet used to it, although we had not permitted ourselves to do otherwise since the day she prophesied that wretched traitor's death and he was straightway drowned, thus confirming many previous signs that she was indeed an ambassador commissioned of God, commanded us to sit; then the Sieur de Metz said to Joan:

"The King has got the letter, but they will not let us have speech with him."

"Who is it that forbids?"

"None forbids, but there be three or four that are nearest his person—schemers and traitors every one—that put obstructions in the way, and seek all ways, by lies and pretexts, to make delay. Chiefest of these are Georges de la Tremouille and that plotting fox the Archbishop of Rheims. While they keep the King idle and in bondage to his sports and follies, they are great and their importance grows; whereas if ever he assert himself and rise and strike for crown and country like a man, their reign is done. So they but thrive they care not if the crown go to destruction and the King with it."

"You have spoken with others besides these?"

"Not of the Court, no—the Court are the meek slaves of those reptiles, and watch their mouths and their actions, acting as they act, thinking as they think, saying as they say: wherefore they are cold to us, and turn aside and go another way when we appear. But we have spoken with the commissioners from Orleans. They said with heat: 'It is a marvel that any man in such desperate case as is the King can moon around in this torpid way, and see his all go to ruin without lifting a finger to stay the disaster. What a most strange spectacle it is! Here he is, shut up in this wee corner of the realm

like a rat in a trap; his royal shelter this huge gloomy tomb of
a castle, with wormy rags for upholstery and crippled furniture for use, a very house of desolation; in his treasury forty
francs, and not a farthing more, God be witness! no army,
nor any shadow of one; and by contrast with this hungry
poverty you behold this crownless pauper and his shoals of
fools and favorites tricked out in the gaudiest silks and velvets
you shall find in any Court in Christendom. And look you, he
knows that when our city falls—as fall it surely will except
succor come swiftly—*France* falls; he knows that when that
day comes he will be an outlaw and a fugitive, and that behind him the English flag will float unchallenged over every
acre of his great heritage; he knows these things, he knows
that our faithful city is fighting all solitary and alone against
disease, starvation, and the sword to stay this awful calamity,
yet he will not strike one blow to save her, he will not hear
our prayers, he will not even look upon our faces.' That is
what the commissioners said, and they are in despair."

Joan said, gently—

"It is pity, but they must not despair. The Dauphin will
hear them presently. Tell them so."

She almost always called the King the Dauphin. To her
mind he was not King yet, not being crowned.

"We will tell them so, and it will content them, for they
believe you come from God. The Archbishop and his confederate have for backer that veteran soldier Raoul de Gaucourt,
Grand Master of the Palace, a worthy man but simply a soldier, with no head for any greater matter. He cannot make
out to see how a country girl, ignorant of war, can take a
sword in her small hand and win victories where the trained
generals of France have looked for defeats only, for fifty
years—and always found them. And so he lifts his frosty
mustache and scoffs."

"When God fights it is but small matter whether the hand
that bears His sword is big or little. He will perceive this in
time. Is there none in that Castle of Chinon who favors us?"

"Yes, the King's mother-in-law, Yolande, Queen of Sicily,
who is wise and good. She spoke with the Sieur Bertrand."

"She favors us, and she hates those others, the King's be-
guilers," said Bertrand. "She was full of interest, and asked a

thousand questions, all of which I answered according to my ability. Then she sat thinking over these replies until I thought she was lost in a dream and would wake no more. But it was not so. At last she said, slowly, and as if she were talking to herself: 'A child of seventeen—a girl—country bred—untaught—ignorant of war, the use of arms, and the conduct of battles—modest, gentle, shrinking—yet throws away her shepherd's crook and clothes herself in steel, and fights her way through a hundred and fifty leagues of hostile territory, never losing heart or hope and never showing fear, and comes—she to whom a king must be a dread and awful presence—and will stand up before such an one and say, Be not afraid, God has sent me to save you! Ah, whence could come a courage and conviction so sublime as this *but* from very God Himself!' She was silent again awhile, thinking, and making up her mind; then she said, 'And whether she comes of God or no, there is that in her heart that raises her above men—high above all men that breathe in France to-day—for in her is that mysterious something that puts heart into soldiers, and turns mobs of cowards into armies of fighters that forget what fear is when they are in that presence—fighters who go into battle with joy in their eyes and songs on their lips, and sweep over the field like a storm—that is the spirit that can save France, and that alone, come it whence it may! It is in her, I do truly believe, for what else could have borne up that child on that great march, and made her despise its dangers and fatigues? The King must see her face to face—and shall!' She dismissed me with those good words, and I know her promise will be kept. They will delay her all they can—those animals—but she will not fail, in the end."

"Would *she* were King!" said the other knight, fervently. "For there is little hope that the King himself can be stirred out of his lethargy. He is wholly without hope, and is only thinking of throwing away everything and flying to some foreign land. The commissioners say there is a spell upon him that makes him hopeless—yes, and that it is shut up in a mystery which they cannot fathom."

"I know the mystery," said Joan, with quiet confidence; "I know it, and he knows it, but no other but God. When I see him I will tell him a secret that will drive away his trouble, then he will hold up his head again."

I was miserable with curiosity to know what it was that she would tell him, but she did not say, and I did not expect she would. She was but a child, it is true; but she was not a chatterer to tell great matters and make herself important to little people; no, she was reserved, and kept things to herself, as the truly great always do.

The next day Queen Yolande got one victory over the King's keepers, for in spite of their protestations and obstructions she procured an audience for our two knights, and they made the most they could out of their opportunity. They told the King what a spotless and beautiful character Joan was, and how great and noble a spirit animated her, and they implored him to trust in her, believe in her, and have faith that she was sent to save France. They begged him to consent to see her. He was strongly moved to do this, and promised that he would not drop the matter out of his mind, but would consult with his council about it. This began to look encouraging. Two hours later there was a great stir below, and the inn-keeper came flying up to say a commission of illustrious ecclesiastics was come from the King—from the King his very self, understand!—think of this vast honor to his humble little hostelry!—and he was so overcome with the glory of it that he could hardly find breath enough in his excited body to put the facts into words. They were come from the King to speak with the Maid of Vaucouleurs. Then he flew downstairs, and presently appeared again, backing into the room and bowing to the ground with every step, in front of four imposing and austere bishops and their train of servants.

Joan rose, and we all stood. The bishops took seats, and for a while no word was said, for it was their prerogative to speak first, and they were so astonished to see what a child it was that was making such a noise in the world and degrading personages of their dignity to the base function of ambassadors to her in her plebeian tavern, that they could not find any words to say, at first. Then presently their spokesman told Joan they were aware that she had a message for the King, wherefore she was now commanded to put it into words, briefly and without waste of time or embroideries of speech.

As for me, I could hardly contain my joy—our message was to reach the King at last! And there was the same joy and pride and exultation in the faces of our knights, too, and in those of Joan's brothers. And I knew that they were all praying—as I was—that the awe which we felt in the presence of these great dignitaries, and which would have tied our tongues and locked our jaws, would not affect her in the like degree, but that she would be enabled to word her message well, and with little stumbling, and so make a favorable impression here, where it would be so valuable and so important.

Ah dear, how little we were expecting what happened then! We were aghast to hear her say what she said. She was standing in a reverent attitude, with her head down and her hands clasped in front of her; for she was always reverent toward the consecrated servants of God. When the spokesman had finished, she raised her head and set her calm eye on those faces, not any more disturbed by their state and grandeur than a princess would have been, and said, with all her ordinary simplicity and modesty of voice and manner:

"Ye will forgive me, reverend sirs, but I have no message save for the King's ear alone."

Those surprised men were dumb for a moment, and their faces flushed darkly; then the spokesman said:

"Hark ye, do you fling the King's command in his face and refuse to deliver this message of yours to his servants appointed to receive it?"

"God has appointed one to receive it, and another's commandment may not take precedence of that. I pray you let me have speech of his grace the Dauphin."

"Forbear this folly, and come at your message! Deliver it, and waste no more time about it."

"You err indeed, most reverend fathers in God, and it is not well. I am not come hither to talk, but to deliver Orleans, and lead the Dauphin to his good city of Rheims, and set the crown upon his head."

"Is that the message you send to the King?"

But Joan only said, in the simple fashion which was her wont:

"Ye will pardon me for reminding you again—but I have no message to send to any one."

The King's messengers rose in deep anger and swept out of the place without further words, we and Joan kneeling as they passed.

Our countenances were vacant, our hearts full of a sense of disaster. Our precious opportunity was thrown away; we could not understand Joan's conduct, she who had been so wise until this fatal hour. At last the Sieur Bertrand found courage to ask her why she had let this great chance to get her message to the King go by.

"Who sent them here?" she asked.

"The King."

"Who moved the King to send them?" She waited for an answer; none came, for we began to see what was in her mind—so she answered herself: "The Dauphin's council moved him to it. Are they enemies to me and to the Dauphin's weal, or are they friends?"

"Enemies," answered the Sieur Bertrand.

"If one would have a message go sound and ungarbled, does one choose traitors and tricksters to send it by?"

I saw that we had been fools, and she wise. They saw it too, so none found anything to say. Then she went on:

"They had but small wit that contrived this trap. They thought to get my message and seem to deliver it straight, yet deftly twist it from its purpose. You know that one part of my message is but this—to move the Dauphin by argument and reasonings to give me men-at-arms and send me to the siege. If an enemy carried these in the right words, the exact words, and no word missing, yet left out the persuasions of gesture and supplicating tone and beseeching looks that inform the words and make them live, where were the value of that argument—whom could it convince? Be patient, the Dauphin will hear me presently; have no fear."

The Sieur de Metz nodded his head several times, and muttered as to himself:

"She was right and wise, and we are but dull fools, when all is said."

It was just my thought; I could have said it myself; and indeed it was the thought of all there present. A sort of awe crept over us, to think how that untaught girl, taken suddenly and unprepared, was yet able to penetrate the cunning devices of a King's trained advisers and defeat them. Marvelling over this, and astonished at it, we fell silent and spoke no more. We had come to know that she was great in courage, fortitude, endurance, patience, conviction, fidelity to all duties —in all things, indeed, that make a good and trusty soldier and perfect him for his post; now we were beginning to feel that maybe there were greatnesses in her brain that were even greater than these great qualities of the heart. It set us thinking.

What Joan did that day bore fruit the very day after. The King was obliged to respect the spirit of a young girl who could hold her own and stand her ground like that, and he asserted himself sufficiently to put his respect into an act instead of into polite and empty words. He moved Joan out of that poor inn, and housed her, with us her servants, in the Castle of Courdray, personally confiding her to the care of Madame de Bellier, wife of old Raoul de Gaucourt, Master of the Palace. Of course this royal attention had an immediate result: all the great lords and ladies of the Court began to flock there to see and listen to the wonderful girl-soldier that all the world was talking about, and who had answered the King's mandate with a bland refusal to obey. Joan charmed them every one with her sweetness and simplicity and unconscious eloquence, and all the best and capablest among them recognized that there was an indefinable something about her that testified that she was not made of common clay, that she was built on a grander plan than the mass of mankind, and moved on a loftier plane. These spread her fame. She always made friends and advocates that way; neither the high nor the low could come within the sound of her voice and the sight of her face and go out from her presence indifferent.

Chapter VI

WELL, anything to make delay. The King's council advised him against arriving at a decision in our matter too precipitately. *He* arrive at a decision too precipitately! So they sent a committee of priests—always priests—into Lorraine to inquire into Joan's character and history—a matter which would consume several weeks, of course. You see how fastidious they were. It was as if people should come to put out the fire when a man's house was burning down, and they waited till they could send into another country to find out if he had always kept the Sabbath or not, before letting him try.

So the days poked along; dreary for us young people in some ways, but not in all, for we had one great anticipation in front of us; we had never seen a king, and now some day we should have that prodigious spectacle to see and to treasure in our memories all our lives; so we were on the lookout, and always eager and watching for the chance. The others were doomed to wait longer than I, as it turned out. One day great news came—the Orleans commissioners, with Yolande and our knights, had at last turned the council's position and persuaded the King to see Joan.

Joan received the immense news gratefully but without losing her head, but with us others it was otherwise; we could not eat or sleep or do any rational thing for the excitement and the glory of it. During two days our pair of noble knights were in distress and trepidation on Joan's account, for the audience was to be at night, and they were afraid that Joan would be so paralyzed by the glare of light from the long files of torches, the solemn pomps and ceremonies, the great concourse of renowned personages, the brilliant costumes, and the other splendors of the Court, that she, a simple country maid, and all unused to such things, would be overcome by these terrors and make a piteous failure.

No doubt I could have comforted them, but I was not free to speak. Would Joan be disturbed by this cheap spectacle, this tinsel show, with its small King and his butterfly dukelets? —she who had spoken face to face with the princes of heaven, the familiars of God, and seen their retinue of angels stretching back into the remoteness of the sky, myriads upon myriads, like a measureless fan of light, a glory like the glory of the sun streaming from each of those innumerable heads, the massed radiance filling the deeps of space with a blinding splendor? I thought not.

Queen Yolande wanted Joan to make the best possible impression upon the King and the Court, so she was strenuous to have her clothed in the richest stuffs, wrought upon the princeliest pattern, and set off with jewels; but in that she had to be disappointed, of course, Joan not being persuadable to it, but begging to be simply and sincerely dressed, as became a servant of God, and one sent upon a mission of a serious sort and grave political import. So then the gracious Queen imagined and contrived that simple and witching costume which I have described to you so many times, and which I cannot think of even now in my dull age without being moved just as rhythmical and exquisite music moves one; for *that* was music, that dress—that is what it was—music that one saw with the eyes and felt in the heart. Yes, she was a poem, she was a dream, she was a spirit when she was clothed in that.

She kept that raiment always, and wore it several times upon occasions of state, and it is preserved to this day in the Treasury of Orleans, with two of her swords, and her banner, and other things now sacred because they had belonged to her.

At the appointed time the Count of Vendôme, a great lord of the court, came richly clothed, with his train of servants and assistants, to conduct Joan to the King, and the two knights and I went with her, being entitled to this privilege by reason of our official positions near her person.

When we entered the great audience hall, there it all was, just as I have already painted it. Here were ranks of guards in shining armor and with polished halberds; two sides of the hall were like flower-gardens for variety of color and the magnificence of the costumes; light streamed upon these masses of color from two hundred and fifty flambeaux. There was a wide free space down the middle of the hall, and at the end of it was a throne royally canopied, and upon it sat a crowned and sceptred figure nobly clothed and blazing with jewels.

It is true that Joan had been hindered and put off a good while, but now that she was admitted to an audience at last, she was received with honors granted to only the greatest personages. At the entrance door stood four heralds in a row, in splendid tabards, with long slender silver trumpets at their mouths, with square silken banners depending from them embroidered with the arms of France. As Joan and the Count passed by, these trumpets gave forth in unison one long rich note, and as we moved down the hall under the pictured and gilded vaulting, this was repeated at every fifty feet of our progress—six times in all. It made our good knights proud and happy, and they held themselves erect, and stiffened their stride, and looked fine and soldierly. They were not expecting this beautiful and honorable tribute to our little country maid.

Joan walked two yards behind the Count, we three walked two yards behind Joan. Our solemn march ended when we were as yet some eight or ten steps from the throne. The Count made a deep obeisance, pronounced Joan's name, then bowed again and moved to his place among a group of officials near the throne. I was devouring the crowned personage with all my eyes, and my heart almost stood still with awe.

The eyes of all others were fixed upon Joan in a gaze of wonder which was half worship, and which seemed to say, "How sweet—how lovely—how divine!" All lips were parted and motionless, which was a sure sign that those people, who seldom forget themselves, had forgotten themselves now, and were not conscious of anything but the one object they were gazing upon. They had the look of people who are under the enchantment of a vision.

Then they presently began to come to life again, rousing themselves out of the spell and shaking it off as one drives away little by little a clinging drowsiness or intoxication. Now they fixed their attention upon Joan with a strong new interest of another sort; they were full of curiosity to see what she would do—they having a secret and particular reason for this curiosity. So they watched. This is what they saw:

She made no obeisance, nor even any slight inclination of

her head, but stood looking toward the throne in silence. That was all there was to see, at present.

I glanced up at De Metz, and was shocked at the paleness of his face. I whispered and said—

"What is it man, what is it?"

His answering whisper was so weak I could hardly catch it—

"They have taken advantage of the hint in her letter to play a trick upon her! She will err, and they will laugh at her. That is not the King that sits there."

Then I glanced at Joan. She was still gazing steadfastly toward the throne, and I had the curious fancy that even her shoulders and the back of her head expressed bewilderment. Now she turned her head slowly, and her eye wandered along the lines of standing courtiers till it fell upon a young man who was very quietly dressed; then her face lighted joyously, and she ran and threw herself at his feet, and clasped his knees, exclaiming in that soft melodious voice which was her birthright and was now charged with deep and tender feeling—

"God of his grace give you long life, O dear and gentle Dauphin!"

In his astonishment and exultation De Metz cried out—

"By the shadow of God, it is an amazing thing!" Then he mashed all the bones of my hand in his grateful grip, and added, with a proud shake of his mane, "*Now*, what have these painted infidels to say!"

Meantime the young person in the plain clothes was saying to Joan—

"Ah, you mistake, my child, I am not the King. There he is," and he pointed to the throne.

The knight's face clouded, and he muttered in grief and indignation—

"Ah, it is a shame to use her so. But for this lie she had gone through safe. I will go and proclaim to all the house what—"

"Stay where you are!" whispered I and the Sieur Bertrand in a breath, and made him stop in his place.

Joan did not stir from her knees, but still lifted her happy face toward the King, and said—

"No, gracious liege, you are he, and none other."

De Metz's troubles vanished away, and he said—

"Verily, she was not guessing, she *knew*. Now, how could she know? It is a miracle. I am content, and will meddle no more, for I perceive that she is equal to her occasions, having that in her head that cannot profitably be helped by the vacancy that is in mine."

This interruption of his lost me a remark or two of the other talk; however, I caught the King's next question:

"But tell me who you are, and what would you?"

"I am called Joan the Maid, and am sent to say that the King of Heaven wills that you be crowned and consecrated in your good city of Rheims, and be thereafter Lieutenant of the Lord of Heaven, who is King of France. And He willeth also that you set me at my appointed work and give me men-at-arms." After a slight pause she added, her eye lighting at the sound of her words, "For then will I raise the siege of Orleans and break the English power!"

The young monarch's amused face sobered a little when this martial speech fell upon that sick air like a breath blown from embattled camps and fields of war, and his trifling smile presently faded wholly away and disappeared. He was grave, now, and thoughtful. After a little he waved his hand lightly and all the people fell away and left those two by themselves in a vacant space. The knights and I moved to the opposite side of the hall and stood there. We saw Joan rise at a sign, then she and the King talked privately together.

All that host had been consumed with curiosity to see what Joan would do. Well, they had seen, and now they were full of astonishment to see that she had really performed that strange miracle according to the promise in her letter; and they were fully as much astonished to find that she was not overcome by the pomps and splendors about her, but was even more tranquil and at her ease in holding speech with a monarch than ever they themselves had been, with all their practice and experience.

As for our two knights, they were inflated beyond measure with pride in Joan, but nearly dumb, as to speech, they not being able to think out any way to account for her managing to carry herself through this imposing ordeal without ever a mistake or an awkwardness of any kind to mar the grace and credit of her great performance.

The talk between Joan and the King was long and earnest, and held in low voices. We could not hear, but we had our eyes and could note effects; and presently we and all the house noted one effect which was memorable and striking, and has been set down in memoires and histories and in testimony at the Process of Rehabilitation by some who witnessed it; for all knew it was big with meaning, though none knew what that meaning was at that time, of course. For suddenly we saw the King shake off his indolent attitude and straighten up like a man, and at the same time look immeasurably astonished. It was as if Joan had told him something almost too wonderful for belief, and yet of a most uplifting and welcome nature.

It was long before we found out the secret of this conversation, but we know it now, and all the world knows it. That part of the talk was like this—as one may read in all histories. The perplexed King asked Joan for a sign. He wanted to believe in her and her mission, and that her Voices were supernatural and endowed with knowledge hidden from mortals, but how could he do this unless these Voices could prove their claim in some absolutely unassailable way? It was then that Joan said—

"I will give you a sign, and you shall no more doubt. There is a secret trouble in your heart which you speak of to none—a doubt which wastes away your courage, and makes you dream of throwing all away and fleeing from your realm. Within this little while you have been praying, in your own breast, that God of his grace would resolve that doubt, even if the doing of it must show you that no kingly right is lodged in you."

It was that that amazed the King, for it was as she had said: his prayer was the secret of his own breast, and none but God could know about it. So he said:

"The sign is sufficient. I know, now, that these Voices are of God. They have said true in this matter; if they have said more, tell it me—I will believe."

"They have resolved that doubt, and I bring their very words, which are these: Thou art lawful heir to the King thy father, and true heir of France. God has spoken it. Now lift up thy head, and doubt no more, but give me men-at-arms and let me get about my work."

Telling him he was of lawful birth was what straightened him up and made a man of him for a moment, removing his doubts upon that head and convincing him of his royal right; and if any could have hanged his hindering and pestiferous council and set him free, he would have answered Joan's prayer and set her in the field. But no, those creatures were only checked, not checkmated; they could invent some more delays.

We had been made proud by the honors which had so distinguished Joan's entrance into that place—honors restricted to personages of very high rank and worth—but that pride was as nothing compared with the pride we had in the honor done her upon leaving it. For whereas those first honors were shown only to the great, these last, up to this time, had been shown only to the royal. The King himself led Joan by the hand down the great hall to the door, the glittering multitude standing and making reverence as they passed, and the silver trumpets sounding those rich notes of theirs. Then he dismissed her with gracious words, bending low over her hand and kissing it. Always—from all companies, high or low— she went forth richer in honor and esteem than when she came.

And the King did another handsome thing by Joan, for he sent us back to Courdray Castle torch-lighted and in state, under escort of his own troop—his guard of honor—the only soldiers he had; and finely equipped and bedizened they were, too, though they hadn't seen the color of their wages since they were children, as a body might say. The wonders which Joan had been performing before the King had been carried all around by this time, so the road was so packed with people who wanted to get a sight of her that we could hardly dig through; and as for talking together, we couldn't, all attempts at talk being drowned in the storm of shoutings and huzzas that broke out all along as we passed, and kept abreast of us like a wave the whole way.

Chapter VII

W E WERE doomed to suffer tedious waits and delays, and we settled ourselves down to our fate and bore it with a dreary patience, counting the slow hours and the dull days and hoping for a turn when God should please to send it. The Paladin was the only exception—that is to say, he was the only one who was happy and had no heavy times. This was partly owing to the satisfaction he got out of his clothes. He bought them when he first arrived. He bought them at second hand—a Spanish cavalier's complete suit, wide-brimmed hat with flowing plumes, lace collar and cuffs, faded velvet doublet and trunks, short cloak hung from the shoulder, funnel-topped buskins, long rapier, and all that—a graceful and picturesque costume, and the Paladin's great frame was the right place to hang it for effect. He wore it when off duty; and when he swaggered by with one hand resting on the hilt of his rapier, and twirling his new mustache with the other, everybody stopped to look and admire; and well they might, for he was a fine and stately contrast to the small French gentleman of the day squeezed into the trivial French costume of the time.

He was king bee of the little village that snuggled under the shelter of the frowning towers and bastions of Courdray Castle, and acknowledged lord of the tap-room of the inn. When he opened his mouth there, he got a hearing. Those simple artisans and peasants listened with deep and wondering interest; for he was a traveller and had seen the world—all of it that lay between Chinon and Domremy, at any rate—and that was a wide stretch more of it than they might ever hope to see; and he had been in battle, and knew how to paint its shock and struggle, its perils and surprises, with an art that was all his own. He was cock of that walk, hero of that hostelry; he drew custom as honey draws flies; so he was the pet of the inn-keeper, and of his wife and daughter, and they were his obliged and willing servants.

Most people who have the narrative gift—that great and rare endowment—have with it the defect of telling their choice things over the same way every time, and this injures them and causes them to sound stale and wearisome after several repetitions; but it was not so with the Paladin, whose art was of a finer sort; it was more stirring and interesting to hear him tell about a battle the tenth time than it was the first time, because he did not tell it twice the same way, but always made a new battle of it and a better one, with more casualties on the enemy's side each time, and more general wreck and disaster all around, and more widows and orphans and suffering in the neighborhood where it happened. He could not tell his battles apart himself, except by their names; and by the time he had told one of them ten times he had to lay it aside and start a new one in its place, because it had grown so that there wasn't room enough in France for it any more, but was lapping over the edges. But up to that point the audience would not allow him to substitute a new battle, knowing that the old ones were the best, and sure to improve as long as France could hold them; and so, instead of saying to him as they would have said to another, "Give us something fresh, we are fatigued with that old thing," they would say, with one voice and with a strong interest, "Tell about the surprise at Beaulieu again—tell it three or four times!" That is a compliment which few narrative experts have heard in their lifetime.

At first when the Paladin heard us tell about the glories of the Royal Audience he was broken-hearted because he was not taken with us to it; next, his talk was full of what he would have done if he had been there; and within two days he was telling what he *did* do when he *was* there. His mill was fairly started, now, and could be trusted to take care of its affair. Within three nights afterwards all his battles were taking a rest, for already his worshippers in the tap-room were so infatuated with the great tale of the Royal Audience that they would have nothing else, and so besotted with it were they that they would have cried if they could not have gotten it.

Noël Rainguesson hid himself and heard it, and came and told me, and after that we went together to listen, bribing the inn hostess to let us have her little private parlor, where we could stand at the wickets in the door and see and hear.

The tap-room was large, yet had a snug and cosey look,

with its inviting little tables and chairs scattered irregularly over its red brick floor, and its great fire flaming and crackling in the wide chimney. It was a comfortable place to be in on such chilly and blustering March nights as these, and a goodly company had taken shelter there, and were sipping their wine in contentment and gossiping one with another in a neighborly way while they waited for the historian. The host, the hostess, and their pretty daughter were flying here and there and yonder among the tables and doing their best to keep up with the orders. The room was about forty feet square, and a space or aisle down the centre of it had been kept vacant and reserved for the Paladin's needs. At the end of it was a platform ten or twelve feet wide, with a big chair and a small table on it, and three steps leading up to it.

Among the wine-sippers were many familiar faces: the cobbler, the farrier, the blacksmith, the wheelwright, the armorer, the maltster, the weaver, the baker, the miller's man with his dusty coat, and so on; and conspicuous and important, as a matter of course, was the barber-surgeon, for he is that in all villages. As he has to pull everybody's teeth, and purge and bleed all the grown people once a month to keep their health sound, he knows everybody, and by constant contact with all sorts of folk becomes a master of etiquette and manners and a conversationalist of large facility. There were plenty of carriers, drovers, and their sort, and journeymen artisans.

When the Paladin presently came sauntering indolently in, he was received with a cheer, and the barber bustled forward and greeted him with several low and most graceful and courtly bows, also taking his hand and touching his lips to it. Then he called in a loud voice for a stoup of wine for the Paladin, and when the host's daughter brought it up on to the platform and dropped her courtesy and departed, the barber called after her, and told her to add the wine to his score. This won him ejaculations of approval, which pleased him very much and made his little rat-eyes shine; and such applause is right and proper, for when we do a liberal and gallant thing it is but natural that we should wish to see notice taken of it.

The barber called upon the people to rise and drink the Paladin's health, and they did it with alacrity and affectionate heartiness, clashing their metal flagons together with a simultaneous crash, and heightening the effect with a resounding cheer. It was a fine thing to see how that young swashbuckler had made himself so popular in a strange land in so little a while, and without other helps to his advancement than just his tongue and the talent to use it given him by God—a talent which was but one talent in the beginning, but was now become ten through husbandry and the increment and usufruct that do naturally follow that and reward it as by a law.

The people sat down and began to hammer on the tables with their flagons and call for "the King's Audience!—the King's Audience!—the King's Audience!" The Paladin stood there in one of his best attitudes, with his plumed great hat tipped over to the left, the folds of his short cloak drooping from his shoulder, and the one hand resting upon the hilt of his rapier and the other lifting his beaker. As the noise died down he made a stately sort of a bow, which he had picked up somewhere, then fetched his beaker with a sweep to his lips and tilted his head back and drained it to the bottom. The barber jumped for it and set it upon the Paladin's table. Then the Paladin began to walk up and down his platform with a great deal of dignity and quite at his ease; and as he walked he talked, and every little while stopped and stood facing his house and so standing continued his talk.

We went three nights in succession. It was plain that there was a charm about the performance that was apart from the mere interest which attaches to lying. It was presently discoverable that this charm lay in the Paladin's sincerity. He was not lying consciously; he believed what he was saying. To him, his initial statements were facts, and whenever he enlarged a statement, the enlargement became a fact too. He put his heart into his extravagant narrative, just as a poet puts his heart into a heroic fiction, and his earnestness disarmed criticism—disarmed it as far as he himself was concerned. Nobody believed his narrative, but all believed that he believed it.

He made his enlargements without flourish, without emphasis, and so casually that often one failed to notice that a change had been made. He spoke of the governor of Vaucouleurs, the first night, simply as the governor of Vaucouleurs; he spoke of him the second night as his uncle the governor of Vaucouleurs; the third night he was his father. He did not seem to know that he was making these extraordinary changes; they dropped from his lips in a quite natural and effortless way. By his first night's account the governor merely attached him to the Maid's military escort in a general and unofficial way; the second night his uncle the governor sent him with the Maid as lieutenant of her rear guard; the third night his father the governor put the whole command, Maid and all, in his especial charge. The first night the governor spoke of him as a youth without name or ancestry, but "destined to achieve both"; the second night his uncle the governor spoke of him as the latest and worthiest lineal descendant of the chiefest and noblest of the Twelve Paladins of Charlemagne; the third night he spoke of him as the lineal descendant of the whole dozen. In three nights he promoted the Count of Vendôme from a fresh acquaintance to schoolmate, and then brother-in-law.

At the King's Audience everything grew, in the same way. First the four silver trumpets were twelve, then thirty-five, finally ninety-six; and by that time he had thrown in so many drums and cymbals that he had to lengthen the hall from five hundred feet to nine hundred to accommodate them. Under his hand the people present multiplied in the same large way.

The first two nights he contented himself with merely describing and exaggerating the chief dramatic incident of the Audience, but the third night he added illustration to description. He throned the barber in his own high chair to represent the sham King; then he told how the Court watched the Maid with intense interest and suppressed merriment, expecting to see her fooled by the deception and get herself swept permanently out of credit by the storm of scornful laughter which would follow. He worked this scene up till he got his house in a burning fever of excitement and anticipation, then came his climax. Turning to the barber, he said:

"But mark you what she did. She gazed steadfastly upon that sham's villain face as I now gaze upon yours—this being her noble and simple attitude, just as I stand now—then turned she—thus—to me, and stretching her arm out—so—

and pointing with her finger, she said, in that firm, calm tone which she was used to use in directing the conduct of a battle, 'Pluck me this false knave from the throne!' I, striding forward as I do now, took him by the collar and lifted him out and held him aloft—thus—as if he had been but a child." (The house rose, shouting, stamping, and banging with their flagons, and went fairly mad over this magnificent exhibition of strength—and there was not the shadow of a laugh anywhere, though the spectacle of the limp but proud barber hanging there in the air like a puppy held by the scruff of its neck was a thing that had nothing of solemnity about it.) "Then I set him down upon his feet—thus—being minded to get him by a better hold and heave him out of the window, but she bid me forbear, so by that error he escaped with his life.

"Then she turned her about and viewed the throng with those eyes of hers, which are the clear-shining windows whence her immortal wisdom looketh out upon the world, resolving its falsities and coming at the kernel of truth that is hid within them, and presently they fell upon a young man modestly clothed, and him she proclaimed for what he truly was, saying, 'I am thy servant—thou art the King!' Then all were astonished, and a great shout went up, the whole six thousand joining in it, so that the walls rocked with the volume and the tumult of it."

He made a fine and picturesque thing of the march-out from the Audience, augmenting the glories of it to the last limit of the impossibilities; then he took from his finger and held up a brass nut from a bolt-head which the head-ostler at the castle had given him that morning, and made his conclusion—thus:

"Then the King dismissed the Maid most graciously—as indeed was her desert—and turning to me, said, 'Take this signet-ring, son of the Paladins, and command me with it in your day of need; and look you,' said he, touching my temple, 'preserve this brain, France has use for it; and look well to its casket also, for I foresee that it will be hooped with a ducal coronet one day.' I took the ring, and knelt and kissed his hand, saying, 'Sire, where glory calls, there will I be found; where danger and death are thickest, that is my native air;

when France and the throne need help—well, I say nothing, for I am not of the talking sort—let my deeds speak for me, it is all I ask.'

"So ended that most fortunate and memorable episode, so big with future weal for the crown and the nation, and unto God be the thanks! Rise! Fill your flagons! Now—to France and the King—drink!"

They emptied them to the bottom, then burst into cheers and huzzas, and kept it up as much as two minutes, the Paladin standing at stately ease the while and smiling benignantly from his platform.

Chapter VIII

WHEN Joan told the King what that deep secret was that was torturing his heart, his doubts were cleared away; he believed she was sent of God, and if he had been let alone he would have set her upon her great mission at once. But he was not let alone. Tremouille and the holy fox of Rheims knew their man. All they needed to say was this—and they said it:

"Your Highness says her Voices have revealed to you, by her mouth, a secret known only to yourself and God. How can you know that her Voices are not of Satan, and she his mouthpiece?—for does not Satan know the secrets of men and use his knowledge for the destruction of their souls? It is a dangerous business, and your Highness will do well not to proceed in it without probing the matter to the bottom."

That was enough. It shrivelled up the King's little soul like a raisin, with terrors and apprehensions, and straightway he privately appointed a commission of bishops to visit and question Joan daily until they should find out whether her supernatural helps hailed from heaven or from hell.

The King's relative, the Duke of Alençon, three years prisoner of war to the English, was in these days released from captivity through promise of a great ransom; and the name and fame of the Maid having reached him—for the same filled all mouths now, and penetrated to all parts—he came to Chinon to see with his own eyes what manner of creature she might be. The King sent for Joan and introduced her to the Duke. She said, in her simple fashion:

"You are welcome; the more of the blood of France that is joined to this cause, the better for the cause and it."

Then the two talked together, and there was just the usual result: when they parted, the Duke was her friend and advocate.

Joan attended the King's mass the next day, and afterward dined with the King and the Duke. The King was learning to prize her company and value her conversation; and that might well be, for, like other Kings, he was used to getting nothing out of people's talk but guarded phrases, colorless and non-committal, or carefully tinted to tally with the color of what he said himself; and so this kind of conversation only vexes and bores, and is wearisome; but Joan's talk was fresh and free, sincere and honest, and unmarred by timorous self-watching and constraint. She said the very thing that was in her mind, and said it in a plain, straightforward way. One can believe that to the King this must have been like fresh cold water from the mountains to parched lips used to the water of the sun-baked puddles of the plain.

After dinner Joan so charmed the Duke with her horsemanship and lance-practice in the meadows by the Castle of Chinon, whither the King also had come to look on, that he made her a present of a great black war-steed.

Every day the commission of bishops came and questioned Joan about her Voices and her mission, and then went to the King with their report. These pryings accomplished but little. She told as much as she considered advisable, and kept the rest to herself. Both threats and trickeries were wasted upon her. She did not care for the threats, and the traps caught nothing. She was perfectly frank and childlike about these things. She knew the bishops were sent by the King, that their questions were the King's questions, and that by all law and custom a King's questions *must* be answered; yet she told the King in her naïve way at his own table one day that she answered only such of those questions as suited her.

The bishops finally concluded that they couldn't tell whether Joan was sent by God or not. They were cautious, you see. There were two powerful parties at Court; therefore to make a decision either way would infallibly embroil them with one of those parties; so it seemed to them wisest to roost on the fence and shift the burden to other shoulders. And that is what they did. They made final report that Joan's case was beyond their powers, and recommended that it be put into the hands of the learned and illustrious doctors of the University of Poitiers. Then they retired from the field, leaving behind them this little item of testimony, wrung from them by Joan's wise reticence: they said she was a "gentle and simple little shepherdess, very candid, *but not given to talking*."

It was quite true—in their case. But if they could have
looked back and seen her with us in the happy pastures of
Domremy, they would have perceived that she had a tongue
that could go fast enough when no harm could come of her
words.

So we travelled to Poitiers, to endure there three weeks of
tedious delay while this poor child was being daily questioned and badgered before a great bench of—what? Military experts?—since what she had come to apply for was an
army and the privilege of leading it to battle against the
enemies of France. Oh no; it was a great bench of priests
and monks—profoundly learned and astute casuists—renowned professors of theology! Instead of setting a military
commission to find out if this valorous little soldier could
win victories, they set a company of holy hair-splitters and
phrase-mongers to work to find out if the soldier was sound
in her piety and had no doctrinal leaks. The rats were devouring the house, but instead of examining the cat's teeth
and claws, they only concerned themselves to find out if it
was a holy cat. If it was a pious cat, a moral cat, all right,
never mind about the other capacities, they were of no consequence.

Joan was as sweetly self-possessed and tranquil before this
grim tribunal, with its robed celebrities, its solemn state and
imposing ceremonials, as if she were but a spectator and not
herself on trial. She sat there, solitary on her bench, untroubled, and disconcerted the science of the sages with her sublime ignorance—an ignorance which was a fortress; arts,
wiles, the learning drawn from books, and all like missiles
rebounded from its unconscious masonry and fell to the
ground harmless; they could not dislodge the garrison which
was within—Joan's serene great heart and spirit, the guards
and keepers of her mission.

She answered all questions frankly, and she told all the
story of her visions and of her experiences with the angels and
what they said to her; and the manner of the telling was so
unaffected, and so earnest and sincere, and made it all seem so
life-like and real, that even that hard practical court forgot
itself and sat motionless and mute, listening with a charmed
and wondering interest to the end. And if you would have

other testimony than mine, look in the histories and you will find where an eye-witness, giving sworn testimony in the Rehabilitation process, says that she told that tale "with a noble dignity and simplicity," and as to its effect, says in substance what I have said. Seventeen, she was—seventeen, and all alone on her bench by herself; yet was not afraid, but faced that great company of erudite doctors of law and theology, and by the help of no art learned in the schools, but using only the enchantments which were hers by nature, of youth, sincerity, a voice soft and musical, and an eloquence whose source was the heart, not the head, she laid that spell upon them. Now was not that a beautiful thing to see? If I could, I would put it before you just as I saw it; then I know what you would say.

As I have told you, she could not read. One day they harried and pestered her with arguments, reasonings, objections and other windy and wordy trivialities, gathered out of the works of this and that and the other great theological authority, until at last her patience vanished, and she turned upon them sharply and said—

"I don't know A from B; but I know this: that I am come by command of the Lord of Heaven to deliver Orleans from the English power and crown the King at Rheims, and the matters ye are puttering over are of no consequence!"

Necessarily those were trying days for her, and wearing for everybody that took part; but her share was the hardest, for she had no holidays, but must be always on hand and stay the long hours through, whereas this, that, and the other inquisitor could absent himself and rest up from his fatigues when he got worn out. And yet she showed no wear, no weariness, and but seldom let fly her temper. As a rule she put her day through calm, alert, patient, fencing with those veteran masters of scholarly sword-play and coming out always without a scratch.

One day a Dominican sprung upon her a question which made everybody cock up his ears with interest; as for me, I trembled, and said to myself she is caught this time, poor Joan, for there is no way of answering this. The sly Dominican began in this way—in a sort of indolent fashion, as if the thing he was about was a matter of no moment:

"You assert that God has willed to deliver France from this English bondage?"

"Yes, He has willed it."

"You wish for men-at-arms, so that you may go to the relief of Orleans, I believe?"

"Yes—and the sooner the better."

"God is all-powerful, and able to do whatsoever thing He wills to do, is it not so?"

"Most surely. None doubts it."

The Dominican lifted his head suddenly, and sprung that question I have spoken of, with exultation:

"Then answer me this. If He has willed to deliver France, and is able to do whatsoever He wills, where is the need for men-at-arms?"

There was a fine stir and commotion when he said that, and a sudden thrusting forward of heads and putting up of hands to ears to catch the answer; and the Dominican wagged his head with satisfaction, and looked about him collecting his applause, for it shone in every face. But Joan was not disturbed. There was no note of disquiet in her voice when she answered:

"He helps who help themselves. The sons of France will fight the battles, but *He* will give the victory!"

You could see a light of admiration sweep the house from face to face like a ray from the sun. Even the Dominican himself looked pleased, to see his master-stroke so neatly parried, and I heard a venerable bishop mutter, in the phrasing common to priest and people in that robust time, "By God, the child has said true. He willed that Goliath should be slain, and He sent a child like this to do it!"

Another day, when the inquisition had dragged along until everybody looked drowsy and tired but Joan, Brother Séguin, professor of theology in the University of Poitiers, who was a sour and sarcastic man, fell to plying Joan with all sorts of nagging questions in his bastard Limousin French—for he was from Limoges. Finally he said—

"How is it that you could understand those angels? What language did they speak?"

"French."

"In-deed! How pleasant to know that our language is so honored! Good French?"

"Yes—perfect."

"Perfect, eh? Well, certainly *you* ought to know. It was even better than your own, eh?"

"As to that, I—I believe I cannot say," said she, and was going on, but stopped. Then she added, almost as if she were saying it to herself, "Still, it was an improvement on yours!"

I knew there was a chuckle back of her eyes, for all their innocence. Everybody shouted. Brother Séguin was nettled, and asked brusquely—

"Do you believe in God?"

Joan answered with an irritating nonchalance—

"Oh, well, yes—better than you, it is likely."

Brother Séguin lost his patience, and heaped sarcasm after sarcasm upon her, and finally burst out in angry earnest, exclaiming—

"Very well, I can tell you this, you whose belief in God is so great: God has not willed that any shall believe in you without a sign. Where is your sign?—show it!"

This roused Joan, and she was on her feet in a moment, and flung out her retort with spirit:

"I have not come to Poitiers to show signs and do miracles. Send me to Orleans and you shall have signs enough. Give me men-at-arms—few or many—and let me go!"

The fire was leaping from her eyes—ah, the heroic little figure! can't you see her? There was a great burst of acclamations, and she sat down blushing, for it was not in her delicate nature to like being conspicuous.

This speech and that episode about the French language scored two points against Brother Séguin, while he scored nothing against Joan; yet, sour man as he was, he was a manly man, and honest, as you can see by the histories; for at the Rehabilitation he could have hidden those unlucky incidents if he had chosen, but he didn't do it, but spoke them right out in his evidence.

On one of the later days of that three weeks' session the gowned scholars and professors made one grand assault all along the line, fairly overwhelming Joan with objections and arguments culled from the writings of every ancient and illustrious authority of the Roman Church. She was well-nigh smothered; but at last she shook herself free and struck back, crying out:

"Listen! The Book of God is worth more than all these ye cite, and I stand upon *it*. And I tell ye there are things in that Book that not one among ye can read, with all your learning!"

From the first she was the guest, by invitation, of the dame De Rabateau, wife of a councillor of the Parliament of Poitiers; and to that house the great ladies of the city came nightly to see Joan and talk with her; and not these only, but the old lawyers, councillors, and scholars of the Parliament and the University. And these grave men, accustomed to weigh every strange and questionable thing, and cautiously consider it, and turn it about this way and that and still doubt it, came night after night, and night after night, falling ever deeper and deeper under the influence of that mysterious something, that spell, that elusive and unwordable fascination, which was the supremest endowment of Joan of Arc, that winning and persuasive and convincing something which high and low alike recognized and felt, but which neither high nor low could explain or describe; and one by one they all surrendered, saying, "This child is sent of God."

All day long Joan, in the great court and subject to its rigid rules of procedure, was at a disadvantage; her judges had things their own way; but at night she held court herself, and matters were reversed, she presiding, with her tongue free and her same judges there before her. There could be but one result: all the objections and hindrances they could build around her with their hard labors of the day she would charm away at night. In the end, she carried her judges with her in a mass, and got her great verdict without a dissenting voice.

The court was a sight to see when the president of it read it from his throne, for all the great people of the town were there who could get admission and find room. First there were some solemn ceremonies, proper and usual at such times; then, when there was silence again, the reading followed, penetrating the deep hush so that every word was heard in even the remotest parts of the house:

"It is found, and is hereby declared, that Joan of Arc, called the Maid, is a good Christian and good Catholic; that there is nothing in her person or her words contrary to the faith; and that the King may and ought to accept the succor she offers; for to repel it would be to offend the Holy Spirit, and render him unworthy of the aid of God."

The court rose, and then the storm of plaudits burst forth unrebuked, dying down and bursting forth again and again, and I lost sight of Joan, for she was swallowed up in a great tide of people who rushed to congratulate her and pour out benedictions upon her and upon the cause of France, now solemnly and irrevocably delivered into her little hands.

Chapter IX

Iᴛ ᴡᴀs indeed a great day, and a stirring thing to see.

She had won! It was a mistake of Tremouille and her other ill-wishers to let her hold court those nights.

The commission of priests sent to Lorraine ostensibly to inquire into Joan's character—in fact to weary her with delays and wear out her purpose and make her give it up—arrived back and reported her character perfect. Our affairs were in full career now, you see.

The verdict made a prodigious stir. Dead France woke suddenly to life, wherever the great news travelled. Whereas before, the spiritless and cowed people hung their heads and slunk away if one mentioned war to them, now they came clamoring to be enlisted under the banner of the Maid of Vaucouleurs, and the roaring of war-songs and the thundering of the drums filled all the air. I remembered now what she had said, that time there in our village when I proved by facts and statistics that France's case was hopeless, and nothing could ever rouse the people from their lethargy:

"They will hear the drums—and they will answer, they will march!"

It has been said that misfortunes never come one at a time, but in a body. In our case it was the same with good luck. Having got a start, it came flooding in, tide after tide. Our next wave of it was of this sort. There had been grave doubts among the priests as to whether the Church ought to permit a female soldier to dress like a man. But now came a verdict on that head. Two of the greatest scholars and theologians of the time—one of whom had been Chancellor of the University of Paris—rendered it. They decided that since Joan "must do the work of a man and a soldier, it is just and legitimate that her apparel should conform to the situation."

It was a great point gained, the Church's authority to dress as a man. Oh yes, wave on wave the good luck came sweeping in. Never mind about the smaller waves, let us come to the largest one of all, the wave that swept us small fry quite off our feet and almost drowned us with joy. The day of the great verdict, couriers had been despatched to the King with it, and the next morning bright and early the clear notes of a bugle came floating to us on the crisp air, and we pricked up our ears and began to count them. One—two—three; pause; one—two; pause; one—two—three, again—and out we skipped and went flying; for that formula was used only when the King's herald-at-arms would deliver a proclamation to the people. As we hurried along, people came racing out of every street and house and alley, men, women, and children, all flushed, excited, and throwing lacking articles of clothing on as they ran; still those clear notes pealed out, and still the rush of people increased till the whole town was abroad and streaming along the principal street. At last we reached the square, which was now packed with citizens, and there, high on the pedestal of the great cross, we saw the herald in his brilliant costume, with his servitors about him. The next moment he began his delivery in the powerful voice proper to his office:

"Know all men, and take heed therefore, that the most high, the most illustrious Charles, by the grace of God King of France, hath been pleased to confer upon his well-beloved servant Joan of Arc, called the Maid, the title, emoluments, authorities, and dignity of General-in-Chief of the Armies of France—"

Here a thousand caps flew into the air, and the multitude burst into a hurricane of cheers that raged and raged till it seemed as if it would never come to an end; but at last it did; then the herald went on and finished:

—"and hath appointed to be her lieutenant and chief of staff a prince of his royal house, his grace the Duke of Alençon!"

That was the end, and the hurricane began again, and was split up into innumerable strips by the blowers of it and wafted through all the lanes and streets of the town.

General of the Armies of France, with a prince of the blood for subordinate! Yesterday she was nothing—to-day she was this. Yesterday she was not even a sergeant, not even a corporal, not even a private—to-day, with one step, she was at the top. Yesterday she was less than nobody to the newest recruit —to-day her command was law to La Hire, Saintrailles, the Bastard of Orleans, and all those others, veterans of old renown, illustrious masters of the trade of war. These were the thoughts I was thinking; I was trying to realize this strange and wonderful thing that had happened, you see.

My mind went travelling back, and presently lighted upon a picture—a picture which was still so new and fresh in my memory that it seemed a matter of only yesterday—and indeed its date was no further back than the first days of January. This is what it was. A peasant girl in a far-off village, her seventeenth year not yet quite completed, and herself and her village as unknown as if they had been on the other side of the globe. She had picked up a friendless wanderer somewhere and brought it home—a small gray kitten in a forlorn and starving condition—and had fed it and comforted it and got its confidence and made it believe in her, and now it was curled up in her lap asleep, and she was knitting a coarse stocking and thinking—dreaming—about what, one may never know. And now—the kitten had hardly had time to become a cat, and yet already the girl is General of the Armies of France, with a prince of the blood to give orders to, and out of her village obscurity her name has climbed up like the sun and is visible from all corners of the land! It made me dizzy to think of these things, they were so out of the common order, and seemed so impossible.

Chapter X

JOAN'S first official act was to dictate a letter to the English commanders at Orleans, summoning them to deliver up all strongholds in their possession and depart out of France. She must have been thinking it all out before and arranging it in her mind, it flowed from her lips so smoothly, and framed itself into such vivacious and forcible language. Still, it might not have been so; she always had a quick mind and a capable tongue, and her faculties were constantly developing in these latter weeks. This letter was to be forwarded presently from Blois. Men, provisions, and money were offering in plenty now, and Joan appointed Blois as a recruiting station and depot of supplies, and ordered up La Hire from the front to take charge.

The Great Bastard—him of the ducal house, and governor of Orleans—had been clamoring for weeks for Joan to be sent to him, and now came another messenger, old D'Aulon, a veteran officer, a trusty man and fine and honest. The King kept him, and gave him to Joan to be chief of her household, and commanded her to appoint the rest of her people herself, making their number and dignity accord with the greatness of her office; and at the same time he gave order that they should be properly equipped with arms, clothing, and horses.

Meantime the King was having a complete suit of armor made for her at Tours. It was of the finest steel, heavily plated with silver, richly ornamented with engraved designs, and polished like a mirror.

Joan's Voices had told her that there was an ancient sword hidden somewhere behind the altar of St. Catherine's at Fierbois, and she sent De Metz to get it. The priests knew of no such sword, but a search was made, and sure enough it was found in that place, buried a little way under the ground. It had no sheath and was very rusty, but the priests polished it up and sent it to Tours, whither we were now to come. They also had a sheath of crimson velvet made for it, and the people of Tours equipped it with another one, made of cloth of gold. But Joan meant to carry this sword always in battle; so she laid the showy sheaths away and got one made of leather. It was generally believed that this sword had belonged to Charlemagne, but that was only a matter of opinion. I wanted to sharpen that old blade, but she said it was not necessary, as she should never kill anybody, and should carry it only as a symbol of authority.

At Tours she designed her Standard, and a Scotch painter named James Power made it. It was of the most delicate white *boucassin*, with fringes of silk. For device it bore the image of God the Father throned in the clouds and holding the world in His hand; two angels knelt at His feet, presenting lilies; inscription, JESUS, MARIA; on the reverse the crown of France supported by two angels.

She also caused a smaller standard or pennon to be made, whereon was represented an angel offering a lily to the Holy Virgin.

Everything was humming, there at Tours. Every now and then one heard the bray and crash of military music, every little while one heard the measured tramp of marching men— squads of recruits leaving for Blois; songs and shoutings and huzzas filled the air night and day, the town was full of strangers, the streets and inns were thronged, the bustle of preparation was everywhere, and everybody carried a glad and cheerful face. Around Joan's headquarters a crowd of people was always massed, hoping for a glimpse of the new General, and when they got it, they went wild; but they seldom got it, for she was busy planning her campaign, receiving reports, giving orders, despatching couriers, and giving what odd moments she could spare to the companies of great folk waiting in the drawing-rooms. As for us boys, we hardly saw her at all, she was so occupied.

We were in a mixed state of mind—sometimes hopeful, sometimes not; mostly not. She had not appointed her household yet—that was our trouble. We knew she was being overrun with applications for places in it, and that these applications were backed by great names and weighty influence, whereas we had nothing of the sort to recommend us. She could fill her humblest places with titled folk—folk whose relationships would be a bulwark for her and a valu-

able support at all times. In these circumstances would policy
allow her to consider us? We were not as cheerful as the rest
of the town, but were inclined to be depressed and worried.
Sometimes we discussed our slim chances and gave them as
good an appearance as we could. But the very mention of the
subject was anguish to the Paladin; for whereas we had some
little hope, he had none at all. As a rule, Noël Rainguesson
was quite willing to let the dismal matter alone; but not when
the Paladin was present. Once we were talking the thing over,
when Noël said—

"Cheer up, Paladin; I had a dream last night, and you were
the only one among us that got an appointment. It wasn't a
high one, but it was an appointment, anyway—some kind of
a lackey or body-servant, or something of that kind."

The Paladin roused up and looked almost cheerful; for he
was a believer in dreams, and in anything and everything of a
superstitious sort, in fact. He said, with a rising hopefulness—

"I wish it might come true. Do you think it will come
true?"

"Certainly; I might almost say I know it will, for my
dreams hardly ever fail."

"Noël, I could hug you if that dream could come true, I
could indeed! To be servant to the first General of France and
have all the world hear of it, and the news go back to the
village and make those gawks stare that always said I wouldn't
ever amount to anything—wouldn't it be great! Do you
think it *will* come true, Noël? Don't you believe it will?"

"I do. There's my hand on it."

"Noël, if it comes true I'll never forget you—shake again!
I should be dressed in a noble livery, and the news would go
to the village, and those animals would say, '*Him*, lackey to
the General-in-Chief, with the eyes of the whole world on
him, admiring—well, he has shot up into the sky, now, hasn't
he!'"

He began to walk the floor and pile castles in the air so fast
and so high that we could hardly keep up with him. Then all
of a sudden all the joy went out of his face and misery took its
place, and he said:

"Oh dear, it is all a mistake, it will never come true. I forgot about that foolish business at Toul. I have kept out of her

sight as much as I could, all these weeks, hoping she would forget that and forgive it—but I know she never will. She can't, of course. And after all, I wasn't to blame. I did say she promised to marry me, but they put me up to it and persuaded me, I swear they did!" The vast creature was almost crying. Then he pulled himself together and said, remorsefully, "It was the only lie I've ever told, and—"

He was drowned out with a chorus of groans and outraged exclamations; and before he could begin again, one of D'Aulon's liveried servants appeared and said we were required at headquarters. We rose, and Noël said—

"There—what did I tell you? I have a presentiment—the spirit of prophecy is upon me. She is going to appoint him, and we are to go there and do him homage. Come along!"

But the Paladin was afraid to go, so we left him.

When we presently stood in the presence, in front of a crowd of glittering officers of the army, Joan greeted us with a winning smile, and said she appointed all of us to places in her household, for she wanted her old friends by her. It was a beautiful surprise to have ourselves honored like this when she could have had people of birth and consequence instead, but we couldn't find our tongues to say so, she was become so great and so high above us now. One at a time we stepped forward and each received his warrant from the hand of our chief, D'Aulon. All of us had honorable places: the two knights stood highest; then Joan's two brothers; I was first page and secretary, a young gentleman named Raimond was second page; Noël was her messenger; she had two heralds, and also a chaplain and almoner, whose name was Jean Pasquerel. She had previously appointed a maître d'hôtel and a number of domestics. Now she looked around and said—

"But where is the Paladin?"

The Sieur Bertrand said—

"He thought he was not sent for, your Excellency."

"Now that is not well. Let him be called."

The Paladin entered humbly enough. He ventured no farther than just within the door. He stopped there, looking embarrassed and afraid. Then Joan spoke pleasantly, and said—

"I watched you on the road. You began badly, but improved. Of old you were a fantastic talker, but there is a man in you, and I will bring it out." It was fine to see the Paladin's face light up when she said that. "Will you follow where I lead?"

"Into the fire!" he said; and I said to myself, "By the ring of that, I think she has turned this braggart into a hero. It is another of her miracles, I make no doubt of it."

"I believe you," said Joan. "Here—take my banner. You will ride with me in every field, and when France is saved, you will give it me back."

He took the banner, which is now the most precious of the memorials that remain of Joan of Arc, and his voice was unsteady with emotion when he said—

"If I ever disgrace this trust, my comrades here will know how to do a friend's office upon my body, and this charge I lay upon them, as knowing they will not fail me."

Chapter XI

NOËL and I went back together—silent at first, and impressed. Finally Noël came up out of his thinkings and said—

"The first shall be last and the last first—there's authority for this surprise. But at the same time *wasn't* it a lofty hoist for our big bull!"

"It truly was; I am not over being stunned yet. It was the greatest place in her gift."

"Yes, it was. There are many generals, and she can create more; but there is only one Standard-Bearer."

"True. It is the most conspicuous place in the army, after her own."

"And the most coveted and honorable. Sons of two dukes tried to get it, as we know. And of all people in the world, this majestic windmill carries it off. Well, isn't it a gigantic promotion, when you come to look at it!"

"There's no doubt about it. It's a kind of copy of Joan's own in miniature."

"I don't know how to account for it—do you?"

"Yes—without any trouble at all—that is, I think I do."

Noël was surprised at that, and glanced up quickly, as if to see if I was in earnest. He said—

"I thought you couldn't be in earnest, but I see you are. If you can make me understand this puzzle, do it. Tell me what the explanation is."

"I believe I can. You have noticed that our chief knight says a good many wise things and has a thoughtful head on his shoulders. One day, riding along, we were talking about Joan's great talents, and he said, 'But, greatest of all her gifts, she has the seeing eye.' I said, like an unthinking fool, 'The seeing eye?—I shouldn't count that for much—I suppose we all have it.' 'No,' he said; 'very few have it.' Then he explained, and made his meaning clear. He said the common eye sees only the outside of things, and judges by that, but the seeing eye pierces through and reads the heart and the soul, finding there capacities which the outside didn't indicate or promise, and which the other kind of eye couldn't detect. He said the mightiest military genius must fail and come to nothing if it have not the seeing eye—that is to say, if it cannot read men and select its subordinates with an infallible judgment. It sees as by intuition that this man is good for strategy, that one for dash and dare-devil assault, the other for patient bull-dog persistence, and it appoints each to his right place and wins, while the commander without the seeing eye would give to each the other's place and lose. He was right about Joan, and I saw it. When she was a child and the tramp came one night, her father and all of us took him for a rascal, but she saw the honest man through the rags. When I dined with the governor of Vaucouleurs so long ago, I saw nothing in our two knights, though I sat with them and talked with them two hours; Joan was there five minutes, and neither spoke with them nor heard them speak, yet she marked them for men of worth and fidelity, and they have confirmed her judgment. Whom has she sent for to take charge of this thundering rabble of new recruits at Blois, made up of old disbanded Armagnac raiders, unspeakable hellions, every one? Why, she has sent for Satan himself—that is to say, La Hire—that military hurricane, that godless swashbuckler, that lurid conflagration of blasphemy, that Vesuvius of pro- fanity, forever in eruption. Does he know how to deal with that mob of roaring devils? Better than any man that lives; for he is the head devil of this world his own self, he is the match of the whole of them combined, and probably the father of most of them. She places him in temporary command until she can get to Blois herself—and then! Why, then she will certainly take them in hand personally, or I don't know her as well as I ought to, after all these years of intimacy. That will be a sight to see—that fair spirit in her white armor, deliver- ing her will to that muck-heap, that rag-pile, that abandoned refuse of perdition."

"La Hire!" cried Noël, "our hero of all these years—I do want to see that man!"

"I too. His name stirs me just as it did when I was a little boy."

"I want to hear him swear."

"Of course. I would rather hear him swear than another

man pray. He is the frankest man there is, and the naïvest. Once when he was rebuked for pillaging on his raids, he said it was nothing. Said he, 'If God the Father were a soldier, He would rob.' I judge he is the right man to take temporary charge there at Blois. Joan has cast the seeing eye upon him, you see."

"Which brings us back to where we started. I have an honest affection for the Paladin, and not merely because he is a good fellow, but because he is my child—I made him what he is, the windiest blusterer and most catholic liar in the kingdom. I'm glad of his luck, but I hadn't the seeing eye. I shouldn't have chosen him for the most dangerous post in the army, I should have placed him in the rear to kill the wounded and violate the dead."

"Well, we shall see. Joan probably knows what is in him better than we do. And I'll give you another idea. When a person in Joan of Arc's position tells a man he is brave, he *believes* it; and *believing* it is enough; in fact to believe yourself brave is to *be* brave; it is the one only essential thing."

"Now you've hit it!" cried Noël. "She's got the creating mouth as well as the seeing eye! Ah yes, that is the thing. France was cowed and a coward; Joan of Arc has spoken, and France is marching, with her head up!"

I was summoned now, to write a letter from Joan's dictation. During the next day and night our several uniforms were made by the tailors, and our new armor provided. We were beautiful to look upon now, whether clothed for peace or war. Clothed for peace, in costly stuffs and rich colors, the Paladin was a tower dyed with the glories of the sunset; plumed and sashed and iron-clad for war, he was a still statelier thing to look at.

Orders had been issued for the march towards Blois. It was a clear, sharp, beautiful morning. As our showy great company trotted out in column, riding two and two, Joan and the Duke of Alençon in the lead, D'Aulon and the big standard-bearer next, and so on, we made a handsome spectacle, as you may well imagine; and as we ploughed through the cheering crowds, with Joan bowing her plumed head to left and right and the sun glinting from her silver mail, the spectators realized that the curtain was rolling up before their eyes upon the first act of a prodigious drama, and their rising hopes were expressed in an enthusiasm that increased with each moment, until at last one seemed to even physically feel the concussion of the huzzas as well as hear them. Far down the street we heard the softened strains of wind-blown music, and saw a cloud of lancers moving, the sun glowing with a subdued light upon the massed armor but striking bright upon the soaring lance-heads—a vaguely luminous nebula, so to speak, with a constellation twinkling above it—and that was our guard of honor. It joined us, the procession was complete, the first war-march of Joan of Arc was begun, the curtain was up.

Chapter XII

W E WERE at Blois three days. Oh, that camp, it is one of the treasures of my memory! Order? There was no more order among those brigands than there is among the wolves and the hyenas. They went roaring and drinking about, whooping, shouting, swearing, and entertaining themselves with all manner of rude and riotous horse-play; and the place was full of loud and lewd women, and they were no whit behind the men for romps and noise and fantastics.

It was in the midst of this wild mob that Noël and I had our first glimpse of La Hire. He answered to our dearest dreams. He was of great size and of martial bearing, he was cased in mail from head to heel, with a bushel of swishing plumes on his helmet, and at his side the vast sword of the time.

He was on his way to pay his respects in state to Joan, and as he passed through the camp he was restoring order, and proclaiming that the Maid was come, and he would have no such spectacle as this exposed to the head of the army. His way of creating order was his own, not borrowed. He did it with his great fists. As he moved along swearing and admonishing, he let drive this way, that way, and the other, and wherever his blow landed, a man went down.

"Damn you!" he said, "staggering and cursing around like this, and the Commander-in-Chief in the camp! Straighten up!" and he laid the man flat. What his idea of straightening up was, was his own secret.

We followed the veteran to headquarters, listening, observing, admiring—yes, devouring, you may say, the pet hero of the boys of France from our cradles up to that happy day, and their idol and ours. I called to mind how Joan had once rebuked the Paladin, there in the pastures of Domremy, for uttering lightly those mighty names, La Hire and the Bastard of Orleans, and how she said that if she could but be permitted to stand afar off and let her eyes rest once upon those great men, she would hold it a privilege. They were to her and the other girls just what they were to the boys. Well, here was one of them, at last—and what was his errand? It was hard to realize it, and yet it was true; he was coming to uncover his head before her and take her orders.

While he was quieting a considerable group of his brigands in his soothing way, near headquarters, we stepped on ahead and got a glimpse of Joan's military family, the great chiefs of the army, for they had all arrived now. There they were, six officers of wide renown, handsome men in beautiful armor, but the Lord High Admiral of France was the handsomest of them all and had the most gallant bearing.

When La Hire entered, one could see the surprise in his face at Joan's beauty and extreme youth, and one could see, too, by Joan's glad smile, that it made her happy to get sight of this hero of her childhood at last. La Hire bowed low, with his helmet in his gauntleted hand, and made a bluff but handsome little speech with hardly an oath in it, and one could see that those two took to each other on the spot.

The visit of ceremony was soon over, and the others went away; but La Hire stayed, and he and Joan sat there, and he sipped her wine, and they talked and laughed together like old friends. And presently she gave him some instructions, in his quality as master of the camp, which made his breath stand still. For, to begin with, she said that all those loose women must pack out of the place at once, she wouldn't allow one of them to remain. Next, the rough carousing must stop, drinking must be brought within proper and strictly defined limits, and discipline must take the place of disorder. And finally she climaxed the list of surprises with this—which nearly lifted him out of his armor:

"Every man who joins my standard must confess before the priest and absolve himself from sin; and all accepted recruits must be present at divine service twice a day."

La Hire could not say a word for a good part of a minute, then he said, in deep dejection:

"Oh, sweet child, they were littered in hell, these poor darlings of mine! Attend mass? Why, dear heart, they'll see us both damned first!"

And he went on, pouring out a most pathetic stream of arguments and blasphemy, which broke Joan all up, and made

her laugh as she had not laughed since she played in the
Domremy pastures. It was good to hear.

But she stuck to her point; so the soldier yielded, and said
all right, if such were the orders he must obey, and would do
the best that was in him; then he refreshed himself with a
lurid explosion of oaths, and said that if any man in the camp
refused to renounce sin and lead a pious life, he would knock
his head off. That started Joan off again: she was really having
a good time, you see. But she would not consent to that form
of conversions. She said they must be voluntary.

La Hire said that that was all right, he wasn't going to kill
the voluntary ones, but only the others.

No matter, none of them must be killed—Joan couldn't
have it. She said that to give a man a chance to volunteer, on
pain of death if he didn't, left him more or less trammelled,
and she wanted him to be entirely free.

So the soldier sighed and said he would advertise the mass,
but said he doubted if there was a man in camp that was any
more likely to go to it than he was himself. Then there was
another surprise for him, for Joan said—

"But dear man, *you* are going!"

"I? Impossible! Oh, this is lunacy!"

"Oh no, it isn't. You are going to the service—twice a
day."

"Oh, am I dreaming? Am I drunk—or is my hearing playing me false? Why, I would rather go to—"

"Never mind where. In the morning you are going to begin, and after that it will come easy. Now *don't* look down-
hearted like that. Soon you won't mind it."

La Hire tried to cheer up, but he was not able to do it. He
sighed like a zephyr, and presently said—

"Well, I'll do it for you, but before I would do it for another, I swear I—"

"But don't swear. Break it off."

"Break it off? It is impossible. I beg you to—to— Why—
oh, my General, it is my native speech!"

He begged so hard for grace for his impediment, that Joan
left him one fragment of it; she said he might swear by his
bâton, the symbol of his generalship.

He promised that he would swear only by his bâton when

in her presence, and would try to modify himself elsewhere, but doubted if he could manage it, now that it was so old and stubborn a habit, and such a solace and support to his declining years.

That tough old lion went away from there a good deal tamed and civilized—not to say softened and sweetened, for perhaps those expressions would hardly fit him. Noël and I believed that when he was away from Joan's influence his old aversions would come up so strong in him that he could not master them, and so wouldn't go to mass. But we got up early in the morning to see.

Well, he really went. It was hardly believable, but there he was, striding along, holding himself grimly to his duty, and looking as pious as he could, but growling and cursing like a fiend. It was another instance of the same old thing: whoever listened to the voice and looked into the eyes of Joan of Arc fell under a spell, and was not his own man any more.

Satan was converted, you see. Well, the rest followed. Joan rode up and down that camp, and wherever that fair young form appeared in its shining armor, with that sweet face to grace the vision and perfect it, the rude host seemed to think they saw the god of war in person, descended out of the clouds; and first they wondered, then they worshipped. After that, she could do with them what she would.

In three days it was a clean camp and orderly, and those barbarians were herding to divine service twice a day like good children. The women were gone. La Hire was stunned by these marvels; he could not understand them. He went outside the camp when he wanted to swear. He was that sort of a man—sinful by nature and habit, but full of superstitious respect for holy places.

The enthusiasm of the reformed army for Joan, its devotion to her, and the hot desire she had aroused in it to be led against the enemy, exceeded any manifestations of this sort which La Hire had ever seen before in his long career. His admiration of it all, and his wonder over the mystery and miracle of it, were beyond his power to put into words. He had held this army cheap before, but his pride and confidence in it knew no limits now. He said—

"Two or three days ago it was afraid of a hen-roost; one could storm the gates of hell with it now."

Joan and he were inseparable, and a quaint and pleasant contrast they made. He was so big, she so little; he was so gray and so far along in his pilgrimage of life, she so youthful; his face was so bronzed and scarred, hers so fair and pink, so fresh and smooth; she was so gracious, and he so stern; she was so pure, so innocent, he such a cyclopædia of sin. In her eye was stored all charity and compassion, in his lightnings; when her glance fell upon you it seemed to bring benediction and the peace of God, but with his it was different, generally.

They rode through the camp a dozen times a day, visiting every corner of it, observing, inspecting, perfecting; and wherever they appeared the enthusiasm broke forth. They rode side by side, he a great figure of brawn and muscle, she a little master-work of roundness and grace; he a fortress of rusty iron, she a shining statuette of silver; and when the re-formed raiders and bandits caught sight of them they spoke out, with affection and welcome in their voices, and said—

"There they come—Satan and the Page of Christ!"

All the three days that we were in Blois, Joan worked earnestly and tirelessly to bring La Hire to God—to rescue him from the bondage of sin—to breathe into his stormy heart the serenity and peace of religion. She urged, she begged, she implored him to pray. He stood out, the three days of our stay, begging almost piteously to be let off—to be let off from just that one thing, that impossible thing; he would do anything else—anything—command, and he would obey—he would go through the fire for her if she said the word—but spare him this, only this, for he couldn't pray, had never prayed, he was ignorant of how to frame a prayer, he had no words to put it in.

And yet—can any believe it?—she carried even that point, she won that incredible victory. She made La Hire pray. It shows, I think, that nothing was impossible to Joan of Arc. Yes, he stood there before her and put up his mailed hands and made a prayer. And it was not borrowed, but was his very own; he had none to help him frame it, he made it out of his own head—saying:

"Fair Sir God, I pray you to do by La Hire as he would do by you if you were La Hire and he were God."*

Then he put on his helmet and marched out of Joan's tent as satisfied with himself as any one might be who has arranged a perplexed and difficult business to the content and admiration of all the parties concerned in the matter.

If I had known that he had been praying, I could have understood why he was feeling so superior, but of course I could not know that.

I was coming to the tent at that moment, and saw him come out, and saw him march away in that large fashion, and indeed it was fine and beautiful to see. But when I got to the tent door I stopped and stepped back, grieved and shocked, for I heard Joan crying, as I mistakenly thought—crying as if she could not contain nor endure the anguish of her soul, crying as if she would die. But it was not so, she was laughing—laughing at La Hire's prayer.

It was not until six-and-thirty years afterwards that I found that out, and then—oh, then I only cried when that picture of young care-free mirth rose before me out of the blur and mists of that long-vanished time; for there had come a day between, when God's good gift of laughter had gone out from me to come again no more in this life.

*This prayer has been stolen many times and by many nations in the past four hundred and sixty years, but it originated with La Hire, and the fact is of official record in the National Archives of France. We have the authority of Michelet for this.—TRANSLATOR.

Chapter XIII

W E MARCHED out in great strength and splendor, and took the road toward Orleans. The initial part of Joan's great dream was realizing itself at last. It was the first time that any of us youngsters had ever seen an army, and it was a most stately and imposing spectacle to us. It was indeed an inspiring sight, that interminable column, stretching away into the fading distances, and curving itself in and out of the crookedness of the road like a mighty serpent. Joan rode at the head of it with her personal staff; then came a body of priests singing the *Veni Creator*, the banner of the Cross rising out of their midst; after these the glinting forest of spears. The several divisions were commanded by the great Armagnac generals, La Hire, the Marshal de Boussac, the Sire de Retz, Florent d'Illiers, and Poton de Saintrailles.

Each in his degree was tough, and there were three degrees—tough, tougher, toughest—and La Hire was the last by a shade, but only a shade. They were just illustrious official brigands, the whole party; and by long habits of lawlessness they had lost all acquaintanceship with obedience, if they had ever had any.

The King's strict orders to them had been, "Obey the General-in-Chief in everything; attempt nothing without her knowledge, do nothing without her command."

But what was the good of saying that? These independent birds knew no law. They seldom obeyed the King; they never obeyed him when it didn't suit them to do it. Would they obey the Maid? In the first place they wouldn't know *how* to obey her or anybody else, and in the second place it was of course not possible for them to take her military character seriously—that country girl of seventeen who had been trained for the complex and terrible business of war—how? By tending sheep.

They had no idea of obeying her except in cases where their veteran military knowledge and experience showed them that the thing she required was sound and right when gauged by the regular military standards. Were they to blame for this attitude? I should think not. Old war-worn captains are hard-headed, practical men. They do not easily believe in the ability of ignorant children to plan campaigns and command armies. No general that ever lived could have taken Joan seriously (militarily) before she raised the siege of Orleans and followed it with the great campaign of the Loire.

Did they consider Joan valueless? Far from it. They valued her as the fruitful earth values the sun—they fully believed she could produce the crop, but that it was in their line of business, not hers, to take it off. They had a deep and super-stitious reverence for her as being endowed with a mysterious supernatural something that was able to do a mighty thing which they were powerless to do—blow the breath of life and valor into the dead corpses of cowed armies and turn them into heroes.

To their minds they were everything *with* her, but nothing without her. She could inspire the soldiers and fit them for battle—but fight the battle herself? Oh, nonsense—that was their function. They, the generals, would fight the battles, Joan would give the victory. That was their idea—an uncon-scious paraphrase of Joan's reply to the Dominican.

So they began by playing a deception upon her. She had a clear idea of how she meant to proceed. It was her purpose to march boldly upon Orleans by the north bank of the Loire. She gave that order to her generals. They said to themselves, "The idea is insane—it is blunder No. 1; it is what might have been expected of this child who is ignorant of war." They privately sent the word to the Bastard of Orleans. He also recognized the insanity of it—at least he thought he did—and privately advised the generals to get around the order in some way.

They did it by deceiving Joan. She trusted those people, she was not expecting this sort of treatment, and was not on the lookout for it. It was a lesson to her; she saw to it that the game was not played a second time.

Why was Joan's idea insane, from the generals' point of view, but not from hers? Because her plan was to raise the siege immediately, by fighting, while theirs was to besiege the besiegers and starve them out by closing their commu-nications—a plan which would require months in the con-summation.

The English had built a fence of strong fortresses called bastilles around Orleans—fortresses which closed all the gates of the city but one. To the French generals the idea of trying to fight their way past those fortresses and lead the army into Orleans was preposterous; they believed that the result would be the army's destruction. One may not doubt that their opinion was militarily sound—no, *would* have been, but for one circumstance which they overlooked. That was this: the English soldiers were in a demoralized condition of superstitious terror; they had become satisfied that the Maid was in league with Satan. By reason of this a good deal of their courage had oozed out and vanished. On the other hand the Maid's soldiers were full of courage, enthusiasm, and zeal.

Joan could have marched by the English forts. However, it was not to be. She had been cheated out of her first chance to strike a heavy blow for her country.

In camp that night she slept in her armor on the ground. It was a cold night, and she was nearly as stiff as her armor itself when we resumed the march in the morning, for iron is not good material for a blanket. However, her joy in being now so far on her way to the theatre of her mission was fire enough to warm her, and it soon did it.

Her enthusiasm and impatience rose higher and higher with every mile of progress; but at last we reached Olivet, and down it went, and indignation took its place. For she saw the trick that had been played upon her—the river lay between us and Orleans.

She was for attacking one of the three bastilles that were on our side of the river and forcing access to the bridge which it guarded (a project which, if successful, would raise the siege instantly), but the long-ingrained fear of the English came upon her generals and they implored her not to make the attempt. The soldiers wanted to attack, but had to suffer disappointment. So we moved on and came to a halt at a point opposite Chécy, six miles above Orleans.

Dunois, Bastard of Orleans, with a body of knights and citizens, came up from the city to welcome Joan. Joan was still burning with resentment over the trick that had been put upon her, and was not in the mood for soft speeches, even to revered military idols of her childhood. She said—

"Are you the Bastard of Orleans?"

"Yes, I am he, and am right glad of your coming."

"And did you advise that I be brought by this side of the river instead of straight to Talbot and the English?"

Her high manner abashed him and he was not able to answer with anything like a confident promptness, but with many hesitations and partial excuses he managed to get out the confession that for what he and the council had regarded as imperative military reasons they had so advised.

"In God's name," said Joan, "my Lord's counsel is safer and wiser than yours. You thought to deceive me, but you have deceived yourselves, for I bring you the best help that ever knight or city had; for it is God's help, not sent for love of me, but by God's pleasure. At the prayer of St. Louis and St. Charlemagne He has had pity on Orleans, and will not suffer the enemy to have both the Duke of Orleans and his city. The provisions to save the starving people are here, the boats are below the city, the wind is contrary, they cannot come up hither. Now then tell me, in God's name, you who are so wise, what that council of yours was thinking about, to invent this foolish difficulty."

Dunois and the rest fumbled around the matter a moment, then gave in and conceded that a blunder had been made.

"Yes, a blunder has been made," said Joan, "and except God take your proper work upon Himself and change the wind and correct your blunder for you, there is none else that can devise a remedy."

Some of those people began to perceive that with all her technical ignorance she had practical good sense, and that with all her native sweetness and charm she was not the right kind of a person to play with.

Presently God did take the blunder in hand, and by His grace the wind did change. So the fleet of boats came up and went away loaded with provisions and cattle, and conveyed that welcome succor to the hungry city, managing the matter successfully under protection of a sortie from the walls against the bastille of St. Loup. Then Joan began on the Bastard again:

"You see here the army?"

"Yes."

"It is here on this side by advice of your council?"

"Yes."

"Now, in God's name, can that wise council explain why it is better to have it here than it would be to have it in the bottom of the sea?"

Dunois made some wandering attempts to explain the inexplicable and excuse the inexcusable, but Joan cut him short and said—

"Answer me this, good sir—has the army any value on this side of the river?"

The Bastard confessed that it hadn't—that is, in view of the plan of campaign which she had devised and decreed.

"And yet, knowing this, you had the hardihood to disobey my orders. Since the army's place is on the other side, will you explain to me how it is to get there?"

The whole size of the needless muddle was apparent. Evasions were of no use; therefore Dunois admitted that there was no way to correct the blunder but to send the army all the way back to Blois, and let it begin over again and come up on the other side this time, according to Joan's original plan.

Any other girl, after winning such a triumph as this over a veteran soldier of old renown, might have exulted a little and been excusable for it, but Joan showed no disposition of this sort. She dropped a word or two of grief over the precious time that must be lost, then began at once to issue commands for the march back. She sorrowed to see her army go; for she said its heart was great and its enthusiasm high, and that with it at her back she did not fear to face all the might of England.

All arrangements having been completed for the return of the main body of the army, she took the Bastard and La Hire and a thousand men and went down to Orleans, where all the town was in a fever of impatience to have sight of her face. It was eight in the evening when she and the troops rode in at the Burgundy gate, with the Paladin preceding her with her standard. She was riding a white horse, and she carried in her hand the sacred sword of Fierbois. You should have seen Orleans then. What a picture it was! Such black seas of people, such a starry firmament of torches, such roaring whirlwinds of welcome, such booming of bells and thundering of cannon! It was as if the world was come to an end. Everywhere in the glare of the torches one saw rank upon rank of upturned white faces, the mouths wide open, shouting, and the unchecked tears running down; Joan forged her slow way through the solid masses, her mailed form projecting above the pavement of heads like a silver statue. The people about her struggled along, gazing up at her through their tears with the rapt look of men and women who believe they are seeing one who is divine; and always her feet were being kissed by grateful folk, and such as failed of that privilege touched her horse and then kissed their fingers.

Nothing that Joan did escaped notice; everything she did was commented upon and applauded. You could hear the remarks going all the time.

"There—she's smiling—see!"

"Now she's taking her little plumed cap off to somebody—ah, it's fine and graceful!"

"She's patting that woman on the head with her gauntlet."

"Oh, she was born on a horse—see her turn in her saddle, and kiss the hilt of her sword to the ladies in the window that threw the flowers down."

"Now there's a poor woman lifting up a child—she's kissed it—oh, she's divine!"

"What a dainty little figure it is, and what a lovely face—and such color and animation!"

Joan's slender long banner streaming backward had an accident—the fringe caught fire from a torch. She leaned forward and crushed the flame in her hand.

"She's not afraid of fire nor anything!" they shouted, and delivered a storm of admiring applause that made everything quake.

She rode to the cathedral and gave thanks to God, and the people crammed the place and added their devotions to hers; then she took up her march again and picked her slow way through the crowds and the wilderness of torches to the house of Jacques Boucher, treasurer of the Duke of Orleans, where she was to be the guest of his wife as long as she stayed in the city, and have his young daughter for comrade and room-mate. The delirium of the people went on the rest of the night, and with it the clamor of the joy-bells and the welcoming cannon.

Joan of Arc had stepped upon her stage at last, and was ready to begin.

Chapter XIV

S HE was ready, but must sit down and wait until there was an army to work with.

Next morning, Saturday, April 30, 1429, she set about inquiring after the messenger who carried her proclamation to the English from Blois—the one which she had dictated at Poitiers. Here is a copy of it. It is a remarkable document, for several reasons: for its matter-of-fact directness, for its high spirit and forcible diction, and for its naïve confidence in her ability to achieve the prodigious task which she had laid upon herself, or which had been laid upon her—which you please. All through it you seem to see the pomps of war and hear the rumbling of the drums. In it Joan's warrior soul is revealed, and for the moment the soft little shepherdess has disappeared from your view. This untaught country damsel, unused to dictating anything at all to anybody, much less documents of state to kings and generals, poured out this procession of vigorous sentences as fluently as if this sort of work had been her trade from childhood:

"JESUS MARIA

"King of England, and you Duke of Bedford who call yourself Regent of France; William de la Pole, Earl of Suffolk; and you Thomas Lord Scales, who style yourselves lieutenants of the said Bedford—do right to the King of Heaven. Render to the Maid who is sent by God the keys of all the good towns you have taken and violated in France. She is sent hither by God to restore the blood royal. She is very ready to make peace if you will do her right by giving up France and paying for what you have held. And you archers, companions of war, noble and otherwise, who are before the the good city of Orleans, begone into your own land in God's name, or expect news from the Maid who will shortly go to see you to your very great hurt. King of England, if you do not so, I am chief of war, and wherever I shall find your people in France I will drive them out, willing or not willing; and if they do not obey I will slay them all, but if they obey, I will have them to mercy. I am come hither by God, the King of Heaven, body for body, to put you out of France, in spite of those who would work treason and mischief against the kingdom. Think not you shall ever hold the kingdom from the King of Heaven, the Son of the blessed Mary; King Charles shall hold it, for God wills it so, and has revealed it to him by the Maid. If you believe not the news sent by God through the Maid, wherever we shall meet you we will strike boldly and make such a noise as has not been in France these thousand years. Be sure that God can send more strength to the Maid than you can bring to any assault against her and her good men-at-arms; and then we shall see who has the better right, the King of Heaven, or you. Duke of Bedford, the Maid prays you not to bring about your own destruction. If you do her right, you may yet go in her company where the French shall do the finest deed that has ever been done in Christendom, and if you do not, you shall be reminded shortly of your great wrongs."

In that closing sentence she invites them to go on crusade with her to rescue the Holy Sepulchre.

No answer had been returned to this proclamation, and the messenger himself had not come back. So now she sent her two heralds with a new letter warning the English to raise the siege and requiring them to restore that missing messenger. The heralds came back without him. All they brought was notice from the English to Joan that they would presently catch her and burn her if she did not clear out now while she had a chance, and "go back to her proper trade of minding cows."

She held her peace, only saying it was a pity that the English would persist in inviting present disaster and eventual destruction when she was "doing all she could to get them out of the country with their lives still in their bodies."

Presently she thought of an arrangement that might be acceptable, and said to the heralds, "Go back and say to Lord Talbot this, from me: 'Come out of your bastilles with your host, and I will come with mine; if I beat you, go in peace out of France; if you beat me, burn me, according to your desire.' "

I did not hear this, but Dunois did, and spoke of it. The challenge was refused.

Sunday morning her Voices or some instinct gave her a warning, and she sent Dunois to Blois to take command of the army and hurry it to Orleans. It was a wise move, for he found Regnault de Chartres and some more of the King's pet rascals there trying their best to disperse the army, and crippling all the efforts of Joan's generals to head it for Orleans. They were a fine lot, those miscreants. They turned their attention to Dunois, now, but he had balked Joan once, with unpleasant results to himself, and was not minded to meddle in that way again. He soon had the army moving.

Chapter XV

WE OF the personal staff were in fairy-land, now, during the few days that we waited for the return of the army. We went into society. To our two knights this was not a novelty, but to us young villagers it was a new and wonderful life. Any position of any sort near the person of the Maid of Vaucouleurs conferred high distinction upon the holder and caused his society to be courted; and so the D'Arc brothers, and Noël, and the Paladin, humble peasants at home, were gentlemen here, personages of weight and influence. It was fine to see how soon their country diffidences and awkwardnesses melted away under this pleasant sun of deference and disappeared, and how lightly and easily they took to their new atmosphere. The Paladin was as happy as it was possible for any one in this earth to be. His tongue went all the time, and daily he got new delight out of hearing himself talk. He began to enlarge his ancestry and spread it out all around, and ennoble it right and left, and it was not long until it consisted almost entirely of Dukes. He worked up his old battles and tricked them out with fresh splendors; also with new terrors, for he added artillery now. We had seen cannon for the first time at Blois—a few pieces—here there was plenty of it, and now and then we had the impressive spectacle of a huge English bastille hidden from sight in a mountain of smoke from its own guns, with lances of red flame darting through it; and this grand picture, along with the quaking thunders pounding away in the heart of it, inflamed the Paladin's imagination and enabled him to dress out those ambuscade-skirmishes of ours with a sublimity which made it impossible for any to recognize them at all except people who had not been there.

You may suspect that there was a special inspiration for these great efforts of the Paladin's, and there was. It was the daughter of the house, Catherine Boucher, who was eighteen, and gentle and lovely in her ways, and very beautiful. I think she might have been as beautiful as Joan herself, if she had had Joan's eyes. But that could never be. There was never but that one pair, there will never be another. Joan's eyes were deep and rich and wonderful beyond anything merely earthly. They spoke all the languages—they had no need of words. They produced all effects—and just by a glance, just a single glance: a glance that could convict a liar of his lie and make him confess it; that could bring down a proud man's pride and make him humble; that could put courage into a coward and strike dead the courage of the bravest; that could appease resentments and real hatreds; that could speak peace to storms of passion and be obeyed; that could make the doubter believe and the hopeless hope again; that could purify the impure mind; that could persuade—ah, there it is—*persuasion!* that is the word; what or who is it that it couldn't persuade? The maniac of Domremy—the fairy-banishing priest—the reverend tribunal of Toul—the doubting and superstitious Laxart—the obstinate veteran of Vaucouleurs—the characterless heir of France—the sages and scholars of the Parliament and University of Poitiers—the darling of Satan, La Hire—the masterless Bastard of Orleans, accustomed to acknowledge no way as right and rational but his own—these were the trophies of that great gift that made her the wonder and mystery that she was.

We mingled companionably with the great folk who flocked to the big house to make Joan's acquaintance, and they made much of us and we lived in the clouds, so to speak. But what we preferred even to this happiness was the quieter occasions, when the formal guests were gone and the family and a few dozen of its familiar friends were gathered together for a social good time. It was then that we did our best, we five youngsters, with such fascinations as we had, and the chief object of them was Catherine. None of us had ever been in love before, and now we had the misfortune to all fall in love with the same person at the same time—which was the first moment we saw her. She was a merry heart, and full of life, and I still remember tenderly those few evenings that I was permitted to have my share of her dear society and of comradeship with that little company of charming people.

The Paladin made us all jealous the first night, for when he got fairly started on those battles of his he had everything to himself, and there was no use in anybody else's trying to get any attention. Those people had been living in the midst of real war for seven months; and to hear this windy giant lay out his imaginary campaigns and fairly swim in blood and spatter it all around, entertained them to the verge of the grave. Catherine was like to die, for pure enjoyment. She didn't laugh loud—we, of course, wished she would—but kept in the shelter of a fan, and shook until there was danger that she would unhitch her ribs from her spine. Then when the Paladin had got done with a battle and we began to feel thankful and hope for a change, she would speak up in a way that was so sweet and persuasive that it rankled in me, and ask him about some detail or other in the early part of his battle which she said had greatly interested her, and would he be so good as to describe that part again and with a little more particularity?—which of course precipitated the whole battle on us again, with a hundred lies added that had been overlooked before.

I do not know how to make you realize the pain I suffered. I had never been jealous before, and it seemed intolerable that this creature should have this good fortune which he was so ill entitled to, and I have to sit and see myself neglected when I was so longing for the least little attention out of the thousand that this beloved girl was lavishing upon him. I was near her, and tried two or three times to get started on some of the things that *I* had done in those battles—and I felt ashamed of myself, too, for stooping to such a business—but she cared for nothing but his battles, and could not be got to listen; and presently when one of my attempts caused her to lose some precious rag or other of his mendacities and she asked him to repeat, thus bringing on a new engagement of course and increasing the havoc and carnage tenfold, I felt so humiliated by this pitiful miscarriage of mine that I gave up and tried no more.

The others were as outraged by the Paladin's selfish conduct as I was—and by his grand luck, too, of course—perhaps, indeed, that was the main hurt. We talked our trouble over together, which was but natural, for rivals become brothers when a common affliction assails them and a common enemy bears off the victory.

Each of us could do things that would please and get notice if it were not for this person, who occupied all the time and gave others no chance. I had made a poem, taking a whole night to it—a poem in which I most happily and delicately celebrated that sweet girl's charms, without mentioning her name, but any one could see who was meant; for the bare title—"The Rose of Orleans" would reveal that, as it seemed to me. It pictured this pure and dainty white rose as growing up out of the rude soil of war and looking abroad out of its tender eyes upon the horrid machinery of death, and then— note this conceit—it blushes for the sinful nature of man, and *turns red* in a single night. Becomes a red rose, you see—a rose that was white before. The idea was my own, and quite new. Then it sent its sweet perfume out over the embattled city, and when the beleaguring forces smelt it they *laid down their arms and wept*. This was also my own idea, and new. That closed that part of the poem; then I put her into the similitude of the firmament—not the whole of it, but only part. That is to say, she was the moon, and all the constellations were following her about, their hearts in flames for love of her, but she would not halt, she would not listen, for 'twas thought she loved another. 'Twas thought she loved a poor unworthy suppliant who was upon the earth, facing danger, death, and possible mutilation in the bloody field, waging relentless war against a heartless foe to save her from an all too early grave, and her city from destruction. And when the sad pursuing constellations came to know and realize the bitter sorrow that was come upon them—note this idea—their hearts broke and their tears gushed forth, filling the vault of heaven with a fiery splendor, for those tears were *falling stars*. It was a rash idea, but beautiful; beautiful and pathetic; wonderfully pathetic, the way I had it, with the rhyme and all to help. At the end of each verse there was a two-line refrain pitying the poor earthly lover separated so far, and perhaps forever, from her he loved so well, and growing always paler and weaker and thinner in his agony as he neared the cruel grave—the most touching thing—even the boys themselves could hardly keep back their tears, the way Noël said those lines. There were eight four-line stanzas in the first end of the poem—the end about the rose, the horticultural end, as you may say, if that is not too large a name for such a little poem—and eight in the astronomical end—sixteen stanzas altogether, and I could have made it a hundred and fifty if I had wanted to, I was so inspired and so all swelled up with beautiful thoughts and fancies; but that would have been too many to sing or recite before a company, that way, whereas sixteen was just right, and could be done over again, if desired.

The boys were amazed that I could make such a poem as that out of my own head, and so was I, of course, it being as much a surprise to me as it could be to anybody, for I did not know that it was in me. If any had asked me a single day before if it was in me, I should have told them frankly no, it was not.

That is the way with us; we may go on half of our life not knowing such a thing is in us, when in reality it was there all the time, and all we needed was something to turn up that would call for it. Indeed, it was always so with our family. My grandfather had a cancer, and they never knew what was the matter with him till he died, and he didn't himself. It is wonderful how gifts and diseases can be concealed that way. All that was necessary in my case was for this lovely and inspiring girl to cross my path, and out came the poem, and no more trouble to me to word it and rhyme it and perfect it than it is to stone a dog. No, I should have said it was not in me; but it was.

The boys couldn't say enough about it, they were so charmed and astonished. The thing that pleased them the most was the way it would do the Paladin's business for him. They forgot everything in their anxiety to get him shelved and silenced. Noël Rainguesson was clear beside himself with admiration of the poem, and wished *he* could do such a thing, but it was out of his line and he couldn't, of course. He had it by heart in half an hour, and there was never anything so pathetic and beautiful as the way he recited it. For that was just his gift—that and mimicry. He could recite anything better than anybody in the world, and he could take off La Hire to the very life—or anybody else, for that matter. Now I never could recite worth a farthing; and when I tried with this poem the boys wouldn't let me finish; they would have nobody but Noël. So then, as I wanted the poem to make the best possible impression on Catherine and the company, I told Noël he might do the reciting. Never was anybody so delighted. He could hardly believe that I was in earnest, but I was. I said that to have them know that I was the author of it would be enough for me. The boys were full of exultation, and Noël said if he could just get one chance at those people it would be all he would ask; he would make them realize that there was something higher and finer than war-lies to be had here.

But how to get the opportunity—that was the difficulty. We invented several schemes that promised fairly, and at last we hit upon one that was sure. That was, to let the Paladin get a good start in a manufactured battle, and then send in a false call for him, and as soon as he was out of the room, have Noël take his place and finish the battle himself in the Paladin's own style, imitated to a shade. That would get great applause, and win the house's favor and put it in the right mood to hear the poem. The two triumphs together would finish the Standard-Bearer—modify him, anyway, to a certainty, and give the rest of us a chance for the future.

So the next night I kept out of the way until the Paladin had got his start and was sweeping down upon the enemy like a whirlwind at the head of his corps, then I stepped within the door in my official uniform and announced that a messenger from General La Hire's quarters desired speech with the Standard-Bearer. He left the room, and Noël took his place and said that the interruption was to be deplored, but that fortunately he was personally acquainted with the details of the battle himself, and if permitted would be glad to state them to the company. Then without waiting for the permission he turned himself into the Paladin—a dwarfed Paladin, of course—with manner, tones, gestures, attitudes, everything exact, and went right on with the battle, and it would be impossible to imagine a more perfectly and minutely ridiculous imitation than he furnished to those shrieking people. They went into spasms, convulsions, frenzies of laughter, and the tears flowed down their cheeks in rivulets. The more they laughed, the more inspired Noël grew with his theme and the greater the marvels he worked, till really the laughter was not properly laughing any more, but screaming. Blessedest feature of all, Catherine Boucher was dying with ecstasies, and

presently there was little left of her but gasps and suffocations. Victory? It was a perfect Agincourt.

The Paladin was gone only a couple of minutes; he found
out at once that a trick had been played on him, so he came
back. When he approached the door he heard Noël ranting in
there and recognized the state of the case; so he remained
near the door but out of sight, and heard the performance
through to the end. The applause Noël got when he finished
was wonderful; and they kept it up and kept it up, clapping
their hands like mad, and shouting to him to do it over again.

But Noël was clever. He knew the very best background for
a poem of deep and refined sentiment and pathetic melancholy was one where great and satisfying merriment has prepared the spirit for the powerful contrast.

So he paused until all was quiet, then his face grew grave
and assumed an impressive aspect, and at once all faces sobered in sympathy and took on a look of wondering and expectant interest. Now he began in a low but distinct voice the
opening verses of The Rose. As he breathed the rhythmic
measures forth, and one gracious line after another fell upon
those enchanted ears in that deep hush, one could catch, on
every hand, half-audible ejaculations of "How lovely—how
beautiful—how exquisite."

By this time the Paladin, who had gone away for a moment
with the opening of the poem, was back again, and had
stepped within the door. He stood there, now, resting his
great frame against the wall and gazing toward the reciter like
one entranced. When Noël got to the second part, and that
heart-breaking refrain began to melt and move all listeners,
the Paladin began to wipe away tears with the back of first
one hand and then the other. The next time the refrain was
repeated he got to snuffling, and sort of half sobbing, and
went to wiping his eyes with the sleeves of his doublet. He
was so conspicuous that he embarrassed Noël a little, and also
had an ill effect upon the audience. With the next repetition
he broke quite down and began to cry like a calf, which ruined all the effect and started many in the audience to laughing. Then he went on from bad to worse, until I never saw
such a spectacle; for he fetched out a towel from under his
doublet and began to swab his eyes with it and let go the

most infernal bellowings mixed up with sobbings and groanings and retchings and barkings and coughings and snortings
and screamings and howlings—and he twisted himself about
on his heels and squirmed this way and that, still pouring out
that brutal clamor and flourishing his towel in the air and
swabbing again and wringing it out. Hear? You couldn't hear
yourself think. Noël was wholly drowned out and silenced,
and those people were laughing the very lungs out of themselves. It was the most degrading sight that ever was. Now I
heard the clankety-clank that plate-armor makes when the
man that is in it is running, and then alongside my head there
burst out the most inhuman explosion of laughter that ever
rent the drum of a person's ear, and I looked, and it was La
Hire; and he stood there with his gauntlets on his hips and
his head tilted back and his jaws spread to that degree to let
out his hurricanes and his thunders that it amounted to indecent exposure, for you could see everything that was in him.
Only one thing more and worse could happen, and it happened: at the other door I saw the flurry and bustle and bow-
ings and scrapings of officials and flunkeys which means that
some great personage is coming—then Joan of Arc stepped
in, and the house rose! Yes, and tried to shut its indecorous
mouth and make itself grave and proper; but when it saw the
Maid herself go to laughing, it thanked God for this mercy
and the earthquake followed.

Such things make life a bitterness, and I do not wish to
dwell upon them. The effect of the poem was spoiled.

Chapter XVI

THIS EPISODE disagreed with me and I was not able to leave my bed the next day. The others were in the same condition. But for this, one or another of us might have had the good luck that fell to the Paladin's share that day; but it is observable that God in His compassion sends the good luck to such as are ill equipped with gifts, as compensation for their defect, but requires such as are more fortunately endowed to get by labor and talent what those others get by chance. It was Noël who said this, and it seemed to me to be well and justly thought.

The Paladin, going about the town all the day in order to be followed and admired and overhear the people say in an awed voice, "Ssh!—look, it is the Standard-Bearer of Joan of Arc!" had speech with all sorts and conditions of folk, and he learned from some boatmen that there was a stir of some kind going on in the bastilles on the other side of the river; and in the evening, seeking further, he found a deserter from the fortress called the "Augustins," who said that the English were going to send men over to strengthen the garrisons on our side during the darkness of the night, and were exulting greatly, for they meant to spring upon Dunois and the army when it was passing the bastilles and destroy it: a thing quite easy to do, since the "Witch" would not be there, and without her presence the army would do like the French armies of these many years past—drop their weapons and run when they saw an English face.

It was ten at night when the Paladin brought this news and asked leave to speak to Joan, and I was up and on duty then. It was a bitter stroke to me to see what a chance I had lost. Joan made searching inquiries, and satisfied herself that the word was true, then she made this annoying remark:

"You have done well, and you have my thanks. It may be that you have prevented a disaster. Your name and service shall receive official mention."

Then he bowed low, and when he rose he was eleven feet high. As he swelled out past me he covertly pulled down the corner of his eye with his finger and muttered part of that defiled refrain, "Oh tears, ah tears, oh sad sweet tears!—name in General Orders—personal mention to the King, you see!"

I wished Joan could have seen his conduct, but she was busy thinking what she would do. Then she had me fetch the knight Jean de Metz, and in a minute he was off for La Hire's quarters with orders for him and the Lord de Villars and Florent d'Iliers to report to her at five o'clock next morning with five hundred picked men well mounted. The histories say half-past four, but it is not true, I heard the order given.

We were on our way at five to the minute, and encountered the head of the arriving column between six and seven, a couple of leagues from the city. Dunois was pleased, for the army had begun to get restive and show uneasiness now that it was getting so near to the dreaded bastilles. But that all disappeared now, as the word ran down the line, with a huzzah that swept along the length of it like a wave, that the Maid was come. Dunois asked her to halt and let the column pass in review, so that the men could be sure that the report of her presence was not a ruse to revive their courage. So she took position at the side of the road with her staff, and the battalions swung by with a martial stride, huzzahing. Joan was armed, except her head. She was wearing the cunning little velvet cap with the mass of curved white ostrich plumes tumbling over its edges which the city of Orleans had given her the night she arrived—the one that is in the picture that hangs in the Hôtel de Ville at Rouen. She was looking about fifteen. The sight of soldiers always set her blood to leaping, and lit the fires in her eyes and brought the warm rich color to her cheeks; it was then that you saw that she was too beautiful to be of the earth, or at any rate that there was a subtle something somewhere about her beauty that differed it from the human types of your experience and exalted it above them.

In the train of wains laden with supplies a man lay on top of the goods. He was stretched out on his back, and his hands were tied together with ropes, and also his ankles. Joan signed to the officer in charge of that division of the train to come to her, and he rode up and saluted.

"What is he that is bound, there?" she asked.

"A prisoner, General."

"What is his offence?"

"He is a deserter."

"What is to be done with him?"

"He will be hanged, but it was not convenient on the march, and there was no hurry."

"Tell me about him."

"He is a good soldier, but he asked leave to go and see his wife who was dying, he said, but it could not be granted; so he went without leave. Meanwhile the march began, and he only overtook us yesterday evening."

"Overtook you? Did he come of his own will?"

"Yes, it was of his own will."

"*He* a deserter! Name of God! Bring him to me."

The officer rode forward and loosed the man's feet and brought him back with his hands still tied. What a figure he was—a good seven feet high, and built for business! He had a strong face; he had an unkempt shock of black hair which showed up in a striking way when the officer removed his morion for him; for weapon he had a big axe in his broad leathern belt. Standing by Joan's horse, he made Joan look littler than ever, for his head was about on a level with her own. His face was profoundly melancholy; all interest in life seemed to be dead in the man. Joan said—

"Hold up your hands."

The man's head was down. He lifted it when he heard that soft friendly voice, and there was a wistful something in his face which made one think that there had been music in it for him and that he would like to hear it again. When he raised his hands Joan laid her sword to his bonds, but the officer said with apprehension—

"Ah, madam—my General!"

"What is it?" she said.

"He is under sentence!"

"Yes, I know. I am responsible for him"; and she cut the bonds. They had lacerated his wrists, and they were bleeding. "Ah, pitiful!" she said; "blood—I do not like it"; and she shrank from the sight. But only for a moment. "Give me something, somebody, to bandage his wrists with."

The officer said—

"Ah, my General! it is not fitting. Let me bring another to do it."

"Another? De par le Dieu! You would seek far to find one that can do it better than I, for I learned it long ago among both men and beasts. And I can tie better than those that did this; if I had tied him the ropes had not cut his flesh."

The man looked on, silent, while he was being bandaged, stealing a furtive glance at Joan's face occasionally, such as an animal might that is receiving a kindness from an unexpected quarter and is gropingly trying to reconcile the act with its source. All the staff had forgotten the huzzahing army drifting by in its rolling clouds of dust, to crane their necks and watch the bandaging as if it was the most interesting and absorbing novelty that ever was. I have often seen people do like that—get entirely lost in the simplest trifle, when it is something that is out of their line. Now there in Poitiers, once, I saw two bishops and a dozen of those grave and famous scholars grouped together watching a man paint a sign on a shop; they didn't breathe, they were as good as dead; and when it began to sprinkle they didn't know it at first; then they noticed it, and each man hove a deep sigh, and glanced up with a surprised look as wondering to see the others there, and how he came to be there himself—but that is the way with people, as I have said. There is no way of accounting for people. You have to take them as they are.

"There," said Joan at last, pleased with her success; "another could have done it no better—not as well, I think. Tell me—what is it you did? Tell me all."

The giant said:

"It was this way, my angel. My mother died, then my three little children, one after the other, all in two years. It was the famine; others fared so—it was God's will. I saw them die; I had that grace; and I buried them. Then when my poor wife's fate was come, I begged for leave to go to her—she who was so dear to me—she who was all I had; I begged on my knees. But they would not let me. Could I let her die, friendless and alone? Could I let her die believing I would not come? Would she let *me* die and *she* not come—with her feet free to do it if she would, and no cost upon it but only her life? Ah, she would come—she would come through the fire! So I went. I saw her. She died in my arms. I buried her. Then the army was gone. I had trouble to overtake it, but my legs are long and there are many hours in a day; I overtook it last night."

Joan said, musingly, and as if she were thinking aloud—

"It sounds true. If true, it were no great harm to suspend the law this one time—any would say that. It may not be true, but if it *is* true—" She turned suddenly to the man and said, "I would see your eyes—look up!" The eyes of the two met, and Joan said to the officer, "The man is pardoned. Give you good-day; you may go." Then she said to the man, "Did you know it was death to come back to the army?"

"Yes," he said, "I knew it."

"Then why did you do it?"

The man said, quite simply—

"*Because* it was death. She was all I had. There was nothing left to love."

"Ah, yes, there was—France! The children of France have always their mother—*they* cannot be left with nothing to love. You shall live—and you shall serve France—"

"I will serve *you!*"

"—you shall fight for France—"

"I will fight for *you!*"

"You shall be France's soldier—"

"I will be *your* soldier!"

"—you shall give all your heart to France—"

"I will give all my heart to *you*—and all my soul, if I have one—and all my strength, which is great—for I was dead and am alive again; I had nothing to live for, but now I have! You are France for me. You are my France, and I will have no other."

Joan smiled, and was touched and pleased at the man's grave enthusiasm—solemn enthusiasm, one may call it, for the manner of it was deeper than mere gravity—and she said—

"Well, it shall be as you will. What are you called?"

The man answered with unsmiling simplicity—

"They call me the Dwarf, but I think it is more in jest than otherwise."

It made Joan laugh, and she said—

"It has something of that look, truly! What is the office of that vast axe?"

The soldier replied with the same gravity—which must have been born to him, it sat upon him so naturally—

"It is to persuade persons to respect France."

Joan laughed again, and said—

"Have you given many lessons?"

"Ah, indeed yes—many."

"The pupils behaved to suit you, afterwards?"

"Yes; it made them quiet—quite pleasant and quiet."

"I should think it would happen so. Would you like to be my man-at-arms?—orderly, sentinel, or something like that?"

"If I may!"

"Then you shall. You shall have proper armor, and shall go on teaching your art. Take one of those led horses there, and follow the staff when we move."

That is how we came by the Dwarf; and a good fellow he was. Joan picked him out on sight, but it wasn't a mistake; no one could be faithfuler than he was, and he was a devil and the son of a devil when he turned himself loose with his axe. He was so big that he made the Paladin look like an ordinary man. He liked to like people, therefore people liked him. He liked us boys from the start; and he liked the knights, and liked pretty much everybody he came across; but he thought more of a paring of Joan's finger-nail than he did of all the rest of the world put together.

Yes, that is where we got him—stretched on the wain, going to his death, poor chap, and nobody to say a good word for him. He was a good find. Why, the knights treated him almost like an equal—it is the honest truth; that is the sort of a man he was. They called him the Bastille, sometimes, and sometimes they called him Hellfire, which was on account of his warm and sumptuous style in battle, and you know they wouldn't have given him pet names if they hadn't had a good deal of affection for him.

To the Dwarf, Joan was France, the spirit of France made flesh—he never got away from that idea that he had started with; and God knows it was the true one. That was a humble eye to see so great a truth where some others failed. To me that seems quite remarkable. And yet, after all, it was, in a way, just what nations do. When they love a great and noble thing, they embody it—they want it so that they can see it with their eyes; like Liberty, for instance. They are not content with the cloudy abstract idea, they make a beautiful statue of it, and then their beloved idea is substantial and they can look at it and worship it. And so it is as I say; to the Dwarf, Joan was our country embodied, our country made visible flesh cast in a gracious form. When she stood before others, they saw Joan of Arc, but he saw France.

Sometimes he would speak of her by that name. It shows you how the idea was imbedded in his mind, and how real it was to him. The world has called our kings by it, but I know of none of them who has had so good a right as she to that sublime title.

When the march past was finished, Joan returned to the front and rode at the head of the column. When we began to file past those grim bastilles and could glimpse the men within, standing to their guns and ready to empty death into our ranks, such a faintness came over me and such a sickness that all things seemed to turn dim and swim before my eyes; and the other boys looked droopy too, I thought—including the Paladin, although I do not know this for certain, because he was ahead of me and I had to keep my eyes out toward the bastille side, because I could wince better when I saw what to wince at.

But Joan was at home—in Paradise, I might say. She sat up straight, and I could see that she was feeling different from me. The awfulest thing was the silence, there wasn't a sound but the screaking of the saddles, the measured tramplings, and the sneezing of the horses, afflicted by the smothering dust-clouds which they kicked up. I wanted to sneeze myself, but it seemed to me that I would rather go unsneezed, or suffer even a bitterer torture, if there is one, than attract attention to myself.

I was not of a rank to make suggestions, or I would have suggested that if we went faster we should get by sooner. It seemed to me that it was an ill-judged time to be taking a walk. Just as we were drifting in that suffocating stillness past a great cannon that stood just within a raised portcullis, with nothing between me and it but the moat, a most uncommon jackass in there split the world with his bray, and I fell out of the saddle. Sir Bertrand grabbed me as I went, which was well, for if I had gone to the ground in my armor I could not have gotten up again by myself. The English warders on the battlements laughed a coarse laugh, forgetting that every one must begin, and that there had been a time when they themselves would have fared no better when shot by a jackass.

The English never uttered a challenge nor fired a shot. It was said afterwards that when their men saw the Maid riding at the front and saw how lovely she was, their eager courage cooled down in many cases and vanished in the rest, they feeling certain that that creature was not mortal, but the very child of Satan, and so the officers were prudent and did not try to make them fight. It was said also that some of the officers were affected by the same superstitious fears. Well, in any case, they never offered to molest us, and we poked by all the grisly fortresses in peace. During the march I caught up on my devotions, which were in arrears; so it was not all loss and no profit for me, after all.

It was on this march that the histories say Dunois told Joan that the English were expecting reinforcements under the command of Sir John Falstaff, and that she turned upon him and said—

"Bastard, Bastard, in God's name I warn you to let me know of his coming as soon as you hear of it; for if he passes without my knowledge you shall lose your head!"

It may be so; I don't deny it; but I didn't hear it. If she really said it I think she only meant she would take off his official head—degrade him from his command. It was not like her to threaten a comrade's life. She did have her doubts of her generals, and was entitled to them, for she was all for storm and assault, and they were for holding still and tiring the English out. Since they did not believe in her way and were experienced old soldiers, it would be natural for them to prefer their own and try to get around carrying hers out.

But I did hear something that the histories didn't mention and don't know about. I heard Joan say that now that the garrisons on the other side had been weakened to strengthen those on our side, the most effective point of operations had shifted to the south shore; so she meant to go over there and storm the forts which held the bridge end, and that would open up communication with our own dominions and raise the siege. The generals began to balk, privately, right away, but they only baffled and delayed her, and that for only four days.

All Orleans met the army at the gate and huzzahed it through the bannered streets to its various quarters, but nobody had to rock it to sleep; it slumped down dog-tired, for Dunois had rushed it without mercy, and for the next twenty-four hours it would be quiet, all but the snoring.

Chapter XVII

WHEN we got home, breakfast for us minor fry was waiting in our mess-room and the family honored us by coming in to eat it with us. The nice old treasurer, and in fact all three were flatteringly eager to hear about our adventures. Nobody asked the Paladin to begin, but he did begin, because now that his specially ordained and peculiar military rank set him above everybody on the personal staff but old D'Aulon, who didn't eat with us, he didn't care a farthing for the knights' nobility nor mine, but took precedence in the talk whenever it suited him, which was all the time, because he was born that way. He said:

"God be thanked, we found the army in admirable condition. I think I have never seen a finer body of animals."

"Animals?" said Miss Catherine.

"I will explain to you what he means," said Noël. "He—"

"I will trouble you not to trouble yourself to explain anything for me," said the Paladin, loftily. "I have reason to think—"

"That is his way," said Noël; "always when he thinks he has reason to think, he thinks he does think, but this is an error. He didn't see the army. I noticed him, and he didn't see it. He was troubled by his old complaint."

"What is his old complaint?" Catherine asked.

"Prudence," I said, seeing my chance to help.

But it was not a fortunate remark, for the Paladin said:

"It probably isn't your turn to criticise people's prudence— you who fall out of the saddle when a donkey brays."

They all laughed, and I was ashamed of myself for my hasty smartness. I said:

"It isn't quite fair for you to say I fell out on account of the donkey's braying. It was emotion, just ordinary emotion."

"Very well, if you want to call it that, I am not objecting. What would you call it, Sir Bertrand?"

"Well, it—well, whatever it was, it was excusable, I think. All of you have learned how to behave in hot hand-to-hand engagements, and you don't need to be ashamed of your record in that matter; but to walk along in front of death, with one's hands idle, and no noise, no music, and nothing going on, is a very trying situation. If I were you, De Conte, I would name the emotion; it's nothing to be ashamed of."

It was as straight and sensible a speech as ever I heard, and I was grateful for the opening it gave me; so I came out and said:

"It was fear—and thank you for the honest idea, too."

"It was the cleanest and best way out," said the old trea-surer; "you've done well, my lad."

That made me comfortable, and when Miss Catherine said, "It's what I think, too," I was grateful to myself for getting into that scrape.

Sir Jean de Metz said—

"We were all in a body together when the donkey brayed, and it was dismally still at the time. I don't see how any young campaigner could escape some little touch of that emotion."

He looked about him with a pleasant expression of inquiry on his good face, and as each pair of eyes in turn met his the head they were in nodded a confession. Even the Paladin delivered his nod. That surprised everybody, and saved the Standard-Bearer's credit. It was clever of him; nobody be-lieved he could tell the truth that way without practice, or would tell that particular sort of a truth either with or with-out practice. I suppose he judged it would favorably impress the family. Then the old treasurer said—

"Passing the forts in that trying way required the same sort of nerve that a person must have when ghosts are about him in the dark, I should think. What does the Standard-Bearer think?"

"Well, I don't quite know about that, sir. I've often thought I would like to see a ghost if I—"

"Would you?" exclaimed the young lady. "We've got one! Would you try that one? Will you?"

She was so eager and pretty that the Paladin said straight out that he would; and then as none of the rest had bravery enough to expose the fear that was in him, one volunteered after the other with a prompt mouth and a sick heart till all were shipped for the voyage; then the girl clapped her hands in glee, and the parents were gratified too, saying that the ghosts of their house had been a dread and a misery to them and their forebears for generations, and nobody had ever been found yet who was willing to confront them and find out what their trouble was, so that the family could heal it and content the poor spectres and beguile them to tranquillity and peace.

Chapter XVIII

About noon I was chatting with Madame Boucher; nothing was going on, all was quiet, when Catherine Boucher suddenly entered in great excitement, and said—

"Fly, sir, fly! The Maid was dozing in her chair in my room, when she sprang up and cried out, 'French blood is flowing!—my arms, give me my arms!' Her giant was on guard at the door, and he brought D'Aulon, who began to arm her, and I and the giant have been warning the staff. Fly!—and stay by her; and if there really is a battle, keep her out of it—don't let her risk herself—there is no need—if the men know she is near and looking on, it is all that is necessary. Keep her out of the fight—don't fail of this!"

I started on a run, saying, sarcastically—for I was always fond of sarcasm, and it was said that I had a most neat gift that way—

"Oh yes, nothing easier than that—I'll attend to it!"

At the furthest end of the house I met Joan, fully armed, hurrying toward the door, and she said—

"Ah, French blood is being spilt, and you did not tell me."

"Indeed I did not know it," I said; "there are no sounds of war; everything is quiet, your Excellency."

"You will hear war-sounds enough in a moment," she said, and was gone.

It was true. Before one could count five there broke upon the stillness the swelling rush and tramp of an approaching multitude of men and horses, with hoarse cries of command; and then out of the distance came the muffled deep *boom!—boom-boom!—boom!* of cannon, and straightway that rushing multitude was roaring by the house like a hurricane.

Our knights and all our staff came flying, armed, but with no horses ready, and we burst out after Joan in a body, the Paladin in the lead with the banner. The surging crowd was made up half of citizens and half of soldiers, and had no recognized leader. When Joan was seen a huzzah went up, and she shouted—

"A horse—a horse!"

A dozen saddles were at her disposal in a moment. She mounted, a hundred people shouting—

"Way, there—way for the MAID OF ORLEANS!" The first time that that immortal name was ever uttered—and I, praise God, was there to hear it! The mass divided itself like the waters of the Red Sea, and down this lane Joan went skimming like a bird, crying "Forward, French hearts—follow me!" and we came winging in her wake on the rest of the borrowed horses, the holy standard streaming above us, and the lane closing together in our rear.

This was a different thing from the ghastly march past the dismal bastilles. No, we felt fine, now, and all a-whirl with enthusiasm. The explanation of this sudden uprising was this. The city and the little garrison, so long hopeless and afraid, had gone wild over Joan's coming, and could no longer restrain their desire to get at the enemy; so, without orders from anybody, a few hundred soldiers and citizens had plunged out at the Burgundy gate on a sudden impulse and made a charge on one of Lord Talbot's most formidable fortresses—St. Loup—and were getting the worst of it. The news of this had swept through the city and started this new crowd that we were with.

As we poured out at the gate we met a force bringing in the wounded from the front. The sight moved Joan, and she said—

"Ah, French blood; it makes my hair rise to see it!"

We were soon on the field, soon in the midst of the turmoil. Joan was seeing her first real battle, and so were we.

It was a battle in the open field; for the garrison of St. Loup had sallied confidently out to meet the attack, being used to victories when "witches" were not around. The sally had been re-enforced by troops from the "Paris" bastille, and when we approached the French were getting whipped and were falling back. But when Joan came charging through the disorder with her banner displayed, crying "Forward, men— follow me!" there was a change; the French turned about and surged forward like a solid wave of the sea, and swept the English before them, hacking and slashing, and being hacked and slashed, in a way that was terrible to see.

In the field the Dwarf had no assignment; that is to say, he

was not under orders to occupy any particular place, therefore
he chose his place for himself, and went ahead of Joan and
made a road for her. It was horrible to see the iron helmets fly
into fragments under his dreadful axe. He called it cracking
nuts, and it looked like that. He made a good road, and paved
it well with flesh and iron. Joan and the rest of us followed it
so briskly that we outspeeded our forces and had the English
behind us as well as before. The knights commanded us to
face outwards around Joan, which we did, and then there was
work done that was fine to see. One was obliged to respect
the Paladin, now. Being right under Joan's exalting and transforming eye, he forgot his native prudence, he forgot his diffidence in the presence of danger, he forgot what fear was,
and he never laid about him in his imaginary battles in a more
tremendous way than he did in this real one; and wherever he
struck there was an enemy the less.

We were in that close place only a few minutes; then our
forces to the rear broke through with a great shout and joined
us, and then the English fought a retreating fight, but in a
fine and gallant way, and we drove them to their fortress foot
by foot, they facing us all the time, and their reserves on the
walls raining showers of arrows, cross-bow bolts, and stone
cannon-balls upon us.

The bulk of the enemy got safely within the works and left
us outside with piles of French and English dead and
wounded for company—a sickening sight, an awful sight to
us youngsters, for our little ambush fights in February had
been in the night, and the blood and the mutilations and the
dead faces were mercifully dim, whereas we saw these things
now for the first time in all their naked ghastliness.

Now arrived Dunois from the city, and plunged through
the battle on his foam-flecked horse and galloped up to Joan,
saluting, and uttering handsome compliments as he came. He
waved his hand toward the distant walls of the city, where a
multitude of flags were flaunting gayly in the wind, and said
the populace were up there observing her fortunate performance and rejoicing over it, and added that she and the forces
would have a great reception now.

"*Now?* Hardly now, Bastard. Not yet!"

"Why not yet? Is there more to be done?"

"More, Bastard? We have but begun! We will take this for-tress."

"Ah, you can't be serious! We can't take this place; let me urge you not to make the attempt; it is too desperate. Let me order the forces back."

Joan's heart was overflowing with the joys and enthusiasms of war, and it made her impatient to hear such talk. She cried out—

"Bastard, Bastard, will ye play *always* with these English? Now verily I tell you we will not budge until this place is ours. We will carry it by storm. Sound the charge!"

"Ah, my General—"

"Waste no more time, man—let the bugles sound the as-sault!" and we saw that strange deep light in her eye which we named the battle-light, and learned to know so well in later fields.

The martial notes pealed out, the troops answered with a yell, and down they came against that formidable work, whose outlines were lost in its own cannon smoke, and whose sides were spouting flame and thunder.

We suffered repulse after repulse, but Joan was here and there and everywhere encouraging the men, and she kept them to their work. During three hours the tide ebbed and flowed, flowed and ebbed; but at last La Hire, who was now come, made a final and resistless charge, and the bastille St. Loup was ours. We gutted it, taking all its stores and artillery, and then destroyed it.

When all our host was shouting itself hoarse with rejoic-ings, and there went up a cry for the General, for they wanted to praise her and glorify her and do her homage for her vic-tory, we had trouble to find her; and when we did find her, she was off by herself, sitting among a ruck of corpses, with her face in her hands, crying—for she was a young girl, you know, and her hero-heart was a young girl's heart too, with the pity and the tenderness that are natural to it. She was thinking of the mothers of those dead friends and enemies.

Among the prisoners were a number of priests, and Joan took these under her protection and saved their lives. It was urged that they were most probably combatants in disguise, but she said—

"As to that, how can any tell? They wear the livery of God, and if even one of these wears it rightfully, surely it were better that all the guilty should escape than that we have upon our hands the blood of that innocent man. I will lodge them where I lodge, and feed them, and send them away in safety."

We marched back to the city with our crop of cannon and prisoners on view and our banners displayed. Here was the first substantial bit of war-work the imprisoned people had seen in the seven months that the siege had endured, the first chance they had had to rejoice over a French exploit. You may guess that they made good use of it. They and the bells went mad. Joan was their darling now, and the press of people struggling and shouldering each other to get a glimpse of her was so great that we could hardly push our way through the streets at all. Her new name had gone all about, and was on everybody's lips. The Holy Maid of Vaucouleurs was a forgotten title; the city had claimed her for its own, and she was the MAID OF ORLEANS now. It is a happiness to me to remember that I heard that name the first time it was ever uttered. Between that first utterance and the last time it will be uttered on this earth—ah, think how many mouldering ages will lie in that gap!

The Boucher family welcomed her back as if she had been a child of the house, and saved from death against all hope or probability. They chided her for going into the battle and exposing herself to danger during all those hours. They could not realize that she had meant to carry her warriorship so far, and asked her if it had really been her purpose to go right into the turmoil of the fight, or hadn't she got swept into it by accident and the rush of the troops? They begged her to be more careful another time. It was good advice, maybe, but it fell upon pretty unfruitful soil.

Chapter XIX

BEING WORN OUT with the long fight, we all slept the rest of the afternoon away and two or three hours into the night. Then we got up refreshed, and had supper. As for me, I could have been willing to let the matter of the ghost drop; and the others were of a like mind no doubt, for they talked diligently of the battle and said nothing of that other thing. And indeed it was fine and stirring to hear the Paladin rehearse his deeds and see him pile his dead, fifteen here, eighteen there, and thirty-five yonder; but this only postponed the trouble; it could not do more. He could not go on forever; when he had carried the bastille by assault and eaten up the garrison there was nothing for it but to stop, unless Catherine Boucher would give him a new start and have it all done over again—as we hoped she would, this time—but she was otherwise minded. As soon as there was a good opening and a fair chance, she brought up her unwelcome subject, and we faced it the best we could.

We followed her and her parents to the haunted room at eleven o'clock, with candles, and also with torches to place in the sockets on the walls. It was a big house, with very thick walls, and this room was in a remote part of it which had been left unoccupied for nobody knew how many years, because of its evil repute.

This was a large room, like a salon, and had a big table in it of enduring oak and well preserved; but the chairs were worm-eaten and the tapestry on the walls was rotten and discolored by age. The dusty cobwebs under the ceiling had the look of not having had any business for a century.

Catherine said—

"Tradition says that these ghosts have never been seen—they have merely been heard. It is plain that this room was once larger than it is now, and that the wall at this end was built in some bygone time to make and fence off a narrow room there. There is no communication anywhere with that narrow room, and if it exists—and of that there is no reasonable doubt—it has no light and no air, but is an absolute dungeon. Wait where you are, and take note of what happens."

That was all. Then she and her parents left us. When their footfalls had died out in the distance down the empty stone corridors an uncanny silence and solemnity ensued which was dismaller to me than the mute march past the bastilles. We sat looking vacantly at each other, and it was easy to see that no one there was comfortable. The longer we sat so, the more deadly still that stillness got to be; and when the wind began to moan around the house presently, it made me sick and miserable, and I wished I had been brave enough to be a coward this time, for indeed it is no proper shame to be afraid of ghosts, seeing how helpless the living are in their hands. And then these ghosts were invisible, which made the matter the worse, as it seemed to me. They might be in the room with us at that moment—we could not know. I felt airy touches on my shoulders and my hair, and I shrank from them and cringed, and was not ashamed to show this fear, for I saw the others doing the like, and knew that they were feeling those faint contacts too. As this went on—oh, eternities it seemed, the time dragged so drearily—all those faces became as wax, and I seemed sitting with a congress of the dead.

At last, faint and far and weird and slow, came a "boom! —boom!—boom!"—a distant bell tolling midnight. When the last stroke died, that depressing stillness followed again, and as before I was staring at those waxen faces and feeling those airy touches on my hair and my shoulders once more.

One minute—two minutes—three minutes of this, then we heard a long deep groan, and everybody sprang up and stood, with his legs quaking. It came from that little dungeon. There was a pause, then we heard muffled sobbings, mixed with pitiful ejaculations. Then there was a second voice, low and not distinct, and the one seemed trying to comfort the other; and so the two voices went on, with moanings, and soft sobbings, and, ah, the tones were so full of compassion and sorrow and despair! Indeed, it made one's heart sore to hear it.

But those sounds were so real and so human and so moving

that the idea of ghosts passed straight out of our minds, and Sir Jean de Metz spoke out and said—

"Come! we will smash that wall and set those poor captives free. Here, with your axe!"

The Dwarf jumped forward, swinging his great axe with both hands, and others sprang for the torches and brought them. Bang!—whang!—slam!—smash went the ancient bricks, and there was a hole an ox could pass through. We plunged within and held up the torches.

Nothing there but vacancy! On the floor lay a rusty sword and a rotten fan.

Now you know all that I know. Take the pathetic relics, and weave about them the romance of the dungeon's long-vanished inmates as best you can.

Chapter XX

THE NEXT DAY Joan wanted to go against the enemy again, but it was the feast of the Ascension, and the holy council of bandit generals were too pious to be willing to profane it with bloodshed. But privately they profaned it with plottings, a sort of industry just in their line. They decided to do the only thing proper to do now in the new circumstances of the case—feign an attack on the most important bastille on the Orleans side, and then, if the English weakened the far more imporatnt fortresses on the other side of the river to come to its help, cross in force and capture those works. This would give them the bridge and free communication with the Sologne, which was French territory. They decided to keep this latter part of the programme secret from Joan.

Joan intruded and took them by surprise. She asked them what they were about and what they had resolved upon. They said they had resolved to attack the most important of the English bastilles on the Orleans side next morning—and there the spokesman stopped. Joan said—

"Well, go on."

"There is nothing more. That is all."

"Am I to believe this? That is to say, am I to believe that you have lost your wits?" She turned to Dunois, and said, "Bastard, you have sense, answer me this: if this attack is made and the bastille taken, how much better off would we be than we are now?"

The Bastard hesitated, and then began some rambling talk not quite germane to the question. Joan interrupted him and said—

"That will do, good Bastard, you have answered. Since the Bastard is not able to mention any advantage to be gained by taking that bastille and stopping there, it is not likely that any of you could better the matter. You waste much time here in inventing plans that lead to nothing, and making delays that are a damage. Are you concealing something from me? Bastard, this council has a general plan, I take it; without going into details, what is it?"

"It is the same it was in the beginning, seven months ago —to get provisions in for a long siege, and then sit down and tire the English out."

"In the name of God! As if seven months was not enough, you want to provide for a year of it. Now ye shall drop these pusillanimous dreams—the English shall go in three days!"

Several exclaimed—

"Ah, General, General, be prudent!"

"Be prudent and starve? Do ye call that war? I tell you this, if you do not already know it: The new circumstances have changed the face of matters. The true point of attack has shifted; it is on the other side of the river, now. One must take the fortifications that command the bridge. The English know that if we are not fools and cowards we will try to do that. They are grateful for your piety in wasting this day. They will re-enforce the bridge forts from this side to-night, knowing what ought to happen to-morrow. You have but lost a day and made our task harder, for we *will* cross and take the bridge forts. Bastard, tell me the truth—does not this council know that there is no other course for us than the one I am speaking of?"

Dunois conceded that the council did know it to be the most desirable, but considered it impracticable; and he excused the council as well as he could by saying that inasmuch as nothing was really and rationally to be hoped for but a long continuance of the siege and wearying out of the English, they were naturally a little afraid of Joan's impetuous notions. He said—

"You see, we are sure that the waiting game is the best, whereas you would carry everything by storm."

"That I would!—and moreover that I will! You have my orders—here and now. We will move upon the forts of the south bank to-morrow at dawn."

"And carry them by storm?"

"Yes, carry them by storm!"

La Hire came clanking in, and heard the last remark. He cried out—

"By *my baton*, that is the music I love to hear! Yes, that is the right tune and the beautiful words, my General—we will carry them by storm!"

He saluted in his large way and came up and shook Joan by the hand.

Some member of the council was heard to say—

"It follows, then, that we must begin with the bastille St. John, and that will give the English time to—"

Joan turned and said—

"Give yourselves no uneasiness about the bastille St. John. The English will know enough to retire from it and fall back on the bridge bastilles when they see us coming." She added, with a touch of sarcasm, "Even a war-council would know enough to do that, itself."

Then she took her leave. La Hire made this general remark to the council:

"She is a child, and that is all ye seem to see. Keep to that superstition if you must, but you perceive that this child understands this complex game of war as well as any of you; and if you want my opinion without the trouble of asking for it, here you have it without ruffles or embroidery—by God, I think she can teach the best of you how to *play* it!"

Joan had spoken truly; the sagacious English saw that the policy of the French had undergone a revolution; that the policy of paltering and dawdling was ended; that in place of taking blows, blows were to be struck, now; therefore they made ready for the new state of things by transferring heavy re-enforcements to the bastilles of the south bank from those of the north.

The city learned the great news that once more in French history, after all these humiliating years, France was going to take the offensive; that France, so used to retreating, was going to advance; that France, so long accustomed to skulking, was going to face about and strike. The joy of the people passed all bounds. The city walls were black with them to see the army march out in the morning in that strange new position—its front, not its tail, toward an English camp. You shall imagine for yourselves what the excitement was like and how it expressed itself, when Joan rode out at the head of the host with her banner floating above her.

We crossed the river in strong force, and a tedious long job it was, for the boats were small and not numerous. Our landing on the island of St. Aignan was not disputed. We threw a bridge of a few boats across the narrow channel thence to the south shore and took up our march in good order and unmolested; for although there was a fortress there—St. John—the English vacated and destroyed it and fell back on the bridge forts below as soon as our first boats were seen to leave the Orleans shore; which was what Joan had said would happen, when she was disputing with the council.

We moved down the shore and Joan planted her standard before the bastille of the Augustins, the first of the formidable works that protected the end of the bridge. The trumpets sounded the assault, and two charges followed in handsome style; but we were too weak, as yet, for our main body was still lagging behind. Before we could gather for a third assault the garrison of St. Privé were seen coming up to re-enforce the big bastille. They came on a run, and the Augustins sallied out, and both forces came against us with a rush, and sent our small army flying in a panic, and followed us, slashing and slaying, and shouting jeers and insults at us.

Joan was doing her best to rally the men, but their wits were gone, their hearts were dominated for the moment by the old-time dread of the English. Joan's temper flamed up, and she halted and commanded the trumpets to sound the advance. Then she wheeled about and cried out—

"If there is but a dozen of you that are not cowards, it is enough—follow me!"

Away she went, and after her a few dozen who had heard her words and been inspired by them. The pursuing force was astonished to see her sweeping down upon them with this handful of men, and it was their turn now to experience a grisly fright—surely this *is* a witch, this is a child of Satan! That was their thought—and without stopping to analyze the matter they turned and fled in a panic.

Our flying squadrons heard the bugle and turned to look; and when they saw the Maid's banner speeding in the other direction and the enemy scrambling ahead of it in disorder, their courage returned and they came scouring after us.

La Hire heard it and hurried his force forward and caught up with us just as we were planting our banner again before the ramparts of the Augustins. We were strong enough now. We had a long and tough piece of work before us, but we carried it through before night, Joan keeping us hard at it, and she and La Hire saying we were able to take that big bastille, and *must*. The English fought like—well, they fought like the English; when that is said, there is no more to say. We made assault after assault, through the smoke and flame and the deafening cannon-blasts, and at last as the sun was sinking we carried the place with a rush, and planted our standard on its walls.

The Augustins was ours. The Tourelles must be ours too, if we would free the bridge and raise the siege. We had achieved one great undertaking, Joan was determined to accomplish the other. We must lie on our arms where we were, hold fast to what we had got, and be ready for business in the morning. So Joan was not minded to let the men be demoralized by pillage and riot and carousings; she had the Augustins burned, with all its stores in it, excepting the artillery and ammunition.

Everybody was tired out with this long day's hard work, and of course this was the case with Joan; still, she wanted to stay with the army before the Tourelles, to be ready for the assault in the morning. The chiefs argued with her, and at last persuaded her to go home and prepare for the great work by taking proper rest, and also by having a leech look to a wound which she had received in her foot. So we crossed with them and went home.

Just as usual, we found the town in a fury of joy, all the bells clanging, everybody shouting, and several people drunk. We never went out or came in without furnishing good and sufficient reasons for one of these pleasant tempests, and so the tempest was always on hand. There had been a blank absence of reasons for this sort of upheavals for the past seven months, therefore the people took to the upheavals with all the more relish on that account.

Chapter XXI

To get away from the usual crowd of visitors and have a rest, Joan went with Catherine straight to the apartment which the two occupied together, and there they took their supper and there the wound was dressed. But then, instead of going to bed, Joan, weary as she was, sent the Dwarf for me, in spite of Catherine's protests and persuasions. She said she had something on her mind, and must send a courier to Domremy with a letter for our old Père Fronte to read to her mother. I came, and she began to dictate. After some loving words and greetings to her mother and the family, came this:

"But the thing which moves me to write now, is to say that when you presently hear that I am wounded, you shall give yourself no concern about it, and refuse faith to any that shall try to make you believe it is serious."

She was going on, when Catherine spoke up and said:

"Ah, but it will fright her so to read these words. Strike them out, Joan, strike them out, and wait only one day—two days at most—then write and say your foot *was* wounded but is well again—for it will surely be well then, or very near it. Don't distress her, Joan; do as I say."

A laugh like the laugh of the old days, the impulsive free laugh of an untroubled spirit, a laugh like a chime of bells, was Joan's answer; then she said—

"My foot? Why should I write about such a scratch as that? I was not thinking of it, dear heart."

"Child, have you another wound and a worse, and have not spoken of it? What have you been dreaming about, that you—"

She had jumped up, full of vague fears, to have the leech called back at once, but Joan laid her hand upon her arm and made her sit down again, saying—

"There, now, be tranquil, there is no other wound, as yet; I am writing about one which I shall get when we storm that bastille to-morrow."

Catherine had the look of one who is trying to understand a puzzling proposition but cannot quite do it. She said, in a distraught fashion—

"A wound which you are *going* to get? But—but why grieve your mother when it—when it may not happen?"

"*May* not? Why, it *will*."

The puzzle was a puzzle still. Catherine said in that same abstracted way as before—

"*Will*. It is a strong word. I cannot seem to—my mind is not able to take hold of this. Oh, Joan, such a presentiment is a dreadful thing—it takes one's peace and courage all away. Cast it from you!—drive it out! It will make your whole night miserable, and to no good; for we will hope—"

"But it isn't a presentiment—it is a fact. And it will not make me miserable. It is uncertainties that do that, but this is not an uncertainty."

"Joan, do you *know* it is going to happen?"

"Yes, I know it. My Voices told me."

"Ah," said Catherine, resignedly, "if *they* told you— But are you sure it was they?—quite sure?"

"Yes, quite. It will happen—there is no doubt."

"It is dreadful! Since when have you known it?"

"Since—I think it is several weeks." Joan turned to me. "Louis, you will remember. How long is it?"

"Your Excellency spoke of it first to the King, in Chinon," I answered; "that was as much as seven weeks ago. You spoke of it again the 20th of April, and also the 22d, two weeks ago, as I see by my record here."

These marvels disturbed Catherine profoundly, but I had long ceased to be surprised at them. One can get used to anything in this world. Catherine said—

"And it is to happen to-morrow?—always to-morrow? Is it the same date always? There has been no mistake, and no confusion?"

"No," Joan said, "the 7th of May is the date—there is no other."

"Then you shall not go a step out of this house till that awful day is gone by! You will not dream of it, Joan, *will* you?—promise that you will stay with us."

But Joan was not persuaded. She said—

"It would not help the matter, dear good friend. The wound is to come, and come to-morrow. If I do not seek it, it will seek me. My duty calls me to that place to-morrow; I should have to go if my death were waiting for me there; shall I stay away for only a wound? Oh no, we must try to do better than that."

"Then you are determined to go?"

"Of a certainty, yes. There is only one thing that I can do for France—hearten her soldiers for battle and victory." She thought a moment, then added, "However, one should not be unreasonable, and I would do much to please you, who are so good to me. Do you love France?"

I wondered what she might be contriving now, but I saw no clew. Catherine said, reproachfully—

"Ah, what have I done to deserve this question?"

"Then you do love France. I had not doubted it, dear. Do not be hurt, but answer me—have you ever told a lie?"

"In my life I have not wilfully told a lie—fibs, but no lies."

"That is sufficient. You love France and do not tell lies; therefore I will trust you. I will go or I will stay, as you shall decide."

"Oh, I thank you from my heart, Joan! How good and dear it is of you to do this for me! Oh, you shall stay, and not go!"

In her delight she flung her arms about Joan's neck and squandered endearments upon her the least of which would have made me rich, but as it was, they only made me realize how poor I was—how miserably poor in what I would most have prized in this world. Joan said—

"Then you will send word to my headquarters that I am not going?"

"Oh, gladly. Leave that to me."

"It is good of you. And how will you word it?—for it must have proper official form. Shall I word it for you?"

"Oh, do—for you know about these solemn procedures and stately proprieties, and I have had no experience."

"Then word it like this: 'The chief of staff is commanded to make known to the King's forces in garrison and in the field, that the General-in-Chief of the Armies of France will not face the English on the morrow, she being afraid she may get hurt. Signed, JOAN OF ARC, by the hand of CATHERINE BOUCHER, who loves France.' "

There was a pause—a silence of the sort that tortures one into stealing a glance to see how the situation looks, and I did that. There was a loving smile on Joan's face, but the color was mounting in crimson waves into Catherine's, and her lips were quivering and the tears gathering; then she said—

"Oh, I am so ashamed of myself!—and you are so noble and brave and wise, and I am so paltry—so paltry and such a fool!" and she broke down and began to cry, and I did so want to take her in my arms and comfort her, but Joan did it, and of course I said nothing. Joan did it well, and most sweetly and tenderly, but I could have done it as well, though I knew it would be foolish and out of place to suggest such a thing, and might make an awkwardness too, and be embarrassing to us all, so I did not offer, and I hope I did right and for the best, though I could not know, and was many times tortured with doubts afterwards as having perhaps let a chance pass which might have changed all my life and made it happier and more beautiful than, alas, it turned out to be. For this reason I grieve yet, when I think of that scene, and do not like to call it up out of the deeps of my memory because of the pangs it brings.

Well, well, a good and wholesome thing is a little harmless fun in this world; it tones a body up and keeps him human and prevents him from souring. To set that little trap for Catherine was as good and effective a way as any to show her what a grotesque thing she was asking of Joan. It *was* a funny idea, now, wasn't it, when you look at it all around? Even Catherine dried up her tears and laughed when she thought of the English getting hold of the French Commander-in-Chief's reason for staying out of a battle. She granted that they could have a good time over a thing like that.

We got to work on the letter again, and of course did not have to strike out the passage about the wound. Joan was in fine spirits; but when she got to sending messages to this, that, and the other old playmate and friend, it brought our village and the Fairy Tree and the flowery plain and the browsing sheep and all the peaceful beauty of our old humble home-place back, and the familiar names began to tremble on her lips; and when she got to Haumette and Little Mengette it was no use, her voice broke and she couldn't go on. She waited a moment, then said—

"Give them my love—my warm love—my deep love—oh, out of my heart of hearts! I shall never see our home any more."

Now came Pasquerel, Joan's confessor, and introduced a gallant knight, the Sire de Rais, who had been sent with a message. He said he was instructed to say that the council had decided that enough had been done for the present; that it would be safest and best to be content with what God had already done; that the city was now well victualled and able to stand a long siege; that the wise course must necessarily be to withdraw the troops from the other side of the river and re-sume the defensive—therefore they had decided accordingly.

"The incurable cowards!" exclaimed Joan. "So it was to get me away from my men that they pretended so much solici-tude about my fatigue. Take this message back, not to the council—I have no speeches for those disguised ladies' maids—but to the Bastard and La Hire, who are men. Tell them the army is to remain where it is, and I hold them re-sponsible if this command miscarries. And say the offensive will be resumed in the morning. You may go, good sir."

Then she said to her priest—

"Rise early, and be by me all the day. There will be much work on my hands, and I shall be hurt between my neck and my shoulder."

Chapter XXII

W E WERE up at dawn, and after mass we started. In the hall we met the master of the house, who was grieved, good man, to see Joan going breakfastless to such a day's work, and begged her to wait and eat, but she couldn't afford the time—that is to say, she couldn't afford the patience, she being in such a blaze of anxiety to get at that last remaining bastille which stood between her and the completion of the first great step in the rescue and redemption of France. Boucher put in another plea:

"But think—we poor beleaguered citizens who have hardly known the flavor of fish for these many months, have spoil of that sort again, and we owe it to you. There's a noble shad for breakfast; wait—be persuaded."

Joan said—

"Oh, there's going to be fish in plenty; when this day's work is done the whole river-front will be yours to do as you please with."

"Ah, your Excellency will do well, *that* I know; but we don't require quite that much, even of you; you shall have a month for it in place of a day. Now be beguiled—wait and eat. There's a saying that he that would cross a river twice in the same day in a boat, will do well to eat fish for luck, lest he have an accident."

"That doesn't fit my case, for to-day I cross but once in a boat."

"Oh, don't say that. Aren't you coming back to us?"

"Yes, but not in a boat."

"How, then?"

"By the bridge."

"Listen to that—by the bridge! Now stop this jesting, dear General, and do as I would have you. It's a noble fish."

"Be good, then, and save me some for supper; and I will bring one of those Englishmen with me and he shall have his share."

"Ah, well, have your way if you must. But he that fasts must attempt but little and stop early. When shall you be back?"

"When I've raised the siege of Orleans. FORWARD!"

We were off. The streets were full of citizens and of groups and squads of soldiers, but the spectacle was melancholy. There was not a smile anywhere, but only universal gloom. It was as if some vast calamity had smitten all hope and cheer dead. We were not used to this, and were astonished. But when they saw the Maid, there was an immediate stir, and the eager question flew from mouth to mouth—

"Where is she going? Whither is she bound?"

Joan heard it, and called out—

"Whither would ye suppose? I am going to take the Tourelles."

It would not be possible for any to describe how those few words turned that mourning into joy—into exaltation—into frenzy; and how a storm of huzzahs burst out and swept down the streets in every direction and woke those corpse-like multitudes to vivid life and action and turmoil in a moment. The soldiers broke from the crowd and came flocking to our standard, and many of the citizens ran and got pikes and halberds and joined us. As we moved on, our numbers increased steadily, and the hurrahing continued—yes, we moved through a solid cloud of noise, as you may say, and all the windows on both sides contributed to it, for they were filled with excited people.

You see, the council had closed the Burgundy gate and placed a strong force there, under that stout soldier Raoul de Gaucourt, Bailly of Orleans, with orders to prevent Joan from getting out and resuming the attack on the Tourelles, and this shameful thing had plunged the city into sorrow and despair. But that feeling was gone now. They believed the Maid was a match for the council, and they were right.

When we reached the gate, Joan told Gaucourt to open it and let her pass.

He said it would be impossible to do this, for his orders were from the council and were strict. Joan said—

"There is no authority above mine but the King's. If you have an order from the King, produce it."

"I cannot claim to have an order from him, General."

"Then make way, or take the consequences!"

He began to argue the case, for he was like the rest of the

tribe, always ready to fight with words, not acts; but in the midst of his gabble Joan interrupted with the terse order—

"Charge!"

We came with a rush, and brief work we made of that small job. It was good to see the Bailly's surprise. He was not used to this unsentimental promptness. He said afterwards that he was cut off in the midst of what he was saying—in the midst of an argument by which he could have proved that he could not let Joan pass—an argument which Joan could not have answered.

"Still, it appears she did answer it," said the person he was talking to.

We swung through the gate in great style, with a vast accession of noise, the most of which was laughter, and soon our van was over the river and moving down against the Tourelles.

First we must take a supporting work called a boulevard, and which was otherwise nameless, before we could assault the great bastille. Its rear communicated with the bastille by a drawbridge, under which ran a swift and deep strip of the Loire. The boulevard was strong, and Dunois doubted our ability to take it, but Joan had no such doubt. She pounded it with artillery all the forenoon, then about noon she ordered an assault and led it herself. We poured into the fosse through the smoke and a tempest of missiles, and Joan, shouting encouragements to her men, started to climb a scaling-ladder, when that misfortune happened which we knew was to happen—the iron bolt from an arbalest struck between her neck and her shoulder, and tore its way down through her armor. When she felt the sharp pain and saw her blood gushing over her breast, she was frightened, poor girl, and as she sank to the ground she began to cry, bitterly.

The English sent up a glad shout and came surging down in strong force to take her, and then for a few minutes the might of both adversaries was concentrated upon that spot. Over her and about her, English and French fought with desperation—for she stood for France, indeed she *was* France to both sides—whichever won her won France, *and could keep it forever*. Right there in that small spot, and in ten minutes by the clock, the fate of France, for all time, was to be decided, and *was* decided.

If the English had captured Joan then, Charles VII. would have flown the country, the Treaty of Troyes would have held good, and France, already English property, would have become, without further dispute, an English province, to so remain until the Judgment Day. A nationality and a kingdom were at stake there, and no more time to decide it in than it takes to hard-boil an egg. It was the most momentous ten minutes that the clock has ever ticked in France, or ever will. Whenever you read in histories about hours or days or weeks in which the fate of one or another nation hung in the balance, do not you fail to remember, nor your French hearts to beat the quicker for the remembrance, the ten minutes that France, called otherwise Joan of Arc, lay bleeding in the fosse that day, with two nations struggling over her for her possession.

And you will not forget the Dwarf. For he stood over her, and did the work of any six of the others. He swung his axe with both hands; whenever it came down, he said those two words, "For France!" and a splintered helmet flew like eggshells, and the skull that carried it had learned its manners and would offend the French no more. He piled a bulwark of iron-clad dead in front of him and fought from behind it; and at last when the victory was ours we closed about him, shielding him, and he ran up a ladder with Joan as easily as another man would carry a child, and bore her out of the battle, a great crowd following and anxious, for she was drenched with blood to her feet, half of it her own and the other half English, for bodies had fallen across her as she lay and had poured their red life-streams over her. One couldn't see the white armor now, with that awful dressing over it.

The iron bolt was still in the wound—some say it projected out behind the shoulder. It may be—I did not wish to see, and did not try to. It was pulled out, and the pain made Joan cry again, poor thing. Some say she pulled it out herself because others refused, saying they could not bear to hurt her. As to this I do not know; I only know it was pulled out, and that the wound was treated with oil and properly dressed.

Joan lay on the grass, weak and suffering, hour after hour, but still insisting that the fight go on. Which it did, but not to much purpose, for it was only under her eye that men were heroes and not afraid. They were like the Paladin; I think he was afraid of his shadow—I mean in the afternoon, when it was very big and long; but when he was under Joan's eye and the inspiration of her great spirit, what was he afraid of? Nothing in this world—and that is just the truth.

Toward night Dunois gave it up. Joan heard the bugles.

"What!" she cried. "Sounding the retreat!"

Her wound was forgotten in a moment. She countermanded the order, and sent another, to the officer in command of a battery, to stand ready to fire five shots in quick succession. This was a signal to a force on the Orleans side of the river under La Hire, who was not, as some of the histories say, with *us*. It was to be given whenever Joan should feel sure the boulevard was about to fall into her hands—then that force must make a counter-attack on the Tourelles by way of the bridge.

Joan mounted her horse, now, with her staff about her, and when our people saw us coming they raised a great shout, and were at once eager for another assault on the boulevard. Joan rode straight to the fosse where she had received her wound, and standing there in the rain of bolts and arrows, she ordered the Paladin to let her long standard blow free, and to note when its fringes should touch the fortress. Presently he said—

"It touches."

"Now, then," said Joan to the waiting battalions, "the place is yours—enter in! Bugles, sound the assault! Now, then—all together—*go!*"

And go it was. You never saw anything like it. We swarmed up the ladders and over the battlements like a wave—and the place was our property. Why, one might live a thousand years and never see so gorgeous a thing as that again. There, hand to hand, we fought like wild beasts, for there was no give-up to those English—there was no way to convince one of those people but to kill him, and even then he doubted. At least so it was thought, in those days, and maintained by many.

We were busy and never heard the five cannon-shots fired, but they *were* fired a moment after Joan had ordered the assault; and so, while we were hammering and being hammered in the smaller fortress, the reserve on the Orleans side poured across the bridge and attacked the Tourelles from that side. A fire-boat was brought down and moored under the drawbridge which connected the Tourelles with our boulevard; wherefore, when at last we drove our English ahead of us and they tried to cross that drawbridge and join their friends in the Tourelles, the burning timbers gave way under them and emptied them in a mass into the river in their heavy armor—and a pitiful sight it was to see brave men die such a death as that.

"Ah, God, pity them!" said Joan, and wept to see that sorrowful spectacle. She said those gentle words and wept those compassionate tears although one of those perishing men had grossly insulted her with a coarse name three days before, when she had sent him a message asking him to surrender. That was their leader, Sir William Glasdale, a most valorous knight. He was clothed all in steel; so he plunged under the water like a lance, and of course came up no more.

We soon patched a sort of bridge together and threw ourselves against the last stronghold of the English power that barred Orleans from friends and supplies. Before the sun was quite down, Joan's forever memorable day's work was finished, her banner floated from the fortress of the Tourelles, her promise was fulfilled, she had raised the siege of Orleans!

The seven months' beleaguerment was ended, the thing which the first generals of France had called impossible was accomplished; in spite of all that the King's ministers and war-councils could do to prevent it, this little country maid of seventeen had carried her immortal task through, and had done it in four days!

Good news travels fast, sometimes, as well as bad. By the time we were ready to start homewards by the bridge the whole city of Orleans was one red flame of bonfires, and the heavens blushed with satisfaction to see it; and the booming and bellowing of cannon and the banging of bells surpassed by great odds anything that even Orleans had attempted before in the way of noise.

When we arrived—well, there is no describing that. Why, those acres of people that we ploughed through shed tears enough to raise the river; there was not a face in the glare of those fires that hadn't tears streaming down it; and if Joan's feet had not been protected by iron they would have kissed them off of her. "Welcome! welcome to the Maid of Orleans!" That was the cry; I heard it a hundred thousand times. "Welcome to *our* Maid!" some of them worded it.

No other girl in all history has ever reached such a summit of glory as Joan of Arc reached that day. And do you think it turned her head, and that she sat up to enjoy that delicious music of homage and applause? No; another girl would have done that, but not this one. That was the greatest heart and the simplest that ever beat. She went straight to bed and to sleep, like any tired child; and when the people found she was wounded and would rest, they shut off all passage and traffic in that region and stood guard themselves the whole night through, to see that her slumbers were not disturbed. They said, "She has given us peace, she shall have peace herself."

All knew that that region would be empty of English next day, and all said that neither the present citizens nor their posterity would ever cease to hold that day sacred to the memory of Joan of Arc. That word has been true for more than sixty years; it will continue so always. Orleans will never forget the 8th of May, nor ever fail to celebrate it. It is Joan of Arc's day—and holy.*

*It is still celebrated every year with civic and military pomps and solemnities. — Translator.

Chapter XXIII

IN THE earliest dawn of the morning, Talbot and his English forces evacuated their bastilles and marched away, not stopping to burn, destroy, or carry off anything, but leaving their fortresses just as they were, provisioned, armed, and equipped for a long siege. It was difficult for the people to believe that this great thing had really happened; that they were actually free once more, and might go and come through any gate they pleased, with none to molest or forbid; that the terrible Talbot, that scourge of the French, that man whose mere name had been able to annul the effectiveness of French armies, was gone, vanquished, retreating—driven away by a girl.

The city emptied itself. Out of every gate the crowds poured. They swarmed about the English bastilles like an invasion of ants, but noisier than those creatures, and carried off the artillery and stores, then turned all those dozen fortresses into monster bonfires, imitation volcanoes whose lofty columns of thick smoke seemed supporting the arch of the sky.

The delight of the children took another form. To some of the younger ones seven months was a sort of lifetime. They had forgotten what grass was like, and the velvety green meadows seemed paradise to their surprised and happy eyes after the long habit of seeing nothing but dirty lanes and streets. It was a wonder to them—those spacious reaches of open country to run and dance and tumble and frolic in, after their dull and joyless captivity; so they scampered far and wide over the fair regions on both sides of the river, and came back at eventide weary, but laden with flowers and flushed with new health drawn from the fresh country air and the vigorous exercise.

After the burnings, the grown folk followed Joan from church to church and put in the day in thanksgivings for the city's deliverance, and at night they fêted her and her generals and illuminated the town, and high and low gave themselves up to festivities and rejoicings. By the time the populace were

743

fairly in bed, toward dawn, we were in the saddle and away toward Tours to report to the King.

That was a march which would have turned any one's head but Joan's. We moved between emotional ranks of grateful country people all the way. They crowded about Joan to touch her feet, her horse, her armor, and they even knelt in the road and kissed her horse's hoof-prints.

The land was full of her praises. The most illustrious chiefs of the Church wrote to the King extolling the Maid, comparing her to the saints and heroes of the Bible, and warning him not to let "unbelief, ingratitude, or other injustice" hinder or impair the divine help sent through her. One might think there was a touch of prophecy in that, and we will let it go at that; but to my mind it had its inspiration in those great men's accurate knowledge of the King's trivial and treacherous character.

The King had come to Tours to meet Joan. At the present day this poor thing is called Charles the Victorious, an account of victories which other people won for him, but in our time we had a private name for him which described him better, and was sanctified to him by personal deserving— Charles the Base. When we entered the presence he sat throned, with his tinselled snobs and dandies around him. He looked like a forked carrot, so tightly did his clothing fit him from his waist down; he wore shoes with a rope-like pliant toe a foot long that had to be hitched up to the knee to keep it out of the way; he had on a crimson velvet cape that came no lower than his elbows; on his head he had a tall felt thing like a thimble, with a feather in its jewelled band that stuck up like a pen from an inkhorn, and from under that thimble his bush of stiff hair stuck down to his shoulders, curving outwards at the bottom, so that the cap and the hair together made the head like a shuttlecock. All the materials of his dress were rich, and all the colors brilliant. In his lap he cuddled a miniature greyhound that snarled, lifting its lip and showing its white teeth whenever any slight movement disturbed it. The King's dandies were dressed in about the same fashion as himself, and when I remembered that Joan had called the war-council of Orleans "disguised ladies' maids," it reminded me of people who squander all their money on a trifle and then haven't anything to invest when they come across a better chance; that name ought to have been saved for these creatures.

Joan fell on her knees before the majesty of France, and the other frivolous animal in his lap—a sight which it pained me to see. What had that man done for his country or for anybody in it, that she or any other person should kneel to him? But she—she had just done the only great deed that had been done for France in fifty years, and had consecrated it with the libation of her blood. The positions should have been reversed.

However, to be fair, one must grant that Charles acquitted himself very well for the most part, on that occasion—very much better than he was in the habit of doing. He passed his pup to a courtier, and took off his cap to Joan as if she had been a queen. Then he stepped from his throne and raised her, and showed quite a spirited and manly joy and gratitude in welcoming her and thanking her for her extraordinary achievement in his service. My prejudices are of a later date than that. If he had continued as he was at that moment, I should not have acquired them.

He acted handsomely. He said—

"You shall not kneel to me, my matchless General; you have wrought royally, and royal courtesies are your due." Noticing that she was pale, he said, "But you must not stand; you have lost blood for France, and your wound is yet green—come." He led her to a seat and sat down by her. "Now, then, speak out frankly, as to one who owes you much and freely confesses it before all this courtly assemblage. What shall be your reward? Name it."

I was ashamed of him. And yet that was not fair, for how could he be expected to know this marvellous child in these few weeks, when we who thought we had known her all her life were daily seeing the clouds uncover some new altitudes of her character whose existence was not suspected by us before? But we are all that way: when *we* know a thing we have only scorn for other people who don't happen to know it. And I was ashamed of these courtiers, too, for the way they licked their chops, so to speak, as envying Joan her great chance, they not knowing her any better than the King did. A blush began to rise in Joan's cheeks at the thought that she was working for her country for pay, and she dropped her head and tried to hide her face, as girls always do when they find themselves blushing; no one knows why they do, but they do, and the more they blush the more they fail to get reconciled to it, and the more they can't bear to have people look at them when they are doing it. The King made it a great deal worse by calling attention to it, which is the unkindest thing a person can do when a girl is blushing; sometimes, when there is a big crowd of strangers, it is even likely to make her cry if she is as young as Joan was. God knows the reason for this, it is hidden from men. As for me, I would as soon blush as sneeze; in fact, I would rather. However, these meditations are not of consequence: I will go on with what I was saying. The King rallied her for blushing, and this brought up the rest of the blood and turned her face to fire. Then he was sorry, seeing what he had done, and tried to make her comfortable by saying the blush was exceedingly becoming to her and not to mind it—which caused even the dog to notice it now, so of course the red in Joan's face turned to purple, and the tears overflowed and ran down—I could have told anybody that that would happen. The King was distressed, and saw that the best thing to do would be to get away from this subject, so he began to say the finest kind of things about Joan's capture of the Tourelles, and presently when she was more composed he mentioned the reward again and pressed her to name it. Everybody listened with anxious interest to hear what her claim was going to be, but when her answer came their faces showed that the thing she asked for was not what they had been expecting.

"Oh, dear and gracious Dauphin, I have but one desire—only one. If—"

"Do not be afraid, my child—name it."

"That you will not delay a day. My army is strong and valiant, and eager to finish its work—march with me to Rheims and receive your crown."

You could see the indolent King shrink, in his butterfly clothes.

"To Rheims—oh, impossible, my General! *We* march through the heart of England's power?"

Could those be French faces there? Not one of them lighted in response to the girl's brave proposition, but all promptly showed satisfaction in the King's objection. Leave this silken idleness for the rude contact of war? None of these butterflies desired that. They passed their jewelled comfit-boxes one to another and whispered their content in the head butterfly's practical prudence. Joan pleaded with the King, saying—

"Ah, I pray you do not throw away this perfect opportunity. Everything is favorable—everything. It is as if the circumstances were specially made for it. The spirits of our army are exalted with victory, those of the English forces depressed by defeat. Delay will change this. Seeing us hesitate to follow up our advantage, our men will wonder, doubt, lose confidence, and the English will wonder, gather courage, and be bold again. Now is the time—prithee let us march!"

The King shook his head, and La Tremouille, being asked for an opinion, eagerly furnished it:

"Sire, all prudence is against it. Think of the English strongholds along the Loire; think of those that lie between us and Rheims!"

He was going on, but Joan cut him short, and said, turning to him—

"If we wait, they will all be strengthened, re-enforced. Will that advantage us?"

"Why—no."

"Then what is your suggestion?—what is it that you would propose to do?"

"My judgment is to wait."

"Wait for what?"

The minister was obliged to hesitate, for he knew of no explanation that would sound well. Moreover, he was not used to being catechised in this fashion, with the eyes of a crowd of people on him, so he was irritated, and said—

"Matters of state are not proper matters for public discussion."

Joan said, placidly—

"I have to beg your pardon. My trespass came of ignorance. I did not know that matters connected with your department of the government were matters of state."

The minister lifted his brow in amused surprise, and said, with a touch of sarcasm—

"I am the King's chief minister, and yet you had the impression that matters connected with my department are not matters of state? Pray how is that?"

Joan replied, indifferently—

"Because there is no state."

"No state!"

"No, sir, there is no state, and no use for a minister. France is shrunk to a couple of acres of ground; a sheriff's constable could take care of it; its affairs are not matters of state. The term is too large."

The King did not blush, but burst into a hearty, careless laugh, and the court laughed too, but prudently turned its head and did it silently. La Tremouille was angry, and opened his mouth to speak, but the King put up his hand, and said—

"There—I take her under the royal protection. She has spoken the truth, the ungilded truth—how seldom I hear it! With all this tinsel on me and all this tinsel about me, I am but a sheriff after all—a poor shabby two-acre sheriff—and you are but a constable," and he laughed his cordial laugh again. "Joan, my frank, honest General, *will* you name your reward? I would ennoble you. You shall quarter the crown and the lilies of France for blazon, and with them your victorious sword to defend them—speak the word."

It made an eager buzz of surprise and envy in the assemblage, but Joan shook her head and said—

"Ah, I cannot, dear and noble Dauphin. To be allowed to work for France, to spend one's self for France, is itself so supreme a reward that nothing can add to it—nothing. Give me the one reward I ask, the dearest of all rewards, the highest in your gift—march with me to Rheims and receive your crown. I will beg it on my knees."

But the King put his hand on her arm, and there was a really brave awakening in his voice and a manly fire in his eye when he said—

"No; sit. You have conquered me—it shall be as you—"

But a warning sign from his minister halted him, and he added, to the relief of the Court—

"Well, well, we will think of it, we will think it over and see. Does that content you, impulsive little soldier?"

The first part of the speech sent a glow of delight to Joan's face, but the end of it quenched it and she looked sad, and the tears gathered in her eyes. After a moment she spoke out with what seemed a sort of terrified impulse, and said—

"Oh, use me; I beseech you, use me—there is but little time!"

"But little time?"

"Only a year—I shall last only a year."

"Why, child, there are fifty good years in that compact little body yet."

"Oh, you err, indeed you do. In one little year the end will come. Ah, the time is so short, so short; the moments are flying, and so much to be done. Oh, use me, and quickly—it is life or death for France."

Even those insects were sobered by her impassioned words. The King looked very grave—grave, and strongly impressed. His eyes lit suddenly with an eloquent fire, and he rose and drew his sword and raised it aloft; then he brought it slowly down upon Joan's shoulder and said:

"Ah, thou art so simple, so true, so great, so noble—and by this accolade I join thee to the nobility of France, thy fitting place! And for thy sake I do hereby ennoble all thy family and all thy kin; and all their descendants born in wedlock, not only in the male but also in the female line. And more!—more! To distinguish thy house and honor it above all others, we add a privilege never accorded to any before in the history of these dominions: the females of thy line shall have and hold the right to ennoble their husbands when these shall be of inferior degree." [Astonishment and envy flared up in every countenance when the words were uttered which conferred this extraordinary grace. The King paused and looked around upon these signs with quite evident satisfaction.] "Rise, Joan of Arc, now and henceforth surnamed *Du Lis*, in grateful acknowledgment of the good blow which you have struck for the lilies of France; and they, and the royal crown, and your own victorious sword, fit and fair company for each other, shall be grouped in your escutcheon and be and remain the symbol of your high nobility forever."

As my lady Du Lis rose, the gilded children of privilege pressed forward to welcome her to their sacred ranks and call her by her new name; but she was troubled, and said these honors were not meet for one of her lowly birth and station, and by their kind grace she would remain simple Joan of Arc, nothing more—and so be called.

Nothing more! As if there *could* be anything more, anything higher, anything greater! My lady Du Lis—why, it was tinsel, petty, perishable. But—JOAN OF ARC! The mere sound of it sets one's pulses leaping.

Chapter XXIV

IT WAS vexatious to see what a to-do the whole town, and next the whole country, made over the news. Joan of Arc ennobled by the King! People went dizzy with wonder and delight over it. You cannot imagine how she was gaped at, stared at, envied. Why, one would have supposed that some great and fortunate thing had happened to her. But *we* did not think any great things of it. To our minds no mere human hand could add a glory to Joan of Arc. To us she was the sun soaring in the heavens, and her new nobility a candle atop of it; to us it was swallowed up and lost in her own light. And she was as indifferent to it and as unconscious of it as the other sun would have been.

But it was different with her brothers. They were proud and happy in their new dignity, which was quite natural. And Joan was glad it had been conferred, when she saw how pleased they were. It was a clever thought in the King to outflank her scruples by marching on them under shelter of her love for her family and her kin.

Jean and Pierre sported their coat-of-arms right away; and their society was courted by everybody, the nobles and commons alike. The Standard-bearer said, with some touch of bitterness, that he could see that they just felt good to be alive, they were so soaked with the comfort of their glory; and didn't like to sleep at all, because when they were asleep they didn't know they were noble, and so sleep was a clean loss of time. And then he said—

"They can't take precedence of me in military functions and state ceremonies, but when it comes to civil ones and society affairs I judge they'll cuddle coolly in behind you and the knights, and Noël and I will have to walk behind *them*— hey?"

"Yes," I said, "I think you are right."

"I was just afraid of it—just afraid of it," said the Standard-bearer, with a sigh. "Afraid of it? I'm talking like a fool: of course I *knew* it. Yes, I was talking like a fool."

Noël Rainguesson said, musingly—

"Yes, I noticed something natural about the tone of it."

We others laughed.

"Oh, you did, did you? You think you are very clever, don't you? I'll take and wring your neck for you one of these days, Noël Rainguesson."

The Sieur de Metz said—

"Paladin, your fears haven't reached the top notch. They are away below the grand possibilities. Didn't it occur to you that in civil and society functions they will take precedence of *all* the rest of the personal staff—every individual of us?"

"Oh, come!"

"You'll find it's so. Look at their escutcheon. Its chiefest feature is the lilies of France. It's royal, man, royal—do you understand the size of that? The lilies are there by authority of the King—do you understand the size of *that*? Though not in detail and in entirety, they do nevertheless substantially *quarter the arms of France* in their coat. Imagine it! consider it! measure the magnitude of it! *We* walk in front of those boys? Bless you, we've done that for the last time. In my opinion there isn't a lay lord in this whole region that can walk in front of them, except the Duke d'Alençon, prince of the blood."

You could have knocked the Paladin down with a feather. He seemed to actually turn pale. He worked his lips a moment without getting anything out; then it came:

"*I* didn't know that, nor the half of it; how *could* I? I've been an idiot. I see it now—I've been an idiot. I met them this morning, and sung out *hello* to them just as I would to anybody. *I* didn't mean to be ill-mannered, but I didn't know the half of this that you've been telling. I've been an ass. Yes, that is all there is to it—I've been an ass."

Noël Rainguesson said, in a kind of weary way:

"Yes, that is likely enough; but I don't see why you should seem surprised at it."

"You don't, don't you? Well, *why* don't you?"

"Because I don't see any novelty about it. With some people it is a condition which is present all the time. Now you take a condition which is present all the time, and the results of that condition will be uniform; this uniformity of result will in time become monotonous; monotonousness, by the law of its being, is fatiguing. If you had manifested *fatigue* upon noticing that you had been an ass, that would have been logical, that would have been rational; whereas it seems to me that to manifest surprise was to be *again* an ass, because the condition of intellect that can enable a person to be surprised and stirred by inert monotonousness is a—"

"Now that is enough, Noël Rainguesson; stop where you are, before you get yourself into trouble. And don't bother me any more for some days or a week an it please you, for I cannot abide your clack."

"Come, I like that! *I* didn't want to talk. I tried to get out of talking. If you didn't want to hear my clack, what did you keep intruding your conversation on me for?"

"I? I never dreamed of such a thing."

"Well, you did it, anyway. And I have a right to feel hurt, and I do feel hurt, to have you treat me so. It seems to me that when a person goads, and crowds, and in a manner forces another person to talk, it is neither very fair nor very good-mannered to call what he says *clack*."

"Oh, snuffle—do! and break your heart, you poor thing. Somebody fetch this sick doll a sugar-rag. Look you, Sir Jean de Metz, do you feel absolutely certain about that thing?"

"What thing?"

"Why that Jean and Pierre are going to take precedence of all the lay noblesse hereabouts except the Duke d'Alençon?"

"I think there is not a doubt of it."

The Standard-bearer was deep in thoughts and dreams a few moments, then the silk-and-velvet expanse of his vast breast rose and fell with a sigh, and he said—

"Dear, dear, what a lift it is! It just shows what luck can do. Well, I don't care. I shouldn't care to be a painted accident—I shouldn't value it. I am prouder to have climbed up to where I am just by sheer natural merit than I would be to ride the very sun in the zenith and have to reflect that I was nothing but a poor little accident, and got shot up there out of somebody else's catapult. To me, merit is everything—in fact the only thing. All else is dross."

Just then the bugles blew the assembly, and that cut our talk short.

Chapter XXV

T HE DAYS began to waste away—and nothing decided, nothing done. The army was full of zeal, but it was also hungry. It got no pay, the treasury was getting empty, it was becoming impossible to feed it; under pressure of privation it began to fall apart and disperse—which pleased the trifling court exceedingly. Joan's distress was pitiful to see. She was obliged to stand helpless while her victorious army dissolved away until hardly the skeleton of it was left.

At last one day she went to the Castle of Loches, where the King was idling. She found him consulting with three of his councillors, Robert le Maçon, a former Chancellor of France, Christophe d'Harcourt, and Gerard Machet. The Bastard of Orleans was present also, and it is through him that we know what happened. Joan threw herself at the King's feet and embraced his knees, saying:

"Noble Dauphin, prithee hold no more of these long and numerous councils, but come, and come quickly, to Rheims and receive your crown."

Christophe d'Harcourt asked—

"Is it your Voices that command you to say that to the King?"

"Yes, and urgently."

"Then will you not tell us in the King's presence in what way the Voices communicate with you?"

It was another sly attempt to trap Joan into indiscreet admissions and dangerous pretensions. But nothing came of it. Joan's answer was simple and straightforward, and the smooth Bishop was not able to find any fault with it. She said that when she met with people who doubted the truth of her mission she went aside and prayed, complaining of the distrust of these, and then the comforting Voices were heard at her ear saying, soft and low, "Go forward, Daughter of God, and I will help thee." Then she added, "When I hear that, the joy in my heart, oh, it is insupportable!"

The Bastard said that when she said these words her face lit up as with a flame, and she was like one in an ecstasy.

Joan pleaded, persuaded, reasoned; gaining ground little by little, but opposed step by step by the council. She begged, she implored, leave to march. When they could answer nothing further, they granted that perhaps it had been a mistake to let the army waste away, but how could we help it now? how could we march without an army?

"Raise one!" said Joan.

"But it will take six weeks."

"No matter—begin! let us begin!"

"It is too late. Without doubt the Duke of Bedford has been gathering troops to push to the succor of his strong-holds on the Loire."

"Yes, while we have been disbanding ours—and pity 'tis. But we must throw away no more time; we must bestir ourselves."

The King objected that he could not venture toward Rheims with those strong places on the Loire in his path. But Joan said:

"We will break them up. Then you can march."

With *that* plan the king was willing to venture assent. He could sit around out of danger while the road was being cleared.

Joan came back in great spirits. Straightway everything was stirring. Proclamations were issued calling for men, a recruiting camp was established at Selles in Berry, and the commons and the nobles began to flock to it with enthusiasm.

A deal of the month of May had been wasted; and yet by the 6th of June Joan had swept together a new army and was ready to march. She had eight thousand men. Think of that. Think of gathering together such a body as that in that little region. And these were veteran soldiers, too. In fact most of the men in France were soldiers, when you came to that; for the wars had lasted generations now. Yes, most Frenchmen were soldiers; and admirable runners, too, both by practice and inheritance; they had done next to nothing but run for near a century. But that was not their fault. They had had no fair and proper leadership—at least leaders with a fair and proper chance. Away back, King and Court got the habit of being treacherous to the leaders; then the leaders easily got the habit of disobeying the King and going their own way, each for himself and nobody for the lot. Nobody could win victories that way. Hence, running became the habit of the French troops, and no wonder. Yet all that those troops needed in order to be good fighters was a leader who would attend strictly to business—a leader with *all* authority in his hands in place of a tenth of it along with nine other generals equipped with an equal tenth apiece. They had a leader rightly clothed with authority now, and with a head and heart bent on war of the most intensely business-like and earnest sort—and there would be *results*. No doubt of that. They had Joan of Arc; and under that leadership their legs would lose the art and mystery of running.

Yes, Joan was in great spirits. She was here and there and everywhere, all over the camp, by day and by night, pushing things. And wherever she came charging down the lines, reviewing the troops, it was good to hear them break out and cheer. And nobody could help cheering, she was such a vision of young bloom and beauty and grace, and such an incarnation of pluck and life and go! She was growing more and more ideally beautiful every day, as was plain to be seen—and these were days of development; for she was well past seventeen, now—in fact she was getting close upon seventeen and a half—indeed, just a little woman, as you may say.

The two young Counts de Laval arrived one day—fine young fellows allied to the greatest and most illustrious houses of France; and they could not rest till they had seen Joan of Arc. So the King sent for them and presented them to her, and you may believe she filled the bill of their expectations. When they heard that rich voice of hers they must have thought it was a flute; and when they saw her deep eyes and her face, and the soul that looked out of that face, you could see that the sight of her stirred them like a poem, like lofty eloquence, like martial music. One of them wrote home to his people, and in his letter he said, "It seemed something divine to see her and hear her." Ah, yes, and it was a true word. Truer word was never spoken.

He saw her when she was ready to begin her march and open the campaign, and this is what he said about it:

"She was clothed all in white armor save her head, and in her hand she carried a little battle-axe; and when she was ready to mount her great black horse he reared and plunged and would not let her. Then she said, 'Lead him to the cross.' This cross was in front of the church close by. So they led him there. Then she mounted, and he never budged, any more than if he had been tied. Then she turned toward the door of the church and said, in her soft womanly voice, 'You, priests and people of the Church, make processions and pray to God for us!' Then she spurred away, under her standard, with her little axe in her hand, crying 'Forward—march!' One of her brothers, who came eight days ago, departed with her; and he also was clad all in white armor."

I was there, and I saw it too; saw it all, just as he pictures it. And I see it yet—the little battle-axe, the dainty plumed cap, the white armor—all in the soft June afternoon; I see it just as if it were yesterday. And I rode with the staff—the personal staff—the staff of Joan of Arc.

That young Count was dying to go too, but the King held him back for the present. But Joan had made him a promise. In his letter he said:

"She told me that when the King starts for Rheims I shall go with him. But God grant I may not have to wait till then, but may have a part in the battles!"

She made him that promise when she was taking leave of my lady the Duchess d'Alençon. The Duchess was exacting a promise, so it seemed a proper time for others to do the like. The Duchess was troubled for her husband, for she foresaw desperate fighting; and she held Joan to her breast, and stroked her hair lovingly, and said:

"You must watch over him, dear, and take care of him, and send him back to me safe. I require it of you; I will not let you go till you promise."

Joan said:

"I give you the promise with all my heart; and it is not just words, it *is* a promise: you shall have him back without a hurt. Do you believe? And are you satisfied with me now?"

The Duchess could not speak, but she kissed Joan on the forehead; and so they parted.

We left on the 6th and stopped over at Romorantin; then on the 9th Joan entered Orleans in state, under triumphal arches, with the welcoming cannon thundering and seas of welcoming flags fluttering in the breeze. The Grand Staff rode with her, clothed in shining splendors of costume and decorations: the Duke d'Alençon; the Bastard of Orleans; the Sire de Boussac, Marshal of France; the Lord de Graville, Master of the Crossbowmen; the Sire de Culan, Admiral of France; Ambroise de Loré; Étienne de Vignoles, called La Hire; Gautier de Brusac, and other illustrious captains.

It was grand times: the usual shoutings, and packed multitudes, the usual crush to get sight of Joan; but at last we crowded through to our old lodgings, and I saw old Boucher and the wife and that dear Catherine gather Joan to their hearts and smother her with kisses—and my heart ached so! for I could have kissed Catherine better than anybody, and more and longer; yet was not thought of for that office, and I so famished for it. Ah, she was so beautiful, and oh, so sweet! I had loved her the first day I ever saw her, and from that day forth she was sacred to me. I have carried her image in my heart for sixty-three years—all lonely there, yes, solitary, for it never has had company—and I am grown so old, so old: but it, oh, it is as fresh and young and merry and mischievous and lovely and sweet and pure and witching and divine as it was when it crept in there, bringing benediction and peace to its habitation so long ago, so long ago—for it has not aged a day!

Chapter XXVI

THIS TIME, as before, the King's last command to the generals was this: *"See to it that you do nothing without the sanction of the Maid."* And this time the command was obeyed; and would continue to be obeyed all through the coming great days of the Loire campaign.

That was a change! That was new! It broke the traditions. It shows you what sort of a reputation as a commander-in-chief the child had made for herself in ten days in the field. It was a conquering of men's doubts and suspicions and a capturing and solidifying of men's belief and confidence such as the grayest veteran on the Grand Staff had not been able to achieve in thirty years. Don't you remember that when at sixteen Joan conducted her own case in a grim court of law and won it, the old judge spoke of her as "this marvellous child?" It was the right name, you see.

These veterans were not going to branch out and do things without the sanction of the Maid—that is true; and it was a great gain. But at the same time there were some among them who still trembled at her new and dashing war-tactics and earnestly desired to modify them. And so, during the 10th, while Joan was slaving away at her plans and issuing order after order with tireless industry, the old-time consultations and arguings and speechifyings were going on among certain of the generals.

In the afternoon of that day they came in a body to hold one of these councils of war; and while they waited for Joan to join them they discussed the situation. Now this discussion is not set down in the histories; but I was there, and I will speak of it, as knowing you will trust me, I not being given to beguiling you with lies.

Gautier de Brusac was spokesman for the timid ones; Joan's side was resolutely upheld by D'Alençon, the Bastard, La Hire, the Admiral of France, the Marshal de Boussac, and all the other really important chiefs.

De Brusac argued that the situation was very grave; that Jargeau, the first point of attack, was formidably strong; its imposing walls bristling with artillery; with 7000 picked English veterans behind them, and at their head the great Earl of Suffolk and his two redoubtable brothers the De la Poles. It seemed to him that the proposal of Joan of Arc to try to take such a place by storm was a most rash and over-daring idea, and she ought to be persuaded to relinquish it in favor of the soberer and safer procedure of investment by regular siege. It seemed to him that this fiery and furious new fashion of hurling masses of men against impregnable walls of stone, in defiance of the established laws and usages of war, was—

But he got no further. La Hire gave his plumed helm an impatient toss and burst out with—

"By God she knows her trade, and none can teach it her!"

And before he could get out anything more, D'Alençon was on his feet, and the Bastard of Orleans, and half a dozen others, all thundering at once, and pouring out their indignant displeasure upon any and all that might hold, secretly or publicly, distrust of the wisdom of the Commander-in-Chief. And when they had said their say, La Hire took a chance again, and said:

"There are some that never know how to change. Circumstances may change, but those people are never able to see that *they* have got to change too, to meet those circumstances. All that they know is the one beaten track that their fathers and grandfathers have followed and that they themselves have followed in their turn. If an earthquake come and rip the land to chaos, and that beaten track now lead over precipices and into morasses, those people *can't* learn that they must strike out a new road—no; they will march stupidly along and follow the old one to death and perdition. Men, there's a new state of things; and a surpassing military genius has perceived it with her clear eye. And a new road is required, and that same clear eye has noted where it must go, and has marked it out for us. The man does not live, never has lived, never *will* live, that can improve upon it! The old state of things was defeat, defeat, defeat—and by consequence we had troops with no dash, no heart, no hope. Would you assault stone walls with such? No—there was but one way, with that kind: sit down before a place and wait, wait—starve it out, if you could. The new case is the very opposite; it is this: men all on fire with pluck and dash and vim and fury and energy—a restrained conflagration! What would you do with it? Hold it down and let it smoulder and perish and go out? What would Joan of Arc do with it? Turn it *loose*, by the Lord God of heaven and earth, and let it swallow up the foe in the whirl-wind of its fires! Nothing shows the splendor and wisdom of her military genius like her instant comprehension of the size of the change which has come about, and her instant percep-tion of the right and only right way to take advantage of it. With her is no sitting down and starving out; no dilly-dallying and fooling around; no lazying, loafing, and going to sleep; no, it is storm! storm! storm! and still storm! storm! storm! and forever storm! storm! storm! hunt the enemy to his hole, then turn her French hurricanes loose and carry him by storm! And that is *my* sort! Jargeau? What of Jargeau, with its battlements and towers, its devastating artillery, its seven thousand picked veterans? Joan of Arc is to the fore, and by the splendor of God its fate is sealed!"

Oh, he carried them. There was not another word said about persuading Joan to change her tactics. They sat talking comfortably enough after that.

By-and-by Joan entered, and they rose and saluted with their swords, and she asked what their pleasure might be. La Hire said:

"It is settled, my General. The matter concerned Jargeau. There were some who thought we could not take the place."

Joan laughed her pleasant laugh; her merry, care-free laugh; the laugh that rippled so buoyantly from her lips and made old people feel young again to hear it; and she said to the company—

"Have no fears—indeed there is no need nor any occasion for them. We will strike the English boldly by assault, and you will see." Then a far-away look came into her eyes, and I think that a picture of her home drifted across the vision of her mind; for she said very gently, and as one who muses, "But that I know God guides us and will give us success, I had liefer keep sheep than endure these perils."

We had a homelike farewell supper that evening—just the personal staff and the family. Joan had to miss it; for the city had given a banquet in her honor, and she had gone there in state with the Grand Staff, through a riot of joy-bells and a sparkling Milky Way of illuminations.

After supper some lively young folk whom we knew came in, and we presently forgot that we were soldiers, and only remembered that we were boys and girls and full of animal spirits and long-pent fun; and so there was dancing, and games, and romps, and screams of laughter—just as extravagant and innocent and noisy a good time as ever I had in my life. Dear, dear, how long ago it was!—and I was young then. And outside, all the while, was the measured tramp of marching battalions, belated odds and ends of the French power gathering for the morrow's tragedy on the grim stage of war. Yes, in those days we had those contrasts side by side. And as I passed along to bed there was another one: the big Dwarf, in brave new armor, sat sentry at Joan's door—the stern Spirit of War made flesh, as it were—and on his ample shoulder was curled a kitten asleep.

Chapter XXVII

WE MADE a gallant show next day when we filed out through the frowning gates of Orleans, with banners flying and Joan and the Grand Staff in the van of the long column. Those two young De Lavals were come, now, and were joined to the Grand Staff. Which was well; war being their proper trade, for they were grandsons of that illustrious fighter Bertrand du Guesclin, Constable of France in earlier days. Louis de Bourbon, the Marshal de Rais, and the Vidame de Chartres were added also. We had a right to feel a little uneasy, for we knew that a force of five thousand men was on its way under Sir John Fastolfe to reinforce Jargeau, but I think we were not uneasy, nevertheless. In truth that force was not yet in our neighborhood. Sir John was loitering; for some reason or other he was not hurrying. He was losing precious time—four days at Étampes, and four more at Janville.

We reached Jargeau and began business at once. Joan sent forward a heavy force which hurled itself against the outworks in handsome style, and gained a footing and fought hard to keep it; but it presently began to fall back before a sortie from the city. Seeing this, Joan raised her battle-cry and led a new assault herself under a furious artillery fire. The Paladin was struck down at her side, wounded, but she snatched her standard from his failing hand and plunged on through the ruck of flying missiles, cheering her men with encouraging cries, and then for a good time one had turmoil, and clash of steel, and collision and confusion of struggling multitudes, and the hoarse bellowing of the guns; and then the hiding of it all under a rolling firmament of smoke; a firmament through which veiled vacancies appeared for a moment now and then, giving fitful dim glimpses of the wild tragedy enacting beyond; and always at these times one caught sight of that slight figure in white mail which was the centre and soul of our hope and trust, and whenever we saw that, with its back to us and its face to the fight, we knew that all was well. At last a great shout went up—a joyous roar of

763

shoutings, in fact—and that was sign sufficient that the fau-
bourgs were ours.

Yes, they were ours; the enemy had been driven back
within the walls. On the ground which Joan had won, we
camped; for night was coming on.

Joan sent a summons to the English, promising that if they
surrendered she would allow them to go in peace and take
their horses with them. Nobody knew that she could take that
strong place, but she knew it—knew it well; yet she offered
that grace—offered it in a time when such a thing was unknown in war; in a time when it was custom and usage to
massacre the garrison and the inhabitants of captured cities
without pity or compunction—yes, even to the harmless
women and children sometimes. There are neighbors all
about you who well remember the unspeakable atrocities
which Charles the Bold inflicted upon the men and women
and children of Dinant when he took that place some years
ago. It was a unique and kindly grace which Joan offered that
garrison; but that was her way, that was her loving and merciful nature—she always did her best to save her enemy's life
and his soldierly pride when she had the mastery of him.

The English asked fifteen days' armistice to consider the
proposal in. And Fastolfe coming with five thousand men!
Joan said no. But she offered another grace: they might take
both their horses and their side-arms—but they must go
within the hour.

Well, those bronzed English veterans were pretty hard-
headed folk. They declined again. Then Joan gave command
that her army be made ready to move to the assault at nine in
the morning. Considering the deal of marching and fighting
which the men had done that day, D'Alençon thought the
hour rather early; but Joan said it was best so, and so must be
obeyed. Then she burst out with one of those enthusiasms
which were always burning in her when battle was imminent,
and said:

"Work! work! and God will work with us!"

Yes, one might say that her motto was "Work! stick to it;
keep on working!" for in war she never knew what indolence
was. And whoever will take that motto and live by it will be
likely to succeed. There's many a way to win, in this world,

but none of them is worth much without good hard work back of it.

I think we should have lost our big Standard-Bearer that day, if our bigger Dwarf had not been at hand to bring him out of the mêlée when he was wounded. He was unconscious, and would have been trampled to death by our own horse, if the Dwarf had not promptly rescued him and haled him to the rear and safety. He recovered, and was himself again after two or three hours; and then he was happy and proud, and made the most of his wound, and went swaggering around in his bandages showing off like an innocent big child—which was just what he was. He was prouder of being wounded than a really modest person would be of being killed. But there was no harm in his vanity, and nobody minded it. He said he was hit by a stone from a catapult—a stone the size of a man's head. But the stone grew, of course. Before he got through with it he was claiming that the enemy had flung a building at him.

"Let him alone," said Noël Rainguesson. "Don't interrupt his processes. To-morrow it will be a cathedral."

He said that privately. And, sure enough, to-morrow it *was* a cathedral. I never saw anybody with such an abandoned imagination.

Joan was abroad at the crack of dawn, galloping here and there and yonder, examining the situation minutely, and choosing what she considered the most effective positions for her artillery; and with such accurate judgment did she place her guns that her Lieutenant-General's admiration of it still survived in his memory when his testimony was taken at the Rehabilitation, a quarter of a century later.

In this testimony the Duke d'Alençon said that at Jargeau that morning of the 12th of June she made her dispositions not like a novice, but "with the sure and clear judgment of a trained general of twenty or thirty years' experience."

The veteran captains of the armies of France said she was great in war in all ways, but greatest of all in her genius for posting and handling artillery.

Who taught the shepherd girl to do these marvels—she who could not read, and had had no opportunity to study the complex arts of war? I do not know any way to solve such a baffling riddle as that, there being no precedent for it, nothing in history to compare it with and examine it by. For in history there is no great general, however gifted, who arrived at success otherwise than through able teaching and hard study and some experience. It is a riddle which will never be guessed. *I* think these vast powers and capacities were born in her, and that she applied them by an intuition which could not err.

At eight o'clock all movement ceased, and with it all sounds, all noise. A mute expectancy reigned. The stillness was something awful—because it meant so much. There was no air stirring. The flags on the towers and ramparts hung straight down like tassels. Wherever one saw a person, that person had stopped what he was doing, and was in a waiting attitude, a listening attitude. We were on a commanding spot, clustered around Joan. Not far from us, on every hand, were the lanes and humble dwellings of these outlying suburbs. Many people were visible—all were listening, not one was moving. A man had placed a nail; he was about to fasten something with it to the door-post of his shop—but he had stopped. There was his hand reaching up holding the nail; and there was his other hand in the act of striking with the hammer; but he had forgotten everything—his head was turned aside, listening. Even children unconsciously stopped in their play; I saw a little boy with his hoop-stick pointed slanting toward the ground in the act of steering the hoop around the corner; and so he had stopped and was listening—the hoop was rolling away, doing its own steering. I saw a young girl prettily framed in an open window, a watering-pot in her hand and window-boxes of red flowers under its spout—but the water had ceased to flow; the girl was listening. Everywhere were these impressive petrified forms; and everywhere was suspended movement and that awful stillness.

Joan of Arc raised her sword in the air. At the signal, the silence was torn to rags: cannon after cannon vomited flames and smoke and delivered its quaking thunders; and we saw answering tongues of fire dart from the towers and walls of the city, accompanied by answering deep thunders, and in a minute the walls and the towers disappeared, and in their place stood vast banks and pyramids of snowy smoke, motionless in the dead air. The startled girl dropped her watering-pot and clasped her hands together, and at that moment a stone cannon-ball crashed through her fair body.

The great artillery duel went on, each side hammering away with all its might; and it was splendid for smoke and noise, and most exalting to one's spirits. The poor little town around about us suffered cruelly. The cannon-balls tore through its slight buildings, wrecking them as if they had been built of cards; and every moment or two one would see a huge rock come curving through the upper air above the smoke clouds and go plunging down through the roofs. Fire broke out, and columns of flame and smoke rose toward the sky.

Presently the artillery concussions changed the weather. The sky became overcast, and a strong wind rose and blew away the smoke that hid the English fortresses.

Then the spectacle was fine: turreted gray walls and towers, and streaming bright flags, and jets of red fire and gushes of white smoke in long rows, all standing out with sharp vividness against the deep leaden background of the sky; and then the whizzing missiles began to knock up the dirt all around us, and I felt no more interest in the scenery. There was one English gun that was getting our position down finer and finer all the time. Presently Joan pointed to it and said:

"Fair Duke, step out of your tracks, or that machine will kill you."

The Duke d'Alençon did as he was bid; but Monsieur du Lude rashly took his place, and that cannon tore his head off in a moment.

Joan was watching all along for the right time to order the assault. At last, about nine o'clock, she cried out—

"Now—to the assault!" and the buglers blew the charge.

Instantly we saw the body of men that had been appointed to this service move forward toward a point where the concentrated fire of our guns had crumbled the upper half of a broad stretch of wall to ruins; we saw this force descend into the ditch and begin to plant the scaling-ladders. We were soon with them. The Lieutenant-General thought the assault premature. But Joan said:

"Ah, gentle Duke, are you afraid? Do you not know that I have promised to send you home safe?"

It was warm work in the ditches. The walls were crowded with men, and they poured avalanches of stones down upon us. There was one gigantic Englishman who did us more hurt than any dozen of his brethren. He always dominated the places easiest of assault, and flung down exceedingly trouble-some big stones which smashed men and ladders both—then he would near burst himself with laughing over what he had done. But the Duke settled accounts with him. He went and found the famous cannoneer Jean le Lorrain, and said—

"Train your gun—kill me this demon."

He did it with the first shot. He hit the Englishman fair in the breast and knocked him backwards into the city.

The enemy's resistance was so effective and so stubborn that our people began to show signs of doubt and dismay. Seeing this, Joan raised her inspiring battle-cry and descended into the fosse herself, the Dwarf helping her and the Paladin sticking bravely at her side with the standard. She started up a scaling-ladder, but a great stone flung from above came crash-ing down upon her helmet and stretched her, wounded and stunned, upon the ground. But only for a moment. The Dwarf stood her upon her feet, and straightway she started up the ladder again, crying—

"To the assault, friends, to the assault—the English are ours! It is the appointed hour!"

There was a grand rush, and a fierce roar of war-cries, and we swarmed over the ramparts like ants. The garrison fled, we pursued; Jargeau was ours!

The Earl of Suffolk was hemmed in and surrounded, and the Duke d'Alençon and the Bastard of Orleans demanded that he surrender himself. But he was a proud nobleman and came of a proud race. He refused to yield his sword to subor-dinates, saying—

"I will die rather. I will surrender to the Maid of Orleans alone, and to no other."

And so he did; and was courteously and honorably used by her.

His two brothers retreated, fighting step by step, toward the bridge, we pressing their despairing forces and cutting them down by scores. Arrived on the bridge, the slaughter still continued. Alexander de la Pole was pushed overboard or fell over, and was drowned. Eleven hundred men had fallen; John de la Pole decided to give up the struggle. But he was nearly as proud and particular as his brother of Suffolk as to whom he would surrender to. The French officer nearest at hand was Guillaume Renault, who was pressing him closely. Sir John said to him—

"Are you a gentleman?"

"Yes."

"And a knight?"

"No."

Then Sir John knighted him himself, there on the bridge, giving him the accolade with English coolness and tranquillity in the midst of that storm of slaughter and mutilation; and then bowing with high courtesy took the sword by the blade and laid the hilt of it in the man's hand in token of surrender. Ah, yes, a proud tribe, those De la Poles.

It was a grand day, a memorable day, a most splendid victory. We had a crowd of prisoners, but Joan would not allow them to be hurt. We took them with us and marched into Orleans next day through the usual tempest of welcome and joy.

And this time there was a new tribute to our leader. From everywhere in the packed streets the new recruits squeezed their way to her side to touch the sword of Joan of Arc and draw from it somewhat of that mysterious quality which made it invincible.

Chapter XXVIII

THE TROOPS must have a rest. Two days would be allowed for this.

The morning of the 14th I was writing from Joan's dictation in a small room which she sometimes used as a private office when she wanted to get away from officials and their interruptions. Catherine Boucher came in and sat down and said—

"Joan, dear, I want you to talk to me."

"Indeed I am not sorry for that, but glad. What is in your mind?"

"This. I scarcely slept, last night, for thinking of the dangers you are running. The Paladin told me how you made the Duke stand out of the way when the cannon-balls were flying all about, and so saved his life."

"Well, that was right, wasn't it?"

"Right? Yes; but you stayed there yourself. Why will you do like that? It seems such a wanton risk."

"Oh, no, it was not so. I was not in any danger."

"How can you say that, Joan, with those deadly things flying all about you?"

Joan laughed, and tried to turn the subject, but Catherine persisted. She said—

"It was horribly dangerous, and it could not be necessary to stay in such a place. And you led an assault again. Joan, it is tempting Providence. I want you to make me a promise. I want you to promise me that you will let others lead the assaults, if there *must* be assaults, and that you will take better care of yourself in those dreadful battles. Will you?"

But Joan fought away from the promise and did not give it. Catherine sat troubled and discontented awhile, then she said—

"Joan, are you going to be a soldier always? These wars are so long—so long. They last forever and ever and ever."

There was a glad flash in Joan's eye as she cried—

"This campaign will do all the really hard work that is in front of it in the next four days. The rest of it will be gentler

—oh, far less bloody. Yes, in four days France will gather another trophy like the redemption of Orleans and make her second long step toward freedom!"

Catherine started (and so did I); then she gazed long at Joan like one in a trance, murmuring "four days—four days," as if to herself and unconsciously. Finally she asked, in a low voice that had something of awe in it:

"Joan, tell me—how is it that you know that? For you do know it, I think."

"Yes," said Joan, dreamily, "I know—I know. I shall strike —and strike again. And before the fourth day is finished I shall strike yet again." She became silent. We sat wondering and still. This was for a whole minute, she looking at the floor and her lips moving but uttering nothing. Then came these words, but hardly audible: "And in a thousand years the English power in France will not rise up from that blow."

It made my flesh creep. It was uncanny. She was in a trance again—I could see it—just as she was that day in the pastures of Domremy when she prophesied about us boys in the war and afterward did not know that she had done it. She was not conscious now; but Catherine did not know that, and so she said, in a happy voice—

"Oh, I believe it, I believe it, and I am so glad! Then you will come back and bide with us all your life long, and we will love you so, and so honor you!"

A scarcely perceptible spasm flitted across Joan's face, and the dreamy voice muttered—

"Before two years are sped I shall die a cruel death!"

I sprang forward with a warning hand up. That is why Catherine did not scream. She was going to do that—I saw it plainly. Then I whispered her to slip out of the place, and say nothing of what had happened. I said Joan was asleep— asleep and dreaming. Catherine whispered back, and said—

"Oh, I am so grateful that it is only a dream! It sounded like prophecy." And she was gone.

Like prophecy! I knew it *was* prophecy; and I sat down crying, as knowing we should lose her. Soon she started, shivering slightly, and came to herself, and looked around and saw me crying there, and jumped out of her chair and ran to me all in a whirl of sympathy and compassion, and put her hand on my head, and said—

"My poor boy! What is it? Look up, and tell me."

I had to tell her a lie; I grieved to do it, but there was no other way. I picked up an old letter from my table, written by Heaven knows who, about some matter Heaven knows what, and told her I had just gotten it from Père Fronte, and that in it it said the children's Fairy Tree had been chopped down by some miscreant or other, and—

I got no further. She snatched the letter from my hand and searched it up and down and all over, turning it this way and that, and sobbing great sobs, and the tears flowing down her cheeks, and ejaculating all the time, "Oh, cruel, cruel! how could any be so heartless? Ah, poor Arbre Fée de Bourlemont gone—and we children loved it so! Show me the place where it says it!"

And I, still lying, showed her the pretended fatal words on the pretended fatal page, and she gazed at them through her tears, and said she could see, herself, that they were hateful, ugly words—they "had the very look of it."

Then we heard a strong voice down the corridor announcing—

"His Majesty's messenger—with despatches for her Excellency the Commander-in-Chief of the armies of France!"

Chapter XXIX

I knew she had seen the vision of the Tree. But when? I could not know. Doubtless before she had lately told the King to use her, for that she had but one year left to work in. It had not occurred to me at the time, but the conviction came upon me now that at that time she had already seen the Tree. It had brought her a welcome message; that was plain, otherwise she could not have been so joyous and light-hearted as she had been these latter days. The death-warning had nothing dismal about it for her; no, it was remission of exile, it was leave to come home.

Yes, she had seen the Tree. No one had taken the prophecy to heart which she made to the King; and for a good reason, no doubt: no one *wanted* to take it to heart; all wanted to banish it away and forget it. And all had succeeded, and would go on to the end placid and comfortable. All but me alone. I must carry my awful secret without any to help me. A heavy load, a bitter burden; and would cost me a daily heartbreak. She was to die; and so soon. I had never dreamed of that. How could I, and she so strong and fresh and young, and every day earning a new right to a peaceful and honored old age? For at that time I thought old age valuable. I do not know why, but I thought so. All young people think it, I believe, they being ignorant and full of superstitions. She had seen the Tree. All that miserable night those ancient verses went floating back and forth through my brain:

> "And when in exile wand'ring we
> Shall fainting yearn for glimpse of thee,
>   O rise upon our sight!"

But at dawn the bugles and the drums burst through the dreamy hush of the morning, and it was turn out all! mount and ride. For there was red work to be done.

We marched to Meung without halting. There we carried the bridge by assault, and left a force to hold it, the rest of the army marching away next morning toward Beaugency, where the lion Talbot, the terror of the French, was in command.

When we arrived at that place, the English retired into the castle and we sat down in the abandoned town.

Talbot was not at the moment present in person, for he had gone away to watch for and welcome Fastolfe and his re-enforcement of five thousand men.

Joan placed her batteries and bombarded the castle till night. Then some news came: Richemont, Constable of France, this long time in disgrace with the King, largely because of the evil machinations of La Tremouille and his party, was approaching with a large body of men to offer his services to Joan—and very much she needed them, now that Fastolfe was so close by. Richemont had wanted to join us before, when we first marched on Orleans; but the foolish King, slave of those paltry advisers of his, warned him to keep his distance and refused all reconciliation with him.

I go into these details because they are important. Important because they lead up to the exhibition of a new gift in Joan's extraordinary mental make-up—statesmanship. It is a sufficiently strange thing to find that great quality in an ignorant country girl of seventeen and a half, but she had it.

Joan was for receiving Richemont cordially, and so was La Hire and the two young Lavals and other chiefs, but the Lieutenant-General, D'Alençon, strenuously and stubbornly opposed it. He said he had absolute orders from the King to deny and defy Richemont, and that if they were overridden he would leave the army. This would have been a heavy disaster indeed. But Joan set herself the task of persuading him that the salvation of France took precedence of all minor things—even the commands of a sceptred ass; and she accomplished it. She persuaded him to disobey the King in the interest of the nation, and to be reconciled to Count Richemont and welcome him. That was statesmanship; and of the highest and soundest sort. Whatever thing men call great, look for it in Joan of Arc, and there you will find it.

In the early morning, June 17th, the scouts reported the approach of Talbot and Fastolfe with Fastolfe's succoring force. Then the drums beat to arms; and we set forth to meet the English, leaving Richemont and his troops behind to watch the castle of Beaugency and keep its garrison at home.

By-and-by we came in sight of the enemy. Fastolfe had tried to convince Talbot that it would be wisest to retreat and not risk a battle with Joan at this time, but distribute the new levies among the English strongholds of the Loire, thus securing them against capture; then be patient and wait—wait for more levies from Paris; let Joan exhaust her army with fruitless daily skirmishing; then at the right time fall upon her in resistless mass and annihilate her. He was a wise old experienced general, was Fastolfe. But that fierce Talbot would hear of no delay. He was in a rage over the punishment which the Maid had inflicted upon him at Orleans and since, and he swore by God and Saint George that he would have it out with her if he had to fight her all alone. So Fastolfe yielded, though he said they were now risking the loss of everything which the English had gained by so many years' work and so many hard knocks.

The enemy had taken up a strong position, and were waiting, in order of battle, with their archers to the front and a stockade before them.

Night was coming on. A messenger came from the English with a rude defiance and an offer of battle. But Joan's dignity was not ruffled, her bearing was not discomposed. She said to the herald—

"Go back and say it is too late to meet to-night; but to-morrow, please God and our Lady, we will come to close quarters."

The night fell dark and rainy. It was that sort of light steady rain which falls so softly and brings to one's spirit such serenity and peace. About ten o'clock D'Alençon, the Bastard of Orleans, La Hire, Pothon of Saintrailles, and two or three other generals came to our headquarters tent, and sat down to discuss matters with Joan. Some thought it was a pity that Joan had declined battle, some thought not. Then Pothon asked her why she had declined it. She said—

"There was more than one reason. These English are ours —they cannot get away from us. Wherefore there is no need to take risks, as at other times. The day was far spent. It is good to have much time and the fair light of day when one's force is in a weakened state—nine hundred of us yonder

keeping the bridge of Meung under the Marshal de Rais, fifteen hundred with the Constable of France keeping the
bridge and watching the castle of Beaugency."

Dunois said—

"I grieve for this depletion, Excellency, but it cannot be
helped. And the case will be the same the morrow, as to that."

Joan was walking up and down, just then. She laughed her
affectionate, comrady laugh, and stopping before that old
war-tiger she put her small hand above his head and touched
one of his plumes, saying—

"Now tell me, wise man, which feather is it that I touch?"

"In sooth, Excellency, that I cannot."

"Name of God, Bastard, Bastard! You cannot tell me this
small thing, yet are bold to name a large one—telling us what
is in the stomach of the unborn morrow: that we shall not
have those men. Now it is my thought that they will be with
us."

That made a stir. All wanted to know why she thought
that. But La Hire took the word and said—

"Let be. If she thinks it, that is enough. It will happen."

Then Pothon of Saintrailles said—

"There were other reasons for declining battle, according
to the saying of your Excellency?"

"Yes. One was that we being weak and the day far gone,
the battle might not be decisive. When it is fought it *must* be
decisive. And shall be."

"God grant it, and amen. There were still other reasons?"

"One other—yes." She hesitated a moment, then said:
"This was not the day. To-morrow is the day. It is so
written."

They were going to assail her with eager questionings, but
she put up her hand and prevented them. Then she said—

"It will be the most noble and beneficient victory that God
has vouchsafed to France at any time. I pray you question me
not as to whence or how I know this thing, but be content
that it is so."

There was pleasure in every face, and conviction and high
confidence. A murmur of conversation broke out, but was
interrupted by a messenger from the outposts who brought
news—namely, that for an hour there had been stir and

movement in the English camp of a sort unusual at such a time and with a resting army, he said. Spies had been sent under cover of the rain and darkness to inquire into it. They had just come back and reported that large bodies of men had been dimly made out who were slipping stealthily away in the direction of Meung.

The generals were very much surprised, as any might tell from their faces.

"It is a retreat," said Joan.

"It has that look," said D'Alençon.

"It certainly has," observed the Bastard and La Hire.

"It was not to be expected," said Louis de Bourbon, "but one can divine the purpose of it."

"Yes," responded Joan. "Talbot has reflected. His rash brain has cooled. He thinks to take the bridge of Meung and escape to the other side of the river. He knows that this leaves his garrison of Beaugency at the mercy of fortune, to escape our hands if it can; but there is no other course if he would avoid this battle, and that he also knows. But he shall not get the bridge. We will see to that."

"Yes," said D'Alençon, "we must follow him, and take care of that matter. What of Beaugency?"

"Leave Beaugency to me, gentle Duke; I will have it in two hours, and at no cost of blood."

"It is true, Excellency. You will but need to deliver this news there and receive the surrender."

"Yes. And I will be with you at Meung with the dawn, fetching the Constable and his fifteen hundred; and when Talbot knows that Beaugency has fallen it will have an effect upon him."

"By the mass, yes!" cried La Hire. "He will join his Meung garrison to his army and break for Paris. Then we shall have our bridge force with us again, along with our Beaugency-watchers, and be stronger for our great day's work by four-and-twenty hundred able soldiers, as was here promised within the hour. Verily this Englishman is doing our errands for us and saving us much blood and trouble. Orders, Excellency—give us our orders!"

"They are simple. Let the men rest three hours longer. At one o'clock the advance-guard will march, under your command, with Pothon of Saintrailles as second; the second division will follow at two under the Lieutenant-General. Keep well in the rear of the enemy, and see to it that you avoid an engagement. I will ride under guard to Beaugency and make so quick work there that I and the Constable of France will join you before dawn with his men."

She kept her word. Her guard mounted and we rode off through the puttering rain, taking with us a captured English officer to confirm Joan's news. We soon covered the journey and summoned the castle. Richard Guétin, Talbot's lieutenant, being convinced that he and his five hundred men were left helpless, conceded that it would be useless to try to hold out. He could not expect easy terms, yet Joan granted them nevertheless. His garrison could keep their horses and arms, and carry away property to the value of a silver mark per man. They could go whither they pleased, but must not take arms against France again under ten days.

Before dawn we were with our army again, and with us the Constable and nearly all his men, for we left only a small garrison in Beaugency castle. We heard the dull booming of cannon to the front, and knew that Talbot was beginning his attack on the bridge. But some time before it was yet light the sound ceased and we heard it no more.

Guétin had sent a messenger through our lines under a safe-conduct given by Joan, to tell Talbot of the surrender. Of course this poursuivant had arrived ahead of us. Talbot had held it wisdom to turn, now, and retreat upon Paris. When daylight came he had disappeared; and with him Lord Scales and the garrison of Meung.

What a harvest of English strongholds we had reaped in those three days!—strongholds which had defied France with quite cool confidence and plenty of it until we came.

Chapter XXX

WHEN THE MORNING broke at last on that forever memorable 18th of June, there was no enemy discoverable anywhere, as I have said. But that did not trouble me. I knew we should find him, and that we should strike him; strike him the promised blow—the one from which the English power in France would not rise up in a thousand years, as Joan had said in her trance.

The enemy had plunged into the wide plains of La Beauce—a roadless waste covered with bushes, with here and there bodies of forest trees—a region where an army would be hidden from view in a very little while. We found the trail in the soft wet earth and followed it. It indicated an orderly march; no confusion, no panic.

But we had to be cautious. In such a piece of country we could walk into an ambush without any trouble. Therefore Joan sent bodies of cavalry ahead under La Hire, Poton, and other captains, to feel the way. Some of the other officers began to show uneasiness; this sort of hide-and-go-seek business troubled them and made their confidence a little shaky. Joan divined their state of mind and cried out impetuously—

"Name of God, what would you? We must smite these English, and we will. They shall not escape us. Though they were hung to the clouds we would get them!"

By-and-by we were nearing Patay; it was about a league away. Now at this time our reconnoisance, feeling its way in the bush, frightened a deer, and it went bounding away and was out of sight in a moment. Then hardly a minute later a dull great shout went up in the distance toward Patay. It was the English soldiery. They had been shut up in garrison so long on mouldy food that they could not keep their delight to themselves when this fine fresh meat came springing into their midst. Poor creature, it had wrought damage to a nation which loved it well. For the French knew where the English were, now, whereas the English had no suspicion of where the French were.

La Hire halted where he was, and sent back the tidings.
Joan was radiant with joy. The Duke d'Alençon said to her—

"Very well, we have found them; shall we fight them?"

"Have you good spurs, Prince?"

"Why? Will they make us run away?"

"Nenni, en nom de Dieu! These English are ours—they are
lost. They will fly. Who overtakes them will need good spurs.
Forward—close up!"

By the time we had come up with La Hire the English had
discovered our presence. Talbot's force was marching in three
bodies. First his advance-guard; then his artillery; then his
battle corps a good way in the rear. He was now out of the
bush and in a fair open country. He at once posted his artillery, his advance-guard, and five hundred picked archers along
some hedges where the French would be obliged to pass, and
hoped to hold this position till his battle corps could come
up. Sir John Fastolfe urged the battle corps into a gallop. Joan
saw her opportunity and ordered La Hire to advance—which
La Hire promptly did, launching his wild riders like a storm-
wind, his customary fashion.

The Duke and the Bastard wanted to follow, but Joan
said—

"Not yet—wait."

So they waited—impatiently, and fidgeting in their saddles. But she was steady—gazing straight before her, measuring, weighing, calculating—by shades, minutes, fractions of
minutes, seconds—with all her great soul present, in eye, and
set of head, and noble pose of body—but patient, steady,
master of herself—master of herself and of the situation.

And yonder, receding, receding, plumes lifting and falling,
lifting and falling, streamed the thundering charge of La
Hire's godless crew, La Hire's great figure dominating it and
his sword stretched aloft like a flag-staff.

"O, Satan and his Hellions, see them go!" Somebody muttered it in deep admiration.

And now he was closing up—closing up on Fastolfe's
rushing corps.

And now he struck it—struck it hard, and broke its order.
It lifted the Duke and the Bastard in their saddles to see it;
and they turned, trembling with excitement, to Joan, saying—

"Now!"

But she put up her hand, still gazing, weighing, calculating, and said again—

"Wait—not yet."

Fastolfe's hard-driven battle corps raged on like an avalanche toward the waiting advance-guard. Suddenly these conceived the idea that it was flying in panic before Joan; and so in that instant it broke and swarmed away in a mad panic itself, with Talbot storming and cursing after it.

Now was the golden time. Joan drove her spurs home and waved the advance with her sword. "Follow me!" she cried, and bent her head to her horse's neck and sped away like the wind!

We swept down into the confusion of that flying rout, and for three long hours we cut and hacked and stabbed. At last the bugles sang "Halt!"

The Battle of Patay was won.

Joan of Arc dismounted, and stood surveying that awful field, lost in thought. Presently she said—

"The praise is to God. He has smitten with a heavy hand this day." After a little she lifted her face, and looking afar off, said, with the manner of one who is thinking aloud, "In a thousand years—a thousand years—the English power in France will not rise up from this blow." She stood again a time, thinking, then she turned toward her grouped generals, and there was a glory in her face and a noble light in her eye; and she said—

"O, friends, friends, do you know?—do you comprehend? *France is on the way to be free!*"

"And had never been, but for Joan of Arc!" said La Hire, passing before her and bowing low, the others following and doing likewise; he muttering as he went, "I will say it though I be damned for it." Then battalion after battalion of our victorious army swung by, wildly cheering. And they shouted "Live forever, Maid of Orleans, live forever!" while Joan, smiling, stood at the salute with her sword.

This was not the last time I saw the Maid of Orleans on the red field of Patay. Toward the end of the day I came upon her where the dead and dying lay stretched all about in heaps and winrows; our men had mortally wounded an English prisoner who was too poor to pay a ransom, and from a distance she had seen that cruel thing done; and had galloped to the place and sent for a priest, and now she was holding the head of her dying enemy in her lap, and easing him to his death with comforting soft words, just as his sister might have done; and the womanly tears running down her face all the time.*

*Lord Ronald Gower (*Joan of Arc*, p. 82) says: "Michelet discovered this story in the deposition of Joan of Arc's page, Louis de Conte, who was prob- ably an eye-witness of the scene." This is true. It was a part of the testimony of the author of these "Personal Recollections of Joan of Arc," given by him in the Rehabilitation proceedings of 1456.—TRANSLATOR.

Chapter XXXI

JOAN had said true: France was on the way to be free.

The war called the Hundred Years' War was very sick to-day. Sick on its English side—for the very first time since its birth, ninety-one years gone by.

Shall we judge battles by the numbers killed and the ruin wrought? Or shall we not rather judge them by the results which flowed from them? Any one will say that a battle is only truly great or small according to its results. Yes, any one will grant that, for it is the truth.

Judged by results, Patay's place is with the few supremely great and imposing battles that have been fought since the peoples of the world first resorted to arms for the settlement of their quarrels. So judged, it is even possible that Patay has no peer among that few just mentioned, but stands alone, as the supremest of historic conflicts. For when it began France lay gasping out the remnant of an exhausted life, her case wholly hopeless in the view of all political physicians; when it ended, three hours later, she was convalescent. Convalescent, and nothing requisite but time and ordinary nursing to bring her back to perfect health. The dullest physician of them all could see this, and there was none to deny it.

Many death-sick nations have reached convalescence through a series of battles, a procession of battles, a weary tale of wasting conflicts stretching over years, but only one has reached it in a single day and by a single battle. That nation is France, and that battle Patay.

Remember it and be proud of it; for you are French, and it is the stateliest fact in the long annals of your country. There it stands, with its head in the clouds! And when you grow up you will go on pilgrimage to the field of Patay, and stand uncovered in the presence of—what? A monument with *its* head in the clouds? Yes. For all nations in all times have built monuments on their battle-fields to keep green the memory of the perishable deed that was wrought there and of the perishable name of him who wrought it; and will France neglect Patay and Joan of Arc? Not for long. And will she build a monument scaled to their rank as compared with the world's other fields and heroes? Perhaps—if there be room for it under the arch of the sky.

But let us look back a little, and consider certain strange and impressive facts. The Hundred Years' War began in 1337. It raged on and on, year after year and year after year; and at last England stretched France prone with that fearful blow at Crécy. But she rose and struggled on, year after year, and at last again she went down under another devastating blow—Poitiers. She gathered her crippled strength once more, and the war raged on, and on, and still on, year after year, decade after decade. Children were born, grew up, married, died—the war raged on; *their* children in turn grew up, married, died—the war raged on; *their* children, growing, saw France struck down again; this time under the incredible disaster of Agincourt—and still the war raged on, year after year, and in time *these* children married in their turn.

France was a wreck, a ruin, a desolation. The half of it belonged to England, with none to dispute or deny the truth; the other half belonged to nobody—in three months would be flying the English flag: the French King was making ready to throw away his crown and flee beyond the seas.

Now came the ignorant country maid out of her remote village and confronted this hoary war, this all-consuming conflagration that had swept the land for three generations. Then began the briefest and most amazing campaign that is recorded in history. In seven weeks it was finished. In seven weeks she hopelessly crippled that gigantic war that was ninety-one years old. At Orleans she struck it a staggering blow; on the field of Patay she broke its back.

Think of it. Yes, one can do that; but *understand* it? Ah, that is another matter; none will ever be able to comprehend that stupefying marvel.

Seven weeks—with here and there a little bloodshed. Perhaps the most of it, in any single fight, at Patay, where the English began six thousand strong and left two thousand dead upon the field. It is said and believed that in three battles alone—Crécy, Poitiers, and Agincourt—near a hundred thousand Frenchmen fell, without counting the thousand other fights of that long war. The dead of that war make a mournful long list—an interminable list. Of men slain in the field the count goes by tens of thousands; of innocent women and children slain by bitter hardship and hunger it goes by that appalling term, millions.

It was an ogre, that war; an ogre that went about for near a hundred years, crunching men and dripping blood from his jaws. And with her little hand that child of seventeen struck him down; and yonder he lies stretched on the field of Patay, and will not get up any more while this old world lasts.

Chapter XXXII

THE GREAT NEWS of Patay was carried over the whole of France in twenty hours, people said. I do not know as to that; but one thing is sure, anyway: the moment a man got it he flew shouting and glorifying God and told his neighbor; and that neighbor flew with it to the next homestead; and so on and so on without resting the word travelled; and when a man got it in the night, at what hour soever, he jumped out of his bed and bore the blessed message along. And the joy that went with it was like the light that flows across the land when an eclipse is receding from the face of the sun; and indeed you may say that France had lain in an eclipse this long time; yes, buried in a black gloom which these benefi-cent tidings were sweeping away, now, before the on-rush of their white splendor.

The news beat the flying enemy to Yeuville, and the town rose against its English masters and shut the gates against their brethren. It flew to Mont Pipeau, to Saint Simon, and to this, that, and the other English fortress; and straightway the garrison applied the torch and took to the fields and the woods. A detachment of our army occupied Meung and pil-laged it.

When we reached Orleans that town was as much as fifty times insaner with joy than we had ever seen it before— which is saying much. Night had just fallen, and the illumina-tions were on so wonderful a scale that we seemed to plough through seas of fire; and as to the noise—the hoarse cheering of the multitude, the thundering of cannon, the clash of bells—indeed there was never anything like it. And every-where rose a new cry that burst upon us like a storm when the column entered the gates, and nevermore ceased: "Wel-come to Joan of Arc—way for the SAVIOR OF FRANCE!" And there was another cry: "Crécy is avenged! Poitiers is avenged! Agincourt is avenged!—Patay shall live forever!"

Mad? Why, you never could imagine it in the world. The prisoners were in the centre of the column. When that came along and the people caught sight of their masterful old enemy Talbot, that had made them dance so long to his grim war-music, you may imagine what the uproar was like if you can, for I cannot describe it. They were so glad to see him that presently they wanted to have him out and hang him; so Joan had him brought up to the front to ride in her protection. They made a striking pair.

Chapter XXXIII

Yes, Orleans was in a delirium of felicity. She invited the King, and made sumptuous preparations to receive him, but—he didn't come. He was simply a serf at that time, and La Tremouille was his master. Master and serf were visiting together at the master's castle of Sully-sur-Loire.

At Beaugency Joan had engaged to bring about a reconciliation between the Constable Richemont and the King. She took Richemont to Sully-sur-Loire and made her promise good.

The great deeds of Joan of Arc are five:

1. The Raising of the Siege.
2. The Victory of Patay.
3. The Reconciliation at Sully-sur-Loire.
4. The Coronation of the King.
5. The Bloodless March.

We shall come to the Bloodless March presently; (and the Coronation). It was the victorious long march which Joan made through the enemy's country from Gien to Rheims, and thence to the gates of Paris, capturing every English town and fortress that barred the road, from the beginning of the journey to the end of it; and this by the mere force of her name, and without shedding a drop of blood—perhaps the most extraordinary campaign in this regard in history—this is the most glorious of her military exploits.

The Reconciliation was one of Joan's most important achievements. No one else could have accomplished it; and in fact no one else of high consequence had any disposition to try. In brains, in scientific warfare, and in statesmanship the Constable Richemont was the ablest man in France. His loyalty was sincere; his probity was above suspicion—(and it made him sufficiently conspicuous in that trivial and conscienceless Court).

In restoring Richemont to France, Joan made thoroughly secure the successful completion of the great work which she had begun. She had never seen Richemont until he came to her with his little army. Was it not wonderful that at a glance she should know him for the one man who could finish and perfect her work and establish it in perpetuity? How was it that that child was able to do this? It was because she had the "seeing eye," as one of our knights had once said. Yes, she had that great gift—almost the highest and rarest that has been granted to man. Nothing of an extraordinary sort was still to be done, yet the remaining work could not safely be left to the King's idiots; for it would require wise statesmanship and long and patient though desultory hammering of the enemy. Now and then, for a quarter of a century yet, there would be a little fighting to do, and a handy man could carry that on with small disturbance to the rest of the country; and little by little, and with progressive certainty, the English would disappear from France.

And that happened. Under the influence of Richemont the King became at a later time a man—a man, a king, a brave and capable and determined soldier. Within six years after Patay he was leading storming parties himself; fighting in fortress ditches up to his waist in water, and climbing scaling-ladders under a furious fire with a pluck that would have satisfied even Joan of Arc. In time he and Richemont cleared away all the English; even from regions where the people had been under their mastership for three hundred years. In such regions wise and careful work was necessary, for the English rule had been fair and kindly; and men who have been ruled in that way are not always anxious for a change.

Which of Joan's five chief deeds shall we call chiefest? It is my thought that each *in its turn* was that. This is saying that, taken as a whole, they *equalized* each other, and neither was then greater than its mate.

Do you perceive? Each was a stage in an ascent. To leave out one of them would defeat the journey; to achieve one of them at the wrong time and in the wrong place would have the same effect.

Consider the Coronation. As a masterpiece of diplomacy, where can you find its superior in our history? Did the King suspect its vast importance? No. Did his ministers? No. Did the astute Bedford, representative of the English crown? No. An advantage of incalculable importance was here under the eyes of the King and of Bedford; the King could get it by a bold stroke, Bedford could get it without an effort; but being ignorant of its value, neither of them put forth his hand. Of all the wise people in high office in France, only one knew the priceless worth of this neglected prize—the untaught child of seventeen, Joan of Arc—and she had known it from the beginning, had spoken of it from the beginning as an essential detail of her mission.

How did she know it? It is simple: she was a peasant. That tells the whole story. She was of the people and knew the people; those others moved in a loftier sphere and knew nothing much about them. We make little account of that vague, formless, inert mass, that mighty underlying force which we call "the people"—an epithet which carries contempt with it. It is a strange attitude; for at bottom we know that the throne which the people support, stands, and that when that support is removed, nothing in this world can save it.

Now, then, consider this fact, and observe its importance. Whatever the parish priest believes, his flock believes; they love him, they revere him; he is their unfailing friend, their dauntless protector, their comforter in sorrow, their helper in their day of need; he has their whole confidence; what he tells them to do, that they will do, with a blind and affectionate obedience, let it cost what it may. Add these facts thoughtfully together, and what is the sum? This: *The parish priest governs the nation.* What is the King, then, if the parish priest withdraw his support and deny his authority? Merely a shadow and no King; let him resign.

Do you get that idea? Then let us proceed. A priest is consecrated to his office by the awful hand of God, laid upon him by his appointed representative on earth. That consecration is final; nothing can undo it, nothing can remove it. Neither the Pope nor any other power can strip the priest of his office; God gave it, and it is forever sacred and secure. The dull parish knows all this. To priest and parish, whosoever is anointed of God bears an office whose authority can no longer be disputed or assailed. To the parish priest, and to his subjects the nation, an uncrowned king is a similitude of a person who has been named for holy orders but has not been consecrated; he has no office, he has not been ordained, another may be appointed in his place. In a word, an uncrowned king is a *doubtful* King; but if God appoint him and His servant the Bishop anoint him, the doubt is annihilated; the priest and the parish are his loyal subjects straightway, and while he lives they will recognize no king but him.

To Joan of Arc the peasant girl, Charles VII. was no King until he was crowned; to her he was only the *Dauphin*; that is to say, the *heir*. If I have ever made her call him King, it was a mistake; she called him the Dauphin, and nothing else until after the Coronation. It shows you as in a mirror—for Joan was a mirror in which the lowly hosts of France were clearly reflected—that to all that vast underlying force called "the people" he was no King but only Dauphin before his crowning, and was indisputably and irrevocably King *after* it.

Now you understand what a colossal move on the political chess-board the Coronation was. Bedford realized this by-and-by, and tried to patch up his mistake by crowning *his* King; but what good could that do? None in the world.

Speaking of chess, Joan's great acts may be likened to that game. Each move was made in its proper order, and it was great and effective because it *was* made in its proper order and not out of it. Each, at the time made, seemed the greatest move; but the final result made them all recognizable as equally essential and equally important. This is the game, as played:

1. Joan moves Orleans and Patay—*check*.
2. Then moves the Reconciliation—but does not proclaim check, it being a move for position, and to take effect later.
3. Next she moves the Coronation—*check*.
4. Next, the Bloodless March—*check*.
5. Final move (after her death) the reconciled Constable Richemont to the French King's elbow—*checkmate*.

Chapter XXXIV

THE Campaign of the Loire had as good as opened the road to Rheims. There was no sufficient reason now why the Coronation should not take place. The Coronation would complete the mission which Joan had received from heaven, and then she would be forever done with war, and would fly home to her mother and her sheep, and never stir from the hearth-stone and happiness any more. That was her dream; and she could not rest, she was so impatient to see it fulfilled. She became so possessed with this matter that I began to lose faith in her two prophecies of her early death—and of course when I found that faith wavering I encouraged it to waver all the more.

The King was afraid to start to Rheims, because the road was mile-posted with English fortresses, so to speak. Joan held them in light esteem and not things to be afraid of in the existing modified condition of English confidence.

And she was right. As it turned out, the march to Rheims was nothing but a holiday excursion. Joan did not even take any artillery along, she was so sure it would not be necessary. We marched from Gien twelve thousand strong. This was the 29th of June. The Maid rode by the side of the King; on his other side was the Duke d'Alençon. After the Duke followed three other princes of the blood. After these followed the Bastard of Orleans, the Marshal de Boussac, and the Admiral of France. After these came La Hire, Saintrailles, Tremouille, and a long procession of knights and nobles.

We rested three days before Auxerre. The city provisioned the army, and a deputation waited upon the King, but we did not enter the place.

Saint-Florentin opened its gates to the King.

On the 4th of July we reached Saint-Fal, and yonder lay Troyes before us—a town which had a burning interest for us boys; for we remembered how seven years before, in the pastures of Domremy, the Sunflower came with his black flag and brought us the shameful news of the Treaty of Troyes—that treaty which gave France to England, and a daughter of our royal line in marriage to the Butcher of Agincourt. That poor town was not to blame, of course; yet we flushed hot with that old memory, and hoped there would be a misunderstanding here, for we dearly wanted to storm the place and burn it. It was powerfully garrisoned by English and Burgundian soldiery, and was expecting re-enforcements from Paris. Before night we camped before its gates and made rough work with a sortie which marched out against us.

Joan summoned Troyes to surrender. Its commandant, seeing that she had no artillery, scoffed at the idea, and sent her a grossly insulting reply. Five days we consulted and negotiated. No result. The King was about to turn back now, and give up. He was afraid to go on, leaving this strong place in his rear. Then La Hire put in a word, with a slap in it for some of his Majesty's advisers:

"The Maid of Orleans undertook this expedition of her own motion; and it is my mind that it is her judgment that should be followed here, and not that of any other, let him be of whatsoever breed and standing he may."

There was wisdom and righteousness in that. So the King sent for the Maid, and asked her how she thought the prospect looked. She said, without any tone of doubt or question in her voice:

"In three days' time the place is ours."

The smug Chancellor put in a word now:

"If we were sure of it we would wait here six days."

"Six days, forsooth! Name of God, man, we will enter the gates to-morrow!"

Then she mounted, and rode her lines, crying out—

"Make preparation—to your work, friends, to your work! We assault at dawn!"

She worked hard that night; slaving away with her own hands like a common soldier. She ordered fascines and fagots to be prepared and thrown into the fosse, thereby to bridge it; and in this rough labor she took a man's share.

At dawn she took her place at the head of the storming force and the bugles blew the assault. At that moment a flag of truce was flung to the breeze from the walls, and Troyes surrendered without firing a shot.

The next day the King with Joan at his side and the Paladin

bearing her banner entered the town in state at the head of the army. And a goodly army it was, now, for it had been growing ever bigger and bigger from the first.

And now a curious thing happened. By the terms of the treaty made with the town the garrison of English and Burgundian soldiery were to be allowed to carry away their "goods" with them. This was well, for otherwise how would they buy the wherewithal to live? Very well; these people were all to go out by the one gate, and at the time set for them to depart we young fellows went to that gate, along with the Dwarf, to see the march-out. Presently here they came in an interminable file, the foot-soldiers in the lead. As they approached one could see that each bore a burden of a bulk and weight to sorely tax his strength; and we said among ourselves, truly these folk are well off for poor common soldiers. When they were come nearer, what do you think? Every rascal of them had a French prisoner on his back! They were carrying away their "goods," you see—their property— strictly according to the permission granted by the treaty.

Now think how clever that was, how ingenious. What could a body say? what could a body do? For certainly these people were within their right. These prisoners were property; nobody could deny that. My dears, if those had been *English* captives, conceive of the richness of that booty! For English prisoners had been scarce and precious for a hundred years; whereas it was a different matter with French prisoners. They had been over-abundant for a century. The possessor of a French prisoner did not hold him long for ransom as a rule, but presently killed him to save the cost of his keep. This shows you how small was the value of such a possession in those times. When we took Troyes a calf was worth thirty francs, a sheep sixteen, a French prisoner eight. It was an enormous price for those other animals—a price which naturally seems incredible to you. It was the war, you see. It worked two ways: it made meat dear and prisoners cheap.

Well, here were these poor Frenchmen being carried off. What could we do? Very little of a permanent sort, but we did what we could. We sent a messenger flying to Joan, and we and the French guards halted the procession for a parley—to gain time, you see. A big Burgundian lost his temper and swore a great oath that none should stop *him*; he would go, and would take his prisoner with him. But we blocked him off, and he saw that he was mistaken about going—he couldn't do it. He exploded into the maddest cursings and revilings, then, and unlashing his prisoner from his back, stood him up, all bound and helpless; then drew his knife, and said to us with a light of sarcastic triumph in his eye—

"I may not carry him away, you say—yet he is mine, none will dispute it. Since I may not convey him hence, this property of mine, there is another way. Yes, I can kill him; not even the dullest among you will question *that* right. Ah, you had not thought of that—vermin!"

That poor starved fellow begged us with his piteous eyes to save him; then spoke, and said he had a wife and little children at home. Think how it wrung our heartstrings. But what could we do? The Burgundian was within his right. We could only beg and plead for the prisoner. Which we did. And the Burgundian enjoyed it. He stayed his hand to hear more of it, and laugh at it. That stung. Then the Dwarf said—

"Prithee, young sirs, let me beguile him; for when a matter requiring persuasion is to the fore, I have indeed a gift in that sort, as any will tell you that know me well. You smile; and that is punishment for my vanity, and fairly earned, I grant it you. Still, if I may toy a little, just a little—" saying which he stepped to the Burgundian and began a fair soft speech, all of goodly and gentle tenor; and in the midst he mentioned the Maid; and was going on to say how she out of her good heart would prize and praise this compassionate deed which he was about to—

It was as far as he got. The Burgundian burst into his smooth oration with an insult levelled at Joan of Arc. We sprang forward, but the Dwarf, his face all livid, brushed us aside and said, in a most grave and earnest way—

"I crave your patience. Am not I her guard of honor? This is my affair."

And saying this he suddenly shot his right hand out and gripped the great Burgundian by the throat, and so held him upright on his feet. "You have insulted the Maid," he said; "and the Maid is France. The tongue that does that earns a long furlough."

One heard the muffled cracking of bones. The Burgundian's eyes began to protrude from their sockets and stare with a leaden dulness at vacancy. The color deepened in his face and became an opaque purple. His hands hung down limp, his body collapsed with a shiver, every muscle relaxed its tension and ceased from its function. The Dwarf took away his hand and the column of inert mortality sank mushily to the ground.

We struck the bonds from the prisoner and told him he was free. His crawling humbleness changed to frantic joy in a moment, and his ghastly fear to a childish rage. He flew at that dead corpse and kicked it, spat in its face; danced upon it, crammed mud into its mouth, laughing, jeering, cursing and volleying forth indecencies and bestialities like a drunken fiend. It was a thing to be expected: soldiering makes few saints. Many of the on-lookers laughed, others were indifferent, none was surprised. But presently in his mad caperings the freed man capered within reach of the waiting file, and another Burgundian promptly slipped a knife through his neck, and down he went with a death-shriek, his brilliant artery-blood spurting ten feet as straight and bright as a ray of light. There was a great burst of jolly laughter all around from friend and foe alike; and thus closed one of the pleasantest incidents of my checkered military life.

And now came Joan hurrying, and deeply troubled. She considered the claim of the garrison, then said:—

"You have right upon your side. It is plain. It was a careless word to put in the treaty, and covers too much. But ye may not take these poor men away. They are French, and I will not have it. The King shall ransom them, every one. Wait till I send you word from him; and hurt no hair of their heads; for I tell you, I who speak, that that would cost you very dear."

That settled it. The prisoners were safe for one while, anyway. Then she rode back eagerly and required that thing of the King, and would listen to no paltering and no excuses. So the King told her to have her way, and she rode straight back and bought the captives free in his name and let them go.

Chapter XXXV

It was here that we saw again the Grand Master of the King's Household, in whose castle Joan was guest when she tarried at Chinon in those first days of her coming out of her own country. She made him Bailiff of Troyes, now, by the King's permission.

And now we marched again; Châlons surrendered to us; and there by Châlons in a talk, Joan being asked if she had no fears for the future, said yes, one—treachery. Who could believe it? who could dream it? And yet in a sense it was prophecy. Truly man is a pitiful animal.

We marched, marched, kept on marching; and at last on the 16th of July we came in sight of our goal, and saw the great cathedral towers of Rheims rise out of the distance! Huzzah after huzzah swept the army from van to rear; and as for Joan of Arc, there where she sat her horse gazing, clothed all in white armor, dreamy, beautiful, and in her face a deep, deep joy, a joy not of earth, oh, she was not flesh, she was a spirit! Her sublime mission was closing—closing in flawless triumph. To-morrow she could say, "It is finished—let me go free."

We camped, and the hurry and rush and turmoil of the grand preparations began. The Archbishop and a great deputation arrived; and after these came flock after flock, crowd after crowd, of citizens and country folk hurrahing in, with banners and music, and flowed over the camp, one rejoicing inundation after another, everybody drunk with happiness. And all night long Rheims was hard at work, hammering away, decorating the town, building triumphal arches, and clothing the ancient cathedral within and without in a glory of opulent splendors.

We moved betimes in the morning: the coronation ceremonies would begin at nine and last five hours. We were aware that the garrison of English and Burgundian soldiers had given up all thought of resisting the Maid, and that we should find the gates standing hospitably open and the whole city ready to welcome us with enthusiasm.

It was a delicious morning, brilliant with sunshine but cool and fresh and inspiring. The army was in great form, and fine to see, as it uncoiled from its lair fold by fold, and stretched away on the final march of the peaceful Coronation Campaign.

Joan, on her black horse, with the Lieutenant-General and the personal staff grouped about her, took post for a final review and a good-bye; for she was not expecting to ever be a soldier again, or ever serve with these or any other soldiers any more after this day. The army knew this, and believed it was looking for the last time upon the girlish face of its invincible little Chief, its pet, its pride, its darling, whom it had ennobled in its private heart with nobilities of its own creation, calling her "Daughter of God," "Savior of France," "Victory's Sweetheart," "the Page of Christ," together with still softer titles which were simply naïf and frank endearments such as men are used to confer upon children whom they love. And so one saw a new thing now; a thing bred of the emotion that was present there on both sides. Always before, in the march-past, the battalions had gone swinging by in a storm of cheers, heads up and eyes flashing, the drums rolling, the bands braying pæans of victory; but now there was nothing of that. But for one impressive sound, one could have closed his eyes and imagined himself in a world of the dead. That one sound was all that visited the ear in the summer stillness—just that one sound—the muffled tread of the marching host. As the serried masses drifted by, the men put their right hands up to their temples, palms to the front, in military salute, turning their eyes upon Joan's face in mute God-bless-you and farewell, and keeping them there while they could. They still kept their hands up in reverent salute many steps after they had passed by. Every time Joan put her handkerchief to her eyes you could see a little quiver of emotion crinkle along the faces of the files.

The march-past after a victory is a thing to drive the heart mad with jubilation; but this one was a thing to break it.

We rode now to the King's lodging, which was the Archbishop's country palace; and he was presently ready, and we galloped off and took position at the head of the army. By this time the country people were arriving in multitudes from every direction and massing themselves on both sides of the road to get sight of Joan—just as had been done every day since our first day's march began. Our march now lay through the grassy plain, and those peasants made a dividing double border for that plain. They stretched right down through it, a broad belt of bright colors on each side of the road; for every peasant girl and woman in it had a white jacket on her body and a crimson skirt on the rest of her. Endless borders made of poppies and lilies stretching away in front of us—that is what it looked like. And that is the kind of lane we had been marching through all these days. Not a lane between multitudinous flowers standing upright on their stems—no, these flowers were always kneeling; kneeling, these human flowers, with their hands and faces lifted toward Joan of Arc, and the grateful tears streaming down. And all along, those closest to the road hugged her feet and kissed them and laid their wet cheeks fondly against them. I never, during all those days, saw any of either sex stand while she passed, nor any man keep his head covered. Afterwards in the Great Trial these touching scenes were used as a weapon against her. She had been made an object of adoration by the people, and this was proof that she was a heretic—so claimed that unjust court.

As we drew near the city the curving long sweep of ramparts and towers was gay with fluttering flags and black with masses of people; and all the air was vibrant with the crash of artillery and gloomed with drifting clouds of smoke. We entered the gates in state and moved in procession through the city, with all the guilds and industries in holiday costume marching in our rear with their banners; and all the route was hedged with a huzzahing crush of people, and all the windows were full and all the roofs; and from the balconies hung costly stuffs of rich colors; and the waving of handkerchiefs, seen in perspective through a long vista, was like a snowstorm.

Joan's name had been introduced into the prayers of the Church—an honor theretofore restricted to royalty. But she had a dearer honor and an honor more to be proud of, from a humbler source: the common people had had leaden medals struck which bore her effigy and her escutcheon, and these they wore as charms. One saw them everywhere.

From the Archbishop's Palace, where we halted, and where the King and Joan were to lodge, the King sent to the Abbey Church of St. Remi, which was over toward the gate by which we had entered the city, for the *Sainte Ampoule*, or flask of holy oil. This oil was not earthly oil; it was made in heaven; the flask also. The flask, with the oil in it, was brought down from heaven by a dove. It was sent down to St. Remi just as he was going to baptize King Clovis, who had become a Christian. I know this to be true. I had known it long before; for Père Fronte told me in Domremy. I cannot tell you how strange and awful it made me feel when I saw that flask and knew I was looking with my own eyes upon a thing which had actually been in heaven; a thing which had been seen by angels, perhaps; and by God Himself of a cer- tainty, for He sent it. And I was looking upon it—I. At one time I could have touched it. But I was afraid; for I could not know but that God had touched it. It is most probable that He had.

From this flask Clovis had been anointed; and from it all the Kings of France had been anointed since. Yes, ever since the time of Clovis; and that was nine hundred years. And so, as I have said, that flask of holy oil was sent for, while we waited. A coronation without that would not have been a coronation at all, in my belief.

Now in order to get the flask, a most ancient ceremonial had to be gone through with; otherwise the Abbé of St. Remi, hereditary guardian in perpetuity of the oil, would not deliver it. So, in accordance with custom, the King deputed five great nobles to ride in solemn state and richly armed and accoutred, they and their steeds, to the Abbey Church as a guard of honor to the Archbishop of Rheims and his canons, who were to bear the King's demand for the oil. When the five great lords were ready to start, they knelt in a row and put up their mailed hands before their faces, palm joined to palm, and swore upon their lives to conduct the sacred vessel safely, and safely restore it again to the Church of St. Remi after the anointing of the King. The Archbishop and his sub-

ordinates, thus nobly escorted, took their way to St. Remi.
The Archbishop was in grand costume, with his mitre on his
head and his cross in his hand. At the door of St. Remi they
halted and formed, to receive the holy phial. Soon one heard
the deep tones of the organ and of chanting men; then one
saw a long file of lights approaching through the dim church.
And so came the Abbot, in his sacerdotal panoply, bearing
the phial, with his people following after. He delivered it,
with solemn ceremonies, to the Archbishop; then the march
back began, and it was most impressive; for it moved, the
whole way, between two multitudes of men and women who
lay flat upon their faces and prayed in dumb silence and in
dread while that awful thing went by that had been in heaven.

This august company arrived at the great west door of the
cathedral; and as the Archbishop entered a noble anthem rose
and filled the vast building. The cathedral was packed with
people—people in thousands. Only a wide space down the
centre had been kept free. Down this space walked the Archbishop and his canons, and after them followed those five
stately figures in splendid harness, each bearing his feudal
banner—and riding!

Oh, that was a magnificent thing to see. Riding down the
cavernous vastness of the building through the rich lights
streaming in long rays from the pictured windows—oh, there
was never anything so grand!

They rode clear to the choir—as much as four hundred feet
from the door, it was said. Then the Archbishop dismissed
them, and they made deep obeisance till their plumes touched
their horses' necks, then made those proud prancing and
mincing and dancing creatures go backwards all the way to
the door—which was pretty to see, and graceful; then they
stood them on their hind-feet and spun them around and
plunged away and disappeared.

For some minutes there was a deep hush, a waiting pause;
a silence so profound that it was as if all those packed thousands there were steeped in dreamless slumber—why, you
could even notice the faintest sounds, like the drowsy buzzing
of insects; then came a mighty flood of rich strains from four
hundred silver trumpets, and then, framed in the pointed
archway of the great west door, appeared Joan and the King.

They advanced slowly, side by side, through a tempest of welcome—explosion after explosion of cheers and cries, mingled
with the deep thunders of the organ and rolling tides of
triumphant song from chanting choirs. Behind Joan and the
King came the Paladin with the Banner displayed; and a majestic figure he was, and most proud and lofty in his bearing,
for he knew that the people were marking him and taking
note of the gorgeous state dress which covered his armor.

At his side was the Sire d'Albret, proxy for the Constable of
France, bearing the Sword of State.

After these, in order of rank, came a body royally attired
representing the lay peers of France; it consisted of three
princes of the blood, and La Tremouille and the young De
Laval brothers.

These were followed by the representatives of the ecclesiastical peers—the Archbishop of Rheims, and the Bishops of
Laon, Châlons, Orleans, and one other.

Behind these came the Grand Staff, all our great generals
and famous names, and everybody was eager to get a sight of
them. Through all the din one could hear shouts, all along,
that told you where two of them were: "Live the Bastard of
Orléans!" "Satan La Hire forever!"

The august procession reached its appointed place in time,
and the solemnities of the Coronation began. They were long
and imposing—with prayers, and anthems, and sermons, and
everything that is right for such occasions; and Joan was at
the King's side all these hours, with her Standard in her hand.
But at last came the grand act: the King took the oath, he was
anointed with the sacred oil; a splendid personage, followed
by train-bearers and other attendants, approached, bearing
the Crown of France upon a cushion, and kneeling offered it.
The King seemed to hesitate—in fact *did* hesitate; for he put
out his hand and then stopped with it there in the air over the
crown, the fingers in the attitude of taking hold of it. But that
was for only a moment—though a moment is a notable
something when it stops the heart-beat of twenty thousand
people and makes them catch their breath. Yes, only a moment; then he caught Joan's eye, and she gave him a look with
all the joy of her thankful great soul in it, then he smiled, and

took the Crown of France in his hand, and right finely and right royally lifted it up and set it upon his head.

Then what a crash there was! All about us cries and cheers, and the chanting of the choirs and groaning of the organ; and outside the clamoring of the bells and the booming of the cannon.

The fantastic dream, the incredible dream, the impossible dream of the peasant child stood fulfilled: the English power was broken, the Heir of France was crowned.

She was like one transfigured, so divine was the joy that shone in her face as she sank to her knees at the King's feet and looked up at him through her tears. Her lips were quivering, and her words came soft and low and broken:

"Now, oh gentle King, is the pleasure of God accomplished according to his command that you should come to Rheims and receive the crown that belongeth of right to you, and unto none other. My work which was given me to do is finished; give me your peace, and let me go back to my mother, who is poor and old, and has need of me."

The King raised her up, and there before all that host he praised her great deeds in most noble terms; and there he confirmed her nobility and titles, making her the equal of a count in rank, and also appointed a household and officers for her according to her dignity; and then he said:

"You have saved the crown. Speak—require—demand; and whatsoever grace you ask it shall be granted, though it make the kingdom poor to meet it."

Now that was fine, that was royal. Joan was on her knees again straightway, and said:

"Then, oh gentle King, if out of your compassion you will speak the word, I pray you give commandment that my village, poor and hard pressed by reason of the war, may have its taxes remitted."

"It is so commanded. Say on."

"That is all."

"All? Nothing but that?"

"It is all. I have no other desire."

"But that is nothing—less than nothing. Ask—do not be afraid."

"Indeed I cannot, gentle King. Do not press me. I will not have aught else, but only this alone."

The King seemed nonplussed, and stood still a moment, as if trying to comprehend and realize the full stature of this strange unselfishness. Then he raised his head and said:

"She has won a kingdom and crowned its King; and all she asks and all she will take is this poor grace—and even this is for others, not for herself. And it is well; her act being pro-portioned to the dignity of one who carries in her head and heart riches which outvalue any that any King could add, though he gave his all. She shall have her way. Now therefore it is decreed that from this day forth Domremy, natal village of Joan of Arc, Deliverer of France, called the Maid of Or-leans, is freed from all taxation *forever*." Whereat the silver horns blew a jubilant blast.

There, you see, she had had a vision of this very scene the time she was in a trance in the pastures of Domremy, and we asked her to name the boon she would demand of the King if he should ever chance to tell her she might claim one. But whether she had the vision or not, this act showed that after all the dizzy grandeurs that had come upon her, she was still the same simple unselfish creature that she was that day.

Yes, Charles VII. remitted those taxes "forever." Often the gratitude of kings and nations fades and their promises are forgotten or deliberately violated; but you, who are children of France, should remember with pride that France has kept this one faithfully. Sixty-three years have gone by since that day. The taxes of the region wherein Domremy lies have been collected sixty-three times since then, and all the villages of that region have paid except that one—Domremy. The tax-gatherer never visits Domremy. Domremy has long ago for-gotten what that dreaded sorrow-sowing apparition is like. Sixty-three tax-books have been filled meantime, and they lie yonder with the other public records, and any may see them that desire it. At the top of every page in the sixty-three books stands the name of a village, and below that name its weary burden of taxation is figured out and displayed; in the case of all save one. It is true, just as I tell you. In each of the sixty-three books there is a page headed "Domremi," but under that name not a figure appears. Where the figures should be, there are three words written; and the same words have been written every year for all these years; yes, it is a blank page, with always those grateful words lettered across the face of it—a touching memorial. Thus:

DOMREMI

RIEN—LA PUCELLE

"NOTHING—THE MAID OF ORLEANS." How brief it is; yet how much it says! It is the nation speaking. You have the spectacle of that unsentimental thing, a Government, making reverence to that name and saying to its agent, *"Uncover, and pass on; it is France that commands."* Yes, the promise has been kept; it will be kept always; "forever" was the King's word.*

At two o'clock in the afternoon the ceremonies of the Coronation came at last to an end; then the procession formed once more, with Joan and the King at its head, and took up its solemn march through the midst of the church, all instruments and all people making such clamor of rejoicing noises as was indeed a marvel to hear. And so ended the third of the great days of Joan's life. And how close together they stand—May 8th, June 18th, July 17th!

*It was faithfully kept during three hundred and sixty years and more; then the over-confident octogenarian's prophecy failed. During the tumult of the French Revolution the promise was forgotten and the grace withdrawn. It has remained in disuse ever since. Joan never asked to be remembered, but France has remembered her with an inextinguishable love and reverence; Joan never asked for a statue, but France has lavished them upon her; Joan never asked for a church for Domremy, but France is building one; Joan never asked for saintship, but even that is impending. Everything which Joan of Arc did not ask for has been given her, and with a noble profusion; but the one humble little thing which she did ask for and get, has been taken away from her. There is something infinitely pathetic about this. France owes Domremy a hundred years of taxes, and could hardly find a citizen within her borders who would vote against the payment of the debt.—NOTE BY THE TRANSLATOR.

Chapter XXXVI

W E MOUNTED and rode, a spectacle to remember, a most noble display of rich vestments and nodding plumes, and as we moved between the banked multitudes they sank down all along abreast of us as we advanced, like grain before the reaper, and kneeling hailed with a rousing welcome the consecrated King and his companion the Deliverer of France. But by-and-by when we had paraded about the chief parts of the city and were come near to the end of our course, we being now approaching the Archbishop's palace, one saw on the right, hard by the inn that is called the Zebra, a strange thing—two men not kneeling but *standing!* Standing in the front rank of the kneelers; unconscious, transfixed, staring. Yes, and clothed in the coarse garb of the peasantry, these two. Two halberdiers sprang at them in a fury to teach them better manners; but just as they seized them Joan cried out "Forbear!" and slid from her saddle and flung her arms about one of those peasants, calling him by all manner of endearing names, and sobbing. For it was her father; and the other was her uncle Laxart.

The news flew everywhere, and shouts of welcome were raised, and in just one little moment those two despised and unknown plebeians were become famous and popular and envied, and everybody was in a fever to get sight of them and be able to say, all their lives long, that they had seen the father of Joan of Arc and the brother of her mother. How easy it was for her to do miracles like to this! She was like the sun; on whatsoever dim and humble object her rays fell, that thing was straightway drowned in glory.

All graciously the King said:

"Bring them to me."

And she brought them; she radiant with happiness and affection, they trembling and scared, with their caps in their shaking hands; and there before all the world the King gave them his hand to kiss, while the people gazed in envy and admiration; and he said to old D'Arc—

"Give God thanks for that you are father to this child, this dispenser of immortalities. You who bear a name that will still live in the mouths of men when all the race of Kings has been forgotten, it is not meet that you bare your head before the fleeting fames and dignities of a day—cover yourself!" And truly he looked right fine and princely when he said that. Then he gave order that the Bailly of Rheims be brought; and when he was come, and stood bent low and bare, the King said to him, "These two are guests of France"; and bade him use them hospitably.

I may as well say now as later, that Papa D'Arc and Laxart were stopping in that little Zebra inn, and that there they remained. Finer quarters were offered them by the Bailly, also public distinctions and brave entertainment; but they were frightened at these projects, they being only humble and ignorant peasants: so they begged off, and had peace. They could not have enjoyed such things. Poor souls, they did not even know what to do with their hands, and it took all their attention to keep from treading on them. The Bailly did the best he could in the circumstances. He made the innkeeper place a whole floor at their disposal, and told him to provide everything they might desire, and charge all to the city. Also the Bailly gave them a horse apiece, and furnishings; which so overwhelmed them with pride and delight and astonishment that they couldn't speak a word; for in their lives they had never dreamed of wealth like this, and could not believe, at first, that the horses were real and would not dissolve to a mist and blow away. They could not unglue their minds from those grandeurs, and were always wrenching the conversation out of its groove and dragging the matter of animals into it, so that they could say "my horse" here, and "my horse" there and yonder and all around, and taste the words and lick their chops over them, and spread their legs and hitch their thumbs in their armpits, and feel as the good God feels when He looks out on His fleets of constellations ploughing the awful deeps of space and reflects with satisfaction that they are His—all His. Well, they *were* the happiest old children one ever saw, and the simplest.

The city gave a grand banquet to the King and Joan in mid-afternoon, and to the Court and the Grand Staff; and about the middle of it Père d'Arc and Laxart were sent for,

but would not venture until it was promised that they might
sit in a gallery and be all by themselves and see all that was to
be seen and yet be unmolested. And so they sat there and
looked down upon the splendid spectacle, and were moved
till the tears ran down their cheeks to see the unbelievable
honors that were paid to their small darling, and how naïvely
serene and unafraid she sat there with those consuming
glories beating upon her.

But at last her serenity was broken up. Yes, it stood the
strain of the King's gracious speech; and of D'Alençon's
praiseful words, and the Bastard's; and even La Hire's
thunder-blast, which took the place by storm; but at last, as I
have said, they brought a force to bear which was too strong
for her. For at the close the King put up his hand to command silence, and so waited, with his hand up, till every
sound was dead and it was as if one could almost *feel* the
stillness, so profound it was. Then out of some remote corner
of that vast place there rose a plaintive voice, and in tones
most tender and sweet and rich came floating through that
enchanted hush our poor old simple song "L'Arbre Fée de
Bourlemont!" and then Joan broke down and put her face in
her hands and cried. Yes, you see, all in a moment the pomps
and grandeurs dissolved away and she was a little child again
herding her sheep with the tranquil pastures stretched about
her, and war and wounds and blood and death and the mad
frenzy and turmoil of battle a dream. Ah, that shows you the
power of music, that magician of magicians; who lifts his
wand and says his mysterious word and all things real pass
away and the phantoms of your mind walk before you
clothed in flesh.

That was the King's invention, that sweet and dear surprise. Indeed, he had fine things hidden away in his nature,
though one seldom got a glimpse of them, with that scheming Tremouille and those others always standing in the light,
and he so indolently content to save himself fuss and argument and let them have their way.

At the fall of night we the Domremy contingent of the
personal staff were with the father and uncle at the inn, in
their private parlor, brewing generous drinks and breaking
ground for a homely talk about Domremy and the neighbors,

when a large parcel arrived from Joan to be kept till she came; and soon she came herself and sent her guard away, saying she would take one of her father's rooms and sleep under his roof, and so be at home again. We of the staff rose and stood, as was meet, until she made us sit. Then she turned and saw that the two old men had gotten up too, and were standing in an embarrassed and unmilitary way; which made her want to laugh, but she kept it in, as not wishing to hurt them; and got them to their seats and snuggled down between them, and took a hand of each of them upon her knees and nestled her own hands in them, and said—

"Now we will have no more ceremony, but be kin and playmates as in other times; for I am done with the great wars, now, and you two will take me home with you, and I shall see—" She stopped, and for a moment her happy face sobered, as if a doubt or a presentiment had flitted through her mind; then it cleared again, and she said, with a passionate yearning, "Oh, if the day were but come and we could start!"

The old father was surprised, and said—

"Why, child, are you in earnest? Would you leave doing these wonders that make you to be praised by everybody while there is still so much glory to be won; and would you go out from this grand comradeship with princes and generals to be a drudging villager again and a nobody? It is not rational."

"No," said the uncle, Laxart, "it is amazing to hear, and indeed not understandable. It is a stranger thing to hear her say she will stop the soldiering than it was to hear her say she would begin it; and I who speak to you can say in all truth that that was the strangest word that ever I had heard till this day and hour. I would it could be explained."

"It is not difficult," said Joan. "I was not ever fond of wounds and suffering, nor fitted by my nature to inflict them; and quarrelings did always distress me, and noise and tumult were against my liking, my disposition being toward peace and quietness, and love for all things that have life; and being made like this, how could I bear to think of wars and blood, and the pain that goes with them, and the sorrow and mourning that follow after? But by his angels God laid His great

commands upon me, and could I disobey? I did as I was bid. Did he command me to do many things? No; only two: to raise the siege of Orleans, and crown the King at Rheims. The task is finished, and I am free. Has ever a poor soldier fallen in my sight, whether friend or foe, and I not felt his pain in my own body, and the grief of his home-mates in my own heart? No, not one; and, oh, it is such bliss to know that my release is won, and that I shall not any more see these cruel things or suffer these tortures of the mind again! Then why should I not go to my village and be as I was before? It is heaven! and ye wonder that I desire it. Ah, ye are men—just men! My mother would understand."

They didn't quite know what to say; so they sat still awhile, looking pretty vacant. Then old D'Arc said—

"Yes, your mother—that is true. I never saw such a woman. She worries, and worries, and worries; and wakes nights, and lies so, thinking—that is, worrying; worrying about you. And when the night-storms go raging along, she moans and says, 'Ah, God pity her, she is out in this with her poor wet soldiers.' And when the lightning glares and the thunder crashes she wrings her hands and trembles, saying, 'It is like the awful cannon and the flash, and yonder somewhere she is riding down upon the spouting guns and I not there to protect her.' "

"Ah, poor mother, it is pity, it is pity!"

"Yes, a most strange woman, as I have noticed a many times. When there is news of a victory and all the village goes mad with pride and joy, she rushes here and there in a mani-acal frenzy till she finds out the one only thing she cares to know—that you are safe; then down she goes on her knees in the dirt and praises God as long as there is any breath left in her body; and all on your account, for she never mentions the battle once. And always she says, '*Now* it is over—*now* France is saved—*now* she will come home'—and always is disappointed and goes about mourning."

"Don't, father! it breaks my heart. I will be so good to her when I get home. I will do her work for her, and be her comfort, and she shall not suffer any more through me."

There was some more talk of this sort, then Uncle Laxart said—

"You have done the will of God, dear, and are quits; it is true, and none may deny it; but what of the King? You are his best soldier; what if he command you to stay?"

That was a crusher—and sudden! It took Joan a moment or two to recover from the shock of it; then she said, quite simply and resignedly:

"The King is my Lord; I am his servant." She was silent and thoughtful a little while, then she brightened up and said, cheerily, "But let us drive such thoughts away—this is no time for them. Tell me about home."

So the two old gossips talked and talked; talked about everything and everybody in the village; and it was good to hear. Joan out of her kindness tried to get *us* into the conversation, but that failed, of course. She was the Commander-in-Chief, we were nobodies; her name was the mightiest in France, we were invisible atoms; she was the comrade of princes and heroes, we of the humble and obscure; she held rank above all Personages and all Puissances whatsoever in the whole earth, by right of bearing her commission direct from God. To put it in one word, she was JOAN OF ARC—and when that is said, all is said. To us she was divine. Between her and us lay the bridgeless abyss which that word implies. We could not be familiar with her. No, you can see yourselves that that would have been impossible.

And yet she was so human, too, and so good and kind and dear and loving and cheery and charming and unspoiled and unaffected! Those are all the words I think of now, but they are not enough; no, they are too few and colorless and meagre to tell it all, or tell the half. Those simple old men didn't realize her; they couldn't; they had never known any people but human beings, and so they had no other standard to measure her by. To them, after their first little shyness had worn off, she was just a girl—that was all. It was amazing. It made one shiver, sometimes, to see how calm and easy and comfortable they were in her presence, and hear them talk to her exactly as they would have talked to any other girl in France.

Why, that simple old Laxart sat up there and droned out the most tedious and empty tale one ever heard, and neither he nor Papa D'Arc ever gave a thought to the badness of the etiquette of it, or ever suspected that that foolish tale was anything but dignified and valuable history. There was not an atom of value in it; and whilst they thought it distressing and pathetic, it was in fact not pathetic at all, but actually ridiculous. At least it seemed so to me, and it seems so yet. Indeed I know it was, because it made Joan laugh; and the more sorrowful it got the more it made her laugh; and the Paladin said that he could have laughed himself if she had not been there, and Noël Rainguesson said the same. It was about old Laxart going to a funeral there at Domremy two or three weeks back. He had spots all over his face and hands, and he got Joan to rub some healing ointment on them, and while she was doing it, and comforting him, and trying to say pitying things to him, he told her how it happened. And first he asked her if she remembered that black bull calf that she left behind when she came away, and she said indeed she did, and he was a dear, and she loved him so, and was he well?—and just drowned him in questions about that creature. And he said it was a young bull now, and very frisky; and he was to bear a principal hand at a funeral; and she said, "The bull?" and he said "No, myself"; but said the bull *did* take a hand, but not because of his being invited, for he wasn't; but anyway he was away over beyond the Fairy Tree, and fell asleep on the grass with his Sunday funeral clothes on, and a long black rag on his hat and hanging down his back; and when he woke he saw by the sun how late it was, and not a moment to lose; and jumped up terribly worried, and saw the young bull grazing there, and thought maybe he could ride part way on him and gain time; so he tied a rope around the bull's body to hold on by, and put a halter on him to steer with, and jumped on and started; but it was all new to the bull, and he was discontented with it, and scurried around and bellowed and reared and pranced, and Uncle Laxart was satisfied, and wanted to get off and go by the next bull or some other way that was quieter, but he didn't dare try; and it was getting very warm for him, too, and disturbing and wearisome, and not proper for Sunday; but by-and-by the bull lost all his temper, and went tearing down the slope with his tail in the air and bellowing in the most awful way; and just in the edge of the village he knocked down some bee-hives, and the bees turned out and joined the excursion, and soared along in a black cloud that nearly hid those other two from sight, and prodded them both, and jabbed them and speared them and spiked them, and made them bellow and shriek, and shriek and bellow; and here they came roaring through the village like a hurricane, and took the funeral procession right in the centre, and sent that section of it sprawling, and galloped over it, and the rest scattered apart and fled screeching in every direction, every person with a layer of bees on him, and not a rag of that funeral left but the corpse; and finally the bull broke for the river and jumped in, and when they fished Uncle Laxart out he was nearly drowned, and his face looked like a pudding with raisins in it. And then he turned around, this old simpleton, and looked a long time in a dazed way at Joan where she had her face in a cushion, dying, apparently, and says—

"What do you reckon she is laughing at?"

And old D'Arc stood looking at her the same way, sort of absently scratching his head; but had to give it up, and said *he* didn't know—"must have been something that happened when we weren't noticing."

Yes, both of those old people thought that that tale was pathetic; whereas to my mind it was purely ridiculous, and not in any way valuable to any one. It seemed so to me then, and it seems so to me yet. And as for history, it does not resemble history, for the office of history is to furnish serious and important facts that *teach*; whereas this strange and use-less event teaches nothing; nothing that I can see, except not to ride a bull to a funeral; and surely no reflecting person needs to be taught that.

Chapter XXXVII

NOW THESE were nobles, you know, by decree of the King!—these precious old infants. But they did not realize it; they could not be called conscious of it; it was an abstraction, a phantom; to them it had no substance; their minds could not take hold of it. No, they did not bother about their nobility; they lived in their horses. The horses were solid; they were visible facts, and would make a mighty stir in Domremy. Presently something was said about the Coronation, and old D'Arc said it was going to be a grand thing to be able to say, when they got home, that they were present in the very town itself when it happened. Joan looked troubled, and said—

"Ah, that reminds me. You were here and you didn't send me word. In the town, indeed! Why, you could have sat with the other nobles, and been welcome; and could have looked upon the crowning itself, and carried *that* home to tell. Ah, why did you use me so, and send me no word?"

The old father was embarrassed, now, quite visibly embarrassed, and had the air of one who does not quite know what to say. But Joan was looking up in his face, her hands upon his shoulders—waiting. He had to speak; so presently he drew her to his breast, which was heaving with emotion; and he said, getting out his words with difficulty—

"There, hide your face, child, and let your old father humble himself and make his confession. I—I—don't you see, don't you understand?—I could not know that these grandeurs would not turn your young head—it would be only natural. I might shame you before these great per—"

"Father!"

"And then I was afraid, as remembering that cruel thing I said once in my sinful anger. Oh, appointed of God to be a soldier, and the greatest in the land! and in my ignorant anger I said I would drown you with my own hands if you unsexed yourself and brought shame to your name and family. Ah, how could I ever have said it, and you so good and dear and

814

innocent! I was afraid; for I was guilty. You understand it now, my child, and you forgive?"

Do you see? Even that poor groping old land-crab, with his skull full of pulp, had pride. Isn't it wonderful? And more—he had conscience; he had a sense of right and wrong, such as it was; he was able to feel remorse. It looks impossible, it looks incredible, but it is not. I believe that some day it will be found out that peasants are people. Yes, beings in a great many respects like ourselves. And I believe that some day *they* will find this out, too—and then! Well, then I think they will rise up and demand to be regarded as part of the race, and that by consequence there will be trouble. Whenever one sees in a book or in a king's proclamation those words "the nation," they bring before us the upper classes; only those; we know no other "nation"; for us and the kings no other "nation" exists. But from the day that I saw old D'Arc the peasant acting and feeling just as I should have acted and felt myself, I have carried the conviction in my heart that our peasants are not merely animals, beasts of burden put here by the good God to produce food and comfort for the "nation," but something more and better. You look incredulous. Well, that is your training; it is the training of everybody; but as for me, I thank that incident for giving me a better light, and I have never forgotten it.

Let me see—where was I? One's mind wanders around here and there and yonder, when one is old. I think I said Joan comforted him. Certainly, that is what she would do— there was no need to say that. She coaxed him and petted him and caressed him, and laid the memory of that old hard speech of his to rest. Laid it to rest until she should be dead. Then he would remember it again—yes, yes! Lord, how those things sting, and burn, and gnaw—the things which we did against the innocent dead! And we say in our anguish, "If they could only come back!" Which is all very well to say, but as far as I can see, it doesn't profit anything. In my opinion the best way is not to do the thing in the first place. And I am not alone in this; I have heard our two knights say the same thing; and a man there in Orleans—no, I believe it was at Beaugency, or one of those places—it seems more as if it was at Beaugency than the others—this man said the same thing exactly; almost the same words; a dark man with a cast in his eye and one leg shorter than the other. His name was—was—it is singular that I can't call that man's name; I had it in my mind only a moment ago, and I know it begins with—no, I don't remember what it begins with; but never mind, let it go; I will think of it presently, and then I will tell you.

Well, pretty soon the old father wanted to know how Joan felt when she was in the thick of a battle, with the bright blades hacking and flashing all around her, and the blows rapping and slatting on her shield, and blood gushing on her from the cloven ghastly face and broken teeth of the neighbor at her elbow, and the perilous sudden back surge of massed horses upon a person when the front ranks give way before a heavy rush of the enemy, and men tumble limp and groaning out of saddles all around, and battle-flags falling from dead hands wipe across one's face and hide the tossing turmoil a moment, and in the reeling and swaying and laboring jumble one's horse's hoofs sink into soft substances and shrieks of pain respond, and presently—panic! rush! swarm! flight! and death and hell following after! And the old fellow got ever so much excited; and strode up and down, his tongue going like a mill, asking question after question and never waiting for an answer; and finally he stood Joan up in the middle of the room and stepped off and scanned her critically, and said—

"No—I don't understand it. You are so little. So little and slender. When you had your armor on, to-day, it gave one a sort of notion of it; but in these pretty silks and velvets, you are only a dainty page, not a league-striding war-colossus, moving in clouds and darkness and breathing smoke and thunder. I would God I might see you at it and go tell your mother! *That* would help her sleep, poor thing! Here—teach me the arts of the soldier, that I may explain them to her."

And she did it. She gave him a pike, and put him through the manual of arms; and made him do the steps, too. His marching was incredibly awkward and slovenly, and so was his drill with the pike; but he didn't know it, and was wonderfully pleased with himself, and mightily excited and charmed with the ringing, crisp words of command. I am obliged to say that if looking proud and happy when one is marching were sufficient, he would have been the perfect soldier.

And he wanted a lesson in sword-play, and got it. But of course that was beyond him; he was too old. It was beautiful to see Joan handle the foils, but the old man was a bad failure. He was afraid of the things, and skipped and dodged and scrambled around like a woman who has lost her mind on account of the arrival of a bat. He was of no good as an exhibition. But if La Hire had only come in, that would have been another matter. Those two fenced often; I saw them many times. True, Joan was easily his master, but it made a good show for all that, for La Hire was a grand swordsman. What a swift creature Joan was! You would see her standing erect with her ankle-bones together and her foil arched over her head, the hilt in one hand and the button in the other—the old general opposite, bent forward, left hand reposing on his back, his foil advanced, slightly wiggling and squirming, his watching eye boring straight into hers—and all of a sudden she would give a spring forward, and back again; and there she was, with the foil arched over her head as before. La Hire had been hit, but all that the spectator saw of it was a something like a thin flash of light in the air, but nothing distinct, nothing definite.

We kept the drinkables moving, for that would please the Bailly and the landlord; and old Laxart and D'Arc got to feeling quite comfortable, but without being what you could call tipsy. They got out the presents which they had been buying to carry home—humble things and cheap, but they would be fine there, and welcome. And they gave to Joan a present from Père Fronte and one from her mother—the one a little leaden image of the Holy Virgin, the other half a yard of blue silk ribbon; and she was as pleased as a child; and touched, too, as one could see plainly enough. Yes, she kissed those poor things over and over again, as if they had been something costly and wonderful; and she pinned the Virgin on her doublet, and sent for her helmet and tied the ribbon on that; first one way, then another; then a new way, then another new way; and with each effort perching the helmet on her hand and holding it off this way and that, and canting her head to one side and then the other, examining the effect, as a bird does when it has got a new bug. And she said she could almost wish she was going to the wars again; for then she would fight with the better courage, as having always with her something which her mother's touch had blessed.

Old Laxart said he hoped she would go to the wars again, but home first, for that all the people there were cruel anxious to see her—and so he went on:

"They are proud of you, dear. Yes, prouder than any village ever was of anybody before. And indeed it is right and rational; for it is the first time a village has ever had anybody like you to be proud of and call its own. And it is strange and beautiful how they try to give your name to every creature that has a set that is convenient. It is but half a year since you began to be spoken of and left us, and so it is surprising to see how many babies there are already in that region that are named for you. First it was just Joan; then it was Joan-Orleans; then Joan-Orleans-Beaugency-Patay; and now the next ones will have a lot of towns and the Coronation added, of course. Yes, and the animals the same. They know how you love animals, and so they try to do you honor and show their love for you by naming all those creatures after you; insomuch that if a body should step out and call 'Joan of Arc—come!' there would be a landslide of cats and all such things, each supposing it was the one wanted, and all willing to take the benefit of the doubt, anyway, for the sake of the food that might be on delivery. The kitten you left behind—the last estray you fetched home—bears your name, now, and belongs to Père Fronte, and is the pet and pride of the village; and people have come miles to look at it and pet it and stare at it and wonder over it because it was Joan of Arc's cat. Everybody will tell you that; and one day when a stranger threw a stone at it, not knowing it was your cat, the village rose against him as one man and hanged him! And but for Père Fronte—"

There was an interruption. It was a messenger from the King, bearing a note for Joan, which I read to her, saying he had reflected, and had consulted his other generals, and was obliged to ask her to remain at the head of the army and withdraw her resignation. Also, would she come immediately and attend a council of war? Straightway, at a little distance, military commands and the rumble of drums broke on the still night, and we knew that her guard was approaching.

Deep disappointment clouded her face for just one moment and no more—it passed, and with it the homesick girl, and she was Joan of Arc, Commander-in-Chief again, and ready for duty.

Chapter XXXVIII

IN MY double quality of page and secretary I followed Joan
to the council. She entered that presence with the bearing
of a grieved goddess. What was become of the volatile child
that so lately was enchanted with a ribbon and suffocated
with laughter over the distresses of a foolish peasant who had
stormed a funeral on the back of a bee-stung bull? One may
not guess. Simply it was gone, and had left no sign. She
moved straight to the council-table, and stood. Her glance
swept from face to face there, and where it fell, these it lit as
with a torch, those it scorched as with a brand. She knew
where to strike. She indicated the generals with a nod, and
said—

"My business is not with you. You have not craved a council of war." Then she turned toward the King's privy council,
and continued: "No; it is with you. A council of war! It is
amazing. There is but one thing to do, and only one, and lo,
ye call a council of war! Councils of war have no value but to
decide between two or several doubtful courses. But a council
of war when there is only *one* course? Conceive of a man in a
boat and his family in the water, and he goes out among his
friends to ask what he would better do? A council of war,
name of God! To determine what?"

She stopped, and turned till her eyes rested upon the face
of La Tremouille; and so she stood, silent, measuring him,
the excitement in all faces burning steadily higher and higher,
and all pulses beating faster and faster; then she said, with de-
liberation—

"Every sane man—whose loyalty to his King is not a show
and a pretence—knows that there is but one rational thing
before us—*the march upon Paris!*"

Down came the fist of La Hire with an approving crash
upon the table. La Tremouille turned white with anger, but
he pulled himself firmly together and held his peace. The
King's lazy blood was stirred and his eye kindled finely, for
the spirit of war was away down in him somewhere, and a
frank bold speech always found it and made it tingle glad-

somely. Joan waited to see if the chief minister might wish to defend his position; but he was experienced and wise, and not a man to waste his forces where the current was against him. He would wait; the King's private ear would be at his disposal by-and-by.

That pious fox the Chancellor of France took the word now. He washed his soft hands together, smiling persuasively, and said to Joan:

"Would it be courteous, your Excellency, to move abruptly from here without waiting for an answer from the Duke of Burgundy? You may not know that we are negotiating with his Highness, and that there is likely to be a fortnight's truce between us; and on his part a pledge to deliver Paris into our hands without cost of a blow or the fatigue of a march thither."

Joan turned to him and said, gravely—

"This is not a confessional, my lord. You were not obliged to expose that shame here."

The Chancellor's face reddened, and he retorted—

"Shame? What is there shameful about it?"

Joan answered in level, passionless tones—

"One may describe it without hunting far for words. I knew of this poor comedy, my lord, although it was not intended that I should know. It is to the credit of the devisers of it that they tried to conceal it—this comedy whose text and impulse are describable in two words."

The Chancellor spoke up with a fine irony in his manner:

"Indeed? And will your Excellency be good enough to utter them?"

"Cowardice and treachery!"

The fists of all the generals came down this time, and again the King's eye sparkled with pleasure. The Chancellor sprang to his feet and appealed to his Majesty—

"Sire, I claim your protection."

But the King waved him to his seat again, saying—

"Peace. She had a right to be consulted before that thing was undertaken, since it concerned war as well as politics. It is but just that she be heard upon it now."

The Chancellor sat down trembling with indignation, and remarked to Joan—

"Out of charity I will consider that you did not know who devised this measure which you condemn in so candid language."

"Save your charity for another occasion, my lord," said Joan, as calmly as before. "Whenever anything is done to injure the interests and degrade the honor of France, all but the dead know how to name the two conspirators-in-chief."

"Sire, sire! this insinuation—"

"It is not an insinuation, my lord," said Joan, placidly, "it is a charge. I bring it against the King's chief minister and his Chancellor."

Both men were on their feet now, insisting that the King modify Joan's frankness; but he was not minded to do it. His ordinary councils were stale water—his spirit was drinking wine, now, and the taste of it was good. He said—

"Sit—and be patient. What is fair for one must in fairness be allowed the other. Consider—and be just. When have you two spared her? What dark charges and harsh names have you withheld when you spoke of her?" Then he added, with a veiled twinkle in his eye, "If these are offences I see no particular difference between them, except that she says her hard things to your faces, whereas you say yours behind her back."

He was pleased with that neat shot and the way it shrivelled those two people up, and made La Hire laugh out loud and the other generals softly quake and chuckle. Joan tranquilly resumed—

"From the first, we have been hindered by this policy of shilly-shally; this fashion of counselling and counselling and counselling where no counselling is needed, but only fighting. We took Orleans on the 8th of May, and could have cleared the region round about in three days and saved the slaughter of Patay. We could have been in Rheims six weeks ago, and in Paris now; and would see the last Englishman pass out of France in half a year. But we struck no blow after Orleans, but went off into the country—what for? Ostensibly to hold councils; really to give Bedford time to send re-enforcements to Talbot—which he did; and Patay had to be fought. After Patay, more counselling, more waste of precious time. O my King, I would that you would be persuaded!" She began to warm up, now. "Once more we have our opportunity. If we rise and strike, all is well. Bid me march upon Paris. In twenty days it shall be yours, and in six months all France! Here is half a year's work before us; if this chance be wasted, I give you twenty years to do it in. Speak the word, O gentle King—speak but the one—"

"I cry you mercy!" interrupted the Chancellor, who saw a dangerous enthusiasm rising in the King's face. "March upon Paris? Does your Excellency forget that the way bristles with English strongholds?"

"*That* for your English strongholds!" and Joan snapped her fingers scornfully. "Whence have we marched in these last days? From Gien. And whither? To Rheims. What bristled between? English strongholds. What are they now? French ones—and they never cost a blow!" Here applause broke out from the group of generals, and Joan had to pause a moment to let it subside. "Yes, English strongholds bristled before us; now French ones bristle behind us. What is the argument? A child can read it. The strongholds between us and Paris are garrisoned by no new breed of English, but by the same breed as those others—with the same fears, the same questionings, the same weaknesses, the same disposition to see the heavy hand of God descending upon them. We have but to march!—on the instant—and they are ours, Paris is ours, France is ours! Give the word, O my King, command your servant to—"

"Stay!" cried the Chancellor. "It would be madness to put this affront upon his Highness the Duke of Burgundy. By the treaty which we have every hope to make with him—"

"O, the treaty which we hope to make with him! He has scorned you for years, and defied you. Is it your subtle persuasions that have softened his manners and beguiled him to listen to proposals? No; it was *blows*!—the blows which *we* gave him! That is the only teaching that that sturdy rebel can understand. What does he care for *wind*? The treaty which we hope to make with him—alack! *He* deliver Paris! There is no pauper in the land that is less able to do it. He deliver Paris! Ah, but that would make great Bedford smile! Oh, the pitiful pretext! the blind can see that this thin pourparler with its fifteen-day truce has no purpose but to give Bedford time to hurry forward his forces against us. More treachery—always treachery! We call a council of war—with nothing to counsel about; but Bedford calls no council to teach him what our one course is. He knows what he would do in our place. *He would hang his traitors and march upon Paris!* O gentle King, rouse! The way is open, Paris beckons, France implores. Speak and we—"

"Sire, it is madness, sheer madness! Your Excellency, we cannot, we must not go back from what we have done; we have proposed to treat, we *must* treat with the Duke of Burgundy."

"And we *will!*" said Joan.

"Ah? How?"

"At the point of the lance!"

The house rose, to a man—all that had French hearts—and let go a crash of applause—and kept it up; and in the midst of it one heard La Hire growl out: "At the point of the lance! By God, that is the music!" The King was up, too, and drew his sword, and took it by the blade and strode to Joan and delivered the hilt of it into her hand, saying—

"There, the King surrenders. Carry it to Paris."

And so the applause burst out again, and the historical council of war that has bred so many legends was over.

Chapter XXXIX

IT WAS away past midnight, and had been a tremendous day in the matter of excitement and fatigue, but that was no matter to Joan when there was business on hand. She did not think of bed. The generals followed her to her official quarters, and she delivered her orders to them as fast as she could talk, and they sent them off to their different commands as fast as delivered; wherefore the messengers galloping hither and thither raised a world of clatter and racket in the still streets; and soon were added to this the music of distant bugles and the roll of drums—notes of preparation; for the vanguard would break camp at dawn.

The generals were soon dismissed, but I wasn't; nor Joan; for it was my turn to work, now. Joan walked the floor and dictated a summons to the Duke of Burgundy to lay down his arms and make peace and exchange pardons with the King; or, if he *must* fight, go fight the Saracens. "Pardonnez-vous l'un à l'autre de bon cœur, entièrement, ainsi que doivent faire loyaux chrétiens, et, s'il vous plait de guerroyer, allez contre les Sarrasins." It was long, but it was good, and had the sterling ring to it. It is my opinion that it was as fine and simple and straightforward and eloquent a state paper as she ever uttered.

It was delivered into the hands of a courier, and he galloped away with it. Then Joan dismissed me, and told me to go to the inn and stay; and in the morning give to her father the parcel which she had left there. It contained presents for the Domremy relatives and friends and a peasant dress which she had bought for herself. She said she would say good-bye to her father and uncle in the morning if it should still be their purpose to go, instead of tarrying awhile to see the city.

I didn't say anything, of course; but I could have said that wild horses couldn't keep those men in that town half a day. *They* waste the glory of being the first to carry the great news to Domremy—*the taxes remitted forever!*—and hear the bells clang and clatter, and the people cheer and shout? Oh, not they. Patay and Orleans and the Coronation were events

which in a vague way these men understood to be colossal;
but they were colossal mists, films, abstractions: *this* was a
gigantic reality!

When I got there, do you suppose they were abed! Quite
the reverse. They and the rest were as mellow as mellow could
be; and the Paladin was doing his battles over in great style,
and the old peasants were endangering the building with their
applause. He was doing Patay now; and was bending his big
frame forward and laying out the positions and movements
with a rake here and a rake there of his formidable sword on
the floor, and the peasants were stooped over with their
hands on their spread knees observing with excited eyes and
ripping out ejaculations of wonder and admiration all along:

"Yes, here we were, waiting—waiting for the word; our
horses fidgeting and snorting and dancing to get away, we
lying back on the bridles till our bodies fairly slanted to the
rear; the word rang out at last—*'Go!'* and we went!

"Went? There was nothing like it ever seen! Where we
swept by squads of scampering English, the mere wind of our
passage laid them flat in piles and rows! Then we plunged
into the ruck of Fastolfe's frantic battle-corps and tore
through it like a hurricane, leaving a causeway of the dead
stretching far behind; no tarrying, no slacking rein, but on!
on! on! far yonder in the distance lay *our* prey—Talbot and
his host looming vast and dark like a storm-cloud brooding
on the sea! Down we swooped upon them, glooming all the
air with a quivering pall of dead leaves flung up by the whirlwind of our flight. In another moment we should have struck
them as world strikes world when disorbited constellations
crash into the Milky Way, but by misfortune and the inscrutable dispensation of God I was recognized! Talbot turned
white, and shouting, 'Save yourselves, it is the Standard-
bearer of Joan of Arc!' drove his spurs home till they met in
the middle of his horse's entrails, and fled the field with his
billowing multitudes at his back! I could have cursed myself
for not putting on a disguise. I saw reproach in the eyes of
her Excellency, and was bitterly ashamed. I had caused what
seemed an irreparable disaster. Another might have gone
aside to grieve, as not seeing any way to mend it; but I thank
God I am not of those. Great occasions only summon as with

a trumpet-call the slumbering reserves of my intellect. I saw my opportunity in an instant—in the next I was away! Through the woods I vanished—*fst!*—like an extinguished light! Away around through the curtaining forest I sped, as if on wings, none knowing what was become of me, none suspecting my design. Minute after minute passed, on and on I flew; on, and still on; and at last with a great cheer I flung my Banner to the breeze and burst out in *front* of Talbot! Oh, it was a mighty thought! That weltering chaos of distracted men whirled and surged backward like a tidal wave which has struck a continent, and the day was ours! Poor helpless creatures, they were in a trap; they were surrounded; they could not escape to the rear, for there was our army; they could not escape to the front, for there was I. Their hearts shrivelled in their bodies, their hands fell listless at their sides. They stood still, and at our leisure we slaughtered them to a man; all except Talbot and Fastolfe, whom I saved and brought away, one under each arm."

Well, there is no denying it, the Paladin was in great form that night. Such style! such noble grace of gesture, such grandeur of attitude, such energy when he got going! such steady rise, on such sure wing, such nicely graduated expenditures of voice according to weight of matter, such skilfully calculated approaches to his surprises and explosions, such belief-compelling sincerity of tone and manner, such a climaxing peal from his brazen lungs, and such a lightning-vivid picture of his mailed form and flaunting banner when he burst out before that despairing army! And oh, the gentle art of the last half of his last sentence—delivered in the careless and indolent tone of one who has finished his real story, and only adds a colorless and inconsequential detail because it has happened to occur to him in a lazy way.

It was a marvel to see those innocent peasants. Why, they went all to pieces with enthusiasm, and roared out applauses fit to raise the roof and wake the dead. When they had cooled down at last and there was silence but for their heaving and panting, old Laxart said, admiringly—

"As it seems to me, you are an army in your single person."

"Yes, that is what he is," said Noël Rainguesson, convincingly. "He is a terror; and not just in *this* vicinity. His mere

name carries a shudder with it to distant lands—just his mere
name; and when he frowns, the shadow of it falls as far as
Rome, and the chickens go to roost an hour before schedule
time. Yes; and some say—"

"Noël Rainguesson, you are preparing yourself for trouble.
I will say just one word to you, and it will be to your advantage to—"

I saw that the usual thing had got a start. No man could
prophesy when it would end. So I delivered Joan's message
and went off to bed.

Joan made her good-byes to those old fellows in the morning, with loving embraces and many tears, and with a packed
multitude for sympathizers, and they rode proudly away on
their precious horses to carry their great news home. I had
seen better riders, I will say that; for horsemanship was a new
art to them.

The vanguard moved out at dawn and took the road, with
bands braying and banners flying; the second division followed at eight. Then came the Burgundian ambassadors, and
lost us the rest of that day and the whole of the next. But Joan
was on hand, and so they had their journey for their pains.
The rest of us took the road at dawn, next morning, July 20th.
And got how far? Six leagues. Tremouille was getting in his
sly work with the vacillating King, you see. The King stopped
at St. Marcoul and prayed three days. Precious time lost—for
us; precious time gained for Bedford. He would know how
to use it.

We could not go on without the King; that would be to
leave him in the conspirators' camp. Joan argued, reasoned,
implored; and at last we got under way again.

Joan's prediction was verified. It was not a campaign, it was
only another holiday excursion. English strongholds lined our
route; they surrendered without a blow; we garrisoned them
with Frenchmen and passed on. Bedford was on the march
against us with his new army by this time, and on the 25th of
July the hostile forces faced each other and made preparation
for battle; but Bedford's good judgment prevailed, and he
turned and retreated toward Paris. Now was our chance. Our
men were in great spirits.

Will you believe it? Our poor stick of a King allowed his worthless advisers to persuade him to start back for Gien, whence we had set out when we first marched for Rheims and the Coronation! And we actually did start back. The fifteen-day truce had just been concluded with the Duke of Burgundy, and we would go and tarry at Gien until he should deliver Paris to us without a fight.

We marched to Bray; then the King changed his mind once more, and with it his face toward Paris. Joan dictated a letter to the citizens of Rheims to encourage them to keep heart in spite of the truce, and promising to stand by them. She furnished them the news herself that the King had made this truce; and in speaking of it she was her usual frank self. She said she was not satisfied with it, and didn't know whether she would keep it or not; that if she kept it, it would be solely out of tenderness for the King's honor. All French children know those famous words. How naïve they are! "De cette trève qui a été faite, je ne suis pas contente, et je ne sais si je la tiendrai. Si je la tiens, ce sera seulement pour garder l'honneur du roi." But in any case, she said, she would not allow the blood royal to be abused, and would keep the army in good order and ready for work at the end of the truce.

Poor child, to have to fight England, Burgundy, and a French conspiracy all at the same time—it was too bad. She was a match for the others, but a conspiracy—ah, nobody is a match for that, when the victim that is to be injured is weak and willing. It grieved her, these troubled days, to be so hindered and delayed and baffled, and at times she was sad and the tears lay near the surface. Once, talking with her good old faithful friend and servant the Bastard of Orleans, she said—

"Ah, if it might but please God to let me put off this steel raiment and go back to my father and my mother, and tend my sheep again with my sister and my brothers, who would be so glad to see me!"

By the 12th of August we were camped near Dampmartin. Later we had a brush with Bedford's rear-guard, and had hopes of a big battle on the morrow, but Bedford and all his force got away in the night and went on toward Paris.

Charles sent heralds and received the submission of Beauvais. The Bishop Pierre Cauchon, that faithful friend and slave of the English, was not able to prevent it, though he did his best. He was obscure then, but his name was to travel round the globe presently, and live forever in the curses of France! Bear with me now, while I spit in fancy upon his grave.

Compiègne surrendered, and hauled down the English flag. On the 14th we camped two leagues from Senlis. Bedford turned and approached, and took up a strong position. We went against him, but all our efforts to beguile him out from his intrenchments failed, though he had promised us a duel in the open field. Night shut down. Let him look out for the morning! But in the morning he was gone again.

We entered Compiègne the 18th of August, turning out the English garrison and hoisting our own flag.

On the 23d Joan gave command to move upon Paris. The King and the clique were not satisfied with this, and retired sulking to Senlis, which had just surrendered. Within a few days many strong places submitted—Creil, Pont-Saint-Maxence, Choisy, Gournay-sur-Aronde, Remy, La Neufville-en-Hez, Moguay, Chantilly, Saintines. The English power was tumbling, crash after crash! And still the King sulked and disapproved, and was afraid of our movement against the capital.

On the 26th of August, 1429, Joan camped at Saint Denis; in effect, under the walls of Paris.

And still the King hung back and was afraid. If we could but have had him there to back us with his authority! Bedford had lost heart and decided to waive resistance and go and concentrate his strength in the best and loyalest province remaining to him—Normandy. Ah, if we could only have persuaded the King to come and countenance us with his presence and approval at this supreme moment!

Chapter XL

COURIER after courier was despatched to the King, and he promised to come, but didn't. The Duke d'Alençon went to him and got his promise again, which he broke again. Nine days were lost thus; then he came, arriving at St. Denis September 7th.

Meantime the enemy had begun to take heart: the spiritless conduct of the King could have no other result. Preparations had now been made to defend the city. Joan's chances had been diminished, but she and her generals considered them plenty good enough yet. Joan ordered the attack for eight o'clock next morning, and at that hour it began.

Joan placed her artillery and began to pound a strong work which protected the gate St. Honoré. When it was sufficiently crippled the assault was sounded at noon, and it was carried by storm. Then we moved forward to storm the gate itself, and hurled ourselves against it again and again, Joan in the lead with her standard at her side, the smoke enveloping us in choking clouds, and the missiles flying over us and through us as thick as hail.

In the midst of our last assault, which would have carried the gate sure and given us Paris and in effect France, Joan was struck down by a crossbow bolt, and our men fell back instantly and almost in a panic—for what were they without her? *She* was the army, herself.

Although disabled, she refused to retire, and begged that a new assault be made, saying it *must* win; and adding, with the battle-light rising in her eyes, "I will take Paris now or die!" She had to be carried away by force, and this was done by Gaucourt and the Duke d'Alençon.

But her spirits were at the very top notch, now. She was brimming with enthusiasm. She said she would be carried before the gate in the morning, and in half an hour Paris would be ours without any question. She could have kept her word. About this there is no doubt. But she forgot one factor—the King, shadow of that substance named La Tremouille. The King forbade the attempt!

You see, a new Embassy had just come from the Duke of Burgundy, and another sham private trade of some sort was on foot.

You would know, without my telling you, that Joan's heart was nearly broken. Because of the pain of her wound and the pain at her heart she slept little that night. Several times the watchers heard muffled sobs from the dark room where she lay at St. Denis, and many times the grieving words "It could have been taken!—it could have been taken!" which were the only ones she said.

She dragged herself out of bed a day later with a new hope. D'Alençon had thrown a bridge across the Seine near St. Denis. Might she not cross by that and assault Paris at another point? But the King got wind of it and broke the bridge down! And more—he declared the campaign ended! And more still—he had made a new truce and a long one, in which he had agreed to leave Paris unthreatened and unmolested, and go back to the Loire whence he had come!

Joan of Arc, who had never been defeated by the enemy, was defeated by her own King. She had said once that all she feared for her cause was treachery. It had struck its first blow now. She hung up her white armor in the royal basilica of St. Denis, and went and asked the King to relieve her of her functions and let her go home. As usual, she was wise. Grand combinations, far-reaching great military moves were at an end, now; for the future, when the truce should end, the war would be merely a war of random and idle skirmishes, apparently; work suitable for subalterns, and not requiring the supervision of a sublime military genius. But the King would not let her go. The truce did not embrace all France; there were French strongholds to be watched and preserved; he would need her. Really, you see, Tremouille wanted to keep her where he could balk and hinder her.

Now came her Voices again. They said, *"Remain at St. Denis."* There was no explanation. They did not say why. That was the voice of God; it took precedence of the command of the King; Joan resolved to stay. But that filled La Tremouille with dread. She was too tremendous a force to be left to herself; she would surely defeat all his plans. He beguiled the King to use compulsion. Joan had to submit—because she was wounded and helpless. In the Great Trial she said she was carried away against her will; and that if she had not been wounded it could not have been accomplished. Ah, she had a spirit, that slender girl! a spirit to brave all earthly powers and defy them. We shall never know why the Voices ordered her to stay. We only know this: that if she could have obeyed, the history of France would not be as it now stands written in the books. Yes, well we know that.

On the 13th of September the army, sad and spiritless, turned its face toward the Loire, and marched—without music! Yes, one noted that detail. It was a funeral march; that is what it was. A long, dreary funeral march, with never a shout or a cheer; friends looking on in tears, all the way, enemies laughing. We reached Gien at last—that place whence we had set out on our splendid march toward Rheims less than three months before, with flags flying, bands playing, the victory-flush of Patay glowing in our faces, and the massed multitudes shouting and praising and giving us God-speed. There was a dull rain falling now, the day was dark, the heavens mourned, the spectators were few, we had no welcome but the welcome of silence, and pity, and tears.

Then the King disbanded that noble army of heroes; it furled its flags, it stored its arms: the disgrace of France was complete. La Tremouille wore the victor's crown; Joan of Arc, the unconquerable, was conquered.

Chapter XLI

Yes, it was as I have said: Joan had Paris and France in her grip, and the Hundred Years' War under her heel, and the King made her open her fist and take away her foot.

Now followed about eight months of drifting about with the King and his council, and his gay and showy and dancing and flirting and hawking and frolicking and serenading and dissipating court—drifting from town to town and from castle to castle—a life which was pleasant to us of the personal staff, but not to Joan. However, she only *saw* it, she didn't live it. The King did his sincerest best to make her happy, and showed a most kind and constant anxiety in this matter. All others had to go loaded with the chains of an exacting court etiquette, but she was free, she was privileged. So that she paid her duty to the King once a day and passed the pleasant word, nothing further was required of her. Naturally, then, she made herself a hermit, and grieved the weary days through in her own apartments, with her thoughts and devotions for company, and the planning of now forever unrealizable military combinations for entertainment. In fancy she moved bodies of men from this and that and the other point, so calculating the distances to be covered, the time required for each body, and the nature of the country to be traversed, as to have them appear in sight of each other on a given day or at a given hour and concentrate for battle. It was her only game, her only relief from her burden of sorrow and inaction. She played it hour after hour, as others play chess; and lost herself in it, and so got repose for her mind and healing for her heart.

She never complained, of course. It was not her way. She was the sort that endure in silence. But—she was a caged eagle just the same, and pined for the free air and the alpine heights and the fierce joys of the storm.

France was full of rovers—disbanded soldiers ready for anything that might turn up. Several times, at intervals, when Joan's dull captivity grew too heavy to bear, she was allowed to gather a troop of cavalry and make a health-

restoring dash against the enemy. These things were like a
bath to her spirits.

It was like old times, there at Saint-Pierre-le-Moutier, to
see her lead assault after assault, be driven back again and
again, but always rally and charge anew, all in a blaze of eagerness and delight; till at last the tempest of missiles rained
so intolerably thick that old D'Aulon, who was wounded,
sounded the retreat (for the King had charged him on his
head to let no harm come to Joan); and away everybody
rushed after him—as he supposed; but when he turned and
looked, there were we of the staff still hammering away;
wherefore he rode back and urged her to come, saying she
was mad to stay there with only a dozen men. Her eye danced
merrily, and she turned upon him crying out—

"A dozen men! name of God, I have fifty thousand, and
will never budge till this place is taken! Sound the charge!"

Which he did, and over the walls we went, and the fortress
was ours. Old D'Aulon thought her mind was wandering;
but all she meant was, that she felt the might of fifty thousand
men surging in her heart. It was a fanciful expression; but, to
my thinking, truer word was never said.

Then there was the affair near Lagny, where we charged
the intrenched Burgundians through the open field four
times, the last time victoriously; the best prize of it Franquet
d'Arras, the freebooter and pitiless scourge of the region
roundabout.

Now and then other such affairs; and at last, away toward
the end of May, 1430, we were in the neighborhood of
Compiègne, and Joan resolved to go to the help of that place,
which was being besieged by the Duke of Burgundy.

I had been wounded lately, and was not able to ride without help; but the good Dwarf took me on behind him, and I
held on to him and was safe enough. We started at midnight,
in a sullen downpour of warm rain, and went slowly and
softly and in dead silence, for we had to slip through the
enemy's lines. We were challenged only once; we made no
answer, but held our breath and crept steadily and stealthily
along, and got through without any accident. About three or
half past we reached Compiègne, just as the gray dawn was
breaking in the east.

Joan set to work at once, and concerted a plan with Guillaume de Flavy, captain of the city—a plan for a sortie toward evening against the enemy, who was posted in three bodies on the other side of the Oise, in the level plain. From our side one of the city gates communicated with a bridge. The end of this bridge was defended on the other side of the river by one of those fortresses called a boulevard; and this boulevard also commanded a raised road, which stretched from its front across the plain to the village of Marguy. A force of Burgundians occupied Marguy; another was camped at Clairoix, a couple of miles *above* the raised road; and a body of English was holding Venette, a mile and a half *below* it. A kind of bow-and-arrow arrangement, you see: the causeway the arrow, the boulevard at the feather-end of it, Marguy at the barb, Venette at one end of the bow, Clairoix at the other.

Joan's plan was to go straight per causeway against Marguy, carry it by assault, then turn swiftly upon Clairoix, up to the right, and capture that camp in the same way, then face to the rear and be ready for heavy work, for the Duke of Burgundy lay behind Clairoix with a reserve. Flavy's lieutenant, with archers and the artillery of the boulevard, was to keep the English troops from coming up from below and seizing the causeway and cutting off Joan's retreat in case she should have to make one. Also, a fleet of covered boats was to be stationed near the boulevard as an additional help in case a retreat should become necessary.

It was the 24th of May. At four in the afternoon Joan moved out at the head of six hundred cavalry—on her last march in this life!

It breaks my heart. I had got myself helped up on to the walls, and from there I saw much that happened, the rest was told me long afterwards by our two knights and other eyewitnesses. Joan crossed the bridge, and soon left the boulevard behind her and went skimming away over the raised road with her horsemen clattering at her heels. She had on a brilliant silver-gilt cape over her armor, and I could see it flap and flare and rise and fall like a little patch of white flame.

It was a bright day, and one could see far and wide over that plain. Soon we saw the English force advancing, swiftly and in handsome order, the sunlight flashing from its arms.

Joan crashed into the Burgundians at Marguy and was repulsed. Then we saw the other Burgundians moving down
from Clairoix. Joan rallied her men and charged again, and
was again rolled back. Two assaults occupy a good deal of
time—and time was precious here. The English were approaching the road, now, from Venette, but the boulevard
opened fire on them and they were checked. Joan heartened
her men with inspiring words and led them to the charge
again in great style. This time she carried Marguy with a hurrah. Then she turned at once to the right and plunged into
the plain and struck the Clairoix force, which was just arriving; then there was heavy work, and plenty of it, the two
armies hurling each other backward turn about and about,
and victory inclining first to the one, then to the other. Now
all of a sudden there was a panic on our side. Some say one
thing caused it, some another. Some say the cannonade made
our front ranks think retreat was being cut off by the English,
some say the rear ranks got the idea that Joan was killed. Anyway our men broke, and went flying in a wild rout for the
causeway. Joan tried to rally them and face them around, crying to them that victory was sure, but it did no good, they
divided and swept by her like a wave. Old D'Aulon begged
her to retreat while there was yet a chance for safety, but she
refused; so he seized her horse's bridle and bore her along
with the wreck and ruin in spite of herself. And so along the
causeway they came swarming, that wild confusion of fren-
zied men and horses—and the artillery had to stop firing, of
course; consequently the English and Burgundians closed in
in safety, the former in front, the latter behind their prey.
Clear to the boulevard the French were washed in this enveloping inundation; and there, cornered in an angle formed by
the flank of the boulevard and the slope of the causeway, they
bravely fought a hopeless fight, and sank down one by one.

Flavy, watching from the city wall, ordered the gate to be
closed and the drawbridge raised. This shut Joan out.

The little personal guard around her thinned swiftly. Both
of our good knights went down, disabled; Joan's two brothers
fell wounded; then Noël Rainguesson—all wounded while
loyally sheltering Joan from blows aimed at her. When only
the Dwarf and the Paladin were left, they would not give up,

but stood their ground stoutly, a pair of steel towers streaked and splashed with blood; and where the axe of the one fell, and the sword of the other, an enemy gasped and died. And so fighting, and loyal to their duty to the last, good simple souls, they came to their honorable end. Peace to their memories! they were very dear to me.

Then there was a cheer and a rush, and Joan, still defiant, still laying about her with her sword, was seized by her cape and dragged from her horse. She was borne away a prisoner to the Duke of Burgundy's camp, and after her followed the victorious army roaring its joy.

The awful news started instantly on its round; from lip to lip it flew; and wherever it came it struck the people as with a sort of paralysis; and they murmured over and over again, as if they were talking to themselves, or in their sleep, "The Maid of Orleans taken! . . . Joan of Arc a prisoner! . . . the Savior of France lost to us!"—and would keep saying that over, as if they couldn't understand how it could be, or how God could permit it, poor creatures!

You know what a city is like when it is hung from eaves to pavement with rustling black? Then you know what Tours was like, and some other cities. But can any man tell you what the mourning in the hearts of the peasantry of France was like? No, nobody can tell you that; and, poor dumb things, they could not have told you themselves; but it was there— indeed yes. Why, it was the spirit of a whole nation hung with crape!

The 24th of May. We will draw down the curtain, now, upon the most strange, and pathetic, and wonderful military drama that has been played upon the stage of the world. Joan of Arc will march no more.

Chapter I

I CANNOT bear to dwell at great length upon the shameful history of the summer and winter following the capture. For a while I was not much troubled, for I was expecting every day to hear that Joan had been put to ransom, and that the King—no, not the King, but grateful France—had come eagerly forward to pay it. By the laws of war she could not be denied the privilege of ransom. She was not a rebel; she was a legitimately constituted soldier, head of the armies of France by her King's appointment, and guilty of no crime known to military law; therefore she could not be detained upon any pretext, if ransom were proffered.

But day after day dragged by and no ransom was offered! It seems incredible, but it is true. Was that reptile Tremouille busy at the King's ear? All we know is, that the King was silent, and made no offer and no effort in behalf of this poor girl who had done so much for him.

But unhappily there was alacrity enough in another quarter. The news of the capture reached Paris the day after it happened, and the glad English and Burgundians deafened the world all the day and all the night with the clamor of their joy-bells and the thankful thunder of their artillery; and the next day the Vicar General of the Inquisition sent a message to the Duke of Burgundy requiring the delivery of the prisoner into the hands of the Church to be tried as an idolater.

The English had seen their opportunity, and it was the English power that was really acting, not the Church. The Church was being used as a blind, a disguise; and for a forcible reason: the Church was not only able to take the life of Joan of Arc, but to blight her influence and the valor-breeding inspiration of her name, whereas the English power could but kill her body; that would not diminish or destroy the influence of her name; it would magnify it and make it permanent. Joan of Arc was the only power in France that the English did not despise, the only power in France that they considered formidable. If the Church could be brought to take her life, or to proclaim her an idolater, a heretic, a witch, sent from Satan, not from heaven, it was believed that the English supremacy could be at once reinstated.

The Duke of Burgundy listened—but waited. He could not doubt that the French King or the French people would come forward presently and pay a higher price than the English. He kept Joan a close prisoner in a strong fortress, and continued to wait, week after week. He was a French Prince, and was at heart ashamed to sell her to the English. Yet with all his waiting no offer came to him from the French side.

One day Joan played a cunning trick on her jailer, and not only slipped out of her prison, but locked him up in it. But as she fled away she was seen by a sentinel, and was caught and brought back.

Then she was sent to Beaurevoir, a stronger castle. This was early in August, and she had been in captivity more than two months, now. Here she was shut up in the top of a tower which was sixty feet high. She ate her heart there for another long stretch—about three months and a half. And she was aware, all these weary five months of captivity, that the English, under cover of the Church, were dickering for her as one would dicker for a horse or a slave, and that France was silent, the King silent, all her friends the same. Yes, it was pitiful.

And yet when she heard at last that Compiègne was being closely besieged and likely to be captured, and that the enemy had declared that no inhabitant of it should escape massacre, not even children of seven years of age, she was in a fever at once to fly to our rescue. So she tore her bed-clothes to strips and tied them together and descended this frail rope in the night, and it broke and she fell and was badly bruised, and remained three days insensible, meantime neither eating nor drinking.

And now came relief to us, led by the Count of Vendôme, and Compiègne was saved and the siege raised. This was a disaster to the Duke of Burgundy. He had to have money, now. It was a good time for a new bid to be made for Joan of Arc. The English at once sent a French Bishop—that forever

infamous Pierre Cauchon of Beauvais. He was partly promised the Archbishopric of Rouen, which was vacant, if he
should succeed. He claimed the right to preside over Joan's
ecclesiastical trial because the battle-ground where she was
taken was within his diocese.

By the military usage of the time the ransom of a royal
Prince was 10,000 livres of gold, which is 61,125 francs—a
fixed sum, you see. It must be accepted, when offered; it
could not be refused.

Cauchon brought the offer of this very sum from the English—a royal Prince's ransom for the poor little peasant girl
of Domremy. It shows in a striking way the English idea of
her formidable importance. It was accepted. For that sum
Joan of Arc the Savior of France was sold; sold to her enemies; to the enemies of her country; enemies who had lashed
and thrashed and thumped and trounced France for a century
and made holiday sport of it; enemies who had forgotten,
years and years ago, what a Frenchman's face was like, so used
were they to seeing nothing but his back; enemies whom she
had whipped, whom she had cowed, whom she had taught to
respect French valor, new-born in her nation by the breath of
her spirit; enemies who hungered for her life as being the
only puissance able to stand between English triumph and
French degradation. Sold to a French priest by a French
Prince, with the French King and the French nation standing
thankless by and saying nothing.

And she—what did she say? Nothing. Not a reproach
passed her lips. She was too great for that—she was Joan of
Arc; and when that is said, all is said.

As a soldier, her record was spotless. She could not be
called to account for anything under that head. A subterfuge
must be found, and, as we have seen, was found. She must be
tried by priests for crimes against religion. If none could be
discovered, some must be invented. Let the miscreant Cauchon alone to contrive those.

Rouen was chosen as the scene of the trial. It was in the
heart of the English power; its population had been under
English dominion so many generations that they were hardly
French now, save in language. The place was strongly garrisoned. Joan was taken there near the end of December, 1430,

and flung into a dungeon. Yes, and clothed in chains, that free spirit!

Still France made no move. How do I account for this? I think there is only one way. You will remember that whenever Joan was not at the front, the French held back and ventured nothing; that whenever she led, they swept everything before them, so long as they could see her white armor or her banner; that every time she fell wounded or was reported killed—as at Compiègne—they broke in panic and fled like sheep. I argue from this that they had undergone no real transformation as yet; that at bottom they were still under the spell of a timorousness born of generations of unsuccess, and a lack of confidence in each other and in their leaders born of old and bitter experience in the way of treacheries of all sorts—for their kings had been treacherous to their great vassals and to their generals, and these in turn were treacherous to the head of the state and to each other. The soldiery found that they could depend utterly on Joan, and upon her alone. With her gone, everything was gone. She was the sun that melted the frozen torrents and set them boiling; with that sun removed, they froze again, and the army and all France became what they had been before, mere dead corpses—that and nothing more; incapable of thought, hope, ambition, or motion.

Chapter II

M Y WOUND gave me a great deal of trouble clear into the first part of October; then the fresher weather renewed my life and strength. All this time there were reports drifting about that the King was going to ransom Joan. I believed these, for I was young and had not yet found out the littleness and meanness of our poor human race, which brags about itself so much, and thinks it is better and higher than the other animals.

In October I was well enough to go out with two sorties, and in the second one, on the 23d, I was wounded again. My luck had turned, you see. On the night of the 25th the besiegers decamped, and in the disorder and confusion one of their prisoners escaped and got safe into Compiègne, and hobbled into my room as pallid and pathetic an object as you would wish to see.

"What? Alive? Nöel Rainguesson!"

It was indeed he. It was a most joyful meeting, that you will easily know; and also as sad as it was joyful. We could not speak Joan's name. One's voice would have broken down. We knew who was meant when she was mentioned; we could say "she" and "her," but we could not speak the name.

We talked of the personal staff. Old D'Aulon, wounded and a prisoner, was still with Joan and serving her, by permission of the Duke of Burgundy. Joan was being treated with the respect due to her rank and to her character as a prisoner of war taken in honorable conflict. And this was continued—as we learned later—until she fell into the hands of that bastard of Satan, Pierre Cauchon, Bishop of Beauvais.

Nöel was full of noble and affectionate praises and appreciations of our old boastful big Standard-bearer, now gone silent forever, his real and imaginary battles all fought, his work done, his life honorably closed and completed.

"And think of his luck!" burst out Nöel, with his eyes full of tears. "Always the pet child of luck! See how it followed him and stayed by him, from his first step all through, in the field or out of it; always a splendid figure in the public eye, courted and envied everywhere; always having a chance to do fine things and always doing them; in the beginning called the Paladin in joke, and called it afterwards in earnest because he magnificently made the title good; and at last—supremest luck of all—died in the field! died with his harness on; died faithful to his charge, the Standard in his hand; died—oh, think of it—with the approving eye of Joan of Arc upon him! He drained the cup of glory to the last drop, and went jubilant to his peace, blessedly spared all part in the disaster which was to follow. What luck, what luck! And we? What was our sin that we are still here, we who have also earned our place with the happy dead?"

And presently he said:

"They tore the sacred Standard from his dead hand and carried it away, their most precious prize after its captured owner. But they haven't it now. A month ago we put our lives upon the risk—our two good knights, my fellow-prisoners, and I—and stole it, and got it smuggled by trusty hands to Orleans, and there it is now, safe for all time in the Treasury."

I was glad and grateful to learn that. I have seen it often since, when I have gone to Orleans on the 8th of May to be the petted old guest of the city and hold the first place of honor at the banquets and in the processions—I mean since Joan's brothers passed from this life. It will still be there, sacredly guarded by French love, a thousand years from now—yes, as long as any shred of it hangs together.*

Two or three weeks after this talk came the tremendous

---

*It remained there three hundred and sixty years, and then was destroyed in a public bonfire, together with two swords, a plumed cap, several suits of state apparel, and other relics of the Maid, by a mob in the time of the Revolution. Nothing which the hand of Joan of Arc is known to have touched now remains in existence except a few preciously guarded military and state papers which she signed, her pen being guided by a clerk or her secretary Louis de Conte. A bowlder exists from which she is known to have mounted her horse when she was once setting out upon a campaign. Up to a quarter of a century ago there was a single hair from her head still in existence. It was drawn through the wax of a seal attached to the parchment of a state document. It was surreptitiously snipped out, seal and all, by some vandal relic-hunter, and carried off. Doubtless it still exists, but only the thief knows where.—TRANSLATOR.

news like a thunder-clap, and we were aghast—Joan of Arc sold to the English!

Not for a moment had we ever dreamed of such a thing. We were young, you see, and did not know the human race, as I have said before. We had been so proud of our country, so sure of her nobleness, her magnanimity, her gratitude. We had expected little of the King, but of France we had expected everything. Everybody knew that in various towns patriot priests had been marching in procession urging the people to sacrifice money, property, everything, and buy the freedom of their heaven-sent deliverer. That the money would be raised we had not thought of doubting.

But it was all over, now, all over. It was a bitter time for us. The heavens seemed hung with black; all cheer went out from our hearts. Was this comrade here at my bedside really Noël Rainguesson, that light-hearted creature whose whole life was but one long joke, and who used up more breath in laughter than in keeping his body alive? No, no; *that* Noël I was to see no more. This one's heart was broken. He moved grieving about, and absently, like one in a dream; the stream of his laughter was dried at its source.

Well, that was best. It was my own mood. We were company for each other. He nursed me patiently through the dull long weeks, and at last, in January, I was strong enough to go about again. Then he said:

"Shall we go, now?"

"Yes."

There was no need to explain. Our hearts were in Rouen, we would carry our bodies there. All that we cared for in this life was shut up in that fortress. We could not help her, but it would be some solace to us to be near her, to breathe the air that she breathed, and look daily upon the stone walls that hid her. What if we should be made prisoners there? Well, we could but do our best, and let luck and fate decide what should happen.

And so we started. We could not realize the change which had come upon the country. We seemed able to choose our own route and go wherever we pleased, unchallenged and unmolested. When Joan of Arc was in the field, there was a sort of panic of fear everywhere; but now that she was out of the way, fear had vanished. Nobody was troubled about you or afraid of you, nobody was curious about you or your business, everybody was indifferent.

We presently saw that we could take to the Seine, and not weary ourselves out with land travel. So we did it, and were carried in a boat to within a league of Rouen. Then we got ashore; not on the hilly side, but on the other, where it is as level as a floor. Nobody could enter or leave the city without explaining himself. It was because they feared attempts at a rescue of Joan.

We had no trouble. We stopped in the plain with a family of peasants and stayed a week, helping them with their work for board and lodging, and making friends of them. We got clothes like theirs, and wore them. When we had worked our way through their reserves and gotten their confidence, we found that they secretly harbored French hearts in their bodies. Then we came out frankly and told them everything, and found them ready to do anything they could to help us. Our plan was soon made, and was quite simple. It was to help them drive a flock of sheep to the market of the city. One morning early we made the venture in a melancholy drizzle of rain, and passed through the frowning gates unmolested. Our friends had friends living over a humble wine-shop in a quaint tall building situated in one of the narrow lanes that run down from the cathedral to the river, and with these they bestowed us; and the next day they smuggled our own proper clothing and other belongings to us. The family that lodged us—the Pierrons—were French in sympathy, and we needed to have no secrets from them.

Chapter III

I T WAS NECESSARY for me to have some way to gain bread for Noël and myself; and when the Pierrons found that I knew how to write, they applied to their confessor in my behalf, and he got a place for me with a good priest named Manchon, who was to be the chief recorder in the Great Trial of Joan of Arc now approaching. It was a strange position for me—clerk to the recorder—and dangerous if my sympathies and late employment should be found out. But there was not much danger. Manchon was at bottom friendly to Joan and would not betray me; and my name would not, for I had discarded my surname and retained only my given one, like a person of low degree.

I attended Manchon constantly straight along, out of January and into February, and was often in the citadel with him —in the very fortress where Joan was imprisoned, though not in the dungeon where she was confined, and so did not see her, of course.

Manchon told me everything that had been happening before my coming. Ever since the purchase of Joan, Cauchon had been busy packing his jury for the destruction of the Maid—weeks and weeks he had spent in this bad industry. The University of Paris had sent him a number of learned and able and trusty ecclesiastics of the stripe he wanted; and he had scraped together a clergyman of like stripe and great fame here and there and yonder, until he was able to construct a formidable court numbering half a hundred distinguished names. French names they were, but their interests and sympathies were English.

A great officer of the Inquisition was also sent from Paris, for the accused must be tried by the forms of the Inquisition; but this was a brave and righteous man, and he said squarely that this court had no power to try the case, wherefore he refused to act; and the same honest talk was uttered by two or three others.

The Inquisitor was right. The case as here resurrected against Joan had already been tried long ago at Poitiers, and decided in her favor. Yes, and by a higher tribunal than this one, for at the head of it was an Archbishop—he of Rheims—Couchon's own metropolitan. So here, you see, a lower court was impudently preparing to re-try and re-decide a cause which had already been decided by its superior, a court of higher authority. Imagine it! No, the case could not properly be tried again. Cauchon could not properly preside in this new court, for more than one reason: Rouen was not in his diocese; Joan had not been arrested in her domicile, which was still Domremy; and finally this proposed judge was the prisoner's outspoken enemy, and therefore he was incompetent to try her. Yet all these large difficulties were gotten rid of. The territorial Chapter of Rouen finally granted territorial letters to Cauchon—though only after a struggle and under compulsion. Force was also applied to the Inquisitor, and he was obliged to submit.

So, then, the little English King, by his representative, formally delivered Joan into the hands of the court, but with this reservation: *if the court failed to condemn her, he was to have her back again!*

Ah, dear, what chance was there for that forsaken and friendless child? Friendless indeed—it is the right word. For she was in a black dungeon, with half a dozen brutal common soldiers keeping guard night and day in the room where her cage was—for she was in a cage; an iron cage, and chained to her bed by neck and hands and feet. Never a person near her whom she had ever seen before; never a woman at all. Yes, this was indeed friendlessness.

Now it was a vassal of Jean de Luxembourg who captured Joan at Compiègne, and it was Jean who sold her to the Duke of Burgundy. Yet this very De Luxembourg was shameless enough to go and show his face to Joan in her cage. He came with two English earls, Warwick and Stafford. He was a poor reptile. He told her he would get her set free if she would promise not to fight the English any more. She had been in that cage a long time now, but not long enough to break her spirit. She retorted scornfully—

"Name of God, you but mock me. I know that you have neither the power nor the will to do it."

He insisted. Then the pride and dignity of the soldier rose

in Joan, and she lifted her chained hands and let them fall with a clash, saying—

"See these! They know more than you, and can prophesy better. I know that the English are going to kill me, for they think that when I am dead they can get the Kingdom of France. It is not so. Though there were a hundred thousand of them they would never get it."

This defiance infuriated Stafford, and he—now think of it—he a free, strong man, she a chained and helpless girl—he drew his dagger and flung himself at her to stab her. But Warwick seized him and held him back. Warwick was wise. Take her life in that way? Send her to Heaven stainless and undisgraced? It would make her the idol of France, and the whole nation would rise and march to victory and emancipation under the inspiration of her spirit. No, she must be saved for another fate than that.

Well, the time was approaching for the Great Trial. For more than two months Cauchon had been raking and scraping everywhere for any odds and ends of evidence or suspicion or conjecture that might be made usable against Joan, and carefully suppressing all evidence that came to hand in her favor. He had limitless ways and means and powers at his disposal for preparing and strengthening the case for the prosecution, and he used them all.

But Joan had no one to prepare her case for her, and she was shut up in those stone walls and had no friend to appeal to for help. And as for witnesses, she could not call a single one in her defence; they were all far away, under the French flag, and this was an English court; they would have been seized and hanged if they had shown their faces at the gates of Rouen. No, the prisoner must be the *sole* witness—witness for the prosecution, witness for the defence; and with a verdict of death resolved upon before the doors were opened for the court's first sitting.

When she learned that the court was made up of ecclesiastics in the interest of the English, she begged that in fairness an equal number of priests of the French party should be added to these. Cauchon scoffed at her message, and would not even deign to answer it.

By the law of the Church—she being a minor under

twenty-one—it was her right to have counsel to conduct her case, advise her how to answer when questioned, and protect her from falling into traps set by cunning devices of the prosecution. She probably did not know that this was her right, and that she could demand it and require it, for there was none to tell her that; but she begged for this help at any rate. Cauchon refused it. She urged and implored, pleading her youth and her ignorance of the complexities and intricacies of the law and of legal procedure. Cauchon refused again, and said she must get along with her case as best she might by herself. Ah, his heart was a stone.

Cauchon prepared the *proces verbal*. I will simplify that by calling it the Bill of Particulars. It was a detailed list of the charges against her, and formed the basis of the trial. Charges? It was a list of *suspicions and public rumors*—those were the words used. It was merely charged that she was suspected of having been guilty of heresies, witchcraft, and other such offences against religion.

Now by law of the Church, a trial of that sort could not be begun until a searching inquiry had been made into the history and character of the accused, and it was essential that the result of this inquiry be added to the *proces verbal* and form a part of it. You remember that that was the first thing they did before the trial at Poitiers. They did it again, now. An ecclesiastic was sent to Domremy. There and all about the neighborhood he made an exhaustive search into Joan's history and character, and came back with his verdict. It was very clear. The searcher reported that he found Joan's character to be in every way what he "would like his own sister's character to be." Just about the same report that was brought back to Poitiers, you see. Joan's was a character which could endure the minutest examination.

This verdict was a strong point for Joan, you will say. Yes, it *would* have been if it could have seen the light; but Cauchon was awake, and it disappeared from the *proces verbal* before the trial. People were prudent enough not to inquire what became of it.

One would imagine that Cauchon was ready to begin the trial by this time. But no, he devised one more scheme for poor Joan's destruction, and it promised to be a deadly one.

One of the great personages picked out and sent down by the University of Paris was an ecclesiastic named Nicholas Loyseleur. He was tall, handsome, grave, of smooth soft speech and courteous and winning manners. There was no seeming of treachery or hypocrisy about him, yet he was full of both. He was admitted to Joan's prison by night, disguised as a cobbler; he pretended to be from her own country; he professed to be secretly a patriot; he revealed the fact that he was a priest. She was filled with gladness to see one from the hills and plains that were so dear to her; happier still to look upon a priest and disburden her heart in confession, for the offices of the Church were the bread of life, the breath of her nostrils to her, and she had been long forced to pine for them in vain. She opened her whole innocent heart to this creature, and in return he gave her advice concerning her trial which could have destroyed her if her deep native wisdom had not protected her against following it.

You will ask, what value could this scheme have, since the secrets of the confessional are sacred and cannot be revealed? True—but suppose another person should overhear them? That person is not bound to keep the secret. Well, that is what happened. Cauchon had previously caused a hole to be bored through the wall; and he stood with his ear to that hole and heard all. It is pitiful to think of these things. One wonders how they could treat that poor child so. She had not done them any harm.

Chapter IV

O N Tuesday the 20th of February, whilst I sat at my
master's work in the evening, he came in, looking sad,
and said it had been decided to begin the trial at eight o'clock
the next morning, and I must get ready to assist him.

Of course I had been expecting such news every day for
many days; but no matter, the shock of it almost took my
breath away and set me trembling like a leaf. I suppose that
without knowing it I had been half imagining that at the last
moment something would happen, something that would
stop this fatal trial: maybe that La Hire would burst in at the
gates with his hellions at his back; maybe that God would
have pity and stretch forth His mighty hand. But now—now
there was no hope.

The trial was to begin in the chapel of the fortress and
would be public. So I went sorrowing away and told Noël, so
that he might be there early and secure a place. It would give
him a chance to look again upon the face which we so revered
and which was so precious to us. All the way, both going and
coming, I ploughed through chattering and rejoicing multitudes of English soldiery and English-hearted French citizens.
There was no talk but of the coming event. Many times I
heard the remark, accompanied by a pitiless laugh—

"The fat Bishop has got things as he wants them at last,
and says he will lead the vile witch a merry dance and a short
one."

But here and there I glimpsed compassion and distress in a
face, and it was not always a French one. English soldiers
feared Joan, but they admired her for her great deeds and her
unconquerable spirit.

In the morning Manchon and I went early, yet as we approached the vast fortress we found crowds of men already
there and still others gathering. The chapel was already full
and the way barred against further admissions of unofficial
persons. We took our appointed places. Throned on high sat
the president, Cauchon, Bishop of Beauvais, in his grand
robes, and before him in rows sat his robed court—fifty dis-

tinguished ecclesiastics, men of high degree in the Church, of clear-cut intellectual faces, men of deep learning, veteran adepts in strategy and casuistry, practised setters of traps for ignorant minds and unwary feet. When I looked around upon this army of masters of legal fence, gathered here to find just one verdict and no other, and remembered that Joan must fight for her good name and her life single-handed against them, I asked myself what chance an ignorant poor country girl of nineteen could have in such an unequal conflict; and my heart sank down low, very low. When I looked again at that obese president, puffing and wheezing there, his great belly distending and receding with each breath, and noted his three chins, fold above fold, and his knobby and knotty face, and his purple and splotchy complexion, and his repulsive cauliflower nose, and his cold and malignant eyes—a brute, every detail of him—my heart sank lower still. And when I noted that all were afraid of this man, and shrank and fidgeted in their seats when his eye smote theirs, my last poor ray of hope dissolved away and wholly disappeared.

There was one unoccupied seat in this place, and only one. It was over against the wall, in view of every one. It was a little wooden bench without a back, and it stood apart and solitary on a sort of dais. Tall men-at-arms in morion, breast-plate, and steel gauntlets stood as stiff as their own halberds on each side of this dais, but no other creature was near by it. A pathetic little bench to me it was, for I knew whom it was for; and the sight of it carried my mind back to the great court at Poitiers, where Joan sat upon one like it and calmly fought her cunning fight with the astonished doctors of the Church and Parliament, and rose from it victorious and ap-plauded by all, and went forth to fill the world with the glory of her name.

What a dainty little figure she was, and how gentle and innocent, how winning and beautiful in the fresh bloom of her seventeen years! Those were grand days. And so recent—for she was but just nineteen now—and how much she had seen since, and what wonders she had accomplished!

But now—oh, all was changed, now. She had been lan-guishing in dungeons, away from light and air and the cheer of friendly faces, for nearly three-quarters of a year—she, born child of the sun, natural comrade of the birds and of all happy free creatures. She would be weary, now, and worn with this long captivity, her forces impaired; despondent, perhaps, as knowing there was no hope. Yes, all was changed.

All this time there had been a muffled hum of conversation, and rustling of robes and scraping of feet on the floor, a combination of dull noises which filled all the place. Suddenly—

"Produce the accused!"

It made me catch my breath. My heart began to thump like a hammer. But there was silence, now—silence absolute. All those noises ceased, and it was as if they had never been. Not a sound; the stillness grew oppressive; it was like a weight upon one. All faces were turned towards the door; and one could properly expect that, for most of the people there suddenly realized, no doubt, that they were about to see, in actual flesh and blood, what had been to them before only an embodied prodigy, a word, a phrase, a world-girdling Name.

The stillness continued. Then, far down the stone-paved corridors, one heard a vague slow sound approaching: *clank* . . . . . . clink . . clank—Joan of Arc, Deliverer of France, in chains!

My head swam; all things whirled and spun about me. Ah, *I* was realizing, too.

Chapter V

I GIVE YOU my honor, now, that I am not going to distort or discolor the facts of this miserable trial. No, I will give them to you honestly, detail by detail, just as Manchon and I set them down daily in the official record of the court, and just as one may read them in the printed histories. There will be only this difference: that in talking familiarly with you I shall use my right to comment upon the proceedings and explain them as I go along, so that you can understand them better; also, I shall throw in trifles which came under our eyes and have a certain interest for you and me, but were not important enough to go into the official record.*

To take up my story, now, where I left off. We heard the clanking of Joan's chains down the corridors; she was approaching.

Presently she appeared; a thrill swept the house, and one heard deep breaths drawn. Two guardsmen followed her at a short distance to the rear. Her head was bowed a little, and she moved slowly, she being weak and her irons heavy. She had on men's attire—all black; a soft woollen stuff, intensely black, funereally black, not a speck of relieving color in it from her throat to the floor. A wide collar of this same black stuff lay in radiating folds upon her shoulders and breast; the sleeves of her doublet were full, down to the elbows, and tight thence to her manacled wrists; below the doublet, tight black hose down to the chains on her ankles.

Half-way to her bench she stopped, just where a wide shaft of light fell slanting from a window, and slowly lifted her face. Another thrill!—it was totally colorless, white as snow; a face of gleaming snow set in vivid contrast upon that slender statue of sombre unmitigated black. It was smooth and pure and girlish, beautiful beyond belief, infinitely sad and sweet. But, dear, dear! when the challenge of those untamed eyes fell upon that judge, and the droop vanished from her

---

*He kept his word. His account of the Great Trial will be found to be in strict and detailed accordance with the sworn facts of history.—TRANS-LATOR.

form and it straightened up soldierly and noble, my heart leaped for joy; and I said, all is well, all is well—they have not broken her, they have not conquered her, she is Joan of Arc still! Yes, it was plain to me, now, that there was one spirit there which this dreaded judge could not quell nor make afraid.

She moved to her place and mounted the dais and seated herself upon her bench, gathering her chains into her lap and nestling her little white hands there. Then she waited in tranquil dignity, the only person there who seemed unmoved and unexcited. A bronzed and brawny English soldier, standing at martial ease in the front rank of the citizen spectators, did now most gallantly and respectfully put up his great hand and give her the military salute; and she, smiling friendly, put up hers and returned it; whereat there was a sympathetic little break of applause, which the judge sternly silenced.

Now the memorable inquisition called in history the Great Trial began. Fifty experts against a novice, and no one to help the novice!

The judge summarized the circumstances of the case and the public reports and suspicions upon which it was based; then he required Joan to kneel and make oath that she would answer with exact truthfulness to all questions asked her.

Joan's mind was not asleep. It suspected that dangerous possibilities might lie hidden under this apparently fair and reasonable demand. She answered with the simplicity which so often spoiled the enemy's best-laid plans in the trial at Poitiers, and said,

"No; for I do not know what you are going to ask me; you might ask of me things which I would not tell you."

This incensed the Court, and brought out a brisk flurry of angry exclamations. Joan was not disturbed. Cauchon raised his voice and began to speak in the midst of this noise, but he was so angry that he could hardly get his words out. He said—

"With the divine assistance of our Lord we require you to expedite these proceedings for the welfare of your conscience. Swear, with your hands upon the Gospels, that you will answer true to the questions which shall be asked you!" and he brought down his fat hand with a crash upon his official table.

Joan said, with composure—

"As concerning my father and mother, and the faith, and what things I have done since my coming into France, I will gladly answer; but as regards the revelations which I have received from God, my Voices have forbidden me to confide them to any save my King—"

Here there was another angry outburst of threats and expletives, and much movement and confusion; so she had to stop, and wait for the noise to subside; then her waxen face flushed a little and she straightened up and fixed her eye on the judge, and finished her sentence in a voice that had the old ring in it—

"—and I will never reveal these things though you cut my head off!"

Well, maybe you know what a deliberative body of Frenchmen is like. The judge and half the court were on their feet in a moment, and all shaking their fists at the prisoner and all storming and vituperating at once, so that you could hardly hear yourself think. They kept this up several minutes; and because Joan sat untroubled and indifferent, they grew madder and noisier all the time. Once she said, with a fleeting trace of the old-time mischief in her eye and manner—

"Prithee speak one at a time, fair lords, then I will answer all of you."

At the end of three whole hours of furious debating over the oath, the situation had not changed a jot. The Bishop was still requiring an unmodified oath, Joan was refusing for the twentieth time to take any except the one which she had herself proposed. There was a physical change apparent, but it was confined to court and judge; they were hoarse, droopy, exhausted by their long frenzy, and had a sort of haggard look in their faces, poor men, whereas Joan was still placid and reposeful and did not seem noticeably tired.

The noise quieted down; there was a waiting pause of some moments' duration. Then the judge surrendered to the prisoner, and with bitterness in his voice told her to take the oath after her own fashion. Joan sunk at once to her knees; and as she laid her hands upon the Gospels, that big English soldier set free his mind:

"By God if she were but English, she were not in this place another half a second!"

It was the soldier in him responding to the soldier in her. But what a stinging rebuke it was, what an arraignment of French character and French royalty! Would that he could have uttered just that one phrase in the hearing of Orleans! I know that that grateful city, that adoring city, would have risen, to the last man and the last woman, and marched upon Rouen. Some speeches—speeches that shame a man and humble him—burn themselves into the memory and remain there. That one is burnt into mine.

After Joan had made oath, Cauchon asked her her name, and where she was born, and some questions about her family; also what her age was. She answered these. Then he asked her how much education she had.

"I have learned from my mother the Pater Noster, the Ave Maria, and the Belief. All that I know was taught me by my mother."

Questions of this unessential sort dribbled on for a considerable time. Everybody was tired out by now, except Joan. The tribunal prepared to rise. At this point Cauchon forbade Joan to try to escape from prison, upon pain of being held guilty of the crime of heresy—singular logic! She answered simply—

"I am not bound by this prohibition. If I could escape I would not reproach myself, for I have given no promise, and I shall not."

Then she complained of the burden of her chains, and asked that they might be removed, for she was strongly guarded in that dungeon and there was no need of them. But the Bishop refused, and reminded her that she had broken out of prison twice before. Joan of Arc was too proud to insist. She only said, as she rose to go with the guard—

"It is true I have wanted to escape, and I do want to escape." Then she added, in a way that would touch the pity of anybody, I think, "It is the right of every prisoner."

And so she went from the place in the midst of an impressive stillness, which made the sharper and more distressful to me the clank of those pathetic chains.

What presence of mind she had! One could never surprise her out of it. She saw Noël and me there when she first took her seat on her bench; and we flushed to the forehead with excitement and emotion, but her face showed nothing, betrayed nothing. Her eyes sought us fifty times that day, but they passed on and there was never any ray of recognition in them. Another would have started upon seeing us, and then—why then there could have been trouble for us, of course.

We walked slowly home together, each busy with his own grief and saying not a word.

Chapter VI

T HAT NIGHT Manchon told me that all through the day's proceedings Cauchon had had some clerks concealed in the embrasure of a window who were to make a special report garbling Joan's answers and twisting them from their right meaning. Ah, that was surely the cruelest man and the most shameless that has lived in this world. But his scheme failed. Those clerks had human hearts in them, and their base work revolted them, and they turned to and boldly made a straight report, whereupon Cauchon cursed them and ordered them out of his presence with a threat of drowning, which was his favorite and most frequent menace. The matter had gotten abroad and was making great and unpleasant talk, and Cauchon would not try to repeat this shabby game right away. It comforted me to hear that.

When we arrived at the citadel next morning, we found that a change had been made. The chapel had been found too small. The court had now removed to a noble chamber situated at the end of the great hall of the castle. The number of judges was increased to sixty-two—one ignorant girl against such odds, and none to help her.

The prisoner was brought in. She was as white as ever, but she was looking no whit worse than she looked when she had first appeared the day before. Isn't it a strange thing? Yesterday she had sat five hours on that backless bench with her chains in her lap, baited, badgered, persecuted by that unholy crew, without even the refreshment of a cup of water—for she was never offered anything, and if I have made you know her by this time you will know without my telling you that she was not a person likely to ask favors of those people. And she had spent the night caged in her wintry dungeon with her chains upon her; yet here she was, as I say, collected, unworn, and ready for the conflict; yes, and the only person there who showed no signs of the wear and worry of yesterday. And her eyes—ah, you should have seen them and broken your hearts. Have you seen that veiled deep glow, that pathetic hurt dignity, that unsubdued and unsubduable spirit that burns and

smoulders in the eye of a caged eagle and makes you feel
mean and shabby under the burden of its mute reproach? Her
eyes were like that. How capable they were, and how wonderful! Yes, at all times and in all circumstances they could express as by print every shade of the wide range of her moods.
In them were hidden floods of gay sunshine, the softest and
peacefulest twilights, and devastating storms and lightnings.
Not in this world have there been others that were compara-
ble to them. Such is my opinion, and none that had the privilege to see them would say otherwise than this which I have
said concerning them.

The seance began. And how did it begin, should you think?
Exactly as it began before—with that same tedious thing
which had been settled once, after so much wrangling. The
Bishop opened thus:

"You are required, now, to take the oath pure and simple,
to answer truly all questions asked you."

Joan replied placidly—

"I have made oath yesterday, my lord; let that suffice."

The Bishop insisted and insisted, with rising temper; Joan
but shook her head and remained silent. At last she said—

"I made oath yesterday; it is sufficient." Then she sighed
and said, "Of a truth, you do burden me too much."

The Bishop still insisted, still commanded, but he could not
move her. At last he gave it up and turned her over for the
day's inquest to an old hand at tricks and traps and deceptive
plausibilities—Beaupere, a doctor of theology. Now notice
the form of this sleek strategist's first remark—flung out in
an easy, off-hand way that would have thrown any unwatch-
ful person off his guard—

"Now, Joan, the matter is very simple; just speak up and
frankly and truly answer the questions which I am going to
ask you, as you have sworn to do."

It was a failure. Joan was not asleep. She saw the artifice.
She said—

"No. You could ask me things which I could not tell you—
and would not." Then, reflecting upon how profane and out
of character it was for these ministers of God to be prying
into matters which had proceeded from His hands under the
awful seal of His secrecy, she added, with a warning note in

her tone, "If you were well informed concerning me you would wish me out of your hands. I have done nothing but by revelation."

Beaupere changed his attack, and began an approach from another quarter. He would slip upon her, you see, under cover of innocent and unimportant questions.

"Did you learn any trade at home?"

"Yes, to sew and to spin." Then the invincible soldier, victor of Patay, conqueror of the lion Talbot, deliverer of Orleans, restorer of a king's crown, commander-in-chief of a nation's armies, straightened herself proudly up, gave her head a little toss, and said with naïve complacency, "And when it comes to that, I am not afraid to be matched against any woman in Rouen!"

The crowd of spectators broke out with applause—which pleased Joan—and there was many a friendly and petting smile to be seen. But Cauchon stormed at the people and warned them to keep still and mind their manners.

Beaupere asked other questions. Then—

"Had you other occupations at home?"

"Yes. I helped my mother in the household work and went to the pastures with the sheep and the cattle."

Her voice trembled a little, but one could hardly notice it. As for me, it brought those old enchanted days flooding back to me, and I could not see what I was writing for a little while.

Beaupere cautiously edged along up with other questions toward the forbidden ground, and finally repeated a question which she had refused to answer a little while back—as to whether she had received the Eucharist in those days at other festivals than that of Easter. Joan merely said—

"*Passez outre.*" Or, as one might say, "Pass on to matters which you are privileged to pry into."

I heard a member of the court say to a neighbor—

"As a rule, witnesses are but dull creatures, and an easy prey—yes, and easily embarrassed, easily frightened—but truly one can neither scare this child nor find her dozing."

Presently the house pricked up its ears and began to listen eagerly, for Beaupere began to touch upon Joan's Voices, a matter of consuming interest and curiosity to everybody. His purpose was, to trick her into heedless sayings that could indicate that the Voices had sometimes given her evil advice—hence that they had come from Satan, you see. To have dealings with the devil—well, that would send her to the stake in brief order, and that was the deliberate end and aim of this trial.

"When did you first hear these Voices?"

"I was thirteen when I first heard a Voice coming from God to help me to live well. I was frightened. It came at mid-day, in my father's garden in the summer."

"Had you been fasting?"

"Yes."

"The day before?"

"No."

"From what direction did it come?"

"From the right—from toward the church."

"Did it come with a bright light?"

"Oh, indeed yes. It was brilliant. When I came into France I often heard the Voices very loud."

"What did the Voice sound like?"

"It was a noble Voice, and I thought it was sent to me from God. The third time I heard it I recognized it as being an angel's."

"You could understand it?"

"Quite easily. It was always clear."

"What advice did it give you as to the salvation of your soul?"

"It told me to live rightly, and be regular in attendance upon the services of the Church. And it told me that I must go to France."

"In what species of form did the Voice appear?"

Joan looked suspiciously at the priest a moment, then said, tranquilly—

"As to that, I will not tell you."

"Did the Voice seek you often?"

"Yes. Twice or three times a week, saying, 'Leave your village and go to France.'"

"Did your father know about your departure?"

"No. The Voice said, 'Go to France'; therefore I could not abide at home any longer."

"What else did it say?"

"That I should raise the siege of Orleans."

"Was that all?"

"No, I was to go to Vaucouleurs, and Robert de Baudricourt would give me soldiers to go with me to France; and I answered, saying that I was a poor girl who did not know how to ride, neither how to fight."

Then she told how she was baulked and interrupted at Vaucouleurs, but finally got her soldiers, and began her march.

"How were you dressed?"

The court of Poitiers had distinctly decided and decreed that as God had appointed her to do a man's work, it was meet and no scandal to religion that she should dress as a man; but no matter, this court was ready to use any and all weapons against Joan, even broken and discredited ones, and much was going to be made of this one before this trial should end.

"I wore a man's dress, also a sword which Robert de Baudricourt gave me, but no other weapon."

"Who was it that advised you to wear the dress of a man?"

Joan was suspicious again. She would not answer.

The question was repeated.

She refused again.

"Answer. It is a command!"

"*Passez outre,*" was all she said.

So Beaupere gave up the matter for the present.

"What did Baudricourt say to you when you left?"

"He made them that were to go with me promise to take charge of me, and to me he said, 'Go, and let happen what may!' " (*Advienne que pourra!*)

After a good deal of questioning upon other matters she was asked again about her attire. She said it was necessary for her to dress as a man.

"Did your Voice advise it?"

Joan merely answered placidly—

"I believe my Voice gave me good advice."

It was all that could be got out of her, so the questions wandered to other matters, and finally to her first meeting with the King at Chinon. She said she chose out the King, who was unknown to her, by the revelation of her Voices. All that happened at that time was gone over. Finally—

"Do you still hear those Voices?"

"They come to me every day."

"What do you ask of them?"

"I have never asked of them any recompense but the salvation of my soul."

"Did the Voice always urge you to follow the army?"

He is creeping upon her again. She answered—

"It required me to remain behind at St. Denis. I would have obeyed if I had been free, but I was helpless by my wound, and the knights carried me away by force."

"When were you wounded?"

"I was wounded in the moat before Paris, in the assault."

The next question reveals what Beaupere had been leading up to—

"Was it a feast day?"

You see? The suggestion is that a voice coming from God would hardly advise or permit the violation, by war and bloodshed, of a sacred day.

Joan was troubled a moment, then she answered yes, it was a feast day.

"Now then, tell me this: did you hold it right to make the attack on such a day?"

This was a shot which might make the first breach in a wall which had suffered no damage thus far. There was immediate silence in the court and intense expectancy noticeable all about. But Joan disappointed the house. She merely made a slight little motion with her hand, as when one brushes away a fly, and said with reposeful indifference—

"Passez outre."

Smiles danced for a moment in some of the sternest faces there, and several even laughed outright. The trap had been long and laboriously prepared; it fell, and was empty.

The court rose. It had sat for hours, and was cruelly fatigued. Most of the time had been taken up with apparently idle and purposeless inquiries about the Chinon events, the exiled Duke of Orleans, Joan's first proclamation, and so on, but all this seemingly random stuff had really been sown thick with hidden traps. But Joan had fortunately escaped them all, some by the protecting luck which attends upon ignorance and innocence, some by happy accident, the others by force of her best and surest helper, the clear vision and lightning intuitions of her extraordinary mind.

Now then, this daily baiting and badgering of this friendless girl, a captive in chains, was to continue a long, long time—dignified sport, a kennel of mastiffs and blood-hounds harassing a kitten!—and I may as well tell you, upon sworn testimony, what it was like from the first day to the last. When poor Joan had been in her grave a quarter of a century, the Pope called together that great court which was to re-examine her history, and whose just verdict cleared her illustrious name from every spot and stain, and laid upon the verdict and conduct of our Rouen tribunal the blight of its everlasting execrations. Manchon and several of the judges who had been members of our court were among the witnesses who appeared before that Tribunal of Rehabilitation. Recalling these miserable proceedings which I have been telling you about, Manchon testified thus:—here you have it, all in fair print in the official history:

When Joan spoke of her apparitions she was interrupted at almost every word. They wearied her with long and multiplied interrogatories upon all sorts of things. Almost every day the interrogatories of the morning lasted *three or four hours*; then from these morning-interrogatories they extracted the particularly difficult and subtle points, and these served as material for the afternoon-interrogatories, which lasted *two or three hours*. Moment by moment they skipped from one subject to another; yet in spite of this *she always responded with an astonishing wisdom and memory*. She often corrected the judges, saying, "But I have already answered that once before—ask the recorder," referring them to me.

And here is the testimony of one of Joan's judges. Remember, these witnesses are not talking about two or three days, they are talking about a tedious long *procession* of days:

They asked her profound questions, but she extricated herself quite well. Sometimes the questioners changed suddenly and passed to another subject *to see if she would not contradict herself*. They burdened her with long interrogatories of two or three hours, from which *the judges themselves went forth fatigued*. From the snares with which she was beset *the expertest man in the world could not have extricated himself but with difficulty*. She gave her responses with great prudence; indeed to such a degree that during *three weeks I believed she was inspired*.

Ah, had she a mind such as I have described? You see what these priests say under oath—picked men, men chosen for their places in that terrible court on account of their learning, their experience, their keen and practised intellects and their strong bias against the prisoner. They make that poor young country girl out the match, and more than the match, of the sixty-two trained adepts. Isn't it so? They from the University of Paris, she from the sheepfold and the cow-stable! Ah yes, she was great, she was wonderful. It took six thousand years to produce her; her like will not be seen in the earth again in fifty thousand. Such is my opinion.

Chapter VII

The third meeting of the court was in that same spacious chamber, next day, 24th of February.

How did it begin work? In just the same old way. When the preparations were ended, the robed sixty-two massed in their chairs and the guards and order-keepers distributed to their stations, Cauchon spoke from his throne and commanded Joan to lay her hands upon the Gospels and swear to tell the truth concerning everything asked her!

Joan's eyes kindled, and she rose; rose and stood, fine and noble, and faced toward the Bishop and said—

"Take care what you do, my Lord, you who are my judge, for you take a terrible responsibility on yourself and you presume too far."

It made a great stir, and Cauchon burst out upon her with an awful threat—the threat of instant condemnation unless she obeyed. That made the very bones in my body turn cold, and I saw cheeks about me blanch—for it meant fire and the stake! But Joan, still standing, answered him back, proud and undismayed—

"Not all the clergy in Paris and Rouen could condemn me, lacking the right!"

This made a great tumult, and part of it was applause from the spectators. Joan resumed her seat. The Bishop still insisted. Joan said—

"I have already made oath. It is enough."

The Bishop shouted—

"In refusing to swear, you place yourself under suspicion!"

"Let be. I have sworn already. It is enough."

The Bishop continued to insist. Joan answered that "she would tell what she knew—but not all that she knew."

The Bishop plagued her straight along, till at last she said, in a weary tone—

"I came from God; I have nothing more to do here. Return me to God, from whom I came."

It was piteous to hear; it was the same as saying, "You only want my life; take it and let me be at peace."

The Bishop stormed out again—

"Once more I command you to—"

Joan cut in with a nonchalant *"Passez outre,"* and Cauchon retired from the struggle; but he retired with some credit this time, for he offered a compromise, and Joan, always clear-headed, saw protection for herself in it and promptly and willingly accepted it. She was to swear to tell the truth "as touching the matters set down in the *proces verbal.*" They could not sail her outside of definite limits, now; her course was over a charted sea, henceforth. The Bishop had granted more than he had intended, and more than he would honestly try to abide by.

By command, Beaupere resumed his examination of the accused. It being Lent, there might be a chance to catch her neglecting some detail of her religious duties. I could have told him he would fail there. Why, religion was her life!

"Since when have you eaten or drunk?"

If the least thing had passed her lips in the nature of sustenance, neither her youth nor the fact that she was being half starved in her prison could save her from dangerous suspicion of contempt for the commandments of the Church.

"I have done neither since yesterday at noon."

The priest shifted to the Voices again.

"When have you heard your Voice?"

"Yesterday and to-day."

"At what time?"

"Yesterday it was in the morning."

"What were you doing, then?"

"I was asleep and it woke me."

"By touching your arm?"

"No; without touching me."

"Did you thank it? Did you kneel?"

He had Satan in his mind, you see; and was hoping, perhaps, that by-and-by it could be shown that she had rendered homage to the archenemy of God and man.

"Yes, I thanked it; and knelt in my bed where I was chained, and joined my hands and begged it to implore God's help for me so that I might have light and instruction as touching the answers I should give here."

"Then what did the Voice say?"

"It told me to answer boldly, and God would help me."
Then she turned toward Cauchon and said, "You say that you
are my judge; now I tell you again, take care what you do, for
in truth I am sent of God and you are putting yourself in
great danger."

Beaupere asked her if the Voice's counsels were not fickle
and variable.

"No. It never contradicts itself. This very day it has told me
again to answer boldly."

"Has it forbidden you to answer only part of what is asked
you?"

"I will tell you nothing as to that. I have revelations
touching the King my master, and those I will not tell you."
Then she was stirred by a great emotion, and the tears
sprang to her eyes and she spoke out as with strong conviction, saying—

"I believe wholly—as wholly as I believe the Christian faith
and that God has redeemed us from the fires of hell, that God
speaks to me by that Voice!"

Being questioned further concerning the Voice, she said she
was not at liberty to tell all she knew.

"Do you think God would be displeased at your telling the
whole truth?"

"The Voice has commanded me to tell the King certain
things, and not you—and some very lately—even last night;
things which I would he knew. He would be more easy at his
dinner."

"Why doesn't the Voice speak to the King itself, as it did
when you were with him? Would it not if you asked it?"

"I do not know if it be the wish of God." She was pensive,
a moment or two, busy with her thoughts and far away, no
doubt; then she added a remark in which Beaupere, always
watchful, always alert, detected a possible opening—a chance
to set a trap. Do you think he jumped at it instantly, betraying the joy he had in his find, as a young hand at craft and
artifice would do? No, oh, no, you could not tell that he had
noticed the remark at all. He slid indifferently away from it at
once, and began to ask idle questions about other things, so
as to slip around and spring on it from behind, so to speak:
tedious and empty questions as to whether the Voice had told

her she would escape from this prison; and if it had furnished answers to be used by her in to-day's seance; if it was accompanied with a glory of light; if it had eyes, etc. That risky remark of Joan's was this:

"Without the Grace of God I could do nothing."

The court saw the priest's game, and watched his play with a cruel eagerness. Poor Joan was grown dreamy and absent; possibly she was tired. Her life was in imminent danger, and she did not suspect it. The time was ripe now, and Beaupere quietly and stealthily sprung his trap:

"Are you in a state of Grace?"

Ah, we had two or three honorable brave men in that pack of judges; and Jean Lefevre was one of them. He sprang to his feet and cried out—

"It is a terrible question! The accused is not obliged to answer it!"

Cauchon's face flushed black with anger to see this plank flung to the perishing child, and he shouted—

"Silence! and take your seat. The accused will answer the question!"

There was no hope, no way out of the dilemma; for whether she said yes or whether she said no, it would be all the same—a disastrous answer, for the Scriptures had said one *cannot know* this thing. Think what hard hearts they were to set this fatal snare for that ignorant young girl and be proud of such work and happy in it. It was a miserable moment for me while we waited; it seemed a year. All the house showed excitement; and mainly it was glad excitement. Joan looked out upon these hungering faces with innocent untroubled eyes, and then humbly and gently she brought out that immortal answer which brushed the formidable snare away as it had been but a cobweb:

"If I be not in a state of Grace, I pray God place me in it; if I be in it, I pray God keep me so."

Ah, you will never see an effect like that; no, not while you live. For a space there was the silence of the grave. Men looked wondering into each other's faces, and some were awed and crossed themselves; and I heard Lefevre mutter—

"It was beyond the wisdom of man to devise that answer. *Whence* come this child's amazing inspirations?"

Beaupere presently took up his work again, but the humiliation of his defeat weighed upon him, and he made but a rambling and dreary business of it, he not being able to put any heart in it.

He asked Joan a thousand questions about her childhood and about the oak wood, and the fairies, and the children's games and romps under our dear *Arbre Fée de Bourlemont*, and this stirring up of old memories broke her voice and made her cry a little, but she bore up as well as she could, and answered everything.

Then the priest finished by touching again upon the matter of her apparel—a matter which was never to be lost sight of in this still-hunt for this innocent creature's life, but kept always hanging over her, a menace charged with mournful possibilities:

"Would you like a woman's dress?"

"Indeed yes, if I may go out from this prison—but here, no."

Chapter VIII

THE COURT met next on Monday the 27th. Would you believe it? The Bishop ignored the contract limiting the examination to matters set down in the *proces verbal* and again commanded Joan to take the oath without reservations. She said—

"You should be content; I have sworn enough."

She stood her ground, and Cauchon had to yield.

The examination was resumed, concerning Joan's Voices.

"You have said that you recognized them as being the voices of angels the third time that you heard them. What angels were they?"

"St. Catherine and St. Marguerite."

"How did you know that it was those two saints? How could you tell the one from the other?"

"I know it was they; and I know how to distinguish them."

"By what sign?"

"By their manner of saluting me. I have been these seven years under their direction, and I knew who they were because they told me."

"Whose was the first Voice that came to you when you were thirteen years old?"

"It was the Voice of St. Michael. I saw him before my eyes; and he was not alone, but attended by a cloud of angels."

"Did you see the archangel and the attendant angels in the body, or in the spirit?"

"I saw them with the eyes of my body, just as I see you; and when they went away I cried because they did not take me with them."

It made me see that awful shadow again that fell dazzling white upon her that day under *l'Arbre Fée de Bourlemont*, and it made me shiver again, though it was so long ago. It was really not very long gone by, but it seemed so, because so much had happened since.

"In what shape and form did St. Michael appear?"

"As to that, I have not received permission to speak."

"What did the archangel say to you that first time?"

"I cannot answer you to-day."

Meaning, I think, that she would have to get permission of her Voices first.

Presently, after some more questions as to the revelations which had been conveyed through her to the King, she complained of the unnecessity of all this, and said—

"I will say again, as I have said before, many times in these sittings, that I answered all questions of this sort before the court at Poitiers, and I would that you would bring here the record of that court and read from that. Prithee send for that book."

There was no answer. It was a subject that had to be got around and put aside. That book had wisely been gotten out of the way, for it contained things which would be very awkward here. Among them was a decision that Joan's mission was from God, whereas it was the intention of this inferior court to show that it was from the devil; also a decision permitting Joan to wear male attire, whereas it was the purpose of this court to make the male attire do hurtful work against her.

"How was it that you were moved to come into France —by your own desire?"

"Yes; and by command of God. But that it was his will I would not have come. I would sooner have had my body torn in sunder by horses than come, lacking that."

Beaupere shifted once more to the matter of the male attire, now, and proceeded to make a solemn talk about it. That tried Joan's patience; and presently she interrupted and said—

"It is a trifling thing and of no consequence. And I did not put it on by counsel of any man, but by command of God."

"Robert de Baudricourt did not order you to wear it?"

"No."

"Do you think you did well in taking the dress of a man?"

"I did well to do whatsoever thing God commanded me to do."

"But in this particular case do you think you did well in taking the dress of a man?"

"I have done nothing but by command of God."

Beaupere made various attempts to lead her into contradictions of herself; also to put her words and acts in disaccord with the Scriptures. But it was lost time. He did not succeed. He returned to her visions, the light which shone about them, her relations with the King, and so on.

"Was there an angel above the King's head the first time you saw him?"

"By the Blessed Mary!—"

She forced her impatience down, and finished her sentence with tranquillity: "If there was one I did not see it."

"Was there light?"

"There were more than three hundred soldiers there, and five hundred torches, without taking account of spiritual light."

"What made the King believe in the revelations which you brought him?"

"He had signs; also the counsel of the clergy."

"What revelations were made to the King?"

"You will not get that out of me this year." Presently she added: "During three weeks I was questioned by the clergy at Chinon and Poitiers. The King had a sign before he would believe; and the clergy were of opinion that my acts were good and not evil."

The subject was dropped now for a while, and Beaupere took up the matter of the miraculous sword of Fierbois to see if he could not find a chance there to fix the crime of sorcery upon Joan.

"How did you know that there was an ancient sword buried in the ground under the rear of the altar of the church of St. Catherine of Fierbois?"

Joan had no concealments to make as to this:

"I knew the sword was there because my Voices told me so; and I sent to ask that it be given to me to carry in the wars. It seemed to me that it was not very deep in the ground. The clergy of the church caused it to be sought for and dug up; and they polished it, and the rust fell easily off from it."

"Were you wearing it when you were taken in battle at Compiègne?"

"No. But I wore it constantly until I left St. Denis after the attack upon Paris."

This sword, so mysteriously discovered and so long and so

constantly victorious, was suspected of being under the protection of enchantment.

"Was that sword blest? What blessing had been invoked upon it?"

"None. I loved it because it was found in the church of St. Catherine, for I loved that church very dearly."

She loved it because it had been built in honor of one of her angels.

"Didn't you lay it upon the altar, to the end that it might be lucky?" (The altar of St. Denis.)

"No."

"Didn't you pray that it might be made lucky?"

"Truly it were no harm to wish that my harness might be fortunate."

"Then it was not that sword which you wore in the field of Compiègne? What sword did you wear there?"

The sword of the Burgundian Franquet d'Arras, whom I took prisoner in the engagement at Lagny. I kept it because it was a good war-sword—good to lay on stout thumps and blows with."

She said that quite simply; and the contrast between her delicate little self and the grim soldier-words which she dropped with such easy familiarity from her lips made many spectators smile.

"What is become of the other sword? Where is it now?"

"Is that in the *proces verbal*?"

Beaupere did not answer.

"Which do you love best, your banner or your sword?"

Her eye lighted gladly at the mention of her banner, and she cried out—

"I love my banner best—oh, forty times more than the sword! Sometimes I carried it myself when I charged the enemy, to avoid killing any one." Then she added, naïvely, and with again that curious contrast between her girlish little personality and her subject, "I have never killed any one."

It made a great many smile; and no wonder, when you consider what a gentle and innocent little thing she looked. One could hardly believe she had ever even seen men slaughtered, she looked so little fitted for such things.

"In the final assault at Orleans did you tell your soldiers

that the arrows shot by the enemy and the stones discharged from their catapults and cannon would not strike any one but you?"

"No. And the proof is, that more than a hundred of my men were struck. I told them to have no doubts and no fears; that they would raise the siege. I was wounded in the neck by an arrow in the assault upon the bastille that commanded the bridge, but St. Catherine comforted me and I was cured in fifteen days without having to quit the saddle and leave my work."

"Did you know that you were going to be wounded?"

"Yes; and I had told it to the King beforehand. I had it from my Voices."

"When you took Jargeau, why did you not put its commandant to ransom?"

"I offered him leave to go out unhurt from the place, with all his garrison; and if he would not I would take it by storm."

"And you did, I believe."

"Yes."

"Had your Voices counselled you to take it by storm?"

"As to that, I do not remember."

Thus closed a weary long sitting, without result. Every device that could be contrived to trap Joan into wrong thinking, wrong doing, or disloyalty to the Church, or sinfulness as a little child at home or later had been tried, and none of them had succeeded. She had come unscathed through the ordeal.

Was the court discouraged? No. Naturally it was very much surprised, very much astonished, to find its work baffling and difficult instead of simple and easy, but it had powerful allies in the shape of hunger, cold, fatigue, persecution, deception, and treachery; and opposed to this array nothing but a defenceless and ignorant girl who must some time or other surrender to bodily and mental exhaustion or get caught in one of the thousand traps set for her.

And had the court made no progress during these seemingly resultless sittings? Yes. It had been feeling its way, groping here, groping there, and had found one or two vague trails which might freshen by-and-by and lead to something. The male attire, for instance, and the visions and Voices. Of course no one doubted that she had seen supernatural beings and been spoken to and advised by them. And of course no one doubted that by supernatural help miracles had been done by Joan, such as choosing out the King in a crowd when she had never seen him before, and her discovery of the sword buried under the altar. It would have been foolish to doubt these things, for we all know that the air is full of devils and angels that are visible to traffickers in magic on the one hand and to the stainlessly holy on the other; but what many and perhaps most did doubt was, that Joan's visions, voices, and miracles came from God. It was hoped that in time they could be proven to have been of satanic origin. Therefore, as you see, the court's persistent fashion of coming back to that subject every little while and spooking around it and prying into it was not to pass the time—it had a strictly business end in view.

Chapter IX

THE NEXT SITTING opened on Thursday the first of March. Fifty-eight judges present—the others resting.

As usual, Joan was required to take an oath without reservations. She showed no temper this time. She considered herself well buttressed by the *proces verbal* compromise which Cauchon was so anxious to repudiate and creep out of; so she merely refused, distinctly and decidedly; and added, in a spirit of fairness and candor—

"But as to matters set down in the *proces verbal*, I will freely tell the whole truth—yes, as freely and fully as if I were before the Pope."

Here was a chance! We had two or three Popes, then; only one of them could be the true Pope, of course. Everybody judiciously shirked the question of *which* was the true Pope and refrained from naming him, it being clearly dangerous to go into particulars in this matter. Here was an opportunity to trick an unadvised girl into bringing herself into peril, and the unfair judge lost no time in taking advantage of it. He asked, in a plausibly indolent and absent way—

"Which one do you consider to be the true Pope?"

The house took an attitude of deep attention, and so waited to hear the answer and see the prey walk into the trap. But when the answer came it covered the judge with confusion, and you could see many people covertly chuckling. For Joan asked in a voice and manner which almost deceived even me, so innocent it seemed—

"Are there two?"

One of the ablest priests in that body and one of the best swearers there, spoke right out so that half the house heard him, and said—

"By God it was a master stroke!"

As soon as the judge was better of his embarrassment he came back to the charge, but was prudent and passed by Joan's question—

"Is it true that you received a letter from the Count of

Armagnac asking you which of the three Popes he ought to obey?"

"Yes, and answered it."

Copies of both letters were produced and read. Joan said that hers had not been quite strictly copied. She said she had received the Count's letter when she was just mounting her horse; and added—

"So, in dictating a word or two of reply I said I would try to answer him from Paris or somewhere where I could be at rest."

She was asked again which Pope she had considered the right one.

"I was not able to instruct the Count of Armagnac as to which one he ought to obey"; then she added, with a frank fearlessness which sounded fresh and wholesome in that den of trimmers and shufflers, "but as for me, I hold that we are bound to obey our Lord the Pope who is at Rome."

The matter was dropped. Then they produced and read a copy of Joan's first effort at dictating—her proclamation summoning the English to retire from the siege of Orleans and vacate France—truly a great and fine production for an unpractised girl of seventeen.

"Do you acknowledge as your own the document which has just been read?"

"Yes, except that there are errors in it—words which make me give myself too much importance." I saw what was coming; I was troubled and ashamed. "For instance, I did not say 'Deliver up to the Maid' (*rendez a la Pucelle*); I said 'Deliver up to the King' (*rendez au Roi*); and I did not call myself 'Commander-in-Chief' (*chef de guerre*). All those are words which my secretary substituted; or mayhap he misheard me or forgot what I said."

She did not look at me when she said it; she spared me that embarrassment. I hadn't misheard her at all, and hadn't forgotten. I changed her language purposely, for she *was* Commander-in-Chief and entitled to call herself so, and it was becoming and proper, too; and who was going to surrender anything to the King?—at that time a stick, a cipher? If any surrendering was done, it would be to the noble Maid of

Vaucouleurs, already famed and formidable though she had not yet struck a blow.

Ah, there would have been a fine and disagreeable episode (for me) there, if that pitiless court had discovered that the very scribbler of that piece of dictation, secretary to Joan of Arc, was present—and not only present, but helping build the record; and not only that, but destined at a far distant day to testify against lies and perversions smuggled into it by Cauchon and deliver them over to eternal infamy!

"Do you acknowledge that you dictated this proclamation?"

"I do."

"Have you repented of it? Do you retract it?"

Ah, then she was indignant!

"No! Not even these chains"—and she shook them—"not even these chains can chill the hopes that I uttered there. And more!"—she rose, and stood a moment with a divine strange light kindling in her face, then her words burst forth as in a flood—"I warn you now that before seven years a disaster will smite the English, oh, many fold greater than the fall of Orleans! and—"

"Silence! Sit down!"

"—and then, soon after, they will lose all France!"

Now consider these things. The French armies no longer existed. The French cause was standing still, our King was standing still, there was no hint that by-and-by the Constable Richemont would come forward and take up the great work of Joan of Arc and finish it. In face of all this, Joan made that prophecy—made it with perfect confidence—*and it came true*.

For within five years Paris fell—1436—and our King marched into it flying the victor's flag. So the first part of the prophecy was then fulfilled—in fact, almost the entire prophecy; for, with Paris in our hands, the fulfilment of the rest of it was assured.

Twenty years later all France was ours excepting a single town—Calais.

Now that will remind you of an earlier prophecy of Joan's. At the time that she wanted to take Paris and could have done it with ease if our King had but consented, she said that that was the golden time; that with Paris ours, all France would be ours in six months. But if this golden opportunity to recover France was wasted, said she, *"I give you twenty years to do it in."*

She was right. After Paris fell, in 1436, the rest of the work had to be done city by city, castle by castle, and it took twenty years to finish it.

Yes, it was the first day of March, 1431, there in the court, that she stood in the view of everybody and uttered that strange and incredible prediction. Now and then, in this world, somebody's prophecy turns up correct, but when you come to look into it there is sure to be considerable room for suspicion that the prophecy was made after the fact. But here the matter is different. There in that court Joan's prophecy was set down in the official record at the hour and moment of its utterance, years before the fulfilment, and there you may read it to this day. Twenty-five years after Joan's death the record was produced in the great Court of the Rehabilitation and verified under oath by Manchon and me, and surviving judges of our court confirmed the exactness of the record in their testimony.

Joan's startling utterance on that now so celebrated first of March stirred up a great turmoil, and it was some time before it quieted down again. Naturally everybody was troubled, for a prophecy is a grisly and awful thing, whether one thinks it ascends from hell or comes down from heaven. All that these people felt sure of was, that the inspiration back of it was genuine and puissant. They would have given their right hands to know the source of it.

At last the questions began again.

"How do you know that those things are going to happen?"

"I know it by revelation. And I know it as surely as I know that you sit here before me."

This sort of answer was not going to allay the spreading uneasiness. Therefore, after some further dallying the judge got the subject out of the way and took up one which he could enjoy more.

"What language do your Voices speak?"

"French."

"St. Marguerite, too?"

"Verily; why not? She is on our side, not on the English!"

Saints and angels who did not condescend to speak English! a grave affront. They could not be brought into court and punished for contempt, but the tribunal could take silent note of Joan's remark and remember it against her; which they did. It might be useful by-and-by.

"Do your saints and angels wear jewelry?—crowns, rings, ear-rings?"

To Joan, questions like this were profane frivolities and not worthy of serious notice; she answered indifferently. But the question brought to her mind another matter, and she turned upon Cauchon and said—

"I had two rings. They have been taken away from me during my captivity. You have one of them. It is the gift of my brother. Give it back to me. If not to me, then I pray that it be given to the Church."

The judges conceived the idea that maybe these rings were for the working of enchantments. Perhaps they could be made to do Joan a damage.

"Where is the other ring?"

"The Burgundians have it."

"Where did you get it?"

"My father and mother gave it to me."

"Describe it."

"It is plain and simple and has *'Jesus and Mary'* engraved upon it."

Everybody could see that that was not a valuable equipment to do devil's work with. So that trail was not worth following. Still, to make sure, one of the judges asked Joan if she had ever cured sick people by touching them with the ring. She said no.

"Now as concerning the fairies, that were used to abide near by Domremy whereof there are many reports and traditions. It is said that your godmother surprised these creatures on a summer's night dancing under the tree called *L'Arbre Fée de Bourlemont*. Is it not possible that your pretended saints and angels are but those fairies?"

"Is that in your *proces*?"

She made no other answer.

"Have you not conversed with St. Marguerite and St. Catherine under that tree?"

"I do not know."

"Or by the fountain near the tree?"

"Yes, sometimes."

"What promises did they make you?"

"None but such as they had God's warrant for."

"But what promises *did* they make?"

"That is not in your *proces*; yet I will say this much: they told me that the King would become master of his kingdom in spite of his enemies."

"And what else?"

There was a pause; then she said humbly—

"They promised to lead me to Paradise."

If faces do really betray what is passing in men's minds, a fear came upon many in that house, at this time, that maybe, after all, a chosen servant and herald of God was here being hunted to her death. The interest deepened. Movements and whisperings ceased: the stillness became almost painful.

Have you noticed that almost from the beginning the nature of the questions asked Joan showed that in some way or other the questioner very often already knew his fact before he asked his question? Have you noticed that somehow or other the questioners usually knew just how and where to search for Joan's secrets; that they really knew the bulk of her privacies—a fact not suspected by her—and that they had no task before them but to trick her into exposing those secrets?

Do you remember Loyseleur the hypocrite, the treacherous priest, tool of Cauchon? Do you remember that under the sacred seal of the confessional Joan freely and trustingly revealed to him everything concerning her history save only a few things regarding her supernatural revelations which her Voices had forbidden her to tell to any one—and that the unjust judge, Cauchon, was a hidden listener all the time?

Now you understand how the inquisitors were able to devise that long array of minutely prying questions; questions whose subtlety and ingenuity and penetration are astonishing until we come to remember Loyseleur's performance and recognize their source. Ah, Bishop of Beauvais, you are now lamenting this cruel iniquity these many years in hell! Yes verily, unless one has come to your help. There is but one among the redeemed that would do it; and it is futile to hope that that one has not already done it—Joan of Arc.

We will return to the court and the questionings.

"Did they make you still another promise?"

"Yes, but that is not in your *proces*. I will not tell it now, but before three months I will tell it you."

The judge seems to know the matter he is asking about, already; one gets this idea from his next question.

"Did your Voices tell you that you would be liberated before three months?"

Joan often showed a little flash of surprise at the good guessing of the judges, and she showed one this time. I was frequently in terror to find my mind (which *I* could not control) criticising the Voices and saying, "They counsel her to speak boldly—a thing which she would do without any suggestion from *them* or anybody else—but when it comes to telling her any useful thing, such as how these conspirators manage to guess their way so skilfully into her affairs, they are always off attending to some other business." I am reverent by nature; and when such thoughts swept through my head they made me cold with fear, and if there was a storm and thunder at the time, I was so ill that I could but with difficulty abide at my post and do my work.

Joan answered—

"That is not in your *proces*. I do not know when I shall be set free, but some who wish me out of this world will go from it before me."

It made some of them shiver.

"Have your Voices told you that you will be delivered from this prison?"

Without a doubt they had, and the judge knew it before he asked the question.

"Ask me again in three months and I will tell you."

She said it with such a happy look, the tired prisoner! And I? And Noël Rainguesson, drooping yonder?—why, the floods of joy went streaming through us from crown to sole! It was all that we could do to hold still and keep from making fatal exposure of our feelings.

She was to be set free in three months. That was what she meant; we saw it. The Voices had told her so, and told her true—true to the very day—May 30. But we know, now, that they had mercifully hidden from her *how* she was to be set free, but left her in ignorance. Home again! That was our understanding of it—Noël's and mine; that was our dream; and now we would count the days, the hours, the minutes. They would fly lightly along; they would soon be over. Yes, we would carry our idol home; and there, far from the pomps and tumults of the world, we would take up our happy life again and live it out as we had begun it, in the free air and the sunshine, with the friendly sheep and the friendly people for comrades, and the grace and charm of the meadows, the woods, and the river always before our eyes and their deep peace in our hearts. Yes, that was our dream, the dream that carried us bravely through that three months to an exact and awful fulfilment, the thought of which would have killed us, I think, if we had foreknown it and been obliged to bear the burden of it upon our hearts the half of those heavy days.

Our reading of the prophecy was this: We believed the King's soul was going to be smitten with remorse; and that he would privately plan a rescue with Joan's old lieutenants, D'Alençon and the Bastard and La Hire, and that this rescue would take place at the end of the three months. So we made up our minds to be ready and take a hand in it.

In the present and also in later sittings Joan was urged to name the exact day of her deliverance; but she could not do that. She had not the permission of her Voices. Moreover, the Voices themselves did not name the precise day. Ever since the fulfilment of the prophecy, I have believed that Joan had the idea that her deliverance was going to come in the form of death. But not *that* death! Divine as she was, dauntless as she was in battle, she was human also. She was not solely a saint, an angel, she was a clay-made girl also—as human a girl as any in the world, and full of a human girl's sensitivenesses and tendernesses and delicacies. And so, *that* death! No, she could not have lived the three months with that one before her, I think. You remember that the first time she was wounded she was frightened, and cried, just as any other girl of seventeen would have done, although she had known for eighteen days that she was going to be wounded on that very day. No, she was not afraid of any ordinary death, and an ordinary death was what she believed the prophecy of deliverance meant, I think, for her face showed happiness, not horror, when she uttered it.

Now I will explain why I think as I do. Five weeks before she was captured in the battle of Compiègne, her Voices told her what was coming. They did not tell her the day or the place, but said she would be taken prisoner and that it would be before the feast of St. John. She begged that death, certain and swift, should be her fate, and the captivity brief; for she was a free spirit, and dreaded the confinement. The Voices made no promise, but only told her to bear whatever came. Now as they did not *refuse* the swift death, a hopeful young thing like Joan would naturally cherish that fact and make the most of it, allowing it to grow and establish itself in her mind. And so now that she was told she was to be "delivered" in three months, I think she believed it meant that she would die in her bed in the prison, and that that was why she looked happy and content—the gates of Paradise standing open for her, the time so short, you see, her troubles so soon to be over, her reward so close at hand. Yes, that would make her look happy, that would make her patient and bold, and able to fight her fight out like a soldier. Save herself if she could, of course, and try her best, for that was the way she was made; but die with her face to the front if die she must.

Then later, when she charged Cauchon with trying to kill her with a poisoned fish, her notion that she was to be "delivered" by death in the prison—if she had it, and I believe she had—would naturally be greatly strengthened, you see.

But I am wandering from the trial. Joan was asked to definitely name the time that she would be delivered from prison.

"I have always said that I was not permitted to tell you everything. I am to be set free, and I desire to ask leave of my Voices to tell you the day. This is why I wish for delay."

"Do your Voices forbid you to tell the truth?"

"Is it that you wish to know matters concerning the King of France? I tell you again that he will regain his kingdom, and that I know it as well as I know that you sit here before me in this tribunal." She sighed and, after a little pause, added: "I should be dead but for this revelation, which comforts me always."

Some trivial questions were asked her about St. Michael's dress and appearance. She answered them with dignity, but one saw that they gave her pain. After a little she said—

"I have great joy in seeing him, for when I see him I have the feeling that I am not in mortal sin." She added, "Sometimes St. Marguerite and St. Catherine have allowed me to confess myself to them."

Here was a possible chance to set a successful snare for her innocence.

"When you confessed were you in mortal sin, do you think?"

But her reply did her no hurt. So the inquiry was shifted once more to the revelations made to the King—secrets which the court had tried again and again to force out of Joan, but without success.

"Now as to the sign given to the King—"

"I have already told you that I will tell you nothing about it."

"Do you know what the sign was?"

"As to that, you will not find out from me."

All this refers to Joan's secret interview with the King—held apart, though two or three others were present. It was known—through Loyseleur, of course—that this sign was a crown and was a pledge of the verity of Joan's mission. But that is all a mystery until this day—the nature of the crown, I mean—and will remain a mystery to the end of time. We can never know whether a real crown descended upon the King's head, or only a symbol, the mystic fabric of a vision.

"Did you see a crown upon the King's head when he received the revelation?"

"I cannot tell you as to that, without perjury."

"Did the King have that crown at Rheims?"

"I think the King put upon his head a crown which he found there; but a much richer one was brought him afterwards."

"Have you seen that one?"

"I cannot tell you, without perjury. But whether I have seen it or not, I have heard say that it was rich and magnificent."

They went on and pestered her to weariness about that mysterious crown, but they got nothing more out of her. The sitting closed. A long, hard day for all of us.

Chapter X

THE COURT rested a day, then took up work again on Saturday the third of March.

This was one of our stormiest sessions. The whole court was out of patience; and with good reason. These three-score distinguished churchmen, illustrious tacticians, veteran legal gladiators, had left important posts where their super-vision was needed, to journey hither from various regions and accomplish a most simple and easy matter—condemn and send to death a country lass of nineteen who could nei-ther read nor write, knew nothing of the wiles and perplexi-ties of legal procedure, could call not a single witness in her defence, was allowed no advocate or adviser, and must con-duct her case by herself against a hostile judge and a packed jury. In two hours she would be hopelessly entangled, routed, defeated, convicted. Nothing could be more certain than this—so they thought. But it was a mistake. The two hours had strung out into days; what promised to be a skir-mish had expanded into a siege; the thing which had looked so easy had proven to be surprisingly difficult; the light vic-tim who was to have been puffed away like a feather re-mained planted like a rock; and on top of all this, if anybody had a right to laugh it was the country lass and not the court.

She was not doing that, for that was not her spirit; but others were doing it. The whole town was laughing in its sleeve, and the court knew it, and its dignity was deeply hurt. The members could not hide their annoyance.

And so, as I have said, the session was stormy. It was easy to see that these men had made up their minds to force words from Joan to-day which should shorten up her case and bring it to a prompt conclusion. It shows that after all their experi-ence with her they did not know her yet. They went into the battle with energy. They did not leave the questioning to a particular member; no, everybody helped. They volleyed questions at Joan from all over the house, and sometimes so many were talking at once that she had to ask them to deliver

their fire one at a time and not by platoons. The beginning
was as usual:

"You are once more required to take the oath pure and
simple."

"I will answer to what is in the *proces verbal*. When I do
more, I will choose the occasion for myself."

That old ground was debated and fought over inch by inch
with great bitterness and many threats. But Joan remained
steadfast, and the questionings had to shift to other matters.
Half an hour was spent over Joan's apparitions—their dress,
hair, general appearance, and so on—in the hope of fishing
something of a damaging sort out of the replies; but with no
result.

Next, the male attire was reverted to, of course. After many
well-worn questions had been re-asked, one or two new ones
were put forward.

"Did not the King or the Queen sometimes ask you to quit
the male dress?"

"That is not in your *proces*."

"Do you think you would have sinned if you had taken the
dress of your sex?"

"I have done best to serve and obey my sovereign Lord and
Master."

After a while the matter of Joan's Standard was taken up, in
the hope of connecting magic and witchcraft with it.

"Did not your men copy your banner in their pennons?"

"The lancers of my guard did it. It was to distinguish them
from the rest of the forces. It was their own idea."

"Were they often renewed?"

"Yes. When the lances were broken they were renewed."

The purpose of the questions unveils itself in the next one.

"Did you not say to your men that pennons made like your
banner would be lucky?"

The soldier-spirit in Joan was offended at this puerility. She
drew herself up, and said with dignity and fire: "What I said
to them was, 'Ride these English down!' and I did it myself."

Whenever she flung out a scornful speech like that at
these French menials in English livery it lashed them into a
rage; and that is what happened this time. There were ten,
twenty, sometimes even thirty of them on their feet at a time,

storming at the prisoner minute after minute, but Joan was not disturbed.

By-and-by there was peace, and the inquiry was resumed.

It was now sought to turn against Joan the thousand loving honors which had been done her when she was raising France out of the dirt and shame of a century of slavery and castigation.

"Did you not cause paintings and images of yourself to be made?"

"No. At Arras I saw a painting of myself kneeling in armor before the King and delivering him a letter; but I caused no such things to be made."

"Were not masses and prayers said in your honor?"

"If it was done it was not by my command. But if any prayed for me I think it was no harm."

"Did the French people believe you were sent of God?"

"As to that, I know not: but whether they believed it or not, I was not the less sent of God."

"If they thought you were sent of God do you think it was well thought?"

"If they believed it, their trust was not abused."

"What impulse was it, think you, that moved the people to kiss your hands, your feet, and your vestments?"

"They were glad to see me, and so they did those things; and I could not have prevented them if I had had the heart. Those poor people came lovingly to me because I had not done them any hurt, but had done the best I could for them according to my strength."

See what modest little words she uses to describe that touching spectacle, her marches about France walled in on both sides by the adoring multitudes: "They were glad to see me." Glad? Why, they were transported with joy to see her. When they could not kiss her hands or her feet, they knelt in the mire and kissed the hoof-prints of her horse. They worshipped her; and that is what these priests were trying to prove. It was nothing to them that she was not to blame for what other people did. No, if she was worshipped, it was enough; she was guilty of mortal sin. Curious logic, one must say.

"Did you not stand sponsor for some children baptized at Rheims?"

"At Troyes I did, and at St. Denis; and I named the boys Charles, in honor of the King, and the girls I named Joan."

"Did not women touch their rings to those which you wore?"

"Yes, many did, but I did not know their reason for it."

"At Rheims was your Standard carried into the church? Did you stand at the altar with it in your hand at the Coronation?"

"Yes."

"In passing through the country did you confess yourself in the churches and receive the sacrament?"

"Yes."

"In the dress of a man?"

"Yes. But I do not remember that I was in armor."

It was almost a concession! almost a half-surrender of the permission granted her by the Church at Poitiers to dress as a man. The wily court shifted to another matter: to pursue this one at this time might call Joan's attention to her small mistake, and by her native cleverness she might recover her lost ground. The tempestuous session had worn her and drowsed her alertness.

"It is reported that you brought a dead child to life in the church at Lagny. Was that in answer to your prayers?"

"As to that, I have no knowledge. Other young girls were praying for the child, and I joined them and prayed also, doing no more than they."

"Continue."

"While we prayed it came to life, and cried. It had been dead three days, and was as black as my doublet. It was straightway baptized, then it passed from life again and was buried in holy ground."

"Why did you jump from the tower of Beaurevoir by night and try to escape?"

"I would go to the succor of Compiègne."

It was insinuated that this was an attempt to commit the deep crime of suicide to avoid falling into the hands of the English.

"Did you not say that you would rather die than be delivered into the power of the English?"

Joan answered frankly, without perceiving the trap—

"Yes; my words were, that I would rather that my soul be returned unto God than that I should fall into the hands of the English."

It was now insinuated that when she came to, after jumping from the tower, she was angry and blasphemed the name of God; and that she did it again when she heard of the defection of the Commandant of Soissons. She was hurt and indignant at this, and said—

"It is not true. I have never cursed. It is not my custom to swear."

Chapter XI

A HALT was called. It was time. Cauchon was losing ground in the fight, Joan was gaining it. There were signs that here and there in the court a judge was being softened toward Joan by her courage, her presence of mind, her fortitude, her constancy, her piety, her simplicity and candor, her manifest purity, the nobility of her character, her fine intelligence, and the good brave fight she was making, all friendless and alone against unfair odds, and there was grave room for fear that this softening process would spread further and presently bring Cauchon's plans in danger.

Something must be done, and it was done. Cauchon was not distinguished for compassion, but he now gave proof that he had it in his character. He thought it pity to subject so many judges to the prostrating fatigues of this trial when it could be conducted plenty well enough by a handful of them. Oh, gentle Judge! But he did not remember to modify the fatigues for the little captive.

He would let all the judges but a handful go, but he would select the handful himself, and he did. He chose tigers. If a lamb or two got in, it was by oversight, not intention; and he knew what to do with lambs when discovered.

He called a small council, now, and during five days they sifted the huge bulk of answers thus far gathered from Joan. They winnowed it of all chaff, all useless matter—that is, all matter favorable to Joan; they saved up all matter which could be twisted to her hurt, and out of this they constructed a basis for a new trial which should have the semblance of a continuation of the old one. Another change. It was plain that the public trial had wrought damage: its proceedings had been discussed all over the town and had moved many to pity the abused prisoner. There should be no more of that. The sittings should be secret hereafter, and no spectators admitted. So Noël could come no more. I sent this news to him. I had not the heart to carry it myself. I would give the pain a chance to modify before I should see him in the evening.

On the tenth of March the secret trial began. A week had passed since I had seen Joan. Her appearance gave me a great shock. She looked tired and weak. She was listless and far away, and her answers showed that she was dazed and not able to keep perfect run of all that was done and said. Another court would not have taken advantage of her state, seeing that her life was at stake here, but would have adjourned and spared her. Did this one? No; it worried her for hours, and with a glad and eager ferocity, making all it could out of this great chance, the first one it had had.

She was tortured into confusing herself concerning the "sign" which had been given the King, and the next day this was continued hour after hour. As a result, she made partial revealments of particulars forbidden by her Voices; and seemed to me to state as facts things which were but allegories and visions mixed with facts.

The third day she was brighter, and looked less worn. She was almost her normal self again, and did her work well. Many attempts were made to beguile her into saying indiscreet things, but she saw the purpose in view and answered with tact and wisdom.

"Do you know if St. Catherine and St. Marguerite hate the English?"

"They love whom Our Lord loves, and hate whom He hates."

"Does God hate the English?"

"Of the love or the hatred of God toward the English I know nothing." Then she spoke up with the old martial ring in her voice and the old audacity in her words, and added, "But I know this—that God will send victory to the French, and that all the English will be flung out of France but the dead ones!"

"Was God on the side of the English when they were *prosperous* in France?"

"I do not know if God hates the French, but I think that he allowed them to be chastised for their sins."

It was a sufficiently naïve way to account for a chastisement which had now strung out for ninety-six years. But nobody found fault with it. There was nobody there who would not punish a sinner ninety-six years if he could, nor anybody there who would ever dream of such a thing as the Lord's being any shade less stringent than men.

"Have you ever embraced St. Marguerite and St. Catherine?"

"Yes, both of them."

The evil face of Cauchon betrayed satisfaction when she said that.

"When you hung garlands upon *L'Arbre Fée de Bourlemont*, did you do it in honor of your apparitions?"

"No."

Satisfaction again. No doubt Cauchon would take it for granted that she hung them there out of sinful love for the fairies.

"When the saints appeared to you did you bow, did you make reverence, did you kneel?"

"Yes; I did them the most honor and the most reverence that I could."

A good point for Cauchon if he could eventually make it appear that these were no saints to whom she had done reverence, but devils in disguise.

Now there was the matter of Joan's keeping her supernatural commerce a secret from her parents. Much might be made of that. In fact, particular emphasis had been given to it in a private remark written in the margin of the *proces*: "*She concealed her visions from her parents and from every one.*" Possibly this disloyalty to her parents might itself be the sign of the satanic source of her mission.

"Do you think it was right to go away to the wars without getting your parents' leave? It is written one must honor his father and his mother."

"I have obeyed them in all things but that. And for that I have begged their forgiveness in a letter and gotten it."

"Ah, you asked their pardon? So you *knew* you were guilty of sin in going without their leave!"

Joan was stirred. Her eyes flashed, and she exclaimed—

"I was commanded of God, and it was right to go! If I had had a hundred fathers and mothers and been a king's daughter to boot I would have gone."

"Did you never ask your Voices if you might tell your parents?"

"They were willing that I should tell them, but I would not for anything have given my parents that pain."

To the minds of the questioners this headstrong conduct savored of pride. That sort of pride would move one to seek sacrilegious adorations.

"Did not your Voices call you Daughter of God?"

Joan answered with simplicity, and unsuspiciously—

"Yes; before the siege of Orleans and since, they have several times called me Daughter of God."

Further indications of pride and vanity were sought.

"What horse were you riding when you were captured? Who gave it you?"

"The King."

"You had other things—riches—of the King?"

"For myself I had horses and arms, and money to pay the service in my household."

"Had you not a treasury?"

"Yes. Ten or twelve thousand crowns." Then she said with naïveté, "It was not a great sum to carry on a war with."

"You have it yet?"

"No. It is the King's money. My brothers hold it for him."

"What were the arms which you left as an offering in the church of St. Denis?"

"My suit of silver mail and a sword."

"Did you put them there in order that they might be adored?"

"No. It was but an act of devotion. And it is the custom of men of war who have been wounded to make such offering there. I had been wounded before Paris."

Nothing appealed to those stony hearts, those dull imaginations—not even this pretty picture, so simply drawn, of the wounded girl-soldier hanging her toy harness there in curious companionship with the grim and dusty iron mail of the historic defenders of France. No, there was nothing in it for them; nothing, unless evil and injury for that innocent creature could be gotten out of it somehow.

"Which aided most—you the Standard, or the Standard you?"

"Whether it was the Standard or whether it was I, is nothing—the victories came from God."

"But did you base your hopes of victory in yourself or in your Standard?"

"In neither. In God, and not otherwhere."

"Was not your Standard waved around the King's head at the Coronation?"

"No. It was not."

"Why was it that *your* Standard had place at the crowning of the King in the Cathedral of Rheims, rather than those of the other captains?"

Then, soft and low, came that touching speech which will live as long as language lives, and pass into all tongues, and move all gentle hearts wheresoever it shall come, down to the latest day:

*"It had borne the burden, it had earned the honor."**

How simple it is, and how beautiful. And how it beggars the studied eloquence of the masters of oratory. Eloquence was a native gift of Joan of Arc; it came from her lips without effort and without preparation. Her words were as sublime as her deeds, as sublime as her character; they had their source in a great heart and were coined in a great brain.

---

*What she said has been many times translated, but never with success. There is a haunting pathos about the original which eludes all efforts to convey it into our tongue. It is as subtle as an odor, and escapes in the transmission. Her words were these:

"Il avait été a la peine, c'etait bien raison qu'il fut a l'honneur."

Monseigneur Ricard, Honorary Vicar-General to the Archbishop of Aix, finely speaks of it (*"Jeanne d'Arc la Vénérable,"* page 197) as "that sublime reply, enduring in the history of celebrated sayings like the cry of a French and Christian soul wounded unto death in its patriotism and its faith." —TRANSLATOR.

Chapter XII

Now as a next move, this small secret court of holy assassins did a thing so base that even at this day, in my old age, it is hard to speak of it with patience.

In the beginning of her commerce with her Voices there at Domremy, the child Joan solemnly devoted her life to God, vowing her pure body and her pure soul to his service. You will remember that her parents tried to stop her from going to the wars by haling her to the court at Toul to compel her to make a marriage which she had never promised to make—a marriage with our poor, good, windy, big, hard-fighting and most dear and lamented comrade the Standard-bearer, who fell in honorable battle and sleeps in God these sixty years, peace to his ashes! And you will remember how Joan, sixteen years old, stood up in that venerable court and conducted her case all by herself, and tore the poor Paladin's case to rags and blew it away with a breath; and how the astonished old judge on the bench spoke of her as "this marvellous child."

You remember all that. Then think what I felt, to see these false priests here in the tribunal wherein Joan had fought a fourth lone fight in three years, deliberately twist that matter entirely around and try to make out that Joan haled the Paladin into court and pretended that he had promised to marry her, and was bent on making him do it.

Certainly there was no baseness that those people were ashamed to stoop to in their hunt for that friendless girl's life. What they wanted to show was this—that she had committed the sin of relapsing from her vow and trying to violate it.

Joan detailed the true history of the case, but lost her temper as she went along, and finished with some words for Cauchon which he remembers yet, whether he is fanning himself in the world he belongs in or has swindled his way into the other.

The rest of this day and part of the next the court labored upon the old theme—the male attire. It was shabby work for those grave men to be engaged in; for they well knew one of

Joan's reasons for clinging to the male dress was, that soldiers of the guard were always present in her room whether she was asleep or awake, and that the male dress was a better protection for her modesty than the other.

The court knew that one of Joan's purposes had been the deliverance of the exiled Duke of Orleans, and they were curious to know how she had intended to manage it. Her plan was characteristically business-like, and her statement of it as characteristically simple and straightforward:

"I would have taken English prisoners enough in France for his ransom; and failing that, I would have invaded England and brought him out by force."

That was just her way. If a thing was to be done, it was love first, and hammer and tongs to follow; but no shilly-shallying between. She added with a little sigh—

"If I had had my freedom three years, I would have delivered him."

"Have you the permission of your Voices to break out of prison whenever you can?"

"I have asked their leave several times, but they have not given it."

I think it is as I have said, she expected the deliverance of death, and within the prison walls, before the three months should expire.

"Would you escape if you saw the doors open?"

She spoke up frankly and said—

"Yes—for I should see in that the permission of Our Lord. God helps who help themselves, the proverb says. But except I thought I had permission, I would not go."

Now, then, at this point, something occurred which convinces me, every time I think of it—and it struck me so at the time—that for a moment, at least, her hopes wandered to the King, and put into her mind the same notion about her deliverance which Noël and I had settled upon—a rescue by her old soldiers. I think the idea of the rescue did occur to her, but only as a passing thought, and that it quickly passed away.

Some remark of the Bishop of Beauvais moved her to remind him once more that he was an unfair judge, and had no right to preside there, and that he was putting himself in great danger.

"What danger?" he asked.

"I do not know. St. Catherine has promised me help, but I do not know the form of it. I do not know whether I am to be delivered from this prison or whether when you send me to the scaffold there will happen a trouble by which I shall be set free. Without much thought as to this matter, I am of the opinion that it may be one or the other." After a pause she added these words, memorable forever—words whose meaning she may have miscaught, misunderstood, as to that we can never know; words which she may have rightly understood; as to that also, we can never know; but words whose mystery fell away from them many a year ago and revealed their real meaning to all the world:

"But what my Voices have said clearest is, that I shall be delivered *by a great victory.*" She paused, my heart was beating fast, for to me that great victory meant the sudden bursting in of our old soldiers with war-cry and clash of steel at the last moment and the carrying off of Joan of Arc in triumph. But oh, that thought had such a short life! For now she raised her head and finished, with those solemn words which men still so often quote and dwell upon—words which filled me with fear, they sounded so like a prediction. "And always they say 'Submit to whatever comes; *do not grieve for your martyrdom*; from it you will ascend into the Kingdom of Paradise.'"

Was she thinking of fire and the stake? I think not. I thought of it myself, but I believe she was only thinking of this slow and cruel martyrdom of chains and captivity and insult. Surely martyrdom was the right name for it.

It was Jean de la Fontaine who was asking the questions. He was willing to make the most he could out of what she had said:

"As the Voices have told you you are going to Paradise, you feel certain that that will happen and that you will not be damned in hell. Is that so?"

"I believe what they told me. I know that I shall be saved."

"It is a weighty answer."

"To me the knowledge that I shall be saved is a great treasure."

"Do you think that after that revelation you could be able to commit mortal sin?"

"As to that, I do not know. My hope for salvation is in holding fast to my oath to keep my body and my soul pure."

"Since you know you are to be saved do you think it necessary to go to confession?"

The snare was ingeniously devised, but Joan's simple and humble answer left it empty—

"One cannot keep his conscience too clean."

We were now arriving at the last day of this new trial. Joan had come through the ordeal well. It had been a long and wearisome struggle for all concerned. All ways had been tried to convict the accused, and all had failed, thus far. The inquisitors were thoroughly vexed and dissatisfied. However, they resolved to make one more effort, put in one more day's work. This was done—March 17th. Early in the sitting a notable trap was set for Joan:

"Will you submit to the determination of the Church all your words and deeds, whether good or bad?"

That was well planned. Joan was in imminent peril now. If she should heedlessly say yes, it would put her mission *itself* upon trial, and one would know how to decide its source and character promptly. If she should say no, she would render herself chargeable with the crime of heresy.

But she was equal to the occasion. She drew a distinct line of separation between the Church's authority over her as a subject member, and the matter of her *mission*. She said she loved the Church and was ready to support the Christian faith with all her strength; but as to the works done under her mission, those must be judged by God alone, who had commanded them to be done.

The judge still insisted that she submit them to the decision of the Church. She said—

"I will submit them to Our Lord who sent me. It would seem to me that He and His Church are one, and that there should be no difficulty about this matter." Then she turned upon the judge and said, "Why do you make a difficulty where there is no room for any?"

Then Jean de la Fontaine corrected her notion that there was but one Church. There were two—the Church Triumphant, which is God, the saints, the angels, and the redeemed, and has its seat in heaven; and the Church Militant, which is our Holy Father the Pope, Vicar of God, the prelates, the clergy and all good christians and catholics, the which Church has its seat in the earth, is governed by the Holy Spirit, and cannot err. "Will you not submit those matters to the Church Militant?"

"I am come to the King of France from the Church Triumphant on high by its commandment, and to that Church I will submit all those things which I have done. For the Church Militant I have no other answer now."

The court took note of this straightly worded refusal, and would hope to get profit out of it; but the matter was dropped for the present, and a long chase was then made over the old hunting-ground—the fairies, the visions, the male attire, and all that.

In the afternoon the satanic Bishop himself took the chair and presided over the closing scenes of the trial. Along toward the finish, this question was asked by one of the judges:

"You have said to my lord the Bishop that you would answer him as you would answer before our Holy Father the Pope, and yet there are several questions which you continually refuse to answer. Would you not answer the Pope more fully than you have answered before my lord of Beauvais? Would you not feel obliged to answer the Pope, who is the Vicar of God, more fully?"

Now fell a thunder-clap out of a clear sky—

"*Take me to the Pope.* I will answer to everything that I ought to."

It made the Bishop's purple face fairly blanch with consternation. If Joan had only known, if she had only known! She had lodged a mine under this black conspiracy able to blow the Bishop's schemes to the four winds of heaven, and she didn't know it. She had made that speech by mere instinct, not suspecting what tremendous forces were hidden in it, and there was none to tell her what she had done. I knew, and Manchon knew; and if she had known how to read writing we could have hoped to get the knowledge to her somehow; but speech was the only way, and none was allowed to approach her near enough for that. So there she sat, once more Joan of Arc the Victorious, but all unconscious of it. She was miserably worn and tired, by the long day's struggle and by illness, or she must have noticed the effect of that speech and divined the reason of it.

She had made many master-strokes, but this was *the* master-stroke. It was *an appeal to Rome*. It was her clear right; and if she had persisted in it Cauchon's plot would have tumbled about his ears like a house of cards, and he would have gone from that place the worst beaten man of the century. He was daring, but he was not daring enough to stand up against that demand if Joan had urged it. But no, she was ignorant, poor thing, and did not know what a blow she had struck for life and liberty.

France was not the Church. Rome had no interest in the destruction of this messenger of God. Rome would have given her a fair trial, and that was all that her cause needed. From that trial she would have gone forth free and honored and blest.

But it was not so fated. Cauchon at once diverted the questions to other matters and hurried the trial quickly to an end.

As Joan moved feebly away, dragging her chains, I felt stunned and dazed, and kept saying to myself, "Such a little while ago she said the saving word and could have gone free; and now, there she goes to her death; yes, it is to her death, I know it, I feel it. They will double the guards; they will never let any come near her now between this and her condemnation, lest she get a hint and speak that word again. This is the bitterest day that has come to me in all this miserable time."

Chapter XIII

S O THE SECOND TRIAL in the prison was over. Over, and no definite result. The character of it I have described to you. It was baser in one particular than the previous one; for this time the charges had not been communicated to Joan, therefore she had been obliged to fight in the dark. There was no opportunity to do any thinking beforehand; there was no foreseeing what traps might be set, and no way to prepare for them. Truly it was a shabby advantage to take of a girl situated as this one was. One day, during the course of it, an able lawyer of Normandy, Maître Lohier, happened to be in Rouen, and I will give you his opinion of that trial, so that you may see that I have been honest with you, and that my partisanship has not made me deceive you as to its unfair and illegal character. Cauchon showed Lohier the *proces* and asked his opinion about the trial. Now this was the opinion which he gave to Cauchon. He said that the whole thing was null and void; for these reasons: 1, because the trial was secret, and full freedom of speech and action on the part of those present not possible; 2, because the trial touched the honor of the King of France, yet he was not summoned to defend himself, nor any one appointed to represent him; 3, because the charges against the prisoner were not communicated to her; 4, because the accused, although young and simple, had been forced to defend her cause without help of counsel, notwithstanding she had so much at stake.

Did that please Bishop Cauchon? It did not. He burst out upon Lohier with the most savage cursings, and swore he would have him drowned. Lohier escaped from Rouen and got out of France with all speed, and so saved his life.

Well, as I have said, the second trial was over, without definite result. But Cauchon did not give up. He could trump up another. And still another and another, if necessary. He had the half-promise of an enormous prize—the Archbishopric of Rouen—if he should succeed in burning the body and damning to hell the soul of this young girl who had never done him any harm; and such a prize as that, to a man like the

Bishop of Beauvais, was worth the burning and damning of fifty harmless girls, let alone one.

So he set to work again straight off, next day; and with high confidence, too, intimating with brutal cheerfulness that he should succeed this time. It took him and the other scavengers nine days to dig matter enough out of Joan's testimony and their own inventions to build up the new mass of charges. And it was a formidable mass indeed, for it numbered sixty-six articles!

This huge document was carried to the castle the next day, March 27th; and there, before a dozen carefully selected judges, the new trial was begun.

Opinions were taken, and the tribunal decided that Joan should hear the articles read, this time. Maybe that was on account of Lohier's remark upon that head; or maybe it was hoped that the reading would kill the prisoner with fatigue—for, as it turned out, this reading occupied several days. It was also decided that Joan should be required to answer squarely to every article, and that if she refused she should be considered *convicted*. You see, Cauchon was managing to narrow her chances more and more all the time; he was drawing the toils closer and closer.

Joan was brought in, and the Bishop of Beauvais opened with a speech to her which ought to have made even himself blush, so laden it was with hypocrisy and lies. He said that this court was composed of holy and pious churchmen whose hearts were full of benevolence and compassion toward her, and that they had no wish to hurt her body, but only a desire to instruct her and lead her into the way of truth and salvation.

Why, this man was born a devil; now think of his describing himself and those hardened slaves of his in such language as that.

And yet, worse was to come. For now, having in mind another of Lohier's hints, he had the cold effrontery to make to Joan a proposition which I think will surprise you when you hear it. He said that this court, recognizing her untaught estate and her inability to deal with the complex and difficult matters which were about to be considered, had determined, out of their pity and their mercifulness, to allow her to choose

one or more persons *out of their own number* to help her with
counsel and advice!

Think of that—a court made up of Loyseleur and his breed
of reptiles. It was granting leave to a lamb to ask help of a
wolf. Joan looked up to see if he was serious, and perceiving
that he was at least pretending to be, she declined, of course.

The Bishop was not expecting any other reply. He had
made a show of fairness and could have it entered on the
minutes, therefore he was satisfied.

Then he commanded Joan to answer straightly to every accusation; and threatened to cut her off from the Church if she
failed to do that or delayed her answers beyond a given length
of time. Yes, he was narrowing her chances down, step by
step.

Thomas de Courcelles began the reading of that interminable document, article by article. Joan answered to each article
in its turn; sometimes merely denying its truth, sometimes by
saying her answer would be found in the records of the previous trials.

What a strange document that was, and what an exhibition
and exposure of the heart of man, the one creature authorized
to boast that he is made in the image of God. To know Joan
of Arc was to know one who was wholly noble, pure, truthful, brave, compassionate, generous, pious, unselfish, modest,
blameless as the very flowers in the fields—a nature fine and
beautiful, a character supremely great. To know her from that
document would be to know her as the exact reverse of all
that. Nothing that she *was* appears in it, everything that she
was *not* appears there in detail.

Consider some of the things it charges against her, and remember who it is it is speaking of. It calls her a sorceress, a
false prophet, an invoker and companion of evil spirits, a
dealer in magic, a person ignorant of the Catholic faith,
a schismatic; she is sacrilegious, an idolator, an apostate, a
blasphemer of God and his saints, scandalous, seditious, a
disturber of the peace; she incites men to war, and to the
spilling of human blood; she discards the decencies and proprieties of her sex, irreverently assuming the dress of a man
and the vocation of a soldier; she beguiles both princes and

people; she usurps divine honors, and has caused herself to be adored and venerated, offering her hands and her vestments to be kissed.

There it is—every fact of her life distorted, perverted, reversed. As a child she had loved the fairies, she had spoken a pitying word for them when they were banished from their home, she had played under their tree and around their fountain—hence she was a comrade of evil spirits. She had lifted France out of the mud and moved her to strike for freedom, and led her to victory after victory—hence she was a disturber of the peace—as indeed she was, and a provoker of war—as indeed she was again! and France will be proud of it and grateful for it for many a century to come. And she had been adored—as if she could help that, poor thing, or was in any way to blame for it. The cowed veteran and the wavering recruit had drunk the spirit of war from her eyes and touched her sword with theirs and moved forward invincible—hence she was a sorceress.

And so the document went on, detail by detail, turning these waters of life to poison, this gold to dross, these proofs of a noble and beautiful life to evidences of a foul and odious one.

Of course the sixty-six articles were just a rehash of the things which had come up in the course of the previous trials, so I will touch upon this new trial but lightly. In fact Joan went but little into detail herself, usually merely saying "That is not true—*passez outre*"; or, "I have answered that before—let the clerk read it in his record", or saying some other brief thing.

She refused to have her mission examined and tried by the earthly Church. The refusal was taken note of.

She denied the accusation of idolatry and that she had sought men's homage. She said—

"If any kissed my hands and my vestments it was not by my desire, and I did what I could to prevent it."

She had the pluck to say to that deadly tribunal that she did not know the fairies to be evil beings. She knew it was a perilous thing to say, but it was not in her nature to speak anything but the truth when she spoke at all. Danger had no weight with her in such things. Note was taken of her remark.

She refused, as always before, when asked if she would put off the male attire if she were given permission to commune. And she added this:

"When one receives the sacrament, the manner of his dress is a small thing and of no value in the eyes of Our Lord."

She was charged with being so stubborn in clinging to her male dress that she would not lay it off even to get the blessed privilege of hearing mass. She spoke out with spirit and said:

"I would rather die than be untrue to my oath to God."

She was reproached with doing man's work in the wars and thus deserting the industries proper to her sex. She answered, with some little touch of soldierly disdain—

"As to the matter of women's work, there's plenty to do it."

It was always a comfort to me to see the soldier-spirit crop up in her. While that remained in her she would be Joan of Arc, and able to look trouble and fate in the face.

"It appears that this mission of yours which you claim you had from God, was to make war and pour out human blood."

Joan replied quite simply, contenting herself with explaining that war was not her first move, but her second:

"To begin with, I demanded that peace should be made. If it was refused, then I would fight."

The judge mixed the Burgundians and English together in speaking of the enemy which Joan had come to make war upon. But she showed that she made a distinction between them by act and word, the Burgundians being Frenchmen and therefore entitled to less brusque treatment than the English. She said:

"As to the Duke of Burgundy, I required of him, both by letters and by his ambassadors, that he make peace with the King. As to the English, the only peace for them was that they leave the country and go home."

Then she said that even with the English she had shown a pacific disposition, since she had warned them away by proclamation before attacking them.

"If they had listened to me," said she, "they would have done wisely." At this point she uttered her prophecy again, saying with emphasis, "Before seven years they will see it themselves."

Then they presently began to pester her again about her male costume, and tried to persuade her to voluntarily promise to discard it. I was never deep, so I think it no wonder that I was puzzled by their persistency in what seemed a thing of no consequence, and could not make out what their reason could be. But we all know, now. We all know now that it was another of their treacherous projects. Yes, if they could but succeed in getting her to formally discard it they could play a game upon her which would quickly destroy her. So they kept at their evil work until at last she broke out and said—

"Peace! Without the permission of God I will not lay it off though you cut off my head!"

At one point she corrected the *proces verbal*, saying—

"It makes me say that everything which I have done was done by the counsel of Our Lord. I did not say that. I said 'all which I have *well* done.'"

Doubt was cast upon the authenticity of her mission because of the ignorance and simplicity of the messenger chosen. Joan smiled at that. She could have reminded these people that Our Lord, who is no respecter of persons, had chosen the lowly for his high purposes even oftener than he had chosen bishops and cardinals; but she phrased her rebuke in simpler terms:

"It is the prerogative of Our Lord to choose His instruments where He will."

She was asked what form of prayer she used in invoking counsel from on high. She said the form was brief and simple; then she lifted her pallid face and repeated it, clasping her chained hands:

"Most dear God, in honor of your holy passion I beseech you, if you love me, that you will reveal to me what I am to answer to these churchmen. As concerns my dress, I know by what command I have put it on, but I know not in what manner I am to lay it off. I pray you tell me what to do."

She was charged with having dared, against the precepts of God and His saints, to assume empire over men and make herself Commander-in-Chief. That touched the soldier in her. She had a deep reverence for priests, but the soldier in her had but small reverence for a priest's opinions about war; so, in her answer to this charge she did not condescend to go into any explanations or excuses, but delivered herself with bland indifference and military brevity.

"If I was Commander-in-Chief, it was to thrash the English!"

Death was staring her in the face here, all the time, but no matter: she dearly loved to make these English-hearted Frenchmen squirm, and whenever they gave her an opening she was prompt to jab her sting into it. She got great refreshment out of these little episodes. Her days were a desert; these were the oases in it.

Her being in the wars with men was charged against her as an indelicacy. She said—

"I had a woman with me when I could—in towns and lodgings. In the field I always slept in my armor."

That she and her family had been ennobled by the King was charged against her as evidence that the source of her deeds were sordid self-seeking. She answered that she had not asked this grace of the King, it was his own act.

This third trial was ended at last. And once again there was no definite result.

Possibly a fourth trial might succeed in defeating this apparently unconquerable girl. So the malignant Bishop set himself to work to plan it.

He appointed a commission to reduce the substance of the sixty-six articles to twelve compact lies, as a basis for the new attempt. This was done. It took several days.

Meantime Cauchon went to Joan's cell one day, with Manchon and two of the judges, Isambard de la Pierre and Martin Ladvenue, to see if he could not manage somehow to beguile Joan into submitting her mission to the examination and decision of the church militant—that is to say, to that part of the church militant which was represented by himself and his creatures.

Joan once more positively refused. Isambard de la Pierre had a heart in his body, and he so pitied this persecuted poor girl that he ventured to do a very daring thing; for he asked her if she would be willing to have her case go before the

Council of Basel, and said it contained as many priests of her party as of the English party.

Joan cried out that she would gladly go before so fairly constructed a tribunal as that, but before Isambard could say another word, Cauchon turned savagely upon him and exclaimed—

"Shut up, in the devil's name!"

Then Manchon ventured to do a brave thing, too, though he did it in great fear for his life. He asked Cauchon if he should enter Joan's submission to the Council of Basel upon the minutes.

"No! It is not necessary."

"Ah," said poor Joan, reproachfully, "you set down everything that is against me, but you will not set down what is for me."

It was piteous. It would have touched the heart of a brute. But Cauchon was more than that.

Chapter XIV

W E WERE now in the first days of April. Joan was ill. She had fallen ill the 29th of March, the day after the close of the third trial, and was growing worse when the scene which I have just described occurred in her cell. It was just like Cauchon to go there and try to get some advantage out of her weakened state.

Let us note some of the particulars in the new indictment —the Twelve Lies.

Part of the first one says Joan asserts that she has found her salvation. She never said anything of the kind. It also says she refuses to submit herself to the Church. Not true. She was willing to submit all her acts to this Rouen tribunal except those done by command of God in fulfilment of her mission. Those she reserved for the judgment of God. She refused to recognize Cauchon and his serfs as the Church, but was willing to go before the Pope or the Council of Basel.

A clause of another of the Twelve says she admits having threatened with death those who would not obey her. Distinctly false. Another clause says she declares that all she has done has been done by command of God. What she really said was, all that she had done *well*—a correction made by herself as you have already seen.

Another of the Twelve says she claims that she has never committed any sin. She never made any such claim.

Another makes the wearing of the male dress a sin. If it was, she had high Catholic authority for committing it—that of the Archbishop of Rheims and the tribunal of Poitiers.

The Tenth Article was resentful against her for "pretending" that St. Catherine and St. Marguerite spoke French and not English, and were French in their politics.

The Twelve were to be submitted first to the learned doctors of theology of the University of Paris for approval. They were copied out and ready by the night of April 4th. Then Manchon did another bold thing: he wrote in the margin that many of the Twelve put statements in Joan's mouth which were the exact opposite of what she had said. *That* fact would not be considered important by the University of Paris, and would not influence its decision or stir its humanity, in case it had any—which it hadn't when acting in a political capacity, as at present—but it was a brave thing for that good Manchon to do, all the same.

The Twelve were sent to Paris next day, April 5th. That afternoon there was a great tumult in Rouen, and excited crowds were flocking through all the chief streets, chattering and seeking for news; for a report had gone abroad that Joan of Arc was sick unto death. In truth these long seances had worn her out, and she was ill indeed. The heads of the English party were in a state of consternation; for if Joan should die uncondemned by the Church and go to the grave unsmirched, the pity and the love of the people would turn her wrongs and sufferings and death into a holy martyrdom, and she would be even a mightier power in France dead, than she had been when alive.

The Earl of Warwick and the English Cardinal (Winchester) hurried to the castle and sent messengers flying for physicians. Warwick was a hard man, a rude coarse man, a man without compassion. There lay the sick girl stretched in her chains in her iron cage—not an object to move man to ungentle speech, one would think; yet Warwick spoke right out in her hearing and said to the physicians—

"Mind you take good care of her. The King of England has no mind to have her die a natural death. She is dear to him, for he bought her dear, and he does not want her to die, save at the stake. Now then, mind you cure her."

The doctors asked Joan what had made her ill. She said the Bishop of Beauvais had sent her a fish and she thought it was that.

Then Jean d'Estivet burst out on her, and called her names and abused her. He understood Joan to be charging the Bishop with poisoning her, you see; and that was not pleasing to him, for he was one of Cauchon's most loving and conscienceless slaves, and it outraged him to have Joan injure his master in the eyes of these great English chiefs, these being men who could ruin Cauchon and would promptly do it if they got the conviction that he was capable of saving Joan from the stake by poisoning her and thus cheating the

English out of all the real value gainable by her purchase from the Duke of Burgundy.

Joan had a high fever, and the doctors proposed to bleed her. Warwick said—

"Be careful about that; she is smart and is capable of killing herself."

He meant that to escape the stake she might undo the bandage and let herself bleed to death.

But the doctors bled her anyway, and then she was better.

Not for long, though. Jean d'Estivet could not hold still, he was so worried and angry about the suspicion of poisoning which Joan had hinted at; so he came back in the evening and stormed at her till he brought the fever all back again.

When Warwick heard of this he was in a fine temper, you may be sure, for here was his prey threatening to escape again, and all through the over-zeal of this meddling fool. Warwick gave D'Estivet a quite admirable cursing—admirable as to strength, I mean, for it was said by persons of culture that the art of it was not good—and after that the meddler kept still.

Joan remained ill more than two weeks; then she grew better. She was still very weak, but she could bear a little persecution now without much danger to her life. It seemed to Cauchon a good time to furnish it. So he called together some of his doctors of theology and went to her dungeon. Manchon and I went along to keep the record—that is, to set down what might be useful to Cauchon, and leave out the rest.

The sight of Joan gave me a shock. Why, she was but a shadow! It was difficult for me to realize that this frail little creature with the sad face and drooping form was the same Joan of Arc that I had so often seen, all fire and enthusiasm, charging through a hail of death and the lightning and thunder of the guns at the head of her battalions. It wrung my heart to see her looking like this.

But Cauchon was not touched. He made another of those conscienceless speeches of his, all dripping with hypocrisy and guile. He told Joan that among her answers had been some which had seemed to endanger religion; and as she was ignorant and without knowledge of the Scriptures, he had brought some good and wise men to instruct her, if she desired it. Said he, "We are churchmen, and disposed by our good will as well as by our vocation to procure for you the salvation of your soul and your body, in every way in our power, just as we would do the like for our nearest kin or for ourselves. In this we but follow the example of Holy Church, who never closes the refuge of her bosom against any that are willing to return."

Joan thanked him for these sayings and said:

"I seem to be in danger of death from this malady; if it be the pleasure of God that I die here, I beg that I may be heard in confession and also receive my Saviour; and that I may be buried in consecrated ground."

Cauchon thought he saw his opportunity at last; this weakened body had the fear of an unblessed death before it and the pains of hell to follow. This stubborn spirit would surrender now. So he spoke out and said—

"Then if you want the Sacraments, you must do as all good Catholics do, and submit to the Church."

He was eager for her answer; but when it came there was no surrender in it, she still stood to her guns. She turned her head away and said wearily—

"I have nothing more to say."

Cauchon's temper was stirred, and he raised his voice threateningly and said that the more she was in danger of death the more she ought to amend her life; and again he refused the things she begged for unless she would submit to the Church. Joan said—

"If I die in this prison I beg you to have me buried in holy ground; if you will not, I cast myself upon my Saviour."

There was some more conversation of the like sort, then Cauchon demanded again, and imperiously, that she submit herself and all her deeds to the Church. His threatening and storming went for nothing. That body was weak, but the spirit in it was the spirit of Joan of Arc; and out of that came the steadfast answer which these people were already so familiar with and detested so sincerely—

"Let come what may, I will neither do nor say any otherwise than I have said already in your tribunals."

Then the good theologians took turn about and worried her with reasonings and arguments and Scriptures; and always they held the lure of the Sacraments before her famishing soul, and tried to bribe her with them to surrender her mission to the Church's judgment—that is to *their* judgment—as if *they* were the Church! But it availed nothing. I could have told them that beforehand, if they had asked me. But they never asked me anything; I was too humble a creature for their notice.

Then the interview closed with a threat; a threat of fearful import; a threat calculated to make a Catholic Christian feel as if the ground were sinking from under him—

"The Church calls upon you to submit; disobey, and she will abandon you as if you were a pagan!"

Think of being abandoned by the Church!—that august Power in whose hands is lodged the fate of the human race; whose sceptre stretches beyond the furthest constellation that twinkles in the sky; whose authority is over the millions that live and over the billions that wait trembling in purgatory for ransom or doom; whose smile opens the gates of Heaven to you, whose frown delivers you to the fires of everlasting hell; a Power whose dominion overshadows and belittles earthly empire as earthly empire overshadows and belittles the pomps and shows of a village. To be abandoned by one's King—yes, that is death, and death is much; but to be abandoned by Rome, to be abandoned by the Church! Ah, death is nothing to that, for that is consignment to endless *life*—and such a life!

I could see the red waves tossing in that shoreless lake of fire, I could see the black myriads of the damned rise out of them and struggle and sink and rise again; and I knew that Joan was seeing what I saw, while she paused musing; and I believed that she must yield now, and in truth I hoped she would, for these men were able to make the threat good and deliver her over to eternal suffering, and I knew that it was in their natures to do it.

But I was foolish to think that thought and hope that hope. Joan of Arc was not made as others are made. Fidelity to principle, fidelity to truth, fidelity to her word, all these were in her bone and in her flesh—they were parts of her. She could not change, she could not cast them out. She was the very genius of Fidelity, she was Steadfastness incarnated. Where she had taken her stand and planted her foot, there she would abide; hell itself could not move her from that place.

Her Voices had not given her permission to make the sort of submission that was required, therefore she would stand fast. She would wait, in perfect obedience, let come what might.

My heart was like lead in my body when I went out from that dungeon; but she—she was serene, she was not troubled. She had done what she believed to be her duty, and that was sufficient; the consequences were not her affair. The last thing she said, that time, was full of this serenity, full of contented repose—

"I am a good Christian born and baptized, and a good Christian I will die."

Chapter XV

Two weeks went by; the second of May was come, the chill was departed out of the air, the wild flowers were springing in the glades and glens, the birds were piping in the woods, all nature was brilliant with sunshine, all spirits were renewed and refreshed, all hearts glad, the world was alive with hope and cheer, the plain beyond the Seine stretched away soft and rich and green, the river was limpid and lovely, the leafy islands were dainty to see, and flung still daintier reflections of themselves upon the shining water; and from the tall bluffs above the bridge Rouen was become again a delight to the eye, the most exquisite and satisfying picture of a town that nestles under the arch of heaven anywhere.

When I say that all hearts were glad and hopeful, I mean it in a general sense. There were exceptions—we who were the friends of Joan of Arc, also Joan of Arc herself, that poor girl shut up there in that frowning stretch of mighty walls and towers: brooding in darkness, so close to the flooding downpour of sunshine yet so impossibly far away from it; so longing for any little glimpse of it, yet so implacably denied it by those wolves in the black gowns who were plotting her death and the blackening of her good name.

Cauchon was ready to go on with his miserable work. He had a new scheme to try, now. He would see what persuasion could do—argument, eloquence, poured out upon the incorrigible captive from the mouth of a trained expert. That was his plan. But the reading of the Twelve Articles to her was not a part of it. No, even Cauchon was ashamed to lay that monstrosity before her; even he had a remnant of shame in him, away down deep, a million fathoms deep, and that remnant asserted itself now and prevailed.

On this fair second of May, then, the black company gathered itself together in the spacious chamber at the end of the great hall of the castle—the Bishop of Beauvais on his throne, and sixty-two minor judges massed before him, with the guards and recorders at their stations and the orator at his desk.

Then we heard the far clank of chains, and presently Joan entered with her keepers and took her seat upon her isolated bench. She was looking well, now, and most fair and beautiful after her fortnight's rest from wordy persecution.

She glanced about and noted the orator. Doubtless she divined the situation.

The orator had written his speech all out, and had it in his hand, though he held it back of him out of sight. It was so thick that it resembled a book. He began flowingly, but in the midst of a flowery period his memory failed him and he had to snatch a furtive glance at his manuscript—which much injured the effect. Again this happened, and then a third time. The poor man's face was red with embarrassment, the whole great house was pitying him, which made the matter worse; then Joan dropped in a remark which completed his trouble. She said:

"*Read your book*—and then I will answer you!"

Why, it was almost cruel the way those mouldy veterans laughed; and as for the orator, he looked so flustered and helpless that almost anybody would have pitied him, and I had difficulty to keep from doing it myself. Yes, Joan was feeling very well after her rest, and the native mischief that was in her lay near the surface. It did not show, when she made the remark, but I knew it was close in there back of the words.

When the orator had gotten back his composure he did a wise thing; for he followed Joan's advice: he made no more attempts at sham impromptu oratory, but read his speech straight from his "book." In the speech he compressed the Twelve Articles into six and made these his text.

Every now and then he stopped and asked questions, and Joan replied. The nature of the church militant was explained, and once more Joan was asked to submit herself to it.

She gave her usual answer.

Then she was asked—

"Do you believe the Church can err?"

"I believe it cannot err; but for those deeds and words of mine which were done and uttered by command of God, I will answer to him alone."

"Will you say that you have no judge upon earth? Is not our Holy Father the Pope your judge?"

"I will say nothing to you about it. I have a good Master who is our Lord and to Him I will submit all."

Then came these terrible words:

"If you do not submit to the Church you will be pronounced a heretic by these judges here present and burned at the stake!"

Ah, that would have smitten you or me dead with fright, but it only roused the lion heart of Joan of Arc, and in her answer rang that martial note which had used to stir her soldiers like a bugle-call—

"I will not say otherwise than I have said already; and if I saw the fire before me I would say it again!"

It was uplifting to hear her battle-voice once more and see the battle-light burn in her eye. Many there were stirred; every man that was a *man* was stirred, whether friend or foe; and Manchon risked his life again, good soul, for he wrote in the margin of the record in good plain letters these brave words: *"Superba responsio!"* and there they have remained these sixty years, and there you may read them to this day.

"Superba responsio!" Yes, it was just that. For this "superb answer" came from the lips of a girl of nineteen with death and hell staring her in the face.

Of course the matter of the male attire was gone over again; and as usual at wearisome length; also, as usual, the customary bribe was offered: if she would discard that dress voluntarily they would let her hear mass. But she answered as she had often answered before—

"I will go in a woman's robe to all services of the church if I may be permitted, but I will resume the other dress when I return to my cell."

They set several traps for her in a tentative form; that is to say, they placed supposititious propositions before her and cunningly tried to commit her to one end of the propositions without committing themselves to the other. But she always saw the game and spoiled it. The trap was in this form—

"Would you be willing to do so and so if we should give you leave?"

Her answer was always in this form or to this effect:

"When you give me leave, then you will know."

Yes, Joan was at her best, that second of May. She had all

her wits about her, and they could not catch her anywhere. It was a long, long session, and all the old ground was fought over again, foot by foot, and the orator-expert worked all his persuasions, all his eloquence; but the result was the familiar one—a drawn battle, the sixty-two retiring upon their base, the solitary enemy holding her original position within her original lines.

Chapter XVI

THE BRILLIANT WEATHER, the heavenly weather, the bewitching weather made everybody's heart to sing, as I have told you; yes, Rouen was feeling light-hearted and gay, and most willing and ready to break out and laugh upon the least occasion; and so when the news went around that the young girl in the tower had scored another defeat against Bishop Cauchon there was abundant laughter—abundant laughter among the citizens of both parties, for they all hated the Bishop. It is true, the English-hearted majority of the people wanted Joan burned, but that did not keep them from laughing at the man they hated. It would have been perilous for anybody to laugh at the English chiefs or at the majority of Cauchon's assistant judges, but to laugh at Cauchon or D'Estivet and Loyseleur was safe—nobody would report it.

The difference between Cauchon and *cochon** was not noticeable in speech, and so there was plenty of opportunity for puns: the opportunities were not thrown away.

Some of the jokes got well worn in the course of two or three months, from repeated use; for every time Cauchon started a new trial the folk said "The sow has littered† again"; and every time the trial failed they said it over again, with its other meaning, "The hog has made a mess of it."

And so, on the third of May, Noël and I, drifting about the town, heard many a wide-mouthed lout let go his joke and his laugh, and then move to the next group, proud of his wit and happy, to work it off again—

" 'Ods blood, the sow has littered five times, and five times has made a mess of it!"

And now and then one was bold enough to say—but he said it softly—

"Sixty-three and the might of England against a girl, and she camps on the field five times!"

Cauchon lived in the great palace of the Archbishop, and it

*Hog, pig.
†*Cochonner*, to litter, to farrow; also, "to make a mess of!"

was guarded by English soldiery; but no matter, there was never a dark night but the walls showed, next morning, that the rude joker had been there with his paint and brush. Yes, he had been there, and had smeared the sacred walls with pictures of hogs in all attitudes except flattering ones; hogs clothed in a Bishop's vestments and wearing a Bishop's mitre irreverently cocked on the side of their heads.

Cauchon raged and cursed over his defeats and his impotence during seven days, then he conceived a new scheme. You shall see what it was; for you have not cruel hearts, and you would never guess it.

On the ninth of May there was a summons, and Manchon and I got our materials together and started. But this time we were to go to one of the other towers—not the one which was Joan's prison. It was round and grim and massive, and built of the plainest and thickest and solidest masonry—a dismal and forbidding structure.*

We entered the circular room on the ground floor, and I saw what turned me sick—the instruments of torture and the executioners standing ready! Here you have the black heart of Cauchon at the blackest, here you have the proof that in his nature there was no such thing as pity. One wonders if he ever knew his mother or ever had a sister.

Cauchon was there, and the Vice-Inquisitor and the Abbot of St. Corneille; also six others, among them that false Loyseleur. The guards were in their places, the rack was there, and by it stood the executioner and his aids in their crimson hose and doublets, meet color for their bloody trade. The picture of Joan rose before me stretched upon the rack, her feet tied to one end of it, her wrists to the other, and those red giants turning the windlass and pulling her limbs out of their sockets. It seemed to me that I could hear the bones snap and the flesh tear apart, and I did not see how that body of anointed servants of the merciful Jesus could sit there and look so placid and indifferent.

After a little, Joan arrived and was brought in. She saw the rack, she saw its attendants, and the same picture which I had

---

*The lower half of it remains to-day just as it was then; the upper half is of a later date.—TRANSLATOR.

been seeing must have risen in her mind; but do you think she quailed, do you think she shuddered? No, there was no sign of that sort. She straightened herself up, and there was a slight curl of scorn about her lip; but as for fear, she showed not a vestige of it.

This was a memorable session, but it was the shortest one of all the list. When Joan had taken her seat a résumé of her "crimes" was read to her. Then Cauchon made a solemn speech. In it he said that in the course of her several trials Joan had refused to answer some of the questions and had answered others with lies, but that now he was going to have the truth out of her, and the whole of it.

His manner was full of confidence this time; he was sure he had found a way at last to break this child's stubborn spirit and make her beg and cry. He would score a victory this time and stop the mouths of the jokers of Rouen. You see, he was only just a man, after all, and couldn't stand ridicule any better than other people. He talked high, and his splotchy face lighted itself up with all the shifting tints and signs of evil pleasure and promised triumph—purple, yellow, red, green—they were all there, with sometimes the dull and spongy blue of a drowned man, the uncanniest of them all. And finally he burst out in a great passion and said—

"There is the rack, and there are its ministers! You will reveal all, now, or be put to the torture. Speak."

Then she made that great answer, which will live forever; made it without fuss or bravado, and yet how fine and noble was the sound of it—

"I will tell you nothing more than I have told you; no, not even if you tear the limbs from my body. And even if in my pain I *did* say something otherwise, I would always say afterwards that it was the torture that spoke and not I."

There was no crushing that spirit. You should have seen Cauchon. Defeated again, and he had not dreamed of such a thing. I heard it said next day, around the town, that he had a full confession, all written out, in his pocket and all ready for Joan to sign. I do not know that that was true, but it probably was, for her mark signed at the bottom of a confession would be the kind of evidence (for effect with the public) which Cauchon and his people would particularly value, you know.

No, there was no crushing that spirit, and no beclouding that clear mind. Consider the depth, the wisdom of that answer, coming from an ignorant girl. Why, there were not six men in the world who had ever reflected that words forced out of a person by horrible tortures were not necessarily words of verity and truth, yet this unlettered peasant girl put her finger upon that flaw with an unerring instinct. I had always supposed that torture brought out the truth—everybody supposed it; and when Joan came out with those simple common-sense words they seemed to flood the place with light. It was like a lightning-flash at midnight which suddenly reveals a fair valley sprinkled over with silver streams and gleaming villages and farmsteads where was only an impenetrable world of darkness before. Manchon stole a sidewise look at me, and his face was full of surprise; and there was the like to be seen in other faces there. Consider—they were old, and deeply cultured, yet here was a village maid able to teach them something which they had not known before. I heard one of them mutter—

"Verily it is a wonderful creature. She has laid her hand upon an accepted truth that is as old as the world, and it has crumbled to dust and rubbish under her touch. Now whence got she that marvellous insight?"

The judges laid their heads together and began to talk low. It was plain, from chance words which one caught now and then, that Cauchon and Loyseleur were insisting upon the application of the torture, and that most of the others were urgently objecting.

Finally Cauchon broke out with a good deal of asperity in his voice and ordered Joan back to her dungeon. That was a happy surprise for me. I was not expecting that the Bishop would yield.

When Manchon came home that night he said he had found out why the torture was not applied. There were two reasons. One was, a fear that Joan might die under the torture, which would not suit the English at all; the other was, that the torture would effect nothing if Joan was going to take back everything she said under its pains; and as to putting her mark to a confession, it was believed that not even the rack could ever make her do that.

So all Rouen laughed again, and kept it up for three days, saying—

"The sow has littered six times, and made six messes of it."

And the palace walls got a new decoration—a mitred hog carrying a discarded rack home on its shoulder, and Loyseleur weeping in its wake. Many rewards were offered for the capture of these painters, but nobody applied. Even the English guard feigned blindness and would not see the artists at work.

The Bishop's anger was very high now. He could not reconcile himself to the idea of giving up the torture. It was the pleasantest idea he had invented yet, and he would not cast it by. So he called in some of his satellites on the twelfth, and urged the torture again. But it was a failure. With some, Joan's speech had wrought an effect; others feared she might die under the torture; others did not believe that any amount of suffering could make her put her mark to a lying confession. There were fourteen men present, including the Bishop. Eleven of them voted dead against the torture, and stood their ground in spite of Cauchon's abuse. Two voted with the Bishop and insisted upon the torture. These two were Loyseleur and the orator—the man whom Joan had bidden to "read his book"—Thomas de Courcelles, the renowned pleader, and master of eloquence.

Age has taught me charity of speech; but it fails me when I think of those three names—Cauchon, Courcelles, Loyseleur.

Chapter XVII

ANOTHER ten days' wait. The great theologians of that treasury of all valuable knowledge and all wisdom, the University of Paris, were still weighing and considering and discussing the Twelve Lies.

I had but little to do, these ten days, so I spent them mainly in walks about the town with Noël. But there was no pleasure in them, our spirits being so burdened with cares, and the outlook for Joan growing so steadily darker and darker all the time. And then we naturally contrasted our circumstances with hers: this freedom and sunshine, with her darkness and chains; our comradeship, with her lonely estate; our alleviations of one sort and another, with her destitution in all. She was used to liberty, but now she had none; she was an out-of-door creature by nature and habit, but now she was shut up day and night in a steel cage like an animal; she was used to the light, but now she was always in a gloom where all objects about her were dim and spectral; she was used to the thousand various sounds which are the cheer and music of a busy life, but now she heard only the monotonous footfall of the sentry pacing his watch; she had been fond of talking with her mates, but now there was no one to talk to; she had had an easy laugh, but it was gone dumb, now; she had been born for comradeship, and blithe and busy work, and all manner of joyous activities, but here were only dreariness, and leaden hours, and weary inaction, and brooding stillness, and thoughts that travel day and night and night and day round and round in the same circle, and wear the brain and break the heart with weariness. It was death in life; yes, death in life, that is what it must have been. And there was another hard thing about it all. A young girl in trouble needs the soothing solace and support and sympathy of persons of her own sex, and the delicate offices and gentle ministries which only these can furnish; yet in all these months of gloomy captivity in her dungeon Joan never saw the face of a girl or a woman. Think how her heart would have leaped to see such a face.

Consider. If you would realize how great Joan of Arc was, remember that it was out of such a place and such circumstances that she came week after week and month after month and confronted the master intellects of France single-handed, and baffled their cunningest schemes, defeated their ablest plans, detected and avoided their secretest traps and pitfalls, broke their lines, repelled their assaults, and camped on the field after every engagement; steadfast always, true to her faith and her ideals; defying torture, defying the stake, and answering threats of eternal death and the pains of hell with a simple "Let come what may, here I take my stand and will abide."

Yes, if you would realize how great was the soul, how profound the wisdom, and how luminous the intellect of Joan of Arc, you must study her there, where she fought out that long fight all alone—and not merely against the subtlest brains and deepest learning of France, but against the ignoblest deceits, the meanest treacheries, and the hardest hearts to be found in any land, pagan or Christian.

She was great in battle—we all know that; great in foresight; great in loyalty and patriotism; great in persuading discontented chiefs and reconciling conflicting interests and passions, great in the ability to discover merit and genius wherever it lay hidden; great in picturesque and eloquent speech; supremely great in the gift of firing the hearts of hopeless men with noble enthusiasms, the gift of turning hares into heroes, slaves and skulkers into battalions that march to death with songs upon their lips. But all these are exalting activities; they keep hand and heart and brain keyed up to their work: there is the joy of achievement, the inspiration of stir and movement, the applause which hails success; the soul is overflowing with life and energy, the faculties are at white heat; weariness, despondency, inertia—these do not exist.

Yes, Joan of Arc was great always, great everywhere, but she was greatest in the Rouen trials. There she rose above the limitations and infirmities of our human nature, and accomplished under blighting and unnerving and hopeless conditions all that her splendid equipment of moral and intellectual forces could have accomplished if they had been supplemented by the mighty helps of hope and cheer and light, the presence of friendly faces, and a fair and equal fight, with the great world looking on and wondering.

Chapter XVIII

OWARD THE END of the ten-day interval the University of
Paris rendered its decision concerning the Twelve Articles. By this finding, Joan was guilty upon all the counts: she
must renounce her errors and make satisfaction, or be abandoned to the secular arm for punishment.

The University's mind was probably already made up before the Articles were laid before it; yet it took it from the
fifth to the eighteenth to produce its verdict. I think the delay
may have been caused by temporary difficulties concerning
two points:

1, As to who the fiends were who were represented in Joan's
Voices;

2, As to whether her saints spoke French only.

You understand, the University decided emphatically that it
was fiends who spoke in those Voices; it would need to prove
that, and it did. It found out who the fiends were, and named
them in the verdict: Belial, Satan, and Behemoth. This has
always seemed a doubtful thing to me, and not entitled to
much credit. I think so for this reason: if the University had
actually known it was those three, it would for very consisten-
cy's sake have told *how* it knew it, and not stopped with the
mere assertion, since it had made Joan explain how she knew
they were *not* fiends. Does not that seem reasonable? To my
mind the University's position was weak, and I will tell you
why. It had claimed that Joan's angels were devils in disguise,
and we all know that devils do disguise themselves as angels;
up to that point the University's position was strong; but you
see yourself that it eats its own argument when it turns
around and pretends that *it* can tell who such apparitions are,
while denying the like ability to a person with as good a
head on her shoulders as the best one the University could
produce.

The doctors of the University had to see those creatures in
order to know; and if Joan was deceived, it is argument that
they in their turn could also be deceived, for their insight and
judgment were surely not clearer than hers.

As to the other point which I have thought may have proved a difficulty and cost the University delay, I will touch but a moment upon that, and pass on. The University decided that it was blasphemy for Joan to say that her saints spoke French and not English, and were on the French side in political sympathies. I think that the thing which troubled the doctors of theology was this: they had decided that the three Voices were Satan and two other devils; but they had also decided that these Voices were *not* on the French side— thereby tacitly asserting that they were on the English side; and if on the English side, then they must be angels and not devils. Otherwise, the situation was embarrassing. You see, the University being the wisest and deepest and most erudite body in the world, it would like to be logical if it could, for the sake of its reputation; therefore it would study and study, days and days, trying to find some good common-sense reason for proving the Voices devils in Article No. 1 and proving them angels in Article No. 10. However, they had to give it up. They found no way out: and so, to this day the University's verdict remains just so—devils in No. 1, angels in No. 10; and no way to reconcile the discrepancy.

The envoys brought the verdict to Rouen, and with it a letter for Cauchon which was full of fervid praise. The University complimented him on his zeal in hunting down this woman "whose venom had infected the faithful of the whole West," and as recompense it as good as promised him "a crown of imperishable glory in heaven." Only *that!*—a crown in heaven; a promissory note and no indorser; always something away off yonder; not a word about the Archbishopric of Rouen, which was the thing Cauchon was destroying his soul for. A crown in heaven; it must have sounded like a sarcasm to him, after all his hard work. What should *he* do in heaven? he did not know anybody there.

On the nineteenth of May a court of fifty judges sat in the archiepiscopal palace to discuss Joan's fate. A few wanted her delivered over to the secular arm at once for punishment, but the rest insisted that she be once more "charitably admonished" first.

So the same court met in the castle on the twenty-third, and Joan was brought to the bar. Pierre Maurice, a canon of

Rouen, made a speech to Joan in which he admonished her to save her life and her soul by renouncing her errors and surrendering to the Church. He finished with a stern threat: if she remained obstinate the damnation of her soul was certain, the destruction of her body probable. But Joan was immovable. She said—

"If I were under sentence, and saw the fire before me, and the executioner ready to light it—more, if I were in the fire itself, I would say none but the things which I have said in these trials; and I would abide by them till I died."

A deep silence followed, now, which endured some moments. It lay upon me like a weight. I knew it for an omen. Then Cauchon, grave and solemn, turned to Pierre Maurice—

"Have you anything further to say?"

The priest bowed low, and said—

"Nothing, my lord."

"Prisoner at the bar, have you anything further to say?"

"Nothing."

"Then the debate is closed. To-morrow, sentence will be pronounced. Remove the prisoner."

She seemed to go from the place erect and noble. But I do not know; my sight was dim with tears.

To-morrow—twenty-fourth of May! Exactly a year since I saw her go speeding across the plain at the head of her troops, her silver helmet shining, her silvery cape fluttering in the wind, her white plumes flowing, her sword held aloft; saw her charge the Burgundian camp three times, and carry it; saw her wheel to the right and spur for the Duke's reserve; saw her fling herself against it in the last assault she was ever to make. And now that fatal day was come again—and see what it was bringing!

Chapter XIX

JOAN had been adjudged guilty of heresy, sorcery, and all the other terrible crimes set forth in the Twelve Articles, and her life was in Cauchon's hands at last. He could send her to the stake at once. His work was finished now, you think? He was satisfied? Not at all. What would his Archbishopric be worth if the people should get the idea into their heads that this faction of interested priests, slaving under the English lash, had wrongly condemned and burned Joan of Arc, Deliverer of France? That would be to make of her a holy martyr. Then her spirit would rise from her body's ashes, a thousand-fold reinforced, and sweep the English domination into the sea, and Cauchon along with it. No, the victory was not complete yet. Joan's guilt must be established by evidence which would satisfy the people. Where was that evidence to be found? There was only one person in the world who could furnish it—*Joan of Arc herself.* She must condemn herself, and in public—at least she must *seem* to do it.

But how was this to be managed? Weeks had been spent already in trying to get her to surrender—time wholly wasted; what was to persuade her now? Torture had been threatened, the fire had been threatened; what was left? Illness, deadly fatigue, and the sight of the fire, the presence of the fire! That was left.

Now that was a shrewd thought. She was but a girl, after all, and, under illness and exhaustion, subject to a girl's weaknesses.

Yes, it was shrewdly thought. She had tacitly said, herself, that under the bitter pains of the rack they would be able to extort a false confession from her. It was a hint worth remembering, and it was remembered.

She had furnished another hint at the same time: that as soon as the pains were gone, she would retract the confession. That hint was also remembered.

She had herself taught them what to do, you see. First, they must wear out her strength, then frighten her with the fire.

Second, while the fright was on her, she must be made to sign a paper.

But she would demand a reading of the paper. They could not venture to refuse this, with the public there to hear. Suppose that during the reading her courage should return? she would refuse to sign, then. Very well, even that difficulty could be got over. They could read a short paper of no importance, then slip a long and deadly one into its place and trick her into signing *that*.

Yet there was still one other difficulty. If they made her seem to abjure, that would free her from the death penalty. They could keep her in a prison of the Church, but they could not kill her. That would not answer; for only her death would content the English. Alive she was a terror, in a prison or out of it. She had escaped from two prisons already.

But even that difficulty could be managed. Cauchon would make promises to her; in return, she would promise to leave off the male dress. He would violate his promises, and that would so situate her that she would not be able to keep hers. Her lapse would condemn her to the stake, and the stake would be ready.

These were the several moves; there was nothing to do but to make them, each in its order, and the game was won. One might almost name the day that the betrayed girl, the most innocent creature in France, and the noblest, would go to her pitiful death.

And the time was favorable—cruelly favorable. Joan's spirit had as yet suffered no decay, it was as sublime and masterful as ever; but her body's forces had been steadily wasting away in those last ten days, and a strong mind needs a healthy body for its rightful support.

The world knows, now, that Cauchon's plan was as I have sketched it to you, but the world did not know it at that time. There are sufficient indications that Warwick and all the other English chiefs except the highest one—the Cardinal of Winchester—were not let into the secret; also, that only Loyseleur and Beaupère, on the French side, knew the scheme. Sometimes I have doubted if even Loyseleur and Beaupère knew the whole of it at first. However, if any did, it was these two.

It is usual to let the condemned pass their last night of life in peace, but this grace was denied to poor Joan, if one may credit the rumors of the time. Loyseleur was smuggled into her presence, and in the character of priest, friend, and secret partisan of France and hater of England, he spent some hours in beseeching her to do "the only right and righteous thing"—submit to the Church, as a good Christian should; and that then she would straightway get out of the clutches of the dreaded English and be transferred to the Church's prison, where she would be honorably used and have women about her for jailers. He knew where to touch her. He knew how odious to her was the presence of her rough and profane English guards; he knew that her Voices had vaguely promised something which she interpreted to be escape, rescue, release of some sort, and the chance to burst upon France once more and victoriously complete the great work which she had been commissioned of Heaven to do. Also there was that other thing: if her failing body could be further weakened by loss of rest and sleep, now, her tired mind would be dazed and drowsy on the morrow, and in ill condition to stand out against persuasions, threats, and the sight of the stake, and also be purblind to traps and snares which it would be swift to detect when in its normal estate.

I do not need to tell you that there was no rest for me that night. Nor for Noël. We went to the main gate of the city before nightfall, with a hope in our minds, based upon that vague prophecy of Joan's Voices which seemed to promise a rescue by force at the last moment. The immense news had flown swiftly far and wide that at last Joan of Arc was condemned, and would be sentenced and burned alive on the morrow; and so, crowds of people were flowing in at the gate, and other crowds were being refused admission by the soldiery; these being people who brought doubtful passes or none at all. We scanned these crowds eagerly, but there was nothing about them to indicate that they were our old war-comrades in disguise, and certainly there were no familiar faces among them. And so, when the gate was closed at last, we turned away grieved, and more disappointed than we cared to admit, either in speech or thought.

The streets were surging tides of excited men. It was difficult to make one's way. Toward midnight our aimless tramp brought us to the neighborhood of the beautiful church of St. Ouen, and there all was bustle and work. The square was a wilderness of torches and people; and through a guarded passage dividing the pack, laborers were carrying planks and timbers and disappearing with them through the gate of the churchyard. We asked what was going forward; the answer was—

"Scaffolds and the stake. Don't you know that the French witch is to be burnt in the morning?"

Then we went away. We had no heart for that place.

At dawn we were at the city gate again; this time with a hope which our wearied bodies and fevered minds magnified into a large probability. We had heard a report that the Abbot of Jumièges with all his monks was coming to witness the burning. Our desire, abetted by our imagination, turned those nine hundred monks into Joan's old campaigners, and their Abbot into La Hire or the Bastard or D'Alençon; and we watched them file in, unchallenged, the multitude respectfully dividing and uncovering while they passed, with our hearts in our throats and our eyes swimming with tears of joy and pride and exultation; and we tried to catch glimpses of the faces under the cowls, and were prepared to give signal to any recognized face that we were Joan's men and ready and eager to kill and be killed in the good cause. How foolish we were; but we were young, you know, and youth hopeth all things, believeth all things.

Chapter XX

IN THE MORNING I was at my official post. It was on a platform raised the height of a man, in the churchyard, under the eaves of St. Ouen. On this same platform was a crowd of priests and important citizens, and several lawyers. Abreast it, with a small space between, was another and larger platform, handsomely canopied against sun and rain, and richly carpeted; also it was furnished with comfortable chairs, and with two which were more sumptuous than the others, and raised above the general level. One of these two was occupied by a prince of the royal blood of England, his Eminence the Cardinal of Winchester; the other by Cauchon, Bishop of Beauvais. In the rest of the chairs sat three bishops, the Vice-Inquisitor, eight abbots, and the sixty-two friars and lawyers who had sat as Joan's judges in her late trials.

Twenty steps in front of the platforms was another—a table-topped pyramid of stone, built up in retreating courses, thus forming steps. Out of this rose that grisly thing the stake; about the stake bundles of fagots and firewood were piled. On the ground at the base of the pyramid stood three crimson figures, the executioner and his assistants. At their feet lay what had been a goodly heap of brands, but was now a smokeless nest of ruddy coals; a foot or two from this was a supplemental supply of wood and fagots compacted into a pile shoulder-high and containing as much as six pack-horse loads. Think of that. We seem so delicately made, so destructible, so insubstantial; yet it is easier to reduce a granite statue to ashes than it is to do that with a man's body.

The sight of the stake sent physical pains tingling down the nerves of my body; and yet, turn as I would, my eyes would keep coming back to it, such fascination has the grewsome and the terrible for us.

The space occupied by the platforms and the stake was kept open by a wall of English soldiery, standing elbow to elbow, erect and stalwart figures, fine and sightly in their polished steel; while from behind them on every hand stretched far away a level plain of human heads; and there was no window and no housetop within our view, howsoever distant, but was black with patches and masses of people.

But there was no noise, no stir; it was as if the world was dead. The impressiveness of this silence and solemnity was deepened by a leaden twilight, for the sky was hidden by a pall of low-hanging storm-clouds; and above the remote horizon faint winkings of heat-lightning played, and now and then one caught the dull mutterings and complainings of distant thunder.

At last the stillness was broken. From beyond the square rose an indistinct sound, but familiar—curt, crisp phrases of command; next I saw the plain of heads dividing, and the steady swing of a marching host was glimpsed between. My heart leaped, for a moment. Was it La Hire and his hellions? No—that was not their gait. No, it was the prisoner and her escort; it was Joan of Arc, under guard, that was coming; my spirits sank as low as they had been before. Weak as she was, they made her walk; they would increase her weakness all they could. The distance was not great—it was but a few hundred yards—but short as it was it was a heavy tax upon one who had been lying chained in one spot for months, and whose feet had lost their powers from inaction. Yes, and for a year Joan had known only the cool damps of a dungeon, and now she was dragging herself through this sultry summer heat, this airless and suffocating void. As she entered the gate, drooping with exhaustion, there was that creature Loyseleur at her side with his head bent to her ear. We knew afterwards that he had been with her again this morning in the prison wearying her with his persuasions and enticing her with false promises, and that he was now still at the same work at the gate, imploring her to yield everything that would be required of her, and assuring her that if she would do this all would be well with her: she would be rid of the dreaded English and find safety in the powerful shelter and protection of the Church. A miserable man, a stony-hearted man!

The moment Joan was seated on the platform she closed her eyes and allowed her chin to fall; and so sat, with her hands nestling in her lap, indifferent to everything, caring for nothing but rest. And she was so white again; white as alabaster.

How the faces of that packed mass of humanity lighted up with interest, and with what intensity all eyes gazed upon this fragile girl! And how natural it was; for these people realized that at last they were looking upon that person whom they had so long hungered to see; a person whose name and fame filled all Europe, and made all other names and all other renowns insignificant by comparison: Joan of Arc, the wonder of the time, and destined to be the wonder of all times! And I could read as by print, in their marvelling countenances, the words that were drifting through their minds: "Can it be true; is it believable, that it is this little creature, this girl, this child with the good face, the sweet face, the beautiful face, the dear and bonny face, that has carried fortresses by storm, charged at the head of victorious armies, blown the might of England out of her path with a breath, and fought a long campaign, solitary and alone, against the massed brains and learning of France—and had won it if the fight had been fair!"

Evidently Cauchon had grown afraid of Manchon because of his pretty apparent leanings toward Joan, for another recorder was in the chief place, here, which left my master and me nothing to do but sit idle and look on.

Well, I supposed that everything had been done which could be thought of to tire Joan's body and mind, but it was a mistake; one more device had been invented. This was to preach a long sermon to her in that oppressive heat.

When the preacher began, she cast up one distressed and disappointed look, then dropped her head again. This preacher was Guillaume Erard, an oratorical celebrity. He got his text from the Twelve Lies. He emptied upon Joan all the calumnies, in detail, that had been bottled up in that mess of venom, and called her all the brutal names that the Twelve were labelled with, working himself into a whirlwind of fury as he went on; but his labors were wasted, she seemed lost in dreams, she made no sign, she did not seem to hear. At last he launched this apostrophe:

"O France, how hast thou been abused! Thou hast always been the home of Christianity; but now, Charles, who calls himself thy King and governor, indorses like the heretic and schismatic that he is, the words and deeds of a worthless and

infamous woman!" Joan raised her head, and her eyes began
to burn and flash. The preacher turned toward her: "It is to
you, Joan, that I speak, and I tell you that your King is schismatic and a heretic!"

Ah, he might abuse *her* to his heart's content; she could
endure that; but to her dying moment she could never hear in
patience a word against that ingrate, that treacherous dog our
King, whose proper place was here, at this moment, sword in
hand, routing these reptiles and saving this most noble servant that ever King had in this world—and he *would* have
been there if he had not been what I have called him. Joan's
loyal soul was outraged, and she turned upon the preacher
and flung out a few words with a spirit which the crowd
recognized as being in accordance with the Joan of Arc
traditions—

"By my faith, sir! I make bold to say and swear, on pain of
death, that he is the most noble Christian of all Christians,
and the best lover of the faith and the Church!"

There was an explosion of applause from the crowd—
which angered the preacher, for he had been aching long to
hear an expression like this, and now that it was come at last
it had fallen to the wrong person: he had done all the work;
the other had carried off all the spoil. He stamped his foot
and shouted to the sheriff—

"Make her shut up!"

That made the crowd laugh.

A mob has small respect for a grown man who has to call
on a sheriff to protect him from a sick girl.

Joan had damaged the preacher's cause more with one sentence than he had helped it with a hundred; so he was much
put out, and had trouble to get a good start again. But he
needn't have bothered; there was no occasion. It was mainly
an English-feeling mob. It had but obeyed a law of our nature—an irresistible law—to enjoy and applaud a spirited
and promptly delivered retort, no matter who makes it. The
mob was with the preacher; it had been beguiled for a moment, but only that; it would soon return. It was there to see
this girl burnt; so that it got that satisfaction—without too
much delay—it would be content.

Presently the preacher formally summoned Joan to submit to the Church. He made the demand with confidence, for he had gotten the idea from Loyseleur and Beaupère that she was worn to the bone, exhausted, and would not be able to put forth any more resistance; and indeed, to look at her it seemed that they must be right. Nevertheless, she made one more effort to hold her ground, and said, wearily—

"As to that matter, I have answered my judges before. I have told them to report all that I have said and done to our holy Father the Pope—to whom, and to God first, I appeal."

Again, out of her native wisdom, she had brought those words of tremendous import, but was ignorant of their value. But they could have availed her nothing in any case, now, with the stake there and these thousands of enemies about her. Yet they made every churchman there blench, and the preacher changed the subject with all haste. Well might those criminals blench, for Joan's appeal of her case to the Pope stripped Cauchon at once of jurisdiction over it, and annulled all that he and his judges had already done in the matter and all that they should do in it thenceforth.

Joan went on presently to reiterate, after some further talk, that she had acted by command of God in her deeds and utterances; then, when an attempt was made to implicate the King, and friends of hers and his, she stopped that. She said—

"I charge my deeds and words upon no one, neither upon my King nor any other. If there is any fault in them, I am responsible and no other."

She was asked if she would not recant those of her words and deeds which had been pronounced evil by her judges. Her answer made confusion and damage again:

"I submit them to God and the Pope."

The Pope once more! It was very embarrassing. Here was a person who was asked to submit her case to the Church, and who frankly consents—offers to submit it to the very head of it. What more could any one require? How was one to answer such a formidably unanswerable answer as that?

The worried judges put their heads together and whispered and planned and discussed. Then they brought forth this sufficiently shambling conclusion—but it was the best they could do, in so close a place: they said the Pope was so far away; and it was not necessary to go to him, anyway, because these present judges had sufficient power and authority to deal with the present case, and were in effect "the Church" to that extent. At another time they could have smiled at this conceit, but not now; they were not comfortable enough, now.

The mob was getting impatient. It was beginning to put on a threatening aspect; it was tired standing, tired of the scorching heat; and the thunder was coming nearer, the lightning was flashing brighter. It was necessary to hurry this matter to a close. Erard showed Joan a written form, which had been prepared and made all ready beforehand, and asked her to abjure.

"Abjure? What is abjure?"

She did not know the word. It was explained to her by Massieu. She tried to understand, but she was breaking, under exhaustion, and she could not gather the meaning. It was all a jumble and confusion of strange words. In her despair she sent out this beseeching cry—

"I appeal to the Church universal whether I ought to abjure or no!"

Erard exclaimed—

"You shall abjure instantly, or instantly be burnt!"

She glanced up, at those awful words, and for the first time she saw the stake and the mass of red coals—redder and angrier than ever, now, under the constantly deepening storm-gloom. She gasped and staggered up out of her seat muttering and mumbling incoherently, and gazed vacantly upon the people and the scene about her like one who is dazed, or thinks he dreams, and does not know where he is.

The priests crowded about her imploring her to sign the paper, there were many voices beseeching and urging her at once, there was great turmoil and shouting and excitement, amongst the populace and everywhere.

"Sign! sign!" from the priests; "sign—sign and be saved!" And Loyseleur was urging at her ear, "Do as I told you—do not destroy yourself!"

Joan said plaintively to these people—

"Ah, you do not do well to seduce me."

The judges joined their voices to the others. Yes, even the iron in *their* hearts melted, and they said—

"Oh, Joan, we pity you so! Take back what you have said, or we must deliver you up to punishment."

And now there was another voice—it was from the other platform—pealing solemnly above the din: Cauchon's—reading the sentence of death!

Joan's strength was all spent. She stood looking about her in a bewildered way a moment, then slowly she sank to her knees, and bowed her head and said—

"I submit."

They gave her no time to reconsider—they knew the peril of that. The moment the words were out of her mouth Massieu was reading to her the abjuration, and she was repeating the words after him mechanically, unconsciously—and *smiling*; for her wandering mind was far away in some happier world.

Then this short paper of six lines was slipped aside and a long one of many pages was smuggled into its place, and she, noting nothing, put her mark to it, saying, in pathetic apology, that she did not know how to write. But a secretary of the King of England was there to take care of that defect; he guided her hand with his own, and wrote her name—*Jehanne*.

The great crime was accomplished. She had signed—what? She did not know—but the others knew. She had signed a paper confessing herself a sorceress, a dealer with devils, a liar, a blasphemer of God and His angels, a lover of blood, a promoter of sedition, cruel, wicked, commissioned of Satan; and this signature of hers bound her to resume the dress of a woman. There were other promises, but that one would answer, without the others; that one could be made to destroy her.

Loyseleur pressed forward and praised her for having done "such a good day's work."

But she was still dreamy, she hardly heard.

Then Cauchon pronounced the words which dissolved the excommunication and restored her to her beloved Church, with all the dear privileges of worship. Ah, she heard that!

You could see it in the deep gratitude that rose in her face and transfigured it with joy.

But how transient was that happiness! For Cauchon, without a tremor of pity in his voice, added these crushing words—

"And that she may repent of her crimes and repeat them no more, she is sentenced to perpetual imprisonment, with the bread of affliction and the water of anguish!"

Perpetual imprisonment! She had never dreamed of that—such a thing had never been hinted to her by Loyseleur or by any other. Loyseleur had distinctly said and promised that "all would be well with her." And the very last words spoken to her by Erard, on that very platform, when he was urging her to abjure, was a straight, unqualified promise—that if she would do it she should *go free from captivity.*

She stood stunned and speechless a moment; then she remembered, with such solacement as the thought could furnish, that by another clear promise—a promise made by Cauchon himself—she would at least be the Church's captive, and have women about her in place of a brutal foreign soldiery. So she turned to the body of priests and said, with a sad resignation—

"Now, you men of the Church, take me to your prison, and leave me no longer in the hands of the English"; and she gathered up her chains and prepared to move.

But alas, now came these shameful words from Cauchon—and with them a mocking laugh:

"Take her to the prison whence she came!"

Poor abused girl! She stood dumb, smitten, paralyzed. It was pitiful to see. She had been beguiled, lied to, betrayed; she saw it all, now.

The rumbling of a drum broke upon the stillness, and for just one moment she thought of the glorious deliverance promised by her Voices—I read it in the rapture that lit her face; then she saw what it was—her prison escort—and that light faded, never to revive again. And now her head began a piteous rocking motion, swaying slowly, this way and that, as is the way when one is suffering unwordable pain, or when one's heart is broken; then drearily she went from us, with her face in her hands, and sobbing bitterly.

Chapter XXI

THERE is no certainty that any one in all Rouen was in the secret of the deep game which Cauchon was playing except the Cardinal of Winchester. Then you can imagine the astonishment and stupefaction of that vast mob gathered there and those crowds of churchmen assembled on the two platforms, when they saw Joan of Arc moving away, alive and whole—slipping out of their grip at last, after all this tedious waiting, all this tantalizing expectancy.

Nobody was able to stir or speak, for a while, so paralyzing was the universal astonishment, so unbelievable the fact that the stake was actually standing there unoccupied and its prey gone. Then suddenly everybody broke into a fury of rage; maledictions and charges of treachery began to fly freely; yes, and even stones: a stone came near killing the Cardinal of Winchester—it just missed his head. But the man who threw it was not to blame, for he was excited, and a person who is excited never can throw straight.

The tumult was very great indeed, for a while. In the midst of it a chaplain of the Cardinal even forgot the proprieties so far as to opprobriously assail the august Bishop of Beauvais himself, shaking his fist in his face and shouting:

"By God, you are a traitor!"

"You lie!" responded the Bishop.

He a traitor! Oh, far from it; he certainly was the last Frenchman that any Briton had a right to bring that charge against.

The Earl of Warwick lost his temper, too. He was a doughty soldier, but when it came to the intellectuals—when it came to delicate chicane, and scheming, and trickery—he couldn't see any further through a millstone than another. So he burst out in his frank warrior fashion, and swore that the King of England was being treacherously used, and that Joan of Arc was going to be allowed to cheat the stake. But they whispered comfort into his ear—

"Give yourself no uneasiness, my lord; we shall soon have her again."

Perhaps the like tidings found their way all around, for
good news travels fast as well as bad. At any rate the ragings
presently quieted down, and the huge concourse crumbled
apart and disappeared. And thus we reached the noon of that
fearful Thursday.

We two youths were happy; happier than any words can
tell—for we were not in the secret any more than the rest.
Joan's life was saved. We knew that, and that was enough.
France would hear of this day's infamous work—and then!
Why, then her gallant sons would flock to her standard by
thousands and thousands, multitudes upon multitudes, and
their wrath would be like the wrath of the ocean when the
storm-winds sweep it; and they would hurl themselves against
this doomed city and overwhelm it like the resistless tides of
that ocean, and Joan of Arc would march again! In six days—
seven days—one short week—noble France, grateful France,
indignant France, would be thundering at these gates—let us
count the hours, let us count the minutes, let us count the
seconds! Oh happy day, oh day of ecstasy, how our hearts
sang in our bosoms!

For we were young, then; yes, we were very young.

Do you think the exhausted prisoner was allowed to rest
and sleep after she had spent the small remnant of her
strength in dragging her tired body back to the dungeon?

No; there was no rest for her, with those sleuth-hounds on
her track. Cauchon and some of his people followed her to
her lair, straightway; they found her dazed and dull, her mental and physical forces in a state of prostration. They told her
she had abjured; that she had made certain promises—among
them, to resume the apparel of her sex; and that if she relapsed, the Church would cast her out for good and all. She
heard the words, but they had no meaning to her. She was
like a person who has taken a narcotic and is dying for sleep,
dying for rest from nagging, dying to be let alone, and who
mechanically does everything the persecutor asks, taking but
dull note of the things done, and but dully recording them in
the memory. And so Joan put on the gown which Cauchon
and his people had brought; and would come to herself by-
and-by, and have at first but a dim idea as to when and how
the change had come about.

Cauchon went away happy and content. Joan had resumed woman's dress without protest; also she had been formally warned against relapsing. He had witnesses to these facts. How could matters be better?

But suppose she should *not* relapse?

Why, then she must be forced to do it.

Did Cauchon hint to the English guards that thenceforth if they chose to make their prisoner's captivity crueler and bitterer than ever, no official notice would be taken of it? Perhaps so; since the guards did begin that policy at once, and no official notice *was* taken of it. Yes, from that moment Joan's life in that dungeon was made almost unendurable. Do not ask me to enlarge upon it. I will not do it.

Chapter XXII

FRIDAY and Saturday were happy days for Noël and me. Our minds were full of our splendid dream of France aroused—France shaking her mane—France on the march—France at the gates—Rouen in ashes, and Joan free! Our imagination was on fire; we were delirious with pride and joy. For we were very young, as I have said.

We knew nothing about what had been happening in the dungeon the yester-afternoon. We supposed that as Joan had abjured and been taken back into the forgiving bosom of the Church, she was being gently used, now, and her captivity made as pleasant and comfortable for her as the circumstances would allow. So, in high contentment, we planned out our share in the great rescue, and fought our part of the fight over and over again during those two happy days—as happy days as ever I have known.

Sunday morning came. I was awake, enjoying the balmy, lazy weather, and thinking. Thinking of the rescue—what else? I had no other thought now. I was absorbed in that, drunk with the happiness of it.

I heard a voice shouting, far down the street, and soon it came nearer, and I caught the words—

"Joan of Arc has relapsed! The witch's time has come!"

It stopped my heart, it turned my blood to ice. That was more than sixty years ago, but that triumphant note rings as clear in my memory to-day as it rang in my ear that long-vanished summer morning. We are so strangely made; the memories that could make us happy pass away; it is the memories that break our hearts that abide.

Soon other voices took up that cry—tens, scores, hundreds of voices; all the world seemed filled with the brutal joy of it. And there were other clamors—the clatter of rushing feet, merry congratulations, bursts of coarse laughter, the rolling of drums, the boom and crash of distant bands profaning the sacred day with the music of victory and thanksgiving.

About the middle of the afternoon came a summons for Manchon and me to go to Joan's dungeon—a summons from

Cauchon. But by that time distrust had already taken posses-sion of the English and their soldiery again, and all Rouen was in an angry and threatening mood. We could see plenty evidences of this from our own windows—fist-shaking, black looks, tumultuous tides of furious men billowing by along the street.

And we learned that up at the castle things were going very badly indeed; that there was a great mob gathered there who considered the relapse a lie and a priestly trick, and among them many half-drunk English soldiers. Moreover, these peo-ple had gone beyond words. They had laid hands upon a number of churchmen who were trying to enter the castle, and it had been difficult work to rescue them and save their lives.

And so Manchon refused to go. He said he would not go a step without a safeguard from Warwick. So next morning Warwick sent an escort of soldiers, and then we went. Matters had not grown peacefuler meantime, but worse. The soldiers protected us from bodily damage, but as we passed through the great mob at the castle we were assailed with insults and shameful epithets. I bore it well enough, though, and said to myself, with secret satisfaction, "In three or four short days, my lads, you will be employing your tongues in a different sort from this—and I shall be there to hear."

To my mind these were as good as dead men. How many of them would still be alive after the rescue that was coming? Not more than enough to amuse the executioner a short half-hour, certainly.

It turned out that the report was true. Joan had relapsed. She was sitting there in her chains, clothed again in her male attire.

She accused nobody. That was her way. It was not in her character to hold a servant to account for what his master had made him do, and her mind had cleared, now, and she knew that the advantage which had been taken of her the previous morning had its origin, not in the subordinate, but in the master—Cauchon.

Here is what had happened. While Joan slept, in the early morning of Sunday, one of the guards stole her female ap-parel and put her male attire in its place. When she woke she asked for the other dress, but the guards refused to give it back. She protested, and said she was forbidden to wear the male dress. But they continued to refuse. She had to have clothing, for modesty's sake; moreover, she saw that she could not save her life if she must fight for it against treacheries like this; so she put on the forbidden garments, knowing what the end would be. She was weary of the struggle, poor thing.

We had followed in the wake of Cauchon, the Vice-Inquisitor, and the others—six or eight—and when I saw Joan sitting there, despondent, forlorn, and still in chains, when I was expecting to find her situation so different, I did not know what to make of it. The shock was very great. I had doubted the relapse, perhaps; possibly I had believed in it, but had not realized it.

Cauchon's victory was complete. He had had a harassed and irritated and disgusted look for a long time, but that was all gone now, and contentment and serenity had taken its place. His purple face was full of tranquil and malicious happiness. He went trailing his robes and stood grandly in front of Joan, with his legs apart, and remained so more than a minute, gloating over her and enjoying the sight of this poor ruined creature, who had won so lofty a place for him in the service of the meek and merciful Jesus, Saviour of the World, Lord of the Universe—in case England kept her promise to him, who kept no promises himself.

Presently the judges began to question Joan. One of them, named Marguerie, who was a man with more insight than prudence, remarked upon Joan's change of clothing, and said—

"There is something suspicious about this. How could it have come about without connivance on the part of others? Perhaps even something worse?"

"Thousand devils!" screamed Cauchon, in a fury. "Will you shut your mouth?"

"Armagnac! Traitor!" shouted the soldiers on guard, and made a rush for Marguerie with their lances levelled. It was with the greatest difficulty that he was saved from being run through the body. He made no more attempts to help the inquiry, poor man. The other judges proceeded with the questionings.

"Why have you resumed this male habit?"

I did not quite catch her answer, for just then a soldier's halberd slipped from his fingers and fell on the stone floor with a crash; but I thought I understood Joan to say that she had resumed it of her own motion.

"But you have promised and sworn that you would not go back to it."

I was full of anxiety to hear her answer to that question; and when it came it was just what I was expecting. She said—quite quietly—

"I have never intended and never understood myself to swear I would not resume it."

There—I had been sure, all along, that she did not know what she was doing and saying on the platform Thursday, and this answer of hers was proof that I had not been mistaken. Then she went on to add this—

"But I had a right to resume it, because the promises made to me have not been kept—promises that I should be allowed to go to mass, and receive the communion, and that I should be freed from the bondage of these chains—but they are still upon me, as you see."

"Nevertheless, you have abjured, and have especially promised to return no more to the dress of a man."

Then Joan held out her fettered hands sorrowfully toward these unfeeling men and said—

"I would rather die than continue so. But if they may be taken off, and if I may hear mass, and be removed to a penitential prison, and have a woman about me, I will be good, and will do what shall seem good to you that I do."

Cauchon sniffed scoffingly at that. Honor the compact which he and his had made with her? Fulfil its conditions? What need of that? Conditions had been a good thing to concede, temporarily, and for advantage; but they had served their turn—let something of a fresher sort and of more consequence be considered. The resumption of the male dress was sufficient for all practical purposes, but perhaps Joan could be led to add something to that fatal crime. So

Cauchon asked her if her Voices had spoken to her since Thursday—and he reminded her of her abjuration.

"Yes," she answered; and then it came out that the Voices had talked with her about the abjuration—*told* her about it, I suppose. She guilelessly reasserted the heavenly origin of her mission, and did it with the untroubled mien of one who was not conscious that she had ever knowingly repudiated it. So I was convinced once more that she had had no notion of what she was doing that Thursday morning on the platform. Finally she said, "My Voices told me I did very wrong to confess that what I had done was not well." Then she sighed, and said with simplicity, "But it was the fear of the fire that made me do so."

That is, fear of the fire had made her sign a paper whose contents she had not understood then, but understood now by revelation of her Voices and by testimony of her persecutors.

She was sane now, and not exhausted; her courage had come back, and with it her inborn loyalty to the truth. She was bravely and serenely speaking it again, knowing that it would deliver her body up to that very fire which had such terrors for her.

That answer of hers was quite long, quite frank, wholly free from concealments or palliations. It made me shudder; I knew she was pronouncing sentence of death upon herself. So did poor Manchon. And he wrote in the margin abreast of it—

RESPONSIO MORTIFERA.

Fatal answer. Yes, all present knew that it was indeed a fatal answer. Then there fell a silence such as falls in a sick-room when the watchers by the dying draw a deep breath and say softly one to another, "All is over."

Here, likewise, all was over; but after some moments Cauchon, wishing to clinch this matter and make it final, put this question—

"Do you still believe that your Voices are St. Marguerite and St. Catherine?"

"Yes—and that they come from God."

"Yet you denied them on the scaffold?"

Then she made direct and clear affirmation that she had never had any intention to deny them; and that if—I noted that *if*—"if she had made some retractions and revocations on the scaffold it was from fear of the fire, and was a violation of the truth."

There it is again, you see. She certainly never knew what it was she had done on the scaffold until she was told of it afterwards by these people and by her Voices.

And now she closed this most painful scene with these words; and there was a weary note in them that was pathetic—

"I would rather do my penance all at once; let me die. I cannot endure captivity any longer."

The spirit born for sunshine and liberty so longed for release that it would take it in any form, even that.

Several among the company of judges went from the place troubled and sorrowful, the others in another mood. In the court of the castle we found the Earl of Warwick and fifty English waiting, impatient for news. As soon as Cauchon saw them he shouted—*laughing*—think of a man destroying a friendless poor girl and then having the heart to laugh at it:

"Make yourselves comfortable—it's all over with her!"

Chapter XXIII

THE YOUNG can sink into abysses of despondency, and it was so with Noël and me, now; but the hopes of the young are quick to rise again, and it was so with ours. We called back that vague promise of the Voices, and said the one to the other that the glorious release was to happen at "the last moment"—"that other time was not the last moment, but this is; it will happen now; the King will come, La Hire will come, and with them our veterans, and behind them all France!" And so we were full of heart again, and could already hear, in fancy, that stirring music—the clash of steel and the war-cries and the uproar of the onset, and in fancy see our prisoner free, her chains gone, her sword in her hand.

But this dream was to pass also, and come to nothing. Late at night, when Manchon came in, he said—

"I am come from the dungeon, and I have a message for you from that poor child."

A message to me! If he had been noticing I think he would have discovered me—discovered that my indifference concerning the prisoner was a pretence; for I was caught off my guard, and was so moved and so exalted to be so honored by her that I must have shown my feeling in my face and manner.

"A message for me, your reverence?"

"Yes. It is something she wishes done. She said she had noticed the young man who helps me, and that he had a good face; and did I think he would do a kindness for her? I said I knew you would, and asked her what it was, and she said a letter—would you write a letter to her mother? And I said you would. But I said I would do it myself, and gladly; but she said no, that my labors were heavy, and she thought the young man would not mind the doing of this service for one not able to do it for herself, she not knowing how to write. Then I would have sent for you, and at that the sadness vanished out of her face. Why, it was as if she was going to see a friend, poor friendless thing. But I was not permitted. I did my best, but the orders remain as strict as ever, the doors are

956

closed against all but officials; as before, none but officials may speak to her. So I went back and told her, and she sighed, and was sad again. Now this is what she begs you to write to her mother. It is partly a strange message, and to me means nothing, but she said her mother would understand. You will 'convey her adoring love to her family and her village friends, and say there will be no rescue, for that this night— and it is the third time in the twelve-month, and is final—she has seen The Vision of the Tree.' "

"How strange!"

"Yes, it *is* strange, but that is what she said; and said her parents would understand. And for a little time she was lost in dreams and thinkings, and her lips moved, and I caught in her mutterings these lines, which she said over two or three times, and they seemed to bring peace and contentment to her. I set them down, thinking they might have some connection with her letter and be useful; but it was not so; they were a mere memory, floating idly in a tired mind, and they have no meaning, at least no relevancy."

I took the piece of paper, and found what I knew I should find:

> "And when in exile wand'ring we
> Shall fainting yearn for glimpse of thee,
> O rise upon our sight!"

There was no hope any more. I knew it now. I knew that Joan's letter was a message to Noël and me, as well as to her family, and that its object was to banish vain hopes from our minds and tell us from her own mouth of the blow that was going to fall upon us, so that we, being her soldiers, would know it for a command to bear it as became us and her, and so submit to the will of God; and in thus obeying, find assuagement of our grief. It was like her, for she was always thinking of others, not of herself. Yes, her heart was sore for us; she could find time to think of us, the humblest of her servants, and try to soften our pain, lighten the burden of our troubles,—she that was drinking of the bitter waters; she that was walking in the Valley of the Shadow of Death.

I wrote the letter. You will know what it cost me, without my telling you. I wrote it with the same wooden stylus which had put upon parchment the first words ever dictated by Joan of Arc—that high summons to the English to vacate France, two years past, when she was a lass of seventeen; it had now set down the last ones which she was ever to dictate. Then I broke it. For the pen that had served Joan of Arc could not serve any that would come after her in this earth without abasement.

The next day, May 29th, Cauchon summoned his serfs, and forty-two responded. It is charitable to believe that the other twenty were ashamed to come. The forty-two pronounced her a relapsed heretic, and condemned her to be delivered over to the secular arm. Cauchon thanked them. Then he sent orders that Joan be conveyed the next morning to the place known as the Old Market; and that she be then delivered to the civil judge, and by the civil judge to the executioner. That meant that she would be burnt.

All the afternoon and evening of Tuesday the 29th the news was flying, and the people of the country-side flocking to Rouen to see the tragedy—all, at least, who could prove their English sympathies and count upon admission. The press grew thicker and thicker in the streets, the excitement grew higher and higher. And now a thing was noticeable again which had been noticeable more than once before—that there was pity for Joan in the hearts of many of these people. Whenever she had been in great danger it had manifested itself, and now it was apparent again—manifest in a pathetic dumb sorrow which was visible in many faces.

Early the next morning, Wednesday, Martin Ladvenu and another friar were sent to Joan to prepare her for death; and Manchon and I went with them—a hard service for me. We tramped through the dim corridors, winding this way and that, and piercing ever deeper and deeper into that vast heart of stone, and at last we stood before Joan. But she did not know it. She sat with her hands in her lap and her head bowed, thinking, and her face was very sad. One might not know what she was thinking of. Of her home, and the peaceful pastures, and the friends she was no more to see? Of her wrongs, and her forsaken estate, and the cruelties which had been put upon her? Or was it of death—the death which she had longed for, and which was now so close? Or was it of the *kind* of death she must suffer? I hoped not; for she feared only one kind, and that one had for her unspeakable terrors. I believed she so feared that one that with her strong will she would shut the thought of it wholly out of her mind, and hope and believe that God would take pity on her and grant her an easier one; and so it might chance that the awful news which we were bringing might come as a surprise to her, at last.

We stood silent awhile, but she was still unconscious of us, still deep in her sad musings and far away. Then Martin Ladvenu said, softly—

"Joan."

She looked up then, with a little start, and a wan smile, and said—

"Speak. Have you a message for me?"

"Yes, my poor child. Try to bear it. Do you think you can bear it?"

"Yes"—very softly, and her head drooped again.

"I am come to prepare you for death."

A faint shiver trembled through her wasted body. There was a pause. In the stillness we could hear our breathings. Then she said, still in that low voice—

"When will it be?"

The muffled notes of a tolling bell floated to our ears out of the distance.

"Now. The time is at hand."

That slight shiver passed again.

"It is so soon—ah, it is so soon!"

There was a long silence. The distant throbbings of the bell pulsed through it, and we stood motionless and listening. But it was broken at last—

"What death is it?"

"By fire!"

"Oh, I knew it, I knew it!" She sprang wildly to her feet, and wound her hands in her hair, and began to writhe and sob, oh, so piteously, and mourn and grieve and lament, and turn to first one and then another of us, and search our faces beseechingly, as hoping she might find help and friendliness there, poor thing—she that had never denied these to any creature, even her wounded enemy on the battle-field.

"Oh, cruel, cruel, to treat me so! And must my body, that has never been defiled, be consumed to-day and turned to ashes? Ah, sooner would I that my head were cut off seven times than suffer this woful death. I had the promise of the Church's prison when I submitted, and if I had but been there, and not left here in the hands of my enemies, this miserable fate had not befallen me. Oh, I appeal to God the Great Judge, against the injustice which has been done me."

There was none there that could endure it. They turned away, with the tears running down their faces. In a moment I was on my knees at her feet. At once she thought only of my danger, and bent and whispered in my ear: "Up!—do not peril yourself, good heart. There—God bless you always!" and I felt the quick clasp of her hand. Mine was the last hand she touched with hers in life. None saw it; history does not know of it or tell of it, yet it is true, just as I have told it. The next moment she saw Cauchon coming, and she went and stood before him and reproached him, saying—

"Bishop, it is by you that I die!"

He was not shamed, not touched; but said, smoothly—

"Ah, be patient, Joan. You die because you have not kept your promise, but have returned to your sins."

"Alas," she said, "if you had put me in the Church's prison, and given me right and proper keepers, as you promised, this would not have happened. And for this I summon you to answer before God!"

Then Cauchon winced, and looked less placidly content than before, and he turned him about and went away.

Joan stood awhile musing. She grew calmer, but occasionally she wiped her eyes, and now and then sobs shook her body; but their violence was modifying now, and the intervals between them were growing longer. Finally she looked up and saw Pierre Maurice, who had come in with the Bishop, and she said to him—

"Master Peter, where shall I be this night?"

"Have you not good hope in God?"

"Yes—and by His grace I shall be in Paradise."

Now Martin Ladvenu heard her in confession; then she begged for the sacrament. But how grant the communion to one who had been publicly cut off from the Church, and was now no more entitled to its privileges than an unbaptized pagan? The brother could not do this, but he sent to Cauchon to inquire what he must do. All laws, human and divine, were alike to that man—he respected none of them. He sent back orders to grant Joan whatever she wished. Her last speech to him had reached his fears, perhaps: it could not reach his heart, for he had none.

The Eucharist was brought now to that poor soul that had yearned for it with such unutterable longing all these desolate months. It was a solemn moment. While we had been in the deeps of the prison, the public courts of the castle had been filling up with crowds of the humbler sort of men and women, who had learned what was going on in Joan's cell, and had come with softened hearts to do—they knew not what; to hear—they knew not what. We knew nothing of this, for they were out of our view. And there were other great crowds of the like caste gathered in masses outside the castle gates. And when the lights and the other accompaniments of the Sacrament passed by, coming to Joan in the prison, all those multitudes kneeled down and began to pray for her, and many wept; and when the solemn ceremony of the communion began in Joan's cell, out of the distance a moving sound was borne moaning to our ears—it was those invisible multitudes chanting the litany for a departing soul.

The fear of the fiery death was gone from Joan of Arc now, to come again no more, except for one fleeting instant—then it would pass, and serenity and courage would take its place and abide till the end.

Chapter XXIV

AT NINE O'CLOCK the Maid of Orleans, Deliverer of France, went forth in the grace of her innocence and her youth to lay down her life for the country she loved with such devotion, and for the King that had abandoned her. She sat in the cart that is used only for felons. In one respect she was treated worse than a felon; for whereas she was on her way to be sentenced by the civil arm, she already bore her judgment inscribed in advance upon a mitre-shaped cap which she wore:

HERETIC, RELAPSED, APOSTATE, IDOLATER.

In the cart with her sat the friar Martin Ladvenu and Maître Jean Massieu. She looked girlishly fair and sweet and saintly in her long white robe, and when a gush of sun-light flooded her as she emerged from the gloom of the prison and was yet for a moment still framed in the arch of the sombre gate, the massed multitudes of poor folk murmured "A vision! a vision!" and sank to their knees praying, and many of the women weeping; and the moving invocation for the dying rose again, and was taken up and borne along, a majestic wave of sound, which accompanied the doomed, solacing and blessing her, all the sorrowful way to the place of death. "Christ have pity! Saint Margaret have pity! Pray for her, all ye saints, archangels, and blessed martyrs, pray for her! Saints and angels intercede for her! From thy wrath, good Lord, deliver her! O Lord God, save her! Have mercy on her, we beseech Thee, good Lord!"

It is just and true, what one of the histories has said: "The poor and the helpless had nothing but their prayers to give Joan of Arc; but these we may believe were not unavailing. There are few more pathetic events recorded in history than this weeping, helpless, praying crowd, holding their lighted candles and kneeling on the pavement beneath the prison walls of the old fortress."

And it was so all the way: thousands upon thousands massed upon their knees and stretching far down the distances, thick-sown with the faint yellow candle-flames, like a field starred with golden flowers.

But there were some that did not kneel; these were the English soldiers. They stood elbow to elbow, on each side of Joan's road, and walled it in, all the way; and behind these living walls knelt the multitudes.

By-and-by a frantic man in priest's garb came wailing and lamenting, and tore through the crowd and the barrier of soldiers and flung himself on his knees by Joan's cart and put up his hands in supplication, crying out—

"O, forgive, forgive!"

It was Loyseleur!

And Joan forgave him; forgave him out of a heart that knew nothing but forgiveness, nothing but compassion, nothing but pity for all that suffer, let their offence be what it might. And she had no word of reproach for this poor wretch who had wrought day and night with deceits and treacheries and hypocrisies to betray her to her death.

The soldiers would have killed him, but the Earl of Warwick saved his life. What became of him is not known. He hid himself from the world somewhere, to endure his remorse as he might.

In the square of the Old Market stood the two platforms and the stake that had stood before in the church-yard of St. Ouen. The platforms were occupied as before, the one by Joan and her judges, the other by great dignitaries, the principal being Cauchon and the English Cardinal—Winchester. The square was packed with people, the windows and roofs of the blocks of buildings surrounding it were black with them.

When the preparations had been finished, all noise and movement gradually ceased, and a waiting stillness followed which was solemn and impressive.

And now, by order of Cauchon, an ecclesiastic named Nicholas Midi preached a sermon, wherein he explained that when a branch of the vine—which is the Church—becomes diseased and corrupt, it must be cut away or it will corrupt and destroy the whole vine. He made it appear that Joan, through her wickedness, was a menace and a peril to the Church's purity and holiness, and her death therefore necessary.

When he was come to the end of his discourse he turned toward her and paused a moment, then he said—

"Joan, the Church can no longer protect you. Go in peace!"

Joan had been placed wholly apart and conspicuous, to signify the Church's abandonment of her, and she sat there in her loneliness, waiting in patience and resignation for the end. Cauchon addressed her now. He had been advised to read the form of her abjuration to her, and had brought it with him; but he changed his mind, fearing that she would proclaim the truth—that she had never knowingly abjured—and so bring shame upon him and eternal infamy. He contented himself with admonishing her to keep in mind her wickednesses, and repent of them, and think of her salvation. Then he solemnly pronounced her excommunicate and cut off from the body of the Church. With a final word he delivered her over to the secular arm for judgment and sentence.

Joan, weeping, knelt and began to pray. For whom? Herself? Oh no—for the King of France. Her voice rose sweet and clear, and penetrated all hearts with its passionate pathos. She never thought of his treacheries to her, she never thought of his desertion of her, she never remembered that it was because he was an ingrate that she was here to die a miserable death; she remembered only that he was her King, that she was his loyal and loving subject, and that his enemies had undermined his cause with evil reports and false charges, and he not by to defend himself. And so, in the very presence of death, she forgot her own troubles to implore all in her hearing to be just to him; to believe that he was good and noble and sincere, and not in any way to blame for any acts of hers, neither advising them nor urging them, but being wholly clear and free of all responsibility for them. Then, closing, she begged in humble and touching words that all here present would pray for her and would pardon her, both her enemies and such as might look friendly upon her and feel pity for her in their hearts.

There was hardly one heart there that was not touched—even the English, even the judges showed it, and there was many a lip that trembled and many an eye that was blurred with tears; yes, even the English Cardinal's—that man with a political heart of stone but a human heart of flesh.

The secular judge who should have delivered judgment and pronounced sentence was himself so disturbed that he forgot his duty, and Joan went to her death unsentenced—thus completing with an illegality what had begun illegally and had so continued to the end. He only said—to the guards—

"Take her"; and to the executioner, "Do your duty."

Joan asked for a cross. None was able to furnish one. But an English soldier broke a stick in two and crossed the pieces and tied them together, and this cross he gave her, moved to it by the good heart that was in him; and she kissed it and put it in her bosom. Then Isambard de la Pierre went to the church near by and brought her a consecrated one; and this one also she kissed, and pressed it to her bosom with rapture, and then kissed it again and again, covering it with tears and pouring out her gratitude to God and the saints.

And so, weeping, and with her cross to her lips, she climbed up the cruel steps to the face of the stake, with the friar Isambard at her side. Then she was helped up to the top of the pile of wood that was built around the lower third of the stake, and stood upon it with her back against the stake, and the world gazing up at her breathless. The executioner ascended to her side and wound chains about her slender body, and so fastened her to the stake. Then he descended to finish his dreadful office; and there she remained alone—she that had had so many friends in the days when she was free, and had been so loved and so dear.

All these things I saw, albeit dimly and blurred with tears; but I could bear no more. I continued in my place, but what I shall deliver to you now I got by others' eyes and others' mouths. Tragic sounds there were that pierced my ears and wounded my heart as I sat there, but it is as I tell you: the latest image recorded by my eyes in that desolating hour was Joan of Arc with the grace of her comely youth still un-marred; and that image, untouched by time or decay, has re-mained with me all my days. Now I will go on.

If any thought that now, in that solemn hour when all transgressors repent and confess, she would revoke her revo-cation and say her great deeds had been evil deeds and Satan and his fiends their source, they erred. No such thought was in her blameless mind. She was not thinking of herself and her troubles, but of others, and of woes that might befall them. And so, turning her grieving eyes about her, where rose the towers and spires of that fair city, she said—

"Oh, Rouen, Rouen, must I die here, and must you be my tomb? Ah, Rouen, Rouen, I have great fear that you will suffer for my death."

A whiff of smoke swept upward past her face, and for one moment terror seized her and she cried out, "Water! Give me holy water!" but the next moment her fears were gone, and they came no more to torture her.

She heard the flames crackling below her, and immediately distress for a fellow-creature who was in danger took possession of her. It was the friar Isambard. She had given him her cross and begged him to raise it toward her face and let her eyes rest in hope and consolation upon it till she was entered into the peace of God. She made him go out from the danger of the fire. Then she was satisfied, and said—

"Now keep it always in my sight until the end."

Not even yet could Cauchon, that man without shame, endure to let her die in peace, but went toward her, all black with crimes and sins as he was, and cried out—

"I am come, Joan, to exhort you for the last time to repent and seek the pardon of God."

"I die through you," she said, and these were the last words she spoke to any upon earth.

Then the pitchy smoke, shot through with red flashes of flame, rolled up in a thick volume and hid her from sight; and from the heart of this darkness her voice rose strong and eloquent in prayer, and when by moments the wind shredded somewhat of the smoke aside, there were veiled glimpses of an upturned face and moving lips. At last a mercifully swift tide of flame burst upward, and none saw that face any more nor that form, and the voice was still.

Yes, she was gone from us: JOAN OF ARC! What little words they are, to tell of a rich world made empty and poor!

Conclusion

JOAN's brother Jacques died in Domremy during the Great Trial at Rouen. This was according to the prophecy which Joan made that day in the pastures the time that she said the rest of us would go to the great wars.

When her poor old father heard of the martyrdom it broke his heart and he died.

The mother was granted a pension by the City of Orleans, and upon this she lived out her days, which were many. Twenty-four years after her illustrious child's death she travelled all the way to Paris in the winter time and was present at the opening of the discussion in the Cathedral of Nôtre Dame which was the first step in the Rehabilitation. Paris was crowded with people, from all about France, who came to get sight of the venerable dame, and it was a touching spectacle when she moved through these reverend wet-eyed multitudes on her way to the grand honors awaiting her at the cathedral. With her were Jean and Pierre, no longer the light-hearted youths who marched with us from Vaucouleurs, but war-worn veterans with hair beginning to show frost.

After the martyrdom Noël and I went back to Domremy, but presently when the Constable Richemont superseded La Tremouille as the King's chief adviser and began the completion of Joan's great work, we put on our harness and returned to the field and fought for the King all through the wars and skirmishes until France was freed of the English. It was what Joan would have desired of us; and, dead or alive, her desire was law for us. All the survivors of the personal staff were faithful to her memory and fought for the King to the end. Mainly we were well scattered, but when Paris fell we happened to be together. It was a great day and a joyous; but it was a sad one at the same time, because Joan was not there to march into the captured capital with us.

Noël and I remained always together, and I was by his side when death claimed him. It was in the last great battle of the war. In that battle fell also Joan's sturdy old enemy, Talbot. He was eighty-five years old, and had spent his whole life in battle. A fine old lion he was, with his flowing white mane and his tameless spirit; yes, and his indestructible energy as well; for he fought as knightly and vigorous a fight that day as the best man there.

La Hire survived the martyrdom thirteen years; and always fighting, of course, for that was all he enjoyed in life. I did not see him in all that time, for we were far apart, but one was always hearing of him.

The Bastard of Orleans and D'Alençon and D'Aulon lived to see France free, and to testify with Jean and Pierre d'Arc and Pasquerel and me at the Rehabilitation. But they are all at rest now, these many years. I alone am left of those who fought at the side of Joan of Arc in the great wars. She said I would live until these wars were forgotten—a prophecy which failed. If I should live a thousand years it would still fail. For whatsoever had touch with Joan of Arc, that thing is immortal.

Members of Joan's family married, and they have left descendants. Their descendants are of the nobility, but their family name and blood bring them honors which no other nobles receive or may hope for. You have seen how everybody along the way uncovered when those children came yesterday to pay their duty to me. It was not because they are noble, it is because they are grandchildren of the brothers of Joan of Arc.

Now as to the Rehabilitation. Joan crowned the King at Rheims. For reward he allowed her to be hunted to her death without making one effort to save her. During the next twenty-three years he remained indifferent to her memory; indifferent to the fact that her good name was under a damning blot put there by the priests because of the deeds which she had done in saving him and his sceptre; indifferent to the fact that France was ashamed, and longed to have the Deliverer's fair fame restored. Indifferent all that time. Then he suddenly changed and was anxious to have justice for poor Joan, himself. Why? Had he become grateful at last? Had remorse attacked his hard heart? No, he had a better reason—a better one for his sort of man. This better reason was that, now that the English had been finally expelled from the country, they were beginning to call attention to the fact that this

King had gotten his crown by the hands of a person proven by the priests to have been in league with Satan and burnt for it by them as a sorceress—therefore, of what value or authority was such a Kingship as that? Of no value at all; no nation could afford to allow such a king to remain on the throne.

It was high time to stir, now, and the King did it. That is how Charles VII. came to be smitten with anxiety to have justice done the memory of his benefactress.

He appealed to the Pope, and the Pope appointed a great commission of churchmen to examine into the facts of Joan's life and award judgment. The Commission sat at Paris, at Domremy, at Rouen, at Orleans, and at several other places, and continued its work during several months. It examined the records of Joan's trials, it examined the Bastard of Orleans, and the Duke d'Alençon, and D'Aulon, and Pasquerel, and Courcelles, and Isambard de la Pierre, and Manchon, and me, and many others whose names I have made familiar to you; also they examined more than a hundred witnesses whose names are less familiar to you—friends of Joan in Domremy, Vaucouleurs, Orleans, and other places, and a number of judges and other people who had assisted at the Rouen trials, the abjuration, and the martyrdom. And out of this exhaustive examination Joan's character and history came spotless and perfect, and this verdict was placed upon record, to remain forever.

I was present upon most of these occasions, and saw again many faces which I have not seen for a quarter of a century; among them some well-beloved faces—those of our generals and that of Catherine Boucher (married, alas!), and also among them certain other faces that filled me with bitterness—those of Beaupère and Courcelles and a number of their fellow-fiends. I saw Haumette and Little Mengette—edging along toward fifty, now, and mothers of many children. I saw Noël's father, and the parents of the Paladin and the Sunflower.

It was beautiful to hear the Duke d'Alençon praise Joan's splendid capacities as a general, and to hear the Bastard indorse these praises with his eloquent tongue and then go on and tell how sweet and good Joan was, and how full of pluck and fire and impetuosity, and mischief, and mirthfulness, and tenderness, and compassion, and everything that was pure and fine and noble and lovely. He made her live again before me, and wrung my heart.

I have finished my story of Joan of Arc, that wonderful child, that sublime personality, that spirit which in one regard has had no peer and will have none—this: its purity from all alloy of self-seeking, self-interest, personal ambition. In it no trace of these motives can be found, search as you may, and this cannot be said of any other person whose name appears in profane history.

With Joan of Arc love of country was more than a sentiment—it was a passion. She was the Genius of Patriotism—she was Patriotism embodied, concreted, made flesh, and palpable to the touch and visible to the eye.

Love, Mercy, Charity, Fortitude, War, Peace, Poetry, Music —these may be symbolized as any shall prefer: by figures of either sex and of any age; but a slender girl in her first young bloom, with the martyr's crown upon her head, and in her hand the sword that severed her country's bonds—shall not this, and no other, stand for PATRIOTISM through all the ages until time shall end?

CHRONOLOGY

NOTE ON THE TEXTS

NOTES

Chronology

1835   Samuel Langhorne Clemens born prematurely on November 30 in Florida, Missouri, fifth surviving child of John Marshall Clemens (b. 1798) and Jane Lampton Clemens (b. 1803). Siblings are brother Orion (b. 1825), sisters Pamela (b. 1827) and Margaret (b. 1830), and brother Benjamin (b. 1832). At time of birth Halley's Comet is still visible in the sky (Clemens will often mention this later in life). Family lives in rented house on South Mill Street and father runs store in partnership with John Adams Quarles, husband of Jane Lampton Clemens' sister, Martha Ann "Patsy" Quarles. (Grandparents Samuel and Pamelia Clemens were slave-owning farmers in Campbell County, Virginia, before moving family to southern bank of Ohio River in Mason County, Virginia—now West Virginia—in 1803 or 1804. Grandmother, widowed in 1805, moved with her five children to Adair County, Kentucky, to live with her brother; she married Simon Hancock in 1809. By 1812 father was supporting himself in a Lynchburg, Virginia, ironworks. After paying debts owed to stepfather Hancock, father and siblings settled their father's estate in 1821; John Clemens' share included three slaves. He then read law with Cyrus Walker in Columbia, Kentucky, received his license to practice in 1822, and in 1823 married Jane Lampton, a cousin of Walker's wife; the daughter of Benjamin and Margaret Casey Lampton, she was born in Columbia and was descended from early English and Irish settlers of Kentucky. They moved to Gainesboro, Tennessee, then Jamestown, Tennessee, where John Clemens built a large house, practiced law, opened a store, and bought 75,000 acres of uncleared land before moving in 1831 to nearby Three Forks of Wolf River, where he bought 200 acres of farmland and built a log house. In 1835 the family moved with their remaining slave, a woman named Jenny, to Florida, Missouri, on the Salt River, where John and Martha Ann Quarles were already established and where grandfather Benjamin Lampton and other members of mother's family also lived. After their arrival in June father quickly acquired 120 acres of government land, and then bought a 2¾-acre homesite for $300.)

1836   Clemens is frequently sick and mother is unsure if he will live. Family buys house in town from grandfather Lampton.

1837   Grandfather dies. Father dissolves partnership with Quarles and sets up his own store; heads committees to improve Salt River navigation, develop railroads, and start an academy. Father becomes Monroe County judge.

1838   Family moves into new house built by father. Brother Henry born July 13.

1839   Clemens walks in his sleep (will often do so for several years). Sister Margaret dies of "bilious fever" August 17. Father earns $5,000 from land sales and then purchases $7,000 worth of property in Hannibal, Missouri, a rapidly growing port village of a thousand inhabitants on the Mississippi, 30 miles from Florida and about 130 miles north of St. Louis by water. Family moves to Hannibal in November; other Florida residents move as well, including family friends Dr. Hugh Meredith and schoolteacher Mary Ann Newcomb. Father opens store and family lives in the Virginia House, former hotel that is part of purchased property.

1840   Clemens enters school taught by Elizabeth Horr and Mary Ann Newcomb (will attend three other schools in Hannibal).

1841   Mother and sister Pamela join Presbyterian church in February. Newcomb, who often eats as a paying guest with the Clemenses, opens her own school in basement of Presbyterian church. Father sells house in Florida to uncle John Quarles in August and transfers title to Virginia House to creditor in October.

1842   Brother Benjamin dies on May 12 after a few days of illness. Orion moves to St. Louis to work as printer. Clemens continues to be sickly, and is doctored with castor oil, calomel, rhubarb, and jalap, as well as poultices, socks full of hot ashes, and various water treatments. Has nightmares and continues to walk in his sleep. Family sells Jenny.

1843   Mother moves children from Methodist to Presbyterian Sunday school. Clemens enjoys visits to the Quarles' family farm in Florida (will spend two or three months a year with them for several years). Takes with him his own trained cat (will have lifelong love of cats). Attends country summer school with cousins once or twice a week and enjoys playing with the slaves on the farm. Becomes especially appreciative of the friendship and counsel of Dann, a slave in his late thirties (emancipated by Quarles in 1855). Father auctions off much of his Hannibal property to pay debts. James C. Clemens, a distant cousin, buys one lot on Hill Street and leases it to father to build house.

1844   During epidemic in spring, Clemens deliberately catches measles from Will Bowen, his closest friend, and nearly dies as a result. Father helps found Hannibal Library Institute (will later head civic committees promoting railroad construction and higher education) and is elected justice of the peace. Clemens is horrified when he finds a corpse in his father's office (body is of an emigrant to California stabbed in a quarrel while in town).

1845   Watches man die in the street after being shot by Hannibal merchant William Owsley (who is later acquitted). Group of friends includes Will Bowen and his brother Sam, John Briggs, Ed Stevens, John Garth, Anna Laura Hawkins, and Tom Blankenship. Health improves, and enjoys swimming, fishing, playing Robin Hood, pirates, and Crusaders. Attends school taught by Samuel Cross.

1846   Mother takes in paying guests for meals. Family sells furniture to help pay debts and moves in with pharmacist Orville Grant; mother supplies him with meals in exchange for rent. In November, father announces candidacy for clerk of the circuit court (becomes favored to win election, held in August 1847). Clemens and friends enjoy watching local volunteer infantry drill for service in Mexican War.

1847   Father dies of pneumonia on March 24. Clemens watches through keyhole as Dr. Meredith performs postmortem examination. Family moves back to frame house at 206 Hill Street. Orion, working as printer in St. Louis, provides main family support, while Pamela gives guitar and piano lessons, mother continues to take in paying guests for meals, and Clemens works at odd jobs, including helping a blacksmith and clerking in a grocery store, a pharmacy, and a bookstore. Begins attending John D. Dawson's school. Witnesses drowning of friend Clint Levering while swimming with a group of friends in the Mississippi in August. While fishing on Sny Island a few days later, Clemens and several friends discover the body of a drowned fugitive slave, whom Bence Blankenship (Tom's older brother) had been secretly supplying with food. Gets job in fall as errand boy and delivers papers for printer Henry La Cossitt at the Hannibal *Gazette*.

1848   Still attending Dawson's school, begins working in late spring in the office of Joseph P. Ament's *Missouri Courier* as chore boy and printer's devil. Lives meagerly in Ament's house as an apprentice. Goes skating late in the year on the Mississippi with friend Tom Nash; when the ice breaks, Clemens manages to get to shore safely, but Nash falls through (illnesses suffered as a result eventually make Nash deaf).

1849   Gold rush emigrants pass through Hannibal en route to California, and 80 Hannibal residents join them, including Dawson, head of the last school Clemens attends, and Samuel Cross. Enjoys company of fellow apprentices Wales McCormick and T. P. "Pet" McMurry. Clemens reads Cooper, Marryat, Dickens, Byron, Scott, and anything else he can find that features knights, pirates, or Crusaders (Henry is considered to be the serious reader in the family).

1850   Joins Cadets of Temperance, briefly gives up smoking and chewing tobacco, and marches in parades with friends. In May, witnesses a poor widow shoot and kill the leader of a group of strangers from Illinois who are trying to force their way into her house. Orion returns to Hannibal from St. Louis and begins publishing weekly newspaper, the *Western Union*.

1851   Clemens leaves *Missouri Courier* and, with Henry, goes to work for Orion as a typesetter and editorial assistant;

although Orion promises Clemens $3.50 a week in wages, no money is ever available. Likes apprentice Jim Wolf, who boards with Clemens family. Publishes first known sketch, "A Gallant Fireman," in the *Western Union* January 16. Cholera epidemic in June kills 24 people in Hannibal. Orion buys Hannibal *Journal* in September. Sister Pamela marries William A. Moffett on September 20 and moves to St. Louis.

1852   Fire destroys *Journal* office, and Orion rents new space. Clemens occasionally writes humorous sketches for the Hannibal *Journal*. "The Dandy Frightening the Squatter" appears in the Boston *Carpet-Bag* and "Hannibal, Missouri" in the Philadelphia *American Courier* in May. Niece Annie Moffett born in July. During Orion's absence on business trips, Clemens becomes responsible for getting paper out. On September 9 signs a sketch "W. Epaminondas Adrastus Perkins," his first known use of a pseudonym.

1853   In January Clemens and Will Bowen give matches to a drunk in the town jail, who later that night sets fire to his cell and burns to death. (Clemens will often recall this incident.) Leaves Hannibal in early June and works as a typesetter in St. Louis for Thomas Watt Ustick, who does the printing for the *Evening News* and other publications. Goes to New York City by steamer and rail in late August. Visits Crystal Palace, center of New York World's Fair. Works for low pay in John A. Gray's large print shop on Cliff Street and boards on Duane Street. Takes pride in his typesetting skill, attends theater, and spends evenings reading in the printers' free library. Has two of his letters from New York printed in Hannibal *Journal* before Orion sells paper in September and moves with mother and brother Henry to Muscatine, Iowa, where Orion buys share in, and becomes co-editor of, the Muscatine *Journal*. Clemens moves to Philadelphia in late October. Works as typesetter, writes letters for the Muscatine *Journal*, and enjoys visiting sites connected with Benjamin Franklin and the Revolution.

1854   Briefly visits Washington, D.C., in February and records his impressions in letter for the Muscatine *Journal*. Returns to Philadelphia for a few weeks, then goes to New York, where he finds high unemployment among printers due to fires that had destroyed Harpers and another publishing house. Goes to Muscatine in spring and works for the *Journal*. Moves to St. Louis in summer and resumes work at the *Evening News*, boarding and lodging with the Paveys from Hannibal at the corner of 4th and Wash streets. Mother moves in with Pamela and William Moffett on Pine Street in St. Louis. Orion marries Mary Eleanor (Mollie) Stotts of Keokuk, Iowa, on December 19.

1855   Writes four letters for the Muscatine *Journal* before Orion sells paper in June and moves to Keokuk, where he sets up the Ben Franklin Book and Job Office, a printing shop. Clemens joins him in mid-June, working for $5 a week and board before becoming a partner in the business (mother remains in St. Louis with the Moffetts). Travels to Hannibal and Palymra in July to collect belongings and arrange for sale of Hill Street house, then goes on to Paris and Florida, Missouri, to settle mother's inheritance from grandfather Benjamin Lampton and great-aunt Diana Lampton. Visits with uncle John Quarles.

1856   Sees mother and Pamela in St. Louis in October, and writes his first "Thomas Jefferson Snodgrass" letter for the Keokuk *Post*. Moves to Cincinnati, where he works as a typesetter and writes two more Snodgrass letters for the *Post*.

1857   Leaves Cincinnati in April by steamboat for New Orleans, intending to seek his fortune in South America, but instead becomes cub riverboat pilot under Horace Bixby for an apprentice fee of $500 (borrows the first $100 from William Moffett, then pays more in installments, though Bixby will not charge him the full amount). Works on several boats and learns Mississippi River between New Orleans and St. Louis. Orion sells Keokuk print shop and goes to Jamestown, Tennessee, where family owns land, to study law and try to survey and sell the property (is unsuccessful in selling land and returns to Keokuk in July 1858 to practice law).

1858   Clemens serves as cub on the *Pennsylvania* under pilot William Brown, whom he considers a tyrant. Arranges job as "mud clerk" (purser's assistant) for brother Henry aboard the boat. Meets and falls in love with Laura M. Wright, the 14-year-old daughter of a Missouri judge (her family does not approve and intercepts letters). Hits Brown after the pilot strikes Henry, then leaves the *Pennsylvania* when no replacement can be found for Brown. Henry remains with crew and is badly injured in a boiler explosion below Memphis on June 13. Clemens arrives in Memphis June 15, and is with Henry when he dies on June 21 (Brown is also among the dead). Feels crazed with grief and guilt. Henry is buried in Hannibal June 25. Clemens resumes apprenticeship and steers for two pilot friends from Hannibal, Bart and Sam Bowen.

1859–60   Receives his pilot's license on April 9, 1859. Becomes steadily employed and well paid for his work. Feels at home in New Orleans and St. Louis, where he sees Pamela and her family. Continues his self-education and studies French. In May 1859 publishes a lampoon of senior pilot Isaiah Sellers (from whom Clemens later claimed he appropriated the pen name "Mark Twain") and writes several other sketches. Orion moves to Memphis to practice law in May 1860.

1861   Clemens becomes member of the Polar Star Lodge 79, a St. Louis Masonic lodge (maintains contact with the lodge until formally resigning in October 1869). Takes mother on a private steamboat excursion from St. Louis to New Orleans and back. In letter to Orion, describes Goldsmith's *The Citizen of the World* and Cervantes' *Don Quixote* as his *"beau ideals"* of fine writing." Is much impressed by Frederick Edwin Church's painting *Heart of the Andes*, on exhibit in St. Louis. Through the influence of St. Louis lawyer Edward Bates, attorney general in the new Lincoln administration, Orion is appointed secretary of Nevada Territory in March. By May outbreak of the Civil War has severely disrupted river traffic. After spending some time with family in St. Louis, fearful of being impressed as gunboat pilot by Union forces, Clemens goes to Hannibal in mid-June and helps form the Marion Rangers, group of Confederate volunteers composed of old Hannibal schoolmates, including Sam Bowen, John L. Robards, Perry Smith, and Ed Stevens. After two weeks of camping and retreating across countryside, half the group decides to disband (Absalom Grimes later carried mail for the Confederacy, John Meredith, son of the Clemenses' doctor, became chief of a guerrilla band, and Perry Smith was killed in battle). Clemens returns to St. Louis in early July and leaves with Orion for Nevada on July 18. Travels on steamer *Sioux City* up the Missouri to St. Joseph, Missouri, then goes by stagecoach through Fort Kearny, Scotts Bluff, South Pass, Fort Bridger, and Salt Lake City, arriving in Carson City, Nevada, on August 14. Meets and becomes friendly with Horatio G. Phillips, Robert Howland, and John D. Kinney. Travels to Aurora, Nevada, in the Esmeralda mining district in early September, where he shares claims with Phillips. Takes trips with Kinney to establish timber claims near Lake Bigler (later Tahoe), and accidentally starts forest fire. Speculates in silver- and gold-mining stocks and serves for $8 a day as Orion's secretary during the fall session of the territorial legislature. Meets Clement T. Rice, who will become close friend and journalistic collaborator. Goes on prospecting trip to Humboldt County, Nevada, with Keokuk friend William H. Clagett in December. Reads and quotes from Dickens' *Dombey and Son*.

1862 Returns to Carson City in late January, then to Aurora in April. Continues prospecting with Phillips without much success and writes occasional letters for the Keokuk *Gate City* and Carson City *Silver Age*; begins sending letters to the Virginia City, Nevada, *Territorial Enterprise* in late April, using pen name "Josh." Clemens and Phillips learn advanced techniques of reducing silver ore from Joshua Eliot Clayton. Has falling-out with Phillips. In July begins to feel restless and wants to move on. Becomes partner in potentially lucrative mining claim and shares cabin for a short time with Calvin H. Higbie (will later dedicate *Roughing It* to him). Nurses Captain John Nye, brother of governor of the Nevada Territory, James Warren Nye, for nine days when he is sick with "inflammatory rheumatism." "Josh" letters to the *Territorial Enterprise* attract the attention of business manager William H. Barstow and editor Joseph T. Goodman, and they offer Clemens a salaried job as reporter ($25 per week) in late July. Takes two-week walking trip through the White Mountains along the Nevada-California border, for pleasure and to look for legendary lost gold "cement" mine. Moves to Virginia

City and begins work as local reporter for the *Territorial Enterprise* in late September; duties include covering fall legislative session in Carson City. Writes "The Petrified Man," a hoax made up to "worry" Judge G. T. Sewall of Humboldt County. Begins lasting friendships with Joseph T. Goodman and Dan De Quille (William Wright), fellow reporter and humorist. Becomes responsible for local reporting when De Quille leaves at end of year on extended visit home to Iowa.

1863   Continues to trade in mining stocks, sometimes receiving free shares in return for favorable mention in the *Enterprise*. Orion serves as acting governor of Nevada during Governor Nye's absence from the territory (Nye returns in July). Clemens goes to Carson City for a week and sends three letters to the *Enterprise*, published February 3, 5, and 8, signing them "Mark Twain," his first known use of the name. Continues his mock feud in print with "the Unreliable," the name he has given to his friend and fellow reporter Clement T. Rice. Leaves Virginia City with Rice early in May to visit San Francisco, where he sees Neil Moss, former classmate and son of the wealthiest man in Hannibal, who has been prospecting without success, and Bill Briggs (brother of his close Hannibal friend John Briggs), who is now running a successful gambling establishment. Enjoys San Francisco, staying at the Occidental Hotel and the Lick House. Makes money selling and trading stocks. Arranges to become Nevada correspondent for the San Francisco *Morning Call*. Returns to Virginia City in July and moves into the new White House hotel; it burns down on July 26 and Clemens loses all his possessions, including his mine stocks. Sick with a severe cold and bronchitis, goes to Lake Bigler with young journalist friend Adair Wilson, and then to Steamboat Springs, nine miles northwest of Virginia City, to try its hot mineral water. When Dan De Quille returns to Virginia City and resumes duties as local editor for the *Enterprise*, Clemens goes to San Francisco for a month. Writes "How to Cure a Cold," his first piece for the *Golden Era*, a San Francisco literary weekly. Returns to Nevada in time to serve as recording secretary of the Washoe Agricultural, Mining, and Mechanical Society Fair, held in Carson City in mid-October. Writes a hoax about a man killing his family, "A Bloody Massacre Near Carson"; when it is uncovered,

other papers that had reported it as a true story are furious
and refuse to reprint news stories from the *Enterprise*.
Clemens offers to resign, but Goodman and De Quille
assure him that the anger will diminish and the story will
be remembered. Rents suite of rooms with De Quille at 25
North B Street in Virginia City. Goes to Carson City to
cover convention drafting first state constitution, then returns to Virginia City in time to meet humorist Artemus
Ward (Charles Farrar Browne), who encourages him to
write for the New York *Mercury*. Enjoys spirited Christmas
Eve dinner with Ward, De Quille, Goodman, and others,
which ends with Ward and Clemens walking across the
rooftops in Virginia City.

1864   Reports on rejection by the voters on January 19 of the
proposed state constitution (clause proposing tax on un-
developed mines is unpopular). Publishes two articles in
the New York *Mercury*, "Doings in Nevada" (February 7)
and "Those Blasted Children" (February 21). Sees Reuel
Gridley, friend from Hannibal, in May when Gridley
tours Nevada raising funds for the Sanitary Commission
Fair in St. Louis (Commission aids sick and wounded
Union soldiers). Joins Gridley in repeatedly auctioning off
flour sack, with different towns and groups in Storey
County competing to outbid one another (county eventually contributes $22,000 to the fair). Writes two contro-
versial pieces for the *Enterprise* in late May; one repeats
rumor that Carson City women were diverting funds intended for the Sanitary Commission to a freedman's society, and the other alleges that the Virginia City *Union* has
not fulfilled its bid in the flour-sack auction. When reply
in the *Union* calls him "an unmitigated *liar, a poltroon and
a puppy*," Clemens challenges its editor, James L. Laird, to
a duel, while publicly and privately apologizing to the
Carson City women. After exchanging several letters with
Laird, Clemens publishes the correspondence on May 24,
then becomes concerned about Nevada law outlawing
dueling challenges. Leaves with Stephen E. Gillis, close
friend and news editor at the *Enterprise*, and Goodman for
San Francisco on May 29 (will become ashamed of this
"dueling" episode in later years). Rooms with Gillis in
several hotels, rooming houses, and private homes. Becomes reporter for the San Francisco *Morning Call* for
$40 a week and continues to contribute pieces to the

Golden Era. Meets the Reverend Henry Whitney Bellows, founder and president of the United States Sanitary Commission, and enjoys his sense of humor. Finds long hours at the *Call* tedious and makes new arrangement to work only during daylight hours for $25 a week. Contracts to write four articles for $50 a month (same amount he had received from the *Golden Era*) for newly established literary magazine, the *Californian*, owned by Charles Henry Webb and edited by Bret Harte. Bored with the *Call*, becomes lax about work; resigns on October 10 at the suggestion of one of the proprietors. Writes several articles for the *Enterprise* criticizing San Francisco police for corruption, incompetence, and mistreatment of Chinese immigrants. When Gillis is charged for his part in a barroom brawl, they decide in early December to go to Jackass Hill in Tuolumne County, California, where Jim and William Gillis, Stephen's brothers, and Dick Stoker have pocketmine claims. Remains in camp after Stephen Gillis returns to Virginia City.

1865   In January goes with Jim Gillis to Angel's Camp in Calaveras County and stays there four weeks (soon joined by Stoker), spending most of the time indoors because of bad weather. Listens to stories told by prospectors, one of which is about a jumping frog, and writes notes in journal. Returns briefly to Jackass Hill and then goes to San Francisco in late February. Moves into the Gillis family rooming house at 44 Minna Street. Writes articles for the *Californian*, and pieces for the *Golden Era*, other California journals, and the *Enterprise*. Befriends Charles Warren Stoddard, another contributor to the *Californian*. Begins writing more often for the *Enterprise* and soon contracts to write a letter a day for $100 a month. Takes on another job with the San Francisco *Dramatic Chronicle* for $40 a week, writing Orion that he is determined to get out of debt. Articles reprinted in New York begin to bring recognition (New York *Round Table* calls him "the foremost among the merry gentlemen of the California press"). Experiences strong earthquake on October 8 that causes significant damage in San Francisco, San Jose, and Santa Cruz. After repeated requests from Artemus Ward for a sketch to include in a book of humorous works, sends "Jim Smiley and His Jumping Frog" to him, but the text arrives too late for inclusion in the book and is published in Henry

Clapp's *Saturday Press*. The story is widely reprinted all over the country.

1866   Stops writing for the *Californian* (both it and the *Golden Era* will reprint articles published in the *Enterprise*). Begins to think of writing a book about the Mississippi, and also reviews his articles, saving some and destroying others. Sails on the *Ajax* on March 7 for the Sandwich Islands (Hawaii) as roving correspondent for the Sacramento *Union*. Arrives in Honolulu on March 18. Explores Oahu on horseback (will also ride on Maui and Hawaii), meets King Kamehameha V, and discovers that he is also a Mason. Goes to Maui by small schooner in mid-April; returns to Honolulu May 22, then sails on May 26 to the island of Hawaii, where he sees the volcano Kilauea erupting. Returns to Oahu June 16. Reads Oliver Wendell Holmes' *Songs in Many Keys* while recovering from saddle boils. Meets Anson Burlingame, American minister to China, in Honolulu and spends time with him and his son Edward. Takes notes while Burlingame interviews survivors of the shipwrecked *Hornet* and writes report for the *Union* that scoops all other papers. Sails for San Francisco July 19 on the *Smyrniote*. Fellow passengers include three *Hornet* survivors; Clemens reads and copies parts of their diaries for article "Forty-three Days in an Open Boat" (published in *Harper's Magazine* in December). Arrives in San Francisco on August 13. Sees Orion and his wife, Mollie, who are in city before sailing for the East Coast. Goes to Sacramento and collects $20 for each week of his trip and $100 for each column of the *Hornet* story. Writes articles for the *Union* and the New York *Weekly Review*, and covers California State Agricultural Society Fair in Sacramento. Delivers first lecture on October 2, speaking on the Sandwich Islands to a large, appreciative audience at Maguire's Academy of Music in San Francisco. Goes on tour, lecturing in Sacramento, Marysville, Grass Valley, Nevada City, Red Dog, and You Bet in California, and then in Virginia City, Carson City, Dayton, Silver City, Washoe City, and Gold City in Nevada. Returns to California and appears in San Francisco, San Jose, Petaluma, and Oakland, concluding tour with a special appearance in San Francisco on December 10 at the request of Frederick F. Low, governor of California, and Henry G. Blasdel, governor of Nevada. Becomes traveling correspondent for the San Francisco *Alta California* and leaves San Francisco December 15 aboard the *America*, captained by Edgar Wakeman. Enjoys company of Wakeman and writes down some of his stories. Crosses Central America by way of Nicaragua.

1867   Arrives in Greytown, Nicaragua, and sails on *San Francisco* to New York. Cholera breaks out and seven passengers die; when ship stops at Key West, a number of fearful passengers disembark. Clemens arrives in New York January 12 and takes rooms at the Metropolitan Hotel (establishment frequented by westerners). Sees old California friends Frank Fuller (who will later manage a series of lectures for Clemens) and Charles Henry Webb, who offers to help him put together a book of sketches (Webb will publish it himself after other publishers turn it down). Through Webb, meets Edward H. House of the New York *Tribune*, Henry Clapp, and John Hay. Sends letters to the *Alta* and makes arrangements to contribute articles to the New York *Sunday Mercury*, the *Evening Express* and the New York *Weekly*. Has no success finding a publisher for the Sandwich Islands letters. Reserves cabin on the *Quaker City* for the first American transatlantic excursion, organized by Henry Ward Beecher's congregation (Beecher and General Sherman are expected to be passengers), then goes to St. Louis to visit family (Pamela's husband had died in August 1865). Publishes three satirical articles on women's suffrage in *Missouri Democrat*. Lectures successfully in St. Louis, Hannibal, Keokuk, and Quincy, Illinois, and sees old friends. Returns to New York on April 15 and soon moves into the Westminster Hotel. *The Celebrated Jumping Frog of Calaveras County, and Other Sketches* published by Webb on April 30 (Clemens is unhappy with Webb's editing and sales are poor). Gives three successful lectures in New York and Brooklyn in May. Accepts assignments to write for the New York *Tribune*, the New York *Herald* (unsigned articles), and the *Alta*. Boards *Quaker City* on June 8. After two days anchored off Brooklyn because of bad weather, the ship sails on June 10 for Europe and the Holy Land. Disappointed by absence of Beecher and Sherman and finds most of the passengers too pious and staid, but makes friends with some, including Daniel Slote, his cabin mate, Moses Sperry Beach, editor of the New York *Sun*, and his daughter Emma, John A. Van Nostrand, Julius Moulton, Dr. Abraham Reeves Jackson, Julia Newell, Solon Long Severance and his wife, Emily, Mary Mason Fairbanks ("Mother Fairbanks"), who becomes one of his closest friends and advisers, and 18-year-old Charles Jervis Langdon, from Elmira, New York, who shows Clemens a picture of his sister, Olivia. Travels to North Africa, Spain, France, Italy, Greece, Russia (where members of the excursion meet with Czar Alexander II at Yalta in the Crimea on August 26), Turkey, the Holy Land, and Egypt. Returns to New York on November 19, and goes to Washington, D.C., where he serves for a few weeks as private secretary to William M. Stewart, Republican senator from Nevada. Acts as Washington correspondent for the *Territorial Enterprise*, *Alta California*, and the New York *Tribune*. Receives several offers from book publishers; prefers one from the American Publishing Company, a subscription firm in Hartford, Connecticut. Returns to New York on Christmas Day and moves in with Dan Slote's family. Invited by Charles Langdon to dine with his family at the St. Nicholas Hotel, meets Olivia Louise (Livy) Langdon (b. Nov. 27, 1845). Goes with the Langdons to hear Charles Dickens read.

1868   Spends New Year's Day visiting with Livy and her friend Alice Hooker. Attends services given by Henry Ward Beecher as guest of *Quaker City* friends, Moses and Emma Beach. Has dinner at Beecher's home and meets his sister, Harriet Beecher Stowe. Returns to Washington on January 8. Delivers lecture "The Frozen Truth," an account of the cruise, and gives a successful toast to "Woman" at the Washington Newspaper Correspondents' Club. Lodges at several addresses, often rooming with John Henry Riley, *Alta* correspondent in Washington. Tries unsuccessfully to obtain Patent Office clerkship for Orion. Stops in New York in late January and arranges to write articles for the *Herald*. Makes agreement in Hartford with Elisha Bliss to have his book on the excursion published by the American Publishing Company. Stays with John Hooker (father of Alice Hooker) and his family in the "Nook Farm" area of Hartford, but is uncomfortable because he cannot smoke openly. Returns to Washington and works on book. Sails for California on March 11 to arrange republication rights for his *Alta* letters from the excursion, which the newspaper had copyrighted. Leaves from New York aboard the *Henry Chauncey*, crosses Panama, boards the *Sacramento*, and arrives in San Francisco on April 2. Sees Anson Burlingame at the Occidental Hotel, where they are both staying. Lectures in San Francisco and interior towns, then travels by train and stagecoach from Sacramento to Virginia City, arriving on April 24. Lectures there and in Carson City. Returns to San Francisco May 5. Reaches agreement with the *Alta* regarding *Quaker City* material. Works intensively on book, revising, arranging, and cutting letters and adding new passages. In June asks Bret Harte to read the manuscript and make suggestions (will remember his help with appreciation). Gives another lecture in San Francisco (reviewed more favorably than the earlier ones). Sails for New York on the *Montana* July 6 and arrives in New York on the *Henry Chauncey* July 29. Stays at the Westminster Hotel, where he again sees Burlingame; writes, with his help, "The Treaty with China," article that is published on the front page of the New York *Tribune*. Goes to Hartford and stays with the Blisses while he works on the book. After brief return to New York City goes to visit the Langdon family in Elmira, New York. (Jervis, b. 1809, and Olivia Lewis Langdon, b. 1810, both natives of New York State, were married in 1832 and lived in a succession of towns in upstate New York, where Jervis worked as a storekeeper. They were ardent abolitionists and "conductors" on the Underground Railroad, and had sheltered Frederick Douglass in Millport in 1842 while he was still a fugitive slave. After settling in Elmira in 1845 the Langdons soon prospered in the lumber business and then became wealthy in the coal trade. Their friends included abolitionists Gerritt Smith, William Lloyd Garrison, Wendell Phillips, and Frederick Douglass, and women's rights advocate Anna E. Dickinson. When Livy was 16 years old, a fall on the ice invalided her for two years. She regained her mobility after being treated by Dr. Newton, a faith healer, although for the remainder of her life she is unable to walk very far.) Clemens falls in love with Livy and proposes to her early in September, but is refused. Leaves on September 8 with Charles Langdon to visit Mary Fairbanks and her husband, Abel, at their home in Cleveland. Goes on alone to see family in

St. Louis. Courts Livy with letters. Visits her again in late September, and then goes to Hartford to work on book. Meets the Reverend Joseph H. Twichell, a Congregational minister who will become one of his closest lifetime friends. Returns to New York in late October and gives lecture, "The American Vandal Abroad," in Cleveland, Pittsburgh, and Elmira in November. Proposes to Livy again and she confesses that she loves him. Promises to reform himself, to become religious, and to stop drinking. Jervis Langdon has a former employee make inquiries in San Francisco about Clemens' past. Resumes lectures in December, appearing in New Jersey, New York (where he again stops in Elmira), Pennsylvania, Michigan, Indiana, and Illinois.

1869   Spends New Year's Day with the Fairbanks in Cleveland. Continues lecture tour through Ohio, Illinois, Michigan, Iowa, Wisconsin, Pennsylvania, and New Jersey. Writes long letters to Livy, and marks up books for her to read, in particular Oliver Wendell Holmes' *The Autocrat of the Breakfast Table* (they call it their "courting-book"); she sends him marked copies of Henry Ward Beecher's sermons. Clemens learns that some Californians have responded unfavorably to Jervis Langdon's inquiries about his character; he tells Langdon that though many people were acquainted with him, only five were close, and that he is no longer the same person he was then. Returns to Elmira; engagement is formally announced February 4. Concerned about earning steady income, investigates buying share in either the Cleveland *Herald*, partly owned by Abel Fairbanks, or the Hartford *Courant*, published in a city where he and Livy have many friends. While working on his book in Hartford in early March, rereads *Gulliver's Travels* and finds that though he had enjoyed it as a boy, he had no idea then how wonderful it was. Writes to Livy about it (and *Don Quixote*, which she is reading) that he "will mark it & tear it until it is fit for your eyes. . . .You are as pure as snow, & I would have you always so— untainted, untouched even by the impure thoughts of others. . . ." Hears Petroleum V. Nasby (David Ross Locke) lecture in Hartford and they become friends. Goes to Boston, where Nasby introduces him to Holmes. Returns to Elmira to read proofs, with Livy's assistance (she will continue to help edit his work). Meets Wendell Phillips in March and Anna E. Dickinson in April when they come to visit the Langdons. Leaves Elmira with Charles Langdon on May 5 and goes to New York and Hartford, where he continues work on book. Engages James Redpath as his lecture agent and begins planning fall tour. Writes articles, including "Personal Habits of the Siamese Twins." Returns to Elmira at the end of May. Finishes reading proofs and goes with Langdon family to the St. Nicholas Hotel in New York, then to Hartford, where they attend the June 17 wedding of Alice Hooker to John Day. Meets Charles Dudley Warner, part-owner of the Hartford *Courant*, at the wedding; he will become a life-long close friend. After a short visit to New York, returns with Livy to Elmira. Unable to buy a share in the Hartford *Courant*, and feeling the price of investing in the Cleveland *Herald* is too high, on the advice of Jervis Langdon buys a one-third interest in the Buffalo *Express* for $25,000 in August (Clemens puts in $2,500, Langdon lends him $12,500, and the remainder is to be paid in installments). Moves to Buffalo and takes lodgings in rooming house at 39 Swan Street, close to the *Express* office. Makes friends with young newlywed couple living there, John James and Esther (Essie) Keeler Norton McWilliams. Changes the typographical look of the *Express*, using smaller type for headlines and saving larger type for important news. Works closely with part-owner and editor-in-chief Josephus Nelson Larned, who becomes lifelong friend. *The Innocents Abroad*, account of *Quaker City* excursion, is published by American Publishing Company on August 15; it receives good reviews and sells well. Visits Elmira whenever possible. Prepares lecture "Our Fellow Savages of the Sandwich Islands" in Elmira and begins tour in Pittsburgh on November 1. Continues lecturing in Massachusetts, Rhode Island, Connecticut, New York, Washington, D.C., and Maine, using Young's Hotel in Boston as his base. Meets other lyceum lecturers, including humorist Josh Billings (Henry Wheeler Shaw). Begins long, close friendship with William Dean Howells, who had enthusiastically reviewed *The Innocents Abroad*. Returns briefly to Hartford to pick up first-quarter royalty check and finds that the Hartford *Courant* is now eager to have him, but is unable to accept because of his commit-

ment to the *Express*. Sees Langdons in New York in early
December. Meets Frederick Douglass in Boston and is impressed by him.

1870   Sends out wedding invitations to old friends, including
Dan De Quille, Charles Warren Stoddard, Horace Bixby,
and informal invitations to California mining friends Jim
Gillis and Dick Stoker. Sees Joseph Goodman when he
comes to New York before sailing for Europe. Elated by
sales of book. No longer drinks, and cuts down on his
smoking. Continues lecturing in New York until January
21. Marries Livy in Elmira on February 2, with Thomas
Beecher (half-brother of Henry Ward Beecher and uncle
of Alice Hooker) and Twichell performing the service.
Sister Pamela and niece Annie Moffett attend. Goes by
private train to Buffalo with Livy and a small party of
guests on February 3. Clemens expects to be moving into
a boarding house and is surprised by gift from Jervis
Langdon of furnished house at 472 Delaware Street, with
three servants, stable, and horse and carriage (worth
more than $40,000). House guests include Pamela and
Annie, the Twichells, friends from Elmira, and Petroleum
V. Nasby. Clemens goes to the *Express* offices only twice a
week. Signs contract in March with *Galaxy* to supply a
monthly humorous column, "Memoranda," for $2,000 a
year, reserving all republication rights to himself (first
column appears in May). Continues writing for the *Express*, but feels that *Galaxy* allows him more freedom.
Livy begins to address him as "Youth" (will do so for the
rest of her life). Becomes close friends with poet and es-
sayist David Gray, part-owner and associate editor of the
Buffalo *Courier*, and his wife, Martha. Mother comes to
visit in April (her first meeting with Livy), while sister
prepares to move to Fredonia, New York, 60 miles from
Buffalo. Jervis Langdon's health deteriorates, and Clemenses go to Elmira for two weeks (will continue to help
nurse Langdon; Clemens often sits at his bedside for
four hours a night). Goes to Washington, D.C., in early
July to lobby for passage of bill to divide Tennessee into
two judicial districts (measure would potentially benefit
both Jervis Langdon's lumber business and Orion's plans
to sell family land near Jamestown). Sees old friends Senator William M. Stewart, Vice-President Schuyler Colfax,
and Thomas Fitch (now congressman from Nevada), and

meets President Ulysses S. Grant. Sees old friend John Henry Riley. Returns to Elmira and signs new contract with Bliss for book on the West for 7½ percent royalty. Jervis Langdon dies August 6 of stomach cancer. Livy is grief-stricken; Clemens gives her opiates to help her sleep. Livy's mother and Emma Nye, Livy's old class-mate, come to visit in Buffalo late in August. Nye imme-diately falls ill with typhoid; Livy cares for her with help of hired nurse. Clemens continues to write *Galaxy* articles and works on western book. Writes Orion expressing his exasperation over Orion's schemes for selling Tennessee land. Delights in making burlesque woodcut, "Fortifica-tions of Paris," for paper. Visits mother, sister, nephew, and niece in Fredonia. Susan Langdon Crane (Livy's fos-ter sister, b. 1836, who was orphaned in 1840 and then adopted by the Langdons) comes to take care of Livy, who is pregnant and exhausted. Clemens gets Orion a job in Hartford as editor of Bliss's new magazine, *Ameri-can Publisher*, for $100 a month (first issue comes out in April 1871). Son Langdon born, one month prematurely, on November 7 and at first is not expected to live. Mary Fairbanks comes to help nurse Livy. Clemens goes to New York to meet Webb about obtaining rights to *Cele-brated Jumping Frog of Calaveras County*, forgoes $600 due in royalties, and pays Webb an additional $800 for rights and plates (will destroy them). Arranges for Riley to go to South Africa and research book on its diamond fields, which Clemens will write; pays Riley's passage and salary ($100 a month). Contracts with Bliss for South Af-rican book and *Mark Twain's Sketches, New & Old*. Son's health continues to be poor.

1871   Attends wedding in Cleveland of Mary Fairbanks' step-daughter, Alice, to William Henry Gaylord (Livy, still un-well, is unable to attend). Hires a wet nurse to care for baby. Livy falls dangerously ill with typhoid in February. Clemens hires nurses and doctors, including Dr. Rachel Brooks Gleason, to care for her and stays up nights watch-ing over her. Susan Crane and Livy's close friend Clara Spaulding assist in nursing. Decides to stop writing for the *Galaxy* in order to work more on books (last "Memo-randa" column appears in April). Has come to "loathe Buffalo" and puts house and interest in the *Express* up for sale, hoping to move to Hartford. When Livy's health improves slightly, takes her to Elmira on March 18, intending never to return to Buffalo. Chagrined by unfavorable reception of pamphlet *Mark Twain's (Burlesque) Autobiography and First Romance*, published by Isaac E. Sheldon, the same firm that published *Galaxy*. Works hard on *Roughing It*, his western book, writing at Quarry Farm, located on a hill outside Elmira and owned by Susan and Theodore Crane. Pleased when Goodman visits in April and works with him on the manuscript. Sells interest in *Express* for $15,000, taking a loss of $10,000. Pamela and her son Samuel Erasmus Moffett stay at Quarry Farm in June to take Elmira Water Cure. Livy's and baby's health improve. Writes lecture on "boys' rights." Arranges another lecture tour with Redpath, but asks that he be paid at least as much as his friend Nasby receives. Has Bliss arrange for George Routledge and Sons to publish and copyright *Roughing It* in England. Clemens writes two more lectures and decides that the third, "Reminiscences of Some Un-Commonplace Characters I Have Chanced to Meet," is the one he wants to deliver. Goes to Hartford in August to complete *Roughing It*. Sees mother and Annie, who have come to visit Orion and Mollie in Hartford, and brings them with him to visit Elmira. Baby is very sick again, and Livy discovers that during her illness he has been given laudanum and other sleeping medicines. Clemens goes to Washington in September to secure patent on "elastic strap" (granted patent for "Improvement in Adjustable and Detachable Straps for Garments"). Leases John and Isabella Beecher Hooker's house in "Nook Farm" area of Hartford. Returns to Buffalo to pack, and moves to Hartford in October. Lectures in Pennsylvania, Washington, D.C., Massachusetts, Vermont, New Hampshire, Maine, and New York. Uses Boston as base when delivering New England lectures, meets Thomas Bailey Aldrich, sees Howells and Bret Harte, and is occasionally accompanied by Ralph Keeler, young writer friend from California. Dislikes his prepared lectures and writes one about Artemus Ward, then writes another one based on *Roughing It*. Goes on to Chicago and is struck by the extent of damage caused by the great fire of October 8–9 ("literally no Chicago *here*"). Stays with *Quaker City* friends Dr. Abraham Reeves Jackson and his second wife, Julia Newell, then continues lecturing in Illinois.

1872   Lectures in Indiana, Ohio, West Virginia, Pennsylvania, and New York, where he sees his friend John Hay. Attends birthday celebration for Horace Greeley, editor of the New York *Tribune*, in New York on February 3; other guests include Hay, Bret Harte, Whitelaw Reid, and P. T. Barnum. *Roughing It* is published in February and sells well. Orion quits as editor of Bliss's *American Publisher* and tells Clemens that Bliss is cheating him on production costs of *Roughing It*. Clemens questions figures, but does not break with Bliss. Returns to Elmira in early March. Daughter Olivia Susan (Susy) born March 19. Visits Fairbanks in Cleveland with Livy and mother in early May. Returns to Elmira, then goes to Hartford. South African book is abandoned when Riley develops fatal cancer of the mouth (he will die in September). Son Langdon dies June 2 of diptheria. In July family goes to stay at Fenwick Hall in New Saybrook, Connecticut, to escape summer heat. Prepares prefaces and makes revisions for English edition of *The Innocents Abroad*, published by Routledge. Devises idea for "Mark Twain's Self-Pasting Scrap-Book" (patented June 24, 1873, it is successfully marketed by his friend Dan Slote). Sails for Liverpool on August 21 on the *Scotia*, intending to write a book on England. Speaks at the Whitefriars, a London literary club, and is made honorary member. Tours Warwickshire in open barouche with American publisher James R. Osgood. Meets humorist Tom Hood, son of the poet, actor Henry Irving, clergyman Moncure Conway, and sees Henry Morton Stanley, whom he had met in St. Louis in 1867. Writes letter to the *Spectator* protesting John Camden Hotten's printing of books attributed to him that include articles he did not write. Speaks at the Savage Club, a literary and artistic club. Overwhelmed by social activities, invitations to private houses, and ceremonial functions, is amazed and flattered by his fame in England. Sails for America on board the *Batavia*, on November 12; impressed when Captain John E. Mouland and crew rescue shipwreck survivors in heavy seas and writes letter to the Royal Humane Society recommending that they be rewarded (among fellow passengers signing letter is Edward Emerson, son of Ralph Waldo Emerson). Arrives in New York on November 25. Begins work on novel *The Gilded Age* with friend and neighbor, Charles Dudley Warner.

1873   Buys large lot in "Nook Farm" area of Hartford, planning to build house on it. Lectures in Hartford to raise money for charity, and in New York and Brooklyn in February on the Sandwich Islands. Made a member of the Lotos Club in New York City. Becomes a director of the American Publishing Company (owns $5,000 stock in it). Livy goes to Elmira late in April and Clemens follows after he and Warner finish *The Gilded Age*. Family, accompanied by Clara Spaulding and recently hired shorthand secretary Samuel Chalmers Thompson, sails for England on the *Batavia* on May 17. They initially stay at Edwards' Hotel in London, but after a few weeks move to the Langham because Clemens misses the billiard room there. Intrigued by trial for perjury of claimant to the Tichborne title (claimant is eventually proved to have committed perjury). Sees Henry Lee, naturalist at Brighton Aquarium, and poet Joaquin Miller, whom he had met in California. Arranges for Routledge to bring out *The Gilded Age* in England. Begins writing letters for the *Herald* on the activities of Nasr-Ed-Din, shah of Persia, during his visit to England and Europe (eventually sends five). Meets Thomas Hughes, Herbert Spencer, Charles Godfrey Leland ("Hans Breitmann"), Anthony Trollope, Robert Browning, and Wilkie Collins, among others. Moncure Conway takes Clemens and Livy to Stratford-on-Avon, where they are guests of the mayor. Meets Scottish writer George MacDonald and his wife, Louise, in July. Discharges Thompson as secretary, goes to Edinburgh, Scotland, and meets Dr. John Brown, who is called in to treat Livy, who is exhausted after the hectic London season; the doctor becomes a lifelong friend. Buys the Abbotsford Edition of Sir Walter Scott's works. Clara Spaulding rejoins them after traveling in France. Visits Belfast, becoming friends there with *Northern Whig* proprietor Francis Dalzell Finlay, goes to Dublin, then returns to London. Sees old friend Charles Warren Stoddard, who is in London as newspaper correspondent. Clemenses go to Paris in late September to buy household items. Having spent more money than expected, Clemens has George Dolby, Dickens' agent, arrange for him to lecture in London in mid-October. Accompanies family home to America, sailing on the *Batavia* October 21 and arriving in New York November 2, where Orion is trying to get work as an editor, proofreader, or typesetter on a newspaper. Clemens leaves for England on November 8 to obtain copyright for *The Gilded Age* and to give further lectures. Arrives in London November 20. Moves into the Langham Hotel but feels lonely and asks Stoddard to join him there as secretary and companion. Lectures in December on the Sandwich Islands for a week, then changes to "Roughing It on the Silver Frontier" for the next two weeks. Writes out after-dinner speeches because he is often called on to give them. Feels oppressed by continuous, unusually heavy fog and coal smoke. Elected honorary member of the Temple Club. Finlay visits for a week. *The Gilded Age* published simultaneously in England and America on December 23. Spends Christmas holiday at Salisbury and visits Stonehenge.

1874   Lectures in Leicester and Liverpool. Sails for Boston on the *Parthia* January 13 and arrives on January 26. Introduces lecture by English clergyman and writer Charles Kingsley at the Essex Institute in Salem, Massachusetts. Works on two plays. Lectures in Boston in March. Mary Fairbanks and her children visit Hartford. Sales of *The Gilded Age* are very good. Buys Orion a small chicken farm outside Keokuk (will begin sending regular payments to Orion, who considers them loans, though he will be unable to repay more than nominal amounts of interest). Goes to Elmira in late April and stays in the Langdon house, then moves to Quarry Farm on May 5, where Susan Crane has built a free-standing octagonal study for him. Daughter Clara Langdon born June 8. Works on five-act play *Colonel Sellers*, dramatization of *The Gilded Age*, and *Tom Sawyer*. Pleased when "A True Story" is accepted by Howells for the *Atlantic* (published November 1874), his first piece to appear there. Stops in New York en route from Elmira to Hartford to help with rehearsals for *Colonel Sellers*; play opens September 16, starring John T. Raymond, at the Park Theatre. Returns to Hartford September 19 and moves into still unfinished house designed by architect Edward T. Potter. With Howells' encouragement, begins writing articles about the Mississippi ("Old Times on the Mississippi," first in series, appears in January 1875 *Atlantic*). Decides in November to walk with Twichell from Hartford to Boston; they cover 28 miles the first day and six miles the next before taking the train the rest of the way. Buys a typewriter and writes to Howells on it (later boasts to friends that he was the first writer to use one). Attends *Atlantic* contributors' dinner in Boston on December 15.

1875 Enjoys new home, spending hours playing billiards in room at top of house; close neighbors are the Warners and Stowes. Describes his taste in reading: "I like history, biography, travels, curious facts & strange happenings, & science. And I detest novels, poetry & theology." Continues writing reminiscences of life as a pilot on the Mississippi (installments appear in the *Atlantic* until August). Pleased with royalties received from *Colonel Sellers*, which is successfully touring the country. Goes to New York to attend Henry Ward Beecher's trial for adultery (it results in a hung jury). Decides not to go to Quarry Farm for the summer. Resumes work on *Tom Sawyer*. Invites Dan De Quille to come to Hartford and helps him get his book *The Big Bonanza* published by Bliss (appears fall 1876). Clemens and Howells frequently visit each other in Hartford and Cambridge. Hires George Griffin as butler; he becomes a family favorite (household includes about seven servants, among them nurses for the children). Receives many visitors, including Joaquin Miller and Bret Harte. Finishes *Tom Sawyer* in July. Goes to Bateman's Point, Newport, Rhode Island, at the end of month and stays through August. *Mark Twain's Sketches, New and Old* published September 25 by Bliss. Moncure Conway visits the Clemenses in Hartford.

1876 Engages Conway as agent for English publication of *Tom Sawyer* (Conway is paid 5 percent of royalty). Clemens is ill for several weeks. Employs private secretary to take dictation and answer letters. Makes revisions in *Tom Sawyer* based on Howells' suggestions. Gives talk, "The Facts Concerning the Recent Carnival of Crime in Connecticut," to the Monday Evening Club, Hartford literary group. Mother and sister visit. Clemens goes to Quarry Farm on June 15 for the summer. *The Adventures of Tom Sawyer* published in England by Chatto & Windus. Begins work on *Huckleberry Finn*. Attends centennial celebration in Philadelphia with other authors and reads eulogy to

Francis Lightfoot Lee. Angered by widespread sales in the United States of pirated Canadian editions of *Tom Sawyer*. Works on scatological tale [*Date, 1601.*] *Conversation, as it Was by the Social Fireside, in the Time of the Tudors* (published privately 1880), and reads it to close friends Twichell, David Gray, Howells, and John Hay. Returns to Hartford September 11. In November gives a series of readings arranged by Redpath. Collaborates with Harte on play, *Ah Sin*, Harte staying at the Clemenses' house for two weeks. Becomes friends with Frank Millet when he comes to Hartford to paint Clemens' portrait. American edition of *Tom Sawyer*, published December 8 by the American Publishing Company, sells moderately well. Tauchnitz firm publishes continental edition of *Tom Sawyer* with his approval (Tauchnitz will continue as his European publisher).

1877　Continues work on play with Harte until late February. Relations with Harte become strained over their financial and publishing ties, and then break off completely when Clemens receives an angry letter from him. Oversees rehearsals of *Ah Sin* in Baltimore in April, then returns home on May 1 (play opens in Washington on May 7). Travels with Twichell to Bermuda for short holiday, then goes with family to Elmira in June. Writes "Some Rambling Notes of an Idle Excursion" about Bermuda trip for the *Atlantic*. Begins work on another play, "Cap'n Simon Wheeler, the Amateur Detective" (never produced or published). Attends New York rehearsals for *Ah Sin* in July (produced by Augustin Daly, the play opens July 31 and runs for five weeks). Reads English and French histories and French novels; likes the elder Dumas' novels of the Revolution, and describes Carlyle's *History of the French Revolution* as "one of the greatest creations that ever flowed from a pen." Tries to persuade cartoonist Thomas Nast to go on a lecture tour with him. At banquet in Boston on December 17 delivers the "Whittier Birthday Speech," a burlesque of three tramps who pass themselves off as Longfellow, Emerson, and Holmes. Many listeners, including Howells, are shocked, and some newspapers are severely critical. Chagrined, sends letters of apology to the three writers, all of whom had attended dinner (will eventually become less embarrassed by this incident).

1878   Works on *The Prince and the Pauper*. Signs contract on March 8 with Elisha Bliss for book about Europe, accepting half of the profits in lieu of royalties (Clemens considers separate agreement with Bliss expedient because Bliss is threatening to leave the American Publishing Company). Visits Elmira and Fredonia (niece Annie is now married to Charles Webster). Sails for Europe April 11 on the *Holsatia* with family, Clara Spaulding, and German nursemaid Rosina (Rosa) Hay. Passengers include Bayard Taylor, on his way to become minister to Germany, and journalist Murat Halstead. Family stops in Hamburg for a week and then travels slowly through Germany to Heidelberg, arriving May 6. Clemens takes excursions into the countryside before they leave on July 23 for Baden-Baden. Twichell arrives August 1 (Clemens is paying for his trip). Clemens and Twichell take "walking tour," traveling by rail, carriage, boat, and foot through the Black Forest and the Swiss Alps to Lausanne and Geneva, from where Twichell returns home in September. Family travels through Italy, staying in Venice, Florence, and Rome until November, then settles in Munich for three months, where they study German. Saddened by news of death of Bayard Taylor in Berlin on December 19.

1879   Family goes to Paris at the end of February. Clemens is very ill with rheumatism and dysentery. Feels better in April and works on *A Tramp Abroad*. Dislikes Paris, but enjoys friends who are also there, including Moncure Conway and the Aldriches. Meets artists and literary men who belong to the Stomach Club, including Edwin Austin Abbey and Augustus Saint-Gaudens, and attends wedding of friend Frank Millet. Has two meetings with Ivan Turgenev, a writer he admires. Family leaves Paris in late July and travels through Belgium and Holland, then spends a month in England. Renews old acquaintances there and meets Charles Darwin at Grasmere in the Lake District. Family sails on the *Gallia* August 23 and arrives in New York on September 3, then goes to Quarry Farm. Clemens visits his family in Fredonia. Returns to Hartford in late October. Installs telephone in his home. Attends reunion banquet of Army of the Tennessee, held in Chicago on November 13 with Ulysses S. Grant as the guest of honor (generals Sherman, Sheridan, Pope, Schofield, and Logan are also present). Responds to toast with speech "The Babies." Becomes friends with orator Robert G. Ingersoll. Attends *Atlantic* breakfast in honor of Oliver Wendell Holmes and gives well-received speech.

1880   Goes to Elmira with Livy, who is exhausted from redecorating house and installing furniture bought in Europe. Works for a short time on *Huckleberry Finn*, then sets it aside. Visits mother, who is not well, in Fredonia. Buys four-fifths interest in Dan Slote's patent in Kaolatype, a chalk-plate process for engraving illustrations, and forms company with himself as president, Charles Perkins (his Hartford lawyer and friend) as secretary, and Slote as treasurer. Agrees to finance company with his own money as needed for three months. *A Tramp Abroad* published in March by the American Publishing Company. It sells well, and Clemens earns more money on each book sold than under previous contracts. Increases payments to Orion, telling him that the money is for his role in making him more aware of the need to obtain better terms from publishers. Works happily on *The Prince and the Pauper* and encourages Orion to write autobiography (Orion will write several chapters, but never finishes manuscript). Daughter Jane Lampton (Jean) born July 26. Elisha Bliss dies on September 28 (death will cause Clemens to seek new publisher). Clemens accompanies Grant to Hartford and delivers welcoming speech. Actively supports James A. Garfield, the Republican presidential nominee.

1881   Writes letter to president-elect Garfield, describing Frederick Douglass as a personal friend and asking that he be retained in the office of marshal of the District of Columbia (Garfield makes Douglass recorder of deeds for the District). Pays support for Paris stay of young Hartford machinist Karl Gerhardt and wife, Hattie, so that Gerhardt can study sculpture. Buys additional land next to house to keep neighbor from building and begins renovations of house and grounds. Disillusioned with Slote, hires Charles Webster, niece Annie's husband, to supervise Slote and the Kaolatype concern, and to be his business agent in other matters. Enjoys reading out loud works of Joel Chandler Harris. Spends June and July at Montowese House, in Branford, Connecticut, before going to Elmira. Makes Webster his legal representative in business aspects of the publication of his books by the American Publishing Company. Upset by the shooting of President Garfield on July 2 and his death on September 19. By now has made numerous investments in various speculative ventures, including the Paige typesetter (will eventually invest at least $190,000 trying to get the machine perfected). Howells reads proofs and suggests revisions of *The Prince and the Pauper*. Clemens and James R. Osgood travel to Canada to issue an edition of the book there (their presence in the country is needed to secure Canadian copyright). Clemens reads Francis Parkman's histories of the Anglo-French conflict in North America. *The Prince and the Pauper* is published by James R. Osgood & Co. in the United States in late December (Clemens pays production costs and Osgood produces and markets the book in return for a 7½ percent royalty).

1882   Dan Slote dies. Old friend Edward House visits in February with his adopted daughter Koto, and House is ill for weeks. Clemens and Howells ask Grant to intercede with President Arthur to keep Howells' father as consul in Toronto (Arthur retains him). Visits the aged Emerson with Howells, and is pleased when Emerson eventually recognizes him. In preparation for expanding 1875 *Atlantic* articles about the Mississippi into a book, Clemens travels with Osgood and shorthand secretary Roswell Phelps to St. Louis, then goes by steamboat to New Orleans, where he meets Joel Chandler Harris, George Washington Cable, and old friend Horace Bixby. Travels up the Mississippi with Bixby in pilothouse, stopping off in Hannibal and Quincy, Illinois. *The Stolen White Elephant*, collection of short pieces, published by Osgood. Trip to Quarry Farm delayed when Jean, Susy, and Clemens get scarlet fever and their house is quarantined. Struggles over writing *Life on the Mississippi*. Beginning to have doubts about Osgood's ability to sell books by subscription, makes Webster his subscription agent for the New York area. Remains in Elmira until September 29. Cable visits.

1883   Finishes book. Livy is sick with diphtheria and other ailments for over a month. Goes again to Canada to safeguard copyright. *Life on the Mississippi* published in May by Osgood (contractual terms are the same as for *The*

Prince and the Pauper). Resumes work on *Huckleberry Finn* and enjoys the writing. Collaborates with Howells on play *Colonel Sellers as Scientist*. Begins work on dramatizations of *Tom Sawyer* and *The Prince and the Pauper*. Family entertains many house guests. Becomes very dissatisfied with sales of books under Osgood's direction. Meets Matthew Arnold in Hartford during his American lecture tour.

1884 Cable visits in January and comes down with mumps; nurse is hired to take care of him. Clemens invests in Howells' father's invention, one-handed grape shears. Tries unsuccessfully to get plays produced. Howells reads typescript of *Huckleberry Finn* and suggests revisions. Clemens has attack of gout. Founds his own publishing company, Charles L. Webster & Co., and signs contract in May with Webster, who acts as publisher. Learns to ride a bicycle. Reads proofs of *Huckleberry Finn* from June through August, with help from Howells. Gerhardt makes bust of Clemens. Needing more money, contracts with Major J. B. Pond to do four-month lecture tour with Cable (Pond receives 10 percent commission, Cable $450 a week and expenses, and Clemens the remainder). Joins other Republican "mugwumps," who consider Republican presidential candidate James G. Blaine to be dishonest, in voting for Democrat Grover Cleveland. Lecture tour begins November 5 in New Haven. Learns from Richard Watson Gilder, editor of *Century Magazine*, that General Grant is writing his memoirs. Visits Grant in New York, tells him that terms offered by Century Company are inadequate, and urges him not to sign any contract until Webster & Co. can make an offer; Grant makes no commitments. On recommendation of Cable, Clemens reads Malory's *Le Morte d'Arthur*. In December, visits president-elect Cleveland in Albany at his invitation. *Century* publishes first of three excerpts from *Huckleberry Finn*. Charles Webster offers Grant $50,000 advance for his memoirs.

1885 Continues lecture tour, which includes Hannibal and Keokuk, where mother is now living with Orion. Charles Webster offers Grant choice of 20 percent royalty or 70 percent of net profits. *Adventures of Huckleberry Finn* published in the United States by Webster & Co. on February

16 (sells 39,000 copies by March 14); Clemens again goes to Canada to protect copyright. Webster & Co. buys rights to books published by Osgood for $3,000. Clemens visits Grant in New York on February 21 and learns that he is dying from throat cancer, but again urges him to accept the Webster offer. Grant signs contract on February 27, choosing to receive 70 percent of the profits. Canvassing for the books begins immediately. Lecture tour ends February 28; is very successful financially, and Clemens likes Cable, but is irritated by his strict observance of the Sabbath. Clemens signs new contract that makes Charles Webster a partner in Webster & Co. and gives him more money. When Concord, Massachusetts, library bans *Huckleberry Finn*, tells Webster that they will sell an extra 20,000 books as a result. Arranges for Gerhardt to make bust of Grant. Concerned about Grant's well-being and worried that he may not live to complete the memoirs, Clemens helps in any way he can, reading proofs as pages are set and praising the writing. By May more than 60,000 two-volume sets have been ordered, and production arrangements become costly and complex. Clemens is pleased when Susy begins writing biography of his life. Learns of Osgood's business failure. Writes account of the Marion Rangers, "The Private History of a Campaign that Failed," and shows it to Grant, who enjoys it immensely (published in *Century Magazine* in December as part of its series on the Civil War). Works on sequel to *Huckleberry Finn*, "Tom and Huck among the Indians" (never finished). Family goes to Elmira. Clemens visits Grant at Mount McGregor, New York, June 29–July 2, working with him on the completion of the second volume. Grant dies July 23, only a few days after finishing his memoirs. Clemens is involved in many ventures, including patents for a historical game, a perpetual calendar, and a "bed-clasp" for keeping babies' blankets in place; his major investment, now costing $3,000 a month, is the Paige typesetter. Reads manuscripts for possible publication by Webster & Co. Touched when Oliver Wendell Holmes, Charles Dudley Warner, and others write tributes in the *Critic* for his fiftieth birthday. In December 325,000 copies of first volume of *Personal Memoirs of U. S. Grant* are bound and shipped (second volume appears in March 1886). Clemens begins paying board of Warner T.

McGuinn, one of the first black students at the Yale Law School, whom he had met during a speaking engagement at Yale in the fall. (Will also support study of Charles Ethan Porter, a black sculptor, and pay tuition of a black undergraduate at Lincoln University. McGuinn graduates from Yale in 1887 and becomes an attorney in Baltimore, where he later serves as local director of the NAACP and wins lawsuit challenging mandated segregation of Baltimore city housing.)

1886   Family continues to entertain lavishly. Howells comes with his daughter Mildred to see staging of *The Prince and the Pauper* dramatized by Livy and performed by the Clemens children and their friends. Clemens frequently goes to New York on publishing business. Charles Webster gives Julia Grant check for $200,000 on February 27 (Grant family eventually receives between $420,000 and $450,000 from sales of *Personal Memoirs*). Clemens makes Frederick J. Hall third partner in Webster & Co. on April 28. Learns in May that after prolonged negotiations, Webster & Co. has signed contract with Bernard O'Reilly, authorized biographer of Pope Leo XIII; Clemens expects that the papal biography will be more successful than Grant's memoirs (is disappointed by sales when book is published in 1887). Reads from his works at U.S. Military Academy at West Point. Resumes work with Howells on play *Colonel Sellers as Scientist* and makes arrangements to have it produced, but at the last moment Howells asks that it be withdrawn. In July, takes family to visit mother, Orion, and Mollie in Keokuk. Hires Frank G. Whitmore as business agent in August, primarily to supervise construction of the Paige typesetting machine at the Pratt & Whitney works in Hartford. Begins work on *A Connecticut Yankee in King Arthur's Court*. Reads Robert Browning steadily ("It takes me much longer to learn how to read a page of Browning than a page of Shakespeare") and enjoys reading his poetry aloud to the "Browning class," a group of Livy's friends who meet in his billiard room once a week. Entertains Henry Morton Stanley in Hartford and gives introduction at Stanley's lecture in Boston.

1887   Attends benefit on March 31 for the Longfellow Memorial Fund in Boston and reads from "English as She Is

Taught," after being introduced by Charles Eliot Norton, who tells anecdote about Darwin keeping Clemens' works on his bedside table (other readers include Howells, Julia Ward Howe, Edward Everett Hale, Oliver Wendell Holmes, Thomas W. Higginson, George W. Curtis, Thomas B. Aldrich, and James R. Lowell). Defends General Grant's grammar against criticism by Matthew Arnold in speech in Hartford on April 27. Clemens financially backs production of *Colonel Sellers as Scientist*, retitled *The American Claimant* and credited solely to Mark Twain, that has a brief run starring A. P. Burbank. With Livy and several Hartford friends, visits artist Frederick Edwin Church and his wife at Olana, New York (Clemens had long admired him). At Quarry Farm, continues to work with pleasure on *A Connecticut Yankee in King Arthur's Court*. *Mark Twain's Library of Humor* (collaboration among Howells, Clemens, and Charles H. Clark, finished a number of years earlier; introduction written by Howells, signed "The Associate Editors") published in late December by Webster & Co.

1888   Signs agreement stating that Webster (who has been suffering increasingly from painful neuralgia) is to withdraw "from business, from all authority, and from the city, till April 1, 1889, & try to get back his health." Frederick Hall takes over his responsibilities. In April Clemens spends afternoon with Robert Louis Stevenson in New York's Washington Square Park. Visits Thomas Edison at his laboratory in West Orange, New Jersey, in June. Awarded honorary Master of Arts degree by Yale. Theodore Crane has partially paralyzing stroke in Elmira on September 6. Writer Grace King stays with the Clemenses at Hartford, October–November. Crane's condition worsens and he is nursed by Susan and Livy in Hartford in December. Hall buys Webster's interest in firm for $12,000.

1889   Success of prototype Paige typesetter thrills Clemens, although technical problems again develop. Writes letter of tribute to Whitman for publication in *Camden's Compliment to Walt Whitman*, edited by Horace Traubel (Clemens had joined others in financially assisting Whitman in 1885 and 1887). Theodore Crane dies at Quarry Farm on July 3. Clemens is charmed by Rudyard Kipling, who visits him in Elmira (will later read and reread Kipling's works with pleasure). Goes to Hartford to work on revisions of *A Connecticut Yankee in King Arthur's Court*. Hoping to live on profits from Paige machine, calls the novel his "swan-song" and his "retirement from literature" in letter to Howells. Unable to read manuscript because of eye trouble, Livy asks Clemens to have Howells read proofs because she trusts Howells to keep Clemens from offending good taste. Certain that the Paige machine will soon be ready for production, Clemens writes Howells that "after patiently & contentedly spending more than $3,000 a month on it for 44 consecutive months" it is "done at last. . . . Come & see this sublime magician of iron & steel work his enchantments." Invites Joseph Goodman to come east and help find investors for machine. Reads and is deeply impressed with Edward Bellamy's *Looking Backward: 2000–1887*. Anticipating that Chatto, his English publisher, will make changes in *A Connecticut Yankee* to avoid offending English sensibilities, writes letter to them refusing to alter text and saying that the book was "written for England." *A Connecticut Yankee in King Arthur's Court*, published in America December 10 by Webster & Co., with illustrations by Daniel Carter Beard, sells moderately well. Dramatization of *The Prince and the Pauper* by Abby Sage Richardson, produced by Belasco and Frohman, opens on Christmas Day in Philadelphia and is fairly successful.

1890   January, Edward Bellamy visits Clemens in Hartford. Financial problems become acute from continued cost of Paige machine and lack of profits from Webster & Co. (unsold books, subscription costs, and expense of producing and distributing 11-volume *Library of American Literature*, an anthology edited by Edmund C. Stedman, create constant cash-flow problems that drain away his book royalties). Edward House brings suit against dramatization of *The Prince and the Pauper* by Richardson, claiming he had been given the rights long ago. Litigation prevents Clemens from receiving royalties from play and ends their friendship. Family goes for the summer to Onteora Park, artists' and writers' colony in the Catskills near Tannersville, New York. With Goodman's help, Clemens travels frequently in search of investors for the Paige machine. Goes to Keokuk in August when mother has stroke. Susy enters Bryn Mawr in October. Clara takes piano lessons in New York twice a week. Mother dies in Keokuk October 27, and Clemens attends funeral in Hannibal on October 30. Goes to Elmira in November, where Livy's mother dies November 28. Clemens rushes back to Hartford because Jean is ill.

1891   Webster & Co. goes deeper into debt. Attempts at raising capital for Paige machine are unsuccessful, and Clemens stops his monthly $3,000 payments in support of project. Writes articles for magazines. Suffering from rheumatism in right arm, finds writing difficult. Works on novel *The American Claimant*. Experiments with dictating into phonograph, but soon gives up. Susy leaves Bryn Mawr in April, too homesick to continue. Charles Webster dies April 26. Clemens signs contract with *McClure's Magazine* to serialize *The American Claimant* in America and Europe for $12,000 and to write six letters from Europe for $1,000 each. No longer able to afford the maintenance of the Hartford home, decides to go to Europe, hoping that baths will help Livy's health (she is developing heart trouble) and relieve rheumatism in his arm, which makes writing almost impossible. They close the house, sell the horses, and find new positions for their servants. Family sails with Susan Crane on June 6 aboard the *Gascogne* and arrives in Le Havre June 14. Stops in Paris before going to take baths at Aix-les-Bains. Susy and Clara attend boarding school in Geneva. Clemens hears Wagner operas at Bayreuth in August. Tries other baths at Marienbad. Settles family in Ouchy, Switzerland, in September, then hires courier, boatman, and flatboat for ten-day trip down the Rhône. Family goes to Berlin for the winter and moves into Körnerstrasse Hotel. Still suffers from pain in arm and continues to find writing difficult. Moves family to better rooms in Hotel Royal on December 31.

1892   Clemens develops pneumonia. Doctors recommend that as soon as he is well enough to travel, Livy and he should go south. Has private dinner with Kaiser William II on February 20. Leaves daughters at school in Berlin and goes with Livy in March to Mentone, France, for three weeks and then to Italy, spending several weeks in Rome and Venice before returning to Berlin. Collection *Merry*

Tales published in April in cheaply bound edition, and *The American Claimant* published in May, both by Webster & Co.; sales are poor. Many Germans and Americans visit, including Sarah Orne Jewett and Annie Fields. Family moves to Bad Nauheim for the summer. Clemens goes to New York in mid-June to check on publishing business and makes quick trip to Chicago, where factory has been established to manufacture the Paige typesetter. Returns to Europe in mid-July. Works on "Those Extraordinary Twins" and then turns to *Tom Sawyer Abroad* (published serially in *St. Nicholas*, November 1893–January 1894, and as a book by Webster & Co. in 1894). Twichells visit in August, and Clemens and Twichell go to Bad Homburg, where they meet Edward, Prince of Wales. Susan Crane returns to America. In September the family goes to Florence, traveling slowly because of Livy's health and stopping in Frankfurt am Main and Lucerne, Switzerland, on the way. Moves into the Villa Viviani, Settignano, Florence, in late September. Family enjoys living there, and Clemens concentrates on writing. Clara returns to Berlin to study music. Livy's health continues to be poor. Clemens reworks "Those Extraordinary Twins" into *Pudd'nhead Wilson*. Meets William James.

1893　Works on *Personal Recollections of Joan of Arc* and articles for magazines. Sails to New York for business reasons, leaving on *Kaiser Wilhelm II* March 22 and arriving in New York April 3. Sees Howells and Kipling and goes with Hall to Chicago, where he checks progress of Paige machine and attends the World's Columbian Exposition. Financial panic in America makes problems at Webster & Co. more severe. Feeling disheartened, leaves for Europe aboard *Kaiser Wilhelm II* May 13. Tries to find buyer for his interest in Webster & Co., then suggests selling *Library of American Literature* to another publisher. In June family goes to Munich and to spas, where Livy continues to take baths. Clemens resumes work on *Pudd'nhead Wilson*. Feels depressed and distraught about financial circumstances. Borrows money and seeks financial advice from Charles Langdon. Sails with Clara from Bremen on the *Spree* August 29, arriving in New York on September 7. Sells "The Esquimau Maiden's Romance" to *Cosmopolitan* for $800, and *Pudd'nhead Wilson* to *Century* for $6,500 (appears December 1893–June 1894). After Clara leaves to visit family in Elmira, Clemens rooms with friend Dr. Clarence C. Rice, then takes a cheap room in the Players' Club on September 29. Tries to borrow money to meet pressing debts of Webster & Co. from friends in Hartford and Wall Street brokers and bankers, but panic has made money tight. Through Rice, meets Henry Huttleston Rogers, vice-president and director of the Standard Oil Company (had briefly met him two years earlier), who immediately takes care of an $8,000 debt owed by Webster & Co., and begins examining the problems of the Paige typesetter company. Rogers arranges for his son-in-law, William E. Benjamin, to buy the *Library of American Literature* from Webster & Co. for $50,000 in October. Clemens sees old friends, dines out constantly, is often called upon for after-dinner speeches, and is touched by warmth of his reception in New York. Richard Watson Gilder and Howells pay tribute to him at dinner given in his honor by the Lotos Club on November 11. Clara returns to Europe to study music. Clemens travels with Rogers on December 21 to Chicago in private railroad car to inspect Paige machine.

1894   Goes to Boston to participate in "Author's Reading and Music for the Poor," and has dinner with Annie Fields, Sarah Orne Jewett, and Oliver Wendell Holmes (Holmes will die in October). Sees Mary Fairbanks in New York in February. Gives two readings with James Whitcomb Riley. Becomes closer to Rogers and his family, and enjoys watching Rogers conduct business in his office in the Standard Oil building at 26 Broadway. Gives Rogers power of attorney over all his affairs on March 6. Sails March 7 and arrives in Paris, where family is now living, on March 15. Rogers assigns Clemens' property, including his copyrights and share in the Paige machine, to Livy. Clemens sails for New York on April 7 and arrives April 14. On advice from Rogers, declares the failure of Webster & Co. on April 18 and assumes his share of its debts, causing his personal bankruptcy, which is widely and sympathetically reported in newspapers. Returns to Paris in May. Howells spends a week with him in June. For sake of Susy's health, family goes to La Bourboule-les-Bains in central France. Clemens plans to return to America at Rogers' request, but his departure is delayed by rioting caused by the assassination of French President Carnot on

June 24. Arrives in New York in early July and remains until mid-August, then rejoins family at Étretat in Normandy. Spends October with family in Rouen; Susy is still ill, with persistent high fever. *The Tragedy of Pudd'nhead Wilson and the Comedy of Those Extraordinary Twins* published in November as subscription book by the American Publishing Company (publisher includes earlier version of story as a separate work). Family returns to Paris, where Clemens is confined to bed with attack of gout. Devastated by news in December that Paige typesetter has failed a test in the offices of the Chicago *Herald* because of broken type. Resolves to reimburse his friends, actor Henry Irving and writer Bram Stoker (Irving's manager), for their investment in the machine (they are repaid in spring 1895).

1895   Works on several short pieces for journals, and writes *Tom Sawyer, Detective* (published by Harper & Brothers in November 1896). Finishes *Personal Recollections of Joan of Arc* and sails from Southampton on February 23 on the *New York*. Arrives in New York in early March; serial publication of *Personal Recollections of Joan of Arc* in *Harper's Magazine* begins in April. In hopes of having the work taken more seriously, asks that installments appear anonymously (his authorship soon becomes known, and book edition, published by Harper & Brothers in May 1896, is credited to Mark Twain). Moved by visit to family home in Hartford, now leased to friends John and Alice Hooker Day. Arranges with Major Pond for cross-country lecture tour (Pond receives 25 percent of fee for lectures between New York and San Francisco, and 20 percent for lectures in San Francisco). Clemens returns to France in late March; also aboard ship is Andrew Carnegie, an old acquaintance. Brings family to New York on May 18, then goes to Quarry Farm. Agrees to contract, signed on May 23, with Harpers that gives them rights to Mark Twain books published by Webster & Co. (negotiations with the American Publishing Company for similar agreement continue; Clemens hopes that Harpers will bring out a uniform edition of his works). Prepares lectures, suffers painful carbuncle on leg, and is forced to stay in bed for over six weeks, unable to stand or put on clothes. Leaving Susy and Jean to stay with Susan Crane at Quarry Farm, Clemens, Livy, and Clara leave on July 14 for first lecture in Cleveland. Travels across country, accompanied by Pond and his wife. Tells reporters in Vancouver that he intends to eventually repay every creditor in full. Sails for Australia aboard the *Warrimoo* on August 23 with Livy and Clara, beginning around-the-world lecture tour arranged by firm of R. S. Smythe, who had earlier managed a similar tour for Henry Morton Stanley. Hopes to stop in Honolulu, but is prevented from landing by outbreak of cholera. Visits Suva in Fiji Islands and arrives in Sydney on September 16. Met by Carlyle Smythe, who will serve as their guide on the tour. Continues to suffer from carbuncles. Appears in Sydney, Melbourne, Adelaide, and other Australian towns before large, responsive audiences, reading from his books and telling stories. Visits gold fields in Victoria. Sails for New Zealand on October 30 and stops in Tasmania before landing at Bluff. Lectures throughout South and North Islands, visiting Dunedin, Christchurch, Wellington, Auckland, and other towns. Leaves Wellington on December 13 and lands in Sydney December 17.

1896   Sails for India with Livy, Clara, and Carlyle Smythe from Albany, Western Australia, on January 4. Enjoys emptiness and calm of Indian Ocean. Stops briefly in Colombo, Ceylon, and arrives in Bombay on January 18. Suffers from persistent bronchial cough. Visits Towers of Silence, where Parsis expose their dead. Lectures in great hall of palace at Baroda on January 31. Finds India fascinating and is warmly received by Indian princes and British officials. Reads reports of Major William Sleeman, the suppressor of the Thugs in the late 1830s, and accounts of the 1857 Sepoy Mutiny. Takes train from Bombay to Allahabad and Benares. Lectures to packed audiences in Calcutta, February 10–13, then goes to Darjeeling in the foothills of the Himalayas. Exhilarated by first stage of descent from Darjeeling, made for 35 miles in open railway handcar. Returns to Calcutta and then visits Lucknow, Kanpur, Agra, Delhi, Lahore, Rawalpindi, and Jaipur. Sails from Calcutta for South Africa at the end of March. Stops in Madras and Ceylon, visits Mauritius April 15–28, and lands on May 6 at Durban in British colony of Natal. Livy and Clara stay in Durban while Clemens gives readings across South Africa. Goes to Pietermaritzburg, Natal capital, Johannesburg, and Pretoria, capital of the Boer Transvaal republic. Visits John Hayes Hammond and other "Reformers" imprisoned for their alleged complicity in 1895 Jameson Raid, an aborted invasion intended to bring the Transvaal under British rule (Mrs. Hammond is a Missourian whom Clemens had met previously). After leaving prison, Clemens makes humorous remark to reporter that is misinterpreted as implying that prisoners are being treated leniently. When their confinement is made harsher, Clemens goes to see President Kruger on May 26 to explain the joke (prisoners are soon released). Goes to Bloemfontein, capital of Orange Free State, and Queenstown and East London, in the British Cape Colony. Visits Kimberly diamond mine on July 1. Sails for England from Cape Town with Livy and Clara July 15 and arrives in Southampton on July 31. Takes a house in Guildford, Surrey, for a month. Rogers arranges contract with American Publishing Company and Harper & Brothers, allowing American Publishing to issue subscription volumes, as well as a uniform subscription edition of the complete works, while Harpers will sell individual books and a less-inclusive uniform edition to the trade. Learns that Susy is ill. Livy and Clara leave for America August 15, Clemens remains in England. Susy dies on August 18 of spinal meningitis. Clemens learns of her death by telegram. Livy returns to England on September 9 with Clara and Jean, whose health problems have recently been diagnosed as epilepsy. Rents house at 23 Tedworth Square, Chelsea, London, where they seclude themselves (family will not celebrate birthdays, Thanksgiving, Christmas, or other holidays for several years afterward). Begins writing travel book, *Following the Equator*. Clemens learns that Helen Keller (whom he had met with Rogers two years earlier at the home of Clemens' good friend Laurence Hutton) has lost financial support for her education, and asks Rogers to help her attend Radcliffe College (Rogers does so).

1897   Livy is deeply depressed. Clemens works long hours on book. In February writes Howells, who has published review praising the first five volumes in Harpers' "Uniform Edition," that his "words stir the dead heart of me" and that he feels "indifferent to nearly everything but work." Finishes *Following the Equator* in May. Made an honorary life member of the Savage Club (only Henry Morton Stanley, Arctic explorer Fridtjof Nansen, and the Prince of

Wales had been given honor since club's founding in 1857). In July family goes to the Villa Bühlegg, Weggis, on Lake Lucerne in Switzerland. Hears the Fisk Jubilee Singers perform in village in August and entertains them at home after their concert; deeply moved, writes Twichell that "their music made all other vocal music cheap." On anniversary of Susy's death, writes poem "In Memoriam, Olivia Susan Clemens" (published in November *Harper's Magazine*). Family moves to the Metropole Hotel in Vienna in late September. Clemens suffers from gout. Interviewers from many newspapers come to the hotel. Fascinated by current political unrest caused by rivalry among nationalities of the Austro-Hungarian Empire. Works for many hours a day, but does not intend to publish much of what he writes. Receives $10,000 advance from Frank Bliss for *Following the Equator*, published in November. Clemens and Clara go out in society and attend operas. Family receives daily callers from 5:00 P.M. on. Clara is accepted as student of famed piano teacher Theodor Leschetizky. Begins work on "The Man That Corrupted Hadleyburg" (published in *Harper's Magazine*, December 1899). Orion dies in Keokuk on December 11.

1898 Meets student of Leschetizky's, Ossip Gabrilowitsch, who comes to dinner. Works for eight or nine hours at a time. Tries writing for the stage again, and translates German plays. Continues to follow Dreyfus case in France and admires Zola for his championing of Dreyfus's cause. Creditors are paid in full, and newspapers compare him to Sir Walter Scott (who had also redeemed himself from bankruptcy). Because of Clara's study of music, meets many prominent musicians and attends operas and concerts. Becomes interested in new investments, including a textile design machine that uses a photographic process and a patent for producing a peat-wool fiber cloth. Rogers' advice dampens his enthusiasm. Sends articles directly to magazine editors; if they reject them, has Rogers try to place them with other publications. Commands high prices for his work. When Spanish-American War begins in late April, believes that freeing Cuba from Spanish domination is a worthy cause. Family goes in late May to Kaltenleutgeben, small hydrotherapy resort outside Vienna. Livy's health does not improve. Writes article about the assassination on September 10 of Elizabeth, Empress of Austria, and watches her funeral. Begins work on early version of *The Mysterious Stranger*. Returns to Vienna in mid-October, moving into the new, luxurious Krantz Hotel (hotels are eager to have Clemens in residence and lower their rates for him). Writes autobiographical passages in November and begins considering publishing an autobiography. Feels more relaxed about financial matters, and is delighted with Rogers' investment of his money. Mary Fairbanks dies on December 8.

1899   Takes family to Budapest for a week when he delivers lecture there. Tells Howells in a letter that "it is a luxury! an intellectual drunk" to write material not intended for publication. Goes with family to London in late May, then to Sanna, Sweden, in July, where they are treated at sanitarium run by Henrik Kellgren (Clemens hopes that Kellgren's methods will be especially beneficial to Jean, who has been having frequent seizures). Writes "Christian Science and the Book of Mrs. Eddy," published October in *Cosmopolitan*. Returns to London in October and moves into apartment at 30, Wellington Court, Knightsbridge, near Dr. Kellgren's London institute, where Jean is treated three times a week (therapy seems to be helpful). Blames outbreak of Boer War in October on Cecil Rhodes and British colonial secretary Joseph Chamberlain. Becomes friends with T. Douglas Murray, who asks him to write introduction to *Jeanne d'Arc: Maid of Orleans*, English translation of the official trial records.

1900   Becomes disillusioned with American policy in the Philippines, and writes to Howells about his divided sympathies concerning the Boer War. Dines out frequently at private dinner parties, including ones given by historian W.E.H. Lecky, whom Clemens greatly admires, and Lady Augusta Gregory. Sees much of Stanley and his wife, Dorothy. Has portrait painted by James McNeill Whistler. In March invests $12,500 in Plasmon, food supplement made from milk by-products, and becomes director of English Plasmon syndicate on April 19 (enthusiastically uses product, and will later invest another $12,500 in venture). Spends summer at Dollis Hill House on northwest outskirts of London. Sympathizes with the Chinese in the Boxer Rebellion. Angry with Murray's "school-girl attempts at 'editing,'" withdraws manuscript of introduction to *Jeanne d'Arc* (it appears as article in *Harper's Magazine*, December 1904). Decides to return to America, having learned that osteopathy, now widely practiced in the United States, is very similar to Kellgren's methods. Family sails October 6 on the *Minnehaha* and arrives in New York on October 15. Receives warm welcome from public, press, and friends. Goes to Hartford to attend funeral of old friend Charles Dudley Warner. Rents house at 14 West 10th Street, New York City. Journalists constantly seek interviews and telephone rings incessantly. Rogers negotiates contract in November with Harpers, giving them first serial rights to Clemens' works for a year at rate of 20 cents per word. Introduces Winston S. Churchill to large New York audience on December 12. Writes "To the Person Sitting in Darkness," denunciation of imperialism, and is encouraged to publish it by Livy and Howells (article appears in *North American Review*, February 1901).

1901   Enjoys company of Howells, who now lives in New York and shares his anti-imperialist views. Clemens attacks missionary propaganda in China, and Tammany machine politics. Frequently invited to make speeches, presides over the Lincoln birthday celebration in Carnegie Hall, February 11. Troubled by attacks of gout. Family leaves on June 21 for summer at Ampersand on Lower Saranac Lake, New York, in the Adirondacks. Visited by Howells' son, John, now an architect. Sails for two weeks with Rogers on his yacht, *Kanawha*, to New Brunswick and Nova Scotia; fellow passengers include Clemens' friends Dr. Clarence Rice and Thomas B. Reed, former Speaker of the House of Representatives. Goes to Elmira for a week. Family finds sad memories make it impossible to live in Hartford. Decides to sell the house there and rents the Appleton mansion overlooking the Hudson in Riverdale, New York. Clemens and Howells receive honorary Doctor of Letters degrees from Yale University on October 23. Livy's health deteriorates. Rogers expresses concern in letter to Clemens about fairness of Ida Tarbell's forthcoming investigative series in *McClure's Magazine* on Standard Oil, saying that she has not approached anyone at the company for comment.

1902   Clemens tells friend at *McClure's* that they should have Tarbell speak with Rogers before running articles (when approached, Rogers agrees to interview; Tarbell will describe him as "candid" in her series). Jean has seizures. Clemens goes on yachting excursions with Rogers, taking an extended cruise to Nassau, Cuba, and Florida. Livy buys a house near Tarrytown, New York, for $45,000, hoping to settle family there. Clara leaves for Paris on April 22 to continue her studies. Clemens receives honorary Doctor of Laws from University of Missouri in Columbia on June 4. Visits Hannibal and St. Louis for the last time. Takes trip on Mississippi with pilot Horace Bixby. Family goes to York Harbor, Maine, for the summer. Because of Livy's fragile health, Rogers puts his yacht at their disposal. Clemens is upset as he witnesses more of Jean's epileptic seizures (had previously seen only three of her attacks, though Livy had been present for many more). Howells' family vacations at nearby Kittery Point. Clemens works on "Was It Heaven? Or Hell?" (published in *Harper's Magazine*, December 1902) and "Tom Sawyer's Conspiracy" (never completed). On August 12 Livy is violently ill, can barely breathe, and has severe heart palpitations; family fears she is dying. She is treated by an osteopath, who comes several times a day, and a regular doctor of medicine, who stays nights. Clara comes from Europe and Susan Crane joins them. Jean's health improves. Clemens hires professional nurse for Livy, but she continues to suffer from attacks and on October 16 returns by private invalid train to Riverdale. Clemens is not allowed to go into her room. Attends large dinner in honor of his 67th birthday, given on November 28 by George Harvey of Harper & Brothers at the Metropolitan Club in New York. Visits Elmira. Jean falls ill with pneumonia on December 23. Clara and nurses keep news from Livy, and Clara takes charge of house. Isabel Lyon, hired as Livy's secretary, now acts as Clemens' secretary. On December 30 Clemens is allowed to see Livy for five minutes. Jean improves.

1903   Sees Livy for five minutes on days when she is feeling better. Rarely goes into city. Livy's health improves during the spring months, and he is allowed to see her for twenty minutes twice a day, and to send her two letters each day. Clemens is forced to stay in bed for a month by attacks of bronchitis, gout, and rheumatism. Sells Hartford house and rents the Tarrytown house (sold December

1904). Visits Rogers, who is recovering from appendectomy, at his Fairhaven, Massachusetts, summer home. Doctors tell Livy she should go to Europe to recover. Family leaves Riverdale on July 1, going down the Hudson on Rogers' yacht to Hoboken, where they take train to Elmira. At Quarry Farm Livy takes rides in carriage, goes out in wheelchair, sits on porch, and resumes household responsibilities. Clemens works in octagonal study on the hill. Goes to New York on October 3 to see publishers. Harper & Brothers buys out the American Publishing Company, and on October 22 Clemens signs contract giving Harpers rights to all his books, receiving guaranteed payments of $25,000 a year for five years, plus royalties above that amount. Family sails for Italy on October 24 aboard the *Princess Irene*, accompanied by Isabel Lyon, their servant Kate Leary, who had been with the family since 1880, and a trained nurse. Goes to Florence, where Livy has chosen to settle, and rents the Villa di Quarto, a large house near the city. Trip is tiring for Livy, but she improves and thinks she no longer needs nurse, who leaves on December 7.

1904   Livy's condition worsens and she is confined to bed. Clemens quickly writes several magazine articles, then turns to autobiography, dictating to Lyon every day. Learns that sister-in-law Mollie Clemens died in Keokuk on January 15 (does not tell Livy, and will also keep from her news of Stanley's death on May 10). Livy has severe attacks on February 22 and April 9. Family dislikes landlady and searches for another villa (search proves beneficial to family's spirits because it encourages them to hope that Livy will live long enough for them to move). Clemens declines to invest money in American Plasmon syndicate, but retains confidence in English branch. Clara sings on concert stage and Clemens is impressed by her professionalism. Livy dies on June 5. Clara breaks down. Jean has first seizure in 13 months, but she soon recovers and plans family's return to America. Forced to wait for a ship, they sail June 28 on the *Prince Oscar*. Charles Langdon, his daughter Julia Langdon Loomis, and her husband meet them at the pier and accompany them to Elmira in Loomis's private railway car. Private funeral services are held in Langdon house, conducted by Twichell. Clemens takes cottage in July at Richard Watson Gilder's summer home in the Berkshires near Lee, Massachusetts (daughters are fond of Gilder). Clara, still suffering from shock, enters a rest-cure establishment in New York City. Jean is hit by a trolley on July 30 while horseback riding; horse is killed, and she is knocked unconscious and suffers torn ankle tendon. Clemens goes to New York on August 10, finds Clara still ill, and is not allowed to see her. Searches for house to live in. Signs three-year lease for house at 21 Fifth Avenue. Stays in the Grosvenor Hotel while furnishings for new house are brought from Hartford. Jean remains in the Berkshires with Isabel Lyon. Spends a few days in late August as guest of George Harvey at Deal Beach, New Jersey, where he sees Henry James, who is also visiting Harvey. Sister Pamela dies in Greenwich, Connecticut, on September 1. Visits Elmira with Jean. Moves in December into Fifth Avenue house, where Jean joins him. Seldom goes out, but is visited by Rogers, Andrew Carnegie, and other old friends.

1905   Troubled by chronic bronchitis. Plays cards with Lyon and listens to music on player organ. Goes with Rogers to Fairhaven in May, then takes house for summer in Dublin, New Hampshire, with Jean. Writes "Eve's Diary" (published in *Harper's Magazine* in December), revises "Adam's Diary," and works on other manuscripts, including "3,000 Years Among the Microbes," and a new version of *The Mysterious Stranger*. Clara goes to Norfolk, Connecticut, to continue rest cure. Jean enjoys summer and visits Clara. Clemens is troubled by gout, dyspepsia, bronchitis, and the summer heat. Visits Clara in August (their first meeting in a year) and finds her well. Returns to Dublin and is forced by gout to stay in bed. Goes to New York in November after visit to Boston. Clara comes to live with him. Sees much of Rogers and his extended family. Attends gala 70th birthday party given in his honor by Harvey at Delmonico's on December 5 (172 guests attend). Relies on Lyon to manage household, financial, and literary matters (Lyon refers to him as "the King").

1906   In January Albert Bigelow Paine, 44-year-old midwestern writer and editor, asks permission to write Clemens' biography. Clemens gives Paine a room in his house to work in, and allows him to go through manuscripts and some letters and to listen as he dictates sections of autobiography to stenographer and typist Josephine Hobby. At request of Booker T. Washington, gives talk at Carnegie Hall on the 25th anniversary of the founding of Tuskegee Institute. Continues to give speeches and readings, but no longer accepts money for them. Encouraged when Howells is "full of praises" after spending an afternoon reading autobiographical writings. Meets H. G. Wells at dinner at Howells' house. Reluctantly withdraws support for Maxim Gorky, who is raising funds for the Russian Social Democratic party, after Gorky is discovered to be traveling with his mistress. Writes essay "William Dean Howells," praising his "perfect English" (appears in July *Harper's Magazine*). Goes to Dublin in May to again spend summer. Continues autobiographical dictations, intending to have some of them published in his lifetime. Returns to New York in late June on publishing business. Spends month in New York and Fairhaven, often sleeping aboard Rogers' yacht. Returns to Dublin in time for Jean's birthday on July 26. Harvey comes to Dublin to edit autobiography for publication (25 installments appear in *North American Review*, September 1906–December 1907). Takes yachting trip in August with Rogers, his son Harry, and Harry's wife, Mary, niece of William E. Benjamin. Commissions John Howells to design and supervise building of house in Redding, Connecticut. *What Is Man?* published anonymously in limited private edition by DeVinne Press in August. Goes yachting again in October, and is charmed by Mary Rogers. Delighted with gift of billiard table from Rogers' wife, Emilie, on October 30. Plays billiards with Paine, Harvey, and Finley Peter Dunne ("Mr. Dooley"), and feels health improves as a result. Jean, who had suffered a number of seizures during the summer, is sent to a sanitarium in Katonah, New York. Clara takes rest cure before beginning concert tour. Clemens goes with Paine to Washington in December to lobby, along with Howells and others, for new copyright bill; wears white suit to Capitol Hill. Speaker Joseph Cannon, an old friend, gives him unusual privilege of his private room to use as office.

1907   Often feels lonely and dislikes Fifth Avenue house. Attends club dinners frequently. Spends week in Bermuda with Twichell. *Christian Science*, critical treatment of Mary

Baker Eddy, published by Harpers in February. Summers in Tuxedo Park, New York, where Harry and Mary Rogers have home. Goes to England to receive honorary Litt.D. from Oxford University. Sails from New York June 8 aboard the *Minneapolis*, accompanied by Ralph W. Ashcroft, former secretary and treasurer of the Plasmon Company of America. At Brown's Hotel in London, makes friends with Frances Nunnally, 16-year-old schoolgirl from Atlanta, taking her with him on social calls. Plunges into social life in London, going to royal garden party at Windsor Castle, Lord Mayor's Banquet, the Savage Club, and a party given in his honor by the proprietors of *Punch*. Lunches with George Bernard Shaw, who has called him the greatest American author and one of the great masters of the English language. Sees old friends, including the Rogers, who are touring Europe. Attends Oxford ceremony on June 26; others honored include Rodin, Saint-Saëns, Kipling, and Prime Minister Henry Campbell-Bannerman. Clemens receives the most attention of those present. While returning to New York on the *Minnetonka*, makes friends with 11-year-old Dorothy Quick (she later visits him in Tuxedo Park). Arrives in New York July 22 and goes to Tuxedo Park. Hires Ashcroft to attend to business affairs. Falls ill with bronchitis. Clara studies music in Boston. Visits Fairhaven (Rogers had suffered a stroke on July 22). Returns to New York in late October. Sees Howells often, attends dinners, but feels lonely. "Extract from Captain Stormfield's Visit to Heaven" appears in *Harper's Magazine* December 1907–January 1908.

1908   Goes to Bermuda with Ashcroft for two weeks, then returns there in late February with Rogers, who is in poor health, and Lyon (Emilie Rogers joins them in mid-March). Clemens makes friends with several schoolgirls, all between 10 and 16 years old and the daughters of friends and acquaintances. Calls them "angelfish," and conceives idea of forming a club called the "Aquarium." Returns to New York on April 11. Has Tiffany & Co. make enamel angelfish, sends each girl one, and keeps up frequent correspondence with them. Clara goes to England in May on concert tour. Rents house for Jean and her two companions in Gloucester, Massachusetts. House at Redding is completed; Clemens sees it for the first time on June 18, is very pleased, and moves in immediately. Names it "Innocence at Home" (at Clara's insistence, changes name to "Stormfield" in October) and calls his billiard room "The Aquarium," decorating it with pictures of his young friends. Praises house as the ideal home in letter to John Howells. Attends the dedication of the Aldrich Memorial at Portsmouth, New Hampshire, with Howells. Enjoys receiving guests, including "angelfish," who stay two to eight days. Establishes free library in Redding, donating books from his collection, and starts fund to construct new library building. Taxes male house guests $1 for the fund. Goes to New York in August to attend funeral of nephew Samuel Moffett, who had drowned, and suffers from heatstroke and fatigue. Clara returns from Europe in September. House is burglarized on September 18. Although thieves are chased and caught after a brief gunfight, household staff quits and new servants must be hired. Installs burglar alarm. Clemens accompanies Jean from Gloucester to New York, where she sails for Europe on September 26 to consult specialist in Berlin. Clara moves to New York, making frequent visits to Redding. Actress Billie Burke visits several times. Forms The Mark Twain Company, corporation designed to keep royalties within the family even after copyrights expire, with himself as president, Ashcroft as secretary and treasurer, and Clara, Jean, and Lyon as directors (later replaces Lyon and Ashcroft with Paine).

1909   Enjoys listening to pianists Ossip Gabrilowitsch and Ethel Newcomb, who visit as Clara's guests. Gratified to learn that Congress has passed new copyright bill, extending holders' ownership for an additional 14 years. Attends celebration in New York of Rogers' 69th birthday (continues to see Rogers in the city, but turns down most invitations to New York events). Still entertains in Redding, but no longer has many visits from "angelfish." Howells visits for the first time in late March. Clara begins to arouse his suspicions that Lyon and Ashcroft, who marry on March 18, are mishandling his business affairs. Attends Clara's vocal recital in Mendelssohn Hall in New York on April 13. Dismisses Lyon and Ashcroft in mid-April and writes lengthy, bitter denunciation of them. Jean comes to live at Stormfield on April 26 and takes over household management, including secretarial duties for Clemens, who is impressed by the quality of her mind. *Is Shakespeare Dead?*, supporting Francis Bacon's authorship of the plays, published by Harpers. Goes to New York on May 19 to visit Rogers, but is met at the train by Clara, who tells him that Rogers has died that day. Attends funeral services on May 20. Travels to Baltimore to give promised talk at graduation from St. Timothy's School of "angelfish" Frances Nunnally. Finds trip tiring and develops symptoms of heart disease, diagnosed as angina pectoris in July. Clara marries Ossip Gabrilowitsch at Stormfield on October 6. Twichell performs ceremony and Clemens wears Oxford gown for the occasion. Troubled by chest pains, goes with Paine to Bermuda in November for several weeks. Clara and Ossip leave for Europe in early December. Writes little for publication, but continues to work on "Letters from the Earth." Writes "The Turning Point of My Life" (published in *Harper's Bazar* February 1910). Returns to Stormfield for the Christmas holidays. Jean dies on the morning of December 24, apparently having suffered heart failure during a seizure in her bathtub. Clemens is too distraught to attend services or to go to Elmira for her burial. Writes "The Death of Jean." Tells Paine: "It is the end of my autobiography. I shall never write any more." Paine and his family move into Stormfield.

1910   Goes to Bermuda on January 5, accompanied by his butler, Claude Benchotte. Stays at Bay House, Hamilton, home of the American vice-consul, William H. Allen, whose daughter Helen is an "angelfish" and who takes dictation for him at times. Plays golf with Woodrow Wilson, then president of Princeton University. Howells' daughter Mildred is also in Bermuda for her health and visits him often. Sees Dorothy Quick. Chest pains grow more frequent and severe. Paine comes to help care for him. Clemens notices that Halley's Comet is again visible in the sky. Leaves Bermuda on April 12 in great pain. Dies at Stormfield at approximately 6:30 P.M. on April 21. Funeral service is held at the Brick Presbyterian Church in New York. Henry Van Dyke gives short sermon and Twichell delivers an emotional prayer. Buried in Elmira, April 24, in family plot with Langdon, Susy, Livy, and Jean.

Note on the Texts

The texts of *The Prince and the Pauper*, edited by Victor Fischer and
Lin Salamo, with the assistance of Mary Jane Jones, and *A Connecticut Yankee in King Arthur's Court*, edited by Bernard L. Stein, presented in this volume are those of The Iowa Center for Textual
Studies edition of *The Works of Mark Twain*, published by the University of California Press (Berkeley, Los Angeles, London, 1979).
These texts were prepared according to the standards established
by—and have received the official approval of—The Center for
Scholarly Editions of the Modern Language Association. The text
presented here of *Personal Recollections of Joan of Arc* is that of the first
American edition, published by Harper & Brothers (New York, 1896).

The textual problems that confronted the editors of *The Prince and
the Pauper* and *A Connecticut Yankee in King Arthur's Court* were
similar. In both cases Mark Twain's complete holograph manuscript
is extant: the manuscript of *The Prince and the Pauper* is in the Henry
E. Huntington Library, San Marino, California, and the manuscript
of *A Connecticut Yankee in King Arthur's Court* is in the Henry W.
and Albert A. Berg Collection of The New York Public Library.
These manuscripts served as the basic texts for the Iowa-California
editions. Intervening documents between manuscript and first edition, such as printer's copy and proofs, have not been found. Pro-
spectuses, set from incompletely revised proofs for the purpose of
soliciting prepublication subscription sales, are extant. In both cases,
the English editions, published by Chatto & Windus slightly before
or simultaneously with the American editions, were set from the
American proof sheets in varying stages of revision. The task of the
editors was to determine, after collation of the documents, which of
the many differences between the manuscripts and the published editions were caused by others in the process of transmission from
manuscript to printer's copy to type and then to plates, and which
were deliberate revisions made by Mark Twain when he read proof.

The editor of *A Connecticut Yankee in King Arthur's Court* had two
other published documents to collate, in addition to those mentioned earlier. First, excerpts from *A Connecticut Yankee in King
Arthur's Court* published in the November 1889 *Century Magazine*
contained many variations from the manuscript, some which were
clearly made by Twain or others solely for the purpose of magazine
publication, but some which seem to be changes Twain would have
inserted into the book if he had had more time. And second, Twain

used the Globe edition of Sir Thomas Malory's *Morte Darthur*, edited by Sir Edward Strachey, at times instructing his typist to copy long passages directly from it; in these cases that text is used for copy by the editor. Transcriptions from *Morte Darthur* made, and sometimes revised, by Twain himself remain as he wrote them in the manuscript. For the text of the Iowa-California editions presented in this volume, obvious errors in the manuscript were corrected, and the changes determined to be made by Twain himself were inserted.

Mark Twain began working on *The Prince and the Pauper* late in 1877 and finished eleven chapters before putting it aside in February 1878. He resumed work on it early in 1880 and by December 1880 had finished a draft, which he gave to friends to read. After receiving their comments and suggestions, he made further revisions. On February 9, 1881, he signed a contract with James R. Osgood and Company for publication of the book, in which it was stipulated that Osgood would supply illustrations, pay all advertising costs, and manufacture the book by November 15, 1881, subject to Twain's approval; Twain was to turn in the completed manuscript no later than April 1, 1881, pay for all production costs, own the plates and stock, retain the copyright, and decide what the retail price and discounts to agents would be. Osgood was to receive a 7 1/2 percent royalty for his services. Arrangements were made with Chatto & Windus for prior publication in England. The manuscript was completed in March 1881 and Osgood had a transcription of it made for printer's copy. Twain did not go over this copy. He read proof in late summer and early fall and complained that the typesetters had not followed his punctuation, which he had insisted they do; despite his objections, nine of the chapters still retained the typesetters' punctuation (Mark Twain's punctuation has been restored by the Iowa-California editors). Twain's friends William Dean Howells and Edward House read proof pages for the book and suggested a number of last-minute revisions, which Twain agreed to make. These changes had to be made in the plates, and not all of them were done in time to appear in the English edition, which was set from the American proofs. Twain went to Montreal to protect his Canadian copyright late in November and authorized a 250-volume edition to be published by Dawson Brothers of Montreal early in December. The English edition was published December 1, 1881, and the American edition was published December 12, 1881, bearing an 1882 date on its title page. Mark Twain made no further revisions to the text.

Mark Twain worked on *A Connecticut Yankee in King Arthur's Court* intermittently from early 1886 to April 1889, when a typescript was made (the first complete typescript produced for any Twain work). Frederick Hall, then acting publisher for Twain's firm, Charles L. Webster and Company, gave the typescript to Edmund Clarence Stedman to read, and Stedman offered several suggestions for revisions. Twain revised the typescript in May and June 1889. Because of difficulties with the intricate illustrations and the urgency of getting proofs to England in time for Chatto & Windus to obtain copyright, Hall devised a complicated production process in which illustration, typesetting, plating, and printing were begun before the full book was proofread, and Twain was unable to read revised page proofs. Meanwhile, Twain prepared the excerpts mentioned above for publication in the November 1889 *Century Magazine*. Howells read page proofs for the book and offered suggestions for revisions, many of which Twain accepted; these late revisions had to be made in the plates, and were therefore too late to be made in the English edition, which had been set from earlier stages of the proofs. The English edition is also lacking the second paragraph of the Preface, which Twain had removed because he did not want to offend English taste. The Canadian edition, published by G. M. Rose and Sons in Toronto, was set from the American plates. The book was published simultaneously in Canada, England, and the United States early in December 1889. No further revisions were made by Twain.

Mark Twain began writing *Personal Recollections of Joan of Arc* while staying in Florence, Italy, in late 1892 and continued work until he finished the section describing the siege of Orleans. He arranged to have the manuscript typed, and then he put it aside. During a business trip to New York in July and August 1894, he negotiated an arrangement with J. Henry Harper to serialize the book pseudonymously in *Harper's Magazine*, agreeing to accept in return less than his usual payment for serial publication. Twain had originally intended to write Joan's life up through her great battles and only to summarize her trial and martyrdom briefly at the end, but he was convinced by Henry Mills Alden, the Harper editor, that the trial and martyrdom were essential to the story. After returning to France in late August 1894 Twain continued work on the book, and by December 1894 realized that the third part was much longer than he had expected and that he would have to cut it drastically for serial publication (in addition to occasional paragraphs, 12 chapters in the third section were cut). *Personal Recollections of Joan of Arc* was completed on February 8, 1895, and Twain brought the typescript with him on his next business trip to New York on February 23, 1895. He returned briefly to Paris in April to help prepare for his family's return to America in May. Typesetting for the magazine had been started earlier; in a letter written to Henry Huttleston Rogers on

April 29, 1895, Twain reported that he was reading proof for the September installment. Serial publication of *Personal Recollections of Joan of Arc* began in the April 1895 *Harper's Magazine* with "the Sieur Louis de Conte" given as the author and "Jean François Alden" credited as the translator. Twain continued to read proof in Elmira, N.Y., for both the book and abridged magazine versions. Arrangements were made to have the book published immediately after the last serial installment in April 1896. In August 1895, Twain left the United States with his family to begin his world lecture tour and therefore was unable to read book page proofs. The book was published by Harper & Brothers in New York on May 1, 1896, with Mark Twain's name prominently displayed on the book's cover and spine but not on the title page. The English edition, set from American proofs, was published simultaneously with the American edition by Chatto & Windus; it credited Mark Twain as "editor" on the title page. Except for adding a dedication to his wife in a later printing, Twain made no further revisions in the book. The text of the first American edition is printed here.

This volume presents the texts of the printings chosen for inclusion here, but it does not attempt to reproduce features of their typographic design, such as the display capitalization of chapter openings. Page reference numbers in the originals have been changed to conform to the pages of the present volume. Otherwise, the texts are reproduced without change, except for the correction of typographical errors. Spelling, punctuation, and capitalization often are expressive features and they are not altered, even when inconsistent or irregular. The following is a list of typographical errors corrected, cited by page and line number: 478.5, strees (this error will be corrected in later printings of the Iowa-California edition); 587.9, upon out; 626.37, you?' ; 641.6, "Ah; 716.11, Catharine; 731.17, Catharine; 742.6, Welcome; 823.7, King; 823.17, once; 860.5, Jean's; 883.3, English?"; 934.29, reserves; 956.11, music the.

Notes

In the notes below, the reference numbers denote page and line of the present volume (the line count includes chapter headings). No note is made for material included in standard desk-reference books such as Webster's *Ninth New Collegiate*, *Biographical*, and *Geographical* dictionaries. Footnotes in the texts and the notes on pages 207–12 are Mark Twain's own. For more detailed notes and references to other studies, see *The Works of Mark Twain* (Berkeley: University of California Press, 1979): *Volume 6, The Prince and The Pauper*, ed. Victor Fischer, Lin Salamo, et al., *Volume 9, A Connecticut Yankee in King Arthur's Court*, ed. Bernard L. Stein et al.

For further biographical background, see *Mark Twain's Letters*, 2 vols. (New York: Harper & Brothers, 1917), ed. Albert Bigelow Paine; *The Love Letters of Mark Twain* (New York: Harper & Brothers, 1949), ed. Dixon Wecter; *Mark Twain to Mrs. Fairbanks* (San Marino: Huntington Library, 1949), ed. Dixon Wecter; *Mark Twain –Howells Letters*, 2 vols. (Cambridge: Harvard University Press, 1960), ed. Henry Nash Smith and William M. Gibson; *Mark Twain's Letters to His Publishers 1867–1894* (Berkeley: University of California Press, 1967), ed. Hamlin Hill; *Mark Twain's Correspondence with Henry Huttleston Rogers 1893–1909* (Berkeley: University of California Press, 1969), ed. Lewis Leary; *Mark Twain's Letters* (Berkeley: University of California Press, 1988–1991), *Volume 1 1853–1866*, ed. Edgar Marquess Branch, Michael B. Frank, and Kenneth M. Sanderson, *Volume 2 1867–1868*, ed. Harriet Elinor Smith and Richard Bucci, *Volume 3 1869*, ed. Victor Fischer, Michael B. Frank, and Dahlia Armon; *Mark Twain's Aquarium: The Samuel Clemens Angelfish Correspondence 1905–1910* (Athens: University of Georgia Press, 1991), ed. John Cooley; *Mark Twain's Notebook* (New York: Harper & Brothers, 1935), ed. Albert Bigelow Paine; *Mark Twain's Notebooks & Journals* (Berkeley: University of California Press, 1975–1979), *Volume I 1855–1873*, ed. Frederick Anderson, Michael B. Frank, and Kenneth M. Sanderson, *Volume II 1877–1883*, ed. Frederick Anderson, Lin Salamo, and Bernard L. Stein, *Volume III 1883–1891*, ed. Robert Pack Browning, Michael B. Frank, and Lin Salamo; Albert Bigelow Paine, *Mark Twain: A Biography* (New York: Harper & Brothers, 1912); Clara Clemens, *My Father Mark Twain* (New York: Harper & Brothers, 1931); *Mark Twain, Business Man* (Boston: Little, Brown and Company, 1946), ed. Samuel Charles Webster; and Dixon Wecter, *Sam Clemens of Hannibal* (Boston: Houghton Mifflin Company, 1952).

THE PRINCE AND THE PAUPER

3.8   *inter vicinos*]   Among neighbors.

3.21   *ne optimum . . . depravetur*]   "Let it not be that he distorts the best part of his natural ability through the best education."

17.9   Temple Bar]   Western gate into the City of London; it was removed in 1878.

23.36   *See Note . . . volume.]   Mark Twain's notes are on pp. 207–12 in this volume.

27.11–12   Norfolk . . . captivity.]   Thomas Howard (1473–1554), duke of Norfolk, and his son Henry Howard (1517?–47), earl of Surrey, were arrested for treason in December 1546. Surrey was beheaded on January 19, 1547; Norfolk was released after the accession of Mary I in 1553.

59.24–25   Old Jewry]   The street took its name from a synagogue that stood there before Edward I expelled the Jews from England in 1291.

61.23   Don Caesar de Bazan]   A ruined 17th-century Spanish count in Victor Hugo's play *Ruy Blas* (1838).

107.38–108.6   "Bien . . . trine."]   "Good night then, Ale Wife and House, / The good Fellow's going away, / On Gallows to hang by the malice of Gents / For his long sleep at last. / Go out pretty Women and watch, and watch, / Go out of London go, / And watch the Fellow that stole your duds, / Upon the Gallows to hang."

125.15–16   Alfred . . . cakes burn."]   Legend has it that King Alfred the Great (849–899), while hiding from the invading Danes, took shelter in a cowherd's hut. Meditating on the war, he allowed the cakes to burn and was duly scolded by the cowherd's wife.

205.9   Confessor's tomb]   King Edward the Confessor (1003?–66) is interred in Westminster Abbey.

A CONNECTICUT YANKEE IN KING ARTHUR'S COURT

255.34   Hampton Court Cartoons]   The cartoons (drawings done on stout paper as models for another work) were executed 1515–16 for tapestries for the Sistine Chapel. They were displayed in a gallery of Hampton Court Palace from the 17th to mid-19th centuries.

269.11–270.23   THEN . . . would not.]   From Malory's *Morte D'Arthur* (1485), Bk. 7, ch. 28.

279.25   Moder]   Middle English for "mother."

284.39   "Go up . . . prophet;]   Cf. 2 Kings 2:23–24.

311.10   Corporation . . . Test]   The Corporation Act of 1661 included a requirement that elected officials in incorporated towns in England and Wales take communion according to the rites of the Church of England. Under the Test Act of 1673, all civil and military officers were required to take Anglican communion; in 1678 an additional Test Act excluded Roman Catholics from both houses of parliament. The religious restrictions contained in the Corporation and Test acts were repealed in 1828–29.

317.9–10   "In the Sweet By and By"]   Popular song composed in 1868 by Joseph P. Webster, lyrics by Sanford Fillmore Bennett.

328.4–5   Casanova . . . enemy.]   In his *Mémoires*, Casanova de Seingalt described the sexual activity of two of his aristocratic companions while they were watching from a crowded Paris window the slow torture and execution of attempted regicide Robert François Damiens (1714–57).

333.27   castle d'If]   Sixteenth-century castle on the island of If near Marseilles that was used as a state prison; Huguenots, political prisoners including "the man in the iron mask," and the fictional hero of Dumas' *Count of Monte Cristo* were imprisoned there.

366.14–15   Lives . . . Lecky]   Alban Butler's *Lives of the Saints* (1756–59) is cited by William Lecky in his *History of European Morals from Augustus to Charlemagne* (1869), vol. 2.

371.33   "**Constantinopol** . . . **gesellschafft!**"]   "The Bagpipe Manufacturers Company of Constantinople"; this and the following combinations are German tongue twisters.

372.7–8   "**Nihilisten** . . . **versuchungen!**"]   "Outrageous attempts by nihilists to blow up the strong-box of a theater with dynamite."

372.12–13   "**Transvaal** . . . **tragoedie!**"]   "The lamentable tragedy of the marriage of a dromedary drover in the tropical transport service of the army of the Transvaal."

372.17–19   "**Mekka** . . . **macher!**"]   "A manufacturer of marble monuments commemorating the Moorish mother of the assassins who perpetrated the general massacre of Mohammedans at Mecca."

389.3   Norroy King-at-Arms!]   A principal member of the College of Arms, or Heralds' College.

427.21   labrick]   Clemens defined labrick, a term in use in Missouri during his childhood, as "a little stronger than ass, & not quite as strong as idiot."

516.37–517.30   Then the king . . . oft-times.]   From *Morte D'Arthur*, Bk. 21, ch. 4.

PERSONAL RECOLLECTIONS OF JOAN OF ARC

See pp. 1030 and 1031 for maps of France and Orléans during the time of Joan of Arc.

557.14   three Popes at once]   In 1423–25 the authority of the canonical pope, Martin V, was challenged by the election of an antipope, Clement VIII, and a counter-antipope, Benedict XIV.

621.2   Battle of the Herrings]   The French had attacked an English wagon train taking provisions to the army besieging Orléans but were repulsed by Sir John Fastolf's men, who fought from behind a barricade made from barrels of herring.

641.24   Archbishop of Rheims.]   Regnault de Chartres.

649.28   Count of Vendôme]   Louis de Bourbon (c. 1376–1446).

709.3   De par le Dieu]   Colloquially, "In God's name."

713.23   Sir John Falstaff]   Sir John Fastolf, or Fastolfe (1378?–1459); some people believe that Shakespeare's Falstaff in *Henry IV* was based on him.

763.9–10   the Vidame de Chartres]   A *vidame* was an officer of a bishop, who represented him in temporal matters such as military service.

825.17–20   "Pardonnez-vous . . . Sarrasins."]   "Forgive one another profoundly, completely, thus only will you become loyal Christians, and, if you want to go to war, go fight the Saracens."

913.1   Council of Basel]   Called by Pope Martin V in 1431. Church councils, which include bishops, theologians, and other representatives of the whole church, consider and rule on matters such as doctrine, administration, and discipline.

928.20–22   torture. . . . Courcelles]   Courcelles was charged by Cauchon with translating the minutes of Joan's trial into Latin. At the Rehabilitation, he claimed that he could not recall recommending torture, and while editing the minutes, following the Rehabilitation, removed his name wherever possible.

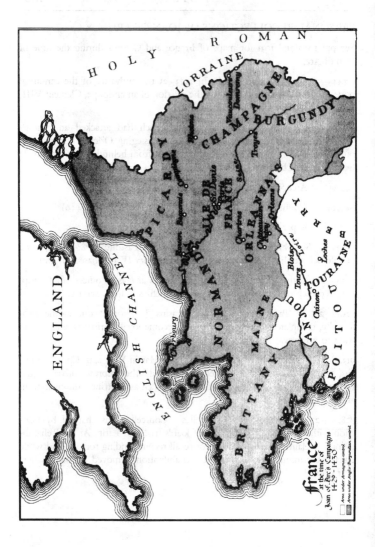

France

at the time of
Joan of Arc's Campaigns
1429-1430

Areas under Armagnac control

Areas under Anglo-Burgundian control

HOLY R O M A N

LORRAINE

CHAMPAGNE

BURGUNDY

PICARDY

ILE DE FRANCE

ORLEANNAIS

NORMANDY

BRITTANY

MAINE

ANJOU

TOURAINE

POITOU

BERRY

ENGLAND

ENGLISH CHANNEL

Troyes

Seine

Orléans

Loire

Tours

Blois

Chinon

Loches

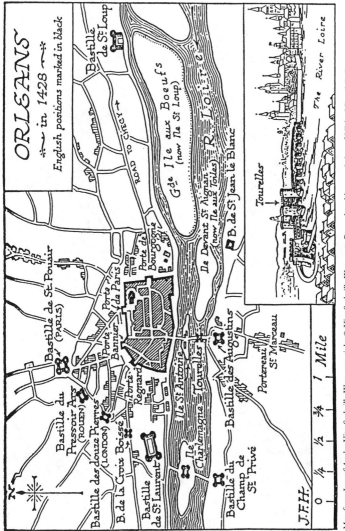

ORLEANS in 1428

English positions marked in black

Bastille de St Pouair (PARIS)

Bastille du Pressoir Ars (ROUEN)

Bastille des douze Pierres (LONDON)

B. de la Croix Boissé

Bastille de St Laurent

Ile Charlemagne

Bastille du Champ de St Privé

Bastille des Augustins

Porte Bannier

Porte de Paris

Porte Renard

Porte Regnard

Ile St Antoine

Tourelles

Porteau St Marceau

Portereau St Marceau

Porte de Bourgogne

ROAD TO CHECY

Bastille de St Loup

Gde Ile aux Boeufs (now Ile St Loup)

De Derant St Aignan (now Ile aux Toiles)

R. LOIRE

B. de St Jean le Blanc

Tourelles

The River Loire

J.F.H.

0   ¼   ½   ¾   1 Mile

Map from *Joan of Arc* by Vita Sackville-West, copyright © Vita Sackville-West, 1936. Reproduced by permission of Michael Joseph Ltd.

CATALOGING INFORMATION
Twain, Mark, 1835–1910
   [Novels, Selections]
   Historical Romances : The prince and the pauper, A Connecticut Yankee
in King Arthur's court, Personal recollections of Joan of Arc / Mark Twain.
   Edited by Susan K. Harris.

   (The Library of America ; 71)
   1. Edward VI, King of England, 1537–1553—Fiction. 2. Great Britian—
Kings and rulers—Fiction. 3. Joan, of Arc, Saint, 1412–1431—Fiction.
4. Christian women saints—France—Fiction. 5. Arthur, King–Fiction.
6. Arthurian romances—Adaptations. 7. Biographical fiction, American.
8. Historical fiction, American. I. Twain, Mark, 1835–1910. Prince and the
pauper. 1994. II. Twain, Mark, 1835–1910. Connecticut Yankee in King
Arthur's Court. 1994. III. Twain, Mark, 1835–1910. Personal Recollections
of Joan of Arc. 1994. IV. Title. V. Series.
PS1302   1992   93–40246
813'.4–dc20
ISBN 0–940450–82–8 (alk. paper)

THE LIBRARY OF AMERICA SERIES

This book is set in 10 point Linotron Galliard,
a face designed for photocomposition by Matthew Carter
and based on the sixteenth-century face Granjon. The paper
is acid-free Ecusta Nyalite and meets the requirements for perma-
nence of the American National Standards Institute. The binding
material is Brillianta, a 100% woven rayon cloth made by
Van Heek-Scholco Textielfabrieken, Holland. The com-
position is by Haddon Craftsmen, Inc., and The
Clarinda Company. Printing and binding
by R. R. Donnelley & Sons Company.
Designed by Bruce Campbell.